THE D0581116

and Selected Stories

THE AWAKENING
and Selected Stories

◆

Kate Chopin

Introduction and Notes by
STEFANIA CIOCIA

WORDSWORTH CLASSICS

For my husband
ANTHONY JOHN RANSON
with love from your wife, the publisher.
Eternally grateful for your unconditional love.

Readers who are interested in other titles from
Wordsworth Editions are invited to visit our website at
www.wordsworth-editions.com

This edition published 2015 by Wordsworth Editions Limited
8B East Street, Ware, Hertfordshire SG12 9HJ

ISBN 978 1 84022 584 6

Text © Wordsworth Editions Limited 2015
Introduction and Notes © Stefania Ciocia 2015

Wordsworth® is a registered trade mark of
Wordsworth Editions Limited

Wordsworth Editions
is the company founded in 1987 by
MICHAEL TRAYLER

Typeset in Great Britain by Antony Gray
Printed and bound by Clays Ltd, Elcograf S.p.A.

CONTENTS

A NIGHT IN ACADIE

UNCOLLECTED STORIES

GENERAL INTRODUCTION

Wordsworth Classics are inexpensive editions designed to appeal to the general reader and students. We commissioned teachers and specialists to write wide ranging, jargon-free introductions and to provide notes that would assist the understanding of our readers rather than interpret the stories for them. In the same spirit, because the pleasures of reading are inseparable from the surprises, secrets and revelations that all narratives contain, we strongly advise you to enjoy this book before turning to the Introduction.

General Adviser
KEITH CARABINE

INTRODUCTION

Kate Chopin completed 'Wiser Than a God' in June 1889. The earliest of her short stories to appear subsequently in print, this is the tale of a young pianist who turns down a proposal from the man she is manifestly in love with. The woman gives a simple explanation for her choice: marriage ' "doesn't enter into the purpose of my life" ' (p. 420); her life is to be devoted entirely to the pursuit of her art. Ten years after this debut, Chopin would publish *The Awakening*, the novel where she most famously revisits the theme of a woman's endeavour to be true to herself, and where, controversially, this quest for authenticity leads to extreme consequences. After the publication of *The Awakening* to largely hostile reviews, Chopin slowed down her literary production. She had become a professional writer aged thirty-nine; her entire career had thus spanned a little over a decade. Her contemporaries knew Chopin primarily as an accomplished writer of short fiction, through her two collections of stories: *Bayou Folk* (1894) and *A Night in Acadie* (1897). Both texts are included in the present volume, together with a dozen uncollected tales and her masterpiece, *The Awakening*. The titles of the two collections gesture to the distinctive character of life in Louisiana, a region of the southern United States often perceived as exotic and alien, even by its immediate neighbours, because of the uniqueness of its multicultural and multilingual history. Ironically, Chopin's reputation as a regional writer – which had secured her success when she was alive – consigned her to a long period of critical oblivion in the first half of the twentieth century, especially once 'local colour' began to be associated with a somewhat narrow provincialism, rather than being valued – as it had been in the postbellum period – for its potential to promote the reading public's appreciation for a home-grown literary tradition.

Chopin was reclaimed as a writer of enduring significance in the 1970s, and when she finally gained admission into the American literary canon, she did so with a vengeance. The timing of this rediscovery was most felicitous, because it corresponded with a flourishing of the second wave feminist movement, whose championing of Chopin's own feminist credentials has since led to a rise in her fortunes so spectacular as to be probably unparalleled in recent literary history. Such radically changed views of *The Awakening* offer a lesson not so much in the relativity of aesthetic judgements but in the mutability of our ethical values. Chopin *was* ahead of her time in her creation of Edna Pontellier, a woman who finds both marriage and, even more shockingly, mother-hood not to be the necessary conditions for happiness and self-fulfil-ment but instead obstacles to a process of self-discovery. *The Awakening* has an undeniable modern sensitivity with regards to its exploration of the condition of women. That said, like all classics deserving of the title, it speaks of the human predicament at large, regardless of gender, or of geographical or historical location. In fact, rather than indicating a process, Chopin's working title for the novel – *A Solitary Soul* – is highly evocative of our common existential condition. The following pages suggest some possible ways of approaching the adventurous, multifaceted and multilayered body of work which sees in *The Awakening* its crowning glory.

A young woman strolling about alone

Kate Chopin was born Catherine O'Flaherty on 8 February 1850 in St Louis, Missouri. Her parents were the forty-five-year-old Irish businessman Thomas O'Flaherty, a widower who already had a son from his previous marriage, and the twenty-two-year-old Eliza Faris, the eldest daughter of a family of French origin, whose maternal lineage could be traced back to the foundation of St Louis in 1764. Her parents' marriage was very likely motivated, at least in part, by the practical and material advantages that such a union brought to both parties: O'Flaherty was in a position to take care of the Farises' debts, while his association with a 'pedigreed' family helped consolidate his social standing in St Louis. Conveniently placed on the Mississippi River, a positioning which had made it the second largest port in the country after New York, in 1850 the city had already been known for half a century as the 'Gateway to the West' and promised to enhance its reputation as a transport and commercial hub even further with the construction of the Pacific Railroad. It was therefore an ideal location for ambitious entrepreneurs. Unfortunately, Chopin's father was killed in the pursuit of his aspirations: he was one of the thirty victims of an accident on the new Gasconade Bridge during the inaugural train journey from St Louis to Jefferson City in 1855. (The idea of a train crash would later be used to startling effect by Chopin in one of her most cleverly crafted tales, 'The Story of an Hour'.)

O'Flaherty had been a first-generation immigrant to the United States, so the familial influences in Chopin's early life all came from her matrilineal ancestry. It was a lineage full of strong, independent female role models who, more often than not, had had to (and perhaps even chosen to?) live without the presence of a husband. Chopin's mother never remarried, nor did her grandmother Athénaïse Charleville Faris, whose widowhood lasted more than fifty years. (Athénaïse was already living with the O'Flahertys at the time of Thomas's death. Her feckless husband had deserted her and their seven young children, which is probably why her eldest daughter Eliza had married at the relatively early age of sixteen.) Chopin would follow in these women's footsteps and not remarry when she herself became a widow, but it was an older relative who exerted the greatest influence on Kate's childhood: her great-grandmother Victoire Verdon Charleville (who also outlived her husband by a good eighteen years). Chopin's biographer Emily Toth makes a persuasive case for the enduring impact that this formidable matriarch had on the young girl. It was Madame Charleville who taught Kate to speak French and who insisted that she should learn to play the piano; just as importantly, Madame Charleville shared with her great-granddaughter real-life stories of proud, unconventional women: her own parents Marianne Victoire (née Richelet) and Joseph Verdon, for example, were the first couple in St Louis to obtain a legal separation (since divorce was not an option for Roman Catholics) in 1785. Remarkably, in this case it was the wife who 'was given all the property, except for Joseph's gun, bed, clothes, and tools' (Toth, p. 37).[1] Four years later, she gave birth to a son, whom her former husband dutifully recognised as his own, possibly because by then Marianne Victoire had become a highly successful businesswoman. (As Toth suggests, the lack of evidence of a reconciliation between the two spouses opens up the possibility that the child might in fact have been illegitimate.)

In what is possibly a homage to the free spirit of this impressive ancestor (as well as a reference to the French national allegory of liberty?), Marianne is the name that Chopin chose for the fiercely independent heroine of 'The Maid of Saint Phillippe', written in 1891 and published the following year. Chopin's only foray into historical fiction is set at the time of the end of the French and Indian War (1754–63), when France ceded to Britain what was then its Louisiana territory east of the Mississippi River. Chopin alludes to the newly founded St Louis ('Laclède's village' [p. 442]; 'the new village of St Louis' [p. 445]) as a haven for the French colonists seeking to escape the impending British rule. (In actual fact, they did so only to come under Spanish jurisdiction since, with the secret Treaty of Fontainebleau in 1762, France had turned over to Spain the Louisiana lands west of the Mississippi, and the city of New Orleans). Honouring her old father's emotional attachment to his home, Marianne refuses to join the French exodus to the west, and soon the two remained the only inhabitants of the village of Saint Phillippe. Marianne's initial, traditional concession to filial duty (' "My life belongs to my father" ' [p. 443]) eventually gives way to a declaration of feminine self-reliance for, even after the death of her father, the young girl continues to turn down her eager rescuers and suitors. Not only that: in a move that aligns her with a long American tradition of heroic figures, from Leatherstocking to Huckleberry Finn, who eschew the lures of a corrupt 'sivilization' and embrace the ideals of frontier, Marianne turns her back on all three European powers in the region (France, Britain and Spain) and ' "goes to the Cherokees!" ' in pursuit of freedom: ' "but let it be death rather than bondage" ' (p. 447). This extraordinary ending fulfils the promise of the story's opening, where the descripion of Marianne has almost mythical undertones: in her androgynous aspect, and her comparison to a stag (the animal sacred to Artemis/Diana), she appears to be a cross between a modern-day virgin goddess of the hunt and of the wilderness,

---

1 As here, all future references to secondary sources will be given parenthetically in the text, including the author's surname and page number. For full details of the works cited, see the Bibliography following this Introduction.

and a buckskin-clad American pioneer. In this context, it is no wonder that she should take leave of the narrative '[w]ith gun across her shoulder . . . her brave, strong face turned to the rising sun' (p. 447).

At the tender age of thirteen, Chopin too asserted her own independence from unwanted political influences with a gesture that earned her the moniker of St Louis's 'Littlest Rebel' (Toth p. 64). During the Civil War, Missouri was one of the slave states not to secede from the Union; nevertheless, many Missourians were Confederate supporters. St Louis in particular was split along ethnic lines: while its large contingent of recent German immigrants was staunchly against slavery, the old settlers of French descent tended to side with the South. (Chopin's stepbrother George O'Flaherty, for example, joined the Confederate army, dying of typhoid during the conflict.) In 1863, two years into the war, Kate manifested her own Confederate sympathies by tearing down a Yankee flag which had mysteriously appeared in the porch of the family home; for this seditious act, young as she was, she was briefly placed under arrest by the Union authorities. While foregrounding her bravery and defiance, episodes such as this raise inevitable questions about the nature of Chopin's feelings, especially as an adult, towards slavery and racism – an issue I address later on. Less controversially for a modern audience, Chopin's rebellious streak would inform her attitude towards the strictures of social conventions, and of the code of conduct expected of women in particular. As a debutante first, and a young wife and mother afterwards, Chopin expressed in her writing, and displayed in her behaviour, a marked impatience towards those customs that impinged upon her intellectual development and physical freedom. In a diary entry dating from 1869, her first social season, Chopin bemoaned: 'I am invited to a ball and I go. – I dance with people I despise; amuse myself with men whose only talent lies in their feet' (quoted in Toth, p. 91). As another diary entry makes clear, Kate resented the fact that her social engagements were taking her away from activities far more congenial to her: 'parties, operas, concerts, skating and amusements ad infinitum have so taken up all my time that my dear reading and writing that I love so well have suffered much neglect' (quoted in Toth, p. 87).

Still, shortly after her official debut into the polite society of St Louis, Kate met the twenty-five-year-old Oscar Chopin, the son of a wealthy plantation owner and businessman from Louisiana, whom she would marry on 9 June 1870, recorded as 'the happiest day on my life' in her diary (Ewell, p. 11). The couple left for a three-month honeymoon around Europe, during which they visited Germany, Switzerland and

France. Even as a newlywed, Chopin had no intention of curtailing her flair for independence: while in Zurich, possibly for the first time in their European travels, Kate left behind her husband, who was taking a nap in their hotel, and ventured on a solitary expedition. Again, her diary shows that Chopin was aware of the unconventionality of her behaviour: 'I wonder what people thought of me – a young woman strolling about alone' (quoted in Toth, p. 113). On their return to the United States, the Chopins would set up their home in New Orleans, a cosmopolitan, sophisticated city where Kate's individuality would continue to thrive, even in the presence of the responsibilities of family life.

Kate Chopin and Louisiana

Louisiana, Kate Chopin's adoptive state, holds a unique position in the US for its exceptional multicultural heritage, characterised by a blend of French and Spanish influences, dating from the early colonial times, overlaid with elements of Native American and African American cultures. Originally a French colony, after the Treaty of Fontainebleau of 1762 Louisiana – which at the time contained part of present-day Missouri, including St Louis – came under Spanish rule for about forty years. Napoleon regained the region for France at the beginning of the nineteenth century, but soon afterwards turned it over to the United States as part of the Louisiana Purchase of 1803. (The name 'Louisiana Purchase' is somewhat misleading to contemporary ears, because the agreement extended to territories which now form fifteen States of the Union. This momentous event remains the greatest single acquisition of land by the US, which virtually doubled in size in one fell swoop.) To add to its multicultural mix, Louisiana was also home to another distinctive group of people: the Acadians (or Cajuns). These were – indeed, still are – the descendants of French Canadian settlers who had been driven away from Nova Scotia by the British in 1755. At the time when Chopin was writing, they tended to be poorer and less educated than other Louisiana people of French descent, commonly referred to as Creoles.[2] The Louisiana Creoles were to all intents and purposes the cultural and economic elite of the state, and retained a proud attachment to their own traditions, including their language (French)

2 The meaning of the term Creole has gone through several changes in time and – to add to the confusion – is often used to refer to languages as well as to ethnic groups. It 'was originally used to describe the first-generation offspring of European settlers and colonizers born in the New World, later expanding to indicate people of mixed race but then, in the Gilded Age [the late nineteenth century], narrowing down once more to indicate Creoles

and religion (Catholicism). This cultural clash is captured most vividly in 'A Matter of Prejudice', where Chopin sums up the wide-reaching, idiosyncratic dislikes of Madame Carambeau in the pithy observation that '[a]nything not French had, in her opinion, little right of existence' (p. 318). In fact, Madame Carambeau 'had not spoken to her son Henri for ten years because he had married an American girl from Prytania Street' (p. 318). Readers familiar with the topography of New Orleans would have known that the street in question was one of the most affluent in the American section of the city, a more recent urban development than the Vieux Carré (Old Quarter), which was home to the Creole elite. Madame Carambeau's prejudice is thus more a matter of cultural affiliation than of social status – although the two are clearly connected – or even of wealth. The strong sense of a distinctively Creole, rather than American, identity pervades *The Awakening* too, where it is Edna herself – ' "of sound old Presbyterian Kentucky stock" ' (p. 64), thus an outsider, especially in the Creole enclave of the summer resort of Grand Isle – who must negotiate the contrast between the two cultures.

Although not a native of Louisiana, Chopin must have adapted relatively easily to life in New Orleans, coming as she did from another large city, and from a family of French descent. (Nevertheless, her Irish parentage did not endear her to her father-in-law who, renowned for his intolerance, might have provided the inspiration for Madame Carambeau's prejudices [see Toth, p. 122]). In the nine years they spent in New Orleans, the Chopins had five sons, and lived in three different houses, but never in the French Quarter. Kate enjoyed exploring the city, and continued to indulge her passion for long, solitary walks; she also went against societal protocols by smoking in public – an unladylike activity at the best of times. In common with her creator, Edna Pontellier would take pleasure in her lone excursions around the city; in Chapter 36 of *The Awakening*, we see her in one of her favourite, secluded haunts: a private garden in the suburbs where she 'often stopped in her perambulations; sometimes taking a book with her, and sitting an hour or two under the trees when she found the place deserted' (p. 103). A local *mulatresse* is on hand to provide refreshments and, as Edna notes, ' "there's the advantage of being able to smoke with your coffee out here" ' (p. 104). There is no evidence to

---

(and Cajuns, in the lower classes) as "white" ' (Castillo, p. 60). Chopin generally uses the term in this final sense, with some notable exceptions (see, for example, 'Nég Créol').

suggest that Oscar Chopin disapproved of his wife's conduct; in fact, according to Kate's earliest biographer Daniel Rankin – who, writing in 1932, was able to draw on the reminiscences of people acquainted with the couple – it was Oscar who incurred his relatives' censure for letting his wife 'go on, always in her own way' (quoted in Toth, p. 125). By contrast, in *The Awakening* the Pontelliers have an open disagreement when Léonce discovers that Edna has been out on her reception day – the one day of the week when ladies were expected to be at home to receive callers. For Mr Pontellier this breach of etiquette is concerning not merely as an abstract gesture of feminine insubordination against domestic order, but also for more practical reasons: he worries that his wife's perceived snub to a Mrs Belthrop will cost him his good relations with the woman's husband, a wealthy businessman who, as he reminds Edna, ' "could buy and sell us ten times over" ' (p. 50). Later that same evening, having retreated to her room, Edna expresses her rage through an action whose symbolic import requires no comment: ' . . . taking off her wedding ring, [she] flung it upon the carpet. When she saw it lying there, she stamped her heel upon it, striving to crush it' (p. 51).

In the course of the Chopins' own married life, the only difficulties of which there is an undeniable record were, instead, of a financial nature. In 1879, after a series of disappointing crops, Oscar's affairs as a cotton factor took such a turn for the worse that the family decided to relocate to the village of Cloutierville on the Cane River, in Natchitoches parish,[3] where the couple's last child and only daughter was born in 1880. In the small community of Cloutierville, any eccentricities of behaviour came inevitably under greater scrutiny than in a city: Kate cut a memorable figure both for her fashionable clothes, and for her independent ways. After Oscar's death of swamp fever (malaria) in 1882, Kate took over her husband's businesses – a general store and some local plantations – and busied herself with the task of settling the not inconsiderable debts she had been saddled with. She also had to apply to be made the legal guardian of her children – a sad reminder of one of the many ways in which men and women were not equals in the eyes of the law at the time.[4] In the period immediately following the death of

---

3 Louisiana is divided into parishes, rather than counties. Natchitoches ['pronounced Nack-e-tosh', as Chopin glosses in one of her notes to *The Awakening*; see 166] is about 260 miles north-west of New Orleans. Cloutierville (pronounced 'Cloochyville') features in several of Chopin's stories.

her husband – some say when her husband was still alive – Chopin is rumoured to have had an affair with Albert Sampite, a married, handsome plantation owner with a reputation for gambling, drinking too much and being prone to violence, even against his wife. We cannot know whether Chopin decided to leave Cloutierville in spite, or because, of her relationship with Sampite, but in 1884 she returned to St Louis to live with her fifty-six-year-old mother, whom she had remained very close to, and had frequently visited, during her time in Louisiana. Unfortunately, this reunion would last less than a year, for Eliza O'Flaherty died in 1885, leaving her daughter 'literally prostrate with grief' (Rankin, quoted in Toth, p. 174).

'My real growth'

The decade following this huge loss in her life – a loss compounded by her recent widowhood – would prove to be a period of crucial development for Chopin, as she acknowledges in a diary entry in 1894: 'If it were possible for my husband and my mother to come back to earth, I feel that I would unhesitatingly give up everything that has come into my life since they left it and join my existence again with theirs. To do that, I would have to forget the past ten years of my growth – *my real growth*' (quoted in Toth, p. 241; my italics). While, understandably, giving priority to the strength of human affections, Chopin none the less implies in no uncertain terms that her 'real growth' has not been brought about by those moments traditionally marking a rite a passage in a woman's life, such as marriage or motherhood. Four years after her mother's death, Chopin embarked on her career as a professional writer, starting with 'Wiser Than a God': in this story, Paula's artistic vocation flourishes, as we have seen, partly at the expense of her desire to marry, but also partly because work functions as a balm in the face of bereavement ('After the first shock of grief [at the death of her mother] was over, the girl had thrown all her energies into work, with a view of attaining that position in the musical world which her father and mother had dreamed might be hers' (p. 419). It is hard not to see the parallel in Chopin's own experience. By the time of her 1894 diary entry, she had

---

4 Louisiana was one of the last States in the US to repudiate completely – well into the twentieth century – the doctrine of coverture, which stipulated that wives had no legal identity or proprietary rights independent from their husbands. During Chopin's lifetime, married women could not own property in their own right and were, much like their children, under the legal guardianship of their husbands.

seen her first novel, *At Fault*, in print (and written another, *Young Dr Gosse*, now lost); she had placed a significant number of stories in regional and national periodicals, and had published her first collection of short stories to favourable reviews. She had found both a vocation and an audience.

As Alexis de Tocqueville had predicted in *Democracy in America* (1843), the United States have proven, throughout their history, to have a rich market for 'compact' literary forms such as the short story – a genre which lends itself perfectly to capture, in all their strength, the small epiphanies and the life-changing turning points in its characters' lives, as well as, as if in a snapshot, the mood and the regional flavours of an entire community. In the late 1880s and 1890s, fiction and poetry were regular features in periodical publications, particularly those targeted at women and children. Chopin's professional life coincided with the period when the United States were still coming to terms with the legacy of the Civil War (1861–5). In the aftermath of what remains the bloodiest, most divisive conflict in its history, the country was actively seeking to build bridges and encourage a spirit of mutual understanding between the industrial, abolitionist North and the rural, pro-slavery South. For this reason, '[b]y the late 1870s the northern magazines [and publishing houses] were very keen to foster a fresh sense of nationalism, and the major publications adopted a policy of reconciliation that meant deliberately seeking copy from regions hitherto little known or courted for their literary output' (Taylor, pp. 18–19). Chopin was not averse to taking advantage of her obvious connection with this thriving literary market; at the same time, she did try to distance herself from the label of 'local colourist',[5] even as she continued, throughout her career, to write with sharpness, sensitivity and humour about Louisiana and Missouri, the places she knew best. Chopin managed to place her work both in newspapers and magazines with a regional readership (for example, the *St Louis Post–Dispatch*, the St Louis *Mirror* or *Spectator*, and the *New Orleans Times–Democrat*) and in prestigious periodicals with a national circulation, such as *Atlantic Monthly*, *Two Tales*, *Century* (formerly *Scribner's Monthly*), and the

5 See, for example, this statement from an untitled article published in the *St Louis Post–Dispatch* on 26 November 1899: 'I have been taken to spots supposed to be alive with local color. I have been introduced to excruciating characters with frank permission to use them as I liked, but never, in any single instance, has such material been of the slightest service' (reprinted as 'On Certain Bright, Brisk Days', in Koloski, p. 108).

extremely popular children's magazines *Youth's Companion* and *Harper's Young People*. Of all the magazines where she was keen to place her work, only the innovative Chicago-based *Chap Book* would never accept any of her stories. Beginning with the pairing of 'Désirée's Baby' and 'A Visit to Avoyelles' in its inaugural issue in January 1893, the newly-founded *Vogue* instead would go on to print a further seventeen of Chopin's pieces, often providing an outlet for material that other magazines might have found too controversial.

In 'On Certain Brisk, Bright Days', Chopin explained that '[s]tory writing – at least with me – is the spontaneous expression of impressions gathered goodness knows where' (Koloski, p. 107). Later on in the same piece, she continues to downplay the amount of artistry, and authorial control, involved in the act of composition by admitting blithely that in her experience '[t]here are stories that seem to write themselves, and others that positively refuse to be written – which no amount of coaxing can bring to anything' (Koloski, p. 107). While the composition dates that she kept in her logbook, and the testimony of those who knew her, confirm that Chopin could often finish a story in one day, and send it off to a prospective publisher the next,[6] she knew, of course, the frustration of rejections and of subsequent resubmissions to alternative outlets. Although the first drafts of her stories are often very close to their eventual published versions, she did revise her work, albeit – one might say – 'retrospectively', that is either when she was reviewing previously published tales for inclusion in one of her collections, or via handwritten editorial changes to magazine clippings of her own writing in the case of some of her uncollected work. In fact, her facetiousness in 'On Certain Brisk, Bright Days' – where at one point Chopin declares that she writes 'in the morning, when not too strongly drawn to struggle with the intricacies of pattern, and in the afternoon, if the temptation to try a new furniture polish on an old table leg is not too powerful to be denied' (Koloski, p. 107) – belies an obvious impatience with those who perceive, and patronise, women writers as somewhat glorified amateurs in a line of work best left to the

---

6 For example, Chopin wrote 'The Bênitous' Slave' on 7 January 1892; twenty-four hours later, she had also written 'A Turkey Hunt' and the short sketch 'Old Aunt Peggy', and sent off all three to *Harper's Young People*, who accepted the lot the following 28 January (see Toth, p. 206). Her son Felix recalled that she would 'go weeks and weeks without an idea, then suddenly grab her pencil and old lapboard . . . and in a couple of hours her story was complete and off to the publisher' (Seyersted's *Biography*, quoted in Ewell, p. 20).

male professionals when one is looking for serious and lofty literary achievements. That said, in spite of her popularity, Chopin did not and could not have depended solely on the proceeds from her writing in order to support herself and her family, and was lucky that she could draw on the revenues yielded by her properties for her livelihood. Nevertheless, as we have already hinted, she could be very canny in her understanding of the market, while never completely pandering to the literary orthodoxies, and the dictates of literary propriety, of her day, as the reception of *The Awakening* most prominently illustrates.

Of her American contemporaries, Chopin admired in particular three fellow women writers who are no longer as popular as they used to be: Sarah Orne Jewett, Ruth McEnery Stuart and Mary Wilkins Freeman; however, it was Guy de Maupassant, another realist author of the same period (accessible to Chopin in his original French), who provided the most influential role model for her. Of her literary acquaintance with Maupassant, whom she first came across in 1888, Chopin wrote as if of a revelation, or a singular meeting of minds which would inform her subsequent growth:

> I had been in the woods, in the fields, groping around; looking for something big, satisfying, convincing, and finding nothing but – myself; a something neither big nor satisfying but wholly convincing. It was at this period of my emerging from the vast solitude in which I had been making my own acquaintance that I stumbled upon Maupassant. I read his stories and marvelled at them. Here was life, not fiction . . . Here was a man who had escaped from tradition and authority . . . and who, in a direct and simple way, told us what he saw.
> [Koloski, p. 101]

Between 1894 and 1898, she translated eight of his stories – including one called 'Solitude' which may have inspired the working title of *The Awakening*. Maupassant's influence might be one of the reasons behind Chopin's departure from the comparatively buoyant mood, and the decidedly regional flavour, of *Bayou Folk* (1894) for the more sombre, mature offering in *A Night in Acadie* (1897) and of other, uncollected stories written in that period.

Koloski has called *Bayou Folk* 'a young person's book' (p. 14), pointing out how most of its stories either focus on or address that particular demographic group (nine of the twenty-three stories in the volume had previously appeared either in *Harper's Young People* or *Youth's Companion*). The publisher Houghton, Mifflin marketed the collection as comprising 'faithful, spirited representations of unfamiliar characters and customs', and reassured readers that '[t]he dialect of these *semi-aliens* is given, but not at such length as to be tedious; and it distinctly aids in imparting to the stories a genuine "local color" ' (quoted in Toth p. 223; my italics). Flagging up, in its title, one of the most typical geographical features of the Louisiana landscape – a 'bayou' is a slow-moving stream – the volume lives up to this promise, introducing its readers in all but four stories to the Cane River country so well known to Chopin. 'A No-Account Creole', 'In and Out of Old Natchitoches' and 'In Sabine' form an initial triptych about variously mismatched couples, and are further connected by the presence of the three Santien brothers; the search for a suitable partner and – one of Chopin's recurrent themes – the continuous negotiations and compromises that long-lasting partnerships demand return in two of the strongest tales, 'Madame Célestin's Divorce' and 'At the 'Cadian Ball'. Alongside the sense of hope of some of these stories, and the light-hearted cheerfulness (and ostensible simplicity) of humorous sketches like 'Old Aunt Peggy' and 'Boulôt and Boulotte', Chopin presents another side of life in the South: she is careful not to gloss over the painful, lasting legacy of the Civil War in the excellent 'Ma'ame Pelagie' (and, more whimsically, in 'The Return of Alcibiade' and 'A Wizard from Gettysburg') and the tragedy of racial prejudice in the memorable 'Désirée's Baby' and the equally distressing 'La Belle Zoraïde'.

The book was generally well received by the press, although – as Toth meticulously points out – 'charming' and other terms to similar effect were recurrent words in the positive reviews (pp. 225ff.). While not exactly damning by faint praise, these assessments sound – to this reader at least – somewhat belittling in their more or less explicit association of Chopin's writing with the cosy and the picturesque. Chopin complained in her diary that, of the 'more than a hundred press notices' of *Bayou Folk* she had received, only 'a very small number . . . show anything like a worthy critical faculty' (quoted in Toth, p. 228). The favourable reception of the volume – whose initial print-run of 1,250 copies sold out within the year, so that a further 500 copies were issued in 1895 – made Chopin eager to follow it up with a second collection. In reply to her enquiries, in 1897 Horace E. Scudder from Houghton, Mifflin encouraged Chopin to write 'a downright novel' in order to maximise 'her chance of success' (quoted in Toth, p. 296). Shortly afterwards, Chopin did begin to work on the novel that would become *The Awakening*; meanwhile she also placed her second collection with Way & Williams, who suggested that she should rename the opening story 'A Night in Acadie' (dropping the original, less evocative

'In the Vicinity of Marksville'), and make that the title of the entire
volume – its strong connotations of pastoral bliss heightened by
the near-homophony with Arcady (from the ancient Greek region of
'Arcadia', a byword for an idyllic, edenic view of rural life).

A Night in Acadie was not as widely nor as warmly reviewed as its
predecessor because, as past and contemporary critics have observed,
the stories in the new collection had a less traditional flavour than those
in Chopin's earlier selection. They displayed a greater tendency towards
lack of closure and a rejection of linear storylines in their privileging of
the intimate, the quotidian and the lyrical over the dramatic. According
to Barbara Ewell, 'Chopin's bayou world persists, but its romance and
charm seem diminished, its happy endings muted. In fact, there
are both fewer love stories and fewer tragic conclusions than before.
Melodrama, too, has faded, implying a greater moral ambivalence than
in *Bayou Folk*' (Ewell, p. 96). Whatever one may think of the overall
effect of each collection – of their respective coherence, of how their
individual tales balance or contrast with one another – and whether one
might prefer the energy of *Bayou Folk* or the more quiet confidence of
A Night in Acadie, the best stories in both volumes are masterpieces of
the genre. Of particular note in the second volume are two sophisticated
studies of female desire: 'Athénaïse' and 'A Respectable Woman'.
Linked by the presence of the bachelor journalist Gouvernail, who
will also feature in *The Awakening*, these two stories see their female
protagonists – two married women – embrace their own sensual nature
in ways that have a profound, and diametrically opposite, effect on their
rapport with their respective husbands. But we will return to the discussion of these and other stories about gender relations after a brief
overview of Chopin's treatment of race and racial prejudice.

Race and racial prejudice in Chopin's work

Admirers of her work are obliged to recognise that Chopin was a
product of her time: the representation of African Americans in her
fiction is not altogether unproblematic for the contemporary reader.
Having gone so far as to state that Chopin was 'politically conservative
and – to a modern sensitivity – deeply racist' (p. xiii), Helen Taylor calls
to task the critics who, 'inevitably uncomfortable with her racism', 'have
evaded its full implications' (Taylor, p. 155). One suspects that the
main reason behind this evasiveness might be the fact that Chopin is
usually much more interesting, and insightful, when she writes about
gender than when she writes about race. In contrast to Taylor, Toth
instead chooses to emphasise that 'Chopin's description of black

people – jarring to current sensibilities – would have been considered liberal in her day' (p. 269), while Ewell and Koloski both acknowledge the reliance on racial stereotypes in some stories, and single out the radical charge of some others.[7] In St Louis, the O'Flaherties had kept slaves (until the Civil War, when the slaves ran off) and, with her marriage to Oscar, Kate joined a family whose stake in the perpetuation of racial divides was even higher. Her father-in-law – a violent man, known to have been cruel to his wife – mistreated his slaves on the Red River plantation, the very same land that had previously belonged to Robert McAlpin (the alleged model for the brutal Simon Legree in *Uncle Tom's Cabin*), so that the reputation of the two men became somewhat intertwined. Oscar refused to follow suit when his father appointed him, still a young boy, as the overseer of the plantation; aged fourteen, he left the paternal home and went to live with some relatives. This does not mean that Oscar could boast spotless liberal credentials; on the contrary, he joined the Crescent White City League, a white supremacist group, which took control of New Orleans for three days following the Battle of Liberty Place on 14 September 1874. (One of the secessionist states, Louisiana remained occupied by federal troops throughout the period known as Reconstruction, from 1865 to 1877.) It is impossible to know to what extent (if any) Kate shared Oscar's political views; biographers and critics have looked in vain for evidence of her direct involvement with any reformist movement – including, we might add, those campaigning for female suffrage or women's rights in general. (In this, Chopin could not be more different from her near-contemporary Charlotte Perkins Gilman, the feminist charge of whose writing accompanied a life-long active political engagement.)

In her work, Chopin did not always rise above simplistic, condescending representations of black characters; this is true of 'The Bênitous' Slave', a sentimental sketch about Old Uncle Oswald: years after his emancipation, 'there was no getting the notion out of his head' (p. 180) that he no longer belongs to his beloved original owners, but that he is, in fact, a free man. 'For Marse Chouchoute' is marred by a similar sentimentality, significantly aggravated by the story's ending, in which we witness the unbounded selflessness of the 'very black, and slightly deformed' (p. 210) young Wash on behalf of the

7 See, for example: 'Some of her stories about blacks do little more than reflect Southern attitudes in the 1890s. But some – 'Nég Créol', 'Tante Cat'rinette', 'La Belle Zoraïde', 'Beyond the Bayou', 'Désirée's Baby', and a few others – do much more . . . They are a treasure for readers today' (Koloski, p. 47).

irresponsible title character. The jovial, humorous tone that underpins both stories enhances – instead of undercutting – their reliance on the stereotype of the loyal slave and the benevolent white master. Conversely, Chopin is successful in rescuing 'Old Aunt Peggy' from a similar fate: although based on virtually the same premise as the other two stories, this sketch is prevented from turning into a patronising caricature by a final injection of unexpected comedy, a tongue-in-cheek turn of the screw in which the narrator implicitly invites us to take sides with the redoubtable, life-affirming protagonist, and to celebrate her self-mythologising along with her resilience. 'Nég Créol' also complicates the stock characterisation of the unstintingly faithful ex-slave by making it obvious that reverence for one's former owners is inextricably tied in with the servant's sense of his or her own dignity; hardly a manifestation of irrational obsequiousness, Chicot's fierce pride in his association with the Boisduré household is an essential manifestation of his self-respect. On her part, the impoverished Mamzelle Aglaé Boisduré keeps her end of the bargain, her obstinate self-importance a necessary counterpart to Chicot's understated generosity. It is in light of the symbiotic nature of this relationship that we ought to read Chicot's apparent about-turn in his denial of Mamzelle Aglaé when she finally becomes just 'a woman who had died in St Philip Street' (p. 338). Elsewhere, in 'In and Out of Old Natchitoches', we encounter a white man suffering the disapproval of his peers – and of the woman he will come to love – because of (entirely justified) rumours that 'he was entirely too much at home with the free mulattoes' (p. 137).[8] It is true that the Giestin family – the free mulattoes in question – become collateral damage in the aftermath of the skirmish between Mr Laballiére and Mademoiselle St Denys Godolph. Whether the Giestins' disappearance in a self-imposed exile to 'l'Isle des Mulâtres' (p. 141) is a missed opportunity for Chopin, or a deliberate, provocative detail in her story – which, after all, exposes how contentious inter-racial relations were, even without the shadow of slavery – it is up to the reader to decide.

The stories where Chopin is most successful in offering a nuanced,

---

8 Chopin herself glosses this as: 'A term still applied in Louisiana to mulattoes who were never in slavery and whose families in most instances were themselves slave owners.' Louisiana was home to a 'significant number of *gens de couleur libre* – mulattoes who had owned land and slaves since the early nineteenth century, supported the Confederacy, but had been thoroughly displaced and disenfranchised since the war' (Taylor, p. 145).

sympathetic portrayal of the black characters and other victims of racial prejudice all involve mothers – biological or otherwise. In 'Beyond the Bayou', La Folle, whose irrational fear of crossing the river is a legacy of the trauma of war, overcomes her 'morbid and insane dread' (p. 161) in order to save the life of Chéri. That the love of a black woman should have fastened on to a white child – who owes to her the affectionate nickname by which he is known by everybody – is a reminder of what had used to be a painful necessity for many slaves, whose children were separated from their mothers at birth. The inabilities of slaves to choose even their own partner, let alone enjoy a loving family, is the subject of 'La Belle Zoraïde'; the eponymous protagonist feigns lack of interest in marriage because she detests '"the little mulatto, with his shining whiskers like a white man's"' (p. 243), whom her mistress has singled out as her prospective husband. In reality, Zoraïde is in love with another man; she ' "had seen le beau Mézor dance the Bamboula in Congo Square . . . proud-looking as a king. His body, bare to the waist, was like a column of ebony"' (p. 243). Prized for her light-skin, Zoraïde in vain asks for the right to marry the man of her choice and, in doing so, to embrace and celebrate her blackness and her African roots, much to the horror of her mistress. Chopin accentuates the poignancy of her protagonist's predicament in several ways: the 'logic' of racism is especially heart-wrenching and perverse when we consider that Madame Delarivière acts not merely out of selfishness, but also out of concern (!) for Zoraïde's happiness, even when she takes away the child conceived by the slave with Mézor. What is more, this harrowing tale is embedded within a narrative frame; it is the story that Manna Loulou decides to tell one night as part of her mistress's bedtime routine. We thus see another white woman incapable of realising the complete devastation visited upon Zoraïde; her sympathy only extends to the pathetic, less unambiguously 'innocent' figure of the abandoned child.

A similarly shocking, painful ending – better left undisclosed, so as not to spoil the reader's appreciation of Chopin's craft – characterises 'Désirée's Baby' (first published as 'The Father of Désirée's Baby' in *Vogue* in 1893 and later included in *Bayou Folk*), a story about the horrific consequences and the absurdity of the fear of miscegenation. Once again Chopin exposes the destructiveness of racial prejudice, and how it strikes at the heart of – and is capable of poisoning – what we hold most dear, our closest relationships. The chilling revelation upon which the story hinges is so carefully built up as to appear inevitable on a second reading, and yet is not altogether predictable in the first instance. This brief, perfectly calibrated narrative – with a startling emotional punch to boot – was one of a handful of stories for which Chopin continued to be known to the reading public in the first half of the twentieth century; as early as 1907, it had been recognised 'one of the most perfect short stories in English' (Koloski, p. 25). With its piercing combination of great craftsmanship and powerful subject matter, 'Désirée's Baby' is an achievement that, by itself, is surely sufficient to have secured any writer's posterity.

Gender and sexuality in Chopin's work

If her contemporaries may have been taken aback either by such themes in her writing as abusive relationships, adultery and venereal disease, or by the rawness and impropriety of the feelings of some of her characters, to a twenty-first-century reader it ought to be obvious that Chopin, while not shrinking away from being provocative, is anything but dogmatic in her portrayal of gender relations and their attendant power struggles. She was clearly suspicious, to say the least, of certain cultural orthodoxies and social conventions – marriage, and the idea that it might constitute the most desirable state for a woman, immediately spring to mind – but she was always nuanced in her critique, and very astute in distinguishing between, say, the inherent flaws of an institution, and the characters' own individual responsibility for the decisions they choose, or fail, to make. For example, as we have seen, *The Awakening* exposes the socio-economic contract that underwrites marriage as a patriarchal institution: Mr Pontellier is happy to provide for his wife, but demands in exchange that she should fulfil her many roles including – to use a modern terminology – the one of 'public relations officer' for the family and, by extension, for his business. While it would be a stretch to argue that Mr Pontellier is a sympathetic figure, Chopin is very careful to give us a clear view of his perspective, without absolving him of all blame. In fact, early on in the narrative, Chopin draws our attention to Edna's own complicity with the more mercenary side of marriage: when Léonce gives her half of his winnings from a game of cards, we are also told, matter-of-fact, that Edna 'liked money as well as most women, and accepted it with no little satisfaction' (p. 6). And when, a few days and a couple of paragraphs later, Edna receives from him a box full of expensive delicacies, she must concede – echoing her friends – that 'Mr Pontellier was the best husband in the world' (p. 7). Indeed Edna is – refreshingly or alarmingly, depending on one's romantic propensities – devoid of any self-delusions when it comes to her reasons for marrying Pontellier; hers is a pragmatic choice, a sensible match to put an end to a series of idealised, impossible infatuations: 'As the devoted wife of a man who worshipped her, [Edna] felt she would take her place with a certain dignity in the world of reality, closing the portals for ever behind her upon the realm of romance and dreams' (p. 17).

Edna's profound self-awareness extends to her motives, her feelings, and even her contradictions: 'At a very early period she had apprehended instinctively the dual life – that outward existence which conforms, the inward life which questions' (p. 13).[9] It is important to notice how earlier, on the previous page, Edna's development is configured in non-gender specific terms: 'Mrs Pontellier was beginning to realise her position in the universe *as a human being*, and to recognise her relations as an individual to the world within and about her' (p. 12, my italics). Her resolution, two-thirds into the novel, 'never again to belong to another than herself' (p. 78) and her declaration, closer to the ending, that she is ' "no longer one of Mr Pontellier's possessions to dispose of or not" ' (p. 106) are, of course, most immediately directed against the strictures of patriarchy, but Edna is conscious both of her previous compromises and of our common, fundamental solitude: 'There was no human being whom she wanted near her except Robert [the man she loves instead of her husband]; and she even realised that the day would come when he, too, and the thought of him would melt out of her existence, leaving her alone' (p. 112). Crucial details such as these render *The Awakening* a novel of much wider breadth, and more exquisite complexity, than a tragedy of doomed love and adulterous passion, or a mere critique of marriage – although this institution comes under much scrutiny both here and in several other stories, but always with great equanimity.

For example, in 'Wiser Than a God', whose title (from a Latin proverb) suggests the incompatibility of love and wisdom, Chopin leaves the door open for a conclusion where marriage might in the end flourish, though not at the expense of Paula's art. In other words, Chopin holds her characters accountable for the necessary realisations, and negotiations, that will lead them to find contentment in their lives, but she is not prescriptive in her accounts of where this elusive balance may lie. In 'A Point at Issue!', the very first story she ever published, Chopin portrays a couple bent on living up to their progressive view of

9 See, by contrast, Edna's good friend Adèle Ratignolle who, amazing as she is as a glowing 'mother-woman', remains comparatively monolithical and devoid of any great depth, with 'nothing subtle or hidden about her charms' (p. 7).

marriage as a genuine partnership of two individuals coming together in full 'readiness to meet the consequences of reciprocal liberty' (p. 424). Amid the scepticism and the disapproval of their peers, Eleanor and Charles Faraday decide to live apart for a while, each pursuing their own intellectual development, until a mutual, unfounded jealousy compels them to revert to a more conventional *ménage*. In poking gentle fun at Mr Faraday, Chopin's quick, ironic ending is a reminder that men and women are really not that different, equally prone to irrational behaviour, and the pang of uncontrollable feelings, as they are. Jealousy is also the engine of 'At the 'Cadian Ball', a story where the pairing of two sets of lovers according to their rightful social status is momentarily derailed. Furious at the prim reaction of his cousin Clarisse to his sanguine advances, the Creole Alcée Laballière makes his way to the 'Cadian ball, where he soon turns to the 'vixen' (p. 233) Calixta, of 'Cadian and Cuban ancestry, for consolation. The story is a treasure of observations about what is socially condoned, or tolerated, in people of different gender and social class with regard to where one may go and whom one may associate with without causing scandal. For this reason, when Clarisse crosses the invisible boundary which should keep her away from the 'Cadian ball, as – quite literally – a lower-class form of entertainment, the sheer scale of her transgression gives Alcée a reliable measure of her true feelings for him. On her part, humiliated by Alcée's public rejection, Calixta falls back on her more humble admirer Bobinôt, and holds him to his past proposal with a carelessness that does not bode too well for their marriage (and that Bobinôt either wilfully ignores or is incapable of noticing). The social conservativism of this conclusion is punctured in the story's sequel 'The Storm' (not included in the present volume for copyright reasons), a narrative so bold in its explicit allusion to sex that Chopin never tried to publish it.[10] In this story, Alcée and Calixta finally give in to their mutual attraction, in a fleeting, passionate encounter which is presented by Chopin with complete moral detachment. Short of interfering with the harmony of their respective marriages, the lovers' indiscretion makes them better disposed, and capable of renewed affection, towards their partners.

Chopin's lack of prudishness about sex is refreshing and is evident in

---

10   In fact, when Per Seyersted rediscovered it in the 1960s among Chopin's papers, and suggested that the *Missouri Historical Society Bulletin* should publish it, the journal declined his offer on account of the story's eroticism; 'The Storm' thus first came out in print in Seyersted's *The Complete Works of Kate Chopin* in 1969, seventy-one years after its composition.

the playful, symbolic import of the broom so often to be found in the hands of the title character of 'Madame Célestin's Divorce'. After much deliberation, Madame Célestin suddenly has second thoughts about filing for divorce, following her husband's unexpected return home to her one night. It is probably something more than his promise that '"he's going to turn ova a new leaf"' (p. 191) that prompts Madame to give Célestin another chance. A further story that flirts with the promise of sexual gratification is the aptly-titled 'A Respectable Woman', where it is intimated that Mrs Baroda's fierce dislike for her husband's great friend Gouvernail might disguise a less admissible truth. As in 'Madame Célestin's Divorce', here too the wife undergoes a sudden change of heart: '"This time I shall be very nice to him"' (p. 406), says she, gleefully assenting to her husband's desire that Gouvernail should come and stay with them again. This pronouncement, on which the story (not so) ambiguously closes, leaves everything open to the reader's imagination. A sensuous awakening of a different kind is what we find in 'Athénaïse', one of the longest stories ever written by Chopin. In a 1898 review of *A Night in Acadie*, 'Athénaïse' was simultaneously praised as an example of Chopin's 'delicacy and understanding of both man and woman', and criticised for being 'marred by one or two slight and unnecessary coarsenesses' (quoted in Toth, p. 299). The story's subject matter is very sensitive indeed, for the young Athénaïse voices her regrets about marriage in terms that combine an abstract abhorrence for the institution and a much more concrete, physical revulsion for her husband Cazeau, and for certain vulgar parts of the male body: '"It's jus' being married that I detes' an' despise . . . I can't stan' to live with a man; to have him always there; his coats an' pantaloons hanging in my room; his ugly bare feet – washing them in my tub befo' my very eyes, ugh!"' (p. 276). Uncompromising in her aversion, Athénaïse leaves the marital home along the Cane River, and relocates to a boarding house in New Orleans, where she makes the acquaintance of her fellow lodger Gouvernail, a free-thinking bachelor who soon starts waiting for the day when the woman might reciprocate his feelings for her ('So long as she did not want him, he had no right to her – no more than her husband had', p. 294). The story, however, ends with the surprising reconciliation between Athénaïse and Cazeau, when the protagonist realises that she is carrying his child.

The conventionality of such an ending – disappointing to some readers – is tempered by Chopin's focus on the physical intensity of Athénaïse's new feelings for her husband, summed up in this account of her epiphany: 'As she thought of him, the first purely sensuous tremor of her life swept over her . . . She was impatient to be with him. Her whole passionate nature was aroused as if by a miracle' (pp. 295–6). Athénaïse's maturation is both sexual and emotional, and it finds a significant counterpart in Cazeau's own independent journey of development. Unbeknownst to his wife, Cazeau relinquishes any proprietorial claims to her, acknowledging – as Gouvernail does all along – that relationships between the sexes ought to proceed from mutual affection, respect and desire. This brief summary, of course, does not do justice to the many nuances in the story, to Athénaïse's beautifully paced process of self-discovery, and to Chopin's masterful portrayal of the supporting characters. Even if the trajectories of their respective plots head in different directions, it is easy to see that Athénaïse anticipates Edna Pontellier, Chopin's most fully rounded and thought-provoking female character.

The Awakening

It is fair to say that Kate Chopin did not have an easy life as a novelist: in 1890 she self-published *At Fault* – one of the earliest American novels to focus on divorce, and to feature a female alcoholic – to benign but rather unenthusiastic reviews; a year later she suffered several rejections of *Young Dr Gosse*, which would never appear in print and which she eventually destroyed in manuscript. While her career as a short-story writer was taking off, Chopin would concede, 'The novel does not seem to me now be [*sic*] my natural form of expression' (Toth, p. 245). And yet in 1897 she began to work on *A Solitary Soul*, which was completed as *The Awakening* and accepted for publication in 1898 by Way & Williams, who also agreed to bring out Chopin's planned third short-story collection, *A Vocation and a Voice*. By the end of that same year, however, Way & Williams were taken over by Herbert S. Stone & Company, and it was with them that Chopin's second novel came out in print on 22 April 1899. In June 1899, within a couple of months of its publication, *The Awakening* had already garnered several reviews; they generally praised the author's writing skills, but – to a greater or lesser extent – they all lamented her choice of subject matter. In the *St Louis Post–Dispatch*, C. L. Deyo wrote, diplomatically: 'There may be many opinions touching other aspects of Mrs Chopin's novel *The Awakening*, but all must concede its flawless art . . . There is no uncertainty in the lines, so surely and firmly drawn. Complete mastery is apparent on every page' (reprinted in Culley, p. 164). When reiterating this point later in the piece, though, Deyo also alludes to the novel's challenging content: 'It is sad and mad and bad, but it is all consummate art. The theme is difficult, but it is handled with a cunning craft' (p. 165).

Other critics were much more explicit in deprecating the author's squandering of her talent on what they regarded as an unsuitable, morally dangerous story. For example, the *Chicago Times–Herald* remarked that ' . . . it was not necessary for a writer of so great refinement and poetic grace to enter the overworked field of sex fiction' (reprinted in Culley, p. 166). This feeling was echoed in *Literature*: 'One cannot refrain from regret that so beautiful a style and so much refinement of taste have been spent by Miss Chopin on an essentially vulgar story' (reprinted in Culley, p. 168), while *The Outlook* further elaborated on the unpalatable repercussions of Chopin's misguided choice of subject matter: '[Chopin] has put her cleverness to very bad use in writing *The Awakening* . . . The worst of such stories is that they will fall into the hands of youth, leading them to dwell on things that only matured persons can understand, and promoting unholy imaginations and unclean desires' (reprinted in Culley, p. 166–7). In July 1899 a young Willa Cather added her voice to this chorus of disapproval in a review for the *Pittsburgh Leader*: 'I shall not attempt to say why Miss Chopin has devoted so sensitive, well-governed a style to so trite and sordid a theme'; she also aptly referred to Mrs Pontellier as a 'Creole Bovary' (reprinted in Culley, p. 170), after the central character in Gustave Flaubert's 1856 masterpiece. Since then, several other critics have compared *The Awakening* to *Madame Bovary*; the connections between the two novels are pronounced, and too numerous to be discussed here – although it has to be said that their respective heroines are also profoundly different, and that a quick glance at the superficial parallels in the two plots – the adulterous relationships, the tragic ending – will inevitably overlook the very different course of Edna's and Emma's journeys, and the reasons behind their various transgressions.

In response to the critics' moral reservations about her novel, Chopin published an undaunted retort, ironically denying all responsibility for her protagonist's behaviour: 'I never dreamed of Mrs Pontellier making such a mess of things and working out her own damnation as she did. If I had had the slightest intimation of such a thing I would have excluded her from the company. But when I found out what she was up to, the play was half over and it was then too late' (reprinted in Culley, p. 178). In February 1900, Herbert S. Stone & Company decided not to go ahead with *A Vocation and a Voice*, Chopin's third collection of short stories. The publishing house was aiming to reduce its list of titles; it is hard to say whether the decision about Chopin's volume was at all influenced by the poor reception of *The Awakening* – just as we cannot know whether Chopin was aware of the wider context in which this cull was made. Chopin's literary production slowed down until her sudden death of a cerebral haemorrhage in 1904, but the claim that *The Awakening* brought about a radical reversal of fortune and ruined her reputation is a blatant exaggeration, fuelled by a long-standing, but now dispelled, myth that the book was banned from various libraries.[11] It is true that Daniel Rankin's 1932 study of Chopin, the first major work to try and rescue her from oblivion, continued to be critical about *The Awakening*, but this says more about Rankin and his moral outlook – he was a Catholic priest – than about the novel itself. It would be up to two non-American scholars to kick-start Chopin's revival. The Frenchman Cyrille Arnavon approached Chopin's work as an example of realist, rather than regionalist, writing, placing her alongside authors like Gustave Flaubert and Theodore Dreiser, instead of the local colourists she had been previously compared to. Arnavon also translated *The Awakening* into French in 1953, but it would be another decade before the novel was published again in the US – under Kenneth Eble's editorship in 1964. Five years later, the Norwegian Per Seyersted laid the foundations for all ensuing scholarship on Chopin with the publication of *Kate Chopin. A Critical Biography* and of his two-volume edition of *The Complete Works of Kate Chopin*, a compendium of ninety-six stories, two novels, twenty poems and a selection of essays. With these seminal texts, Seyersted single-handedly brought her to the attention of the academic community and, by extension, of the general public. Since then, *The Awakening* has become part of the canon of American literature, and of women's writing in particular, attracting the attention of major feminist critics such as, among others, Elaine Showalter and Sandra Gilbert. Showalter identifies *The Awakening* as nothing less than a 'revolutionary book . . . the first aesthetically successful novel to have been written by an American woman'; she argues that 'Chopin went boldly beyond the work of her precursors [in the US female literary tradition] in writing about women's longing for sexual and personal emancipation' (Showalter, p. 34).

In the summer resort of Grand Isle, Edna is surrounded by, and set up in opposition to, the 'mother-women' who 'idolised their children,

---

11 In fact, in 1900 Chopin was included in the first edition of *Who's Who in America* and, throughout her life, she continued to be honoured for her literary achievements.

worshipped their husbands, and esteemed it a holy privilege to efface themselves as individuals and grow wings as ministering angels' (p. 7). Adèle Ratignolle is one such character, but she is also obviously configured as somebody who has embraced this role with enthusiasm, and has found complete fulfilment in it – a fulfilment that extends to, and enhances, her sensuous nature. Adèle relishes her role as a mother-woman in ways that to Edna – whose Presbyterian background is decidedly uptight compared to freer, more open Creole mores – suggests an enjoyment of the sexual dimension of life. Compared to 'the bygone heroine of romance and the fair lady of our dreams' (p. 7), Adèle is possessed of a radiant magnificence and an innate dignity, but even these somewhat lofty, idealised traits throw her lush eroticism into relief. The effect of her friend's presence on Edna is described unambiguously as an early, important catalyst for the latter's awakening: 'The excessive physical charm of the Creole had first attracted her, for Edna had a sensuous susceptibility to beauty' (p. 13). In contrast, the other significant female influence on Edna is almost the polar opposite of Adèle: the bristly, unattractive, elderly Mademoiselle Reisz is introduced as a 'disagreeable little woman' (p. 24) with a difficult, 'imperious' (p. 24) character, and yet she is endowed with great talent and sensitivity as a pianist. Once more, Edna has a physical response to Mademoiselle Reisz and the intensity of her music: 'the very passions themselves were aroused within [Edna's] soul, swaying it, lashing it, as the waves daily beat upon her splendid body. She trembled, she was choking, and the tears blinded her' (p. 25). Mademoiselle Reisz provides an example of fierce independence, but also a reminder of the cost of such self-sufficiency – she lives alone, in rather dingy circumstances – and of the uncompromising pursuit of one's calling: when Edna, an amateur painter, playfully claims that she is becoming an artist, her friend is provoked by these '"pretensions"' and retorts that '"to succeed, the artist must possess the courageous soul"' (p. 62). Later in the narrative, having guessed Edna's feelings for Robert, Mademoiselle also seems to intuit the deeper turmoil and dissatisfaction in which this romance has found fertile soil. In this context, the early appeal to courage resonates as a call for sincerity, and authenticity, which Edna can be seen to respond to in her dealings with Robert, and in her actions upon her return to Grand Isle when Mademoiselle Reisz's words echo again in her mind.

In *The Awakening* the world is represented in richly physical terms, full as it is of experiences that stimulate the senses: from the fabric of the women's clothes to the frequent references to delicious food and vibrant colours, from Mademoiselle's stirring music to the 'everlasting voice of the sea' (p. 5) – an important refrain in the text, alongside the sea's 'seductive odour' (p. 11) and its 'sensuous' touch, 'enfolding the body in its soft, close embrace' (p. 12). Towards the end of the story, Edna presides over a luxurious feast at the dinner party she throws to celebrate both her twenty-ninth birthday and her move from the family home on Esplanade Street to a small, snug pigeon-house not too far away. Rife with decadent allusions and underpinned by a growing melancholy which gestures to the novel's conclusion, the dinner party highlights some of the contradictions in Edna's journey towards emancipation: at the moment of her triumph as 'the regal woman, the one who rules, who looks on, who stands alone' (p. 87), Edna is none the less conforming, in a way, to the traditional feminine role as the society hostess, letting her (absent) husband foot her extravagant bills. Edna's privileged class status – her gilded prison, as suggested by the image of the caged parrot that opens the narrative – is also emphasised by the silent presence of marginalised female figures like the mixed-race nursemaid who relieves her of the care of her children; as Michele Birnbaum observes, 'Edna's agency is measured against – indeed is contingent upon – the necessarily mute quadroon' (Birnbaum, p. 305).

Stylistically, *The Awakening* can be described as a proto-modernist novel, given its impressionistic prose, its blend of realism and symbolism, and the almost mythical scope of some of its recurrent images and key passages, such as the interlude on Chênière Caminada – a place already redolent with legends of pirates and buried treasure – where time slows down almost to a standstill. We thus enter the temporality outside the history of myths and fairy tales, with Edna a modern Sleeping Beauty ('"How many years have I slept?"' [p. 37]) attended to by Robert in the guise of a mundane Prince Charming, ready to feed her, rather than sweep her off her feet, when she spontaneously wakes up. In an influential reading of the novel, Sandra Gilbert perceptively sees in Edna a reincarnation of the goddess Aphrodite, to whom she is indeed compared in a recollection of her dinner party ('Venus rising from the foam could have presented no more entrancing a spectacle than Mrs Pontellier, blazing with beauty and diamonds at the head of the board' [p. 110]) and with whom she shares, among other things, an elemental relationship with the sea. Like Venus/Aphrodite, in the end Edna is not defined by her familial roles as wife, mother, daughter – nor is she identified as a lover, or a mistress. None of the men in her life – the pragmatic Léonce Pontellier, the sentimental Robert Lebrun or the roué Alcée Arobin – holds the key to Edna's quest; her children too – both young boys – appear as 'antagonists who had overcome her'

(p. 112) rather than essential figures in Edna's self-definition, although elsewhere she is shown to enjoy their company and to rejoice at her reunion with them after a long absence. Edna is not devoid of maternal feelings – it is 'with a wrench and a pang' (p. 93) that she leaves her children again – but she refuses to be subsumed within her status as a mother. Her paradoxes and conflicting impulses are precisely what makes her such a compelling character.

The novel's intricate pattern of correspondences, counterpoints and recurrent images is too detailed to be discussed in any greater length in this Introduction; the meaning of the text, especially in its conclusion, ricochets in different directions depending in part on how we choose to interpret the many suggestive symbols and ambiguities with which the entire narrative is interspersed. The very open-endedness of the text is another sign of its modernist sensitivity: does the conclusion signal Edna's definitive triumph or a relinquishing of the self? The fact that *The Awakening* hovers between these two (mutually exclusive?) interpretations is one of Chopin's greatest gifts to her readers, who find in the pages of this short novel countless opportunities for enjoyment and reflection.

Uncollected Stories

A Vocation and a Voice, Chopin's third collection of short stories, would have marked an unmistakable departure from the 'local colour' tradition: of the twenty-three pieces that she planned to include in the volume, only three (and scenes from the title story) are set in Louisiana, while several others take place in an undetermined locale, as if to signal unequivocally a shift in focus from regional to psychological concerns. The manuscript was returned by Herbert S. Stone to Chopin, unpublished, in February 1900, and only came out in print with Penguin in 1991, under the editorship of Emily Toth. About half of the stories in the collection had been written before the publication of *A Night in Acadie*, and seventeen had appeared – or would appear in the author's lifetime – in periodicals; of these, ten were published by *Vogue*, always receptive to Chopin's most experimental work. The rest would have to wait to be unearthed amongst Chopin's papers by Per Seyersted. For the present volume, I have selected a dozen uncollected stories from those that Chopin was able to see in print before her death. Of some of them – 'Wiser Than a God', 'The Maid of Saint Phillippe', 'A Point at Issue!' – I have already had occasion to speak; on the others I will now offer a quick word of introduction. 'Mrs. Mobry's Reason' (1893) and the short 'Dr Chevalier's Lie' (1893) are both remarkable for their treatment of themes suggestive of sexual impropriety, such as venereal disease and prostitution. Particularly affecting is the ending of the first story, which reveals the pun hitherto hidden in its title. Exploiting the connotations of Paris as a licentious city, 'Lilacs' (1896) also deals with a 'scandalous' protagonist in Adrienne Farival, a professional singer and woman of the world – inspired, according to Koloski, by the French actress Sarah Bernhardt (1844–1923) – who each year seeks refuge in the innocent environment of the convent where she had been brought up. The story is notable for its focus on the strong female friendship between Adrienne and Sister Agathe, which of course brings to mind Chopin's own lifelong connection with Kitty Gareshé. (Kate and Kitty had met as fellow-pupils at the Sacred Heart Academy in St Louis. Later in life, Kitty took the vows and joined the convent of the Sacred Heart as a nun.) A number of critics have pointed out the presence of lesbian motifs in this story, as well as in the much shorter 'Fedora' (1897) – and, indeed, in *The Awakening*. All three texts allow for a reading of 'sexuality and desire' as 'a continuum' unbound by heteronormative conventions, to paraphrase Karen Day (p. 116). With its insouciant, coquettish protagonist, 'The Kiss' (1894) is a light-hearted vignette which shows how women can unashamedly take advantage of marriage to improve their circumstances, while looking elsewhere for sexual gratification. 'Her Letters' (1895), instead, is a much more serious study of the repercussions of adultery, and offers an interesting counterpart to *The Awakening*, some of whose motifs and concerns it anticipates, if only in embryonic form.

'A Pair of Silk Stockings' and 'An Egyptian Cigarette', both published in *Vogue* in 1897, are strikingly modern, albeit in different ways. The former follows Mrs Sommers, who has known 'better days' (p. 476), on an impromptu spending spree in the aftermath of a modest windfall; her initial, sensible plans about how to use her money soon give way to the temptations of consumer culture, but Chopin does not seem to be critical of her protagonist, focusing instead on the intensely sensual pleasure, and renewed self-respect, that Mrs Sommers's one-off extra-vagances afford her: 'Her stockings and boots and well-fitting gloves had worked marvels in her bearing – had given her a feeling of assurance, a sense of belonging to the well-dressed multitudes' (p. 478). Most of us are likely to identify with the sense of empowerment that Mrs Sommers experiences, having revived her worn garments with a few choice accessories. The second story is even more decadent and self-indulgent in its account of a nameless woman's heady enjoyment of the Egyptian cigarette of the title, which leaves her shaken by the hallucinatory, Oriental vision it triggers. Also published in *Vogue*, in 1894, is 'The Story of an Hour', possibly the most famous of the uncollected tales. At a mere three pages, and with a truly unforgettable, mischievous ending, this piece might appear at first glance to be little more than a vignette pervaded with black humour. In fact, it is a perfect example of the wonderful economy of Chopin's best writing, of her wit, of her keen desire to probe the hidden, often unspeakable depths of human nature with great generosity of spirit. The story offers yet another critique of the institution of marriage, while holding both spouses responsible for the heavy demands they make on each other (see the telling remark on 'that blind persistence with which men and women believe they have a right to impose a private will upon a fellow-creature', p. 450). Indeed, 'The Story of an Hour' gives us the essence of Chopin in concentrated form. Rightly championed by feminist critics, in this and other stories, Chopin speaks to men and women alike as individuals acting within the constraints of social conventions, but none the less accountable for their personal choices. As we venture deeper into the twenty-first century, her work continues to be relevant, and very readable, with its surprising revelations, poignant moments of self-awareness and insightful observations about human nature.

BIBLIOGRAPHY

Birnbaum, Michele A., ' "Alien Hands": Kate Chopin and the Colonization of Race', *American Literature*, 66.2 (1994), pp. 301–23

Castillo, Susan, ' "Race" and Ethnicity in Kate Chopin's Fiction', in Janet Beer (ed.), *The Cambridge Companion to Kate Chopin*, Cambridge University Press, Cambridge, 2008, pp. 59–72

Culley, Margo (ed.), *The Awakening: An Authoritative Text, Biographical and Historical Contexts, Criticism*, 2nd edn, Norton, New York, 1994

Day, Karen, 'The "Elsewhere" of Female Sexuality and Desire in Kate Chopin's *A Vocation and a Voice*', in *Louisiana Literature: A Review of Literature and Humanities*, 11.1, 1994, pp. 108–17

Ewell, Barbara C., *Kate Chopin*, Ungar Publishing Company, New York, 1986

Gilbert, Susan, 'The Second Coming of Aphrodite: Kate Chopin's Fantasy of Desire', in *The Kenyon Review*, 5.3, 1983, pp. 42–66

Griffin Wolff, Cynthia, 'Un-Utterable Longing: The Discourse of Feminine Sexuality in *The Awakening*', in *Studies in American Fiction*, 24.1, 1996

Knights, Pamela (ed.), *The Awakening and Other Stories*, Oxford University Press, Oxford, 2000

Koloski, Bernard, *Kate Chopin. A Study of the Short Fiction*, Twayne Publishers, New York, 1996

Showalter, Elaine, 'Tradition and the Female Talent: *The Awakening* as a Solitary Book', in *New Essays on The Awakening*, Wendy Martin (ed.), Cambridge University Press, Cambridge, 1988, pp. 33–57

Taylor, Helen, *Gender, Race, and Region in the Writings of Grace King, Ruth McEnery Stuart, and Kate Chopin*, Louisiana State University Press, Baton Rouge and London, 1989

Toth, Emily, *Kate Chopin: A Life of the Author of The Awakening*, Random Century, London, 1990

Walker, Nancy A. (ed.), *The Awakening*, Bedford Books of St Martin's Press, Boston; Macmillan, Basingstoke, 1993

The Awakening

A GREEN AND YELLOW PARROT, which hung in a cage outside the door, kept repeating over and over: '*Allez vous-en! Allez vous-en! Sapristi!*[1] That's all right!'

He could speak a little Spanish, and also a language which nobody understood, unless it was the mockingbird that hung on the other side of the door, whistling his fluty notes out upon the breeze with maddening persistence.

Mr Pontellier, unable to read his newspaper with any degree of comfort, arose with an expression and an exclamation of disgust. He walked down the gallery and across the narrow 'bridges' which connected the Lebrun cottages one with the other. He had been seated before the door of the main house. The parrot and the mockingbird were the property of Madame Lebrun, and they had the right to make all the noise they wished. Mr Pontellier had the privilege of quitting their society when they ceased to be entertaining.

He stopped before the door of his own cottage, which was the fourth one from the main building and next to the last. Seating himself in a wicker rocker which was there, he once more applied himself to the task of reading the newspaper. The day was Sunday; the paper was a day old. The Sunday papers had not yet reached Grand Isle.[2] He was already acquainted with the market reports, and he glanced restlessly over the editorials and bits of news which he had not had time to read before quitting New Orleans the day before.

Mr Pontellier wore eye-glasses. He was a man of forty, of medium height and rather slender build; he stooped a little. His hair was brown and straight, parted on one side. His beard was neatly and closely trimmed.

Once in a while he withdrew his glance from the newspaper and looked about him. There was more noise than ever over at the house. The main building was called 'the house', to distinguish it from the cottages. The chattering and whistling birds were still at it. Two young girls, the Farival twins, were playing a duet from *Zampa*[3] upon the piano. Madame Lebrun[4] was bustling in and out, giving orders in a high key to a yard-boy whenever she got inside the house, and directions in an equally high voice to a dining-room servant whenever she got outside. She was a fresh, pretty woman, clad always in white with elbow sleeves. Her starched skirts crinkled as she came and went. Farther down, before one of the cottages, a lady in black was walking demurely up and down, telling her beads.[5] A good many persons of the *pension* had gone over to the Chênière Caminada[6] in Beaudelet's lugger[7] to hear mass. Some young people were out under the water-oaks playing croquet. Mr Pontellier's two children were there – sturdy little fellows of four and five. A quadroon[8] nurse followed them about with a faraway, meditative air.

Mr Pontellier finally lit a cigar and began to smoke, letting the paper drag idly from his hand. He fixed his gaze upon a white sunshade that was advancing at snail's pace from the beach. He could see it plainly between the gaunt trunks of the water-oaks and across the stretch of yellow camomile. The Gulf looked far away, melting hazily into the blue of the horizon. The sunshade continued to approach slowly. Beneath its pink-lined shelter were his wife, Mrs Pontellier, and young Robert Lebrun. When they reached the cottage, the two seated themselves with some appearance of fatigue upon the upper step of the porch, facing each other, each leaning against a supporting post.

'What folly! to bathe at such an hour in such heat!' exclaimed Mr Pontellier. He himself had taken a plunge at daylight. That was why the morning seemed long to him.

'You are burnt beyond recognition,' he added, looking at his wife as one looks at a valuable piece of personal property which has suffered some damage. She held up her hands, strong, shapely hands, and surveyed them critically, drawing up her lawn sleeves above the wrists. Looking at them reminded her of her rings, which she had given to her husband before leaving for the beach. She silently reached out to him, and he, understanding, took the rings from his vest pocket and dropped them into her open palm. She slipped them upon her fingers; then clasping her knees, she looked across at Robert and began to laugh. The rings sparkled upon her fingers. He sent back an answering smile.

'What is it?' asked Pontellier, looking lazily and amused from one to the other. It was some utter nonsense; some adventure out there in the water, and they both tried to relate it at once. It did not seem half so amusing when told. They realised this, and so did Mr Pontellier. He yawned and stretched himself. Then he got up, saying he had half a mind to go over to Klein's hotel and play a game of billiards.

'Come go along, Lebrun,' he proposed to Robert. But Robert admitted quite frankly that he preferred to stay where he was and talk to Mrs Pontellier.

'Well, send him about his business when he bores you, Edna,' instructed her husband as he prepared to leave.

'Here, take the umbrella,' she exclaimed, holding it out to him. He accepted the sunshade, and lifting it over his head descended the steps and walked away.

'Coming back to dinner?' his wife called after him. He halted a moment and shrugged his shoulders. He felt in his vest pocket; there was a ten-dollar bill there. He did not know: perhaps he would return for the early dinner and perhaps he would not. It all depended upon the company which he found over at Klein's and the size of 'the game'. He did not say this, but she understood it, and laughed, nodding goodbye to him.

Both children wanted to follow their father when they saw him starting out. He kissed them and promised to bring them back bonbons and peanuts.

2

Mrs Pontellier's eyes were quick and bright; they were a yellowish brown, about the colour of her hair. She had a way of turning them swiftly upon an object and holding them there as if lost in some inward maze of contemplation or thought.

Her eyebrows were a shade darker than her hair. They were thick and almost horizontal, emphasising the depth of her eyes. She was rather handsome than beautiful. Her face was captivating by reason of a certain frankness of expression and a contradictory subtle play of features. Her manner was engaging.

Robert rolled a cigarette. He smoked cigarettes because he could not afford cigars, he said. He had a cigar in his pocket which Mr Pontellier had presented him with, and he was saving it for his after-dinner smoke.

This seemed quite proper and natural on his part. In colouring he was not unlike his companion. A clean-shaved face made the re-semblance more pronounced than it would otherwise have been. There rested no shadow of care upon his open countenance. His eyes gathered in and reflected the light and languor of the summer day.

Mrs Pontellier reached over for a palm-leaf fan that lay on the porch and began to fan herself, while Robert sent between his lips light puffs from his cigarette. They chatted incessantly: about the things around them; about their amusing adventure out in the water – it had again assumed its entertaining aspect; about the wind, the trees, the people who had gone to the Chênière; about the children playing croquet under the oaks, and the Farival twins, who were now performing the overture to *The Poet and the Peasant*.[9]

Robert talked a good deal about himself. He was very young, and did not know any better. Mrs Pontellier talked a little about herself for the same reason. Each was interested in what the other said. Robert spoke of his intention to go to Mexico in the autumn, where fortune awaited him. He was always intending to go to Mexico, but some way never got there. Meanwhile he held on to his modest position in a mercantile house in New Orleans, where an equal familiarity with English, French and Spanish gave him no small value as a clerk and correspondent.

He was spending his summer vacation, as he always did, with his mother at Grand Isle. In former times, before Robert could remember, 'the house' had been a summer luxury of the Lebruns. Now, flanked by its dozen or more cottages, which were always filled with exclusive visitors from the *Quartier Français*,[10] it enabled Madame Lebrun to maintain the easy and comfortable existence which appeared to be her birthright.

Mrs Pontellier talked about her father's Mississippi plantation and her girlhood home in the old Kentucky blue-grass country. She was an American woman, with a small infusion of French which seemed to have been lost in dilution. She read a letter from her sister, who was away in the East, and who had engaged herself to be married. Robert was interested, and wanted to know what manner of girls the sisters were, what the father was like and how long the mother had been dead.

When Mrs Pontellier folded the letter it was time for her to dress for the early dinner.

'I see Léonce isn't coming back,' she said, with a glance in the direction whence her husband had disappeared. Robert supposed he was not, as there were a good many New Orleans club men over at Klein's.

When Mrs Pontellier left him to enter her room, the young man descended the steps and strolled over towards the croquet players, where, during the half-hour before dinner, he amused himself with the little Pontellier children, who were very fond of him.

3

It was eleven o'clock that night when Mr Pontellier returned from Klein's hotel. He was in an excellent humour, in high spirits, and very talkative. His entrance awoke his wife, who was in bed and fast asleep when he came in. He talked to her while he undressed, telling her anecdotes and bits of news and gossip that he had gathered during the day. From his trouser pockets he took a fistful of crumpled bank notes and a good deal of silver coin, which he piled on the bureau indiscriminately with keys, knife, handkerchief and whatever else happened to be in his pockets. She was overcome with sleep, and answered him with little half utterances.

He thought it very discouraging that his wife, who was the sole object of his existence, evinced so little interest in things which concerned him, and valued so little his conversation.

Mr Pontellier had forgotten the bonbons and peanuts for the boys. Notwithstanding he loved them very much, and went into the adjoining room where they slept to take a look at them and make sure that they were resting comfortably. The result of his investigation was far from satisfactory. He turned and shifted the youngsters about in bed. One of them began to kick and talk about a basket full of crabs.

Mr Pontellier returned to his wife with the information that Raoul had a high fever and needed looking after. Then he lit a cigar and went and sat near the open door to smoke it.

Mrs Pontellier was quite sure Raoul had no fever. He had gone to bed perfectly well, she said, and nothing had ailed him all day. Mr Pontellier was too well acquainted with fever symptoms to be mistaken. He assured her the child was consuming at that moment in the next room.

He reproached his wife with her inattention, her habitual neglect of the children. If it was not a mother's place to look after children, whose on earth was it? He himself had his hands full with his brokerage business. He could not be in two places at once; making a living for his family on the street, and staying at home to see that no harm befell them. He talked in a monotonous, insistent way.

Mrs Pontellier sprang out of bed and went into the next room. She soon came back and sat on the edge of the bed, leaning her head down on the pillow. She said nothing, and refused to answer her husband when he questioned her. When his cigar was smoked out he went to bed, and in half a minute he was fast asleep.

Mrs Pontellier was by that time thoroughly awake. She began to cry a little, and wiped her eyes on the sleeve of her *peignoir*. Blowing out the candle, which her husband had left burning, she slipped her bare feet into a pair of satin mules[11] at the foot of the bed and went out on the porch, where she sat down in the wicker chair and began to rock gently to and fro.

It was then past midnight. The cottages were all dark. A single faint light gleamed out from the hallway of the house. There was no sound abroad except the hooting of an old owl in the top of a water-oak, and the everlasting voice of the sea, that was not uplifted at that soft hour. It broke like a mournful lullaby upon the night.

The tears came so fast to Mrs Pontellier's eyes that the damp sleeve of her *peignoir* no longer served to dry them. She was holding the back of her chair with one hand; her loose sleeve had slipped almost to the shoulder of her uplifted arm. Turning, she thrust her face, steaming and wet, into the bend of her arm, and she went on crying there, not caring any longer to dry her face, her eyes, her arms. She could not have told why she was crying. Such experiences as the foregoing were not uncommon in her married life. They seemed never before to have weighed much against the abundance of her husband's kindness and a uniform devotion which had come to be tacit and self-understood.

An indescribable oppression, which seemed to generate in some unfamiliar part of her consciousness, filled her whole being with a vague anguish. It was like a shadow, like a mist passing across her soul's summer day. It was strange and unfamiliar; it was a mood. She did not sit there inwardly upbraiding her husband, lamenting at Fate, which had directed her footsteps to the path which they had taken. She was just having a good cry all to herself. The mosquitoes made merry over her, biting her firm, round arms and nipping at her bare insteps.

The little stinging, buzzing imps succeeded in dispelling a mood which might have held her there in the darkness half a night longer.

The following morning Mr Pontellier was up in good time to take the rockaway[12] which was to convey him to the steamer at the wharf. He was returning to the city to his business, and they would not see him again at the Island till the coming Saturday. He had regained his composure, which seemed to have been somewhat impaired the night before. He was eager to be gone, as he looked forward to a lively week in Carondelet Street.[13]

Mr Pontellier gave his wife half of the money which he had brought away from Klein's hotel the evening before. She liked money as well as most women, and accepted it with no little satisfaction.

'It will buy a handsome wedding present for Sister Janet!' she exclaimed, smoothing out the bills as she counted them one by one.

'Oh! we'll treat Sister Janet better than that, my dear,' he laughed, as he prepared to kiss her goodbye.

The boys were tumbling about, clinging to his legs, imploring that numerous things be brought back to them. Mr Pontellier was a great favourite, and ladies, men, children, even nurses, were always on hand to say goodbye to him. His wife stood smiling and waving, the boys shouting, as he disappeared in the old rockaway down the sandy road.

A few days later a box arrived for Mrs Pontellier from New Orleans. It was from her husband. It was filled with *friandises*, with luscious and toothsome bits – the finest of fruits, *pâtés*, a rare bottle or two, delicious syrups, and bonbons in abundance.

Mrs Pontellier was always very generous with the contents of such a box; she was quite used to receiving them when away from home. The *pâtés* and fruit were brought to the dining-room; the bonbons were passed around. And the ladies, selecting with dainty and discriminating fingers and a little greedily, all declared that Mr Pontellier was the best husband in the world. Mrs Pontellier was forced to admit that she knew of none better.

4

It would have been a difficult matter for Mr Pontellier to define to his own satisfaction or anyone else's wherein his wife failed in her duty towards their children. It was something which he felt rather than perceived, and he never voiced the feeling without subsequent regret and ample atonement.

If one of the little Pontellier boys took a tumble while at play, he was not apt to rush crying to his mother's arms for comfort; he would more likely pick himself up, wipe the water out of his eyes and the sand out of his mouth, and go on playing. Tots as they were, they pulled together and stood their ground in childish battles with doubled fists and uplifted voices, which usually prevailed against the other mother-tots. The quadroon nurse was looked upon as a huge encumbrance, only good to button up waists and panties and to brush and part hair; since it seemed to be a law of society that hair must be parted and brushed.

In short, Mrs Pontellier was not a mother-woman. The mother-women seemed to prevail that summer at Grand Isle. It was easy to know them, fluttering about with extended, protecting wings when any harm, real or imaginary, threatened their precious brood. They were women who idolised their children, worshipped their husbands, and esteemed it a holy privilege to efface themselves as individuals and grow wings as ministering angels.

Many of them were delicious in the role; one of them was the embodiment of every womanly grace and charm. If her husband did not adore her, he was a brute, deserving of death by slow torture. Her name was Adèle Ratignolle. There are no words to describe her save the old ones that have served so often to picture the bygone heroine of romance and the fair lady of our dreams. There was nothing subtle or hidden about her charms; her beauty was all there, flaming and apparent: the spun-gold hair that comb nor confining pin could restrain; the blue eyes that were like nothing but sapphires; two lips that pouted, that were so red one could only think of cherries or some other delicious crimson fruit in looking at them. She was growing a little stout, but it did not seem to detract an iota from the grace of every step, pose, gesture. One would not have wanted her white neck a mite less full or her beautiful arms more slender. Never were hands more exquisite than hers, and it was a joy to look at them when she threaded her needle or adjusted her gold thimble to her taper middle finger as she sewed away on the little night-drawers or fashioned a bodice or a bib.

Madame Ratignolle was very fond of Mrs Pontellier, and often she took her sewing and went over to sit with her in the afternoons. She was sitting there the afternoon of the day the box arrived from New Orleans. She had possession of the rocker, and she was busily engaged in sewing upon a diminutive pair of night-drawers.

She had brought the pattern of the drawers for Mrs Pontellier to cut out – a marvel of construction, fashioned to enclose a baby's body so effectually that only two small eyes might look out from the garment, like an Eskimo's. They were designed for winter wear, when treacherous drafts came down chimneys and insidious currents of deadly cold found their way through keyholes.

Mrs Pontellier's mind was quite at rest concerning the present material needs of her children, and she could not see the use of anticipating and making winter night garments the subject of her summer meditations. But she did not want to appear unamiable and uninterested, so she had brought forth newspapers, which she spread upon the floor of the gallery, and under Madame Ratignolle's directions she had cut a pattern of the impervious garment.

Robert was there, seated as he had been the Sunday before, and Mrs Pontellier also occupied her former position on the upper step, leaning listlessly against the post. Beside her was a box of bonbons, which she held out at intervals to Madame Ratignolle.

That lady seemed at a loss to make a selection, but finally settled upon a stick of nougat, wondering if it were not too rich; whether it could possibly hurt her. Madame Ratignolle had been married seven years. About every two years she had a baby. At that time she had three babies, and was beginning to think of a fourth one. She was always talking about her 'condition'. Her 'condition' was in no way apparent, and no one would have known a thing about it but for her persistence in making it the subject of conversation.

Robert started to reassure her, asserting that he had known a lady who had subsisted upon nougat during the entire – but seeing the colour mount into Mrs Pontellier's face he checked himself and changed the subject.

Mrs Pontellier, though she had married a Creole,[14] was not thoroughly at home in the society of Creoles; never before had she been thrown so intimately among them. There were only Creoles that summer at Lebrun's. They all knew each other, and felt like one large family, among whom existed the most amicable relations. A characteristic which distinguished them and which impressed Mrs Pontellier most forcibly was their entire absence of prudery. Their freedom of expression was at first incomprehensible to her, though she had no difficulty in reconciling it with a lofty chastity which in the Creole woman seems to be inborn and unmistakable.

Never would Edna Pontellier forget the shock with which she heard Madame Ratignolle relating to old Monsieur Farival the harrowing story of one of her *accouchements*,[15] withholding no intimate detail. She was growing accustomed to like shocks, but she could not keep the mounting colour back from her cheeks. Oftener than once her coming had interrupted the droll story with which Robert was entertaining some amused group of married women.

A book had gone the rounds of the *pension*. When it came her turn to read it, she did so with profound astonishment. She felt moved to read the book in secret and solitude, though none of the others had done so – to hide it from view at the sound of approaching footsteps. It was openly criticised and freely discussed at table. Mrs Pontellier gave over being astonished, and concluded that wonders would never cease.

5

They formed a congenial group sitting there that summer afternoon – Madame Ratignolle sewing away, often stopping to relate a story or incident with much expressive gesture of her perfect hands; Robert and Mrs Pontellier sitting idle, exchanging occasional words, glances or smiles which indicated a certain advanced stage of intimacy and *camaraderie*.

He had lived in her shadow during the past month. No one thought anything of it. Many had predicted that Robert would devote himself to Mrs Pontellier when he arrived. Since the age of fifteen, which was eleven years before, Robert each summer at Grand Isle had constituted himself the devoted attendant of some fair dame or damsel. Sometimes it was a young girl, again a widow; but as often as not it was some interesting married woman.

For two consecutive seasons he lived in the sunlight of Mademoiselle

Duvigné's[16] presence. But she died between summers; then Robert posed as an inconsolable, prostrating himself at the feet of Madame Ratignolle for whatever crumbs of sympathy and comfort she might be pleased to vouchsafe.

Mrs Pontellier liked to sit and gaze at her fair companion as she might look upon a faultless Madonna.

'Could anyone fathom the cruelty beneath that fair exterior?' murmured Robert. 'She knew that I adored her once, and she let me adore her. It was, "Robert, come; go; stand up; sit down; do this; do that; see if the baby sleeps; my thimble, please, that I left God knows where. Come and read Daudet[17] to me while I sew." '

'*Par exemple!* I never had to ask. You were always there under my feet, like a troublesome cat.'

'You mean like an adoring dog. And just as soon as Ratignolle appeared on the scene, then it *was* like a dog. "*Passez! Adieu! Allez vous-en!*"[18]

'Perhaps I feared to make Alphonse jealous,' she interjoined, with excessive naïvety. That made them all laugh. The right hand jealous of the left! The heart jealous of the soul! But for that matter, the Creole husband is never jealous; with him the gangrene passion is one which has become dwarfed by disuse.

Meanwhile Robert, addressing Mrs Pontellier, continued to tell of his one time hopeless passion for Madame Ratignolle; of sleepless nights, of consuming flames till the very sea sizzled when he took his daily plunge. While the lady at the needle kept up a little running, contemptuous comment: '*Blagueur – farceur – gros bête, va!*'[19]

He never assumed this serio-comic tone when alone with Mrs Pontellier. She never knew precisely what to make of it; at that moment it was impossible for her to guess how much of it was jest and what proportion was earnest. It was understood that he had often spoken words of love to Madame Ratignolle, without any thought of being taken seriously. Mrs Pontellier was glad he had not assumed a similar role towards herself. It would have been unacceptable and annoying.

Mrs Pontellier had brought her sketching materials, which she sometimes dabbled with in an unprofessional way. She liked the dabbling. She felt in it satisfaction of a kind which no other employment afforded her.

She had long wished to try herself on Madame Ratignolle. Never had that lady seemed a more tempting subject than at that moment, seated there like some sensuous Madonna, with the gleam of the fading day enriching her splendid colour.

Robert crossed over and seated himself upon the step below Mrs

Pontellier, that he might watch her work. She handled her brushes with a certain ease and freedom which came, not from long and close acquaintance with them, but from a natural aptitude. Robert followed her work with close attention, giving forth little ejaculatory expressions of appreciation in French, which he addressed to Madame Ratignolle.

'*Mais ce n'est pas mal! Elle s'y connait, elle a de la force, oui.*'[20]

During his oblivious attention he once quietly rested his head against Mrs Pontellier's arm. As gently she repulsed him. Once again he repeated the offence. She could not but believe it to be thoughtlessness on his part; yet that was no reason she should submit to it. She did not remonstrate, except again to repulse him quietly but firmly. He offered no apology.

The picture completed bore no resemblance to Madame Ratignolle. She was greatly disappointed to find that it did not look like her. But it was a fair enough piece of work, and in many respects satisfying.

Mrs Pontellier evidently did not think so. After surveying the sketch critically she drew a broad smudge of paint across its surface, and crumpled the paper between her hands.

The youngsters came tumbling up the steps, the quadroon following at the respectful distance which they required her to observe. Mrs Pontellier made them carry her paints and things into the house. She sought to detain them for a little talk and some pleasantry. But they were greatly in earnest. They had only come to investigate the contents of the bonbon box. They accepted without murmuring what she chose to give them, each holding out two chubby hands scoop-like, in the vain hope that they might be filled; and then away they went.

The sun was low in the west, and the breeze soft and languorous that came up from the south, charged with the seductive odour of the sea. Children, freshly befurbelowed,[21] were gathering for their games under the oaks. Their voices were high and penetrating.

Madame Ratignolle folded her sewing, placing thimble, scissors and thread all neatly together in the roll, which she pinned securely. She complained of faintness. Mrs Pontellier flew for the cologne water and a fan. She bathed Madame Ratignolle's face with cologne, while Robert plied the fan with unnecessary vigour.

The spell was soon over, and Mrs Pontellier could not help wondering if there were not a little imagination responsible for its origin, for the rose tint had never faded from her friend's face.

She stood watching the fair woman walk down the long line of galleries with the grace and majesty which queens are sometimes supposed to possess. Her little ones ran to meet her. Two of them clung about her white skirts, the third she took from its nurse and with a thousand endearments bore it along in her own fond, encircling arms. Though, as everybody well knew, the doctor had forbidden her to lift so much as a pin!

'Are you going bathing?' asked Robert of Mrs Pontellier. It was not so much a question as a reminder.

'Oh, no,' she answered, with a tone of indecision. 'I'm tired; I think not.' Her glance wandered from his face away towards the Gulf, whose sonorous murmur reached her like a loving but imperative entreaty.

'Oh, come!' he insisted. 'You mustn't miss your bathe. Come on. The water must be delicious; it will not hurt you. Come.'

He reached up for her big, rough straw hat that hung on a peg outside the door, and put it on her head. They descended the steps, and walked away together towards the beach. The sun was low in the west and the breeze was soft and warm.

6

Edna Pontellier could not have told why, wishing to go to the beach with Robert, she should in the first place have declined, and in the second place have followed in obedience to one of the two contradictory impulses which impelled her.

A certain light was beginning to dawn dimly within her – the light which, showing the way, forbids it.

At that early period it served but to bewilder her. It moved her to dreams, to thoughtfulness, to the shadowy anguish which had overcome her the midnight when she had abandoned herself to tears.

In short, Mrs Pontellier was beginning to realise her position in the universe as a human being, and to recognise her relations as an individual to the world within and about her. This may seem like a ponderous weight of wisdom to descend upon the soul of a young woman of twenty-eight – perhaps more wisdom than the Holy Ghost is usually pleased to vouchsafe to any woman.

But the beginning of things, of a world especially, is necessarily vague, tangled, chaotic and exceedingly disturbing. How few of us ever emerge from such beginning! How many souls perish in its tumult!

The voice of the sea is seductive; never ceasing, whispering, clamouring, murmuring, inviting the soul to wander for a spell in abysses of solitude; to lose itself in mazes of inward contemplation.

The voice of the sea speaks to the soul. The touch of the sea is sensuous, enfolding the body in its soft, close embrace.

7

Mrs Pontellier was not a woman given to confidences, a characteristic hitherto contrary to her nature. Even as a child she had lived her own small life all within herself. At a very early period she had apprehended instinctively the dual life – that outward existence which conforms, the inward life which questions.

That summer at Grand Isle she began to loosen a little the mantle of reserve that had always enveloped her. There may have been – there must have been – influences both subtle and apparent, working in their several ways to induce her to do this; but the most obvious was the influence of Adèle Ratignolle. The excessive physical charm of the Creole had first attracted her, for Edna had a sensuous susceptibility to beauty. Then the candour of the woman's whole existence, which everyone might read, and which formed so striking a contrast to her own habitual reserve – this might have furnished a link. Who can tell what metals the gods use in forging the subtle bond which we call sympathy, which we might as well call love.

The two women went away one morning to the beach together, arm in arm, under the huge white sunshade. Edna had prevailed upon Madame Ratignolle to leave the children behind, though she could not induce her to relinquish a diminutive roll of needlework, which Adèle begged to be allowed to slip into the depths of her pocket. In some unaccountable way they had escaped from Robert.

The walk to the beach was no inconsiderable one, consisting as it did of a long, sandy path, upon which a sporadic and tangled growth that bordered it on either side made frequent and unexpected inroads. There were acres of yellow camomile reaching out on either hand. Further away still, vegetable gardens abounded, with frequent small plantations of orange or lemon trees intervening. The dark green clusters glistened from afar in the sun.

The women were both of goodly height, Madame Ratignolle possessing the more feminine and matronly figure. The charm of Edna Pontellier's physique stole insensibly upon you. The lines of her body were long, clean and symmetrical; it was a body which occasionally fell into splendid poses; there was no suggestion of the trim, stereotyped fashion-plate about it. A casual and indiscriminating observer, in passing, might not cast a second glance upon the figure. But with more feeling and discernment he would have recognised the noble beauty of its modelling, and the graceful severity of poise and movement, which made Edna Pontellier different from the crowd.

She wore a cool muslin that morning – white, with a waving vertical line of brown running through it; also a white linen collar and the big straw hat which she had taken from the peg outside the door. The hat rested any way on her yellow-brown hair, that waved a little, was heavy, and clung close to her head.

Madame Ratignolle, more careful of her complexion, had twined a gauze veil about her head. She wore dogskin gloves, with gauntlets that protected her wrists. She was dressed in pure white, with a fluffiness of ruffles that became her. The draperies and fluttering things which she wore suited her rich, luxuriant beauty as a greater severity of line could not have done.

There were a number of bath-houses along the beach, of rough but solid construction, built with small, protecting galleries facing the water. Each house consisted of two compartments, and each family at Lebrun's possessed a compartment for itself, fitted out with all the essential paraphernalia for a bathe and whatever other conveniences the owners might desire. The two women had no intention of bathing; they had just strolled down to the beach for a walk and to be alone and near the water. The Pontellier and Ratignolle compartments adjoined one another under the same roof.

Mrs Pontellier had brought down her key through force of habit. Unlocking the door of her bathroom she went inside, and soon emerged bringing a rug, which she spread upon the floor of the gallery, and two huge hair pillows covered with crash,²² which she placed against the front of the building.

The two seated themselves there in the shade of the porch, side by side, with their backs against the pillows and their feet extended. Madame Ratignolle removed her veil, wiped her face with a rather delicate handkerchief, and fanned herself with the fan which she always carried suspended somewhere about her person by a long, narrow ribbon. Edna removed her collar and opened her dress at the throat. She took the fan from Madame Ratignolle and began to fan both herself and her companion. It was very warm, and for a while they did nothing but exchange remarks about the heat, the sun, the glare. But there was a breeze blowing, a choppy, stiff wind that whipped the water into froth. It fluttered the skirts of the two women and kept them for a while engaged in adjusting, readjusting, tucking in, securing hairpins and hatpins. A few persons were sporting some distance away in the water. The beach was very still of human sound at that hour. The lady in black was reading her morning devotions on the porch of a neighbouring bath-house. Two young lovers were exchanging their hearts' yearnings beneath the children's tent, which they had found unoccupied.

Edna Pontellier, casting her eyes about, had finally kept them at rest upon the sea. The day was clear and carried the gaze out as far as the blue sky went; there were a few white clouds suspended idly over the horizon. A lateen[23] sail was visible in the direction of Cat Island,[24] and others to the south seemed almost motionless in the far distance.

'Of whom – of what are you thinking?' asked Adèle of her companion, whose countenance she had been watching with a little amused attention, arrested by the absorbed expression which seemed to have seized and fixed every feature into a statuesque repose.

'Nothing,' returned Mrs Pontellier, with a start, adding at once: 'How stupid! But it seems to me it is the reply we make instinctively to such a question. Let me see,' she went on, throwing back her head and narrowing her fine eyes till they shone like two vivid points of light. 'Let me see. I was really not conscious of thinking of anything; but perhaps I can retrace my thoughts.'

'Oh! never mind!' laughed Madame Ratignolle. 'I am not quite so exacting. I will let you off this time. It is really too hot to think, especially to think about thinking.'

'But for the fun of it,' persisted Edna. 'First of all, the sight of the water stretching so far away, those motionless sails against the blue sky, made a delicious picture that I just wanted to sit and look at. The hot wind beating in my face made me think – without any connection that I can trace – of a summer day in Kentucky, of a meadow that seemed as big as the ocean to the very little girl walking through the grass, which was higher than her waist. She threw out her arms as if swimming when she walked, beating the tall grass as one strikes out in the water. Oh, I see the connection now!'

'Where were you going that day in Kentucky, walking through the grass?'

'I don't remember now. I was just walking diagonally across a big field. My sun-bonnet obstructed the view. I could see only the stretch of green before me, and I felt as if I must walk on for ever, without coming to the end of it. I don't remember whether I was frightened or pleased. I must have been entertained.

'Likely as not it was Sunday,' she laughed; 'and I was running away from prayers, from the Presbyterian service, read in a spirit of gloom by my father that chills me yet to think of.'

'And have you been running away from prayers ever since, *ma chère*?' asked Madame Ratignolle, amused.

'No! oh, no!' Edna hastened to say. 'I was a little unthinking child in those days, just following a misleading impulse without question. On the contrary, during one period of my life religion took a firm hold upon me; after I was twelve and until – until – why, I suppose until now, though, just driven along by habit, I never thought much about it. But do you know,' she broke off, turning her quick eyes upon Madame Ratignolle and leaning forward a little so as to bring her face quite close to that of her companion, 'sometimes I feel this summer as if I were walking through the green meadow again: idly, aimlessly, unthinking and unguided.'

Madame Ratignolle laid her hand over that of Mrs Pontellier, which was near her. Seeing that the hand was not withdrawn, she clasped it firmly and warmly. She even stroked it a little, fondly, with the other hand, murmuring in an undertone, '*Pauvre chérie.*'

The action was at first a little confusing to Edna, but she soon lent herself readily to the Creole's gentle caress. She was not accustomed to an outward and spoken expression of affection, either in herself or in others. She and her younger sister, Janet, had quarrelled a good deal through force of unfortunate habit. Her older sister, Margaret, was matronly and dignified, probably from having assumed matronly and housewifely responsibilities too early in life, their mother having died when they were quite young. Margaret was not effusive; she was practical. Edna had had an occasional girl friend, but whether accidentally or not, they seemed to have been all of one type – the self-contained. She never realised that the reserve of her own character had much, perhaps everything, to do with this. Her most intimate friend at school[25] had been one of rather exceptional intellectual gifts, who wrote fine-sounding essays, which Edna admired and strove to imitate; and with her she talked and glowed over the English classics, and sometimes held religious and political controversies.

Edna often wondered at one propensity which sometimes had inwardly disturbed her without causing any outward show or manifestation on her part. At a very early age – perhaps it was when she traversed the ocean of waving grass – she remembered that she had been passionately enamoured of a dignified and sad-eyed cavalry officer who visited her father in Kentucky. She could not leave his presence when he was there, nor remove her eyes from his face, which was something like Napoleon's,[26] with a lock of black hair falling across the forehead. But the cavalry officer melted imperceptibly out of her existence.

At another time her affections were deeply engaged by a young gentleman who visited a lady on a neighbouring plantation. It was after they went to Mississippi to live. The young man was engaged to be married to the young lady, and they sometimes called upon Margaret, driving over of afternoons in a buggy. Edna was a little miss, just merging into her teens; and the realisation that she herself was nothing, nothing, nothing to the engaged young man was a bitter affliction to her. But he, too, went the way of dreams.

She was a grown young woman when she was overtaken by what she supposed to be the climax of her fate. It was when the face and figure of a great tragedian began to haunt her imagination and stir her senses. The persistence of the infatuation lent it an aspect of genuineness. The hopelessness of it coloured it with the lofty tones of a great passion.

The picture of the tragedian stood enframed upon her desk. Anyone may possess the portrait of a tragedian without exciting suspicion or comment. (This was a sinister reflection which she cherished.) In the presence of others she expressed admiration for his exalted gifts, as she handed the photograph around and dwelt upon the fidelity of the likeness. When alone she sometimes picked it up and kissed the cold glass passionately.

Her marriage to Léonce Pontellier was purely an accident, in this respect resembling many other marriages which masquerade as the decrees of Fate. It was in the midst of her secret great passion that she met him. He fell in love, as men are in the habit of doing, and pressed his suit with an earnestness and an ardour which left nothing to be desired. He pleased her; his absolute devotion flattered her. She fancied there was a sympathy of thought and taste between them, in which fancy she was mistaken. Add to this the violent opposition of her father and her sister Margaret to her marriage with a Catholic, and we need seek no further for the motives which led her to accept Monsieur Pontellier for her husband.

The acme of bliss, which would have been a marriage with the tragedian, was not for her in this world. As the devoted wife of a man who worshipped her, she felt she would take her place with a certain dignity in the world of reality, closing the portals for ever behind her upon the realm of romance and dreams.

But it was not long before the tragedian had gone to join the cavalry officer and the engaged young man and a few others; and Edna found herself face to face with the realities. She grew fond of her husband, realising with some unaccountable satisfaction that no trace of passion or excessive and fictitious warmth coloured her affection, thereby threatening its dissolution.

She was fond of her children in an uneven, impulsive way. She would sometimes gather them passionately to her heart; she would sometimes forget them. The year before they had spent part of the summer with their grandmother Pontellier in Iberville.[27] Feeling secure regarding their happiness and welfare, she did not miss them except with an occasional intense longing. Their absence was a sort of relief, though she did not admit this, even to herself. It seemed to free her of a responsibility which she had blindly assumed and for which Fate had not fitted her.

Edna did not reveal so much as all this to Madame Ratignolle that summer day when they sat with faces turned to the sea. But a good part of it escaped her. She had put her head down on Madame Ratignolle's shoulder. She was flushed and felt intoxicated with the sound of her own voice and the unaccustomed taste of candour. It muddled her like wine, or like a first breath of freedom.

There was the sound of approaching voices. It was Robert, surrounded by a troop of children, searching for them. The two little Pontelliers were with him, and he carried Madame Ratignolle's little girl in his arms. There were other children beside, and two nursemaids followed, looking disagreeable and resigned.

The women at once rose and began to shake out their draperies and relax their muscles. Mrs Pontellier threw the cushions and rug into the bath-house. The children all scampered off to the awning, and they stood there in a line, gazing upon the intruding lovers, still exchanging their vows and sighs. The lovers got up, with only a silent protest, and walked slowly away somewhere else.

The children possessed themselves of the tent, and Mrs Pontellier went over to join them.

Madame Ratignolle begged Robert to accompany her to the house; she complained of cramp in her limbs and stiffness of the joints. She leaned draggingly upon his arm as they walked.

8

'Do me a favour, Robert,' spoke the pretty woman at his side, almost as soon as she and Robert had started on their slow, homeward way. She looked up in his face, leaning on his arm beneath the encircling shadow of the umbrella which he had lifted.

'Granted; as many as you like,' he returned, glancing down into her eyes that were full of thoughtfulness and some speculation.

'I only ask for one; let Mrs Pontellier alone.'

'*Tiens!*' he exclaimed, with a sudden, boyish laugh. '*Voilà que Madame Ratignolle est jalouse!*'[28]

'Nonsense! I'm in earnest; I mean what I say. Let Mrs Pontellier alone.'

'Why?' he asked; himself growing serious at his companion's solicitation.

'She is not one of us; she is not like us. She might make the unfortunate blunder of taking you seriously.'

His face flushed with annoyance, and taking off his soft hat he began to beat it impatiently against his leg as he walked. 'Why shouldn't she take me seriously?' he demanded sharply. 'Am I a comedian, a clown, a jack-in-the-box? Why shouldn't she? You Creoles! I have no patience with you! Am I always to be regarded as a feature of an amusing programme? I hope Mrs Pontellier does take me seriously. I hope she has discernment enough to find in me something besides the *blagueur*. If I thought there was any doubt – '

'Oh, enough, Robert!' she broke into his heated outburst. 'You are not thinking of what you are saying. You speak with about as little reflection as we might expect from one of those children down there playing in the sand. If your attentions to any married woman here were ever offered with any intention of being convincing, you would not be the gentleman we all know you to be, and you would be unfit to associate with the wives and daughters of the people who trust you.'

Madame Ratignolle had spoken what she believed to be the law and the gospel. The young man shrugged his shoulders impatiently.

'Oh! well! That isn't it,' slamming his hat down vehemently upon his head. 'You ought to feel that such things are not flattering to say to a fellow.'

'Should our whole intercourse consist of an exchange of compliments? *Ma foi!*'

'It isn't pleasant to have a woman tell you – ' he went on, unheedingly, but breaking off suddenly: 'Now if I were like Arobin[29] – you remember Alcée Arobin and that story of the consul's wife at Biloxi?'[30] And he related the story of Alcée Arobin and the consul's wife; and another about the tenor of the French Opera, who received letters which should never have been written; and still other stories, grave and gay, till Mrs Pontellier and her possible propensity for taking young men seriously was apparently forgotten.

Madame Ratignolle, when they had regained her cottage, went in to take the hour's rest which she considered helpful. Before leaving her, Robert begged her pardon for the impatience – he called it rudeness – with which he had received her well-meant caution.

'You made one mistake, Adèle,' he said, with a light smile; 'there is no earthly possibility of Mrs Pontellier ever taking me seriously. You should have warned me against taking myself seriously. Your advice might then have carried some weight and given me subject for some reflection. *Au revoir.* But you look tired,' he added, solicitously. 'Would you like a cup of *bouillon*? Shall I stir you a toddy? Let me mix you a toddy with a drop of Angostura.'[31]

She acceded to the suggestion of *bouillon*, which was grateful and acceptable. He went himself to the kitchen, which was a building apart from the cottages and lying to the rear of the house. And he himself brought her the golden-brown bouillon, in a dainty Sèvres cup, with a flaky cracker or two on the saucer.

She thrust a bare, white arm from the curtain which shielded her open door, and received the cup from his hands. She told him he was a *bon garçon*, and she meant it. Robert thanked her and turned away towards 'the house'.

The lovers were just entering the grounds of the *pension*. They were leaning towards each other as the water-oaks bent from the sea. There was not a particle of earth beneath their feet. Their heads might have been turned upside-down, so absolutely did they tread upon blue ether. The lady in black, creeping behind them, looked a trifle paler and more jaded than usual. There was no sign of Mrs Pontellier and the children. Robert scanned the distance for any such apparition. They would doubtless remain away till the dinner hour. The young man ascended to his mother's room. It was situated at the top of the house, made up of odd angles and a queer sloping ceiling. Two broad dormer windows looked out towards the Gulf, and as far across it as a man's eye might reach. The furnishings of the room were light, cool, and practical.

Madame Lebrun was busily engaged at the sewing-machine. A little black girl sat on the floor and with her hands worked the treadle of the machine. The Creole woman does not take any chances which may be avoided of imperilling her health.

Robert went over and seated himself on the broad sill of one of the dormer windows. He took a book from his pocket and began energetically to read it, judging by the precision and frequency with which he turned the leaves. The sewing-machine made a resounding clatter in the room; it was of a ponderous, bygone make. In the lulls, Robert and his mother exchanged bits of desultory conversation.

'Where is Mrs Pontellier?'

'Down at the beach with the children.'

'I promised to lend her the Goncourt.[32] Don't forget to take it down when you go; it's there on the bookshelf over the small table.' Clatter, clatter, bang! for the next five or eight minutes.

'Where is Victor going with the rockaway?'

'The rockaway? Victor?'

'Yes; down there in front. He seems to be getting ready to drive away somewhere.'

'Call him.' Clatter, clatter!

Robert uttered a shrill, piercing whistle which might have been heard back at the wharf.

'He won't look up.'

Madame Lebrun flew to the window. She called 'Victor!' She waved a handkerchief and called again. The young fellow below got into the vehicle and started the horse off at a gallop.

Madame Lebrun went back to the machine, crimson with annoyance. Victor was the younger son and brother – a *tête montée*,[33] with a temper which invited violence and a will which no axe could break.

'Whenever you say the word I'm ready to thrash any amount of reason into him that he's able to hold.'

'If your father had only lived!' Clatter, clatter, clatter, clatter, bang! It was a fixed belief with Madame Lebrun that the conduct of the universe and all things pertaining thereto would have been manifestly of a more intelligent and higher order had not Monsieur Lebrun been removed to other spheres during the early years of their married life.

'What do you hear from Montel?' Montel was a middle-aged gentleman whose vain ambition and desire for the past twenty years had been to fill the void which Monsieur Lebrun's taking off had left in the Lebrun household. Clatter, clatter, bang, clatter!

'I have a letter somewhere,' looking in the machine drawer and finding the letter in the bottom of the work-basket. 'He says to tell you he will be in Vera Cruz[34] the beginning of next month' – clatter, clatter! – 'and if you still have the intention of joining him . . . ' – bang! clatter, clatter, bang!

'Why didn't you tell me so before, mother? You know I wanted – ' Clatter, clatter, clatter!

'Do you see Mrs Pontellier starting back with the children? She will be in late to luncheon again. She never starts to get ready for luncheon till the last minute.' Clatter, clatter! 'Where are you going?'

'Where did you say the Goncourt was?'

9

Every light in the hall was ablaze; every lamp turned as high as it could be without smoking the chimney or threatening explosion. The lamps were fixed at intervals against the wall, encircling the whole room. Someone had gathered orange and lemon branches, and with these fashioned graceful festoons between. The dark green of the branches stood out and glistened against the white muslin curtains which draped the windows, and which puffed, floated and flapped at the capricious will of a stiff breeze that swept up from the Gulf.

It was Saturday night a few weeks after the intimate conversation held between Robert and Madame Ratignolle on their way from the beach. An unusual number of husbands, fathers and friends had come down to stay over Sunday; and they were being suitably entertained by their families, with the material help of Madame Lebrun. The dining tables had all been removed to one end of the hall, and the chairs ranged about in rows and in clusters. Each little family group had had its say and exchanged its domestic gossip earlier in the evening. There was now an apparent disposition to relax; to widen the circle of confidences and give a more general tone to the conversation.

Many of the children had been permitted to sit up beyond their usual bedtime. A small band of them were lying on their stomachs on the floor looking at the coloured sheets of the comic papers which Mr Pontellier had brought down.

The little Pontellier boys were permitting them to do so, and making their authority felt.

Music, dancing and a recitation or two were the entertainments furnished, or rather, offered. But there was nothing systematic about the programme, no appearance of prearrangement nor even premeditation.

At an early hour in the evening the Farival twins were prevailed upon to play the piano. They were girls of fourteen, always clad in the Virgin's colours, blue and white, having been dedicated to the Blessed Virgin at their baptism. They played a duet from *Zampa*, and at the earnest solicitation of everyone present followed it with the overture to *The Poet and the Peasant*.

'*Allez vous-en! Sapristi!*'[35] shrieked the parrot outside the door. He was the only being present who possessed sufficient candour to admit that he was not listening to these gracious performances for the first time that summer. Old Monsieur Farival, grandfather of the twins, grew indignant over the interruption, and insisted upon having the bird removed and consigned to regions of darkness. Victor Lebrun objected; and his decrees were as immutable as those of Fate. The parrot fortunately offered no further interruption to the entertainment, the whole venom of his nature apparently having been cherished up and hurled against the twins in that one impetuous outburst.

Later a young brother and sister gave recitations, which everyone present had heard many times at winter-evening entertainments in the city.

A little girl performed a skirt dance in the centre of the floor. The mother played her accompaniments and at the same time watched her daughter with greedy admiration and nervous apprehension. She need have had no apprehension. The child was mistress of the situation. She had been properly dressed for the occasion in black tulle and black silk tights. Her little neck and arms were bare, and her hair, artificially crimped, stood out like fluffy black plumes over her head. Her poses were full of grace, and her little black-shod toes twinkled as they shot out and upward with a rapidity and suddenness which were bewildering.

But there was no reason why everyone should not dance. Madame Ratignolle could not, so it was she who gaily consented to play for the others. She played very well, keeping excellent waltz time and infusing an expression into the strains which was indeed inspiring. She was keeping up her music on account of the children, she said; because she and her husband both considered it a means of brightening the home and making it attractive.

Almost everyone danced but the twins, who could not be induced to separate during the brief period when one or the other should be whirling around the room in the arms of a man. They might have danced together, but they did not think of it.

The children were sent to bed. Some went submissively; others with shrieks and protests as they were dragged away. They had been permitted to sit up till after the ice-cream which naturally marked the limit of human indulgence.

The ice-cream was passed around with cake – gold and silver cake arranged on platters in alternate slices; it had been made and frozen during the afternoon back of the kitchen by two black women, under the supervision of Victor. It was pronounced a great success – excellent if it had only contained a little less vanilla or a little more sugar, if it had been frozen a degree harder, and if the salt might have been kept out of portions of it. Victor was proud of his achievement and went about recommending it and urging everyone to partake of it to excess.

After Mrs Pontellier had danced twice with her husband, once with

Robert, and once with Monsieur Ratignolle, who was thin and tall and swayed like a reed in the wind when he danced, she went out on the gallery and seated herself on the low window-sill, where she commanded a view of all that went on in the hall and could look out towards the Gulf. There was a soft effulgence in the east. The moon was coming up, and its mystic shimmer was casting a million lights across the distant, restless water.

'Would you like to hear Mademoiselle Reisz play?' asked Robert, coming out on the porch where she was. Of course Edna would like to hear Mademoiselle Reisz play; but she feared it would be useless to entreat her.

'I'll ask her,' he said. 'I'll tell her that you want to hear her. She likes you. She will come.' He turned and hurried away to one of the far cottages, where Mademoiselle Reisz was shuffling away. She was dragging a chair in and out of her room, and at intervals objecting to the crying of a baby, which a nurse in the adjoining cottage was endeavouring to put to sleep. She was a disagreeable little woman, no longer young, who had quarrelled with almost everyone, owing to a temper which was self-assertive and a disposition to trample upon the rights of others. Robert prevailed upon her without any too great difficulty.

She entered the hall with him during a lull in the dance. She made an awkward, imperious little bow as she went in. She was a homely woman, with a small wizened face and body and eyes that glowed. She had absolutely no taste in dress, and wore a batch of rusty black lace with a bunch of artificial violets pinned to the side of her hair.

'Ask Mrs Pontellier what she would like to hear me play,' she requested of Robert. She sat perfectly still before the piano, not touching the keys, while Robert carried her message to Edna at the window. A general air of surprise and genuine satisfaction fell upon everyone as they saw the pianist enter. There was a settling down, and a prevailing air of expectancy everywhere. Edna was a trifle embarrassed at being thus singled out for the imperious little woman's favour. She would not dare to choose, and begged that Mademoiselle Reisz would please herself in her selections.

Edna was what she herself called very fond of music. Musical strains, well rendered, had a way of evoking pictures in her mind. She sometimes liked to sit in the room of mornings when Madame Ratignolle played or practised. One piece which that lady played Edna had entitled 'Solitude'.[36] It was a short, plaintive, minor strain. The name of the piece was something else, but she called it 'Solitude'. When she heard it there came before her imagination the figure of a man standing beside a desolate rock on the seashore. He was naked. His attitude was one of hopeless resignation as he looked towards a distant bird winging its flight away from him. Another piece called to her mind a dainty young woman clad in an Empire gown, taking mincing dancing steps as she came down a long avenue between tall hedges. Again, another reminded her of children at play, and still another of nothing on earth but a demure lady stroking a cat.

The very first chords which Mademoiselle Reisz struck upon the piano sent a keen tremor down Mrs Pontellier's spinal column. It was not the first time she had heard an artist at the piano. Perhaps it was the first time she was ready, perhaps the first time her being was tempered to take an impress of the abiding truth.

She waited for the material pictures which she thought would gather and blaze before her imagination. She waited in vain. She saw no pictures of solitude, of hope, of longing or of despair. But the very passions themselves were aroused within her soul, swaying it, lashing it, as the waves daily beat upon her splendid body. She trembled, she was choking, and the tears blinded her.

Mademoiselle had finished. She arose, and bowing her stiff, lofty bow, she went away, stopping for neither thanks nor applause. As she passed along the gallery she patted Edna upon the shoulder.

'Well, how did you like my music?' she asked. The young woman was unable to answer; she pressed the hand of the pianist convulsively. Mademoiselle Reisz perceived her agitation and even her tears.

She patted her again upon the shoulder as she said: 'You are the only one worth playing for. Those others? Bah!' and she went shuffling and sidling on down the gallery towards her room.

But she was mistaken about 'those others'. Her playing had aroused a fever of enthusiasm. 'What passion!' 'What an artist!' 'I have always said no one could play Chopin[37] like Mademoiselle Reisz!' 'That last prelude! Bon Dieu! It shakes a man!'

It was growing late, and there was a general disposition to disband. But someone, perhaps it was Robert, thought of a bathe at that mystic hour and under that mystic moon.

10

At all events Robert proposed it, and there was not a dissenting voice. There was not one but was ready to follow when he led the way. He did not lead the way, however, he directed the way; and he himself loitered behind with the lovers, who had betrayed a disposition to linger and hold themselves apart. He walked between them, whether with malicious or mischievous intent was not wholly clear, even to himself.

The Pontelliers and Ratignolles walked ahead; the women leaning upon the arms of their husbands. Edna could hear Robert's voice behind them, and could sometimes hear what he said. She wondered why he did not join them. It was unlike him not to. Of late he had sometimes held away from her for an entire day, redoubling his devotion upon the next and the next, as though to make up for hours that had been lost. She missed him the days when some pretext served to take him away from her, just as one misses the sun on a cloudy day without having thought much about the sun when it was shining.

The people walked in little groups towards the beach. They talked and laughed; some of them sang. There was a band playing down at Klein's hotel, and the strains reached them faintly, tempered by the distance. There were strange, rare odours abroad – a tangle of the sea smell and of weeds and damp, new-ploughed earth, mingled with the heavy perfume of a field of white blossoms somewhere near. But the night sat lightly upon the sea and the land. There was no weight of darkness; there were no shadows. The white light of the moon had fallen upon the world like the mystery and the softness of sleep.

Most of them walked into the water as though into a native element. The sea was quiet now, and swelled lazily in broad billows that melted into one another and did not break except upon the beach in little foamy crests that coiled back like slow, white serpents.

Edna had attempted all summer to learn to swim. She had received instructions from both the men and women; in some instances from the children. Robert had pursued a system of lessons almost daily; and he was nearly at the point of discouragement in realising the futility of his efforts. A certain ungovernable dread hung about her when in the water, unless there was a hand near by that might reach out and reassure her.

But that night she was like the little tottering, stumbling, clutching child, who of a sudden realises its powers, and walks for the first time alone, boldly and with over-confidence. She could have shouted for joy. She did shout for joy, as with a sweeping stroke or two she lifted her body to the surface of the water.

A feeling of exultation overtook her, as if some power of significant import had been given her to control the working of her body and her soul. She grew daring and reckless, overestimating her strength. She wanted to swim far out, where no woman had swum before.

Her unlooked-for achievement was the subject of wonder, applause and admiration. Each one congratulated himself that his special teachings had accomplished this desired end.

'How easy it is!' she thought. 'It is nothing,' she said aloud; 'why did I not discover before that it was nothing. Think of the time I have lost splashing about like a baby!' She would not join the groups in their sports and bouts, but intoxicated with her newly conquered power, she swam out alone.

She turned her face seaward to gather in an impression of space and solitude, which the vast expanse of water, meeting and melting with the moonlit sky, conveyed to her excited fancy. As she swam, she seemed to be reaching out for the unlimited in which to lose herself.

Once she turned and looked towards the shore, towards the people she had left there. She had not gone any great distance – that is, what would have been a great distance for an experienced swimmer. But to her unaccustomed vision the stretch of water behind her assumed the aspect of a barrier which her unaided strength would never be able to overcome.

A quick vision of death smote her soul, and for a second of time appalled and enfeebled her senses. But by an effort she rallied her staggering faculties and managed to regain the land.

She made no mention of her encounter with death and her flash of terror, except to say to her husband, 'I thought I should have perished out there alone.'

'You were not so very far, my dear; I was watching you,' he told her.

Edna went at once to the bath-house, and she had put on her dry clothes and was ready to return home before the others had left the water. She started to walk away alone. They all called to her and shouted to her. She waved a dissenting hand, and went on, paying no further heed to their renewed cries which sought to detain her.

'Sometimes I am tempted to think that Mrs Pontellier is capricious,' said Madame Lebrun, who was amusing herself immensely and feared that Edna's abrupt departure might put an end to the pleasure.

'I know she is,' assented Mr Pontellier; 'sometimes, not often.'

Edna had not traversed a quarter of the distance on her way home before she was overtaken by Robert.

'Did you think I was afraid?' she asked him, without a shade of annoyance.

'No; I knew you weren't afraid.'

'Then why did you come? Why didn't you stay out there with the others?'

'I never thought of it.'

'Thought of what?'

'Of anything. What difference does it make?'

'I'm very tired,' she uttered, complainingly.

'I know you are.'

'You don't know anything about it. Why should you know? I never was so exhausted in my life. But it isn't unpleasant. A thousand emotions have swept through me tonight. I don't comprehend half of them. Don't mind what I'm saying; I am just thinking aloud. I wonder if I shall ever be stirred again as Mademoiselle Reisz's playing moved me tonight. I wonder if any night on earth will ever again be like this one. It is like a night in a dream. The people about me are like some uncanny, half-human beings. There must be spirits abroad tonight.'

'There are,' whispered Robert. 'Didn't you know this was the twenty-eighth of August?'

'The twenty-eighth of August?'

'Yes. On the twenty-eighth of August, at the hour of midnight, and if the moon is shining – the moon must be shining – a spirit that has haunted these shores for ages rises up from the Gulf. With its own penetrating vision the spirit seeks some one mortal worthy to hold him company, worthy of being exalted for a few hours into realms of the semi-celestials. His search has always hitherto been fruitless, and he has sunk back, disheartened, into the sea. But tonight he found Mrs Pontellier. Perhaps he will never wholly release her from the spell. Perhaps she will never again suffer a poor, unworthy earthling to walk in the shadow of her divine presence.'

'Don't banter me,' she said, wounded at what appeared to be his flippancy. He did not mind the entreaty, but the tone with its delicate note of pathos was like a reproach. He could not explain; he could not tell her that he had penetrated her mood and understood. He said nothing except to offer her his arm, for, by her own admission, she was exhausted. She had been walking alone with her arms hanging limp, letting her white skirts trail along the dewy path. She took his arm, but she did not lean upon it. She let her hand lie listlessly, as though her thoughts were elsewhere – somewhere in advance of her body, and she was striving to overtake them.

Robert assisted her into the hammock which swung from the post before her door out to the trunk of a tree.

'Will you stay out here and wait for Mr Pontellier?' he asked.

'I'll stay out here. Good-night.'

'Shall I get you a pillow?'

'There's one here,' she said, feeling about, for they were in the shadow.

'It must be soiled; the children have been tumbling it about.'

'No matter.' And having discovered the pillow, she adjusted it beneath her head. She extended herself in the hammock with a deep breath of relief. She was not a supercilious or an over-dainty woman. She was not much given to reclining in the hammock, and when she did so it was with no catlike suggestion of voluptuous ease, but with a beneficent repose which seemed to invade her whole body.

'Shall I stay with you till Mr Pontellier comes?' asked Robert, seating himself on the outer edge of one of the steps and taking hold of the hammock rope which was fastened to the post.

'If you wish. Don't swing the hammock. Will you get my white shawl which I left on the window-sill over at the house?'

'Are you chilly?'

'No; but I shall be presently.'

'Presently?' he laughed. 'Do you know what time it is? How long are you going to stay out here?'

'I don't know. Will you get the shawl?'

'Of course I will,' he said, rising. He went over to the house, walking along the grass. She watched his figure pass in and out of the strips of moonlight. It was past midnight. It was very quiet.

When he returned with the shawl she took it and kept it in her hand. She did not put it around her.

'Did you say I should stay till Mr Pontellier came back?'

'I said you might if you wished to.'

He seated himself again and rolled a cigarette, which he smoked in silence. Neither did Mrs Pontellier speak. No multitude of words could have been more significant than those moments of silence, or more pregnant with the first-felt throbbings of desire.

When the voices of the bathers were heard approaching, Robert said good-night. She did not answer him. He thought she was asleep. Again she watched his figure pass in and out of the strips of moonlight as he walked away.

11

'What are you doing out here, Edna? I thought I should find you in bed,' said her husband, when he discovered her lying there. He had walked up with Madame Lebrun and left her at the house. His wife did not reply.

'Are you asleep?' he asked, bending down close to look at her.

'No,' Her eyes gleamed bright and intense, with no sleepy shadows, as they looked into his.

'Do you know it is past one o'clock? Come on,' and he mounted the steps and went into their room.

'Edna!' called Mr Pontellier from within, after a few moments had gone by.

'Don't wait for me,' she answered. He thrust his head through the door.

'You will take cold out there,' he said, irritably. 'What folly is this? Why don't you come in?'

'It isn't cold; I have my shawl.'

'The mosquitoes will devour you.'

'There are no mosquitoes.'

She heard him moving about the room; every sound indicating impatience and irritation. Another time she would have gone in at his request. She would, through habit, have yielded to his desire; not with any sense of submission or obedience to his compelling wishes, but unthinkingly, as we walk, move, sit, stand, go through the daily treadmill of the life which has been portioned out to us.

'Edna, dear, are you not coming in soon?' he asked again, this time fondly, with a note of entreaty.

'No; I am going to stay out here.'

'This is more than folly,' he blurted out. 'I can't permit you to stay out there all night. You must come into the house instantly.'

With a writhing motion she settled herself more securely in the hammock. She perceived that her will had blazed up stubborn and resistant. She could not at that moment have done other than denied and resisted. She wondered if her husband had ever spoken to her like that before, and if she had submitted to his command. Of course she had; she remembered that she had. But she could not realise why or how she should have yielded, feeling as she then did.

'Léonce, go to bed,' she said. 'I mean to stay out here. I don't wish to go in, and I don't intend to. Don't speak to me like that again; I shall not answer you.'

Mr Pontellier had prepared for bed, but he slipped on an extra garment. He opened a bottle of wine, of which he kept a small and select supply in a buffet of his own. He drank a glass of the wine and went out on the gallery and offered a glass to his wife. She did not wish any. He drew up the rocker, hoisted his slippered feet on the rail, and proceeded to smoke a cigar. He smoked two cigars; then he went inside and drank another glass of wine. Mrs Pontellier again declined to accept a glass when it was offered to her. Mr Pontellier once more seated himself with elevated feet, and after a reasonable interval of time smoked some more cigars.

Edna began to feel like one who awakens gradually out of a dream, a delicious, grotesque, impossible dream, to feel again the realities pressing into her soul. The physical need for sleep began to overtake her; the exuberance which had sustained and exalted her spirit left her helpless and yielding to the conditions which crowded her in.

The stillest hour of the night had come, the hour before dawn, when the world seems to hold its breath. The moon hung low, and had turned from silver to copper in the sleeping sky. The old owl no longer hooted, and the water-oaks had ceased to moan as they bent their heads.

Edna arose, cramped from lying so long and still in the hammock. She tottered up the steps, clutching feebly at the post before passing into the house.

'Are you coming in, Léonce?' she asked, turning her face towards her husband.

'Yes, dear,' he answered, with a glance following a misty puff of smoke. 'Just as soon as I have finished my cigar.'

12

She slept but a few hours. They were troubled and feverish hours, disturbed with dreams that were intangible, that eluded her, leaving only an impression upon her half-awakened senses of something un-attainable. She was up and dressed in the cool of the early morning. The air was invigorating and steadied somewhat her faculties. However, she was not seeking refreshment or help from any source, either external or from within. She was blindly following whatever impulse moved her, as if she had placed herself in alien hands for direction, and freed her soul of responsibility.

Most of the people at that early hour were still in bed and asleep. A few, who intended to go over to the Chênière for mass, were moving about. The lovers, who had laid their plans the night before, were already strolling towards the wharf. The lady in black, with her Sunday prayer-book, velvet and gold-clasped, and her Sunday silver beads, was following them at no great distance. Old Monsieur Farival was up, and was more than half inclined to do anything that suggested itself. He put on his big straw hat, and taking his umbrella from the stand in the hall, followed the lady in black, never overtaking her.

The little negro girl who worked Madame Lebrun's sewing-machine was sweeping the galleries with long, absent-minded strokes of the broom. Edna sent her up into the house to awaken Robert.

'Tell him I am going to the Chênière. The boat is ready; tell him to hurry.'

He had soon joined her. She had never sent for him before. She had never asked for him. She had never seemed to want him before. She did not appear conscious that she had done anything unusual in commanding his presence. He was apparently equally unconscious of anything extraordinary in the situation. But his face was suffused with a quiet glow when he met her.

They went together back to the kitchen to drink coffee. There was no time to wait for any nicety of service. They stood outside the window and the cook passed them their coffee and a roll, which they drank and ate from the window-sill. Edna said it tasted good. She had not thought of coffee nor of anything. He told her he had often noticed that she lacked forethought.

'Wasn't it enough to think of going to the Chênière and waking you up?' she laughed. 'Do I have to think of everything? – as Léonce says when he's in a bad humour. I don't blame him; he'd never be in a bad humour if it weren't for me.'

They took a short cut across the sands. At a distance they could see the curious procession moving towards the wharf – the lovers, shoulder to shoulder, creeping; the lady in black, gaining steadily upon them; old Monsieur Farival, losing ground inch by inch, and a young barefooted Spanish girl, with a red kerchief on her head and a basket on her arm, bringing up the rear.

Robert knew the girl, and he talked to her a little in the boat. No one present understood what they said. Her name was Mariequita. She had a round, sly, piquant face and pretty black eyes. Her hands were small, and she kept them folded over the handle of her basket. Her feet were broad and coarse. She did not strive to hide them. Edna looked at her feet, and noticed the sand and slime between her brown toes.

Beaudelet grumbled because Mariequita was there, taking up so much room. In reality he was annoyed at having old Monsieur Farival, who considered himself the better sailor of the two. But he would not quarrel with so old a man as Monsieur Farival, so he quarrelled with Mariequita. The girl was deprecatory at one moment, appealing to Robert. She was saucy the next, moving her head up and down, making 'eyes' at Robert and making 'mouths' at Beaudelet.

The lovers were all alone. They saw nothing, they heard nothing. The lady in black was counting her beads for the third time. Old Monsieur Farival talked incessantly of what he knew about handling a boat, and of what Beaudelet did not know on the same subject.

Edna liked it all. She looked Mariequita up and down, from her ugly brown toes to her pretty black eyes, and back again.

'Why does she look at me like that?' enquired the girl of Robert.

'Maybe she thinks you are pretty. Shall I ask her?'

'No. Is she your sweetheart?'

'She's a married lady, and has two children.'

'Oh! well! Francisco ran away with Sylvano's wife, who had four children. They took all his money and one of the children and stole his boat.'

'Shut up!'

'Does she understand?'

'Oh, hush!'

'Are those two married over there – leaning on each other?'

'Of course not,' laughed Robert.

'Of course not,' echoed Mariequita, with a serious, confirmatory bob of the head.

The sun was high up and beginning to bite. The swift breeze seemed to Edna to bury the sting of it into the pores of her face and hands. Robert held his umbrella over her.

As they went cutting sidewise through the water, the sails bellied taut, with the wind filling and overflowing them. Old Monsieur Farival laughed sardonically at something as he looked at the sails, and Beaudelet swore at the old man under his breath.

Sailing across the bay to the Chênière Caminada, Edna felt as if she were being borne away from some anchorage which had held her fast, whose chains had been loosening – had snapped the night before when the mystic spirit was abroad, leaving her free to drift whithersoever she chose to set her sails. Robert spoke to her incessantly; he no longer noticed Mariequita. The girl had shrimps in her bamboo basket. They were covered with Spanish moss.[38] She beat the moss down impatiently, and muttered to herself sullenly.

'Let us go to Grande Terre[39] tomorrow,' said Robert in a low voice.

'What shall we do there?'

'Climb up the hill to the old fort and look at the little wriggling gold snakes, and watch the lizards sun themselves.'

She gazed away towards Grande Terre and thought she would like to be alone there with Robert, in the sun, listening to the ocean's roar and watching the slimy lizards writhe in and out among the ruins of the old fort.

'And the next day or the next we can sail to the Bayou Brulow,'[40] he went on.

'What shall we do there?'

'Anything – cast bait for fish.'

'No; we'll go back to Grande Terre. Let the fish alone.'

'We'll go wherever you like,' he said. 'I'll have Tonie[41] come over and help me patch and trim my boat. We shall not need Beaudelet nor anyone. Are you afraid of the pirogue?'

'Oh, no.'

'Then I'll take you some night in the pirogue when the moon shines. Maybe your Gulf spirit will whisper to you in which of these islands the treasures are hidden – direct you to the very spot, perhaps.'

'And in a day we should be rich!' she laughed. 'I'd give it all to you, the pirate gold[42] and every bit of treasure we could dig up. I think you would know how to spend it. Pirate gold isn't a thing to be hoarded or utilised. It is something to squander and throw to the four winds, for the fun of seeing the golden specks fly.'

'We'd share it, and scatter it together,' he said. His face flushed.

They all went together up to the quaint little Gothic church of Our Lady of Lourdes, gleaming all brown and yellow with paint in the sun's glare. Only Beaudelet remained behind, tinkering at his boat, and Mariequita walked away with her basket of shrimps, casting a look of childish ill-humour and reproach at Robert from the corner of her eye.

13

A feeling of oppression and drowsiness overcame Edna during the service. Her head began to ache, and the lights on the altar swayed before her eyes. Another time she might have made an effort to regain her composure; but her one thought was to quit the stifling atmosphere of the church and reach the open air. She arose, climbing over Robert's feet with a muttered apology. Old Monsieur Farival, flurried, curious, stood up, but upon seeing that Robert had followed Mrs Pontellier, he sank back into his seat. He whispered an anxious enquiry of the lady in black, who did not notice him or reply, but kept her eyes fastened upon the pages of her velvet prayer-book.

'I felt giddy and almost overcome,' Edna said, lifting her hands instinctively to her head and pushing her straw hat up from her forehead. 'I couldn't have stayed through the service.' They were outside in the shadow of the church. Robert was full of solicitude.

'It was folly to have thought of going in the first place, let alone staying. Come over to Madame Antoine's;[43] you can rest there.' He took her arm and led her away, looking anxiously and continuously down into her face.

How still it was, with only the voice of the sea whispering through the reeds that grew in the salt-water pools! The long line of little grey, weather-beaten houses nestled peacefully among the orange trees. It must always have been God's day on that low, drowsy island, Edna thought. They stopped, leaning over a jagged fence made of sea-drift, to ask for water. A youth, a mild-faced Acadian,[44] was drawing water from the cistern, which was nothing more than a rusty buoy, with an opening on one side, sunk in the ground. The water which the youth handed to them in a tin pail was not cold to taste, but it was cool to her heated face, and it greatly revived and refreshed her.

Madame Antoine's cot[45] was at the far end of the village. She welcomed them with all the native hospitality, as she would have opened her door to let the sunlight in. She was fat, and walked heavily and clumsily across the floor. She could speak no English, but when Robert made her understand that the lady who accompanied him was ill and desired to rest, she was all eagerness to make Edna feel at home and to dispose of her comfortably.

The whole place was immaculately clean, and the big, four-posted bed, snow-white, invited one to repose. It stood in a small side room which looked out across a narrow grass plot towards the shed, where there was a disabled boat lying keel upward.

Madame Antoine had not gone to mass. Her son Tonie had, but she supposed he would soon be back, and she invited Robert to be seated and wait for him. But he went and sat outside the door and smoked. Madame Antoine busied herself in the large front room preparing dinner. She was boiling mullets over a few red coals in the huge fireplace.

Edna, left alone in the little side room, loosened her clothes, removing the greater part of them. She bathed her face, her neck and arms in the basin that stood between the windows. She took off her shoes and stockings and stretched herself in the very centre of the high, white bed. How luxurious it felt to rest thus in a strange, quaint bed, with its sweet country odour of laurel lingering about the sheets and mattress! She stretched her strong limbs that ached a little. She ran her fingers through her loosened hair for a while. She looked at her round arms as she held them straight up and rubbed them one after the other, observing closely, as if it were something she saw for the first time, the fine, firm quality and texture of her flesh. She clasped her hands easily above her head, and it was thus she fell asleep.

She slept lightly at first, half awake and drowsily attentive to the things about her. She could hear Madame Antoine's heavy, scraping tread as she walked back and forth on the sanded floor. Some chickens were clucking outside the windows, scratching for bits of gravel in the grass. Later she half heard the voices of Robert and Tonie talking under the shed. She did not stir. Even her eyelids rested numb and heavily over her sleepy eyes. The voices went on – Tonie's slow, Acadian drawl, Robert's quick, soft, smooth French. She understood French imperfectly unless directly addressed, and the voices were only part of the other drowsy, muffled sounds lulling her senses.

When Edna awoke it was with the conviction that she had slept long and soundly. The voices were hushed under the shed. Madame Antoine's step was no longer to be heard in the adjoining room. Even the chickens had gone elsewhere to scratch and cluck. The mosquito bar was drawn over her; the old woman had come in while she slept and let down the bar. Edna arose quietly from the bed, and looking between the curtains of the window, she saw by the slanting rays of the sun that the afternoon was far advanced. Robert was out there under the shed, reclining in the shade against the sloping keel of the overturned boat. He was reading from a book. Tonie was no longer with him. She wondered what had become of the rest of the party. She peeped out at him two or three times as she stood washing herself in the little basin between the windows.

Madame Antoine had laid some coarse, clean towels upon a chair, and had placed a box of *poudre de riz* within easy reach. Edna dabbed the powder upon her nose and cheeks as she looked at herself closely in the little distorted mirror which hung on the wall above the basin. Her eyes were bright and wide awake and her face glowed.

When she had completed her toilet she walked into the adjoining room. She was very hungry. No one was there. But there was a cloth spread upon the table that stood against the wall, and a cover was laid for one, with a crusty brown loaf and a bottle of wine beside the plate. Edna bit a piece from the brown loaf, tearing it with her strong, white teeth. She poured some of the wine into the glass and drank it down. Then she went softly out of doors, and plucking an orange from the low-hanging bough of a tree, threw it at Robert, who did not know she was awake and up.

An illumination broke over his whole face when he saw her and joined her under the orange tree.

'How many years have I slept?' she enquired. 'The whole island seems changed. A new race of beings must have sprung up, leaving only you and me as past relics. How many ages ago did Madame Antoine and Tonie die? and when did our people from Grand Isle disappear from the earth?'

He familiarly adjusted a ruffle upon her shoulder.

'You have slept precisely one hundred years. I was left here to guard your slumbers; and for one hundred years I have been out under the shed reading a book. The only evil I couldn't prevent was to keep a broiled fowl from drying up.'

'If it has turned to stone, still will I eat it,' said Edna, moving with him into the house. 'But really, what has become of Monsieur Farival and the others?'

'Gone hours ago. When they found that you were sleeping they thought it best not to awake you. Anyway, I wouldn't have let them. What was I here for?'

'I wonder if Léonce will be uneasy!' she speculated, as she seated herself at table.

'Of course not; he knows you are with me,' Robert replied, as he busied himself among sundry pans and covered dishes which had been left standing on the hearth.

'Where are Madame Antoine and her son?' asked Edna.

'Gone to vespers, and to visit some friends, I believe. I am to take you back in Tonie's boat whenever you are ready to go.'

He stirred the smouldering ashes till the broiled fowl began to sizzle afresh. He served her with no mean repast, dripping the coffee anew and sharing it with her. Madame Antoine had cooked little else than the mullets, but while Edna slept Robert had foraged the island. He was childishly gratified to discover her appetite, and to see the relish with which she ate the food which he had procured for her.

'Shall we go right away?' she asked, after draining her glass and brushing together the crumbs of the crusty loaf.

'The sun isn't as low as it will be in two hours,' he answered.

'The sun will be gone in two hours.'

'Well, let it go; who cares!'

They waited a good while under the orange trees, till Madame Antoine came back, panting, waddling, with a thousand apologies to explain her absence. Tonie did not dare to return. He was shy, and would not willingly face any woman except his mother.

It was very pleasant to stay there under the orange trees, while the sun dipped lower and lower, turning the western sky to flaming copper and gold. The shadows lengthened and crept out like stealthy, grotesque monsters across the grass.

Edna and Robert both sat upon the ground – that is, he lay upon the ground beside her, occasionally picking at the hem of her muslin gown.

Madame Antoine seated her fat body, broad and squat, upon a bench beside the door. She had been talking all the afternoon, and had wound herself up to the storytelling pitch.

And what stories she told them! But twice in her life she had left the Chênière Caminada, and then for the briefest span. All her years she had squatted and waddled there upon the island, gathering legends of the Baratarians[46] and the sea. The night came on, with the moon to lighten it. Edna could hear the whispering voices of dead men and the click of muffled gold.

When she and Robert stepped into Tonie's boat, with the red lateen sail, misty spirit forms were prowling in the shadows and among the reeds, and upon the water were phantom ships, speeding to cover.

14

The youngest boy, Etienne, had been very naughty, Madame Ratignolle said, as she delivered him into the hands of his mother. He had been unwilling to go to bed and had made a scene; whereupon she had taken charge of him and pacified him as well as she could. Raoul had been in bed and asleep for two hours.

The youngster was in his long white nightgown, that kept tripping him up as Madame Ratignolle led him along by the hand. With the other chubby fist he rubbed his eyes, which were heavy with sleep and ill humour. Edna took him in her arms, and seating herself in the rocker, began to coddle and caress him, calling him all manner of tender names, soothing him to sleep.

It was not more than nine o'clock. No one had yet gone to bed but the children.

Léonce had been very uneasy at first, Madame Ratignolle said, and had wanted to start at once for the Chênière. But Monsieur Farival had assured him that his wife was only overcome with sleep and fatigue, that Tonie would bring her safely back later in the day; and he had thus been dissuaded from crossing the bay. He had gone over to Klein's, looking up some cotton broker whom he wished to see in regard to

securities, exchanges, stocks, bonds or something of the sort, Madame
Ratignolle did not remember what. He said he would not remain away
late. She herself was suffering from heat and oppression, she said. She
carried a bottle of salts and a large fan. She would not consent to remain
with Edna, for Monsieur Ratignolle was alone, and he detested above
all things to be left alone.

When Etienne had fallen asleep Edna bore him into the back room,
and Robert went and lifted the mosquito bar that she might lay the
child comfortably in his bed. The quadroon had vanished. When they
emerged from the cottage Robert bade Edna good-night.

'Do you know we have been together the whole livelong day, Robert –
since early this morning?' she said at parting.

'All but the hundred years when you were sleeping. Good-night.'

He pressed her hand and went away in the direction of the beach. He
did not join any of the others, but walked alone towards the Gulf.

Edna stayed outside, awaiting her husband's return. She had no desire
to sleep or to retire; nor did she feel like going over to sit with the
Ratignolles, or to join Madame Lebrun and a group whose animated
voices reached her as they sat in conversation before the house. She let
her mind wander back over her stay at Grand Isle; and she tried to
discover wherein this summer had been different from any and every
other summer of her life. She could only realise that she herself – her
present self – was in some way different from the other self. That she
was seeing with different eyes and making the acquaintance of new
conditions in herself that coloured and changed her environment in a
way she did not yet suspect.

She wondered why Robert had gone away and left her. It did not
occur to her to think he might have grown tired of being with her the
livelong day. She was not tired, and she felt that he was not. She
regretted that he had gone. It was so much more natural to have him
stay, when he was not absolutely required to leave her.

As Edna waited for her husband she sang low a little song that Robert
had sung as they crossed the bay. It began with '*Ah! si tu savais!*'⁴⁷ and
every verse ended with '*si tu savais*'.

Robert's voice was not pretentious. It was musical and true. The
voice, the notes, the whole refrain haunted her memory.

15

When Edna entered the dining-room one evening a little late, as was
her habit, an unusually animated conversation seemed to be going
on. Several persons were talking at once, and Victor's voice was

predominating, even over that of his mother. Edna had returned late from her bathe, had dressed in some haste, and her face was flushed. Her head, set off by her dainty white gown, suggested a rich, rare blossom. She took her seat at table between old Monsieur Farival and Madame Ratignolle.

As she seated herself and was about to begin to eat her soup, which had been served when she entered the room, several persons informed her simultaneously that Robert was going to Mexico. She laid her spoon down and looked about her bewildered. He had been with her, reading to her all the morning, and had never even mentioned such a place as Mexico. She had not seen him during the afternoon; she had heard someone say he was at the house, upstairs with his mother. This she had thought nothing of, though she was surprised when he did not join her later in the afternoon, when she went down to the beach.

She looked across at him, where he sat beside Madame Lebrun, who presided. Edna's face was a blank picture of bewilderment, which she never thought of disguising. He lifted his eyebrows with the pretext of a smile as he returned her glance. He looked embarrassed and uneasy.

'When is he going?' she asked of everybody in general, as if Robert were not there to answer for himself.

'Tonight!' 'This very evening!' 'Did you ever!' 'What possesses him!' were some of the replies she gathered, uttered simultaneously in French and English.

'Impossible!' she exclaimed. 'How can a person start off from Grand Isle to Mexico at a moment's notice, as if he were going over to Klein's or to the wharf or down to the beach?'

'I said all along I was going to Mexico; I've been saying so for years!' cried Robert, in an excited and irritable tone, with the air of a man defending himself against a swarm of stinging insects.

Madame Lebrun knocked on the table with her knife handle.

'Please let Robert explain why he is going, and why he is going tonight,' she called out. 'Really, this table is getting to be more and more like Bedlam[48] every day, with everybody talking at once. Sometimes – I hope God will forgive me – but positively, sometimes I wish Victor would lose the power of speech.'

Victor laughed sardonically as he thanked his mother for her holy wish, of which he failed to see the benefit to anybody, except that it might afford her a more ample opportunity and licence to talk herself.

Monsieur Farival thought that Victor should have been taken out in mid-ocean in his earliest youth and drowned. Victor thought there would be more logic in thus disposing of people with an established claim for making themselves universally obnoxious. Madame Lebrun grew a trifle hysterical; Robert called his brother some sharp, hard names.

'There's nothing much to explain, mother,' he said; though he explained, nevertheless – looking chiefly at Edna – that he could only meet the gentleman whom he intended to join at Vera Cruz by taking such and such a steamer, which left New Orleans on such a day; that Beaudelet was going out with his lugger-load of vegetables that night, which gave him an opportunity of reaching the city and making his vessel in time.

'But when did you make up your mind to all this?' demanded Monsieur Farival.

'This afternoon,' returned Robert, with a shade of annoyance.

'At what time this afternoon?' persisted the old gentleman, with nagging determination, as if he were cross-questioning a criminal in a court of justice.

At four o'clock this afternoon, Monsieur Farival,' Robert replied, in a high voice and with a lofty air, which reminded Edna of some gentleman on the stage.

She had forced herself to eat most of her soup, and now she was picking the flaky bits of a *courtbouillon*[49] with her fork.

The lovers were profiting by the general conversation on Mexico to speak in whispers of matters which they rightly considered were interesting to no one but themselves. The lady in black had once received a pair of prayer-beads of curious workmanship from Mexico, with very special indulgence attached to them, but she had never been able to ascertain whether the indulgence extended outside the Mexican border. Father Fochel of the cathedral had attempted to explain it; but he had not done so to her satisfaction. And she begged that Robert would interest himself, and discover, if possible, whether she was entitled to the indulgence accompanying the remarkably curious Mexican prayer-beads.

Madame Ratignolle hoped that Robert would exercise extreme caution in dealing with the Mexicans who, she considered, were a treacherous people, unscrupulous and revengeful. She trusted she did them no injustice in thus condemning them as a race. She had known personally but one Mexican, who made and sold excellent tamales,[50] and whom she would have trusted implicitly, so soft-spoken was he. One day he was arrested for stabbing his wife. She never knew whether he had been hanged or not.

Victor had grown hilarious, and was attempting to tell an anecdote about a Mexican girl who served chocolate one winter in a restaurant in Dauphine Street. No one would listen to him but old Monsieur Farival, who went into convulsions over the droll story.

Edna wondered if they had all gone mad, to be talking and clamouring at that rate. She herself could think of nothing to say about Mexico or the Mexicans.

'At what time do you leave?' she asked Robert.

'At ten,' he told her. 'Beaudelet wants to wait for the moon.' .

'Are you all ready to go?'

'Quite ready. I shall only take a handbag, and shall pack my trunk in the city.'

He turned to answer some question put to him by his mother, and Edna, having finished her black coffee, left the table.

She went directly to her room. The little cottage was close and stuffy after leaving the outer air. But she did not mind; there appeared to be a hundred different things demanding her attention indoors. She began to set the toilet-stand to rights, grumbling at the negligence of the quadroon, who was in the adjoining room putting the children to bed. She gathered together stray garments that were hanging on the backs of chairs, and put each where it belonged in closet or bureau drawer. She changed her gown for a more comfortable and commodious wrapper. She rearranged her hair, combing and brushing it with unusual energy. Then she went in and assisted the quadroon in getting the boys to bed.

They were very playful and inclined to talk – to do anything but lie quiet and go to sleep. Edna sent the quadroon away to her supper and told her she need not return. Then she sat and told the children a story. Instead of soothing it excited them, and added to their wakefulness. She left them in heated argument, speculating about the conclusion of the tale which their mother promised to finish the following night.

The little black girl came in to say that Madame Lebrun would like to have Mrs Pontellier go and sit with them over at the house till Mr Robert went away. Edna returned answer that she had already undressed, that she did not feel quite well, but perhaps she would go over to the house later. She started to dress again, and got as far advanced as to remove her *peignoir*. But changing her mind once more she resumed the *peignoir*, and went outside and sat down before her door. She was overheated and irritable, and fanned herself energetically for a while. Madame Ratignolle came down to discover what was the matter.

'All that noise and confusion at the table must have upset me,' replied Edna, 'and moreover, I hate shocks and surprises. The idea of Robert starting off in such a ridiculously sudden and dramatic way! As if it were a matter of life and death! Never saying a word about it all morning when he was with me.'

'Yes,' agreed Madame Ratignolle. 'I think it was showing us all – you especially – very little consideration. It wouldn't have surprised me in any of the others; those Lebruns are all given to heroics. But I must say I should never have expected such a thing from Robert. Are you not coming down? Come on, dear; it doesn't look friendly.'

'No,' said Edna, a little sullenly. 'I can't go to the trouble of dressing again; I don't feel like it.'

'You needn't dress; you look all right; fasten a belt around your waist. Just look at me!'

'No,' persisted Edna; 'but you go on. Madame Lebrun might be offended if we both stayed away.'

Madame Ratignolle kissed Edna good-night, and went away, being in truth rather desirous of joining in the general and animated conversation which was still in progress concerning Mexico and the Mexicans.

Somewhat later Robert came up, carrying his handbag.

'Aren't you feeling well?' he asked.

'Oh, well enough. Are you going right away?'

He lit a match and looked at his watch. 'In twenty minutes,' he said. The sudden and brief flare of the match emphasised the darkness for a while. He sat down upon a stool which the children had left out on the porch.

'Get a chair,' said Edna.

'This will do,' he replied. He put on his soft hat and nervously took it off again, and wiping his face with his handkerchief, complained of the heat.

'Take the fan,' said Edna, offering it to him.

'Oh, no! Thank you. It does no good; you have to stop fanning sometime, and feel all the more uncomfortable afterwards.'

'That's one of the ridiculous things which men always say. I have never known one to speak otherwise of fanning. How long will you be gone?'

'For ever, perhaps. I don't know. It depends upon a good many things.'

'Well, in case it shouldn't be for ever, how long will it be?'

'I don't know.'

'This seems to me perfectly preposterous and uncalled for. I don't like it. I don't understand your motive for silence and mystery, never saying a word to me about it this morning.' He remained silent, not offering to defend himself.

He only said, after a moment: 'Don't part from me in an ill-humour. I never knew you to be out of patience with me before.'

'I don't want to part in any ill-humour,' she said. 'But can't you understand? I've grown used to seeing you, to having you with me all the time, and your action seems unfriendly, even unkind. You don't even offer an excuse for it. Why, I was planning to be together, thinking of how pleasant it would be to see you in the city next winter.'

'So was I,' he blurted. 'Perhaps that's the – ' He stood up suddenly and held out his hand. 'Goodbye, my dear Mrs Pontellier; goodbye. You won't – I hope you won't completely forget me.'

She clung to his hand, striving to detain him. 'Write to me when you get there, won't you, Robert?' she entreated.

'I will, thank you. Goodbye.'

How unlike Robert! The merest acquaintance would have said something more emphatic than, 'I will, thank you; goodbye,' to such a request.

He had evidently already taken leave of the people over at the house for he descended the steps and went to join Beaudelet, who was out there with an oar across his shoulder waiting for Robert. They walked away in the darkness. She could only hear Beaudelet's voice; Robert had apparently not even spoken a word of greeting to his companion.

Edna bit her handkerchief convulsively, striving to hold back and to hide, even from herself as she would have hidden from another, the emotion which was troubling – tearing – her. Her eyes were brimming with tears.

For the first time she recognised anew the symptoms of infatuation which she had felt incipiently as a child, as a girl in her earliest teens, and later as a young woman. The recognition did not lessen the reality, the poignancy of the revelation by any suggestion or promise of instability. The past was nothing to her; offered no lesson which she was willing to heed. The future was a mystery which she never attempted to penetrate. The present alone was significant; was hers, to torture her as it was doing then with the biting conviction that she had lost that which she had held, that she had been denied that which her impassioned, newly awakened being demanded.

16

'Do you miss your friend greatly?' asked Mademoiselle Reisz one morning as she came creeping up behind Edna, who had just left her cottage on her way to the beach. She spent much of her time in the water since she had acquired finally the art of swimming. As their stay at Grand Isle drew near its close, she felt that she could not give too much time to a diversion which afforded her the only real pleasurable moments that she knew. When Mademoiselle Reisz came and touched her upon the shoulder and spoke to her, the woman seemed to echo the thought which was ever in Edna's mind; or, better, the feeling which constantly possessed her.

Robert's going had in some way taken the brightness, the colour, the meaning out of everything. The conditions of her life were in no way changed, but her whole existence was dulled, like a faded garment which seems to be no longer worth wearing. She sought him every-where – in others whom she induced to talk about him. She went up in the mornings to Madame Lebrun's room, braving the clatter of the old sewing-machine. She sat there and chatted at intervals as Robert had done. She gazed around the room at the pictures and photographs hanging upon the wall, and discovered in some corner an old family album, which she examined with the keenest interest, appealing to Madame Lebrun for enlightenment concerning the many figures and faces which she discovered between its pages.

There was a picture of Madame Lebrun with Robert as a baby, seated in her lap, a round-faced infant with a fist in his mouth. The eyes alone in the baby suggested the man. And that was he also in kilts, at the age of five, wearing long curls and holding a whip in his hand. It made Edna laugh, and she laughed, too, at the portrait in his first long trousers; while another interested her, taken when he left for college, looking thin, long-faced, with eyes full of fire, ambition and great intentions. But there was no recent picture, none which suggested the Robert who had gone away five days ago, leaving a void and wilderness behind him.

'Oh, Robert stopped having his pictures taken when he had to pay for them himself! He found wiser use for his money, he says,' explained Madame Lebrun. She had a letter from him, written before he left New Orleans. Edna wished to see the letter, and Madame Lebrun told her to look for it either on the table or the dresser, or perhaps it was on the mantelpiece.

The letter was on the bookshelf. It possessed the greatest interest and attraction for Edna: the envelope, its size and shape, the postmark, the handwriting. She examined every detail of the outside before opening it. There were only a few lines, setting forth that he would leave the city that afternoon, that he had packed his trunk in good shape, that he was well, and sent her his love and begged to be affectionately remembered to all. There was no special message to Edna except a postscript saying that if Mrs Pontellier desired to finish the book which he had been reading to her, his mother would find it in his room, among other books there on the table. Edna experienced a pang of jealousy because he had written to his mother rather than to her.

Everyone seemed to take for granted that she missed him. Even her husband, when he came down the Saturday following Robert's departure, expressed regret that he had gone.

'How do you get on without him, Edna?' he asked.

'It's very dull without him,' she admitted. Mr Pontellier had seen Robert in the city, and Edna asked him a dozen questions or more. Where had they met? On Carondelet Street, in the morning. They had gone 'in' and had a drink and a cigar together. What had they talked about? Chiefly about his prospects in Mexico, which Mr Pontellier thought were promising. How did he look? How did he seem – grave or gay, or how? Quite cheerful, and wholly taken up with the idea of his trip, which Mr Pontellier found altogether natural in a young fellow about to seek fortune and adventure in a strange, queer country.

Edna tapped her foot impatiently, and wondered why the children persisted in playing in the sun when they might be under the trees. She went down and led them out of the sun, scolding the quadroon for not being more attentive.

It did not strike her as in the least grotesque that she should be making Robert the object of conversation and leading her husband to speak of him. The sentiment which she entertained for Robert in no way resembled that which she felt for her husband, or had ever felt, or ever expected to feel. She had all her life long been accustomed to harbour thoughts and emotions which never voiced themselves. They had never taken the form of struggles. They belonged to her and were her own, and she entertained the conviction that she had a right to them and that they concerned no one but herself. Edna had once told Madame Ratignolle that she would never sacrifice herself for her children or for anyone. Then had followed a rather heated argument; the two women did not appear to understand each other or to be talking the same language.

Edna tried to appease her friend, to explain. 'I would give up the unessential: I would give my money, I would give my life for my children; but I wouldn't give myself. I can't make it more clear; it's only something which I am beginning to comprehend, which is revealing itself to me.'

'I don't know what you would call the essential, or what you mean by the unessential,' said Madame Ratignolle, cheerfully; 'but a woman who would give her life for her children could do no more than that – your Bible tells you so. I'm sure I couldn't do more than that.'

'Oh, yes you could!' laughed Edna.

She was not surprised at Mademoiselle Reisz's question the morning that lady, following her to the beach, tapped her on the shoulder and asked if she did not greatly miss her young friend.

'Oh, good-morning, mademoiselle; is it you? Why, of course I miss Robert. Are you going down to bathe?'

'Why should I go down to bathe at the very end of the season when I haven't been in the surf all summer,' replied the woman, disagreeably.

'I beg your pardon,' offered Edna, in some embarrassment, for she should have remembered that Mademoiselle Reisz's avoidance of the water had furnished a theme for much pleasantry. Some among them thought it was on account of her false hair, or the dread of getting the violets wet, while others attributed it to the natural aversion for water sometimes believed to accompany the artistic temperament. Mademoiselle offered Edna some chocolates in a paper bag, which she took from her pocket, by way of showing that she bore no ill feeling. She habitually ate chocolates for their sustaining quality; they contained much nutriment in small compass, she said. They saved her from starvation, as Madame Lebrun's table was utterly impossible; and no one save so impertinent a woman as Madame Lebrun would think of offering such food to people and requiring them to pay for it.

'She must feel very lonely without her son,' said Edna, desiring to change the subject. 'Her favourite son, too. It must have been quite hard to let him go.'

Mademoiselle laughed maliciously.

'Her favourite son! Oh, dear! Who could have been imposing such a tale upon you? Aline Lebrun lives for Victor, and for Victor alone. She has spoiled him into the worthless creature he is. She worships him and the ground he walks on. Robert is very well in a way, to give up all the money he can earn to the family, and keep the barest pittance for himself. Favourite son, indeed! I miss the poor fellow myself, my dear. I liked to see him and to hear him about the place – the only Lebrun who is worth a pinch of salt. He comes to see me often in the city. I like to play to him. That Victor! hanging would be too good for him. It's a wonder Robert hasn't beaten him to death long ago.'

'I thought he had great patience with his brother,' offered Edna, glad to be talking about Robert, no matter what was said.

'Oh! he thrashed him well enough a year or two ago,' said Mademoiselle. 'It was about a Spanish girl, whom Victor considered that he had some sort of claim upon. He met Robert one day talking to the girl, or walking with her, or bathing with her, or carrying her basket – I don't remember what; and he became so insulting and abusive that

Robert gave him a thrashing on the spot that has kept him comparatively in order for a good while. It's about time he was getting another.'

'Was her name Mariequita?' asked Edna.

'Mariequita – yes, that was it; Mariequita. I had forgotten. Oh, she's a sly one, and a bad one, that Mariequita!'

Edna looked down at Mademoiselle Reisz and wondered how she could have listened to her venom so long. For some reason she felt depressed, almost unhappy. She had not intended to go into the water; but she donned her bathing suit, and left Mademoiselle alone, seated under the shade of the children's tent. The water was growing cooler as the season advanced. Edna plunged and swam about with an abandon that thrilled and invigorated her. She remained a long time in the water, half hoping that Mademoiselle Reisz would not wait for her.

But Mademoiselle waited. She was very amiable during the walk back, and raved much over Edna's appearance in her bathing suit. She talked about music. She hoped that Edna would go to see her in the city, and wrote her address with the stub of a pencil on a piece of card which she found in her pocket.

'When do you leave?' asked Edna.

'Next Monday; and you?'

'The following week,' answered Edna, adding, 'It has been a pleasant summer, hasn't it, mademoiselle?'

'Well,' agreed Mademoiselle Reisz, with a shrug, 'rather pleasant, if it hadn't been for the mosquitoes and the Farival twins.'

17

The Pontelliers possessed a very charming home on Esplanade Street[51] in New Orleans. It was a large, double cottage, with a broad front veranda, whose round, fluted columns supported the sloping roof. The house was painted a dazzling white; the outside shutters, or jalousies, were green. In the yard, which was kept scrupulously neat, were flowers and plants of every description which flourishes in South Louisiana. Within doors the appointments were perfect after the conventional type. The softest carpets and rugs covered the floors; rich and tasteful draperies hung at doors and windows. There were paintings, selected with judgement and discrimination, upon the walls. The cut glass, the silver, the heavy damask which daily appeared upon the table were the envy of many women whose husbands were less generous than Mr Pontellier.

Mr Pontellier was very fond of walking about his house examining its various appointments and details, to see that nothing was amiss. He greatly valued his possessions, chiefly because they were his, and derived genuine pleasure from contemplating a painting, a statuette, a rare lace curtain – no matter what – after he had bought it and placed it among his household goods.

On Tuesday afternoons – Tuesday being Mrs Pontellier's reception day[52] – there was a constant stream of callers – women who came in carriages or in the street cars, or walked when the air was soft and distance permitted. A light-coloured mulatto boy, in dress coat and bearing a diminutive silver tray for the reception of cards, admitted them. A maid, in white fluted cap, offered the callers liqueur, coffee or chocolate, as they might desire. Mrs Pontellier, attired in a handsome reception gown, remained in the drawing-room the entire afternoon receiving her visitors. Men sometimes called in the evening with their wives.

This had been the programme which Mrs Pontellier had religiously followed since her marriage, six years before. Certain evenings during the week she and her husband attended the opera or sometimes the play.

Mr Pontellier left his home in the morning between nine and ten o'clock, and rarely returned before half-past six or seven in the evening – dinner being served at half-past seven.

He and his wife seated themselves at table one Tuesday evening, a few weeks after their return from Grand Isle. They were alone together. The boys were being put to bed; the patter of their bare, escaping feet could be heard occasionally, as well as the pursuing voice of the quadroon, lifted in mild protest and entreaty. Mrs Pontellier did not wear her usual Tuesday reception gown; she was in ordinary house dress. Mr Pontellier, who was observant about such things, noticed it, as he served the soup and handed it to the boy in waiting.

'Tired out, Edna? Whom did you have? Many callers?' he asked. He tasted his soup and began to season it with pepper, salt, vinegar, mustard – everything within reach.

'There were a good many,' replied Edna, who was eating her soup with evident satisfaction. 'I found their cards when I got home; I was out.'

'Out!' exclaimed her husband, with something like genuine consternation in his voice as he laid down the vinegar cruet and looked at her through his glasses. 'Why, what could have taken you out on Tuesday? What did you have to do?'

'Nothing. I simply felt like going out, and I went out.'

'Well, I hope you left some suitable excuse,' said her husband, somewhat appeased, as he added a dash of cayenne pepper to the soup.

'No, I left no excuse. I told Joe to say I was out that was all.'

'Why, my dear, I should think you'd understand by this time that people don't do such things; we've got to observe *les convenances*[53] if we ever expect to get on and keep up with the procession. If you felt that you had to leave home this afternoon, you should have left some suitable explanation for your absence.

'This soup is really impossible; it's strange that woman hasn't learned yet to make a decent soup. Any free-lunch stand[54] in town serves a better one. Was Mrs Belthrop here?'

'Bring the tray with the cards, Joe. I don't remember who was here.'

The boy retired and returned after a moment, bringing the tiny silver tray, which was covered with ladies' visiting cards. He handed it to Mrs Pontellier.

'Give it to Mr Pontellier,' she said.

Joe offered the tray to Mr Pontellier, and removed the soup.

Mr Pontellier scanned the names of his wife's callers, reading some of them aloud, with comments as he read.

' "The Misses Delasidas". I worked a big deal in futures for their father this morning; nice girls; it's time they were getting married. "Mrs Belthrop". I tell you what it is, Edna; you can't afford to snub Mrs Belthrop. Why, Belthrop could buy and sell us ten times over. His business is worth a good round sum to me. You'd better write her a note. "Mrs James Highcamp". Hugh! the less you have to do with Mrs Highcamp, the better. "Madame Laforcé". Came all the way from Carrolton,[55] too, poor old soul. "Miss Wiggs", "Mrs Eleanor Boltons".' He pushed the cards aside.

'Mercy!' exclaimed Edna, who had been fuming. 'Why are you taking the thing so seriously and making such a fuss over it?'

'I'm not making any fuss over it. But it's just such seeming trifles that we've got to take seriously; such things count.'

The fish was scorched. Mr Pontellier would not touch it. Edna said she did not mind a little scorched taste. The roast was in some way not to his fancy, and he did not like the manner in which the vegetables were served.

'It seems to me,' he said, 'we spend money enough in this house to procure at least one meal a day which a man could eat and retain his self-respect.'

'You used to think the cook was a treasure,' returned Edna, indifferently.

'Perhaps she was when she first came; but cooks are only human. They need looking after, like any other class of persons that you employ.

Suppose I didn't look after the clerks in my office, just let them run things their own way; they'd soon make a nice mess of me and my business.'

'Where are you going?' asked Edna, seeing that her husband arose from table without having eaten a morsel except a taste of the highly seasoned soup.

'I'm going to get my dinner at the club. Good-night.' He went into the hall, took his hat and stick from the stand, and left the house.

She was somewhat familiar with such scenes. They had often made her very unhappy. On a few previous occasions she had been completely deprived of any desire to finish her dinner. Sometimes she had gone into the kitchen to administer a tardy rebuke to the cook. Once she went to her room and studied the cookbook during an entire evening, finally writing out a menu for the week, which left her harassed with a feeling that, after all, she had accomplished no good that was worth the name.

But that evening Edna finished her dinner alone, with forced deliberation. Her face was flushed and her eyes flamed with some inward fire that lighted them. After finishing her dinner she went to her room, having instructed the boy to tell any other callers that she was indisposed.

It was a large, beautiful room, rich and picturesque in the soft, dim light which the maid had turned low. She went and stood at an open window and looked out upon the deep tangle of the garden below. All the mystery and witchery of the night seemed to have gathered there amid the perfumes and the dusky and tortuous outlines of flowers and foliage. She was seeking herself and finding herself in just such sweet, half-darkness which met her moods. But the voices were not soothing that came to her from the darkness and the sky above and the stars. They jeered and sounded mournful notes without promise, devoid even of hope. She turned back into the room and began to walk to and fro down its whole length, without stopping, without resting. She carried in her hands a thin handkerchief, which she tore into ribbons, rolled into a ball, and flung from her. Once she stopped, and taking off her wedding ring, flung it upon the carpet. When she saw it lying there, she stamped her heel upon it, striving to crush it. But her small boot heel did not make an indenture, not a mark upon the little glittering circlet.

In a sweeping passion she seized a glass vase from the table and flung it upon the tiles of the hearth. She wanted to destroy something. The crash and clatter were what she wanted to hear.

A maid, alarmed at the din of breaking glass, entered the room to discover what was the matter.

'A vase fell upon the hearth,' said Edna. 'Never mind; leave it till morning.'

'Oh! you might get some of the glass in your feet, ma'am,' insisted the young woman, picking up bits of the broken vase that were scattered upon the carpet. 'And here's your ring, ma'am, under the chair.'

Edna held out her hand, and taking the ring, slipped it upon her finger.

18

The following morning Mr Pontellier, upon leaving for his office, asked Edna if she would not meet him in town in order to look at some new fixtures for the library.

'I hardly think we need new fixtures, Léonce. Don't let us get anything new; you are too extravagant. I don't believe you ever think of saving or putting by.'

'The way to become rich is to make money, my dear Edna, not to save it,' he said. He regretted that she did not feel inclined to go with him and select new fixtures. He kissed her goodbye, and told her she was not looking well and must take care of herself She was unusually pale and very quiet.

She stood on the front veranda as he quitted the house and absently picked a few sprays of jessamine that grew upon a trellis near by. She inhaled the odour of the blossoms and thrust them into the bosom of her white morning gown. The boys were dragging along the banquette a small 'express wagon', which they had filled with blocks and sticks. The quadroon was following them with little quick steps, having assumed a fictitious animation and alacrity for the occasion. A fruit vender was crying his wares in the street.

Edna looked straight before her with a self-absorbed expression upon her face. She felt no interest in anything about her. The street, the children, the fruit vender, the flowers growing there under her eyes, were all part and parcel of an alien world which had suddenly become antagonistic.

She went back into the house. She had thought of speaking to the cook concerning her blunders of the previous night; but Mr Pontellier had saved her that disagreeable mission, for which she was so poorly fitted. Mr Pontellier's arguments were usually convincing with those whom he employed. He left home feeling quite sure that he and Edna would sit down that evening, and possibly a few subsequent evenings, to a dinner deserving of the name.

Edna spent an hour or two in looking over some of her old sketches. She could see their shortcomings and defects, which were glaring in her eyes. She tried to work a little, but found she was not in the humour. Finally she gathered together a few of the sketches – those which she considered the least discreditable; and she carried them with her when, a little later, she dressed and left the house. She looked handsome and distinguished in her street gown. The tan of the seashore had left her face, and her forehead was smooth, white and polished beneath her heavy, yellow-brown hair. There were a few freckles on her face, and a small, dark mole near the under lip and one on the temple, half-hidden in her hair.

As Edna walked along the street she was thinking of Robert. She was still under the spell of her infatuation. She had tried to forget him, realising the inutility of remembering. But the thought of him was like an obsession, ever pressing itself upon her. It was not that she dwelt upon details of their acquaintance, or recalled in any special or peculiar way his personality; it was his being, his existence, which dominated her thought, fading sometimes as if it would melt into the mist of the forgotten, reviving again with an intensity which filled her with an incomprehensible longing.

Edna was on her way to Madame Ratignolle's. Their intimacy, begun at Grand Isle, had not declined, and they had seen each other with some frequency since their return to the city. The Ratignolles lived at no great distance from Edna's home, on the corner of a side street, where Monsieur Ratignolle owned and conducted a drug store which enjoyed a steady and prosperous trade. His father had been in the business before him, and Monsieur Ratignolle stood well in the community and bore an enviable reputation for integrity and clear-headedness. His family lived in commodious apartments over the store, having an entrance on the side within the *porte cochère*.[56] There was something which Edna thought very French, very foreign, about their whole manner of living. In the large and pleasant salon which extended across the width of the house, the Ratignolles entertained their friends once a fortnight with a *soirée musicale*, sometimes diversified by card-playing. There was a friend who played upon the cello. One brought his flute and another his violin, while there were some who sang and a number who performed upon the piano with various degrees of taste and agility. The Ratignolles' *soirées musicales* were widely known, and it was considered a privilege to be invited to them.

Edna found her friend engaged in assorting the clothes which had returned that morning from the laundry. She at once abandoned her occupation upon seeing Edna, who had been ushered without ceremony into her presence.

' 'Cité can do it as well as I; it is really her business,' she explained to Edna, who apologised for interrupting her. And she summoned a young black woman, whom she instructed, in French, to be very careful in checking off the list which she handed her. She told her to notice particularly if a fine linen handkerchief of Monsieur Ratignolle's, which was missing last week, had been returned; and to be sure to set to one side such pieces as required mending and darning.

Then placing an arm around Edna's waist she led her to the front of the house, to the salon, where it was cool and sweet with the odour of great roses that stood upon the hearth in jars.

Madame Ratignolle looked more beautiful than ever there at home in a *négligé* which left her arms almost wholly bare and exposed the rich, melting curves of her white throat.

'Perhaps I shall be able to paint your picture someday,' said Edna with a smile when they were seated. She produced the roll of sketches and started to unfold them. 'I believe I ought to work again. I feel as if I wanted to be doing something. What do you think of them? Do you think it worth while to take it up again and study some more? I might study for a while with Laidpore.'

She knew that Madame Ratignolle's opinion in such a matter would be next to valueless, that she herself had not alone decided, but determined; but she sought the words of praise and encouragement that would help her to put heart into her venture.

'Your talent is immense, dear!'

'Nonsense!' protested Edna, well pleased.

'Immense, I tell you,' persisted Madame Ratignolle, surveying the sketches one by one, at close range, then holding them at arm's length, narrowing her eyes, and dropping her head on one side. 'Surely, this Bavarian peasant is worthy of framing; and this basket of apples! never have I seen anything more lifelike. One might almost be tempted to reach out a hand and take one.'

Edna could not control a feeling which bordered upon complacency at her friend's praise, even realising, as she did, its true worth. She retained a few of the sketches, and gave all the rest to Madame Ratignolle, who appreciated the gift far beyond its value and proudly exhibited the pictures to her husband when he came up from the store a little later for his midday dinner.

Mr Ratignolle was one of those men who are called the salt of the earth. His cheerfulness was unbounded, and it was matched by his goodness of heart, his broad charity and common sense. He and his wife spoke English with an accent which was only discernible through its un-English emphasis and a certain carefulness and deliberation. Edna's husband spoke English with no accent whatever. The Ratignolles understood each other perfectly. If ever the fusion of two human beings into one has been accomplished on this sphere it was surely in their union.

As Edna seated herself at table with them she thought, 'Better a dinner of herbs,'[57] though it did not take her long to discover that it was no dinner of herbs, but a delicious repast, simple, choice, and in every way satisfying.

Monsieur Ratignolle was delighted to see her, though he found her looking not so well as at Grand Isle, and he advised a tonic. He talked a good deal on various topics, a little politics, some city news and neighbourhood gossip. He spoke with an animation and earnestness that gave an exaggerated importance to every syllable he uttered. His wife was keenly interested in everything he said, laying down her fork the better to listen, chiming in, taking the words out of his mouth.

Edna felt depressed rather than soothed after leaving them. The little glimpse of domestic harmony which had been offered her, gave her no regret, no longing. It was not a condition of life which fitted her, and she could see in it but an appalling and hopeless ennui. She was moved by a kind of commiseration for Madame Ratignolle – a pity for that colourless existence which never uplifted its possessor beyond the region of blind contentment, in which no moment of anguish ever visited her soul, in which she would never have the taste of life's delirium. Edna vaguely wondered what she meant by 'life's delirium'. It had crossed her thought like some unsought, extraneous impression.

19

Edna could not help but think that it was very foolish, very childish, to have stamped upon her wedding ring and smashed the crystal vase upon the tiles. She was visited by no more outbursts moving her to such futile expedients. She began to do as she liked and to feel as she liked. She completely abandoned her Tuesdays at home, and did not return the visits of those who had called upon her. She made no ineffectual efforts to conduct her household *en bonne ménagère*,[58] going and coming as it suited her fancy, and, so far as she was able, lending herself to any passing caprice.

Mr Pontellier had been a rather courteous husband so long as he met a certain tacit submissiveness in his wife. But her new and unexpected line of conduct completely bewildered him. It shocked him. Then her absolute disregard for her duties as a wife angered him. When Mr

Pontellier became rude, Edna grew insolent. She had resolved never to take another step backward.

'It seems to me the utmost folly for a woman at the head of a household, and the mother of children, to spend in an atelier[59] days which would be better employed contriving for the comfort of her family.'

'I feel like painting,' answered Edna. 'Perhaps I shan't always feel like it.'

'Then in God's name paint! but don't let the family go to the devil. There's Madame Ratignolle; because she keeps up her music, she doesn't let everything else go to chaos. And she's more of a musician than you are a painter.'

'She isn't a musician, and I'm not a painter. It isn't on account of painting that I let things go.'

'On account of what, then?'

'Oh! I don't know. Let me alone; you bother me.'

It sometimes entered Mr Pontellier's mind to wonder if his wife were not growing a little unbalanced mentally. He could see plainly that she was not herself. That is, he could not see that she was becoming herself and daily casting aside that fictitious self which we assume like a garment with which to appear before the world.

Her husband let her alone as she requested, and went away to his office. Edna went up to her atelier – a bright room in the top of the house. She was working with great energy and interest, without accomplishing anything, however, which satisfied her even in the smallest degree. For a time she had the whole household enrolled in the service of art. The boys posed for her. They thought it amusing at first, but the occupation soon lost its attractiveness when they discovered that it was not a game arranged especially for their entertainment. The quadroon sat for hours before Edna's palette, patient as a savage, while the housemaid took charge of the children, and the drawing-room went undusted. But the housemaid, too, served her term as model when Edna perceived that the young woman's back and shoulders were moulded on classic lines, and that her hair, loosened from its confining cap, became an inspiration. While Edna worked she sometimes sang low the little air '*Ah! si tu savais!*'[60]

It moved her with recollections. She could hear again the ripple of the water, the flapping sail. She could see the glint of the moon upon the bay, and could feel the soft, gusty beating of the hot south wind. A subtle current of desire passed through her body, weakening her hold upon the brushes and making her eyes burn.

There were days when she was very happy without knowing why.

She was happy to be alive and breathing when her whole being seemed to be one with the sunlight, the colour, the odours, the luxuriant warmth of some perfect Southern day. She liked then to wander alone into strange and unfamiliar places. She discovered many a sunny, sleepy corner, fashioned to dream in. And she found it good to dream and be alone and unmolested.

There were days when she was unhappy, she did not know why – when it did not seem worth while to be glad or sorry, to be alive or dead; when life appeared to her like a grotesque pandemonium and humanity like worms struggling blindly towards inevitable annihilation. She could not work on such a day, nor weave fancies to stir her pulses and warm her blood.

20

It was during such a mood that Edna hunted up Mademoiselle Reisz. She had not forgotten the rather disagreeable impression left upon her by their last interview, but she nevertheless felt a desire to see her – above all, to listen while she played upon the piano. Quite early in the afternoon she started upon her quest for the pianist. Unfortunately she had mislaid or lost Mademoiselle Reisz's card, and looking up her address in the city directory, she found that the woman lived on Bienville Street, some distance away. The directory which fell into her hands was a year or more old, however, and upon reaching the number indicated, Edna discovered that the house was occupied by a respectable family of mulattoes who had *chambres garnies* to let. They had been living there for six months, and knew absolutely nothing of a Mademoiselle Reisz. In fact, they knew nothing of any of their neighbours; their lodgers were all people of the highest distinction, they assured Edna. She did not linger to discuss class distinctions with Madame Pouponne, but hastened to a neighbouring grocery store, feeling sure that Mademoiselle would have left her address with the proprietor.

He knew Mademoiselle Reisz a good deal better than he wanted to know her, he informed his questioner. In truth, he did not want to know her at all, or anything concerning her – the most disagreeable and unpopular woman who ever lived in Bienville Street. He thanked heaven she had left the neighbourhood, and was equally thankful that he did not know where she had gone.

Edna's desire to see Mademoiselle Reisz had increased tenfold since these unlooked-for obstacles had arisen to thwart it. She was wondering who could give her the information she sought, when it suddenly occurred to her that Madame Lebrun would be the one most likely to do so. She knew it was useless to ask Madame Ratignolle, who was on the most distant terms with the musician, and preferred to know nothing concerning her. She had once been almost as emphatic in expressing herself upon the subject as the corner grocer.

Edna knew that Madame Lebrun had returned to the city, for it was the middle of November. And she also knew where the Lebruns lived, on Chartres Street.

Their home from the outside looked like a prison, with iron bars before the door and lower windows. The iron bars were a relic of the old *régime*,[61] and no one had ever thought of dislodging them. At the side was a high fence enclosing the garden. A gate or door opening upon the street was locked. Edna rang the bell at this side garden gate, and stood upon the banquette, waiting to be admitted.

It was Victor who opened the gate for her. A black woman, wiping her hands upon her apron, was close at his heels. Before she saw them Edna could hear them in altercation, the woman – plainly an anomaly – claiming the right to be allowed to perform her duties, one of which was to answer the bell.

Victor was surprised and delighted to see Mrs Pontellier, and he made no attempt to conceal either his astonishment or his delight. He was a dark-browed, good-looking youngster of nineteen, greatly resembling his mother, but with ten times her impetuosity. He instructed the black woman to go at once and inform Madame Lebrun that Mrs Pontellier desired to see her. The woman grumbled a refusal to do part of her duty when she had not been permitted to do it all, and started back to her interrupted task of weeding the garden. Whereupon Victor administered a rebuke in the form of a volley of abuse, which, owing to its rapidity and incoherence, was all but incomprehensible to Edna. Whatever it was, the rebuke was convincing, for the woman dropped her hoe and went mumbling into the house.

Edna did not wish to enter. It was very pleasant there on the side porch, where there were chairs, a wicker lounge, and a small table. She seated herself, for she was tired from her long tramp; and she began to rock gently and smooth out the folds of her silk parasol. Victor drew up his chair beside her. He at once explained that the black woman's offensive conduct was all due to imperfect training, as he was not there to take her in hand. He had only come up from the island the morning before, and expected to return next day. He stayed all winter at the island; he lived there, and kept the place in order and got things ready for the summer visitors.

But a man needed occasional relaxation, he informed Mrs Pontellier, and every now and again he drummed up a pretext to bring him to the city. My! but he had had a time of it the evening before! He wouldn't want his mother to know, and he began to talk in a whisper. He was scintillant with recollections. Of course, he couldn't think of telling Mrs Pontellier all about it, she being a woman and not comprehending such things. But it all began with a girl peeping and smiling at him through the shutters as he passed by. Oh! but she was a beauty! Certainly he smiled back, and went up and talked to her. Mrs Pontellier did not know him if she supposed he was one to let an opportunity like that escape him. Despite herself, the youngster amused her. She must have betrayed in her look some degree of interest or entertainment. The boy grew more daring, and Mrs Pontellier might have found herself, in a little while, listening to a highly coloured story but for the timely appearance of Madame Lebrun.

That lady was still clad in white, according to her custom of the summer. Her eyes beamed an effusive welcome. Would not Mrs Pontellier go inside? Would she partake of some refreshment? Why had she not been there before? How was that dear Mr Pontellier and how were those sweet children? Had Mrs Pontellier ever known such a warm November?

Victor went and reclined on the wicker lounge behind his mother's chair, where he commanded a view of Edna's face. He had taken her parasol from her hands while he spoke to her, and he now lifted it and twirled it above him as he lay on his back. When Madame Lebrun complained that it was *so* dull coming back to the city; that she saw *so* few people now; that even Victor, when he came up from the island for a day or two, had *so* much to occupy him and engage his time; then it was that the youth went into contortions on the lounge and winked mischievously at Edna. She somehow felt like a confederate in crime, and tried to look severe and disapproving.

There had been but two letters from Robert, with little in them, they told her. Victor said it was really not worth while to go inside for the letters, when his mother entreated him to go in search of them. He remembered the contents, which in truth he rattled off very glibly when put to the test.

One letter was written from Vera Cruz and the other from the City of Mexico. He had met Montel, who was doing everything towards his advancement. So far, the financial situation was no improvement over the one he had left in New Orleans, but of course the prospects were vastly better. He wrote of the City of Mexico, the buildings, the people and their habits, the conditions of life which he found there. He sent his love to the family. He enclosed a cheque to his mother and hoped she would affectionately remember him to all his friends. That was about the substance of the two letters. Edna felt that if there had been a message for her, she would have received it. The despondent frame of mind in which she had left home began again to overtake her, and she remembered that she wished to find Mademoiselle Reisz.

Madame Lebrun knew where Mademoiselle Reisz lived. She gave Edna the address, regretting that she would not consent to stay and spend the remainder of the afternoon, and pay a visit to Mademoiselle Reisz some other day. The afternoon was already well advanced.

Victor escorted her out upon the banquette, lifted her parasol, and held it over her while he walked to the car with her. He entreated her to bear in mind that the disclosures of the afternoon were strictly confidential. She laughed and bantered him a little, remembering too late that she should have been dignified and reserved.

'How handsome Mrs Pontellier looked!' said Madame Lebrun to her son.

'Ravishing!' he admitted. 'The city atmosphere has improved her. Some way she doesn't seem like the same woman.'

21

Some people contended that the reason Mademoiselle Reisz always chose apartments up under the roof was to discourage the approach of beggars, pedlars and callers. There were plenty of windows in her little front room. They were for the most part dingy, but as they were nearly always open it did not make so much difference. They often admitted into the room a good deal of smoke and soot; but at the same time all the light and air that there was came through them. From her windows could be seen the crescent of the river, the masts of ships and the big chimneys of the Mississippi steamers. A magnificent piano crowded the apartment. In the next room she slept, and in the third and last she harboured a gasoline stove on which she cooked her meals when disinclined to descend to the neighbouring restaurant. It was there also that she ate, keeping her belongings in a rare old buffet, dingy and battered from a hundred years of use.

When Edna knocked at Mademoiselle Reisz's front-room door and entered, she discovered that person standing beside the window, engaged in mending or patching an old prunella gaiter.[62] The little musician laughed all over when she saw Edna. Her laugh consisted of a contortion of the face and all the muscles of the body. She seemed strikingly homely, standing there in the afternoon light. She still wore the shabby lace and the artificial bunch of violets on the side of her head.

'So you remembered me at last,' said Mademoiselle. 'I had said to myself, "Ah, bah! she will never come." '

'Did you want me to come?' asked Edna with a smile.

'I had not thought much about it,' answered Mademoiselle. The two had seated themselves on a little bumpy sofa which stood against the wall. 'I am glad, however, that you came. I have the water boiling back there, and was just about to make some coffee. You will drink a cup with me. And how is *la belle dame*?[63] Always handsome! always healthy! always contented!' She took Edna's hand between her strong wiry fingers, holding it loosely without warmth, and executing a sort of double theme upon the back and palm.

'Yes,' she went on; 'I sometimes thought: "She will never come. She promised as those women in society always do without meaning it. She will not come." For I really don't believe you like me, Mrs Pontellier.'

'I don't know whether I like you or not,' replied Edna, gazing down at the little woman with a quizzical look.

The candour of Mrs Pontellier's admission greatly pleased Mademoiselle Reisz. She expressed her gratification by repairing forthwith to the region of the gasoline stove and rewarding her guest with the promised cup of coffee. The coffee and the biscuit accompanying it proved very acceptable to Edna, who had declined refreshment at Madame Lebrun's and was now beginning to feel hungry. Mademoiselle set the tray which she brought in upon a small table near at hand, and seated herself once again on the lumpy sofa.

'I have had a letter from your friend,' she remarked, as she poured a little cream into Edna's cup and handed it to her.

'My friend?'

'Yes, your friend Robert. He wrote to me from the City of Mexico.'

'Wrote to *you*?' repeated Edna in amazement, stirring her coffee absently.

'Yes to me Why not? Don't stir all the warmth out of your coffee; drink it. Though the letter might as well have been sent to you; it was nothing but Mrs Pontellier from beginning to end.'

'Let me see it,' requested the young woman, entreatingly.

'No; a letter concerns no one but the person who writes it and the one to whom it is written.'

'Haven't you just said it concerned me from beginning to end?'

'It was written about you, not to you. "Have you seen Mrs Pontellier? How is she looking?" he asks. "As Mrs Pontellier says", or "as Mrs

Pontellier once said". "If Mrs Pontellier should call upon you, play for her that Impromptu of Chopin's,[64] my favourite. I heard it here a day or two ago, but not as you play it. I should like to know how it affects her," and so on, as if he supposed we were constantly in each other's society.'

'Let me see the letter.'

'Oh, no.'

'Have you answered it?'

'No.'

'Let me see the letter.'

'No, and again, no.'

'Then play the Impromptu for me.'

'It is growing late; what time do you have to be home?'

'Time doesn't concern me. Your question seems a little rude. Play the Impromptu.'

'But you have told me nothing of yourself. What are you doing?'

'Painting!' laughed Edna. 'I am becoming an artist. Think of it!'

'Ah! an artist! You have pretensions, madame.'

'Why pretensions? Do you think I could not become an artist?'

'I do not know you well enough to say. I do not know your talent or your temperament. To be an artist includes much; one must possess many gifts – absolute gifts – which have not been acquired by one's own effort. And, moreover, to succeed, the artist must possess the courageous soul.'

'What do you mean by the courageous soul?'

'Courageous, ma foi! The brave soul. The soul that dares and defies.'

'Show me the letter and play for me the Impromptu. You see that I have persistence. Does that quality count for anything in art?'

'It counts with a foolish old woman whom you have captivated,' replied Mademoiselle, with her wriggling laugh.

The letter was right there at hand in the drawer of the little table upon which Edna had just placed her coffee cup. Mademoiselle opened the drawer and drew forth the letter, the topmost one. She placed it in Edna's hands, and without further comment arose and went to the piano.

Mademoiselle played a soft interlude. It was an improvisation. She sat low at the instrument, and the lines of her body settled into ungraceful curves and angles that gave it an appearance of deformity. Gradually and imperceptibly the interlude melted into the soft opening minor chords of the Chopin Impromptu.

Edna did not know when the Impromptu began or ended. She sat in the sofa corner reading Robert's letter by the fading light. Mademoiselle had glided from the Chopin into the quivering love-notes of Isolde's song,[65] and back again to the Impromptu with its soulful and poignant longing.

The shadows deepened in the little room. The music grew strange and fantastic – turbulent, insistent, plaintive and soft with entreaty. The shadows grew deeper. The music filled the room. It floated out upon the night, over the housetops, the crescent of the river, losing itself in the silence of the upper air.

Edna was sobbing, just as she had wept one midnight at Grand Isle when strange, new voices awoke in her. She arose in some agitation to take her departure. 'May I come again, Mademoiselle?' she asked at the threshold.

'Come whenever you feel like it. Be careful; the stairs and landings are dark; don't stumble.'

Mademoiselle re-entered and lit a candle. Robert's letter was on the floor. She stooped and picked it up. It was crumpled and damp with tears. Mademoiselle smoothed the letter out, restored it to the envelope, and replaced it in the table drawer.

22

One morning on his way into town Mr Pontellier stopped at the house of his old friend and family physician, Dr Mandelet. The doctor was a semi-retired physician, resting, as the saying is, upon his laurels. He bore a reputation for wisdom rather than skill – leaving the active practice of medicine to his assistants and younger contemporaries – and was much sought for in matters of consultation. A few families, united to him by bonds of friendship, he still attended when they required the services of a physician. The Pontelliers were among these.

Mr Pontellier found the doctor reading at the open window of his study. His house stood rather far back from the street, in the centre of a delightful garden, so that it was quiet and peaceful at the old gentleman's study window. He was a great reader. He stared up disapprovingly over his eye-glasses as Mr Pontellier entered, wondering who had the temerity to disturb him at that hour of the morning.

'Ah, Pontellier! Not sick, I hope. Come and have a seat. What news do you bring this morning?' He was quite portly, with a profusion of grey hair, and small blue eyes which age had robbed of much of their brightness but none of their penetration.

'Oh! I'm never sick, doctor. You know that I come of tough fibre – of that old Creole race of Pontelliers that dry up and finally blow away. I came to consult – no, not precisely to consult – to talk to you about Edna. I don't know what ails her.'

'Madame Pontellier not well?' marvelled the doctor. 'Why, I saw her – I think it was a week ago – walking along Canal Street,[66] the picture of health, it seemed to me.'

'Yes, yes; she seems quite well,' said Mr Pontellier, leaning forward and whirling his stick between his two hands; 'but she doesn't act well. She's odd, she's not like herself. I can't make her out, and I thought perhaps you'd help me.'

'How does she act?' enquired the doctor.

'Well, it isn't easy to explain,' said Mr Pontellier, throwing himself back in his chair. 'She lets the housekeeping go to the dickens.'

'Well, well; women are not all alike, my dear Pontellier. We've got to consider – '

'I know that; I told you I couldn't explain. Her whole attitude – towards me and everybody and everything – has changed. You know I have a quick temper, but I don't want to quarrel or be rude to a woman, especially my wife; yet I'm driven to it, and feel like ten thousand devils after I've made a fool of myself. She's making it devilishly uncomfortable for me,' he went on nervously. 'She's got some sort of notion in her head concerning the eternal rights of women, and – you understand – we meet in the morning at the breakfast table.'

The old gentleman lifted his shaggy eyebrows, protruded his thick nether lip, and tapped the arms of his chair with his cushioned fingertips.

'What have you been doing to her, Pontellier?'

'Doing! *Parbleu!*'

'Has she,' asked the doctor, with a smile, 'has she been associating of late with a circle of pseudo-intellectual women – super-spiritual superior beings? My wife has been telling me about them.'

'That's the trouble,' broke in Mr Pontellier, 'she hasn't been associating with anyone. She has abandoned her Tuesdays at home, has thrown over all her acquaintances, and goes tramping about by herself, moping in the street-cars, getting in after dark. I tell you she's peculiar. I don't like it; I feel a little worried over it.'

This was a new aspect for the doctor. 'Nothing hereditary?' he asked, seriously. 'Nothing peculiar about her family antecedents, is there?'

'Oh, no, indeed! She comes of sound old Presbyterian Kentucky stock. The old gentleman, her father, I have heard, used to atone for his weekday sins with his Sunday devotions. I know for a fact, that his race-horses literally ran away with the prettiest bit of Kentucky farming land I ever laid eyes upon. Margaret – you know Margaret – she has all the Presbyterianism undiluted. And the youngest is something of a vixen. By the way, she gets married in a couple of weeks from now.'

'Send your wife up to the wedding,' exclaimed the doctor, foreseeing a happy solution. 'Let her stay among her own people for a while; it will do her good.'

'That's what I want her to do. She won't go to the marriage. She says a wedding is one of the most lamentable spectacles on earth. Nice thing for a woman to say to her husband!' exclaimed Mr Pontellier, fuming anew at the recollection.

'Pontellier,' said the doctor, after a moment's reflection, 'let your wife alone for a while. Don't bother her, and don't let her bother you. Woman, my dear friend, is a very peculiar and delicate organism – a sensitive and highly organised woman, such as I know Mrs Pontellier to be, is especially peculiar. It would require an inspired psychologist to deal successfully with them. And when ordinary fellows like you and me attempt to cope with their idiosyncrasies the result is bungling. Most women are moody and whimsical. This is some passing whim of your wife, due to some cause or causes which you and I needn't try to fathom. But it will pass happily over, especially if you let her alone. Send her around to see me.'

'Oh! I couldn't do that; there'd be no reason for it,' objected Mr Pontellier.

'Then I'll go around and see her,' said the doctor. 'I'll drop in to dinner some evening *en bon ami*.'

'Do! by all means,' urged Mr Pontellier. 'What evening will you come? Say Thursday. Will you come Thursday?' he asked, rising to take his leave.

'Very well; Thursday. My wife may possibly have some engagement for me Thursday. In case she has, I shall let you know. Otherwise, you may expect me.'

Mr Pontellier turned before leaving to say: 'I am going to New York on business very soon. I have a big scheme on hand, and want to be on the field proper to pull the ropes and handle the ribbons. We'll let you in on the inside if you say so, doctor,' he laughed.

'No, I thank you, my dear sir,' returned the doctor. 'I leave such ventures to you younger men with the fever of life still in your blood.'

'What I wanted to say,' continued Mr Pontellier, with his hand on the knob; 'I may have to be absent a good while. Would you advise me to take Edna along?'

'By all means, if she wishes to go. If not, leave her here. Don't contradict her. The mood will pass, I assure you. It may take a month, two, three months – possibly longer, but it will pass; have patience.'

'Well, goodbye, *à jeudi*,'[67] said Mr Pontellier, as he let himself out.

The doctor would have liked during the course of conversation to ask, 'Is there any man in the case?' but he knew his Creole too well to make such a blunder as that.

He did not resume his book immediately, but sat for a while meditatively looking out into the garden.

23

Edna's father was in the city, and had been with them several days. She was not very warmly or deeply attached to him, but they had certain tastes in common, and when together they were companionable. His coming was in the nature of a welcome disturbance; it seemed to furnish a new direction for her emotions.

He had come to purchase a wedding gift for his daughter Janet, and an outfit for himself in which he might make a creditable appearance at her marriage. Mr Pontellier had selected the bridal gift, as everyone immediately connected with him always deferred to his taste in such matters. And his suggestions on the question of dress – which too often assumes the nature of a problem – were of inestimable value to his father-in-law. But for the past few days the old gentleman had been upon Edna's hands, and in his society she was becoming acquainted with a new set of sensations. He had been a colonel in the Confederate army,[68] and still maintained, with the title, the military bearing which had always accompanied it. His hair and moustache were white and silky, emphasising the rugged bronze of his face. He was tall and thin, and wore his coats padded, which gave a fictitious breadth and depth to his shoulders and chest. Edna and her father looked very distinguished together, and excited a good deal of notice during their perambulations. Upon his arrival she began by introducing him to her atelier and making a sketch of him. He took the whole matter very seriously. If her talent had been tenfold greater than it was, it would not have surprised him, convinced as he was that he had bequeathed to all of his daughters the germs of a masterful capability, which only depended upon their own efforts to be directed towards successful achievement.

Before her pencil he sat rigid and unflinching, as he had faced the cannon's mouth in days gone by. He resented the intrusion of the children, who gaped with wondering eyes at him, sitting so stiff up there in their mother's bright atelier. When they drew near he motioned them away with an expressive action of the foot, loath to disturb the fixed lines of his countenance, his arms or his rigid shoulders.

Edna, anxious to entertain him, invited Mademoiselle Reisz to meet him, having promised him a treat in her piano playing; but

Mademoiselle declined the invitation. So together they attended a *soirée musicale* at the Ratignolles'. Monsieur and Madame Ratignolle made much of the colonel, installing him as the guest of honour and engaging him at once to dine with them the following Sunday, or any day which he might select. Madame coquetted with him in the most captivating and naïve manner, with eyes, gestures, and a profusion of compliments, till the colonel's old head felt thirty years younger on his padded shoulders. Edna marvelled, not comprehending. She herself was almost devoid of coquetry.

There were one or two men whom she observed at the *soirée musicale*; but she would never have felt moved to any kittenish display to attract their notice – to any feline or feminine wiles to express herself towards them. Their personality attracted her in an agreeable way. Her fancy selected them, and she was glad when a lull in the music gave them an opportunity to meet her and talk with her. Often on the street the glance of strange eyes had lingered in her memory, and sometimes had disturbed her.

Mr Pontellier did not attend these *soirées musicales*. He considered them *bourgeois*,[69] and found more diversion at the club. To Madame Ratignolle he said the music dispensed at her *soirées* was too 'heavy', too far beyond his untrained comprehension. His excuse flattered her. But she disapproved of Mr Pontellier's club and she was frank enough to tell Edna so.

'It's a pity Mr Pontellier doesn't stay home more in the evenings. I think you would be more – well, if you don't mind my saying it – more united, if he did.'

'Oh! dear no!' said Edna, with a blank look in her eyes. 'What should I do if he stayed home? We wouldn't have anything to say to each other.'

She had not much of anything to say to her father, for that matter; but he did not antagonise her. She discovered that he interested her, though she realised that he might not interest her long; and for the first time in her life she felt as if she were thoroughly acquainted with him. He kept her busy serving him and ministering to his wants. It amused her to do so. She would not permit a servant or one of the children to do anything for him which she might do herself. Her husband noticed, and thought it was the expression of a deep filial attachment which he had never suspected.

The colonel drank numerous 'toddies' during the course of the day, which left him, however, imperturbed. He was an expert at concocting strong drinks. He had even invented some, to which he had given fantastic names, and for whose manufacture he required diverse ingredients that it devolved upon Edna to procure for him.

When Dr Mandelet dined with the Pontelliers on Thursday he could discern in Mrs Pontellier no trace of that morbid condition which her husband had reported to him. She was excited and in a manner radiant. She and her father had been to the racecourse, and their thoughts when they seated themselves at table were still occupied with the events of the afternoon, and their talk was still of the track. The doctor had not kept pace with turf affairs. He had certain recollections of racing in what he called 'the good old times' when the Lecompte stables[70] flourished, and he drew upon this fund of memories so that he might not be left out and seem wholly devoid of the modern spirit. But he failed to impose upon the colonel, and was even far from impressing him with this trumped-up knowledge of bygone days. Edna had staked her father on his last venture, with the most gratifying results to both of them. Besides, they had met some very charming people, according to the colonel's impressions. Mrs Mortimer Merriman and Mrs James Highcamp, who were there with Alcée Arobin, had joined them and had enlivened the hours in a fashion that warmed him to think of.

Mr Pontellier himself had no particular leaning towards horse-racing, and was even rather inclined to discourage it as a pastime, especially when he considered the fate of that blue-grass farm in Kentucky. He endeavoured, in a general way, to express a particular disapproval, and only succeeded in arousing the ire and opposition of his father-in-law. A pretty dispute followed, in which Edna warmly espoused her father's cause and the doctor remained neutral.

He observed his hostess attentively from under his shaggy brows, and noted a subtle change which had transformed her from the listless woman he had known into a being who, for the moment, seemed palpitant with the forces of life. Her speech was warm and energetic. There was no repression in her glance or gesture. She reminded him of some beautiful, sleek animal waking up in the sun.

The dinner was excellent. The claret was warm and the champagne was cold, and under their beneficent influence the threatened unpleasantness melted and vanished with the fumes of the wine.

Mr Pontellier warmed up and grew reminiscent. He told some amusing plantation experiences, recollections of old Iberville and his youth, when he hunted 'possum in company with some friendly darky; thrashed the pecan trees, shot the grosbec, and roamed the woods and fields in mischievous idleness.

The colonel, with little sense of humour and of the fitness of things, related a sombre episode of those dark and bitter days, in which he had acted a conspicuous part and always formed a central figure. Nor was the doctor happier in his selection, when he told the old, ever new and curious story of the waning of a woman's love, seeking strange, new channels, only to return to its legitimate source after days of fierce unrest. It was one of the many little human documents which had been unfolded to him during his long career as a physician. The story did not seem especially to impress Edna. She had one of her own to tell, of a woman who paddled away with her lover one night in a pirogue and never came back. They were lost amid the Baratarian Islands,[71] and no one ever heard of them or found trace of them from that day to this. It was a pure invention. She said that Madame Antoine had related it to her. That, also, was an invention. Perhaps it was a dream she had had. But every glowing word seemed real to those who listened. They could feel the hot breath of the Southern night; they could hear the long sweep of the pirogue through the glistening moonlit water, the beating of birds' wings, rising startled from among the reeds in the salt-water pools, they could see the faces of the lovers, pale, close together, rapt in oblivious forgetfulness, drifting into the unknown.

The champagne was cold, and its subtle fumes played fantastic tricks with Edna's memory that night.

Outside, away from the glow of the fire and the soft lamplight, the night was chill and murky. The doctor doubled his old-fashioned cloak across his breast as he strode home through the darkness. He knew his fellow-creatures better than most men; knew that inner life which so seldom unfolds itself to unanointed eyes. He was sorry he had accepted Pontellier's invitation. He was growing old, and beginning to need rest and an imperturbed spirit. He did not want the secrets of other lives thrust upon him.

'I hope it isn't Arobin,' he muttered to himself as he walked. 'I hope to heaven it isn't Alcée Arobin.'

24

Edna and her father had a warm, and almost violent dispute upon the subject of her refusal to attend her sister's wedding. Mr Pontellier declined to interfere, to interpose either his influence or his authority. He was following Dr Mandelet's advice, and letting her do as she liked. The colonel reproached his daughter for her lack of filial kindness and respect, her want of sisterly affection and womanly consideration. His arguments were laboured and unconvincing. He doubted if Janet would accept any excuse – forgetting that Edna had offered none.

He doubted if Janet would ever speak to her again, and he was sure Margaret would not.

Edna was glad to be rid of her father when he finally took himself off with his wedding garments and his bridal gifts, with his padded shoulders, his Bible reading, his 'toddies' and ponderous oaths.

Mr Pontellier followed him closely. He meant to stop at the wedding on his way to New York and endeavour by every means which money and love could devise to atone somewhat for Edna's incomprehensible action.

'You are too lenient, too lenient by far, Léonce,' asserted the colonel. 'Authority, coercion are what is needed. Put your foot down good and hard; the only way to manage a wife. Take my word for it.'

The colonel was perhaps unaware that he had coerced his own wife into her grave. Mr Pontellier had a vague suspicion of it which he thought it needless to mention at that late day.

Edna was not so consciously gratified at her husband's leaving home as she had been over the departure of her father. As the day approached when he was to leave her for a comparatively long stay, she grew melting and affectionate, remembering his many acts of consideration and his repeated expressions of an ardent attachment. She was solicitous about his health and his welfare. She bustled around, looking after his clothing, thinking about heavy underwear, quite as Madame Ratignolle would have done under similar circumstances. She cried when he went away, calling him her dear, good friend, and she was quite certain she would grow lonely before long and go to join him in New York.

But after all, a radiant peace settled upon her when she at last found herself alone. Even the children were gone. Old Madame Pontellier had come herself and carried them off to Iberville with their quadroon. The old madame did not venture to say she was afraid they would be neglected during Léonce's absence; she hardly ventured to think so. She was hungry for them – even a little fierce in her attachment. She did not want them to be wholly 'children of the pavement', she always said when begging to have them for a space. She wished them to know the country, with its streams, its fields, its woods, its freedom, so delicious to the young. She wished them to taste something of the life their father had lived and known and loved when he, too, was a little child.

When Edna was at last alone, she breathed a big, genuine sigh of relief. A feeling that was unfamiliar but very delicious came over her. She walked all through the house, from one room to another, as if inspecting it for the first time. She tried the various chairs and lounges,

as if she had never sat and reclined upon them before. And she per-
ambulated around the outside of the house, investigating, looking to
see if windows and shutters were secure and in order. The flowers were
like new acquaintances; she approached them in a familiar spirit, and
made herself at home among them. The garden walks were damp, and
Edna called to the maid to bring out her rubber sandals. And there she
stayed, and stooped, digging around the plants, trimming, picking dead,
dry leaves. The children's little dog came out, interfering, getting in her
way. She scolded him, laughed at him, played with him. The garden
smelled so good and looked so pretty in the afternoon sunlight. Edna
plucked all the bright flowers she could find, and went into the house
with them, she and the little dog.

Even the kitchen assumed a sudden interesting character which she
had never before perceived. She went in to give directions to the cook,
to say that the butcher would have to bring much less meat, that they
would require only half their usual quantity of bread, of milk and
groceries. She told the cook that she herself would be greatly occupied
during Mr Pontellier's absence, and she begged her to take all thought
and responsibility of the larder upon her own shoulders.

That night Edna dined alone. The candelabra, with a few candles in
the centre of the table, gave all the light she needed. Outside the circle
of light in which she sat, the large dining-room looked solemn and
shadowy. The cook, placed upon her mettle, served a delicious repast –
a luscious tenderloin broiled à point.[72] The wine tasted good; the marron
glacé[73] seemed to be just what she wanted. It was so pleasant, too, to
dine in a comfortable peignoir.

She thought a little sentimentally about Léonce and the children, and
wondered what they were doing. As she gave a dainty scrap or two to
the doggie, she talked intimately to him about Etienne and Raoul. He
was beside himself with astonishment and delight over these companionable advances, and showed his appreciation by his little quick,
snappy barks and a lively agitation.

Then Edna sat in the library after dinner and read Emerson[74] until
she grew sleepy. She realised that she had neglected her reading, and
determined to start anew upon a course of improving studies, now that
her time was completely her own to do with as she liked.

After a refreshing bath, Edna went to bed. And as she snuggled
comfortably beneath the eiderdown a sense of restfulness invaded her,
such as she had not known before.

25

When the weather was dark and cloudy Edna could not work. She needed the sun to mellow and temper her mood to the sticking point. She had reached a stage when she seemed to be no longer feeling her way, working, when in the humour, with sureness and ease. And being devoid of ambition, and striving not towards accomplishment, she drew satisfaction from the work in itself.

On rainy or melancholy days Edna went out and sought the society of the friends she had made at Grand Isle. Or else she stayed indoors and nursed a mood with which she was becoming too familiar for her own comfort and peace of mind. It was not despair; but it seemed to her as if life were passing by, leaving its promise broken and unfulfilled. Yet there were other days when she listened, was led on and deceived by fresh promises which her youth held out to her.

She went again to the races, and again. Alcée Arobin and Mrs Highcamp called for her one bright afternoon in Arobin's drag.[75] Mrs Highcamp was a worldly but unaffected, intelligent, slim, tall, blonde woman in the forties, with an indifferent manner and blue eyes that stared. She had a daughter who served her as a pretext for cultivating the society of young men of fashion. Alcée Arobin was one of them. He was a familiar figure at the racecourse, the opera, the fashionable clubs. There was a perpetual smile in his eyes, which seldom failed to awaken a corresponding cheerfulness in anyone who looked into them and listened to his good-humoured voice. His manner was quiet, and at times a little insolent. He possessed a good figure, a pleasing face, not overburdened with depth of thought or feeling; and his dress was that of the conventional man of fashion.

He admired Edna extravagantly, after meeting her at the races with her father. He had met her before on other occasions, but she had seemed to him unapproachable until that day. It was at his instigation that Mrs Highcamp called to ask her to go with them to the Jockey Club to witness the turf event of the season.

There were possibly a few track men out there who knew the race-horse as well as Edna, but there was certainly none who knew it better. She sat between her two companions as one having authority to speak. She laughed at Arobin's pretensions, and deplored Mrs Highcamp's ignorance. The racehorse was a friend and intimate associate of her childhood. The atmosphere of the stables and the breath of the blue-grass paddock revived in her memory and lingered in her nostrils. She did not perceive that she was talking like her father as the sleek geldings ambled in review before them. She played for very high stakes, and fortune favoured her. The fever of the game flamed in her cheeks and eyes, and it got into her blood and into her brain like an intoxicant. People turned their heads to look at her, and more than one lent an attentive ear to her utterances, hoping thereby to secure the elusive but ever-desired 'tip'. Arobin caught the contagion of excitement which drew him to Edna like a magnet. Mrs Highcamp remained, as usual, unmoved, with her indifferent stare and uplifted eyebrows.

Edna stayed and dined with Mrs Highcamp upon being urged to do so. Arobin also remained and sent away his drag.

The dinner was quiet and uninteresting, save for the cheerful efforts of Arobin to enliven things. Mrs Highcamp deplored the absence of her daughter from the races, and tried to convey to her what she had missed by going to the 'Dante[76] reading' instead of joining them. The girl held a geranium leaf up to her nose and said nothing, but looked knowing and noncommittal. Mr Highcamp was a plain, bald-headed man, who only talked under compulsion. He was unresponsive. Mrs Highcamp was full of delicate courtesy and consideration towards her husband. She addressed most of her conversation to him at table. They sat in the library after dinner and read the evening papers together under the drop-light; while the younger people went into the drawing-room near by and talked. Miss Highcamp played some selections from Grieg[77] upon the piano. She seemed to have apprehended all of the composer's coldness and none of his poetry. While Edna listened she could not help wondering if she had lost her taste for music.

When the time came for her to go home, Mr Highcamp grunted a lame offer to escort her, looking down at his slippered feet with tactless concern. It was Arobin who took her home. The car ride was long, and it was late when they reached Esplanade Street. Arobin asked permission to enter for a second to light his cigarette – his match safe was empty. He filled his match safe, but did not light his cigarette until he left her, after she had expressed her willingness to go to the races with him again.

Edna was neither tired nor sleepy. She was hungry again, for the Highcamp dinner, though of excellent quality, had lacked abundance. She rummaged in the larder and brought forth a slice of Gruyère and some crackers. She opened a bottle of beer which she found in the ice-box. Edna felt extremely restless and excited. She vacantly hummed a fantastic tune as she poked at the wood embers on the hearth and munched a cracker.

She wanted something to happen – something, anything; she did not know what. She regretted that she had not made Arobin stay a half-hour to talk over the horses with her. She counted the money she had won. But there was nothing else to do, so she went to bed, and tossed there for hours in a sort of monotonous agitation.

In the middle of the night she remembered that she had forgotten to write her regular letter to her husband; and she decided to do so next day and tell him about her afternoon at the Jockey Club. She lay wide awake composing a letter which was nothing like the one which she wrote next day. When the maid awoke her in the morning Edna was dreaming of Mr Highcamp playing on the piano at the entrance of a music store on Canal Street, while his wife was saying to Alcée Arobin, as they boarded an Esplanade Street car: 'What a pity that so much talent has been neglected! but I must go.'

When, a few days later, Alcée Arobin again called for Edna in his drag, Mrs Highcamp was not with him. He said they would pick her up. But as that lady had not been apprised of his intention of picking her up, she was not at home. The daughter was just leaving the house to attend the meeting of a branch Folk Lore Society, and regretted that she could not accompany them. Arobin appeared nonplussed, and asked Edna if there were anyone else she cared to ask.

She did not deem it worth while to go in search of any of the fashionable acquaintances from whom she had withdrawn herself. She thought of Madame Ratignolle, but knew that her fair friend did not leave the house, except to take a languid walk around the block with her husband after nightfall. Mademoiselle Reisz would have laughed at such a request from Edna. Madame Lebrun might have enjoyed the outing, but for some reason Edna did not want her. So they went alone, she and Arobin.

The afternoon was intensely interesting to her. The excitement came back upon her like a remittent fever. Her talk grew familiar and con-fidential. It was no labour to become intimate with Arobin. His manner invited easy confidence. The preliminary stage of becoming acquainted was one which he always endeavoured to ignore when a pretty and engaging woman was concerned.

He stayed and dined with Edna. He stayed and sat beside the wood fire. They laughed and talked; and before it was time to go he was telling her how different life might have been if he had known her years before. With ingenuous frankness he spoke of what a wicked, ill-disciplined boy he had been, and impulsively drew up his cuff to exhibit upon his wrist the scar from a sabre cut which he had received in a duel outside of Paris when he was nineteen. She touched his hand as she scanned the red cicatrice on the inside of his white wrist. A quick impulse that was somewhat spasmodic impelled her fingers to close in a sort of clutch upon his hand. He felt the pressure of her pointed nails in the flesh of his palm.

She arose hastily and walked towards the mantel.

'The sight of a wound or scar always agitates and sickens me,' she said. 'I shouldn't have looked at it.'

'I beg your pardon,' he entreated, following her; 'it never occurred to me that it might be repulsive.'

He stood close to her, and the effrontery in his eyes repelled the old, vanishing self in her, yet drew all her awakening sensuousness. He saw enough in her face to impel him to take her hand and hold it while he said his lingering good-night.

'Will you go to the races again?' he asked.

'No,' she said. 'I've had enough of the races. I don't want to lose all the money I've won, and I've got to work when the weather is bright, instead of – '

'Yes; work; to be sure. You promised to show me your work. What morning may I come up to your atelier? Tomorrow?'

'No!'

'Day after?'

'No, no.'

'Oh, please don't refuse me! I know something of such things. I might help you with a stray suggestion or two.'

'No. Good-night. Why don't you go after you have said good-night? I don't like you,' she went on in a high, excited pitch, attempting to draw away her hand. She felt that her words lacked dignity and sincerity, and she knew that he felt it.

'I'm sorry you don't like me. I'm sorry I offended you. How have I offended you? What have I done? Can't you forgive me?' And he bent and pressed his lips upon her hand as if he wished never more to withdraw them.

'Mr Arobin,' she complained, 'I'm greatly upset by the excitement of the afternoon; I'm not myself. My manner must have misled you in some way. I wish you to go, please.' She spoke in a monotonous, dull tone. He took his hat from the table, and stood with eyes turned from her, looking into the dying fire. For a moment or two he kept an impressive silence.

'Your manner has not misled me, Mrs Pontellier,' he said finally. 'My own emotions have done that. I couldn't help it. When I'm near you, how could I help it? Don't think anything of it, don't bother, please. You see, I go when you command me. If you wish me to stay away, I shall do so. If you let me come back, I – oh! you will let me come back?'

He cast one appealing glance at her, to which she made no response. Alcée Arobin's manner was so genuine that it often deceived even himself.

Edna did not care or think whether it were genuine or not. When she was alone she looked mechanically at the back of her hand which he had kissed so warmly. Then she leaned her head down on the mantelpiece. She felt somewhat like a woman who in a moment of passion is betrayed into an act of infidelity, and realises the significance of the act without being wholly awakened from its glamour. The thought was passing vaguely through her mind, 'What would he think?'

She did not mean her husband; she was thinking of Robert Lebrun. Her husband seemed to her now like a person whom she had married without love as an excuse.

She lit a candle and went up to her room. Alcée Arobin was absolutely nothing to her. Yet his presence, his manners, the warmth of his glances, and above all the touch of his lips upon her hand had acted like a narcotic upon her.

She slept a languorous sleep, interwoven with vanishing dreams.

26

Alcée Arobin wrote Edna an elaborate note of apology, palpitant with sincerity. It embarrassed her; for in a cooler, quieter moment it appeared to her absurd that she should have taken his action so seriously, so dramatically. She felt sure that the significance of the whole occurrence had lain in her own self-consciousness. If she ignored his note it would give undue importance to a trivial affair. If she replied to it in a serious spirit it would still leave in his mind the impression that she had in a susceptible moment yielded to his influence. After all, it was no great matter to have one's hand kissed. She was provoked at his having written the apology. She answered in as light and bantering a spirit as she fancied it deserved, and said she would be glad to have him look in upon her at work whenever he felt the inclination and his business gave him the opportunity.

He responded at once by presenting himself at her home with all his disarming *naïveté*. And then there was scarcely a day which followed that she did not see him or was not reminded of him. He was prolific in pretexts. His attitude became one of good-humoured subservience and tacit adoration. He was ready at all times to submit to her moods, which were as often kind as they were cold. She grew accustomed to him. They became intimate and friendly by imperceptible degrees, and then by leaps. He sometimes talked in a way that astonished her at first and brought the crimson into her face; in a way that pleased her at last, appealing to the animalism that stirred impatiently within her.

There was nothing which so quieted the turmoil of Edna's senses as a visit to Mademoiselle Reisz. It was then, in the presence of that personality which was offensive to her, that the woman, by her divine art, seemed to reach Edna's spirit and set it free.

It was misty, with heavy, lowering atmosphere, one afternoon, when Edna climbed the stairs to the pianist's apartments under the roof. Her clothes were dripping with moisture. She felt chilled and pinched as she entered the room. Mademoiselle was poking at a rusty stove that smoked a little and warmed the room indifferently. She was endeavouring to heat a pot of chocolate on the stove. The room looked cheerless and dingy to Edna as she entered. A bust of Beethoven,[78] covered with a hood of dust, scowled at her from the mantelpiece.

'Ah! here comes the sunlight!' exclaimed Mademoiselle rising from her knees before the stove. 'Now it will be warm and bright enough; I can let the fire alone.'

She closed the stove door with a bang, and approaching, assisted in removing Edna's dripping mackintosh.

'You are cold; you look miserable. The chocolate will soon be hot. But would you rather have a taste of brandy? I have scarcely touched the bottle which you brought me for my cold.' A piece of red flannel was wrapped around Mademoiselle's throat; a stiff neck compelled her to hold her head on one side.

'I will take some brandy,' said Edna, shivering as she removed her gloves and overshoes. She drank the liquor from the glass as a man would have done. Then flinging herself upon the uncomfortable sofa she said, 'Mademoiselle, I am going to move away from my house on Esplanade Street.'

'Ah!' ejaculated the musician, neither surprised nor especially interested. Nothing ever seemed to astonish her very much. She was endeavouring to adjust the bunch of violets which had become loose from its fastening in her hair. Edna drew her down upon the sofa and taking a pin from her own hair, secured the shabby artificial flowers in their accustomed place.

'Aren't you astonished?'

'Passably. Where are you going? to New York? to Iberville? to your father in Mississippi? where?'

'Just two steps away,' laughed Edna, 'in a little four-room house around the corner. It looks so cosy, so inviting and restful, whenever I pass by; and it's for rent. I'm tired looking after that big house. It never seemed like mine, anyway – like home. It's too much trouble. I have to keep too many servants. I am tired bothering with them.'

'That is not your true reason, *ma belle*. There is no use in telling me lies. I don't know your reason, but you have not told me the truth.'

Edna did not protest or endeavour to justify herself.

'The house, the money that provides for it, are not mine. Isn't that enough reason?'

'They are your husband's,' returned Mademoiselle, with a shrug and a malicious elevation of the eyebrows.

'Oh! I see there is no deceiving you. Then let me tell you: it is a caprice. I have a little money of my own from my mother's estate, which my father sends me by driblets. I won a large sum this winter on the races, and I am beginning to sell my sketches. Laidpore is more and more pleased with my work; he says it grows in force and individuality. I cannot judge of that myself, but I feel that I have gained in ease and confidence. However, as I said, I have sold a good many through Laidpore. I can live in the tiny house for little or nothing, with one servant. Old Celestine, who works occasionally for me, says she will come stay with me and do my work. I know I shall like it, like the feeling of freedom and independence.'

'What does your husband say?'

'I have not told him yet. I only thought of it this morning. He will think I am demented, no doubt. Perhaps you think so.'

Mademoiselle shook her head slowly. 'Your reason is not yet clear to me,' she said.

Neither was it quite clear to Edna herself; but it unfolded itself as she sat for a while in silence. Instinct had prompted her to put away her husband's bounty in casting off her allegiance. She did not know how it would be when he returned. There would have to be an understanding, an explanation. Conditions would some way adjust themselves, she felt; but whatever came, she had resolved never again to belong to another than herself.

'I shall give a grand dinner before I leave the old house!' Edna exclaimed. 'You will have to come to it, mademoiselle. I will give you everything that you like to eat and to drink. We shall sing and laugh and be merry for once.' And she uttered a sigh that came from the very depths of her being.

If Mademoiselle happened to have received a letter from Robert during the interval of Edna's visits, she would give her the letter unsolicited. And she would seat herself at the piano and play as her humour prompted her while the young woman read the letter.

The little stove was roaring; it was red-hot, and the chocolate in the tin sizzled and sputtered. Edna went forward and opened the stove door, and Mademoiselle rising, took a letter from under the bust of Beethoven and handed it to Edna.

'Another! so soon!' she exclaimed, her eyes filled with delight. 'Tell me, mademoiselle, does he know that I see his letters?'

'Never in the world! He would be angry and would never write to me again if he thought so. Does he write to you? Never a line. Does he send you a message? Never a word. It is because he loves you, poor fool, and is trying to forget you, since you are not free to listen to him or to belong to him.'

'Why do you show me his letters, then?'

'Haven't you begged for them? Can I refuse you anything? Oh! you cannot deceive me,' and Mademoiselle approached her beloved instrument and began to play. Edna did not at once read the letter. She sat holding it in her hand, while the music penetrated her whole being like an effulgence, warming and brightening the dark places of her soul. It prepared her for joy and exultation.

'Oh!' she exclaimed, letting the letter fall to the floor. 'Why did you not tell me?' She went and grasped Mademoiselle's hands up from the keys. 'Oh! unkind! malicious! Why did you not tell me?'

'That he was coming back? No great news, *ma foi*. I wonder he did not come long ago.'

'But when, when?' cried Edna, impatiently. 'He does not say when.'

'He says "very soon". You know as much about it as I do; it is all in the letter.'

'But why? Why is he coming? Oh, if I thought – ' and she snatched the letter from the floor and turned the pages this way and that way, looking for the reason, which was left untold.

'If I were young and in love with a man,' said Mademoiselle, turning on the stool and pressing her wiry hands between her knees as she looked down at Edna, who sat on the floor holding the letter, 'it seems to me he would have to be some *grand esprit*;[79] a man with lofty aims and ability to reach them; one who stood high enough to attract the notice of his fellow-men. It seems to me if I were young and in love I should never deem a man of ordinary calibre worthy of my devotion.'

'Now it is you who are telling lies and seeking to deceive me, mademoiselle; or else you have never been in love, and know nothing about it. Why,' went on Edna, clasping her knees and looking up into Mademoiselle's twisted face, 'do you suppose a woman knows why she loves? Does she select? Does she say to herself: "Go to! Here is a distinguished statesman with presidential possibilities; I shall proceed to fall in love with him." Or, "I shall set my heart upon this musician, whose fame is on every tongue?" Or, "This financier, who controls the world's money markets?" '

'You are purposely misunderstanding me, *ma reine*. Are you in love with Robert?'

'Yes,' said Edna. It was the first time she had admitted it, and a glow overspread her face, blotching it with red spots.

'Why?' asked her companion. 'Why do you love him when you ought not to?'

Edna, with a motion or two, dragged herself on her knees before Mademoiselle Reisz, who took the glowing face between her two hands.

'Why? Because his hair is brown and grows away from his temples; because he opens and shuts his eyes, and his nose is a little out of drawing; because he has two lips and a square chin, and a little finger which he can't straighten from having played baseball too energetically in his youth. Because – '

'Because you do, in short,' laughed Mademoiselle. 'What will you do when he comes back?' she asked.

'Do? Nothing, except feel glad and happy to be alive.'

She was already glad and happy to be alive at the mere thought of his return. The murky, lowering sky, which had depressed her a few hours before, seemed bracing and invigorating as she splashed through the streets on her way home.

She stopped at a confectioner's and ordered a huge box of bonbons for the children in Iberville. She slipped a card in the box, on which she scribbled a tender message and sent an abundance of kisses.

Before dinner in the evening Edna wrote a charming letter to her husband, telling him of her intention to move for a while into the little house around the block, and to give a farewell dinner before leaving, regretting that he was not there to share it, to help her out with the menu and assist her in entertaining the guests. Her letter was brilliant and brimming with cheerfulness.

27

'What is the matter with you?' asked Arobin that evening. 'I never found you in such a happy mood.' Edna was tired by that time, and was reclining on the lounge before the fire.

'Don't you know the weather prophet has told us we shall see the sun pretty soon?'

'Well, that ought to be reason enough,' he acquiesced. 'You wouldn't give me another if I sat here all night imploring you.' He sat close to her on a low tabouret,[80] and as he spoke his fingers lightly touched the hair that fell a little over her forehead. She liked the touch of his fingers through her hair, and closed her eyes sensitively.

'One of these days,' she said, 'I'm going to pull myself together for a while and think – try to determine what character of a woman I am; for, candidly, I don't know. By all the codes which I am acquainted with, I am a devilishly wicked specimen of the sex. But some way I can't convince myself that I am. I must think about it.'

'Don't. What's the use? Why should you bother thinking about it when I can tell you what manner of woman you are.' His fingers strayed occasionally down to her warm, smooth cheeks and firm chin, which was growing a little full and double.

'Oh, yes! You will tell me that I am adorable; everything that is captivating. Spare yourself the effort.'

'No; I shan't tell you anything of the sort, though I shouldn't be lying if I did.'

'Do you know Mademoiselle Reisz?' she asked irrelevantly.

'The pianist? I know her by sight. I've heard her play.'

'She says queer things sometimes in a bantering way that you don't notice at the time and you find yourself thinking about afterwards.'

'For instance?'

'Well, for instance, when I left her today, she put her arms around me and felt my shoulder blades, to see if my wings were strong, she said. "The bird that would soar above the level plain of tradition and prejudice must have strong wings. It is a sad spectacle to see the weaklings bruised, exhausted, fluttering back to earth." '

'Whither would you soar?'

'I'm not thinking of any extraordinary flights. I only half comprehend her.'

'I've heard she's partially demented,' said Arobin.

'She seems to me wonderfully sane,' Edna replied.

'I'm told she's extremely disagreeable and unpleasant. Why have you introduced her at a moment when I desired to talk of you?'

'Oh! talk of me if you like,' cried Edna, clasping her hands beneath her head; 'but let me think of something else while you do.'

'I'm jealous of your thoughts tonight. They're making you a little kinder than usual; but some way I feel as if they were wandering, as if they were not here with me.' She only looked at him and smiled. His eyes were very near. He leaned upon the lounge with an arm extended across her while the other hand still rested upon her hair. They continued silently to look into each other's eyes. When he leaned forward and kissed her, she clasped his head, holding his lips to hers.

It was the first kiss of her life to which her nature had really responded. It was a flaming torch that kindled desire.

28

Edna cried a little that night after Arobin left her. It was only one phase of the multitudinous emotions which had assailed her. There was with her an overwhelming feeling of irresponsibility. There was the shock of the unexpected and the unaccustomed. There was her husband's reproach looking at her from the external things around her which he had provided for her external existence. There was Robert's reproach making itself felt by a quicker, fiercer, more overpowering love, which had awakened within her towards him. Above all there was understanding. She felt as if a mist had been lifted from her eyes, enabling her to look upon and comprehend the significance of life, that monster made up of beauty and brutality. But among the conflicting sensations which assailed her, there was neither shame nor remorse. There was a dull pang of regret because it was not the kiss of love which had inflamed her, because it was not love which had held this cup of life to her lips.

29

Without even waiting for an answer from her husband regarding his opinion or wishes in the matter, Edna hastened her preparations for quitting her home on Esplanade Street and moving into the little house around the block. A feverish anxiety attended her every action in that direction. There was no moment of deliberation, no interval of repose between the thought and its fulfilment. Early upon the morning following those hours passed in Arobin's society, Edna set about securing her new abode and hurrying her arrangements for occupying it. Within the precincts of her home she felt like one who has entered and lingered within the portals of some forbidden temple in which a thousand muffled voices bade her begone.

Whatever was her own in the house, everything which she had acquired aside from her husband's bounty, she caused to be transported to the other house, supplying simple and meagre deficiencies from her own resources.

Arobin found her with rolled sleeves, working in company with the housemaid when he looked in during the afternoon. She was splendid and robust, and had never appeared handsomer than in the old blue gown, with a red silk handkerchief knotted at random around her head to protect her hair from the dust. She was mounted upon a high stepladder, unhooking a picture from the wall when he entered. He had found the front door open, and had followed his ring by walking in unceremoniously.

'Come down!' he said. 'Do you want to kill yourself?' She greeted him with affected carelessness, and appeared absorbed in her occupation.

If he had expected to find her languishing, reproachful, or indulging in sentimental tears, he must have been greatly surprised.

He was no doubt prepared for any emergency, ready for any one of the foregoing attitudes, just as he bent himself easily and naturally to the situation which confronted him.

'Please come down,' he insisted, holding the ladder and looking up at her.

'No,' she answered; 'Ellen is afraid to mount the ladder. Joe is working over at the "pigeon-house" – that's the name Ellen gives it, because it's so small and looks like a pigeon-house – and someone has to do this.'

Arobin pulled off his coat, and expressed himself ready and willing to tempt fate in her place. Ellen brought him one of her dust-caps, and went into contortions of mirth, which she found it impossible to control, when she saw him put it on before the mirror as grotesquely as he could. Edna herself could not refrain from smiling when she fastened it at his request. So it was he who in turn mounted the ladder, unhooking pictures and curtains, and dislodging ornaments as Edna directed. When he had finished he took off his dust-cap and went out to wash his hands.

Edna was sitting on the tabouret, idly brushing the tips of a feather duster along the carpet when he came in again.

'Is there anything more you will let me do?' he asked.

'That is all,' she answered. 'Ellen can manage the rest.'

She kept the young woman occupied in the drawing-room, unwilling to be left alone with Arobin.

'What about the dinner?' he asked; 'the grand event, the *coup d'état*?'

'It will be day after tomorrow. Why do you call it the "*coup d'état*"? Oh! it will be very fine; all my best of everything – crystal, silver and gold, Sèvres, flowers, music, and champagne to swim in. I'll let Léonce pay the bills. I wonder what he'll say when he sees the bills.'

'And you ask me why I call it a *coup d'état*?' Arobin had put on his coat, and he stood before her and asked if his cravat was plumb. She told him it was, looking no higher than the tip of his collar.

'When do you go to the "pigeon-house"? – with all due acknowledgement to Ellen.'

'Day after tomorrow, after the dinner. I shall sleep there.'

'Ellen, will you very kindly get me a glass of water?' asked Arobin. 'The dust in the curtains, if you will pardon me for hinting such a thing, has parched my throat to a crisp.'

'While Ellen gets the water,' said Edna, rising, 'I will say goodbye and let you go. I must get rid of this grime, and I have a million things to do and think of.'

'When shall I see you?' asked Arobin, seeking to detain her, the maid having left the room.

'At the dinner, of course. You are invited.'

'Not before? – not tonight or tomorrow morning or tomorrow noon or night? Or the day after morning or noon? Can't you see yourself, without my telling you, what an eternity it is?'

He had followed her into the hall and to the foot of the stairway, looking up at her as she mounted with her face half turned to him.

'Not an instant sooner,' she said. But she laughed and looked at him with eyes that at once gave him courage to wait and made it torture to wait.

30

Though Edna had spoken of the dinner as a very grand affair, it was in truth a very small affair and very select, in so much as the guests invited were few and were selected with discrimination. She had counted upon an even dozen seating themselves at her round mahogany board, forgetting for the moment that Madame Ratignolle was to the last degree *souffrante* and unpresentable, and not foreseeing that Madame Lebrun would send a thousand regrets at the last moment. So there were only ten, after all, which made a cosy, comfortable number.

There were Mr and Mrs Merriman, a pretty, vivacious little woman in the thirties; her husband, a jovial fellow, something of a shallow-pate, who laughed a good deal at other people's witticisms, and had thereby made himself extremely popular. Mrs Highcamp had accompanied them. Of course, there was Alcée Arobin; and Mademoiselle Reisz had consented to come. Edna had sent her a fresh bunch of violets with black lace trimmings for her hair. Monsieur Ratignolle brought himself and his wife's excuses. Victor Lebrun, who happened to be in the city, bent upon relaxation, had accepted with alacrity. There was a Miss

Mayblunt, no longer in her teens, who looked at the world through lorgnettes[81] and with the keenest interest. It was thought and said that she was intellectual; it was suspected of her that she wrote under a *nom de guerre*.[82] She had come with a gentleman by the name of Gouvernail,[83] connected with one of the daily papers, of whom nothing special could be said, except that he was observant and seemed quiet and inoffensive. Edna herself made the tenth, and at half-past eight they seated themselves at table, Arobin and Monsieur Ratignolle on either side of their hostess.

Mrs Highcamp sat between Arobin and Victor Lebrun. Then came Mrs Merriman, Mr Gouvernail, Miss Mayblunt, Mr Merriman, and Mademoiselle Reisz next to Monsieur Ratignolle.

There was something extremely gorgeous about the appearance of the table, an effect of splendour conveyed by a cover of pale yellow satin under strips of lace-work. There were wax candles in massive brass candelabra, burning softly under yellow silk shades; full, fragrant roses, yellow and red, abounded. There were silver and gold, as she had said there would be, and crystal which glittered like the gems which the women wore.

The ordinary stiff dining chairs had been discarded for the occasion and replaced by the most commodious and luxurious which could be collected throughout the house. Mademoiselle Reisz, being exceedingly diminutive, was elevated upon cushions, as small children are sometimes hoisted at table upon bulky volumes.

'Something new, Edna?' exclaimed Miss Mayblunt, with lorgnette directed towards a magnificent cluster of diamonds that sparkled, that almost sputtered, in Edna's hair, just over the centre of her forehead.

'Quite new; "brand" new, in fact; a present from my husband. It arrived this morning from New York. I may as well admit that this is my birthday, and that I am twenty-nine. In good time I expect you to drink to my health. Meanwhile, I shall ask you to begin with this cocktail, composed – would you say "composed"?' with an appeal to Miss Mayblunt – 'composed by my father in honour of Sister Janet's wedding.'

Before each guest stood a tiny glass that looked and sparkled like a garnet gem.

'Then, all things considered,' spoke Arobin, 'it might not be amiss to start out by drinking the colonel's health in the cocktail which he composed, on the birthday of the most charming of women – the daughter whom he invented.'

Mr Merriman's laugh at this sally was such a genuine outburst and so contagious that it started the dinner with an agreeable swing that never slackened.

Miss Mayblunt begged to be allowed to keep her cocktail untouched before her, just to look at. The colour was marvellous! She could compare it to nothing she had ever seen, and the garnet lights which it emitted were unspeakably rare. She pronounced the colonel an artist, and stuck to it.

Monsieur Ratignolle was prepared to take things seriously: the *mets*, the *entre-mets*,[84] the service, the decorations, even the people. He looked up from his pompono[85] and enquired of Arobin if he were related to the gentleman of that name who formed one of the firm of Laitner and Arobin, lawyers. The young man admitted that Laitner was a warm personal friend, who permitted Arobin's name to decorate the firm's letterheads and to appear upon a shingle that graced Perdido Street.[86]

'There are so many inquisitive people and institutions abounding,' said Arobin, 'that one is really forced as a matter of convenience these days to assume the virtue of an occupation if one has it not.'

Monsieur Ratignolle stared a little, and turned to ask Mademoiselle Reisz if she considered the symphony concerts up to the standard which had been set the previous winter. Mademoiselle Reisz answered Monsieur Ratignolle in French, which Edna thought a little rude, under the circumstances, but characteristic. Mademoiselle had only disagreeable things to say of the symphony concerts, and insulting remarks to make of all the musicians of New Orleans, singly and collectively. All her interest seemed to be centred upon the delicacies placed before her.

Mr Merriman said that Mr Arobin's remark about inquisitive people reminded him of a man from Waco the other day at the St Charles Hotel – but as Mr Merriman's stories were always lame and lacking point, his wife seldom permitted him to complete them. She interrupted him to ask if he remembered the name of the author whose book she had bought the week before to send to a friend in Geneva. She was talking 'books' with Mr Gouvernail and trying to draw from him his opinion upon current literary topics. Her husband told the story of the Waco man privately to Miss Mayblunt, who pretended to be greatly amused and to think it extremely clever.

Mrs Highcamp hung with languid but unaffected interest upon the warm and impetuous volubility of her left-hand neighbour, Victor Lebrun. Her attention was never for a moment withdrawn from him after seating herself at table; and when he turned to Mrs Merriman, who was prettier and more vivacious than Mrs Highcamp, she waited with easy indifference for an opportunity to reclaim his attention. There was the occasional sound of music, of mandolins, sufficiently removed to be an agreeable accompaniment rather than an interruption to the conversation. Outside the soft, monotonous splash of a fountain could be heard; the sound penetrated into the room with the heavy odour of jessamine that came through the open windows.

The golden shimmer of Edna's satin gown spread in rich folds on either side of her. There was a soft fall of lace encircling her shoulders. It was the colour of her skin, without the glow, the myriad living tints that one may sometimes discover in vibrant flesh. There was something in her attitude, in her whole appearance when she leaned her head against the high-backed chair and spread her arms, which suggested the regal woman, the one who rules, who looks on, who stands alone.

But as she sat there amid her guests, she felt the old ennui overtaking her; the hopelessness which so often assailed her, which came upon her like an obsession, like something extraneous, independent of volition. It was something which announced itself; a chill breath that seemed to issue from some vast cavern wherein discords wailed. There came over her the acute longing which always summoned into her spiritual vision the presence of the beloved one, overpowering her at once with a sense of the unattainable.

The moments glided on, while a feeling of good fellowship passed around the circle like a mystic cord, holding and binding these people together with jest and laughter. Monsieur Ratignolle was the first to break the pleasant charm. At ten o'clock he excused himself. Madame Ratignolle was waiting for him at home. She was *bien souffrante*, and she was filled with vague dread, which only her husband's presence could allay.

Mademoiselle Reisz arose with Monsieur Ratignolle, who offered to escort her to the car. She had eaten well; she had tasted the good, rich wines, and they must have turned her head, for she bowed pleasantly to all as she withdrew from the table. She kissed Edna upon the shoulder, and whispered: '*Bonne nuit, ma reine; soyez sage*.'[87] She had been a little bewildered upon rising, or rather, descending from her cushions, and Monsieur Ratignolle gallantly took her arm and led her away.

Mrs Highcamp was weaving a garland of roses, yellow and red. When she had finished the garland, she laid it lightly upon Victor's black curls. He was reclining far back in the luxurious chair, holding a glass of champagne to the light.

As if a magician's wand had touched him, the garland of roses transformed him into a vision of oriental beauty. His cheeks were the colour of crushed grapes, and his dusky eyes glowed with a languishing fire.

'*Sapristi!*' exclaimed Arobin.

But Mrs Highcamp had one more touch to add to the picture. She took from the back of her chair a white silken scarf, with which she had covered her shoulders in the early part of the evening. She draped it across the boy in graceful folds, and in a way to conceal his black, conventional evening dress. He did not seem to mind what she did to him, only smiled, showing a faint gleam of white teeth, while he continued to gaze with narrowing eyes at the light through his glass of champagne.

'Oh! to be able to paint in colour rather than in words!' exclaimed Miss Mayblunt, losing herself in a rhapsodic dream as she looked at him.

> 'There was a graven image of Desire
> Painted with red blood on a ground of gold,'[88]

murmured Gouvernail, under his breath.

The effect of the wine upon Victor was to change his accustomed volubility into silence. He seemed to have abandoned himself to reverie, and to be seeing pleasing visions in the amber bead.

'Sing,' entreated Mrs Highcamp. 'Won't you sing to us?'

'Let him alone,' said Arobin.

'He's posing,' offered Mr Merriman; 'let him have it out.'

'I believe he's paralysed,' laughed Mrs Merriman. And leaning over the youth's chair, she took the glass from his hand and held it to his lips. He sipped the wine slowly, and when he had drained the glass she laid it upon the table and wiped his lips with her little filmy handkerchief.

'Yes, I'll sing for you,' he said, turning in his chair towards Mrs Highcamp. He clasped his hands behind his head, and looking up at the ceiling began to hum a little, trying his voice like a musician tuning an instrument. Then, looking at Edna, he began to sing:

> '*Ah! si tu savais!*'

'Stop!' she cried, 'don't sing that. I don't want you to sing it,' and she laid her glass so impetuously and blindly upon the table as to shatter it against a carafe. The wine spilled over Arobin's legs and some of it trickled down upon Mrs Highcamp's black gauze gown. Victor had lost all idea of courtesy, or else he thought his hostess was not in earnest, for he laughed and went on:

> '*Ah! si tu savais*
> *Ce que tes yeux me disent –*'[89]

'Oh! you mustn't! you mustn't,' exclaimed Edna, and pushing back her chair she got up, and going behind him placed her hand over his mouth. He kissed the soft palm that pressed upon his lips.

'No, no, I won't, Mrs Pontellier. I didn't know you meant it,' looking up at her with caressing eyes. The touch of his lips was like a pleasing sting to her hand. She lifted the garland of roses from his head and flung it across the room.

'Come, Victor; you've posed long enough. Give Mrs Highcamp her scarf.'

Mrs Highcamp undraped the scarf from about him with her own hands. Miss Mayblunt and Mr Gouvernail suddenly conceived the notion that it was time to say good-night. And Mr and Mrs Merriman wondered how it could be so late.

Before parting from Victor, Mrs Highcamp invited him to call upon her daughter, who she knew would be charmed to meet him and talk French and sing French songs with him. Victor expressed his desire and intention to call upon Miss Highcamp at the first opportunity which presented itself. He asked if Arobin were going his way. Arobin was not.

The mandolin players had long since stolen away. A profound stillness had fallen upon the broad, beautiful street. The voices of Edna's disbanding guests jarred like a discordant note upon the quiet harmony of the night.

31

'Well?' questioned Arobin, who had remained with Edna after the others had departed.

'Well,' she reiterated, and stood up, stretching her arms, and feeling the need to relax her muscles after having been so long seated.

'What next?' he asked.

'The servants are all gone. They left when the musicians did. I have dismissed them. The house has to be closed and locked, and I shall trot around to the pigeon-house, and shall send Celestine over in the morning to straighten things up.'

He looked around, and began to turn out some of the lights.

'What about upstairs?' he enquired.

'I think it is all right; but there may be a window or two unlatched. We had better look; you might take a candle and see. And bring me my wrap and hat on the foot of the bed in the middle room.'

He went up with the light, and Edna began closing doors and windows. She hated to shut in the smoke and the fumes of the wine.

Arobin found her cape and hat, which he brought down and helped her to put on.

When everything was secured and the lights put out, they left through the front door, Arobin locking it and taking the key, which he carried for Edna. He helped her down the steps.

'Will you have a spray of jessamine?' he asked, breaking off a few blossoms as he passed.

'No; I don't want anything.'

She seemed disheartened, and had nothing to say. She took his arm, which he offered her, holding up the weight of her satin train with the other hand. She looked down, noticing the black line of his leg moving in and out so close to her against the yellow shimmer of her gown. There was the whistle of a railway train somewhere in the distance, and the midnight bells were ringing. They met no one in their short walk.

The 'pigeon-house' stood behind a locked gate, and a shallow *parterre* that had been somewhat neglected. There was a small front porch, upon which a long window and the front door opened. The door opened directly into the parlour; there was no side entry. Back in the yard was a room for servants, in which old Celestine had been ensconced.

Edna had left a lamp burning low upon the table. She had succeeded in making the room look habitable and homelike. There were some books on the table and a lounge near at hand. On the floor was fresh matting, covered with a rug or two; and on the walls hung a few tasteful pictures. But the room was filled with flowers. These were a surprise to her. Arobin had sent them, and had had Celestine distribute them during Edna's absence. Her bedroom was adjoining, and across a small passage were the dining-room and kitchen.

Edna seated herself with every appearance of discomfort.

'Are you tired?' he asked.

'Yes, and chilled, and miserable. I feel as if I had been wound up to a certain pitch – too tight – and something inside of me had snapped.' She rested her head against the table upon her bare arm.

'You want to rest,' he said, 'and to be quiet. I'll go; I'll leave you and let you rest.'

'Yes,' she replied.

He stood up beside her and smoothed her hair with his soft, magnetic hand. His touch conveyed to her a certain physical comfort. She could have fallen quietly asleep there if he had continued to pass his hand over her hair. He brushed the hair upward from the nape of her neck.

'I hope you will feel better and happier in the morning,' he said. 'You have tried to do too much in the past few days. The dinner was the last straw; you might have dispensed with it.'

'Yes,' she admitted; 'it was stupid.'

'No, it was delightful; but it has worn you out.' His hand had strayed to her beautiful shoulders, and he could feel the response of her flesh to his touch. He seated himself beside her and kissed her lightly upon the shoulder.

'I thought you were going away,' she said, in an uneven voice.

'I am, after I have said good-night.'

'Good-night,' she murmured.

He did not answer, except to continue to caress her. He did not say good-night until she had become supple to his gentle, seductive entreaties.

32

When Mr Pontellier learned of his wife's intention to abandon her home and take up her residence elsewhere, he immediately wrote her a letter of unqualified disapproval and remonstrance. She had given reasons which he was unwilling to acknowledge as adequate. He hoped she had not acted upon rash impulse; and he begged her to consider first, foremost, and above all else, what people would say. He was not dreaming of scandal when he uttered this warning; that was a thing which would never have entered into his mind to consider in connection with his wife's name or his own. He was simply thinking of his financial integrity. It might get noised about that the Pontelliers had met with reverses, and were forced to conduct their *ménage*[90] on a humbler scale than heretofore. It might do incalculable mischief to his business prospects.

But remembering Edna's whimsical turn of mind of late, and foreseeing that she had immediately acted upon her impetuous determination, he grasped the situation with his usual promptness and handled it with his well-known business tact and cleverness.

The same mail which brought to Edna his letter of disapproval carried instructions – the most minute instructions – to a well-known architect concerning the remodelling of his home, changes which he had long contemplated, and which he desired carried forward during his temporary absence.

Expert and reliable packers and movers were engaged to convey the furniture, carpets, pictures – everything movable, in short – to places of security. And in an incredibly short time the Pontellier house was turned over to the artisans. There was to be an addition – a small snuggery;[91]

there was to be frescoing, and hardwood flooring was to be put into such rooms as had not yet been subjected to this improvement.

Furthermore, in one of the daily papers appeared a brief notice to the effect that Mr and Mrs Pontellier were contemplating a summer sojourn abroad, and that their handsome residence on Esplanade Street was undergoing sumptuous alterations, and would not be ready for occupancy until their return. Mr Pontellier had saved appearances!

Edna admired the skill of his manoeuvre, and avoided any occasion to balk his intentions. When the situation as set forth by Mr Pontellier was accepted and taken for granted, she was apparently satisfied that it should be so.

The pigeon-house pleased her. It at once assumed the intimate character of a home, while she herself invested it with a charm which it reflected like a warm glow. There was with her a feeling of having descended in the social scale, with a corresponding sense of having risen in the spiritual. Every step which she took towards relieving herself from obligations added to her strength and expansion as an individual. She began to look with her own eyes; to see and to apprehend the deeper undercurrents of life. No longer was she content to 'feed upon opinion' when her own soul had invited her.

After a little while, a few days, in fact, Edna went up and spent a week with her children in Iberville. They were delicious February days, with all the summer's promise hovering in the air.

How glad she was to see the children! She wept for very pleasure when she felt their little arms clasping her; their hard, ruddy cheeks pressed against her own glowing cheeks. She looked into their faces with hungry eyes that could not be satisfied with looking. And what stories they had to tell their mother! About the pigs, the cows, the mules! About riding to the mill behind Gluglu; fishing back in the lake with their Uncle Jasper; picking pecans with Lidie's little black brood, and hauling chips in their express wagon. It was a thousand times more fun to haul real chips for old lame Susie's real fire than to drag painted blocks along the banquette on Esplanade Street!

She went with them herself to see the pigs and the cows, to look at the darkies laying the cane, to thrash the pecan trees, and catch fish in the back lake. She lived with them a whole week long, giving them all of herself, and gathering and filling herself with their young existence. They listened, breathless, when she told them the house in Esplanade Street was crowded with workmen, hammering, nailing, sawing and filling the place with clatter. They wanted to know where their bed was; what had been done with their rocking-horse; and where did Joe sleep, and where had Ellen gone, and the cook? But, above all, they were fired with a desire to see the little house around the block. Was there any place to play? Were there any boys next door? Raoul, with pessimistic foreboding, was convinced that there were only girls next door. Where would they sleep, and where would papa sleep? She told them the fairies would fix it all right.

The old Madame was charmed with Edna's visit, and showered all manner of delicate attentions upon her. She was delighted to know that the Esplanade Street house was in a dismantled condition. It gave her the promise and pretext to keep the children indefinitely.

It was with a wrench and a pang that Edna left her children. She carried away with her the sound of their voices and the touch of their cheeks. All along the journey homeward their presence lingered with her like the memory of a delicious song. But by the time she had regained the city the song no longer echoed in her soul. She was again alone.

33

It happened sometimes when Edna went to see Mademoiselle Reisz that the little musician was absent, giving a lesson or making some small necessary household purchase. The key was always left in a secret hiding-place in the entry, which Edna knew. If Mademoiselle happened to be away, Edna would usually enter and wait for her return.

When she knocked at Mademoiselle Reisz's door one afternoon there was no response; so unlocking the door, as usual, she entered and found the apartment deserted, as she had expected. Her day had been quite filled up, and it was for a rest, for a refuge, and to talk about Robert, that she sought out her friend.

She had worked at her canvas – a young Italian character study – all the morning, completing the work without the model; but there had been many interruptions, some incident to her modest housekeeping and others of a social nature.

Madame Ratignolle had dragged herself over, avoiding the too public thoroughfares, she said. She complained that Edna had neglected her much of late. Besides, she was consumed with curiosity to see the little house and the manner in which it was conducted. She wanted to hear all about the dinner party; Monsieur Ratignolle had left *so* early. What had happened after he left? The champagne and grapes which Edna sent over were *too* delicious. She had so little appetite, they had refreshed and toned her stomach. Where on earth was she going to put Mr Pontellier in that little house, and the boys? And then she made Edna promise to go to her when her hour of trial overtook her.

'At any time – any time of the day or night, dear,' Edna assured her.

Before leaving Madame Ratignolle said: 'In some way you seem to me like a child, Edna. You seem to act without a certain amount of reflection which is necessary in this life. That is the reason I want to say you mustn't mind if I advise you to be a little careful while you are living here alone. Why don't you have someone come and stay with you? Wouldn't Mademoiselle Reisz come?'

'No; she wouldn't wish to come, and I shouldn't want her always with me.'

'Well, the reason – you know how evil-minded the world is – someone was talking of Alcée Arobin visiting you. Of course, it wouldn't matter if Mr Arobin had not such a dreadful reputation. Monsieur Ratignolle was telling me that his attentions alone are considered enough to ruin a woman's name.'

'Does he boast of his successes?' asked Edna, indifferently, squinting at her picture.

'No, I think not. I believe he is a decent fellow as far as that goes. But his character is so well known among the men. I shan't be able to come back and see you; it was very, very imprudent today.'

'Mind the step!' cried Edna

'Don't neglect me,' entreated Madame Ratignolle; 'and don't mind what I said about Arobin, or having someone to stay with you.'

'Of course not,' Edna laughed. 'You may say anything you like to me.' They kissed each other goodbye. Madame Ratignolle had not far to go, and Edna stood on the porch a while watching her walk down the street.

Then in the afternoon Mrs Merriman and Mrs Highcamp had made their 'party call'. Edna felt that they might have dispensed with the formality. They had also come to invite her to play *vingt-et-un*[92] one evening at Mrs Merriman's. She was asked to go early, to dinner, and Mr Merriman or Mr Arobin would take her home. Edna accepted in a half-hearted way. She sometimes felt very tired of Mrs Highcamp and Mrs Merriman.

Late in the afternoon she sought refuge with Mademoiselle Reisz, and stayed there alone, waiting for her, feeling a kind of repose invade her with the very atmosphere of the shabby, unpretentious little room.

Edna sat at the window, which looked out over the housetops and across the river. The window frame was filled with pots of flowers, and she sat and picked the dry leaves from a rose geranium. The day was warm, and the breeze which blew from the river was very pleasant. She removed her hat and laid it on the piano. She went on picking the leaves and digging around the plants with her hat pin. Once she thought she heard Mademoiselle Reisz approaching. But it was a young black girl, who came in, bringing a small bundle of laundry, which she deposited in the adjoining room, and went away.

Edna seated herself at the piano, and softly picked out with one hand the bars of a piece of music which lay open before her. A half-hour went by. There was the occasional sound of people going and coming in the lower hall. She was growing interested in her occupation of picking out the aria, when there was a second rap at the door. She vaguely wondered what these people did when they found Mademoiselle's door locked.

'Come in,' she called, turning her face towards the door. And this time it was Robert Lebrun who presented himself. She attempted to rise; she could not have done so without betraying the agitation which mastered her at sight of him, so she fell back upon the stool, only exclaiming, 'Why, Robert!'

He came and clasped her hand, seemingly without knowing what he was saying or doing.

'Mrs Pontellier! How do you happen – oh! how well you look! Is Mademoiselle Reisz not here? I never expected to see you.'

'When did you come back?' asked Edna in an unsteady voice, wiping her face with her handkerchief. She seemed ill at ease on the piano stool, and he begged her to take the chair by the window. She did so, mechanically, while he seated himself on the stool.

'I returned day before yesterday,' he answered, while he leaned his arm on the keys, bringing forth a crash of discordant sound.

'Day before yesterday!' she repeated, aloud; and went on thinking to herself, 'day before yesterday,' in a sort of an uncomprehending way. She had pictured him seeking her at the very first hour, and he had lived under the same sky since day before yesterday; while only by accident had he stumbled upon her. Mademoiselle must have lied when she said, 'Poor fool, he loves you.'

'Day before yesterday,' she repeated, breaking off a spray of Mademoiselle's geranium; 'then if you had not met me here today you wouldn't – when – that is, didn't you mean to come and see me?'

'Of course, I should have gone to see you. There have been so many things – ' he turned the leaves of Mademoiselle's music nervously. 'I started in at once yesterday with the old firm. After all there is as much chance for me here as there was there – that is, I might find it profitable someday. The Mexicans were not very congenial.'

So he had come back because the Mexicans were not congenial; because business was as profitable here as there; because of any reason, and not because he cared to be near her. She remembered the day she sat on the floor, turning the pages of his letter, seeking the reason which was left untold.

She had not noticed how he looked – only feeling his presence; but she turned deliberately and observed him. After all, he had been absent but a few months, and was not changed. His hair – the colour of hers – waved back from his temples in the same way as before. His skin was not more burned than it had been at Grand Isle. She found in his eyes, when he looked at her for one silent moment, the same tender caress, with an added warmth and entreaty which had not been there before – the same glance which had penetrated to the sleeping places of her soul and awakened them.

A hundred times Edna had pictured Robert's return, and imagined their first meeting. It was usually at her home, whither he had sought her out at once. She always fancied him expressing or betraying in some way his love for her. And here, the reality was that they sat ten feet apart, she at the window, crushing geranium leaves in her hand and smelling them, he twirling around on the piano stool, saying: 'I was very much surprised to hear of Mr Pontellier's absence; it's a wonder Mademoiselle Reisz did not tell me; and your moving – mother told me yesterday. I should think you would have gone to New York with him, or to Iberville with the children, rather than be bothered here with housekeeping. And you are going abroad, too, I hear. We shan't have you at Grand Isle next summer; it won't seem – do you see much of Mademoiselle Reisz? She often spoke of you in the few letters she wrote.'

'Do you remember that you promised to write to me when you went away?' A flush overspread his whole face.

'I couldn't believe that my letters would be of any interest to you.'

'That is an excuse; it isn't the truth.' Edna reached for her hat on the piano. She adjusted it, sticking the hat pin through the heavy coil of hair with some deliberation.

'Are you not going to wait for Mademoiselle Reisz?' asked Robert.

'No; I have found when she is absent this long, she is liable not to come back till late.' She drew on her gloves, and Robert picked up his hat.

'Won't you wait for her?' asked Edna.

'Not if you think she will not be back till late,' he said, adding, as if suddenly aware of some discourtesy in his speech, 'and I should miss the pleasure of walking home with you.' Edna locked the door and put the key back in its hiding-place.

They went together, picking their way across muddy streets and sidewalks encumbered with the cheap display of small tradesmen. Part of the distance they rode in the car, and after disembarking, passed the Pontellier mansion, which looked broken and half torn asunder. Robert had never known the house, and looked at it with interest.

'I never knew you in your home,' he remarked.

'I am glad you did not.'

'Why?' She did not answer. They went on around the corner, and it seemed as if her dreams were coming true after all when he followed her into the little house.

'You must stay and dine with me, Robert. You see I am all alone, and it is so long since I have seen you. There is so much I want to ask you.'

She took off her hat and gloves. He stood irresolute, making some excuse about his mother who expected him; he even muttered something about an engagement. She struck a match and lit the lamp on the table; it was growing dusk. When he saw her face in the lamplight, looking pained, with all the soft lines gone out of it, he threw his hat aside and seated himself.

'Oh! you know I want to stay if you will let me!' he exclaimed. All the softness came back. She laughed, and went and put her hand on his shoulder.

'This is the first moment you have seemed like the old Robert. I'll go tell Celestine.' She hurried away to tell Celestine to set an extra place. She even sent her off in search of some added delicacy which she had not thought of for herself. And she recommended great care in dripping the coffee and having the omelette done to a proper turn.

When she re-entered, Robert was turning over magazines, sketches and things that lay upon the table in great disorder.

He picked up a photograph, and exclaimed: 'Alcée Arobin! What on earth is his picture doing here?'

I tried to make a sketch of his head one day,' answered Edna, 'and he thought the photograph might help me. It was at the other house. I thought it had been left there. I must have packed it up with my drawing materials.'

I should think you would give it back to him if you have finished with it.'

'Oh! I have a great many such photographs. I never think of returning them. They don't amount to anything.' Robert kept on looking at the picture.

'It seems to me – do you think his head worth drawing? Is he a friend of Mr Pontellier's? You never said you knew him.'

'He isn't a friend of Mr Pontellier's; he's a friend of mine. I always knew him – that is, it is only of late that I know him pretty well. But I'd rather talk about you and know what you have been seeing and doing and feeling out there in Mexico.' Robert threw aside the picture.

'I've been seeing the waves and the white beach of Grand Isle; the quiet, grassy street of the Chênière; the old fort at Grande Terre. I've been working like a machine, and feeling like a lost soul. There was nothing interesting.'

She leaned her head upon her hand to shade her eyes from the light.

'And what have you been seeing and doing and feeling all these days?' he asked.

'I've been seeing the waves and the white beach of Grand Isle; the quiet, grassy street of the Chênière Caminada; the old sunny fort at Grande Terre. I've been working with a little more comprehension than a machine, and still feeling like a lost soul. There was nothing interesting.'

'Mrs Pontellier, you are cruel,' he said, with feeling, closing his eyes and resting his head back in his chair. They remained in silence till old Celestine announced dinner.

34

The dining-room was very small. Edna's round mahogany would have almost filled it. As it was there was but a step or two from the little table to the kitchen, to the mantel, the small buffet, and the side door that opened out on the narrow brick-paved yard.

A certain degree of ceremony settled upon them with the announcement of dinner. There was no return to personalities. Robert related incidents of his sojourn in Mexico, and Edna talked of events likely to interest him, which had occurred during his absence. The dinner was of ordinary quality, except for the few delicacies, which she had sent out to purchase. Old Celestine, with a bandana *tignon* twisted about her head, hobbled in and out, taking a personal interest in everything; and she lingered occasionally to talk patois[93] with Robert, whom she had known as a boy.

He went out to a neighbouring cigar stand to purchase cigarette papers, and when he came back he found that Celestine had served the black coffee in the parlour.

'Perhaps I shouldn't have come back,' he said. 'When you are tired of me, tell me to go.'

'You never tire me. You must have forgotten the hours and hours at Grand Isle in which we grew accustomed to each other and used to being together.'

'I have forgotten nothing at Grand Isle,' he said, not looking at her, but rolling a cigarette. His tobacco pouch, which he laid upon the table, was a fantastic embroidered silk affair, evidently the handiwork of a woman.

'You used to carry your tobacco in a rubber pouch,' said Edna, picking up the pouch and examining the needlework.

'Yes; it was lost.'

'Where did you buy this one? In Mexico?'

'It was given to me by a Vera Cruz girl; they are very generous,' he replied, striking a match and lighting his cigarette.

'They are very handsome, I suppose, those Mexican women; very picturesque, with their black eyes and their lace scarves.'

'Some are; others are hideous. Just as you find women everywhere.'

'What was she like – the one who gave you the pouch? You must have known her very well.'

'She was very ordinary. She wasn't of the slightest importance. I knew her well enough.'

'Did you visit at her house? Was it interesting? I should like to know and hear about the people you met, and the impressions they made on you.'

'There are some people who leave impressions not so lasting as the imprint of an oar upon the water.'

'Was she such a one?'

'It would be ungenerous for me to admit that she was of that order and kind.' He thrust the pouch back in his pocket as if to put away the subject with the trifle which had brought it up.

Arobin dropped in with a message from Mrs Merriman to say that the card party was postponed on account of the illness of one of her children.

'How do you do, Arobin?' said Robert, rising from the obscurity.

'Oh! Lebrun. To be sure! I heard yesterday you were back. How did they treat you down in Mexique?'

'Fairly well.'

'But not well enough to keep you there. Stunning girls, though, in Mexico. I thought I should never get away from Vera Cruz when I was down there a couple of years ago.'

'Did they embroider slippers and tobacco pouches and hat-bands and things for you?' asked Edna.

'Oh! my! no! I didn't get so deep in their regard. I fear they made more impression on me than I made on them.'

'You were less fortunate than Robert, then.'

'I am always less fortunate than Robert. Has he been imparting tender confidences?'

'I've been imposing myself long enough,' said Robert, rising and shaking hands with Edna. 'Please convey my regards to Mr Pontellier when you write.'

He shook hands with Arobin and went away.

'Fine fellow, that Lebrun,' said Arobin when Robert had gone. 'I never heard you speak of him.'

'I knew him last summer at Grand Isle,' she replied. 'Here is that photograph of yours. Don't you want it?'

'What do I want with it? Throw it away.' She threw it back on the table.

'I'm not going to Mrs Merriman's,' she said. 'If you see her, tell her so. But perhaps I had better write. I think I shall write now, and say that I am sorry her child is sick, and tell her not to count on me.'

'It would be a good scheme,' acquiesced Arobin. 'I don't blame you; stupid lot!'

Edna opened the blotter, and having procured paper and pen, began to write the note. Arobin lit a cigar and read the evening paper, which he had in his pocket.

'What is the date?' she asked. He told her.

'Will you mail this for me when you go out?'

'Certainly.' He read to her little bits out of the newspaper, while she straightened things on the table.

'What do you want to do?' he asked, throwing aside the paper. 'Do you want to go out for a walk or a drive or anything? It would be a fine night to drive.'

'No; I don't want to do anything but just be quiet. You go away and amuse yourself. Don't stay.'

'I'll go away if I must; but I shan't amuse myself. You know that I only live when I am near you.'

He stood up to bid her good-night.

'Is that one of the things you always say to women?'

'I have said it before, but I don't think I ever came so near meaning it,' he answered with a smile. There were no warm lights in her eyes; only a dreamy, absent look.

'Good-night. I adore you. Sleep well,' he said, and he kissed her hand and went away.

She stayed alone in a kind of reverie – a sort of stupor. Step by step she lived over every instant of the time she had been with Robert after he had entered Mademoiselle Reisz's door. She recalled his words, his looks. How few and meagre they had been for her hungry heart! A vision – a transcendently seductive vision of a Mexican girl arose before her. She writhed with a jealous pang. She wondered when he would come back. He had not said he would come back. She had been with him, had heard his voice and touched his hand. But some way he had seemed nearer to her off there in Mexico.

35

The morning was full of sunlight and hope. Edna could see before her no denial – only the promise of excessive joy. She lay in bed awake, with bright eyes full of speculation. 'He loves you, poor fool.' If she could but get that conviction firmly fixed in her mind, what mattered about the rest? She felt she had been childish and unwise the night before in giving herself over to despondency. She recapitulated the motives which no doubt explained Robert's reserve. They were not insurmountable, they would not hold if he really loved her; they could not hold against her own passion, which he must come to realise in time. She pictured him going to his business that morning. She even saw how he was dressed; how he walked down one street, and turned the corner of another; saw him bending over his desk, talking to people who entered the office, going to his lunch, and perhaps watching for her on the street. He would come to her in the afternoon or evening, sit and roll his cigarette, talk a little, and go away as he had done the night before. But how delicious it would be to have him there with her! She would have no regrets, nor seek to penetrate his reserve if he still chose to wear it.

Edna ate her breakfast only half dressed. The maid brought her a delicious printed scrawl from Raoul, expressing his love, asking her to send him some bonbons, and telling her they had found that morning ten tiny white pigs all lying in a row beside Lidie's big white pig.

A letter also came from her husband, saying he hoped to be back early in March, and then they would get ready for that journey abroad which he had promised her so long, which he felt now fully able to afford; he felt able to travel as people should, without any thought of small economies – thanks to his recent speculations in Wall Street.

Much to her surprise she received a note from Arobin, written at midnight from the club. It was to say good-morning to her, to hope that she had slept well, to assure her of his devotion, which he trusted she in some faintest manner returned.

All these letters were pleasing to her. She answered the children in a cheerful frame of mind, promising them bonbons, and congratulating them upon their happy find of the little pigs.

She answered her husband with friendly evasiveness – not with any fixed design to mislead him, only because all sense of reality had gone out of her life; she had abandoned herself to Fate, and awaited the consequences with indifference.

To Arobin's note she made no reply. She put it under Celestine's stove-lid.

Edna worked several hours with much spirit. She saw no one but a picture dealer, who asked her if it were true that she was going abroad to study in Paris.

She said possibly she might, and he negotiated with her for some Parisian studies to reach him in time for the holiday trade in December.

Robert did not come that day. She was keenly disappointed. He did not come the following day, nor the next. Each morning she awoke with hope, and each night she was a prey to despondency. She was tempted to seek him out. But far from yielding to the impulse, she avoided any occasion which might throw her in his way. She did not go to Mademoiselle Reisz's nor pass by Madame Lebrun's, as she might have done if he had still been in Mexico.

When Arobin, one night, urged her to drive with him, she went – out to the lake, on the Shell Road. His horses were full of mettle, and even a little unmanageable. She liked the rapid gait at which they spun along, and the quick, sharp sound of the horses' hoofs on the hard road. They did not stop anywhere to eat or to drink. Arobin was not needlessly imprudent. But they ate and they drank when they regained Edna's little dining-room – which was comparatively early in the evening.

It was late when he left her. It was getting to be more than a passing whim with Arobin to see her and be with her. He had detected the latent sensuality which unfolded under his delicate sense of her nature's requirements like a torpid, torrid, sensitive blossom.

There was no despondency when she fell asleep that night; nor was there hope when she awoke in the morning.

36

There was a garden out in the suburbs: a small, leafy corner, with a few green tables under the orange trees. An old cat slept all day on the stone step in the sun, and an old *mulatresse* slept her idle hours away in her chair at the open window, till someone happened to knock on one of the green tables. She had milk and cream cheese to sell, and bread and butter. There was no one who could make such excellent coffee or fry a chicken so golden brown as she.

The place was too modest to attract the attention of people of fashion, and so quiet as to have escaped the notice of those in search of pleasure and dissipation. Edna had discovered it accidentally one day when the high board gate stood ajar. She caught sight of a little green table, blotched with the checkered sunlight that filtered through the quivering leaves overhead. Within she had found the slumbering *mulatresse*, the drowsy cat and a glass of milk which reminded her of the milk she had tasted in Iberville.

She often stopped there during her perambulations; sometimes taking a book with her, and sitting an hour or two under the trees when she found the place deserted. Once or twice she took a quiet dinner there alone, having instructed Celestine beforehand to prepare no dinner at home. It was the last place in the city where she would have expected to meet anyone she knew.

Still she was not astonished when, as she was partaking of a modest dinner late in the afternoon, looking into an open book, stroking the cat, which had made friends with her – she was not greatly astonished to see Robert come in at the tall garden gate.

'I am destined to see you only by accident,' she said, shoving the cat off the chair beside her. He was surprised, ill at ease, almost embarrassed at meeting her thus so unexpectedly.

'Do you come here often?' he asked.

'I almost live here,' she said.

'I used to drop in very often for a cup of Catiche's good coffee. This is the first time since I came back.'

'She'll bring you a plate, and you will share my dinner. There's always enough for two – even three.' Edna had intended to be indifferent and as reserved as he when she met him; she had reached the determination by a laborious train of reasoning, incident to one of her despondent moods. But her resolve melted when she saw him before her, seated there beside her in the little garden, as if a designing Providence had led him into her path.

'Why have you kept away from me, Robert?' she asked, closing the book that lay open upon the table.

'Why are you so personal, Mrs Pontellier? Why do you force me to idiotic subterfuges?' he exclaimed with sudden warmth. 'I suppose there's no use telling you I've been very busy, or that I've been sick, or that I've been to see you and not found you at home. Please let me off with any one of these excuses.'

'You are the embodiment of selfishness,' she said. 'You save yourself something – I don't know what – but there is some selfish motive, and in sparing yourself you never consider for a moment what I think, or how I feel your neglect and indifference. I suppose this is what you would call unwomanly; but I have got into a habit of expressing myself. It doesn't matter to me, and you may think me unwomanly if you like.'

'No; I only think you cruel, as I said the other day. Maybe not intentionally cruel; but you seem to be forcing me into disclosures which can result in nothing; as if you would have me bare a wound for the pleasure of looking at it, without the intention or power of healing it.'

'I'm spoiling your dinner, Robert; never mind what I say. You haven't eaten a morsel.'

'I only came in for a cup of coffee.' His sensitive face was all disfigured with excitement.

'Isn't this a delightful place?' she remarked. 'I am so glad it has never actually been discovered. It is so quiet, so sweet, here. Do you notice there is scarcely a sound to be heard? It's so out of the way; and a good walk from the car. However, I don't mind walking. I always feel so sorry for women who don't like to walk; they miss so much – so many rare little glimpses of life; and we women learn so little of life on the whole.

'Catiche's coffee is always hot. I don't know how she manages it, here in the open air. Celestine's coffee gets cold bringing it from the kitchen to the dining-room. Three lumps! How can you drink it so sweet? Take some of the cress with your chop; it's so biting and crisp. Then there's the advantage of being able to smoke[94] with your coffee out here. Now, in the city – aren't you going to smoke?'

'After a while,' he said, laying a cigar on the table.

'Who gave it to you?' she laughed.

'I bought it. I suppose I'm getting reckless; I bought a whole box.' She was determined not to be personal again and make him uncomfortable.

The cat made friends with him, and climbed into his lap when he smoked his cigar. He stroked her silky fur, and talked a little about her. He looked at Edna's book, which he had read; and he told her the end, to save her the trouble of wading through it, he said.

Again he accompanied her back to her home; and it was after dusk when they reached the little 'pigeon-house'. She did not ask him to remain, which he was grateful for, as it permitted him to stay without the discomfort of blundering through an excuse which he had no intention of considering. He helped her to light the lamp; then she went into her room to take off her hat and to bathe her face and hands.

When she came back Robert was not examining the pictures and magazines as before; he sat off in the shadow, leaning his head back on the chair as if in a reverie. Edna lingered a moment beside the table, arranging the books there. Then she went across the room to where he sat. She bent over the arm of his chair and called his name.

'Robert,' she said, 'are you asleep?'

'No,' he answered, looking up at her.

She leaned over and kissed him – a soft, cool, delicate kiss whose voluptuous sting penetrated his whole being – then she moved away from him. He followed, and took her in his arms, just holding her close to him. She put her hand up to his face and pressed his cheek against her own. The action was full of love and tenderness. He sought her lips again. Then he drew her down upon the sofa beside him and held her hand in both of his.

'Now you know,' he said, 'now you know what I have been fighting against since last summer at Grand Isle; what drove me away and drove me back again.'

'Why have you been fighting against it?' she asked. Her face glowed with soft lights.

'Why? Because you were not free; you were Léonce Pontellier's wife. I couldn't help loving you if you were ten times his wife; but so long as I went away from you and kept away I could help telling you so.' She put her free hand up to his shoulder, and then against his cheek, rubbing it softly. He kissed her again. His face was warm and flushed.

'There in Mexico I was thinking of you all the time, and longing for you.'

'But not writing to me,' she interrupted.

'Something put into my head that you cared for me; and I lost my senses. I forgot everything but a wild dream of your some way becoming my wife.'

'Your wife!'

'Religion, loyalty, everything would give way if only you cared.'

'Then you must have forgotten that I was Léonce Pontellier's wife.'

'Oh! I was demented, dreaming of wild, impossible things, recalling men who had set their wives free; we have heard of such things.'

'Yes, we have heard of such things.'

'I came back full of vague, mad intentions. And when I got here – '

'When you got here you never came near me!' She was still caressing his cheek.

'I realised what a cur I was to dream of such a thing, even if you had been willing.'

She took his face between her hands and looked into it as if she would never withdraw her eyes more. She kissed him on the forehead, the eyes, the cheeks and the lips.

'You have been a very, very foolish boy, wasting your time dreaming of impossible things when you speak of Mr Pontellier setting me free! I am no longer one of Mr Pontellier's possessions to dispose of or not. I give myself where I choose. If he were to say, "Here, Robert, take her and be happy; she is yours," I should laugh at you both.'

His face grew a little white. 'What do you mean?' he asked.

There was a knock at the door. Old Celestine came in to say that Madame Ratignolle's servant had come around the back way with a message that Madame had been taken sick and begged Mrs Pontellier to go to her immediately.

'Yes, yes,' said Edna, rising; 'I promised. Tell her yes – to wait for me. I'll go back with her.'

'Let me walk over with you,' offered Robert.

'No,' she said; 'I will go with the servant.' She went into her room to put on her hat, and when she came in again she sat once more upon the sofa beside him. He had not stirred. She put her arms about his neck.

'Goodbye, my sweet Robert. Tell me goodbye.' He kissed her with a degree of passion which had not before entered into his caress, and strained her to him.

'I love you,' she whispered, 'only you; no one but you. It was you who awoke me last summer out of a life-long, stupid dream. Oh! you have made me so unhappy with your indifference. Oh! I have suffered, suffered! Now you are here we shall love each other, my Robert. We shall be everything to each other. Nothing else in the world is of any consequence. I must go to my friend; but you will wait for me? No matter how late; you will wait for me, Robert?'

'Don't go, don't go! Oh! Edna, stay with me,' he pleaded. 'Why should you go? Stay with me, stay with me.'

'I shall come back as soon as I can; I shall find you here.' She buried her face in his neck, and said goodbye again. Her seductive voice, together with his great love for her, had enthralled his senses, had deprived him of every impulse but the longing to hold her and keep her.

37

Edna looked in at the drug store. Monsieur Ratignolle was putting up a mixture himself, very carefully, dropping a red liquid into a tiny glass. He was grateful to Edna for having come; her presence would be a comfort to his wife. Madame Ratignolle's sister, who had always been with her at such trying times, had not been able to come up from the plantation, and Adèle had been inconsolable until Mrs Pontellier so kindly promised to come to her. The nurse had been with them at night for the past week, as she lived a great distance away. And Dr Mandelet had been coming and going all the afternoon. They were then looking for him any moment.

Edna hastened upstairs by a private stairway that led from the rear of the store to the apartments above. The children were all sleeping in a back room. Madame Ratignolle was in the salon, whither she had strayed in her suffering impatience. She sat on the sofa, clad in an ample white *peignoir*, holding a handkerchief tight in her hand with a nervous clutch. Her face was drawn and pinched, her sweet blue eyes haggard and unnatural. All her beautiful hair had been drawn back and plaited. It lay in a long braid on the sofa pillow, coiled like a golden serpent. The nurse, a comfortable looking *Griffe* woman in white apron and cap, was urging her to return to her bedroom.

'There is no use, there is no use,' she said at once to Edna. 'We must get rid of Mandelet he is getting too old and careless. He said he would be here at half-past seven; now it must be eight. See what time it is, Joséphine.'

The woman was possessed of a cheerful nature, and refused to take any situation too seriously, especially a situation with which she was so familiar. She urged Madame to have courage and patience. But Madame only set her teeth hard into her under lip, and Edna saw the sweat gather in beads on her white forehead. After a moment or two she uttered a profound sigh and wiped her face with the handkerchief rolled in a ball. She appeared exhausted. The nurse gave her a fresh handkerchief, sprinkled with cologne water.

'This is too much!' she cried. 'Mandelet ought to be killed! Where is Alphonse? Is it possible I am to be abandoned like this – neglected by everyone?'

'Neglected, indeed!' exclaimed the nurse. Wasn't she there? And here was Mrs Pontellier leaving, no doubt, a pleasant evening at home to devote to her? And wasn't Monsieur Ratignolle coming that very instant through the hall? And Joséphine was quite sure she had heard Dr Mandelet's coupé. Yes, there it was, down at the door.

Adèle consented to go back to her room. She sat on the edge of a little low couch next to her bed.

Dr Mandelet paid no attention to Madame Ratignolle's upbraidings. He was accustomed to them at such times, and was too well convinced of her loyalty to doubt it.

He was glad to see Edna, and wanted her to go with him into the salon and entertain him. But Madame Ratignolle would not consent that Edna should leave her for an instant. Between agonising moments, she chatted a little, and said it took her mind off her sufferings.

Edna began to feel uneasy. She was seized with a vague dread. Her own like experiences seemed far away, unreal, and only half remembered. She recalled faintly an ecstasy of pain, the heavy odour of chloroform, a stupor which had deadened sensation, and an awakening to find a little new life, to which she had given being, added to the great unnumbered multitude of souls that come and go.

She began to wish she had not come; her presence was not necessary. She might have invented a pretext for staying away; she might even invent a pretext now for going. But Edna did not go. With an inward agony, with a flaming, outspoken revolt against the ways of Nature, she witnessed the scene's torture.

She was still stunned and speechless with emotion when later she leaned over her friend to kiss her and softly say goodbye. Adèle, pressing her cheek, whispered in an exhausted voice, 'Think of the children, Edna. Oh think of the children! Remember them!'

38

Edna still felt dazed when she got outside in the open air. The doctor's coupé had returned for him and stood before the *porte cochère*. She did not wish to enter the coupé, and told Dr Mandelet she would walk; she was not afraid, and would go alone. He directed his carriage to meet him at Mrs Pontellier's, and he started to walk home with her.

Up – away up, over the narrow street between the tall houses, the stars were blazing. The air was mild and caressing, but cool with the breath of spring and the night. They walked slowly, the doctor with a heavy, measured tread and his hands behind him; Edna, in an absent-minded way, as she had walked one night at Grand Isle, as if her thoughts had gone ahead of her and she was striving to overtake them.

'You shouldn't have been there, Mrs Pontellier,' he said. 'That was no place for you. Adèle is full of whims at such times. There were a dozen women she might have had with her, unimpressionable women. I felt that it was cruel, cruel. You shouldn't have gone.'

'Oh, well!' she answered, indifferently. 'I don't know that it matters after all. One has to think of the children sometime or other; the sooner the better.'

'When is Léonce coming back?'

'Quite soon. Sometime in March.'

'And you are going abroad?'

'Perhaps – no, I am not going. I'm not going to be forced into doing things. I don't want to go abroad. I want to be let alone. Nobody has any right – except children, perhaps – and even then, it seems to me – or it did seem – ' She felt that her speech was voicing the incoherency of her thoughts, and stopped abruptly.

'The trouble is,' sighed the doctor, grasping her meaning intuitively, 'that youth is given up to illusions. It seems to be a provision of Nature; a decoy to secure mothers for the race. And Nature takes no account of moral consequences, of arbitrary conditions which we create, and which we feel obliged to maintain at any cost.'

'Yes,' she said. 'The years that are gone seem like dreams – if one might go on sleeping and dreaming – but to wake up and find – oh! well! perhaps it is better to wake up after all, even to suffer, rather than to remain a dupe to illusions all one's life.'

'It seems to me, my dear child,' said the doctor at parting, holding her hand, 'you seem to me to be in trouble. I am not going to ask for your confidence. I will only say that if ever you feel moved to give it to me, perhaps I might help you. I know I would understand, and I tell you there are not many who would – not many, my dear.'

'Some way I don't feel moved to speak of things that trouble me. Don't think I am ungrateful or that I don't appreciate your sympathy. There are periods of despondency and suffering which take possession of me. But I don't want anything but my own way. That is wanting a good deal, of course, when you have to trample upon the lives, the hearts, the prejudices of others – but no matter – still, I shouldn't want to trample upon the little lives. Oh! I don't know what I'm saying, doctor. Good-night. Don't blame me for anything.'

'Yes, I will blame you if you don't come and see me soon. We will talk of things you never have dreamt of talking about before. It will do us both good. I don't want you to blame yourself, whatever comes. Good-night, my child.'

She let herself in at the gate, but instead of entering she sat upon the step of the porch. The night was quiet and soothing. All the tearing emotion of the last few hours seemed to fall away from her like a sombre, uncomfortable garment, which she had but to loosen to be rid of. She went back to that hour before Adèle had sent for her; and her senses kindled afresh in thinking of Robert's words, the pressure of his arms, and the feeling of his lips upon her own. She could picture at that moment no greater bliss on earth than possession of the beloved one. His expression of love had already given him to her in part. When she thought that he was there at hand, waiting for her, she grew numb with the intoxication of expectancy. It was so late; he would be asleep perhaps.

She would awaken him with a kiss. She hoped he would be asleep that she might arouse him with her caresses.

Still, she remembered Adèle's voice whispering, 'Think of the children; think of them.' She meant to think of them; that determination had driven into her soul like a death wound – but not tonight. Tomorrow would be time to think of everything.

Robert was not waiting for her in the little parlour. He was nowhere at hand. The house was empty. But he had scrawled on a piece of paper that lay in the lamplight: 'I love you. Goodbye – because I love you.'

Edna grew faint when she read the words. She went and sat on the sofa. Then she stretched herself out there, never uttering a sound. She did not sleep. She did not go to bed. The lamp sputtered and went out. She was still awake in the morning, when Celestine unlocked the kitchen door and came in to light the fire.

39

Victor, with hammer and nails and scraps of scantling,[95] was patching a corner of one of the galleries. Mariequita sat near by, dangling her legs, watching him work, and handing him nails from the tool-box. The sun was beating down upon them. The girl had covered her head with her apron folded into a square pad. They had been talking for an hour or more. She was never tired of hearing Victor describe the dinner at Mrs Pontellier's. He exaggerated every detail, making it appear a veritable Lucullan feast.[96] The flowers were in tubs, he said. The champagne was quaffed from huge golden goblets. Venus[97] rising from the foam could have presented no more entrancing a spectacle than Mrs Pontellier, blazing with beauty and diamonds at the head of the board, while the other women were all of them youthful houris,[98] possessed of incomparable charms.

She got it into her head that Victor was in love with Mrs Pontellier, and he gave her evasive answers, framed so as to confirm her belief. She grew sullen and cried a little, threatening to go off and leave him to his fine ladies. There were a dozen men crazy about her at the Chênière; and since it was the fashion to be in love with married people, why, she could run away any time she liked to New Orleans with Célina's husband.

Célina's husband was a fool, a coward and a pig, and to prove it to her, Victor intended to hammer his head into a jelly the next time he encountered him. This assurance was very consoling to Mariequita. She dried her eyes, and grew cheerful at the prospect.

They were still talking of the dinner and the allurements of city life when Mrs Pontellier herself slipped around the corner of the house. The two youngsters stayed dumb with amazement before what they considered to be an apparition. But it was really she in flesh and blood, looking tired and a little travel-stained.

'I walked up from the wharf,' she said, 'and heard the hammering. I supposed it was you, mending the porch. It's a good thing. I was always tripping over those loose planks last summer. How dreary and deserted everything looks!'

It took Victor some little time to comprehend that she had come in Beaudelet's lugger, that she had come alone, and for no purpose but to rest.

'There's nothing fixed up yet, you see. I'll give you my room; it's the only place.'

'Any corner will do,' she assured him.

'And if you can stand Philomel's cooking,' he went on, 'though I might try to get her mother while you are here. Do you think she would come?' turning to Mariequita.

Mariequita thought that perhaps Philomel's mother might come for a few days, and money enough.

Beholding Mrs Pontellier make her appearance, the girl had at once suspected a lovers' rendezvous. But Victor's astonishment was so genuine, and Mrs Pontellier's indifference so apparent, that the disturbing notion did not lodge long in her brain. She contemplated with the greatest interest this woman who gave the most sumptuous dinners in America, and who had all the men in New Orleans at her feet.

'What time will you have dinner?' asked Edna. 'I'm very hungry; but don't get anything extra.'

'I'll have it ready in little or no time,' he said, bustling and packing away his tools. 'You may go to my room to brush up and rest yourself. Mariequita will show you.'

'Thank you,' said Edna. 'But, do you know, I have a notion to go down to the beach and take a good wash and even a little swim, before dinner?'

'The water is too cold!' they both exclaimed. 'Don't think of it.'

'Well, I might go down and try – dip my toes in. Why, it seems to me the sun is hot enough to have warmed the very depths of the ocean. Could you get me a couple of towels? I'd better go right away, so as to be back in time. It would be a little too chilly if I waited till this afternoon.'

Mariequita ran over to Victor's room, and returned with some towels, which she gave to Edna.

'I hope you have fish for dinner,' said Edna, as she started to walk away; 'but don't do anything extra if you haven't.'

'Run and find Philomel's mother,' Victor instructed the girl. 'I'll go to the kitchen and see what I can do. By Gimminy! Women have no consideration! She might have sent me word.'

Edna walked on down to the beach rather mechanically, not noticing anything special except that the sun was hot. She was not dwelling upon any particular train of thought. She had done all the thinking which was necessary after Robert went away, when she lay awake upon the sofa till morning.

She had said over and over to herself: 'Today it is Arobin; tomorrow it will be someone else. It makes no difference to me, it doesn't matter about Léonce Pontellier – but Raoul and Etienne!' She understood now clearly what she had meant long ago when she said to Adèle Ratignolle that she would give up the unessential, but she would never sacrifice herself for her children.

Despondency had come upon her there in the wakeful night, and had never lifted. There was no one thing in the world that she desired. There was no human being whom she wanted near her except Robert; and she even realised that the day would come when he, too, and the thought of him would melt out of her existence, leaving her alone. The children appeared before her like antagonists who had overcome her; who had overpowered and sought to drag her into the soul's slavery for the rest of her days. But she knew a way to elude them. She was not thinking of these things when she walked down to the beach.

The water of the Gulf stretched out before her, gleaming with the million lights of the sun. The voice of the sea is seductive, never ceasing, whispering, clamouring, murmuring, inviting the soul to wander in abysses of solitude. All along the white beach, up and down, there was no living thing in sight. A bird with a broken wing was beating the air above, reeling, fluttering, circling disabled down, down to the water.

Edna had found her old bathing suit still hanging, faded, upon its accustomed peg.

She put it on, leaving her clothing in the bath-house. But when she was there beside the sea, absolutely alone, she cast the unpleasant, pricking garments from her, and for the first time in her life she stood naked in the open air, at the mercy of the sun, the breeze that beat upon her and the waves that invited her.

How strange and awful it seemed to stand naked under the sky! how delicious! She felt like some new-born creature, opening its eyes in a familiar world that it had never known.

The foamy wavelets curled up to her white feet, and coiled like serpents about her ankles. She walked out. The water was chill, but she walked on. The water was deep, but she lifted her white body and reached out with a long, sweeping stroke. The touch of the sea is sensuous, enfolding the body in its soft, close embrace.

She went on and on. She remembered the night she swam far out, and recalled the terror that seized her at the fear of being unable to regain the shore. She did not look back now, but went on and on, thinking of the blue-grass meadow that she had traversed when a little child, believing that it had no beginning and no end.

Her arms and legs were growing tired.

She thought of Léonce and the children. They were a part of her life. But they need not have thought that they could possess her, body and soul. How Mademoiselle Reisz would have laughed, perhaps sneered, if she knew! 'And you call yourself an artist! What pretensions, madame! The artist must possess the courageous soul that dares and defies.'

Exhaustion was pressing upon and overpowering her.

'Goodbye – because I love you.' He did not know; he did not understand. He would never understand. Perhaps Dr Mandelet would have understood if she had seen him – but it was too late; the shore was far behind her, and her strength was gone.

She looked into the distance, and the old terror flamed up for an instant, then sank again. Edna heard her father's voice and her sister Margaret's. She heard the barking of an old dog that was chained to the sycamore tree. The spurs of the cavalry officer clanged as he walked across the porch. There was the hum of bees, and the musky odour of pinks filled the air.

A No-Account Creole

1

One agreeable afternoon in late autumn two young men stood together on Canal Street,[99] closing a conversation that had evidently begun within the clubhouse which they had just quitted.

'There's big money in it, Offdean,' said the elder of the two. 'I wouldn't have you touch it if there wasn't. Why, they tell me Patchly's pulled a hundred thousand out of the concern a'ready.'

'That may be,' replied Offdean, who had been politely attentive to the words addressed to him, but whose face bore a look indicating that he was closed to conviction. He leaned back upon the clumsy stick which he carried, and continued: 'It's all true, I dare say, Fitch; but a decision of that sort would mean more to me than you'd believe if I were to tell you. The beggarly twenty-five thousand's all I have, and I want to sleep with it under my pillow a couple of months at least before I drop it into a slot.'

'You'll drop it into Harding & Offdean's[100] mill to grind out the pitiful two-and-a-half-per-cent-commission racket; that's what you'll do in the end, old fellow – see if you don't.'

'Perhaps I shall; but it's more than likely I shan't. We'll talk about it when I get back. You know I'm off to north Louisiana in the morning – '

'No! What the deuce – '

'Oh, business of the firm.'

'Write me from Shreveport, then; or wherever it is.'

'Not so far as that. But don't expect to hear from me till you see me. I can't say when that will be.'

Then they shook hands and parted. The rather portly Fitch boarded a Prytania Street car, and Mr Wallace Offdean hurried to the bank in order to replenish his portemonnaie, which had been materially lightened at the club through the medium of unpropitious jackpots and bobtail flushes.

He was a sure-footed fellow, this young Offdean, despite an occasional fall in slippery places. What he wanted, now that he had reached his twenty-sixth year and his inheritance, was to get his feet well planted on solid ground, and to keep his head cool and clear.

With his early youth he had had certain shadowy intentions of shaping his life on intellectual lines. That is, he wanted to; and he meant to use his faculties intelligently, which means more than is at once apparent. Above all, he would keep clear of the maelstroms of sordid work and senseless pleasure in which the average American business man may be said alternately to exist, and which reduce him, naturally, to a rather ragged condition of soul.

Offdean had done, in a temperate way, the usual things which young men do who happen to belong to good society, and are possessed of moderate means and healthy instincts. He had gone to college, had travelled a little at home and abroad, had frequented society and the clubs, and had worked in his uncle's commission-house; in all of which employments he had expended much time and a modicum of energy.

But he felt all through that he was simply in a preliminary stage of being, one that would develop later into something tangible and intelligent, as he liked to tell himself. With his patrimony of twenty-five thousand dollars came what he felt to be the turning-point in his life – the time when it behooved him to choose a course, and to get himself into proper trim to follow it manfully and consistently.

When Messrs Harding & Offdean determined to have someone look after what they called 'a troublesome piece of land on Red River',[101] Wallace Offdean requested to be entrusted with that special commission of land-inspector.

A shadowy, ill-defined piece of land in an unfamiliar part of his native state might, he hoped, prove a sort of closet into which he could retire and take counsel with his inner and better self.

2

What Harding & Offdean had called a piece of land on Red River was better known to the people of Natchitoches [pronounced Nack-e-tosh] parish[102] as 'the old Santien[103] place'.

In the days of Lucien Santien and his hundred slaves, it had been very splendid in the wealth of its thousand acres. But the war did its work, of course. Then Jules Santien was not the man to mend such damage as the war had left. His three sons were even less able than he had been to bear the weighty inheritance of debt that came to them with the dismantled plantation; so it was a deliverance to all when Harding & Offdean, the New Orleans creditors, relieved them of the place with the responsibility and indebtedness which its ownership had entailed.

Hector the eldest and Grégoire the youngest of these Santien boys had gone each his way. Placide alone tried to keep a desultory foothold upon the land which had been his and his forefathers'. But he too was given to wandering – within a radius, however, which rarely took him so far that he could not reach the old place in an afternoon of travel, when he felt so inclined.

There were acres of open land cultivated in a slovenly fashion, but so rich that cotton and corn and weed and 'cocoa-grass' grew rampant if they had only the semblance of a chance. The negro quarters were at the far end of this open stretch, and consisted of a long row of old and very crippled cabins. Directly back of these a dense wood grew, and held much mystery, and witchery of sound and shadow, and strange lights when the sun shone. Of a gin-house there was left scarcely a trace – only so much as could serve as inadequate shelter to the miserable dozen cattle that huddled within it in wintertime.

A dozen rods or more from the Red River bank stood the dwelling-house, and nowhere upon the plantation had time touched so sadly as here. The steep, black, moss-covered roof sat like an extinguisher[104] above the eight large rooms that it covered, and had come to do its office so poorly that not more than half of these were habitable when the rain fell. Perhaps the live-oaks made too thick and close a shelter about it. The verandas were long and broad and inviting; but it was well to know that the brick pillar was crumbling away under one corner, that the railing was insecure at another, and that still another had long ago been condemned as unsafe. But that, of course, was not the corner in which Wallace Offdean sat the day following his arrival at the Santien place. This one was comparatively secure. A *gloire-de-Dijon*,[105] thick-leaved and charged with huge creamy blossoms, grew and spread here like a hardy vine upon the wires that stretched from post to post. The scent of the blossoms was delicious; and the stillness that surrounded Offdean agreeably fitted his humour that asked for rest. His old host, Pierre Manton, the manager of the place, sat talking to him in a soft, rhythmic monotone; but his speech was hardly more of an interruption than the hum of the bees among the roses. He was saying: 'If it would been me myse'f, I would nevair grumb'. W'en a chimbly breck, I take one, two de boys; we patch 'im up bes' we know how. We keep on men' de fence', firs' one place, anudder; an' if it wouldn' be fer dem mule' of Lacroix – *tonnerre!* I don' wan' to talk 'bout dem mule'. But me, I wouldn' grumb'. It's Euphrasie, hair. She say dat's all fool nonsense fer rich man lack Hardin'-Offde'n to let a piece o' lan' goin' lack dat.'

'Euphrasie?' questioned Offdean, in some surprise; for he had not yet heard of any such person.

'Euphrasie, my li'le chile. Escuse me one minute,' Pierre added, remembering that he was in his shirt-sleeves, and rising to reach for his coat, which hung upon a peg near by. He was a small, square man, with mild, kindly face, brown and roughened from healthy exposure. His hair hung grey and long beneath the soft felt hat that he wore.

When he had seated himself, Offdean asked: 'Where is your little child? I haven't seen her,' inwardly marvelling that a little child should have uttered such words of wisdom as those recorded of her.

'She yonder to Mme Duplan[106] on Cane River. I been kine espectin' hair sence yistiday – hair an' Placide,' casting an unconscious glance down the long plantation road. 'But Mme Duplan she nevair want to let Euphrasie go. You know it's hair raise' Euphrasie sence hair po' ma die', Mr Offde'n. She teck dat li'le chile, an' raise it, sem lack she raisin' Ninette. But it's mo' 'an a year now Euphrasie say dat's all fool nonsense to leave me livin' 'lone lack dat, wid nuttin' 'cep' dem nigger' – an' Placide once a w'ile. An' she came yair bossin'! My goodness!' The old man chuckled, 'Dat's hair been writin' all dem letter' to Hardin'-Offde'n. If it would been me myse'f – '

3

Placide seemed to have had a foreboding of ill from the start when he found that Euphrasie began to interest herself in the condition of the plantation. This ill feeling voiced itself partly when he told her it was none of her lookout if the place went to the dogs. 'It's good enough for Joe Duplan to run things *en grand seigneur*, Euphrasie; that's w'at's spoiled you.'

Placide might have done much single-handed to keep the old place in better trim, if he had wished. For there was no one more clever than he to do a hand's turn at anything and everything. He could mend a saddle or bridle while he stood whistling a tune. If a wagon required a brace or a bolt, it was nothing for him to step into a shop and turn out one as deftly as the most skilled blacksmith. Anyone seeing him at work with plane and rule and chisel would have declared him a born carpenter. And as for mixing paints, and giving a fine and lasting coat to the side of a house or barn, he had not his equal in the country.

This last talent he exercised little in his native parish. It was in a neighbouring one, where he spent the greater part of his time, that his fame as a painter was established. There, in the village of Orville, he owned a little shell of a house, and during odd times it was Placide's great delight to tinker at this small home, inventing daily new beauties and conveniences to add to it. Lately it had become a precious possession to him, for in the spring he was to bring Euphrasie there as his wife.

Maybe it was because of his talent and his indifference in turning it to good that he was often called 'a no-account Creole' by thriftier souls than himself. But no-account Creole or not, painter, carpenter, blacksmith, and whatever else he might be at times, he was a Santien always, with the best blood in the country running in his veins. And many thought his choice had fallen in very low places when he engaged himself to marry little Euphrasie, the daughter of old Pierre Manton and a problematic mother a good deal less than nobody.

Placide might have married almost anyone, too; for it was the easiest thing in the world for a girl to fall in love with him – sometimes the hardest thing in the world not to, he was such a splendid fellow, such a careless, happy, handsome fellow. And he did not seem to mind in the least that young men who had grown up with him were lawyers now, and planters, and members of Shakespeare clubs in town. No one ever expected anything quite so humdrum as that of the Santien boys. As youngsters, all three had been the despair of the country schoolmaster; then of the private tutor who had come to shackle them, and had failed in his design. And the state of mutiny and revolt that they had brought about at the college of Grand Coteau when their father, in a moment of weak concession to prejudice, had sent them there, is a thing yet remembered in Natchitoches.

And now Placide was going to marry Euphrasie. He could not recall the time when he had not loved her. Somehow he felt that it began the day when he was six years old, and Pierre, his father's overseer, had called him from play to come and make her acquaintance. He was permitted to hold her in his arms a moment, and it was with silent awe that he did so. She was the first white-faced baby he remembered having seen, and he straightway believed she had been sent to him as a birthday gift to be his little playmate and friend. If he loved her, there was no great wonder; everyone did, from the time she took her first dainty step, which was a brave one, too.

She was the gentlest little lady ever born in old Natchitoches parish, and the happiest and merriest. She never cried or whimpered for a hurt. Placide never did, why should she? When she wept, it was when she did what was wrong, or when he did; for that was to be a coward, she felt. When she was ten, and her mother was dead, Mme Duplan, the Lady Bountiful of the parish, had driven across from her plantation, Les

Chêniers,[107] to old Pierre's very door, and there had gathered up this precious little maid, and carried her away, to do with as she would.

And she did with the child much as she herself had been done by. Euphrasie went to the convent soon, and was taught all gentle things, the pretty arts of manner and speech that the ladies of the 'Sacred Heart' can teach so well. When she quitted them, she left a trail of love behind her; she always did.

Placide continued to see her at intervals, and to love her always. One day he told her so; he could not help it. She stood under one of the big oaks at Les Chêniers. It was midsummer time, and the tangled sunbeams had enmeshed her in a golden fretwork. When he saw her standing there in the sun's glamour, which was like a glory upon her, he trembled. He seemed to see her for the first time. He could only look at her, and wonder why her hair gleamed so, as it fell in those thick chestnut waves about her ears and neck. He had looked a thousand times into her eyes before; was it only today they held that sleepy, wistful light in them that invites love? How had he not seen it before? Why had he not known before that her lips were red, and cut in fine, strong curves? that her flesh was like cream? How had he not seen that she was beautiful? 'Euphrasie,' he said, taking her hands – 'Euphrasie, I love you!'

She looked at him with a little astonishment. 'Yes; I know, Placide.' She spoke with the soft intonation of the Creole.

'No, you don't, Euphrasie. I didn' know myse'f how much tell jus' now.'

Perhaps he did only what was natural when he asked her next if she loved him. He still held her hands. She looked thoughtfully away, unready to answer.

'Do you love anybody better?' he asked jealously. 'Anyone jus' as well as me?'

'You know I love papa better, Placide, an' Maman Duplan jus' as well.'

Yet she saw no reason why she should not be his wife when he asked her to.

Only a few months before this, Euphrasie had returned to live with her father. The step had cut her off from everything that girls of eighteen call pleasure. If it cost her one regret, no one could have guessed it. She went often to visit the Duplans, however; and Placide had gone to bring her home from Les Chêniers the very day of Offdean's arrival at the plantation.

They had travelled by rail to Natchitoches, where they found Pierre's no-top buggy awaiting them, for there was a drive of five miles to be made through the pine woods before the plantation was reached. When they were at their journey's end, and had driven some distance; up the long plantation road that led to the house in the rear, Euphrasie exclaimed: 'W'y, there's someone on the gall'ry with papa, Placide!'

'Yes; I see.'

'It looks like someone f'om town. It mus' be Mr Gus Adams; but I don' see his horse.'

' 'Tain't no one f'om town that I know. It's boun' to be someone f'om the city.'

'Oh, Placide, I shouldn' wonder if Harding & Offdean have sent someone to look after the place at las',' she exclaimed a little excitedly.

They were near enough to see that the stranger was a young man of very pleasing appearance. Without apparent reason, a chilly depression took hold of Placide.

'I tole you it wasn' yo' lookout f'om the firs', Euphrasie,' he said to her.

4

Wallace Offdean remembered Euphrasie at once as a young person whom he had assisted to a very high perch on his clubhouse balcony the previous Mardi Gras[108] night. He had thought her pretty and attractive then, and for the space of a day or two wondered who she might be. But he had not made even so fleeting an impression upon her; seeing which, he did not refer to any former meeting when Pierre introduced them.

She took the chair which he offered her, and asked him very simply when he had come, if his journey had been pleasant, and if he had not found the road from Natchitoches in very good condition.

'Mr Offde'n only come sence yistiday, Euphrasie,' interposed Pierre. 'We been talk' plenty 'bout de place, him an' me. I been tole 'im all 'bout it – va! An' if Mr Offde'n want to escuse me now, I b'lieve I go he'p Placide wid dat hoss an' buggy;' and he descended the steps slowly, and walked lazily with his bent figure in the direction of the shed beneath which Placide had driven after depositing Euphrasie at the door.

'I dare say you find it strange,' began Offdean, 'that the owners of this place have neglected it so long and shamefully. But you see,' he added, smiling, 'the management of a plantation doesn't enter into the routine of a commission merchant's business. The place has already cost them more than they hope to get from it, and naturally they haven't the wish to sink further money in it.' He did not know why he was saying these things to a mere girl, but he went on: 'I'm authorised to sell the plantation if I can get anything like a reasonable price for it.' Euphrasie laughed in a way that made him uncomfortable, and he thought he would say no more at present – not till he knew her better, anyhow.

'Well,' she said in a very decided fashion, 'I know you'll fin' one or two persons in town who'll begin by running down the lan' till you wouldn' want it as a gif', Mr Offdean; and who will en' by offering to take it off yo' han's for the promise of a song, with the lan' as security again.'

They both laughed, and Placide, who was approaching, scowled. But before he reached the steps his instinctive sense of the courtesy due to a stranger had banished the look of ill humour. His bearing was so frank and graceful, and his face such a marvel of beauty, with its dark, rich colouring and soft lines, that the well-clipped and groomed Offdean felt his astonishment to be more than half admiration when they shook hands. He knew that the Santiens had been the former owners of this plantation which he had come to look after, and naturally he expected some sort of cooperation or direct assistance from Placide in his efforts at reconstruction. But Placide proved non-committal, and exhibited an indifference and ignorance concerning the condition of affairs that savoured surprisingly of affectation.

He had positively nothing to say so long as the talk touched upon matters concerning Offdean's business there. He was only a little less taciturn when more general topics were approached, and directly after supper he saddled his horse and went away. He would not wait until morning, for the moon would be rising about midnight, and he knew the road as well by night as by day. He knew just where the best fords were across the bayous, and the safest paths across the hills. He knew for a certainty whose plantations he might traverse, and whose fences he might derail. But, for that matter, he would derail what he liked, and cross where he pleased.

Euphrasie walked with him to the shed when he went for his horse. She was bewildered at his sudden determination, and wanted it explained.

'I don' like that man,' he admitted frankly; 'I can't stan' him. Sen' me word w'en he's gone, Euphrasie.'

She was patting and rubbing the pony, which knew her well. Only their dim outlines were discernible in the thick darkness.

'You are foolish, Placide,' she replied in French. 'You would do better to stay and help him. No one knows the place so well as you – '

'The place isn't mine, and it's nothing to me,' he answered bitterly. He took her hands and kissed them passionately, but stooping, she pressed her lips upon his forehead.

'Oh!' he exclaimed rapturously, 'you do love me, Euphrasie?' His arms were holding her, and his lips brushing her hair and cheeks as they eagerly but ineffectually sought hers.

'Of co'se I love you, Placide. Ain't I going to marry you nex' spring? You foolish boy!' she replied, disengaging herself from his clasp.

When he was mounted, he stooped to say, 'See yere, Euphrasie, don't have too much to do with that d— Yankee.'

'But, Placide, he isn't a – a – "d— Yankee"; he's a Southerner, like you – a New Orleans man.'

'Oh, well, he looks like a Yankee.' But Placide laughed, for he was happy since Euphrasie had kissed him, and he whistled softly as he urged his horse to a canter and disappeared in the darkness.

The girl stood awhile with clasped hands, trying to understand a little sigh that rose in her throat, and that was not one of regret. When she regained the house, she went directly to her room, and left her father talking to Offdean in the quiet and perfumed night.

5

When two weeks had passed, Offdean felt very much at home with old Pierre and his daughter, and found the business that had called him to the country so engrossing that he had given no thought to those personal questions he had hoped to solve in going there.

The old man had driven him around in the no-top buggy to show him how dismantled the fences and barns were. He could see for himself that the house was a constant menace to human life. In the evenings the three would sit out on the gallery and talk of the land and its strong points and its weak ones, till he came to know it as if it had been his own.

Of the rickety condition of the cabins he got a fair notion, for he and Euphrasie passed them almost daily on horseback, on their way to the woods. It was seldom that their appearance together did not rouse comment among the darkies who happened to be loitering about.

La Chatte,[109] a broad black woman with ends of white wool sticking out from under her *tignon*, stood with arms akimbo watching them as they disappeared one day. Then she turned and said to a young woman who sat in the cabin door: 'Dat young man, ef he want to listen to me, he gwine quit dat ar caperin' roun' Miss 'Phrasie.'

The young woman in the doorway laughed, and showed her white teeth, and tossed her head, and fingered the blue beads at her throat, in a way to indicate that she was in hearty sympathy with any question that touched upon gallantry.

'Law! La Chatte, you ain' gwine hinder a gemman f'om payin' intentions to a young lady w'en he a mine to.'

'Dat all I got to say,' returned La Chatte, seating herself lazily and heavily on the doorstep. 'Nobody don' know dem Sanchun boys bettah 'an I does. Didn' I done part raise 'em? W'at you reckon my ha'r all tu'n plumb w'ite dat-a-way ef it warn't dat Placide w'at done it?'

'How come he make yo' ha'r tu'n w'ite, La Chatte?'

'Dev'ment, pu' dev'ment, Rose. Didn' he come in dat same cabin one day, w'en he warn't no bigga 'an dat Pres'dent Hayes[110] w'at you sees gwine 'long de road wid dat cotton sack 'crost 'im? He come an' sets down by de do', on dat same t'ree-laigged stool w'at you's a-settin' on now, wid his gun in his ban', an' he say: "La Chatte, I wants some croquignoles, an' I wants 'em quick, too." I 'low: "G' 'way f'om dah, boy. Don' you see I's flutin' yo' ma's petticoat?" He say: "La Chatte, put 'side dat ar flutin'-i'on an' dat ar petticoat;" an' he cock dat gun an' p'int it to my head. "Dar de ba'el," he say; "git out dat flour, git out dat butta an' dat aigs; step roun' dah, ole 'oman. Dis heah gun don' quit yo' head tell dem croquignoles is on de table, wid a w'ite table-clof an' a cup o' coffee." Ef I goes to de ba'el, de gun's a-p'intin'. Ef I goes to de fiah, de gun's a-p'intin'. W'en I rolls out de dough, de gun's a-p'intin'; an' him neva say nuttin', an' me a-trim'lin' like ole Uncle Noah w'en de mis'ry strike 'im.'

'Lordy! w'at you reckon he do ef he tu'n roun' an' git mad wid dat young gemman f'om de city?'

'I don' reckon nuttin'; I knows w'at he gwine do – same w'at his pa done.'

'W'at his pa done, La Chatte?'

'G' 'long 'bout yo' business; you's axin' too many questions.' And La Chatte arose slowly and went to gather her party-coloured wash that hung drying on the jagged and irregular points of a dilapidated picket-fence.

But the darkies were mistaken in supposing that Offdean was paying attention to Euphrasie. Those little jaunts in the wood were purely of a business character. Offdean had made a contract with a neighbouring mill for fencing, in exchange for a certain amount of uncut timber. He had made it his work – with the assistance of Euphrasie – to decide upon what trees he wanted felled, and to mark such for the woodman's axe.

If they sometimes forgot what they had gone into the woods for, it was because there was so much to talk about and to laugh about. Often, when Offdean had blazed a tree with the sharp hatchet which he carried at his pommel, and had further discharged his duty by calling it 'a fine piece of timber', they would sit upon some fallen and decaying trunk, maybe to listen to a chorus of mocking-birds above their heads, or to exchange confidences, as young people will.

Euphrasie thought she had never heard anyone talk quite so pleasantly as Offdean did. She could not decide whether it was his manner or the tone of his voice, or the earnest glance of his dark and deep-set blue eyes, that gave such meaning to everything he said; for she found herself afterwards thinking of his every word.

One afternoon it rained in torrents, and Rose was forced to drag buckets and tubs into Offdean's room to catch the streams that threatened to flood it. Euphrasie said she was glad of it; now he could see for himself.

And when he had seen for himself, he went to join her out on a corner of the gallery, where she stood with a cloak around her, close up against the house. He leaned against the house, too, and they stood thus together, gazing upon as desolate a scene as it is easy to imagine.

The whole landscape was grey, seen through the driving rain. Far away the dreary cabins seemed to sink and sink to earth in abject misery. Above their heads the live-oak branches were beating with sad monotony against the blackened roof. Great pools of water had formed in the yard, which was deserted by every living thing; for the little darkies had scampered away to their cabins, the dogs had run to their kennels, and the hens were puffing big with wretchedness under the scanty shelter of a fallen wagon-body.

Certainly a situation to make a young man groan with ennui, if he is used to his daily stroll on Canal Street, and pleasant afternoons at the club. But Offdean thought it delightful. He only wondered that he had never known, or someone had never told him, how charming a place an old, dismantled plantation can be – when it rains. But as well as he liked it, he could not linger there for ever. Business called him back to New Orleans, and after a few days he went away.

The interest which he felt in the improvement of this plantation was of so deep a nature, however, that he found himself thinking of it constantly. He wondered if the timber had all been felled, and how the fencing was coming on. So great was his desire to know such things that much correspondence was required between himself and Euphrasie, and he watched eagerly for those letters that told him of her trials and vexations with carpenters, bricklayers and shingle-bearers. But in the midst of it, Offdean suddenly lost interest in the progress of work on the plantation. Singularly enough, it happened simultaneously with the arrival of a letter from Euphrasie which announced in a modest postscript that she was going down to the city with the Duplans for Mardi Gras.

6

When Offdean learned that Euphrasie was coming to New Orleans, he was delighted to think he would have an opportunity to make some return for the hospitality which he had received from her father. He decided at once that she must see everything: day processions and night parades, balls and tableaux, operas and plays. He would arrange for it all, and he went to the length of begging to be relieved of certain duties that had been assigned him at the club, in order that he might feel himself perfectly free to do so.

The evening following Euphrasie's arrival, Offdean hastened to call upon her, away down on Esplanade Street. She and the Duplans were staying there with old Mme Carantelle, Mrs Duplan's mother, a delightfully conservative old lady who had not 'crossed Canal Street'[111] for many years.

He found a number of people gathered in the long high-ceilinged drawing-room – young people and old people, all talking French, and some talking louder than they would have done if Madame Carantelle had not been so very deaf.

When Offdean entered, the old lady was greeting someone who had come in just before him. It was Placide, and she was calling him Grégoire, and wanting to know how the crops were up on Red River. She met everyone from the country with this stereotyped enquiry, which placed her at once on the agreeable and easy footing she liked.

Somehow Offdean had not counted on finding Euphrasie so well provided with entertainment, and he spent much of the evening in trying to persuade himself that the fact was a pleasing one in itself. But he wondered why Placide was with her, and sat so persistently beside her, and danced so repeatedly with her when Mrs Duplan played upon the piano. Then he could not see by what right these young Creoles had already arranged for the Proteus ball, and every other entertainment that he had meant to provide for her.

He went away without having had a word alone with the girl whom he had gone to see. The evening had proved a failure. He did not go to the club as usual, but went to his rooms in a mood which inclined him to read a few pages from a stoic philosopher whom he sometimes affected. But the words of wisdom that had often before helped him over disagreeable places left no impress tonight. They were powerless to banish from his thoughts the look of a pair of brown eyes, or to drown the tones of a girl's voice that kept singing in his soul.

Placide was not very well acquainted with the city; but that made no difference to him so long as he was at Euphrasie's side. His brother Hector, who lived in some obscure corner of the town, would willingly have made his knowledge a more intimate one; but Placide did not choose to learn the lessons that Hector was ready to teach. He asked nothing better than to walk with Euphrasie along the streets, holding her parasol at an agreeable angle over her pretty head, or to sit beside her in the evening at the play, sharing her frank delight.

When the night of the Mardi Gras ball came, he felt like a lost spirit during the hours he was forced to remain away from her. He stood in the dense crowd on the street gazing up at her, where she sat on the clubhouse balcony amid a bevy of gayly dressed women. It was not easy to distinguish her, but he could think of no more agreeable occupation than to stand down there on the street trying to do so.

She seemed during all this pleasant time to be entirely his own, too. It made him very fierce to think of the possibility of her not being entirely his own. But he had no cause whatever to think this. She had grown conscious and thoughtful of late about him and their relationship. She often communed with herself, and as a result tried to act towards him as an engaged girl would towards her fiancé. Yet a wistful look came sometimes into the brown eyes when she walked the streets with Placide, and eagerly scanned the faces of passers-by.

Offdean had written her a note, very studied, very formal, asking to see her on a certain day and at a certain hour, to consult about matters on the plantation, saying he had found it so difficult to obtain a word with her that he was forced to adopt this means, which he trusted would not be offensive.

This seemed perfectly right to Euphrasie. She agreed to see him one afternoon – the day before leaving town – in the long, stately drawing-room, quite alone.

It was a sleepy day, too warm for the season. Gusts of moist air were sweeping lazily through the long corridors, rattling the slats of the half-closed green shutters, and bringing a delicious perfume from the courtyard where old Chariot was watering the spreading palms and brilliant parterres. A group of little children had stood awhile quarrelling noisily under the windows, but had moved on down the street and left quietness reigning.

Offdean had not long to wait before Euphrasie came to him. She had lost some of that ease which had marked her manner during their first acquaintance. Now, when she seated herself before him, she showed a disposition to plunge at once into the subject that had brought him there. He was willing enough that it should play some role, since it had been his pretext for coming; but he soon dismissed it, and with it much restraint that had held him till now. He simply looked into her eyes, with a gaze that made her shiver a little, and began to complain because she was going away next day and he had seen nothing of her; because he had wanted to do so many things when she came – why had she not let him?

'You fo'get I'm no stranger here,' she told him. 'I know many people. I've been coming so often with Mme Duplan. I wanted to see mo' of you, Mr Offdean – '

'Then you ought to have managed it; you could have done so. It's – it's aggravating,' he said, far more bitterly than the subject warranted, 'when a man has so set his heart upon something.'

'But it wasn' anything ver' important,' she interposed; and they both laughed, and got safely over a situation that would soon have been strained, if not critical.

Waves of happiness were sweeping through the soul and body of the girl as she sat there in the drowsy afternoon near the man whom she loved. It mattered not what they talked about, or whether they talked at all. They were both scintillant with feeling. If Offdean had taken Euphrasie's hands in his and leaned forward and kissed her lips, it would have seemed to both only the rational outcome of things that stirred them. But he did not do this. He knew now that overwhelming passion was taking possession of him. He had not to heap more coals upon the fire; on the contrary, it was a moment to put on the brakes, and he was a young gentleman able to do this when circumstances required.

However, he held her hand longer than he needed to when he bade her goodbye. For he got entangled in explaining why he should have to go back to the plantation to see how matters stood there, and he dropped her hand only when the rambling speech was ended.

He left her sitting by the window in a big brocaded armchair. She drew the lace curtain aside to watch him pass in the street. He lifted his hat and smiled when he saw her. Any other man she knew would have done the same thing, but this simple act caused the blood to surge to her cheeks. She let the curtain drop, and sat there like one dreaming. Her eyes, intense with the unnatural light that glowed in them, looked steadily into vacancy, and her lips stayed parted in the half-smile that did not want to leave them.

Placide found her thus, a good while afterwards, when he came in, full of bustle, with theatre tickets in his pocket for the last night. She started up, and went eagerly to meet him.

'W'ere have you been, Placide?' she asked with unsteady voice, placing her hands on his shoulders with a freedom that was new and strange to him.

He appeared to her suddenly as a refuge from something, she did not know what, and she rested her hot cheek against his breast. This made him mad, and he lifted her face and kissed her passionately upon the lips.

She crept from his arms after that, and went away to her room, and locked herself in. Her poor little inexperienced soul was torn and sore. She knelt down beside her bed, and sobbed a little and prayed a little. She felt that she had sinned, she did not know exactly in what; but a fine nature warned her that it was in Placide's kiss.

7

The spring came early in Orville, and so subtly that no one could tell exactly when it began. But one morning the roses were so luscious in Placide's sunny parterres, the peas and bean-vines and borders of strawberries so rank in his trim vegetable patches, that he called out lustily, 'No mo' winta, Judge!' to the staid Judge Blount, who went ambling by on his grey pony.

'There's right smart o' folks don't know it, Santien,' responded the judge, with occult meaning that might be applied to certain indebted clients back on the bayou who had not broken land yet. Ten minutes later the judge observed sententiously, and apropos of nothing, to a group that stood waiting for the post-office to open: 'I see Santien's got that noo fence o' his painted. And a pretty piece o' work it is,' he added reflectively.

'Look lack Placide goin' pent mo' 'an de fence,' sagaciously snickered 'Tit-Edouard, a strolling *maigre-échine*[112] of indefinite occupation. 'I seen 'im, me, pesterin' wid all kine o' pent on a piece o' bo'd yistiday.'

'I knows he gwine paint mo' 'an de fence,' emphatically announced Uncle Abner, in a tone that carried conviction.

'He gwine paint de house; dat what he gwine do. Didn' Marse Luke Williams orda de paints? An' didn' I done kyar' 'em up dah myse'f?'

Seeing the deference with which this positive piece of knowledge was received, the judge coolly changed the subject by announcing that Luke Williams's Durham bull had broken a leg the night before in Luke's new pasture ditch – a piece of news that fell among his hearers with telling, if paralytic effect.

But most people wanted to see for themselves these astonishing things that Placide was doing. And the young ladies of the village strolled slowly by of afternoons in couples and arm in arm. If Placide happened to see them, he would leave his work to hand them a fine rose or a bunch of geraniums over the dazzling white fence. But if it chanced to be 'Tit-Edouard or Luke Williams, or any of the young men of Orville, he pretended not to see them or to hear the ingratiating cough that accompanied their lingering footsteps.

In his eagerness to have his home sweet and attractive for Euphrasie's coming, Placide had gone less frequently than ever before up to Natchitoches. He worked and whistled and sang until the yearning for the girl's presence became a driving need; then he would put away his tools and mount his horse as the day was closing, and away he would go across bayous and hills and fields until he was with her again. She had never seemed to Placide so lovable as she was then. She had grown more womanly and thoughtful. Her cheek had lost much of its colour, and the light in her eyes flashed less often. But her manner had gained a something of pathetic tenderness towards her lover that moved him with an intoxicating happiness. He could hardly wait with patience for that day in early April which would see the fulfilment of his lifelong hopes.

After Euphrasie's departure from New Orleans, Offdean told himself honestly that he loved the girl. But being yet unsettled in life, he felt it was no time to think of marrying, and, like the worldly-wise young gentleman that he was, resolved to forget the little Natchitoches girl. He knew it would be an affair of some difficulty, but not an impossible thing, so he set about forgetting her.

The effort made him singularly irascible. At the office he was gloomy and taciturn; at the club he was a bear. A few young ladies whom he called upon were astonished and distressed at the cynical views of life which he had so suddenly adopted.

When he had endured a week or more of such humour, and inflicted it upon others, he abruptly changed his tactics. He decided not to fight against his love for Euphrasie. He would not marry her – certainly not; but he would let himself love her to his heart's bent, until that love should die a natural death, and not a violent one as he had designed. He abandoned himself completely to his passion, and dreamed of the girl by day and thought of her by night. How delicious had been the scent of her hair, the warmth of her breath, the nearness of her body, that rainy day when they stood close together upon the veranda! He recalled the glance of her honest, beautiful eyes, that told him things which made his heart beat fast now when he thought of them. And then her voice! Was there another like it when she laughed or when she talked! Was there another woman in the world possessed of so alluring a charm as this one he loved!

He was not bearish now, with these sweet thoughts crowding his brain and thrilling his blood; but he sighed deeply, and worked languidly, and enjoyed himself listlessly.

One day he sat in his room puffing the air thick with sighs and smoke, when a thought came suddenly to him – an inspiration, a very message from heaven, to judge from the cry of joy with which he greeted it. He sent his cigar whirling through the window, over the stone paving of the street, and he let his head fall down upon his arms, folded upon the table.

It had happened to him, as it does to many, that the solution of a vexed question flashed upon him when he was hoping least for it. He positively laughed aloud, and somewhat hysterically. In the space of a moment he saw the whole delicious future which a kind fate had mapped out for him: those rich acres upon the Red River his own, bought and embellished with his inheritance; and Euphrasie, whom he loved, his wife and companion throughout a life such as he knew now he had craved for – a life that, imposing bodily activity, admits the intellectual repose in which thought unfolds.

Wallace Offdean was like one to whom a divinity had revealed his vocation in life – no less a divinity because it was love. If doubts assailed him of Euphrasie's consent, they were soon stilled. For had they not spoken over and over to each other the mute and subtle language of reciprocal love – out under the forest trees, and in the quiet night-time on the plantation when the stars shone? And never so plainly as in the stately old drawing-room down on Esplanade Street. Surely no other speech was needed then, save such as their eyes told. Oh, he knew that she loved him; he was sure of it! The knowledge made him all the more eager now to hasten to her, to tell her that he wanted her for his very own.

8

If Offdean had stopped in Natchitoches on his way to the plantation, he would have heard something there to astonish him, to say the very least; for the whole town was talking of Euphrasie's wedding, which was to take place in a few days. But he did not linger. After securing a horse at the stable, he pushed on with all the speed of which the animal was capable, and only in such company as his eager thoughts afforded him.

The plantation was very quiet, with that stillness which broods over broad, clean acres that furnish no refuge for so much as a bird that sings. The negroes were scattered about the fields at work, with hoe and plough, under the sun, and old Pierre, on his horse, was far off in the midst of them.

Placide had arrived in the morning, after travelling all night, and had gone to his room for an hour or two of rest. He had drawn the lounge close up to the window to get what air he might through the closed shutters. He was just beginning to doze when he heard Euphrasie's light footsteps approaching. She stopped and seated herself so near that he could have touched her if he had but reached out his hand. Her nearness banished all desire to sleep, and he lay there content to rest his limbs and think of her.

The portion of the gallery on which Euphrasie sat was facing the river, and away from the road by which Offdean had reached the house. After fastening his horse, he mounted the steps, and traversed the broad hall that intersected the house from end to end, and that was open wide. He found Euphrasie engaged upon a piece of sewing. She was hardly aware of his presence before he had seated himself beside her.

She could not speak. She only looked at him with frightened eyes, as if his presence were that of some disembodied spirit.

'Are you not glad that I have come?' he asked her. 'Have I made a mistake in coming?' He was gazing into her eyes, seeking to read the meaning of their new, and strange expression.

'Am I glad?' she faltered. 'I don' know. W'at has that to do? You've come to see the work, of co'se. It's – it's only half done, Mr Offdean. They wouldn' listen to me or to papa, an' you didn' seem to care.'

'I haven't come to see the work,' he said, with a smile of love and confidence. 'I am here only to see you – to say how much I want you, and need you – to tell you how I love you.'

She rose, half choking with words she could not utter. But he seized her hands and held her there.

'The plantation is mine, Euphrasie – or it will be when you say that you will be my wife,' he went on excitedly. 'I know that you love me – '

'I do not!' she exclaimed wildly. 'W'at do you mean? How do you dare,' she gasped, 'to say such things w'en you know that in two days I shall be married to Placide?' The last was said in a whisper; it was like a wail.

'Married to Placide!' he echoed, as if striving to understand – to grasp some part of his own stupendous folly and blindness. 'I knew nothing of it,' he said hoarsely. 'Married to Placide! I would never have spoken to you as I did, if I had known. You believe me, I hope? Please say that you forgive me.'

He spoke with long silences between his utterances.

'Oh, there isn' anything to fo'give. You've only made a mistake. Please leave me, Mr Offdean. Papa is out in the fiel', I think, if you would like to speak with him. Placide is somew'ere on the place.'

'I shall mount my horse and go see what work has been done,' said Offdean, rising. An unusual pallor had overspread his face, and his mouth was drawn with suppressed pain. 'I must turn my fool's errand to some practical good,' he added, with a sad attempt at playfulness; and with no further word he walked quickly away.

She listened to his going. Then all the wretchedness of the past months, together with the sharp distress of the moment, voiced itself in a sob: 'O God – O my God, he'p me!'

But she could not stay out there in the broad day for any chance comer to look upon her uncovered sorrow.

Placide heard her rise and go to her room. When he had heard the key turn in the lock, he got up, and with quiet deliberation prepared to go out. He drew on his boots, then his coat. He took his pistol from the dressing-bureau, where he had placed it a while before, and after examining its chambers carefully, thrust it into his pocket. He had certain work to do with the weapon before night. But for Euphrasie's presence he might have accomplished it very surely a moment ago, when the hound – as he called him – stood outside his window. He did not wish her to know anything of his movements, and he left his room as quietly as possible, and mounted his horse, as Offdean had done.

'La Chatte,' called Placide to the old woman, who stood in her yard at the washtub, 'w'ich way did that man go?'

'W'at man dat? I isn' studyin' 'bout no mans; I got 'nough to do wid dis heah washin'. 'Fo' God, I don' know w'at man you's talkin' 'bout – '

'La Chatte, w'ich way did that man go? Quick, now!' with the deliberate tone and glance that had always quelled her.

'Ef you's talkin' 'bout dat Noo Orleans man, I could 'a' tole you dat. He done tuck de road to de cocoa-patch,' plunging her black arms into the tub with unnecessary energy and disturbance.

'That's enough. I know now he's gone into the woods. You always was a liar, La Chatte.'

'Dat his own lookout, de smoove-tongue' raskil,' soliloquised the woman a moment later. 'I done said he didn' have no call to come heah, caperin' roun' Miss 'Phrasie.'

Placide was possessed by only one thought, which was a want as well – to put an end to this man who had come between him and his love. It was the same brute passion that drives the beast to slay when he sees the object of his own desire laid hold of by another.

He had heard Euphrasie tell the man she did not love him, but what of that? Had he not heard her sobs, and guessed what her distress was? It needed no very flexible mind to guess as much, when a hundred signs besides, unheeded before, came surging to his memory. Jealousy held him, and rage and despair.

Offdean, as he rode along under the trees in apathetic despondency, heard someone approaching him on horseback, and turned aside to make room in the narrow pathway.

It was not a moment for punctilious scruples, and Placide had not been hindered by such from sending a bullet into the back of his rival. The only thing that stayed him was that Offdean must know why he had to die.

'Mr Offdean,' Placide said, reining his horse with one hand, while he held his pistol openly in the other, 'I was in my room 'w'ile ago, and yeared w'at you said to Euphrasie. I would 'a' killed you then if she hadn' been 'longside o' you. I could 'a' killed you jus' now w'en I come up behine you.'

'Well, why didn't you?' asked Offdean, meanwhile gathering his faculties to think how he had best deal with this madman.

'Because I wanted you to know who done it, an' w'at he done it for.'

'Mr Santien, I suppose to a person in your frame of mind it will make no difference to know that I'm unarmed. But if you make any attempt upon my life, I shall certainly defend myself as best I can.'

'Defen' yo'se'f, then.'

'You must be mad,' said Offdean, quickly, and looking straight into Placide's eyes, 'to want to soil your happiness with murder. I thought a Creole knew better than that how to love a woman.'

'By —! are you goin' to learn me how to love a woman?'

'No, Placide,' said Offdean eagerly, as they rode slowly along; 'your own honour is going to tell you that. The way to love a woman is to think first of her happiness. If you love Euphrasie, you must go to her clean. I love her myself enough to want you to do that. I shall leave this place tomorrow; you will never see me again if I can help it. Isn't that enough for you? I'm going to turn here and leave you. Shoot me in the back if you like; but I know you won't.' And Offdean held out his hand.

'I don' want to shake han's with you,' said Placide sulkily. 'Go 'way f'om me.' He stayed motionless watching Offdean ride away. He looked at the pistol in his hand, and replaced it slowly in his pocket; then he removed the broad felt hat which he wore, and wiped away the moisture that had gathered upon his forehead.

Offdean's words had touched some chord within him and made it vibrant; but they made him hate the man no less.

'The way to love a woman is to think firs' of her happiness,' he muttered reflectively. 'He thought a Creole knew how to love. Does he reckon he's goin' to learn a Creole how to love?'

His face was white and set with despair now. The rage had all left it as he rode deeper on into the wood.

9

Offdean rose early, wishing to take the morning train to the city. But he was not before Euphrasie, whom he found in the large hall arranging the breakfast-table. Old Pierre was there too, walking slowly about with hands folded behind him, and with bowed head.

A restraint hung upon all of them, and the girl turned to her father and asked him if Placide were up, seemingly for want of something to say. The old man fell heavily into a chair, and gazed upon her in the deepest distress.

'Oh, my po' li'le Euphrasie! my po' li'le chile! Mr Offde'n, you ain't no stranger.'

'*Bon Dieu!* Papa!' cried the girl sharply, seized with a vague terror. She quitted her occupation at the table, and stood in nervous apprehension of what might follow.

'I yaired people say Placide was one no-'count Creole. I nevair want to believe dat, me. Now I know dat's true. Mr Offde'n, you ain't no stranger, you.'

Offdean was gazing upon the old man in amazement.

'In de night,' Pierre continued, 'I yaired some noise on de winder. I go open, an' dere Placide, standin' wid his big boot' on, an' his w'ip w'at he knocked wid on de winder, an' his hoss all saddle'. Oh, my po' li'le chile! He say, "Pierre, I yaired say Mr Luke William' want his house pent down in Orville. I reckon I go git de job befo' somebody else teck it." I say, "You come straight back, Placide?" He say, "Don' look fer me." An' w'en I ax 'im w'at I goin' tell to my li'le chile, he say, "Tell Euphrasie Placide know better 'an anybody livin' w'at goin' make her happy." An' he start 'way; den he come back an' say, "Tell dat man" – I don' know who he was talk' 'bout – "tell 'im he ain't goin' learn nuttin' to a Creole." *Mon Dieu! Mon Dieu!* I don' know w'at all dat mean.'

He was holding the half-fainting Euphrasie in his arms, and stroking her hair.

'I always yaired say he was one no-'count Creole. I nevair want to believe dat.'

'Don't – don't say that again, papa,' she whisperingly entreated, speaking in French. 'Placide has saved me!'

'He has save' you f'om w'at, Euphrasie?' asked her father, in dazed astonishment.

'From sin,' she replied to him under her breath.

'I don' know w'at all dat mean,' the old man muttered, bewildered, as he arose and walked out on the gallery.

Offdean had taken coffee in his room, and would not wait for breakfast. When he went to bid Euphrasie goodbye, she sat beside the table with her head bowed upon her arm.

He took her hand and said goodbye to her, but she did not look up.

'Euphrasie,' he asked eagerly, 'I may come back? Say that I may – after a while.'

She gave him no answer, and he leaned down and pressed his cheek caressingly and entreatingly against her soft thick hair.

'May I, Euphrasie?' he begged. 'So long as you do not tell me no, I shall come back, dearest one.'

She still made him no reply, but she did not tell him no.

So he kissed her hand and her cheek – what he could touch of it, that peeped out from her folded arm – and went away.

An hour later, when Offdean passed through Natchitoches, the old town was already ringing with the startling news that Placide had been dismissed by his fiancée, and the wedding was off, information which the young Creole was taking the trouble to scatter broadcast as he went.

In and Out of Old Natchitoches

Precisely at eight o'clock every morning except Saturdays and Sundays, Mademoiselle Suzanne St Denys Godolph would cross the railroad trestle that spanned Bayou Boispourri. She might have crossed in the flat which Mr Alphonse Laballière[113] kept for his own convenience; but the method was slow and unreliable; so, every morning at eight, Mademoiselle St Denys Godolph crossed the trestle.

She taught public school in a picturesque little white frame structure that stood upon Mr Laballière's land, and hung upon the very brink of the bayou.

Laballière himself was comparatively a newcomer in the parish. It was barely six months since he decided one day to leave the sugar and rice to his brother Alcée, who had a talent for their cultivation, and to try his hand at cotton-planting. That was why he was up in Natchitoches parish on a piece of rich, high, Cane River land, knocking into shape a tumbled-down plantation that he had bought for next to nothing.

He had often during his perambulations observed the trim, graceful figure stepping cautiously over the ties, and had sometimes shivered for its safety. He always exchanged a greeting with the girl, and once threw a plank over a muddy pool for her to step upon. He caught but glimpses of her features, for she wore an enormous sun-bonnet to shield her complexion, that seemed marvellously fair; while loosely-fitting leather gloves protected her hands. He knew she was the schoolteacher, and also that she was the daughter of that very pig-headed old Madame St Denys Godolph who was hoarding her barren acres across the bayou as a miser hoards gold. Starving over them, some people said. But that was nonsense; nobody starves on a Louisiana plantation, unless it be with suicidal intent.

These things he knew, but he did not know why Mademoiselle St Denys Godolph always answered his salutation with an air of chilling hauteur that would easily have paralysed a less sanguine man.

The reason was that Suzanne, like everyone else, had heard the stories that were going the rounds about him. People said he was entirely too much at home with the free mulattoes.[114] It seems a dreadful thing to say, and it would be a shocking thing to think of a Laballière; but it wasn't true.

When Laballière took possession of his land, he found the plantation-house occupied by one Giestin and his swarming family. It was past reckoning how long the free mulatto and his people had been there. The house was a six-room, long, shambling affair, shrinking together from decrepitude. There was not an entire pane of glass in the structure, and the Turkey-red curtains flapped in and out of the broken apertures. But there is no need to dwell upon details; it was wholly unfit to serve as a civilised human habitation; and Alphonse Laballière would no sooner have disturbed its contented occupants than he would have scattered a family of partridges nesting in a corner of his field. He established himself with a few belongings in the best cabin he could find on the place, and, without further ado, proceeded to supervise the building of house, of gin, of this, that and the other, and to look into the hundred details that go to set a neglected plantation in good working order. He took his meals at the free mulatto's, quite apart from the family, of course; and they attended, not too skilfully, to his few domestic wants.

Some loafer whom he had snubbed remarked one day in town that Laballière had more use for a free mulatto than he had for a white man. It was a sort of catching thing to say, and suggestive, and was repeated with the inevitable embellishments.

One morning when Laballière sat eating his solitary breakfast, and being waited upon by the queenly Madame Giestin and a brace of her weazened boys, Giestin himself came into the room. He was about half the size of his wife, puny and timid. He stood beside the table, twirling his felt hat aimlessly and balancing himself insecurely on his high-pointed boot-heels.

'Mr Laballière,' he said, 'I reckon I tell you; it's betta you git shed o' me en' my fambly. Jis like you want, yas.'

'What in the name of common sense are you talking about?' asked Laballière, looking up abstractedly from his New Orleans paper. Giestin wriggled uncomfortably.

'It's heap o' story goin' roun' 'bout you, if you want b'lieve me.' And he snickered and looked at his wife, who thrust the end of her shawl into her mouth and walked from the room with a tread like the Empress Eugénie's,[115] in that elegant woman's palmiest days.

'Stories!' echoed Laballière, his face the picture of astonishment. 'Who – where – what stories?'

'Yon'a in town en' all about. It's heap o' tale goin' roun', yas. They say how come you mighty fon' o' mulatta. You done shoshiate wid de mulatta down yon'a on de suga plantation, tell you can't res' lessen it's mulatta roun' you.'

Laballière had a distressingly quick temper. His fist, which was a strong one, came down upon the wobbling table with a crash that sent half of Madame Giestin's crockery bouncing and crashing to the floor. He swore an oath that sent Madame Giestin and her father and grandmother, who were all listening in the next room, into suppressed convulsions of mirth.

'Oh, ho! so I'm not to associate with whom I please in Natchitoches parish. We'll see about that. Draw up your chair, Giestin. Call your wife and your grandmother and the rest of the tribe, and we'll breakfast together. By thunder! if I want to hobnob with mulattoes, or negroes or Choctaw Indians[116] or South Sea[117] savages, whose business is it but my own?'

'I don' know, me. It's jis like I tell you, Mr Laballière,' and Giestin selected a huge key from an assortment that hung against the wall, and left the room.

A half-hour later, Laballière had not yet recovered his senses. He appeared suddenly at the door of the schoolhouse, holding by the shoulder one of Giestin's boys. Mademoiselle St Denys Godolph stood at the opposite extremity of the room. Her sun-bonnet hung upon the wall, now, so Laballière could have seen how charming she was, had he not at the moment been blinded by stupidity. Her blue eyes that were fringed with dark lashes reflected astonishment at seeing him there. Her hair was dark like her lashes, and waved softly about her smooth, white forehead.

'Mademoiselle,' began Laballière at once, 'I have taken the liberty of bringing a new pupil to you.'

Mademoiselle St Denys Godolph paled suddenly and her voice was unsteady when she replied: 'You are too considerate, monsieur. Will you be so kine to give me the name of the scholar whom you desire to int'oduce into this school?' She knew it as well as he.

'What's your name, youngster? Out with it!' cried Laballière, striving to shake the little free mulatto into speech; but he stayed as dumb as a mummy.

'His name is André Giestin. You know him. He is the son – '

'Then, monsieur,' she interrupted, 'permit me to remine you that you have made a se'ious mistake. This is not a school conducted fo' the education of the coloured population. You will have to go elsew'ere with yo' protégé.'

'I shall leave my protégé right here, mademoiselle, and I trust you'll give him the same kind attention you seem to accord to the others;' saying which Laballière bowed himself out of her presence. The little

Giestin, left to his own devices, took only the time to give a quick, wary glance round the room, and the next instant he bounded through the open door, as the nimblest of four-footed creatures might have done.

Mademoiselle St Denys Godolph conducted school during the hours that remained with a deliberate calmness that would have seemed ominous to her pupils had they been better versed in the ways of young women. When the hour for dismissal came, she rapped upon the table to demand attention.

'Chil'ren,' she began, assuming a resigned and dignified mien, 'you all have been witness today of the insult that has been offered to yo' teacher by the person upon whose lan' this schoolhouse stan's. I have nothing further to say on that subjec'. I only shall add that tomorrow yo' teacher shall sen' the key of this schoolhouse, together with her resignation, to the gentlemen who compose the school-boa'd.' There followed visible disturbance among the young people.

'I ketch that li'le m'latta, I make 'im see sight', yas,' screamed one.

'Nothing of the kine, Mathurin, you mus' take no such step, if only out of consideration fo' my wishes. The person who has offered the affront I consider beneath my notice. André, on the other han', is a chile of good impulse, an' by no means to blame. As you all perceive, he has shown mo' taste and judgement than those above him, f'om whom we might have espected good breeding, at least.'

She kissed them all, the little boys and the little girls, and had a kind word for each. '*Et toi, mon petit Numa, j'espère q'un autre*' – [118] She could not finish the sentence, for little Numa, her favourite, to whom she had never been able to impart the first word of English, was blubbering at a turn of affairs which he had only miserably guessed at.

She locked the schoolhouse door and walked away towards the bridge. By the time she reached it, the little 'Cadians had already disappeared like rabbits, down the road and through and over the fences.

Mademoiselle St Denys Godolph did not cross the trestle the following day, nor the next, nor the next. Laballière watched for her; for his big heart was already sore and filled with shame. But more, it stung him with remorse to realise that he had been the stupid instrument in taking the bread, as it were, from the mouth of Mademoiselle St Denys Godolph.

He recalled how unflinchingly and haughtily her blue eyes had challenged his own. Her sweetness and charm came back to him and he dwelt upon them and exaggerated them, till no Venus, so far un-earthed, could in any way approach Mademoiselle St Denys Godolph. He would have liked to exterminate the Giestin family, from the great-grandmother down to the babe unborn.

Perhaps Giesten suspected this unfavourable attitude, for one morning he piled his whole family and all his effects into wagons, and went away; over into that part of the parish known as l'Isle des Mulâtres.[119]

Laballière's really chivalrous nature told him, besides, that he owed an apology, at least, to the young lady who had taken his whim so seriously. So he crossed the bayou one day and penetrated into the wilds where Madame St Denys Godolph ruled.

An alluring little romance formed in his mind as he went; he fancied how easily it might follow the apology. He was almost in love with Mademoiselle St Denys Godolph when he quitted his plantation. By the time he had reached hers, he was wholly so.

He was met by Madame *mère*, a sweet-eyed, faded woman, upon whom old age had fallen too hurriedly completely to efface all traces of youth. But the house was old beyond question; decay had eaten slowly to the heart of it during the hours, the days and years that it had been standing.

'I have come to see your daughter, madame,' began Laballière, all too bluntly; for there is no denying he was blunt.

'Mademoiselle St Denys Godolph is not presently at home, sir,' Madame replied. 'She is at this time in New Orleans. She fills there a place of high trus' an' employment, Monsieur Laballière.'

*

When Suzanne had ever thought of New Orleans, it was always in connection with Hector Santien, because he was the only soul she knew who dwelt there. He had had no share in obtaining for her the position she had secured with one of the leading dry-goods firms; yet it was to him she addressed herself when her arrangements to leave home were completed.

He did not wait for her train to reach the city, but crossed the river and met her at Gretna. The first thing he did was to kiss her, as he had done eight years before when he left Natchitoches parish. An hour later he would no more have thought of kissing Suzanne than he would have tendered an embrace to the Empress of China. For by that time he had realised that she was no longer twelve nor he twenty-four.

She could hardly believe the man who met her to be the Hector of old. His black hair was dashed with grey on the temples; he wore a short, parted beard and a small moustache that curled. From the crown of his glossy silk hat down to his trimly-gaitered feet, his attire was faultless. Suzanne knew her Natchitoches, and she had been to Shreveport and even penetrated as far as Marshall, Texas, but in all her travels she had never met a man to equal Hector in the elegance of his mien.

They entered a cab, and seemed to drive for an interminable time through the streets, mostly over cobblestones that rendered conversation difficult. Nevertheless he talked incessantly, while she peered from the windows to catch what glimpses she could, through the night, of that New Orleans of which she had heard so much. The sounds were bewildering; so were the lights, that were uneven, too, serving to make the patches of alternating gloom more mysterious.

She had not thought of asking him where he was taking her. And it was only after they crossed Canal and had penetrated some distance into Royal Street, that he told her. He was taking her to a friend of his, the dearest little woman in town. That was Maman Chavan, who was going to board and lodge her for a ridiculously small consideration.

Maman Chavan lived within comfortable walking distance of Canal Street, on one of those narrow, intersecting streets between Royal and Chartres. Her house was a tiny, single-storey one, with overhanging gable, heavily shuttered door and windows and three wooden steps leading down to the banquette. A small garden flanked it on one side, quite screened from outside view by a high fence, over which appeared the tops of orange trees and other luxuriant shrubbery.

She was waiting for them – a lovable, fresh-looking, white-haired, black-eyed, small, fat little body, dressed all in black. She understood no English; which made no difference. Suzanne and Hector spoke but French to each other.

Hector did not tarry a moment longer than was needed to place his young friend and charge in the older woman's care. He would not even stay to take a bite of supper with them. Maman Chavan watched him as he hurried down the steps and out into the gloom. Then she said to Suzanne: 'That man is an angel, mademoiselle, *un ange du bon Dieu*.'[120]

*

'Women, my dear Maman Chavan, you know how it is with me in regard to women. I have drawn a circle round my heart, so – at pretty long range, mind you – and there is not one who gets through it, or over it or under it.'

'*Blagueur, va!*' laughed Maman Chavan, replenishing her glass from the bottle of sauterne.[121]

It was Sunday morning. They were breakfasting together on the pleasant side gallery that led by a single step down to the garden. Hector came every Sunday morning, an hour or so before noon, to breakfast with them. He always brought a bottle of sauterne, a paté, or a mess of artichokes or some tempting bit of *charcuterie*.[122] Sometimes he had to wait till the two women returned from hearing mass at the cathedral. He did not go to mass himself. They were both making a novena on that account, and had even gone to the expense of burning a round dozen of candles before the good St Joseph, for his conversion. When Hector accidentally discovered the fact, he offered to pay for the candles, and was distressed at not being permitted to do so.

Suzanne had been in the city more than a month. It was already the close of February, and the air was flower-scented, moist and deliciously mild.

'As I said: women, my dear Maman Chavan – '

'Let us hear no more about women!' cried Suzanne, impatiently. '*Cher Maître!* but Hector can be tiresome when he wants. Talk, talk; to say what in the end?'

'Quite right, my cousin; when I might have been saying how charming you are this morning. But don't think that I haven't noticed it,' and he looked at her with a deliberation that quite unsettled her. She took a letter from her pocket and handed it to him.

'Here, read all the nice things mamma has to say of you, and the love messages she sends to you.' He accepted the several closely written sheets from her and began to look over them.

'Ah, *la bonne tante*,'[123] he laughed, when he came to the tender passages that referred to himself. He had pushed aside the glass of wine that he had only partly filled at the beginning of breakfast and that he had scarcely touched. Maman Chavan again replenished her own. She also lighted a cigarette. So did Suzanne, who was learning to smoke. Hector did not smoke; he did not use tobacco in any form, he always said to those who offered him cigars.

Suzanne rested her elbows on the table, adjusted the ruffles about her wrists, puffed awkwardly at her cigarette that kept going out, and hummed the Kyrie eleison[124] that she had heard so beautifully rendered an hour before at the cathedral while she gazed off into the green depths of the garden. Maman Chavan slipped a little silver medal towards her, accompanying the action with a pantomime that Suzanne readily understood. She, in turn, secretly and adroitly transferred the medal to Hector's coat-pocket. He noticed the action plainly enough, but pretended not to.

'Natchitoches hasn't changed,' he commented. 'The everlasting *cancans*!'[125] when will they have done with them? This isn't little Athénaïse Miché,[126] getting married! *Sapristi!* but it makes one old! And old Papa Jean-Pierre only dead now? I thought he was out of purgatory five years ago. And who is this Laballière? One of the Laballières of St James?'

'St James, *mon cher*. Monsieur Alphonse Laballière; an aristocrat from the "golden coast". But it is a history, if you will believe me. *Figurez vouz*, Maman Chavan – *pensez donc*,[127] *mon ami*' – And with much dramatic fire, during which the cigarette went irrevocably out, she proceeded to narrate her experiences with Laballière.

'Impossible!' exclaimed Hector when the climax was reached; but his indignation was not so patent as she would have liked it to be.

'And to think of an affront like that going unpunished!' was Maman Chavan's more sympathetic comment.

'Oh, the scholars were only too ready to offer violence to poor little André, but that, you can understand, I would not permit. And now, here is mamma gone completely over to him; entrapped, God only knows how!'

'Yes,' agreed Hector, 'I see he has been sending her tamales and *boudin blanc*.'[128]

'*Boudin blanc*, my friend! If it were only that! But I have a stack of letters, so high – I could show them to you – singing of Laballière, Laballière, enough to drive one distracted. He visits her constantly. He is a man of attainment, she says, a man of courage, a man of heart; and the best of company. He has sent her a bunch of fat robins as big as a tub – '

'There is something in that – a good deal in that, mignonne,' piped Maman Chavan, approvingly.

'And now *boudin blanc*! and she tells me it is the duty of a Christian to forgive. Ah, no; it's no use; mamma's ways are past finding out.'

Suzanne was never in Hector's company elsewhere than at Maman Chavan's. Beside the Sunday visit, he looked in upon them sometimes at dusk, to chat for a moment or two. He often treated them to theatre tickets, and even to the opera, when business was brisk. Business meant a little notebook that he carried in his pocket, in which he sometimes dotted down orders from the country people for wine that he sold on commission. The women always went together, unaccompanied by any male escort; trotting along, arm in arm, and brimming with enjoyment.

That same Sunday afternoon Hector walked with them a short distance when they were on their way to vespers. The three walking abreast almost occupied the narrow width of the banquette. A gentleman who had just stepped out of the Hotel Royal stood aside better to enable them to pass. He lifted his hat to Suzanne, and cast a quick glance, that pictured stupefaction and wrath, upon Hector.

'It's he!' exclaimed the girl, melodramatically seizing Maman Chavan's arm.

'Who, he?'

'Laballière!'

'No!'

'Yes!'

'A handsome fellow, all the same,' nodded the little lady, approvingly. Hector thought so too. The conversation again turned upon Laballière, and so continued till they reached the side door of the cathedral, where the young man left his two companions.

In the evening Laballière called upon Suzanne. Maman Chavan closed the front door carefully after he entered the small parlour, and opened the side one that looked into the privacy of the garden. Then she lighted the lamp and retired, just as Suzanne entered.

The girl bowed a little stiffly, if it may be said that she did anything stiffly. 'Monsieur Laballière.' That was all she said.

'Mademoiselle St Denys Godolph,' and that was all he said. But ceremony did not sit easily upon him.

'Mademoiselle,' he began, as soon as seated, 'I am here as the bearer of a message from your mother. You must understand that otherwise I would not be here.'

'I do understan', sir, that you an' maman have become very warm frien's during my absence,' she returned, in measured, conventional tones.

'It pleases me immensely to hear that from you,' he responded, warmly; 'to believe that Madame St Denys Godolph is my friend.'

Suzanne coughed more affectedly than was quite nice, and patted her glossy braids. 'The message, if you please, Mr Laballière.'

'To be sure,' pulling himself together from the momentary abstraction into which he had fallen in contemplating her. 'Well, it's just this; your mother, you must know, has been good enough to sell me a fine bit of land – a deep strip along the bayou – '

'Impossible! *Mais*, w'at sorcery did you use to obtain such a thing of my mother, Mr Laballière? Lan' that has been in the St Denys Godolph family since time untole!'

'No sorcery whatever, mademoiselle, only an appeal to your mother's intelligence and common sense; and she is well supplied with both. She wishes me to say, further, that she desires your presence very urgently and your immediate return home.'

'My mother is unduly impatient, surely,' replied Suzanne, with chilling politeness.

'May I ask, mademoiselle,' he broke in, with an abruptness that was startling, 'the name of the man with whom you were walking this afternoon?'

She looked at him with unaffected astonishment, and told him: 'I hardly understan' yo' question. That gentleman is Mr Hector Santien, of one of the firs' families of Natchitoches; a warm ole frien' an' far distant relative of mine.'

'Oh, that's his name, is it, Hector Santien? Well, please don't walk on the New Orleans streets again with Mr Hector Santien.'

'Yo' remarks would be insulting if they were not so highly amusing, Mr Laballière.'

'I beg your pardon if I am insulting; and I have no desire to be amusing,' and then Laballière lost his head. 'You are at liberty to walk the streets with whom you please, of course,' he blurted, with ill-suppressed passion, 'but if I encounter Mr Hector Santien in your company again, in public, I shall wring his neck, then and there, as I would a chicken; I shall break every bone in his body' – Suzanne had arisen.

'You have said enough, sir. I even desire no explanation of yo' words.'

'I didn't intend to explain them,' he retorted, stung by the insinuation.

'You will escuse me further,' she requested icily, motioning to retire.

'Not till – oh, not till you have forgiven me,' he cried impulsively, barring her exit; for repentance had come swiftly this time.

But she did not forgive him. 'I can wait,' she said. Then he stepped aside and she passed by him without a second glance.

She sent word to Hector the following day to come to her. And when he was there, in the late afternoon, they walked together to the end of the vine-sheltered gallery – where the air was redolent with the odour of spring blossoms.

'Hector,' she began, after a while, 'someone has told me I should not be seen upon the streets of New Orleans with you.'

He was trimming a long rose-stem with his sharp penknife. He did not stop, nor start, nor look embarrassed, nor anything of the sort.

'Indeed!' he said.

'But, you know,' she went on, 'if the saints came down from heaven to tell me there was a reason for it, I couldn't believe them.'

'You wouldn't believe them, *ma petite Suzanne*?' He was getting all the thorns off nicely, and stripping away the heavy lower leaves.

'I want you to look me in the face, Hector, and tell me if there is any reason.'

He snapped the knife-blade and replaced the knife in his pocket; then he looked in her eyes, so unflinchingly that she hoped and believed it presaged a confession of innocence that she would gladly have accepted. But he said indifferently: 'Yes, there are reasons.'

'Then I say there are not,' she exclaimed excitedly; 'you are amusing yourself – laughing at me, as you always do. There are no reasons that I will hear or believe. You will walk the streets with me, will you not, Hector?' she entreated, 'and go to church with me on Sunday; and, and – oh, it's nonsense, nonsense for you to say things like that!'

He held the rose by its long, hardy stem, and swept it lightly and caressingly across her forehead, along her cheek, and over her pretty mouth and chin, as a lover might have done with his lips. He noticed how the red rose left a crimson stain behind it.

She had been standing, but now she sank upon the bench that was there, and buried her face in her palms. A slight convulsive movement of the muscles indicated a suppressed sob.

'Ah, Suzanne, Suzanne, you are not going to make yourself unhappy about a *bon à rien* like me. Come, look at me; tell me that you are not.' He drew her hands down from her face; and held them a while, bidding her goodbye. His own face wore the quizzical look it often did, as if he were laughing at her.

'That work at the store is telling on your nerves, *mignonne*. Promise me that you will go back to the country. That will be best.'

'Oh, yes; I am going back home, Hector.'

'That is right, little cousin,' and he patted her hands kindly, and laid them both down gently into her lap.

He did not return; neither during the week nor the following Sunday. Then Suzanne told Maman Chavan she was going home. The girl was not too deeply in love with Hector: but imagination counts for something, and so does youth.

*

Laballière was on the train with her. She felt, somehow, that he would be. And yet she did not dream that he had watched and waited for her each morning since he parted from her.

He went to her without preliminary of manner or speech, and held out his hand; she extended her own unhesitatingly. She could not understand why, and she was a little too weary to strive to do so. It seemed as though the sheer force of his will would carry him to the goal of his wishes.

He did not weary her with attentions during the time they were together. He sat apart from her, conversing for the most time with friends and acquaintances who belonged in the sugar district through which they travelled in the early part of the day.

She wondered why he had ever left that section to go up into

Natchitoches. Then she wondered if he did not mean to speak to her at all. As if he had read the thought, he went and sat down beside her.

He showed her, away off across the country, where his mother lived, and his brother Alcée, and his cousin Clarisse.

*

On Sunday morning, when Maman Chavan strove to sound the depth of Hector's feeling for Suzanne, he told her again: 'Women, my dear Maman Chavan, you know how it is with me in regard to women,' and he refilled her glass from the bottle of sauterne.

'*Farceur va!*' and Maman Chavan laughed, and her fat shoulders quivered under the white *volante*[129] she wore.

A day or two later, Hector was walking down Canal Street at four in the afternoon. He might have posed, as he was, for a fashion-plate. He looked not to the right nor to the left; not even at the women who passed by. Some of them turned to look at him.

When he approached the corner of Royal, a young man who stood there nudged his companion.

'You know who that is?' he said, indicating Hector.

'No; who?'

'Well, you are an innocent. Why, that's Deroustan, the most notorious gambler in New Orleans.'

In Sabine

The sight of a human habitation, even if it was a rude log cabin with a mud chimney at one end, was a very gratifying one to Grégoire.

He had come out of Natchitoches parish, and had been riding a great part of the day through the big lonesome parish of Sabine. He was not following the regular Texas road, but, led by his erratic fancy, was pushing towards the Sabine River by circuitous paths through the rolling pine forests.

As he approached the cabin in the clearing, he discerned behind a palisade of pine saplings an old negro man chopping wood.

'Howdy, uncle,' called out the young fellow, reining his horse. The negro looked up in blank amazement at so unexpected an apparition, but he only answered: 'How you do, suh,' accompanying his speech by a series of polite nods.

'Who lives yere?'

'Hit's Mas' Bud Aiken w'at live' heah, suh.'

'Well, if Mr Bud Aiken c'n afford to hire a man to chop his wood, I reckon he won't grudge me a bite o' suppa an' a couple hours' res' on his gall'ry. W'at you say, ole man?'

'I say dit Mas' Bud Aiken don't hires me to chop 'ood. Ef I don't chop dis heah, his wife got it to do. Dat w'y I chops 'ood, suh. Go right 'long in, suh; you g'ine fine Mas' Bud some'eres roun', ef he ain't drunk an' gone to bed.'

Grégoire, glad to stretch his legs, dismounted, and led his horse into the small enclosure which surrounded the cabin. An unkempt, vicious-looking little Texas pony stopped nibbling the stubble there to look maliciously at him and his fine sleek horse, as they passed by. Back of the hut, and running plumb up against the pine wood, was a small, ragged specimen of a cotton-field.

Grégoire was rather undersized, with a square, well-knit figure, upon which his clothes sat well and easily. His corduroy trousers were thrust into the legs of his boots; he wore a blue flannel shirt; his coat was thrown across the saddle. In his keen black eyes had come a puzzled expression, and he tugged thoughtfully at the brown moustache that lightly shaded his upper lip.

He was trying to recall when and under what circumstances he had before heard the name of Bud Aiken. But Bud Aiken himself saved Grégoire the trouble of further speculation on the subject. He appeared suddenly in the small doorway, which his big body quite filled; and then Grégoire remembered. This was the disreputable so-called 'Texan' who a year ago had run away with and married Baptiste Choupic's pretty daughter, 'Tite Reine, yonder on Bayou Pierre, in Natchitoches parish. A vivid picture of the girl as he remembered her appeared to him: her trim rounded figure; her piquant face with its saucy black coquettish eyes; her little exacting, imperious ways that had obtained for her the nickname of 'Tite Reine, little queen. Grégoire had known her at the 'Cadian balls that he sometimes had the hardihood to attend.

These pleasing recollections of 'Tite Reine lent a warmth that might otherwise have been lacking to Grégoire's manner, when he greeted her husband.

'I hope I fine you well, Mr Aiken,' he exclaimed cordially, as he approached and extended his hand.

'You find me damn' porely, suh; but you've got the better o' me, ef I may so say.'

He was a big good-looking brute, with a straw-coloured 'horseshoe' moustache quite concealing his mouth, and a several days' growth of stubble on his rugged face. He was fond of reiterating that women's admiration had wrecked his life, quite forgetting to mention the early and sustained influence of 'Pike's Magnolia'[130] and other brands, and wholly ignoring certain inborn propensities capable of wrecking unaided any ordinary existence. He had been lying down, and looked frouzy and half asleep.

'Ef I may so say, you've got the better o' me, Mr – er – '

'Santien, Grégoire Santien. I have the pleasure o' knowin' the lady you married, suh; an' I think I met you befo' – somew'ere o' 'nother,' Grégoire added vaguely.

'Oh,' drawled Aiken, waking up, 'one o' them Red River Sanchuns!' and his face brightened at the prospect before him of enjoying the society of one of the Santien boys. 'Mortimer!' he called in ringing chest tones worthy a commander at the head of his troop. The negro had rested his axe and appeared to be listening to their talk, though he was too far to hear what they said.

'Mortimer, come along here an' take my frien' Mr Sanchun's hoss. Git a move thar, git a move!' Then turning towards the entrance of the cabin he called back through the open door: 'Rain!' it was his way of pronouncing 'Tite Reine's name. 'Rain!' he cried again peremptorily; and turning to Grégoire: 'she's 'tendin' to some or other housekeepin' truck.' 'Tite Reine was back in the yard feeding the solitary pig which they owned, and which Aiken had mysteriously driven up a few days before, saying he had bought it at Many.

Grégoire could hear her calling out as she approached: 'I'm comin', Bud. Yere I come. W'at you want, Bud?' breathlessly, as she appeared in the door frame and looked out upon the narrow sloping gallery where stood the two men. She seemed to Grégoire to have changed a good deal. She was thinner, and her eyes were larger, with an alert, uneasy look in them; he fancied the startled expression came from seeing him there unexpectedly. She wore cleanly homespun garments, the same she had brought with her from Bayou Pierre; but her shoes were in shreds. She uttered only a low, smothered exclamation when she saw Grégoire.

'Well, is that all you got to say to my frien' Mr Sanchun? That's the way with them Cajuns,' Aiken offered apologetically to his guest; 'ain't got sense enough to know a white man when they see one.' Grégoire took her hand.

'I'm mighty glad to see you, 'Tite Reine,' he said from his heart. She had for some reason been unable to speak; now she panted somewhat hysterically: 'You mus' escuse me, Mista Grégoire. It's the truth I didn' know you firs', stan'in' up there.' A deep flush had supplanted the former pallor of her face, and her eyes shone with tears and ill-concealed excitement.

'I thought you all lived yonda in Grant,' remarked Grégoire carelessly, making talk for the purpose of diverting Aiken's attention away from his wife's evident embarrassment, which he himself was at a loss to understand.

'Why, we did live a right smart while in Grant; but Grant ain't no parish to make a livin' in. Then I tried Winn and Caddo a spell; they wasn't no better. But I tell you, suh, Sabine's a damn' sight worse than any of 'em. Why, a man can't git a drink o' whiskey here without going out of the parish fer it, or across into Texas. I'm fixin' to sell out an' try Vernon.'

Bud Aiken's household belongings surely would not count for much in the contemplated 'selling out'. The one room that constituted his home was extremely bare of furnishing – a cheap bed, a pine table, and a few chairs, that was all. On a rough shelf were some paper parcels representing the larder. The mud daubing had fallen out here and there from between the logs of the cabin; and into the largest of these apertures had been thrust pieces of ragged bagging and wisps of cotton. A tin basin outside on the gallery offered the only bathing facilities to be seen. Notwithstanding these drawbacks, Grégoire announced his intention of passing the night with Aiken.

'I'm jus' goin' to ask the privilege o' layin' down yere on yo' gall'ry tonight, Mr Aiken. My hoss ain't in firs'-class trim; an' a night's res' ain't goin' to hurt him o' me either.' He had begun by declaring his intention of pushing on across the Sabine, but an imploring look from 'Tite Reine's eyes had stayed the words upon his lips. Never had he seen in a woman's eyes a look of such heartbroken entreaty. He resolved on the instant to know the meaning of it before setting foot on Texas soil. Grégoire had never learned to steel his heart against a woman's eyes, no matter what language they spoke.

An old patchwork quilt folded double and a moss pillow which 'Tite Reine gave him out on the gallery made a bed that was, after all, not too uncomfortable for a young fellow of rugged habits.

Grégoire slept quite soundly after he lay down upon his improvised bed at nine o'clock. He was awakened towards the middle of the night by someone gently shaking him. It was 'Tite Reine stooping over him; he could see her plainly, for the moon was shining. She had not removed the clothing she had worn during the day; but her feet were bare and looked wonderfully small and white. He arose on his elbow, wide awake at once. 'W'y, 'Tite Reine! w'at the devil you mean? w'ere's yo' husban'?'

'The house kin fall on 'im, 't en goin' wake up Bud w'en he's sleepin'; he drink' too much.' Now that she had aroused Grégoire, she stood up, and sinking her face in her bended arm like a child, began to cry softly. In an instant he was on his feet.

'My God, 'Tite Reine! w'at's the matta? you got to tell me w'at's the matta.' He could no longer recognise the imperious 'Tite Reine, whose will had been the law in her father's household. He led her to the edge of the low gallery and there they sat down.

Grégoire loved women. He liked their nearness, their atmosphere; the tones of their voices and the things they said; their ways of moving and turning about; the brushing of their garments when they passed him by pleased him. He was fleeing now from the pain that a woman had inflicted upon him. When any overpowering sorrow came to Grégoire he felt a singular longing to cross the Sabine River and lose himself in Texas. He had done this once before when his home, the old Santien place, had gone into the hands of creditors. The sight of 'Tite Reine's distress now moved him painfully.

'W'at is it, 'Tite Reine? tell me w'at it is,' he kept asking her. She was attempting to dry her eyes on her coarse sleeve. He drew a handkerchief from his back pocket and dried them for her.

'They all well, yonda?' she asked, haltingly, 'my popa? my moma? the chil'en?' Grégoire knew no more of the Baptiste Choupic family than the post beside him. Nevertheless he answered: 'They all right well, 'Tite Reine, but they mighty lonesome of you.'

'My popa, he got a putty good crop this yea'?'

'He made right smart o' cotton fo' Bayou Pierre.'

'He done haul it to the relroad?'

'No, he ain't quite finish pickin'.'

'I hope they all ent sole Putty Girl?' she enquired solicitously.

'Well, I should say not! Yo' pa says they ain't anotha piece o' hossflesh in the pa'ish he'd want to swap fo' Putty Girl.' She turned to him with vague but fleeting amazement – Putty Girl was a cow!

The autumn night was heavy about them. The black forest seemed to have drawn nearer; its shadowy depths were filled with the gruesome noises that inhabit a southern forest at night time.

'Ain't you 'fraid sometimes yere, 'Tite Reine?' Grégoire asked, as he felt a light shiver run through him at the weirdness of the scene.

'No,' she answered promptly, 'I ent 'fred o' nothin' 'cep' Bud.'

'Then he treats you mean? I thought so!'

'Mista Grégoire,' drawing close to him and whispering in his face, 'Bud's killin' me.' He clasped her arm, holding her near him, while an expression of profound pity escaped him. 'Nobody don' know, 'cep' Unc' Mort'mer,' she went on. 'I tell you, he beats me; my back an' arms – you ought to see – it's all blue. He would 'a' choke' me to death one day w'en he was drunk, if Unc' Mort'mer hadn' make 'im lef go – with his axe ov' his head.' Grégoire glanced back over his shoulder towards the room where the man lay sleeping. He was wondering if it would really be a criminal act to go then and there and shoot the top of Bud Aiken's head off. He himself would hardly have considered it a crime, but he was not sure of how others might regard the act.

'That's w'y I wake you up, to tell you,' she continued. 'Then some-time' he plague me mos' crazy; he tell me 't ent no preacher, it's a Texas drummer w'at marry him an' me; an' w'en I don' know w'at way to turn no mo', he say no, it's a Meth'dis' archbishop, an' keep on laughin' 'bout me, an' I don' know w'at the truth!'

Then again, she told how Bud had induced her to mount the vicious little mustang Buckeye, knowing that the little brute wouldn't carry a woman; and how it had amused him to witness her distress and terror when she was thrown to the ground.

'If I would know how to read an' write, an' had some pencil an' paper, it's long 'go I would wrote to my popa. But it's no pos'-office, it's no relroad – nothin' in Sabine. An' you know, Mista Grégoire, Bud say he's goin' carry me yonda to Vernon, an' fu'ther off yet – 'way yonda, an' he's goin' turn me loose. Oh, don' leave me yere, Mista Grégoire! don' leave me behine you!' she entreated, breaking once more into sobs.

' 'Tite Reine,' he answered, 'do you think I'm such a low-down scound'el as to leave you yere with that —' He finished the sentence mentally, not wishing to offend the ears of 'Tite Reine.

They talked on a good while after that. She would not return to the room where her husband lay; the nearness of a friend had already emboldened her to inward revolt. Grégoire induced her to lie down and rest upon the quilt that she had given to him for a bed. She did so, and broken down by fatigue was soon fast asleep.

He stayed seated on the edge of the gallery and began to smoke cigarettes which he rolled himself of perique tobacco. He might have gone in and shared Bud Aiken's bed, but preferred to stay there near 'Tite Reine. He watched the two horses, tramping slowly about the lot, cropping the dewy wet tufts of grass.

Grégoire smoked on. He only stopped when the moon sank down behind the pine trees, and the long deep shadow reached out and enveloped him. Then he could no longer see and follow the filmy smoke from his cigarette, and he threw it away. Sleep was pressing heavily upon him. He stretched himself full length upon the rough bare boards of the gallery and slept until daybreak.

Bud Aiken's satisfaction was very genuine when he learned that Grégoire proposed spending the day and another night with him. He had already recognised in the young Creole a spirit not altogether uncongenial to his own.

'Tite Reine cooked breakfast for them. She made coffee; of course there was no milk to add to it, but there was sugar. From a meal bag that stood in the corner of the room she took a measure of meal, and with it made a pone of corn bread.[131] She fried slices of salt pork. Then Bud sent her into the field to pick cotton with old Uncle Mortimer. The negro's cabin was the counterpart of their own, but stood quite a distance away hidden in the woods. He and Aiken worked the crop on shares.

Early in the day Bud produced a grimy pack of cards from behind a parcel of sugar on the shelf. Grégoire threw the cards into the fire and replaced them with a spic and span new deck that he took from his saddle-bags. He also brought forth from the same receptacle a bottle of whiskey, which he presented to his host, saying that he himself had no further use for it, as he had 'sworn off' since day before yesterday, when he had made a fool of himself in Cloutierville.[132]

They sat at the pine table smoking and playing cards all the morning, only desisting when 'Tite Reine came to serve them with the gumbo-*filé*[133] that she had come out of the field to cook at noon. She could afford to treat a guest to chicken gumbo, for she owned a half-dozen chickens that Uncle Mortimer had presented to her at various times. There were only two spoons, and 'Tite Reine had to wait till the men had finished before eating her soup. She waited for Grégoire's spoon, though her husband was the first to get through. It was a very childish whim.

In the afternoon she picked cotton again; and the men played cards, smoked, and Bud drank.

It was a very long time since Bud Aiken had enjoyed himself so well, and since he had encountered so sympathetic and appreciative a listener to the story of his eventful career. The story of 'Tite Reine's fall from the horse he told with much spirit, mimicking quite skilfully the way in which she had complained of never being permitted 'to teck a li'le pleasure', whereupon he had kindly suggested horseback riding. Grégoire enjoyed the story amazingly, which encouraged Aiken to relate many more of a similar character. As the afternoon wore on, all formality of address between the two had disappeared: they were 'Bud' and 'Grégoire' to each other, and Grégoire had delighted Aiken's soul by promising to spend a week with him. 'Tite Reine was also touched by the spirit of recklessness in the air; it moved her to fry two chickens for supper. She fried them deliciously in bacon fat. After supper she again arranged Grégoire's bed out on the gallery.

The night fell calm and beautiful, with the delicious odour of the pines floating upon the air. But the three did not sit up to enjoy it. Before the stroke of nine, Aiken had already fallen upon his bed unconscious of everything about him in the heavy drunken sleep that would hold him fast through the night. It even clutched him more relentlessly than usual, thanks to Grégoire's free gift of whiskey.

The sun was high when he awoke. He lifted his voice and called imperiously for 'Tite Reine, wondering that the coffee-pot was not on the hearth, and marvelling still more that he did not hear her voice in quick response with its, 'I'm comin', Bud. Yere I come.' He called again and again. Then he arose and looked out through the back door to see if she were picking cotton in the field, but she was not there. He dragged himself to the front entrance. Grégoire's bed was still on the gallery, but the young fellow was nowhere to be seen.

Uncle Mortimer had come into the yard, not to cut wood this time, but to pick up the axe which was his own property, and lift it to his shoulder.

'Mortimer,' called out Aiken, 'whur's my wife?' at the same time advancing towards the negro. Mortimer stood still, waiting for him. 'Whur's my wife an' that Frenchman? Speak out, I say, before I send you to h—l.'

Uncle Mortimer never had feared Bud Aiken; and with the trusty axe upon his shoulder, he felt a double hardihood in the man's presence. The old fellow passed the back of his black, knotty hand unctuously over his lips, as though he relished in advance the words that were about to pass them.

He spoke carefully and deliberately: 'Miss Reine,' he said, 'I reckon she mus' of done struck Natchitoches pa'ish sometime to'ard de middle o' de night, on dat 'ar swif' hoss o' Mr Sanchun's.'

Aiken uttered a terrific oath. 'Saddle up Buckeye,' he yelled, 'before I count twenty, or I'll rip the black hide off yer. Quick, thar! Thur ain't nothin' four-footed top o' this earth that Buckeye can't run down.' Uncle Mortimer scratched his head dubiously, as he answered: 'Yas, Mas' Bud, but you see, Mr Sanchun, he done cross de Sabine befo' sun-up on Buckeye.'

A Very Fine Fiddle

When the half-dozen little ones were hungry, old Cléophas would take the fiddle from its flannel bag and play a tune upon it. Perhaps it was to drown their cries, or their hunger, or his conscience, or all three. One day Fifine, in a rage, stamped her small foot and clinched her little hands, and declared: 'It's no two way'! I'm goin' smash it, dat fiddle, some day in a t'ousan' piece'!'

'You mus'n' do dat, Fifine,' expostulated her father. 'Dat fiddle been ol'er 'an you an' me t'ree time' put togedder. You done yaird me tell often 'nough 'bout dat Italien[134] w'at give it to me w'en he die, 'long yonder befo' de war. An' he say, "Cléophas, dat fiddle – dat one part my life – w'at goin' live w'en I be dead – *Dieu merci*!"[135] You talkin' too fas', Fifine.'

'Well, I'm goin' do some'in' wid dat fiddle, *va*!' returned the daughter, only half mollified. 'Mine w'at I say.'

So once when there were great carryings-on up at the big plantation – no end of ladies and gentlemen from the city, riding, driving, dancing and making music upon all manner of instruments – Fifine, with the fiddle in its flannel bag, stole away and up to the big house where these festivities were in progress.

No one noticed at first the little barefoot girl seated upon a step of the veranda and watching, lynx-eyed, for her opportunity.

'It's one fiddle I got for sell,' she announced, resolutely, to the first who questioned her.

It was very funny to have a shabby little girl sitting there wanting to sell a fiddle, and the child was soon surrounded.

The lustreless instrument was brought forth and examined, first with amusement, but soon very seriously, especially by three gentlemen: one with very long hair that hung down, another with equally long hair that stood up, the third with no hair worth mentioning.

These three turned the fiddle upside down and almost inside out. They thumped upon it, and listened. They scraped upon it, and listened. They walked into the house with it, and out of the house with it, and into remote corners with it. All this with much putting of heads together, and talking together in familiar and unfamiliar languages. And, finally, they sent Fifine away with a fiddle twice as beautiful as the one she had brought, and a roll of money besides!

The child was dumb with astonishment, and away she flew. But when she stopped beneath a big chinaberry tree, further to scan the roll of money, her wonder was redoubled. There was far more than she could count, more than she had ever dreamed of possessing. Certainly enough to top the old cabin with new shingles; to put shoes on all the little bare feet and food into the hungry mouths. Maybe enough – and Fifine's heart fairly jumped into her throat at the vision – maybe enough to buy Blanchette and her tiny calf that Unc' Siméon wanted to sell!

'It's jis like you say, Fifine,' murmured old Cléophas, huskily, when he had played upon the new fiddle that night. 'It's one fine fiddle; an' like you say, it shine' like satin. But some way or udder, 't ain' de same. Yair, Fifine, take it – put it 'side. I b'lieve, me, I ain' goin' play de fiddle no mo'.'

Beyond the Bayou

The bayou curved like a crescent around the point of land on which La Folle's[136] cabin stood. Between the stream and the hut lay a big abandoned field, where cattle were pastured when the bayou supplied them with water enough. Through the woods that spread back into unknown regions the woman had drawn an imaginary line, and past this circle she never stepped. This was the form of her only mania.

She was now a large, gaunt black woman, past thirty-five. Her real name was Jacqueline, but everyone on the plantation called her La Folle, because in childhood she had been frightened literally 'out of her senses', and had never wholly regained them.

It was when there had been skirmishing and sharpshooting all day in the woods. Evening was near when P'tit Maître, black with powder and crimson with blood, had staggered into the cabin of Jacqueline's mother, his pursuers close at his heels. The sight had stunned her childish reason.

She dwelt alone in her solitary cabin, for the rest of the quarters had long since been removed beyond her sight and knowledge. She had more physical strength than most men, and made her patch of cotton and corn and tobacco like the best of them. But of the world beyond the bayou she had long known nothing, save what her morbid fancy conceived.

People at Bellissime[137] had grown used to her and her way, and they thought nothing of it. Even when 'Old Mis' ' died, they did not wonder that La Folle had not crossed the bayou, but had stood upon her side of it, wailing and lamenting.

P'tit Maître was now the owner of Bellissime. He was a middle-aged man, with a family of beautiful daughters about him, and a little son whom La Folle loved as if he had been her own. She called him Chéri, and so did everyone else because she did.

None of the girls had ever been to her what Chéri was. They had each and all loved to be with her, and to listen to her wondrous stories of things that always happened 'yonda, beyon' de bayou'.

But none of them had stroked her black hand quite as Chéri did, nor rested their heads against her knee so confidingly, nor fallen asleep in her arms as he used to do. For Chéri hardly did such things now, since he had become the proud possessor of a gun, and had had his black curls cut off.

That summer – the summer Chéri gave La Folle two black curls tied with a knot of red ribbon – the water ran so low in the bayou that even the little children at Bellissime were able to cross it on foot, and the cattle were sent to pasture down by the river. La Folle was sorry when they were gone, for she loved these dumb companions well, and liked to feel that they were there, and to hear them browsing by night up to her own enclosure.

It was Saturday afternoon, when the fields were deserted. The men had flocked to a neighbouring village to do their week's trading, and the women were occupied with household affairs – La Folle as well as the others. It was then she mended and washed her handful of clothes, scoured her house and did her baking.

In this last employment she never forgot Chéri. Today she had fashioned croquignoles of the most fantastic and alluring shapes for him. So when she saw the boy come trudging across the old field with his gleaming little new rifle on his shoulder, she called out gayly to him, 'Chéri! Chéri!'

But Chéri did not need the summons, for he was coming straight to her. His pockets all bulged out with almonds and raisins and an orange that he had secured for her from the very fine dinner which had been given that day up at his father's house.

He was a sunny-faced youngster of ten. When he had emptied his pockets, La Folle patted his round red cheek, wiped his soiled hands on her apron, and smoothed his hair. Then she watched him as, with his cakes in his hand, he crossed her strip of cotton back of the cabin, and disappeared into the wood.

He had boasted of the things he was going to do with his gun out there.

'You think they got plenty deer in the wood, La Folle?' he had enquired, with the calculating air of an experienced hunter.

'Non, non!'[138] the woman laughed. 'Don't you look fo' no deer, Chéri. Dat's too big. But you bring La Folle one good fat squirrel fo' her dinner tomorrow, an' she goin' be satisfi'.'

'One squirrel ain't a bite. I'll bring you mo' 'an one, La Folle,' he had boasted pompously as he went away.

When the woman, an hour later, heard the report of the boy's rifle close to the wood's edge, she would have thought nothing of it if a sharp cry of distress had not followed the sound.

She withdrew her arms from the tub of suds in which they had been plunged, dried them upon her apron, and as quickly as her trembling limbs would bear her, hurried to the spot whence the ominous report had come.

It was as she feared. There she found Chéri stretched upon the ground, with his rifle beside him. He moaned piteously: 'I'm dead, La Folle! I'm dead! I'm gone!'

'*Non, non!*' she exclaimed resolutely, as she knelt beside him. 'Put you' arm 'roun' La Folle's nake, Chéri. Dat's nuttin'; dat goin' be nuttin'.' She lifted him in her powerful arms.

Chéri had carried his gun muzzle-downwards. He had stumbled – he did not know how. He only knew that he had a ball lodged somewhere in his leg, and he thought that his end was at hand. Now, with his head upon the woman's shoulder, he moaned and wept with pain and fright.

'Oh, La Folle! La Folle! it hurt so bad! I can' stan' it, La Folle!'

'Don't cry, *mon bébé, mon bébé, mon Chéri!*'[139] the woman spoke soothingly as she covered the ground with long strides. 'La Folle goin' mine you; Dr Bonfils[140] goin' come make *mon Chéri* well agin.'

She had reached the abandoned field. As she crossed it with her precious burden, she looked constantly and restlessly from side to side. A terrible fear was upon her – the fear of the world beyond the bayou, the morbid and insane dread she had been under since childhood.

When she was at the bayou's edge she stood there, and shouted for help as if a life depended upon it: '*Oh, P'tit Maître! P'tit Maître! Venez donc! Au secours! Au secours!*'[141]

No voice responded. Chéri's hot tears were scalding her neck. She called for each and every one upon the place, and still no answer came.

She shouted, she wailed; but whether her voice remained unheard or unheeded, no reply came to her frenzied cries. And all the while Chéri moaned and wept and entreated to be taken home to his mother.

La Folle gave a last despairing look around her. Extreme terror was upon her. She clasped the child close against her breast, where he could feel her heart beat like a muffled hammer. Then shutting her eyes, she ran suddenly down the shallow bank of the bayou, and never stopped till she had climbed the opposite shore.

She stood there quivering an instant as she opened her eyes. Then she plunged into the footpath through the trees.

She spoke no more to Chéri, but muttered constantly, '*Bon Dieu, ayez pitié La Folle! Bon Dieu, ayez pitié moi!*'[142]

Instinct seemed to guide her. When the pathway spread clear and smooth enough before her, she again closed her eyes tightly against the sight of that unknown and terrifying world.

A child, playing in some weeds, caught sight of her as she neared the quarters. The little one uttered a cry of dismay.

'La Folle!' she screamed, in her piercing treble. 'La Folle done cross de bayer!'

Quickly the cry passed down the line of cabins.

'Yonda, La Folle done cross de bayou!'

Children, old men, old women, young ones with infants in their arms, flocked to doors and windows to see this awe-inspiring spectacle. Most of them shuddered with superstitious dread of what it might portend.

'She totin' Chéri!' some of them shouted.

Some of the more daring gathered about her, and followed at her heels, only to fall back with new terror when she turned her distorted face upon them. Her eyes were bloodshot and the saliva had gathered in a white foam on her black lips.

Someone had run ahead of her to where P'tit Maître sat with his family and guests upon the gallery.

'P'tit Maître! La Folle done cross de bayou! Look her! Look her yonda totin' Chéri!' This startling intimation was the first which they had of the woman's approach.

She was now near at hand. She walked with long strides. Her eyes were fixed desperately before her, and she breathed heavily, as a tired ox.

At the foot of the stairway, which she could not have mounted, she laid the boy in his father's arms. Then the world that had looked red to La Folle suddenly turned black – like that day she had seen powder and blood.

She reeled for an instant. Before a sustaining arm could reach her, she fell heavily to the ground.

When La Folle regained consciousness, she was at home again, in her own cabin and upon her own bed. The moon rays, streaming in through the open door and windows, gave what light was needed to the old black mammy who stood at the table concocting a tisane of fragrant herbs. It was very late.

Others who had come, and found that the stupor clung to her, had gone again. P'tit Maître had been there, and with him Dr Bonfils, who said that La Folle might die.

But death had passed her by. The voice was very clear and steady with which she spoke to Tante Lizette, brewing her tisane there in a corner.

'Ef you will give me one good drink tisane, Tante Lizette, I b'lieve I'm goin' sleep, me.'

And she did sleep; so soundly, so healthfully, that old Lizette without compunction stole softly away, to creep back through the moonlit fields to her own cabin in the new quarters.

The first touch of the cool grey morning awoke La Folle. She arose, calmly, as if no tempest had shaken and threatened her existence but yesterday.

She donned her new blue cottonade and white apron, for she remembered that this was Sunday. When she had made for herself a cup of strong black coffee, and drunk it with relish, she quitted the cabin and walked across the old familiar field to the bayou's edge again.

She did not stop there as she had always done before, but crossed with a long, steady stride as if she had done this all her life.

When she had made her way through the brush and scrub cotton-wood trees that lined the opposite bank, she found herself upon the border of a field where the white, bursting cotton, with the dew upon it, gleamed for acres and acres like frosted silver in the early dawn.

La Folle drew a long, deep breath as she gazed across the country. She walked slowly and uncertainly, like one who hardly knows how, looking about her as she went.

The cabins, that yesterday had sent a clamour of voices to pursue her, were quiet now. No one was yet astir at Bellissime. Only the birds that darted here and there from hedges were awake, and singing their matins.

When La Folle came to the broad stretch of velvety lawn that surrounded the house, she moved slowly and with delight over the springy turf that was delicious beneath her tread.

She stopped to find whence came those perfumes that were assailing her senses with memories from a time far gone.

There they were, stealing up to her from the thousand blue violets that peeped out from green, luxuriant beds. There they were, showering down from the big waxen bells of the magnolias far above her head, and from the jessamine clumps around her.

There were roses, too, without number. To right and left palms spread in broad and graceful curves. It all looked like enchantment beneath the sparkling sheen of dew.

When La Folle had slowly and cautiously mounted the many steps that led up to the veranda, she turned to look back at the perilous ascent she had made. Then she caught sight of the river, bending like a silver bow at the foot of Bellissime. Exultation possessed her soul.

La Folle rapped softly upon a door near at hand. Chéri's mother soon cautiously opened it. Quickly and cleverly she dissembled the astonishment she felt at seeing La Folle.

'Ah, La Folle! Is it you, so early?'

'*Oui*, madame. I come ax how my po' li'le Chéri to, 's mo'nin'.'

'He is feeling easier, thank you, La Folle. Dr Bonfils says it will be nothing serious. He's sleeping now. Will you come back when he awakes?'

'*Non*, madame. I'm goin' wait yair tell Chéri wake up.' La Folle seated herself upon the topmost step of the veranda.

A look of wonder and deep content crept into her face as she watched for the first time the sun rise upon the new, the beautiful world beyond the bayou.

Old Aunt Peggy

When the war[143] was over, old Aunt Peggy went to Monsieur, and said: 'Massa, I ain't never gwine to quit yer. I'm gittin' ole an' feeble, an' my days is few in dis heah lan' o' sorrow an' sin. All I axes is a li'le co'ner whar I kin set down an' wait peaceful fu de en'.'

Monsieur and Madame were very much touched at this mark of affection and fidelity from Aunt Peggy. So, in the general reconstruction of the plantation which immediately followed the surrender, a nice cabin, pleasantly appointed, was set apart for the old woman. Madame did not even forget the very comfortable rocking-chair in which Aunt Peggy might 'set down,' as she herself feelingly expressed it, 'an' wait fu de en'.'

She has been rocking ever since.

At intervals of about two years Aunt Peggy hobbles up to the house, and delivers the stereotyped address which has become more than familiar: 'Mist'ess, I's come to take a las' look at you all. Le' me look at you good. Le' me look at de chillun – de big chillun an' de li'le chillun. Le' me look at de picters an' de photygraphts an' de pianny, an' eve'ything 'fo' it's too late. One eye is done gone, an' de udder's a-gwine fas'. Any mo'nin' yo' po' ole Aunt Peggy gwine wake up an' fin' herse'f stone-bline.'

After such a visit Aunt Peggy invariably returns to her cabin with a generously filled apron.

The scruple which Monsieur one time felt in supporting a woman for so many years in idleness has entirely disappeared. Of late his attitude towards Aunt Peggy is simply one of profound astonishment – wonder at the surprising age which an old black woman may attain when she sets her mind to it, for Aunt Peggy is a hundred and twenty-five, so she says.

It may not be true, however. Possibly she is older.

The Return of Alcibiade

Mr Fred Bartner was sorely perplexed and annoyed to find that a wheel and tyre of his buggy threatened to part company.

'Ef you want,' said the negro boy who drove him, 'we kin stop yonda at ole M'sié Jean Ba's an' fix it; he got de bes' blacksmif shop in de pa'ish on his place.'

'Who in the world is old Monsieur Jean Ba,' the young man enquired.

'How come, suh, you don' know old M'sié Jean Baptiste Plochel? He ole, ole. He sorter quare in he head ev' sence his son M'sié Alcibiade got kill' in de wah. Yonda he live'; whar you sees dat che'okee hedge takin' up half de road.'

Little more than twelve years ago, before the 'Texas and Pacific' had joined the cities of New Orleans and Shreveport with its steel bands, it was a common thing to travel through miles of central Louisiana in a buggy. Fred Bartner, a young commission merchant of New Orleans, on business bent, had made the trip in this way by easy stages from his home to a point on Cane River, within a half-day's journey of Natchitoches. From the mouth of Cane River he had passed one plantation after another – large ones and small ones. There was nowhere sight of anything like a town, except the little hamlet of Cloutierville, through which they had sped in the grey dawn. 'Dat town, hit's ole, ole; mos' a hund'ed year' ole, dey say. Uh, uh, look to me like it heap ol'r an' dat,' the darkey had commented. Now they were within sight of Monsieur Jean Ba's towering Cherokee hedge.

It was Christmas morning, but the sun was warm and the air so soft and mild that Bartner found the most comfortable way to wear his light overcoat was across his knees. At the entrance to the plantation he dismounted and the negro drove away towards the smithy which stood on the edge of the field.

From the end of the long avenue of magnolias that led to it, the house which confronted Bartner looked grotesquely long in comparison with its height. It was one storey, of pale yellow stucco; its massive wooden shutters were a faded green. A wide gallery, topped by the overhanging roof, encircled it.

At the head of the stairs a very old man stood. His figure was small and shrunken, his hair long and snow-white. He wore a broad, soft felt hat, and a brown plaid shawl across his bent shoulders. A tall, graceful girl stood beside him; she was clad in a warm-coloured blue stuff gown. She seemed to be expostulating with the old gentleman, who evidently wanted to descend the stairs to meet the approaching visitor. Before Bartner had had time to do more than lift his hat, Monsieur Jean Ba had thrown his trembling arms about the young man and was exclaiming in his quavering old tones: '*À la fin! mon fils! À la fin!*'[144] Tears started to the girl's eyes and she was rosy with confusion. 'Oh, escuse him, sir; please escuse him,' she whisperingly entreated, gently striving to disengage the old gentleman's arms from around the astonished Bartner. But a new line of thought seemed fortunately to take possession of Monsieur Jean Ba, for he moved away and went quickly, pattering like a baby, down the gallery. His fleecy white hair streamed out on the soft breeze, and his brown shawl flapped as he turned the corner.

Bartner, left alone with the girl, proceeded to introduce himself and to explain his presence there.

'Oh! Mr Fred Bartna of New Orleans? The commission merchant!' she exclaimed, cordially extending her hand. 'So well known in Natchitoches parish. Not *our* merchant, Mr Bartna,' she added, naïvely, 'but jus' as welcome, all the same, at my gran'father's.'

Bartner felt like kissing her, but he only bowed and seated himself in the big chair which she offered him. He wondered what was the longest time it could take to mend a buggy tyre.

She sat before him with her hands pressed down into her lap, and with an eagerness and pretty air of being confidential that were extremely engaging, explained the reasons for her grandfather's singular behaviour.

Years ago, her uncle Alcibiade, in going away to the war, with the cheerful assurance of youth, had promised his father that he would return to eat Christmas dinner with him. He never returned. And now, of late years, since Monsieur Jean Ba had begun to fail in body and mind, that old, unspoken hope of long ago had come back to live anew in his heart. Every Christmas Day he watched for the coming of Alcibiade.

'Ah! if you knew, Mr Bartna, how I have endeavour' to distrac' his mine from that thought! Weeks ago, I tole to all the negroes, big and li'le, "If one of you dare to say the words Christmas gif' in the hearing of Monsieur Jean Baptiste, you will have to answer to me." '

Bartner could not recall when he had been so deeply interested in a narration.

'So las' night, Mr Bartna, I said to *grandpère*, "Pépère, you know tomorrow will be the great feas' of la Trinité; we will read our litany together in the morning and say a *chapelet*."[145] He did not answer a word; *il est malin, oui*.[146] But this morning at daylight he was rapping his cane on the back gallery, calling together the negroes. Did they not know it was Christmas Day, an' a great dinner mus' be prepare' for his son Alcibiade, whom he was especting!'

'And so he has mistaken me for his son Alcibiade. It is very unfortunate,' said Bartner, sympathetically. He was a good-looking, honest-faced young fellow.

The girl arose, quivering with an inspiration. She approached Bartner, and in her eagerness laid her hand upon his arm.

'Oh, Mr Bartna, if you will do me a favour! The greates' favour of my life!'

He expressed his absolute readiness.

'Let him believe, jus' for this one Christmas day, that you are his son. Let him have that Christmas dinner with Alcibiade that he has been longing for so many year'.'

Bartner's was not a puritanical conscience, but truthfulness was a habit as well as a principle with him, and he winced. 'It seems to me it would be cruel to deceive him; it would not be' – he did not like to say 'right', but she guessed that he meant it.

'Oh, for that,' she laughed, 'you may stay as w'ite as snow, Mr Bartna. *I* will take all the sin on my conscience. I assume all the responsibility on my shoulder'.'

'Esmée!' the old man was calling as he came trotting back, 'Esmée, my child,' in his quavering French. 'I have ordered the dinner. Go see to the arrangements of the table, and have everything faultless.'

*

The dining-room was at the end of the house, with windows opening upon the side and back galleries. There was a high, simply carved wooden mantelpiece, bearing a wide, slanting, old-fashioned mirror that reflected the table and its occupants. The table was laden with an overabundance. Monsieur Jean Ba sat at one end, Esmée at the other, and Bartner at the side.

Two '*grif*' boys, a big black woman and a little mulatto girl waited upon them; there was a reserve force outside within easy call, and the little black and yellow faces kept bobbing up constantly above the window-sills. Windows and doors were open, and a fire of hickory branches blazed on the hearth.

Monsieur Jean Ba ate little, but that little greedily and rapidly; then he paused in rapt contemplation of his guest.

'You will notice, Alcibiade, the flavour of the turkey,' he said. 'It is dressed with pecans; those big ones from the tree down on the bayou. I had them gathered expressly.' The delicate and rich flavour of the nut was indeed very perceptible.

Bartner had a stupid impression of acting on the stage, and had to pull himself together every now and then to throw off the stiffness of the amateur actor. But this discomposure amounted almost to paralysis when he found Mademoiselle Esmée taking the situation as seriously as her grandfather.

'*Mon Dieu!* Uncle Alcibiade, you are not eating! *Mais* w'ere have you lef' your appetite? Corbeau, fill your young master's glass. Doralise, you are neglecting Monsieur Alcibiade; he is without bread.'

Monsieur Jean Ba's feeble intelligence reached out very dimly; it was like a dream which clothes the grotesque and unnatural with the semblance of reality. He shook his head up and down with pleased approbation of Esmée's 'Uncle Alcibiade', that tripped so glibly on her lips. When she arranged his after-dinner *brûlot* – a lump of sugar in a flaming teaspoonful of brandy, dropped into a tiny cup of black coffee – he reminded her, 'Your Uncle Alcibiade takes two lumps, Esmée. The scamp! he is fond of sweets. Two or three lumps, Esmée.' Bartner would have relished his *brûlot* greatly, prepared so gracefully as it was by Esmée's deft hands, had it not been for that superfluous lump.

After dinner the girl arranged her grandfather comfortably in his big armchair on the gallery, where he loved to sit when the weather permitted. She fastened his shawl about him and laid a second one across his knees. She shook up the pillow for his head, patted his sunken cheek and kissed his forehead under the soft-brimmed hat. She left him there with the sun warming his feet and old shrunken knees.

Esmée and Bartner walked together under the magnolias. In walking they trod upon the violet borders that grew rank and sprawling, and the subtle perfume of the crushed flowers scented the air deliciously. They stooped and plucked handfuls of them. They gathered roses, too, that were blooming yet against the warm south end of the house; and they chattered and laughed like children. When they sat in the sunlight upon the low steps to arrange the flowers they had broken, Bartner's conscience began to prick him anew.

'You know,' he said, 'I can't stay here always, as well as I should like to. I shall have to leave presently; then your grandfather will discover that we have been deceiving him – and you can see how cruel that will be.'

'Mr Bartna,' answered Esmée, daintily holding a rosebud up to her pretty nose, 'w'en I awoke this morning an' said my prayers, I prayed to the good God that He would give one happy Christmas Day to my gran'father. He has answered my prayer; an' He does not sen' his gif's incomplete. He will provide.

'Mr Bartna, this morning I agreed to take all responsibility on my shoulder', you remember? Now, I place all that responsibility on the shoulder' of the blessed Virgin.'

Bartner was distracted with admiration; whether for this beautiful and consoling faith or its charming votary was not quite clear to him.

Every now and then Monsieur Jean Ba would call out, 'Alcibiade, *mon fils!*' and Bartner would hasten to his side. Sometimes the old man had forgotten what he wanted to say. Once it was to ask if the salad had been to his liking, or if he would, perhaps, not have preferred the turkey *aux truffes.*[147]

'Alcibiade, *mon fils!*' Again Bartner amiably answered the summons. Monsieur Jean Ba took the young man's hand affectionately in his, but limply, as children hold hands. Bartner's closed firmly around it. 'Alcibiade, I am going to take a little nap now. If Robert McFarlane comes while I am sleeping, with more talk of wanting to buy Nég Sévérin, tell him I will sell none of my slaves; not the least little *négrillon.*[148] Drive him from the place with the shotgun. Don't be afraid to use the shotgun, Alcibiade – when I am asleep – if he comes.'

Esmée and Bartner forgot that there was such a thing as time, and that it was passing. There were no more calls of 'Alcibiade, *mon fils!*' As the sun dipped lower and lower in the west, its light was creeping, creeping up and illuming the still body of Monsieur Jean Ba. It lighted his waxen hands, folded so placidly in his lap; it touched his shrunken bosom. When it reached his face, another brightness had come there before it – the glory of a quiet and peaceful death.

*

Bartner remained overnight, of course, to add what assistance he could to that which kindly neighbours offered.

In the early morning, before taking his departure, he was permitted to see Esmée. She was overcome with sorrow, which he could hardly hope to assuage, even with the keen sympathy which he felt.

'And may I be permitted to ask, mademoiselle, what will be your plans for the future?'

'Oh,' she moaned, 'I cannot any longer remain upon the ole plantation, which would not be home without *grandpère*. I suppose I shall go to live in New Orleans with my *tante* Clémentine.' The last was spoken in the depths of her handkerchief.

Bartner's heart bounded at this intelligence in a manner which he could not but feel was one of unbecoming levity. He pressed her disengaged hand warmly, and went away.

The sun was again shining brightly, but the morning was crisp and cool; a thin wafer of ice covered what had yesterday been pools or water in the road. Bartner buttoned his coat about him closely. The shrill whistles of steam cotton-gins sounded here and there. One or two shivering negroes were in the field gathering what shreds of cotton were left on the dry, naked stalks. The horses snorted with satisfaction, and their strong hoof-beats rang out against the hard ground.

'Urge the horses,' Bartner said; 'they've had a good rest and we want to push on to Natchitoches.'

'You right, suh. We done los' a whole blesse' day – a plumb day.'

'Why, so we have,' said Bartner, 'I hadn't thought of it.'

A Rude Awakening

'Take de do' an' go! You year me? Take de do'!'

Lolotte's brown eyes flamed. Her small frame quivered. She stood with her back turned to a meagre supper-table, as if to guard it from the man who had just entered the cabin. She pointed towards the door, to order him from the house.

'You mighty cross tonight, Lolotte. You mus' got up wid de wrong foot to's mo'nin'. *Hein*, Veveste? *Bein*, Jacques, w'at you say?'

The two small urchins who sat at table giggled in sympathy with their father's evident good humour.

'I'm we' out, me!' the girl exclaimed, desperately, as she let her arms fall limp at her side. 'Work, work! Fu w'at? Fu feed de lazies' man in Natchitoches pa'ish.'

'Now, Lolotte, you think w'at you sayin',' expostulated her father. 'Sylveste Bordon don' ax nobody to feed 'im.'

'W'en you brought a poun' of suga in de house?' his daughter retorted hotly, 'or a poun' of coffee? W'en did you brought a piece o' meat home, you? An' Nonomme all de time sick. Co'n bread an' po'k, dat's good fu Veveste an' me an' Jacques; but Nonomme? no!'

She turned as if choking, and cut into the round, soggy 'pone' of corn bread which was the main feature of the scanty supper.

'Po' li'le Nonomme; we mus' fine some'in' to break dat fevah. You want to kill a chicken once a w'ile fu Nonomme, Lolotte.' He calmly seated himself at the table.

'Didn' I done put de las' roostah in de pot?' she cried with exasperation. 'Now you come axen me fu kill de hen'! W'ere I goen to fine aigg' to trade wid, w'en de hen' be gone? Is I got one picayune in de house fu trade wid, me?'

'Papa,' piped the young Jacques, 'w'at dat I yeard you drive in de yard, w'ile go?'

'Dat's it! W'en Lolotte wouldn' been talken' so fas', I could tole you 'bout dat job I got fu tomorrow. Dat was Joe Duplan's team of mule' an' wagon, wid t'ree bale' of cotton, w'at you yaird. I got to go soon in de mo'nin' wid dat load to de landin'. An' a man mus' eat w'at got to work; dat's sho.'

Lolotte's bare brown feet made no sound upon the rough boards as she entered the room where Nonomme lay sick and sleeping. She lifted the coarse mosquito net from about him, sat down in the clumsy chair by the bedside, and began gently to fan the slumbering child.

Dusk was falling rapidly, as it does in the South. Lolotte's eyes grew round and big, as she watched the moon creep up from branch to branch of the moss-draped live-oak just outside her window. Presently the weary girl slept as profoundly as Nonomme. A little dog sneaked into the room, and socially licked her bare feet. The touch, moist and warm, awakened Lolotte.

The cabin was dark and quiet. Nonomme was crying softly, because the mosquitoes were biting him. In the room beyond, old Sylveste and the others slept. When Lolotte had quieted the child, she went outside to get a pail of cool, fresh water at the cistern. Then she crept into bed beside Nonomme, who slept again.

Lolotte's dreams that night pictured her father returning from work, and bringing luscious oranges home in his pocket for the sick child.

When at the very break of day she heard him astir in his room, a certain comfort stole into her heart. She lay and listened to the faint noises of his preparations to go out. When he had quitted the house, she waited to hear him drive the wagon from the yard.

She waited long, but heard no sound of horses' tread or wagon-wheel. Anxious, she went to the cabin door and looked out. The big mules were still where they had been fastened the night before. The wagon was there, too.

Her heart sank. She looked quickly along the low rafters supporting the roof of the narrow porch to where her father's fishing pole and pail always hung. Both were gone.

' 'T ain' no use, 't ain' no use,' she said, as she turned into the house with a look of something like anguish in her eyes.

When the spare breakfast was eaten and the dishes cleared away, Lolotte turned with resolute mien to the two little brothers.

'Veveste,' she said to the older, 'go see if dey got co'n in dat wagon fu feed dem mule'.'

'Yes, dey got co'n. Papa done feed 'em, fur I see de co'n-cob in de trough, me.'

'Den you goen he'p me hitch dem mule to de wagon. Jacques, go down de lane an' ax Aunt Minty if she come set wid Nonomme w'ile I go drive dem mule' to de landin'.'

Lolotte had evidently determined to undertake her father's work. Nothing could dissuade her; neither the children's astonishment nor

Aunt Minty's scathing disapproval. The fat black negress came labouring into the yard just as Lolotte mounted upon the wagon.

'Git down f'om dah, chile! Is you plumb crazy?' she exclaimed.

'No, I ain't crazy; I'm hungry, Aunt Minty. We all hungry. Somebody got fur work in dis fam'ly.'

'Dat ain't no work fur a gal w'at ain't bar' seventeen year ole; drivin' Marse Duplan's[149] mules! W'at I gwine tell yo' pa?'

'Fu me, you kin tell 'im w'at you want. But you watch Nonomme. I done cook his rice an' set it 'side.'

'Don't you bodda,' replied Aunt Minty; 'I got somepin heah fur my boy. I gwine 'ten' to him.'

Lolotte had seen Aunt Minty put something out of sight when she came up, and made her produce it. It was a heavy fowl.

'Sence w'en you start raisin' Brahma chickens,[150] you?' Lolotte asked mistrustfully.

'My, but you is a cu'ious somebody! Ev'ything w'at got fedders on its laigs is one Brahma chicken wid you. Dis heah ole hen – '

'All de same, you don't got fur give dat chicken to eat to Nonomme. You don't got fur cook 'im in my house.'

Aunt Minty, unheeding, turned to the house with blustering enquiry for her boy, while Lolotte drove away with great clatter.

She knew, notwithstanding her injunction, that the chicken would be cooked and eaten. Maybe she herself would partake of it when she came back, if hunger drove her too sharply.

'Nax' thing I'm goen be one rogue,' she muttered; and the tears gathered and fell one by one upon her cheeks.

'It *do* look like one Brahma, Aunt Mint,' remarked the small and weazened Jacques, as he watched the woman picking the lusty fowl.

'How ole is you?' was her quiet retort.

'I don' know, me.'

'Den if you don't know dat much, you betta keep yo' mouf shet, boy.'

Then silence fell, but for a monotonous chant which the woman droned as she worked.

Jacques opened his lips once more. 'It *do* look like one o' Ma'me Duplan' Brahma, Aunt Mint.'

'Yonda, whar I come f'om, befo' de wah – '

'Ole Kaintuck, Aunt Mint?'

'Ole Kaintuck.'

'Dat ain't one country like dis yere, Aunt Mint?'

'You mighty right, chile, dat ain't no sech kentry as dis heah. Yonda, in Kaintuck, w'en boys says de words "Brahma chicken", we takes an' gags 'em, an' ties dar han's behines 'em, an' fo'ces 'em ter stan' up watchin' folks settin' down eatin' chicken soup.'

Jacques passed the back of his hand across his mouth; but lest the act should not place sufficient seal upon it, he prudently stole away to go and sit beside Nonomme, and await there as patiently as he could the coming feast.

And what a treat it was! The luscious soup – a great pot of it – golden yellow, thickened with the flaky rice that Lolotte had set carefully on the shelf. Each mouthful of it seemed to carry fresh blood into the veins and a new brightness into the eyes of the hungry children who ate of it.

And that was not all. The day brought abundance with it. Their father came home with glistening perch and trout that Aunt Minty broiled deliciously over glowing embers, and basted with the rich chicken fat.

'You see,' explained old Sylveste, 'w'en I git up to 's mo'nin' an' see it was cloudy, I say to me, "Sylveste, w'en you go wid dat cotton, rememba you got no tarpaulin. Maybe it rain, an' de cotton was spoil. Betta you go yonda to Lafirme Lake, w'ere de trout was bitin' fas'er 'an mosquito, an' so you git a good mess fur de chil'en." Lolotte – w'at she goen do yonda? You ought stop Lolotte, Aunt Minty, w'en you see w'at she was want to do.'

'Didn' I try to stop 'er? Didn' I ax 'er, "W'at I gwine tell yo' pa?" An' she 'low, "Tell 'im to go hang hisse'f, de triflind ole rapscallion! I's de one w'at's runnin' dis heah fambly!" '

'Dat don' soun' like Lolotte, Aunt Minty; you mus' yaird 'er crooked; *hein*, Nonomme?'

The quizzical look in his good-natured features was irresistible. Nonomme fairly shook with merriment.

'My head feel so good,' he declared. 'I wish Lolotte would come, so I could tole 'er.' And he turned in his bed to look down the long, dusty lane, with the hope of seeing her appear as he had watched her go, sitting on one of the cotton bales and guiding the mules.

But no one came all through the hot morning. Only at noon a broad-shouldered young negro appeared in view riding through the dust. When he had dismounted at the cabin door, he stood leaning a shoulder lazily against the jamb.

'Well, heah you is,' he grumbled, addressing Sylveste with no mark of respect.

'Heah you is, settin' down like comp'ny, an' Marse Joe yonda sont me see if you was dead.'

'Joe Duplan boun' to have his joke, him,' said Sylveste, smiling uneasily.

'Maybe it look like a joke to you, but 't aint no joke to him, man, to have one o' his wagons smoshed to kindlin', an' his bes' team tearin' t'rough de country. You don't want to let 'im lay han's on you, joke o' no joke.'

'*Malédiction!*'[151] howled Sylveste, as he staggered to his feet. He stood for one instant irresolute; then he lurched past the man and ran wildly down the lane. He might have taken the horse that was there, but he went tottering on afoot, a frightened look in his eyes, as if his soul gazed upon an inward picture that was horrible.

The road to the landing was little used. As Sylveste went he could readily trace the marks of Lolotte's wagon-wheels. For some distance they went straight along the road. Then they made a track as if a madman had directed their course, over stump and hillock, tearing the bushes and barking the trees on either side.

At each new turn Sylveste expected to find Lolotte stretched senseless upon the ground, but there was never a sign of her.

At last he reached the landing, which was a dreary spot, slanting down to the river and partly cleared to afford room for what desultory freight might be left there from time to time. There were the wagon-tracks, clean down to the river's edge and partly in the water, where they made a sharp and senseless turn. But Sylveste found no trace of his girl.

'Lolotte!' the old man cried out into the stillness. 'Lolotte, *ma fille*, Lolotte!' But no answer came; no sound but the echo of his own voice, and the soft splash of the red water that lapped his feet.

He looked down at it, sick with anguish and apprehension.

Lolotte had disappeared as completely as if the earth had opened and swallowed her. After a few days it became the common belief that the girl had been drowned. It was thought that she must have been hurled from the wagon into the water, during the sharp turn that the wheel-tracks indicated, and carried away by the rapid current.

During the days of search, old Sylveste's excitement kept him up. When it was over, an apathetic despair seemed to settle upon him.

Madame Duplan, moved by sympathy, had taken the little four-year-old Nonomme to the plantation Les Chêniers, where the child was awed by the beauty and comfort of things that surrounded him there. He thought always that Lolotte would come back, and watched for her every day; for they did not tell him the sad tidings of her loss.

The other two boys were placed in the temporary care of Aunt Minty; and old Sylveste roamed like a persecuted being through the country. He who had been a type of indolent content and repose had changed to a restless spirit.

When he thought to eat, it was in some humble negro cabin that he stopped to ask for food, which was never denied him. His grief had clothed him with a dignity that imposed respect.

One morning very early he appeared before the planter with a dishevelled and hunted look.

'M'sieur Duplan,' he said, holding his hat in his hand and looking away into vacancy, 'I been try ev'thing. I been try settin' down still on de sto' gall'ry. I been walk, I been run; 't ain' no use. Dey got al'ays some'in' w'at push me. I go fishin', an' it's some'in' w'at push me worser 'an ever. By gracious! M'sieur Duplan, gi' me some work!'

The planter gave him at once a plough in hand, and no plough on the whole plantation dug so deep as that one, nor so fast. Sylveste was the first in the field, as he was the last one there. From dawn to nightfall he worked, and after, till his limbs refused to do his bidding.

People came to wonder, and the negroes began to whisper hints of demoniacal possession.

When Mr Duplan gave careful thought to the subject of Lolotte's mysterious disappearance, an idea came to him. But so fearful was he to arouse false hopes in the breasts of those who grieved for the girl that to no one did he impart his suspicions save to his wife. It was on the eve of a business trip to New Orleans that he told her what he thought, or what he hoped rather.

Upon his return, which happened not many days later, he went out to where old Sylveste was toiling in the field with frenzied energy.

'Sylveste,' said the planter, quietly, when he had stood a moment watching the man at work, 'have you given up all hope of hearing from your daughter?'

'I don' know, me; I don' know. Le' me work, M'sieur Duplan.'

'For my part, I believe the child is alive.'

'You b'lieve dat, you?' His rugged face was pitiful in its imploring lines.

'I know it,' Mr Duplan muttered, as calmly as he could. 'Hold up! Steady yourself, man! Come; come with me to the house. There is someone there who knows it, too; someone who has seen her.'

The room into which the planter led the old man was big, cool, beautiful, and sweet with the delicate odour of flowers. It was shady, too, for the shutters were half closed; but not so darkened but Sylveste could at once see Lolotte, seated in a big wicker chair.

She was almost as white as the gown she wore. Her neatly shod feet rested upon a cushion, and her black hair, that had been closely cut, was beginning to make little rings about her temples.

'Aie!' he cried sharply, at sight of her, grasping his seamed throat as he did so. Then he laughed like a madman, and then he sobbed.

He only sobbed, kneeling upon the floor beside her, kissing her knees and her hands, that sought his. Little Nonomme was close to her, with a health flush creeping into his cheek. Veveste and Jacques were there, and rather awed by the mystery and grandeur of everything.

'W'ere'bouts you find her, M'sieur Duplan?' Sylveste asked, when the first flush of his joy had spent itself, and he was wiping his eyes with his rough cotton shirt sleeve.

'M'sieur Duplan find me 'way yonda to de city, papa, in de hospital,' spoke Lolotte, before the planter could steady his voice to reply. 'I didn' know who ev'ybody was, me. I didn' know me, myse'f, tell I tu'n roun' one day an' see M'sieur Duplan, w'at stan'en dere.'

'You was boun' to know M'sieur Duplan, Lolotte,' laughed Sylveste, like a child.

'Yes, an' I know right 'way how dem mule was git frighten' w'en de boat w'istle fu stop, an' pitch me plumb on de groun'. An' I rememba it was one *mulâtresse* w'at call herse'f one chembamed, all de time aside me.'

'You must not talk too much, Lolotte,' interposed Madame Duplan, coming to place her hand with gentle solicitude upon the girl's forehead, and to feel how her pulse beat.

Then to save the child further effort of speech, she herself related how the boat had stopped at this lonely landing to take on a load of cotton-seed. Lolotte had been found stretched insensible by the river, fallen apparently from the clouds, and had been taken on board.

The boat had changed its course into other waters after that trip, and had not returned to Duplan's Landing. Those who had tended Lolotte and left her at the hospital supposed, no doubt, that she would make known her identity in time, and they had troubled themselves no further about her.

'An' dah you is!' almost shouted Aunt Minty, whose black face gleamed in the doorway; 'dah you is, settin' down, lookin' jis' like w'ite folks!'

'Ain't I always was w'ite folks, Aunt Mint?' smiled Lolotte, feebly.

'G'long, chile. You knows me. I don' mean no harm.'

'And now, Sylveste,' said Mr Duplan, as he rose and started to walk the floor, with hands in his pockets, 'listen to me. It will be a long time before Lolotte is strong again. Aunt Minty is going to look after things for you till the child is fully recovered. But what I want to say is this: I shall trust these children into your hands once more, and I want you never to forget again that you are their father – do you hear? – that you are a man!'

Old Sylveste stood with his hand in Lolotte's, who rubbed it lovingly against her cheek.

'By gracious! M'sieur Duplan,' he answered, 'w'en God want to he'p me, I'm goen try my bes'!'

The Bênitous Slave

Old Uncle Oswald believed he belonged to the Bênitous, and there was no getting the notion out of his head. Monsieur tried every way, for there was no sense in it. Why, it must have been fifty years since the Bênitous owned him. He had belonged to others since, and had later been freed. Beside, there was not a Bênitou left in the parish now, except one rather delicate woman, who lived with her little daughter in a corner of Natchitoches town, and constructed 'fashionable millinery'. The family had dispersed, and almost vanished, and the plantation as well had lost its identity.

But that made no difference to Uncle Oswald. He was always running away from Monsieur – who kept him out of pure kindness – and trying to get back to those Bênitous.

More than that, he was constantly getting injured in such attempts. Once he fell into the bayou and was nearly drowned. Again he barely escaped being run down by an engine. But another time, when he had been lost two days, and finally discovered in an unconscious and half-dead condition in the woods, Monsieur and Dr Bonfils[152] reluctantly decided that it was time to 'do something' with the old man.

So, one sunny spring morning, Monsieur took Uncle Oswald in the buggy, and drove over to Natchitoches with him, intending to take the evening train for the institution in which the poor creature was to be cared for.

It was quite early in the afternoon when they reached town, and Monsieur found himself with several hours to dispose of before train-time. He tied his horses in front of the hotel – the quaintest old stuccoed house, too absurdly unlike a 'hotel' for anything – and entered. But he left Uncle Oswald seated upon a shaded bench just within the yard.

There were people occasionally coming in and going out; but no one took the smallest notice of the old negro drowsing over the cane that he held between his knees. The sight was common in Natchitoches.

One who passed in was a little girl about twelve, with dark, kind eyes, and daintily carrying a parcel. She was dressed in blue calico, and wore a stiff white sun-bonnet, extinguisher fashion,[153] over her brown curls.

Just as she passed Uncle Oswald again, on her way out, the old man, half asleep, let fall his cane. She picked it up and handed it back to him, as any nice child would have done.

'Oh, thankee, thankee, missy,' stammered Uncle Oswald, all confused at being waited upon by this little lady. 'You is a putty li'le gal. W'at's yo' name, honey?'

'My name's Susanne; Susanne Bênitou,' replied the girl.

Instantly the old negro stumbled to his feet. Without a moment's hesitancy he followed the little one out through the gate, down the street, and around the corner.

It was an hour later that Monsieur, after a distracted search, found him standing upon the gallery of the tiny house in which Madame Bênitou kept 'fashionable millinery'.

Mother and daughter were sorely perplexed to comprehend the intentions of the venerable servitor, who stood, hat in hand, persistently awaiting their orders.

Monsieur understood and appreciated the situation at once, and he has prevailed upon Madame Bênitou to accept the gratuitous services of Uncle Oswald for the sake of the old darky's own safety and happiness.

Uncle Oswald never tries to run away now. He chops wood and hauls water. He cheerfully and faithfully bears the parcels that Susanne used to carry; and makes an excellent cup of black coffee.

I met the old man the other day in Natchitoches, contentedly stumbling down St Denis Street with a basket of figs that someone was sending to his mistress. I asked him his name.

'My name's Oswal', madame; Oswal' – dat's my name. I b'longs to de Bênitous;' and someone told me his story then.

Désirée's Baby

As the day was pleasant, Madame Valmondé drove over to L'Abri[154] to see Désirée and the baby.

It made her laugh to think of Désirée with a baby. Why, it seemed but yesterday that Désirée was little more than a baby herself; when Monsieur in riding through the gateway of Valmondé had found her lying asleep in the shadow of the big stone pillar.

The little one awoke in his arms and began to cry for 'Dada'. That was as much as she could do or say. Some people thought she might have strayed there of her own accord, for she was of the toddling age. The prevailing belief was that she had been purposely left by a party of Texans, whose canvas-covered wagon, late in the day, had crossed the ferry that Coton Maïs kept, just below the plantation. In time Madame Valmondé abandoned every speculation but the one that Désirée had been sent to her by a beneficent Providence to be the child of her affection, seeing that she was without child of the flesh. For the girl grew to be beautiful and gentle, affectionate and sincere – the idol of Valmondé.

It was no wonder, when she stood one day against the stone pillar in whose shadow she had lain asleep, eighteen years before, that Armand Aubigny, riding by and seeing her there, had fallen in love with her. That was the way all the Aubignys fell in love, as if struck by a pistol shot. The wonder was that he had not loved her before; for he had known her since his father brought him home from Paris, a boy of eight, after his mother died there. The passion that awoke in him that day, when he saw her at the gate, swept along like an avalanche, or like a prairie fire, or like anything that drives headlong over all obstacles.

Monsieur Valmondé grew practical and wanted things well considered: that is, the girl's obscure origin. Armand looked into her eyes and did not care. He was reminded that she was nameless. What did it matter about a name when he could give her one of the oldest and proudest in Louisiana? He ordered the *corbeille*[155] from Paris, and contained himself with what patience he could until it arrived; then they were married.

Madame Valmondé had not seen Désirée and the baby for four weeks. When she reached L'Abri she shuddered at the first sight of it, as she always did. It was a sad looking place which for many years had not known the gentle presence of a mistress, old Monsieur Aubigny having married and buried his wife in France, and she having loved her own land too well ever to leave it. The roof came down steep and black like a cowl, reaching out beyond the wide galleries that encircled the yellow stuccoed house. Big, solemn oaks grew close to it, and their thick-leaved, far-reaching branches shadowed it like a pall. Young Aubigny's rule was a strict one, too, and under it his negroes had forgotten how to be gay, as they had been during the old master's easy-going and indulgent lifetime.

The young mother was recovering slowly, and lay full length, in her soft white muslins and laces, upon a couch. The baby was beside her, upon her arm, where he had fallen asleep, at her breast. The yellow nurse woman sat beside a window fanning herself.

Madame Valmondé bent her portly figure over Désirée and kissed her, holding her an instant tenderly in her arms. Then she turned to the child.

'This is not the baby!' she exclaimed, in startled tones. French was the language spoken at Valmondé in those days.

'I knew you would be astonished,' laughed Désirée, 'at the way he has grown. The little *cochon de lait*![156] Look at his legs, mamma, and his hands and fingernails – real fingernails. Zandrine had to cut them this morning. Isn't it true, Zandrine?'

The woman bowed her turbaned head majestically, '*Mais si, Madame.*'

'And the way he cries,' went on Désirée, 'is deafening. Armand heard him the other day as far away as La Blanche's[157] cabin.'

Madame Valmondé had never removed her eyes from the child. She lifted it and walked with it over to the window that was lightest. She scanned the baby narrowly, then looked as searchingly at Zandrine, whose face was turned to gaze across the fields.

'Yes, the child has grown, has changed,' said Madame Valmondé, slowly, as she replaced it beside its mother. 'What does Armand say?'

Désirée's face became suffused with a glow that was happiness itself.

'Oh, Armand is the proudest father in the parish, I believe, chiefly because it is a boy, to bear his name; though he says not – that he would have loved a girl as well. But I know it isn't true. I know he says that to please me. And mamma,' she added, drawing Madame Valmondé's head down to her, and speaking in a whisper, 'he hasn't punished one of them – not one of them – since baby is born. Even Négrillon, who pretended to have burnt his leg that he might rest from work – he only laughed, and said Négrillon was a great scamp. Oh, mamma, I'm so happy; it frightens me.'

What Désirée said was true. Marriage, and later the birth of his son had softened Armand Aubigny's imperious and exacting nature greatly. This was what made the gentle Désirée so happy, for she loved him desperately. When he frowned she trembled, but loved him. When he smiled, she asked no greater blessing of God. But Armand's dark, handsome face had not often been disfigured by frowns since the day he fell in love with her.

When the baby was about three months old, Désirée awoke one day to the conviction that there was something in the air menacing her peace. It was at first too subtle to grasp. It had only been a disquieting suggestion; an air of mystery among the blacks; unexpected visits from far-off neighbours who could hardly account for their coming. Then a strange, an awful change in her husband's manner, which she dared not ask him to explain. When he spoke to her, it was with averted eyes, from which the old love-light seemed to have gone out. He absented himself from home; and when there, avoided her presence and that of her child, without excuse. And the very spirit of Satan seemed suddenly to take hold of him in his dealings with the slaves. Désirée was miserable enough to die.

She sat in her room, one hot afternoon, in her *peignoir*, listlessly drawing through her fingers the strands of her long, silky brown hair that hung about her shoulders. The baby, half naked, lay asleep upon her own great mahogany bed, that was like a sumptuous throne, with its satin-lined half-canopy. One of La Blanche's little quadroon boys – half naked too – stood fanning the child slowly with a fan of peacock feathers. Désirée's eyes had been fixed absently and sadly upon the baby, while she was striving to penetrate the threatening mist that she felt closing about her. She looked from her child to the boy who stood beside him, and back again; over and over. 'Ah!' It was a cry that she could not help; which she was not conscious of having uttered. The blood turned like ice in her veins, and a clammy moisture gathered upon her face.

She tried to speak to the little quadroon boy; but no sound would come, at first. When he heard his name uttered, he looked up, and his mistress was pointing to the door. He laid aside the great, soft fan, and obediently stole away, over the polished floor, on his bare tiptoes.

She stayed motionless, with gaze riveted upon her child, and her face the picture of fright.

Presently her husband entered the room, and without noticing her, went to a table and began to search among some papers which covered it.

'Armand,' she called to him, in a voice which must have stabbed him, if he was human. But he did not notice. 'Armand,' she said again. Then she rose and tottered towards him. 'Armand,' she panted once more, clutching his arm, 'look at our child. What does it mean? Tell me.'

He coldly but gently loosened her fingers from about his arm and thrust the hand away from him. 'Tell me what it means!' she cried despairingly.

'It means,' he answered lightly, 'that the child is not white; it means that you are not white.'

A quick conception of all that this accusation meant for her nerved her with unwonted courage to deny it. 'It is a lie; it is not true, I am white! Look at my hair, it is brown; and my eyes are grey, Armand, you know they are grey. And my skin is fair,' seizing his wrist. 'Look at my hand; whiter than yours, Armand,' she laughed hysterically.

'As white as La Blanche's,' he returned cruelly; and went away leaving her alone with their child.

When she could hold a pen in her hand, she sent a despairing letter to Madame Valmondé.

'My mother, they tell me I am not white. Armand has told me I am not white. For God's sake tell them it is not true. You must know it is not true. I shall die. I must die. I cannot be so unhappy, and live.'

The answer that came was as brief: 'My own Désirée: Come home to Valmondé; back to your mother who loves you. Come with your child.'

When the letter reached Désirée she went with it to her husband's study, and laid it open upon the desk before which he sat. She was like a stone image: silent, white, motionless after she placed it there.

In silence he ran his cold eyes over the written words. He said nothing. 'Shall I go, Armand?' she asked in tones sharp with agonised suspense.

'Yes, go.'

'Do you want me to go?'

'Yes, I want you to go.'

He thought Almighty God had dealt cruelly and unjustly with him; and felt, somehow, that he was paying Him back in kind when he stabbed thus into his wife's soul. Moreover he no longer loved her, because of the unconscious injury she had brought upon his home and his name.

She turned away like one stunned by a blow, and walked slowly towards the door, hoping he would call her back.

'Goodbye, Armand,' she moaned.

He did not answer her. That was his last blow at fate.

Désirée went in search of her child. Zandrine was pacing the sombre gallery with it. She took the little one from the nurse's arms with no word of explanation, and descending the steps, walked away, under the live-oak branches.

It was an October afternoon; the sun was just sinking. Out in the still fields the negroes were picking cotton.

Désirée had not changed the thin white garment nor the slippers which she wore. Her hair was uncovered and the sun's rays brought a golden gleam from its brown meshes. She did not take the broad, beaten road which led to the far-off plantation of Valmondé. She walked across a deserted field, where the stubble bruised her tender feet, so delicately shod, and tore her thin gown to shreds.

She disappeared among the reeds and willows that grew thick along the banks of the deep, sluggish bayou; and she did not come back again.

Some weeks later there was a curious scene enacted at L'Abri. In the centre of the smoothly swept back yard was a great bonfire. Armand Aubigny sat in the wide hallway that commanded a view of the spectacle; and it was he who dealt out to a half-dozen negroes the material which kept this fire ablaze.

A graceful cradle of willow, with all its dainty furbishings, was laid upon the pyre, which had already been fed with the richness of a price-less *layette*.[158] Then there were silk gowns and velvet and satin ones added to these; laces, too, and embroideries; bonnets and gloves; for the *corbeille* had been of rare quality.

The last thing to go was a tiny bundle of letters; innocent little scribblings that Désirée had sent to him during the days of their espousal. There was the remnant of one back in the drawer from which he took them. But it was not Désirée's; it was part of an old letter from his mother to his father. He read it. She was thanking God for the blessing of her husband's love –

'But, above all,' she wrote, 'night and day, I thank the good God for having so arranged our lives that our dear Armand will never know that his mother, who adores him, belongs to the race that is cursed with the brand of slavery.'

A Turkey Hunt

Three of Madame's finest bronze turkeys were missing from the brood. It was nearing Christmas, and that was the reason, perhaps, that even Monsieur grew agitated when the discovery was made. The news was brought to the house by Sévérin's boy, who had seen the troop at noon a half-mile up the bayou three short. Others reported the deficiency as even greater. So, at about two in the afternoon, though a cold drizzle had begun to fall, popular feeling in the matter was so strong that all the household forces turned out to search for the missing gobblers.

Alice, the housemaid, went down the river, and Polisson[159] the yard-boy, went up the bayou. Others crossed the fields, and Artemise was rather vaguely instructed to, 'Go look too.'

Artemise is in some respects an extraordinary person. In age she's anywhere between ten and fifteen, with a head not unlike, in shape and appearance, a dark chocolate-coloured Easter-egg. She talks almost wholly in monosyllables, and has big round glassy eyes, which she fixes upon one with the placid gaze of an Egyptian sphinx.

The morning after my arrival at the plantation, I was awakened by the rattling of cups at my bedside. It was Artemise with the early coffee.

'Is it cold out?' I asked by way of conversation, as I sipped the tiny cup of ink-black coffee.

'Ya, 'm.'

'Where do you sleep, Artemise?' I further enquired, with the same intention as before.

'In uh hole,' was precisely what she said, with a pumplike motion of the arm that she habitually uses to indicate a locality. What she meant was that she slept in the hall.

Again, another time, she came with an armful of wood, and having deposited it upon the hearth, turned to stare fixedly at me, with folded hands.

'Did Madame send you to build a fire, Artemise?' I hastened to ask, feeling uncomfortable under the look.

'Ya, 'm.'

'Very well; make it.'

'Matches!' was all she said.

There happened to be no matches in my room, and she evidently considered that all personal responsibility ceased in face of this first and not very serious obstacle. Pages might be told of her unfathomable ways; but to the turkey hunt.

All afternoon the searching party kept returning, singly and in couples, and in a more or less bedraggled condition. All brought unfavourable reports. Nothing could be seen of the missing fowls. Artemise had been absent probably an hour when she glided into the hall where the family was assembled, and stood with crossed hands and contemplative air beside the fire. We could see by the benign expression of her countenance that she possibly had information to give, if any inducement were offered her in the shape of a question.

'Have you found the turkeys, Artemise?' Madame hastened to ask.

'Ya, 'm.'

'You Artemise!' shouted Aunt Florindy, the cook, who was passing through the hall with a batch of newly baked light bread. 'She's a-lyin', mist'ess, if dey ever was! *You* foun' dem turkeys?' turning upon the child. 'Whar was you at, de whole blesse' time? Warn't you stan'in' plank up agin de back o' de hen-'ous'? Never budged a inch? Don't jaw me down, gal; don't jaw me!' Artemise was only gazing at Aunt Florindy with unruffled calm. 'I warn't gwine tell on 'er, but arter dat untroof, I boun' to.'

'Let her alone, Aunt Florindy,' Madame interfered. 'Where are the turkeys, Artemise?'

'Yon'a,' she simply articulated, bringing the pump-handle motion of her arm into play.

'Where "yonder"?' Madame demanded, a little impatiently.

'In uh hen-'ous'!'

Sure enough! The three missing turkeys had been accidentally locked up in the morning when the chickens were fed.

Artemise, for some unknown reason, had hidden herself during the search behind the hen-house, and had heard their muffled gobble.

Madame Célestin's Divorce

Madame Célestin always wore a neat and snugly fitting calico wrapper when she went out in the morning to sweep her small gallery. Lawyer Paxton thought she looked very pretty in the grey one that was made with a graceful Watteau fold[160] at the back: and with which she invariably wore a bow of pink ribbon at the throat. She was always sweeping her gallery when lawyer Paxton passed by in the morning on his way to his office in St Denis Street.

Sometimes he stopped and leaned over the fence to say good-morning at his ease; to criticise or admire her rose bushes; or, when he had time enough, to hear what she had to say. Madame Célestin usually had a good deal to say. She would gather up the train of her calico wrapper in one hand, and balancing the broom gracefully in the other, would go tripping down to where the lawyer leaned, as comfortably as he could, over her picket fence.

Of course, she had talked to him of her troubles. Everyone knew Madame Célestin's troubles.

'Really, madame,' he told her once, in his deliberate, calculating, lawyer-tone, 'it's more than human nature – woman's nature – should be called upon to endure. Here you are, working your fingers off' – she glanced down at two rosy fingertips that showed through the rents in her baggy doeskin gloves – 'taking in sewing; giving music lessons; doing God knows what in the way of manual labour to support yourself and those two little ones' – Madame Célestin's pretty face beamed with satisfaction at this enumeration of her trials.

'You right, judge. Not a picayune, not one, not one, have I lay my eyes on in the pas' fo' months that I can say Célestin give it to me or sen' it to me.'

'The scoundrel!' muttered lawyer Paxton in his beard.

'An' *pourtant*,'[161] she resumed, 'they say he's making money down roun' Alexandria w'en he wants to work.'

'I dare say you haven't seen him for months?' suggested the lawyer.

'It's good six month' since I see a sight of Célestin,' she admitted.

'That's it, that's what I say; he has practically deserted you; fails to support you. It wouldn't surprise me a bit to learn that he has ill treated you.'

'Well, you know, judge,' with an evasive cough, 'a man that drinks –
w'at can you expec'? An' if you would know the promises he has made
me! Ah, If I had as many dolla' as I had promise from Célestin, I wouldn'
have to work, *je vous garantis*.'[162]

'And in my opinion, madame, you would be a foolish woman to
endure it longer, when the divorce court is there to offer you redress.'

'You spoke about that befo', judge: I'm goin' think about that divo'ce.
I believe you right.'

Madame Célestin thought about the divorce and talked about it, too;
and lawyer Paxton grew deeply interested in the theme.

'You know, about that divo'ce, judge,' Madame Célestin was waiting
for him that morning, 'I been talking to my family an' my frien's, an' it's
me that tells you, they all plumb agains' that divo'ce.'

'Certainly, to be sure; that's to be expected, madame, in this community of Creoles. I warned you that you would meet with opposition,
and would have to face it and brave it.'

'Oh, don't fear, I'm going to face it! Maman says it's a disgrace like
it's neva been in the family. But it's good for Maman to talk, her. W'at
trouble she ever had? She says I mus' go by all means consult with Père
Duchéron – it's my confessor, you undastan' – Well, I'll go, judge, to
please Maman. But all the confessor' in the worl' ent goin' make me put
up with that conduc' of Célestin any longa.'

A day or two later, she was there waiting for him again. 'You know,
judge, about that divo'ce.'

'Yes, yes,' responded the lawyer, well pleased to trace a new determination in her brown eyes and in the curves of her pretty mouth. 'I suppose
you saw Père Duchéron and had to brave it out with him, too.'

'Oh, fo' that, a perfec' sermon, I assho you. A talk of giving scandal
an' bad example that I thought would neva en'! He says, fo' him, he
wash' his hands; I mus' go see the bishop.'

'You won't let the bishop dissuade you, I trust,' stammered the lawyer,
more anxiously than he could well understand.

'You don't know me yet, judge,' laughed Madame Célestin with a
turn of the head and a flirt of the broom which indicated that the
interview was at an end.

'Well, Madame Célestin! And the bishop!' Lawyer Paxton was
standing there holding to a couple of the shaky pickets. She had not
seen him. 'Oh, it's you, judge?' and she hastened towards him with an
empressement[163] that could not but have been flattering.

'Yes, I saw Monseigneur,' she began. The lawyer had already gathered
from her expressive countenance that she had not wavered in her

determination. 'Ah, he's a eloquent man. It's not a mo' eloquent man in Natchitoches parish. I was fo'ced to cry, the way he talked to me about my troubles; how he undastan's them, an' feels for me. It would move even you, judge, to hear how he talk' about that step I want to take; its danga, its temptation. How it is the duty of a Catholic to stan' everything till the las' extreme. An' that life of retirement an' self-denial I would have to lead – he tole me all that.'

'But he hasn't turned you from your resolve, I see,' laughed the lawyer complacently.

'For that, no,' she returned emphatically. 'The bishop don't know w'at it is to be married to a man like Célestin, an' have to endu' that conduc' like I have to endu' it. The Pope himse'f can't make me stan' that any longer, if you say I got the right in the law to sen' Célestin sailing.'

A noticeable change had come over lawyer Paxton. He discarded his work-day coat and began to wear his Sunday one to the office. He grew solicitous as to the shine of his boots, his collar and the set of his tie. He brushed and trimmed his whiskers with a care that had not before been apparent. Then he fell into a stupid habit of dreaming as he walked the streets of the old town. It would be very good to take unto himself a wife, he dreamed. And he could dream of no other than pretty Madame Célestin filling that sweet and sacred office as she filled his thoughts, now. Old Natchitoches would not hold them comfortably, perhaps; but the world was surely wide enough to live in, outside of Natchitoches town.

His heart beat in a strangely irregular manner as he neared Madame Célestin's house one morning and discovered her behind the rose bushes, as usual plying her broom. She had finished the gallery and steps and was sweeping the little brick walk along the edge of the violet border.

'Good-morning, Madame Célestin.'

'Ah, it's you, judge? Good-morning.' He waited. She seemed to be doing the same. Then she ventured, with some hesitancy, 'You know, judge, about that divo'ce. I been thinking – I reckon you betta neva mine about that divo'ce.' She was making deep rings in the palm of her gloved hand with the end of the broom-handle, and looking at them critically. Her face seemed to the lawyer to be unusually rosy; but maybe it was only the reflection of the pink bow at the throat. 'Yes, I reckon you needn' mine. You see, judge, Célestin came home las' night. An' he's promise me on his word an' honour he's going to turn ova a new leaf.'

Love on the Bon-Dieu

Upon the pleasant veranda of Père Antoine's[164] cottage, that adjoined the church, a young girl had long been seated, awaiting his return. It was the eve of Easter Sunday, and since early afternoon the priest had been engaged in hearing the confessions of those who wished to make their Easters the following day. The girl did not seem impatient at his delay; on the contrary, it was very restful to her to lie back in the big chair she had found there and peep through the thick curtain of vines at the people who occasionally passed along the village street.

She was slender, with a frailness that indicated lack of wholesome and plentiful nourishment. A pathetic, uneasy look was in her grey eyes, and even faintly stamped her features, which were fine and delicate. In lieu of a hat, a *barège*[165] veil covered her light brown and abundant hair. She wore a coarse white cotton 'josie',[166] and a blue calico skirt that only half concealed her tattered shoes.

As she sat there, she held carefully in her lap a parcel of eggs securely fastened in a red bandana handkerchief.

Twice already a handsome, stalwart young man in quest of the priest had entered the yard, and penetrated to where she sat. At first they had exchanged the uncompromising 'howdy' of strangers, and nothing more. The second time, finding the priest still absent, he hesitated to go at once. Instead, he stood upon the step, and narrowing his brown eyes, gazed beyond the river, off towards the west, where a murky streak of mist was spreading across the sun.

'It look like mo' rain,' he remarked, slowly and carelessly.

'We done had 'bout 'nough,' she replied, in much the same tone.

'It's no chance to thin out the cotton,' he went on.

'An' the Bon-Dieu,' she resumed, 'it's on'y today you can cross him on foot.'

'You live yonda on the Bon-Dieu, *donc*?' he asked, looking at her for the first time since he had spoken.

'Yas, by Nid d'Hibout, m'sieur.'

Instinctive courtesy held him from questioning her further. But he seated himself on the step, evidently determined to wait there for the priest. He said no more, but sat scanning critically the steps, the porch and pillar beside him, from which he occasionally tore away little pieces of detached wood, where it was beginning to rot at its base.

A click at the side gate that communicated with the churchyard soon announced Père Antoine's return. He came hurriedly across the garden-path, between the tall, lusty rose bushes that lined either side of it, which were now fragrant with blossoms. His long, flapping cassock added something of height to his undersized, middle-aged figure, as did the skullcap which rested securely back on his head. He saw only the young man at first, who rose at his approach.

'Well, Azenor,' he called cheerily in French, extending his hand. 'How is this? I expected you all the week.'

'Yes, monsieur; but I knew well what you wanted with me, and I was finishing the doors for Gros-Léon's new house;' saying which, he drew back, and indicated by a motion and look that someone was present who had a prior claim upon Père Antoine's attention.

'Ah, Lalie!' the priest exclaimed, when he had mounted to the porch, and saw her there behind the vines. 'Have you been waiting here since you confessed? Surely an hour ago!'

'Yes, monsieur.'

'You should rather have made some visits in the village, child.'

'I am not acquainted with anyone in the village,' she returned.

The priest, as he spoke, had drawn a chair, and seated himself beside her, with his hands comfortably clasping his knees. He wanted to know how things were out on the bayou.

'And how is the grandmother?' he asked. 'As cross and crabbed as ever? And with that' – he added reflectively – 'good for ten years yet! I said only yesterday to Butrand – you know Butrand, he works on Le Blôt's Bon-Dieu place – "And that Madame Zidore: how is it with her, Butrand? I believe God has forgotten her here on earth." "It isn't that, your reverence," said Butrand, "but it's neither God nor the Devil that wants her!"' And Père Antoine laughed with a jovial frankness that took all sting of ill-nature from his very pointed remarks.

Lalie did not reply when he spoke of her grandmother; she only pressed her lips firmly together, and picked nervously at the red bandana.

'I have come to ask, Monsieur Antoine,' she began, lower than she needed to speak – for Azenor had withdrawn at once to the far end of the porch – 'to ask if you will give me a little scrap of paper – a piece of writing for Monsieur Chartrand at the store over there. I want new shoes and stockings for Easter, and I have brought eggs to trade for them. He says he is willing, yes, if he was sure I would bring more every week till the shoes are paid for.'

With good-natured indifference, Père Antoine wrote the order that the girl desired. He was too familiar with distress to feel keenly for a girl who was able to buy Easter shoes and pay for them with eggs.

She went immediately away then, after shaking hands with the priest, and sending a quick glance of her pathetic eyes towards Azenor, who had turned when he heard her rise, and nodded when he caught the look. Through the vines he watched her cross the village street.

'How is it that you do not know Lalie, Azenor? You surely must have seen her pass your house often. It lies on her way to the Bon-Dieu.'

'No, I don't know her; I have never seen her,' the young man replied, as he seated himself – after the priest – and kept his eyes absently fixed on the store across the road, where he had seen her enter.

'She is the granddaughter of that Madame Izidore – '

'What! Ma'ame Zidore whom they drove off the island last winter?'

'Yes, yes. Well, you know, they say the old woman stole wood and things – I don't know how true it is – and destroyed people's property out of pure malice.'

'And she lives now on the Bon-Dieu?'

'Yes, on Le Blôt's place, in a perfect wreck of a cabin. You see, she gets it for nothing; not a negro on the place but has refused to live in it.'

'Surely, it can't be that old abandoned hovel near the swamp, that Michon occupied ages ago?'

'That is the one, the very one.'

'And the girl lives there with that old wretch?' the young man marvelled.

'Old wretch to be sure, Azenor. But what can you expect from a woman who never crosses the threshold of God's house – who even tried to hinder the child doing so as well? But I went to her. I said: "See here, Madame Zidore" – you know it's my way to handle such people without gloves – "you may damn your soul if you choose," I told her, "that is a privilege which we all have; but none of us has a right to imperil the salvation of another. I want to see Lalie at mass hereafter on Sundays, or you will hear from me;" and I shook my stick under her nose. Since then the child has never missed a Sunday. But she is half starved, you can see that. You saw how shabby she is – how broken her shoes are? She is at Chartrand's now, trading for new ones with those eggs she brought, poor thing! There is no doubt of her being ill-treated. Butrand says he thinks Madame Zidore even beats the child. I don't know how true it is, for no power can make her utter a word against her grandmother.'

Azenor, whose face was a kind and sensitive one, had paled with distress as the priest spoke; and now at these final words he quivered as though he felt the sting of a cruel blow upon his own flesh.

But no more was said of Lalie, for Père Antoine drew the young man's attention to the carpenter-work which he wished to entrust to him. When they had talked the matter over in all its lengthy details, Azenor mounted his horse and rode away.

A moment's gallop carried him outside the village. Then came a half-mile strip along the river to cover. Then the lane to enter, in which stood his dwelling midway, upon a low, pleasant knoll.

As Azenor turned into the lane, he saw the figure of Lalie far ahead of him. Somehow he had expected to find her there, and he watched her again, as he had done through Père Antoine's vines. When she passed his house, he wondered if she would turn to look at it. But she did not. How could she know it was his? Upon reaching it himself, he did not enter the yard, but stood there motionless, his eyes always fastened upon the girl's figure. He could not see, away off there, how coarse her garments were. She seemed, through the distance that divided them, as slim and delicate as a flower-stalk. He stayed till she reached the turn of the lane and disappeared into the woods.

*

Mass had not yet begun when Azenor tiptoed into church on Easter morning. He did not take his place with the congregation, but stood close to the holy-water font, and watched the people who entered.

Almost every girl who passed him wore a white mull,[167] a dotted swiss or a fresh-starched muslin, at least. They were bright with ribbons that hung from their persons, and flowers that bedecked their hats. Some carried fans and cambric handkerchiefs. Most of them wore gloves, and were odorant of *poudre de riz* and nice toilet-waters; while all carried gay little baskets filled with Easter-eggs.

But there was one who came empty-handed, save for the worn prayer-book which she bore. It was Lalie, the veil upon her head, and wearing the blue print and cotton bodice which she had worn the day before.

He dipped his hand into the holy water when she came, and held it out to her, though he had not thought of doing this for the others. She touched his fingers with the tips of her own, making a slight inclination as she did so; and after a deep genuflection before the Blessed Sacrament, passed on to the side. He was not sure if she had known him. He knew she had not looked into his eyes, for he would have felt it.

He was angered against other young women who passed him, because of their flowers and ribbons, when she wore none. He himself did not care, but he feared she might, and watched her narrowly to see if she did.

But it was plain that Lalie did not care. Her face, as she seated herself, settled into the same restful lines it had worn yesterday, when she sat in Père Antoine's big chair. It seemed good to her to be there. Sometimes she looked up at the little coloured panes through which the Easter sun was streaming; then at the flaming candles, like stars; or at the embowered figures of Joseph and Mary, flanking the central tabernacle which shrouded the risen Christ. Yet she liked just as well to watch the young girls in their spring freshness, or sensuously to inhale the mingled odour of flowers and incense that filled the temple.

Lalie was among the last to quit the church. When she walked down the clean pathway that led from it to the road, she looked with pleased curiosity towards the groups of men and maidens who were gayly matching their Easter-eggs under the shade of the chinaberry trees.

Azenor was among them, and when he saw her coming solitary down the path, he approached her and, with a smile, extended his hat, whose crown was quite lined with the pretty coloured eggs.

'You mus' of forgot to bring aiggs,' he said. 'Take some o' mine.'

'*Non, merci,*' she replied, flushing and drawing back.

But he urged them anew upon her. Much pleased, then, she bent her pretty head over the hat, and was evidently puzzled to make a selection among so many that were beautiful.

He picked out one for her – a pink one, dotted with white-clover leaves.

'Yere,' he said, handing it to her, 'I think this is the pretties'; an' it look' strong too. I'm sho' it will break all of the res'.' And he playfully held out another, half-hidden in his fist, for her to try its strength upon. But she refused to. She would not risk the ruin of her pretty egg. Then she walked away, without once having noticed that the girls, whom Azenor had left, were looking curiously at her.

When he rejoined them, he was hardly prepared for their greeting; it startled him.

'How come you talk to that girl? She's real *canaille*,[168] her,' was what one of them said to him.

'Who say' so? Who say she's *canaille*? If it's a man, I'll smash 'is head!' he exclaimed, livid. They all laughed merrily at this.

'An' if it's a lady, Azenor? W'at you goin' to do 'bout it?' asked another, quizzingly.

'T ain' no lady. No lady would say that 'bout a po' girl, w'at she don't even know.'

He turned away, and emptying all his eggs into the hat of a little urchin who stood near, walked out of the churchyard. He did not stop to exchange another word with anyone; neither with the men who stood all *endimanchés*[169] before the stores, nor the women who were mounting upon horses and into vehicles or walking in groups to their homes.

He took a short cut across the cotton-field that extended back of the town, and walking rapidly, soon reached his home. It was a pleasant house of few rooms and many windows, with fresh air blowing through from every side; his workshop was beside it. A broad strip of greensward, studded here and there with trees, sloped down to the road.

Azenor entered the kitchen, where an amiable old black woman was chopping onion and sage at a table.

'Tranquiline,' he said abruptly, 'they's a young girl goin' to pass yere afta a w'ile. She's got a blue dress an' w'ite josie on, an' a veil on her head. W'en you see her, I want you to go to the road an' make her res' there on the bench, an' ask her if she don't want a cup o' coffee. I saw her go to communion, me; so she didn't eat any breakfas'. Eve'ybody else f'om out o' town, that went to communion, got invited somew'ere another. It's enough to make a person sick to see such meanness.'

'An' you want me ter go down to de gate, jis' so, an' ax 'er pineblank ef she wants some coffee?' asked the bewildered Tranquiline.

'I don't care if you ask her poin' blank o' not; but you do like I say.'

Tranquiline was leaning over the gate when Lalie came along.

'Howdy,' offered the woman.

'Howdy,' the girl returned.

'Did you see a yalla calf wid black spots a t'arin' down de lane, missy?'

'*Non*; not yalla, an' not with black spot'. *Mais* I see one li'le w'ite calf tie by a rope, yonda 'roun' the ben'.'

'Dat warn't hit. Dis heah one was yalla. I hope he done flung hisse'f down de bank an' broke his nake. Sarve 'im right! But whar you come f'om, chile? You look plum wo' out. Set down dah on dat bench, an' le' me fotch you a cup o' coffee.'

Azenor had already in his eagerness arranged a tray, upon which was a smoking cup of *café au lait*. He had buttered and jellied generous slices of bread, and was searching wildly for something when Tranquiline re-entered.

'W'at become o' that half of chicken-pie, Tranquiline, that was yere in the *garde manger*[170] yesterday?'

'W'at chicken-pie? W'at *garde manger*?' blustered the woman.

'Like we got mo' 'en one *garde manger* in the house, Tranquiline!'

'You jis' like ole Ma'ame Azenor use' to be, you is! You 'spec' chicken-

pie gwine las' etarnal? W'en some'pin done sp'ilt, I flings it' way. Dat's
me – dat's Tranquiline!'

So Azenor resigned himself – what else could he do? – and sent the
tray, incomplete, as he fancied it, out to Lalie.

He trembled at thought of what he did; he, whose nerves were usually
as steady as some piece of steel mechanism.

Would it anger her if she suspected? Would it please her if she knew?
Would she say this or that to Tranquiline? And would Tranquiline tell
him truly what she said – how she looked?

As it was Sunday, Azenor did not work that afternoon. Instead, he
took a book out under the trees, as he often did, and sat reading it, from
the first sound of the Vesper bell, that came faintly across the fields, till
the angelus. All that time! He turned many a page, yet in the end did
not know what he had read. With his pencil he had traced 'Lalie' upon
every margin, and was saying it softly to himself.

*

Another Sunday Azenor saw Lalie at mass – and again. Once he walked
with her and showed her the short cut across the cotton-field. She was
very glad that day, and told him she was going to work – her grandmother said she might. She was going to hoe, up in the fields with
Monsieur Le Blôt's hands. He entreated her not to; and when she asked
his reason, he could not tell her, but turned and tore shyly and savagely
at the elder-blossoms that grew along the fence.

Then they stopped where she was going to cross the fence from the
field into the lane. He wanted to tell her that was his house which they
could see not far away; but he did not dare to, since he had fed her there
on the morning she was hungry.

'An' you say yo' gran'ma's goin' to let you work? She keeps you f'om
workin', *donc*?' He wanted to question her about her grandmother, and
could think of no other way to begin.

'Po' ole *grand'mère*!' she answered. 'I don' b'lieve she know mos' time
w'at she's doin'. Sometime she say' I aint no betta an' one nigga, an' she
fo'ce me to work. Then she say she know I'm goin' be one *canaille* like
maman, an' she make me set down still, like she would want to kill me if
I would move. Her, she on'y want' to be out in the wood', day an' night,
day an' night. She ain' got her right head, po' *grand'mère*. I know she
ain't.'

Lalie had spoken low and in jerks, as if every word gave her pain.
Azenor could feel her distress as plainly as he saw it. He wanted to say
something to her – to do something for her. But her mere presence

paralysed him into inactivity – except his pulses, that beat like hammers when he was with her. Such a poor, shabby little thing as she was, too!

'I'm goin' to wait yere nex' Sunday fo' you, Lalie,' he said, when the fence was between them. And he thought he had said something very daring.

But the next Sunday she did not come. She was neither at the appointed place of meeting in the lane, nor was she at mass. Her absence – so unexpected – affected Azenor like a calamity. Late in the afternoon, when he could stand the trouble and bewilderment of it no longer, he went and leaned over Père Antoine's fence. The priest was picking the slugs from his roses on the other side.

'That young girl from the Bon-Dieu,' said Azenor – 'she was not at mass today. I suppose her grandmother has forgotten your warning.'

'No,' answered the priest. 'The child is ill, I hear. Butrand tells me she has been ill for several days from overwork in the fields. I shall go out tomorrow to see about her. I would go today, if I could.'

'The child is ill,' was all Azenor heard or understood of Père Antoine's words. He turned and walked resolutely away, like one who determines suddenly upon action after meaningless hesitation.

He walked towards his home and past it, as if it were a spot that did not concern him. He went on down the lane and into the wood where he had seen Lalie disappear that day.

Here all was shadow, for the sun had dipped too low in the west to send a single ray through the dense foliage of the forest.

Now that he found himself on the way to Lalie's home, he strove to understand why he had not gone there before. He often visited other girls in the village and neighbourhood – why not have gone to her, as well? The answer lay too deep in his heart for him to be more than half-conscious of it. Fear had kept him – dread to see her desolate life face to face. He did not know how he could bear it.

But now he was going to her at last. She was ill. He would stand upon that dismantled porch that he could just remember. Doubtless Ma'ame Zidore would come out to know his will, and he would tell her that Père Antoine had sent to enquire how Mamzelle Lalie was. No! Why drag in Père Antoine? He would simply stand boldly and say, 'Ma'ame Zidore, I learn that Lalie is ill. I have come to know if it is true, and to see her, if I may.'

When Azenor reached the cabin where Lalie dwelt, all sign of day had vanished. Dusk had fallen swiftly after the sunset. The moss that hung heavy from the great live-oak branches was making fantastic silhouettes against the eastern sky that the big, round moon was beginning to light.

Off in the swamp beyond the bayou, hundreds of dismal voices were droning a lullaby. Upon the hovel itself, a stillness like death rested.

Oftener than once Azenor tapped upon the door, which was closed as well as it could be, without obtaining a reply. He finally approached one of the small unglazed windows, in which coarse mosquito-netting had been fastened, and looked into the room.

By the moonlight slanting in he could see Lalie stretched upon a bed; but of Ma'ame Zidore there was no sign. 'Lalie!' he called softly. 'Lalie!'

The girl slightly moved her head upon the pillow. Then he boldly opened the door and entered.

Upon a wretched bed, over which was spread a cover of patched calico, Lalie lay, her frail body only half concealed by the single garment that was upon it. One hand was plunged beneath her pillow; the other, which was free, he touched. It was as hot as flame; so was her head. He knelt sobbing upon the floor beside her, and called her his love and his soul. He begged her to speak a word to him – to look at him. But she only muttered disjointedly that the cotton was all turning to ashes in the fields, and the blades of the corn were in flames.

If he was choked with love and grief to see her so, he was moved by anger as well; rage against himself, against Père Antoine, against the people upon the plantation and in the village, who had so abandoned a helpless creature to misery and maybe death. Because she had been silent – had not lifted her voice in complaint – they believed she suffered no more than she could bear.

But surely the people could not be utterly without heart. There must be one somewhere with the spirit of Christ. Père Antoine would tell him of such a one, and he would carry Lalie to her – out of this atmosphere of death. He was in haste to be gone with her. He fancied every moment of delay was a fresh danger threatening her life.

He folded the rude bed-cover over Lalie's naked limbs, and lifted her in his arms. She made no resistance. She seemed only loath to withdraw her hand from beneath the pillow. When she did, he saw that she held lightly but firmly clasped in her encircling fingers the pretty Easter-egg he had given her! He uttered a low cry of exultation as the full significance of this came over him. If she had hung for hours upon his neck telling him that she loved him, he could not have known it more surely than by this sign. Azenor felt as if some mysterious bond had all at once drawn them heart to heart and made them one.

No need now to go from door to door begging admittance for her. She was his. She belonged to him. He knew now where her place was, whose roof must shelter her, and whose arms protect her.

So Azenor, with his loved one in his arms, walked through the forest, sure-footed as a panther. Once, as he walked, he could hear in the distance the weird chant which Ma'ame Zidore was crooning – to the moon, maybe – as she gathered her wood.

Once, where the water was trickling cool through rocks, he stopped to lave Lalie's hot cheeks and hands and forehead. He had not once touched his lips to her. But now, when a sudden great fear came upon him because she did not know him, instinctively he pressed his lips upon hers that were parched and burning. He held them there till hers were soft and pliant from the healthy moisture of his own.

Then she knew him. She did not tell him so, but her stiffened fingers relaxed their tense hold upon the Easter bauble. It fell to the ground as she twined her arm around his neck; and he understood.

*

'Stay close by her, Tranquiline,' said Azenor, when he had laid Lalie upon his own couch at home. 'I'm goin' for the doctor en' for Père Antoine. Not because she is goin' to die,' he added hastily, seeing the awe that crept into the woman's face at mention of the priest. 'She is goin' to live! Do you think I would let my wife die, Tranquiline?'

Loka

She was a half-breed Indian girl, with hardly a rag to her back. To the ladies of the Band of United Endeavour[171] who questioned her, she said her name was Loka, and she did not know where she belonged, unless it was on Bayou Choctaw.

She had appeared one day at the side door of Frobissaint's 'oyster saloon' in Natchitoches, asking for food. Frobissaint, a practical philanthropist, engaged her on the spot as tumbler-washer.

She was not successful at that; she broke too many tumblers. But, as Frobissaint charged her for the broken glasses, he did not mind, until she began to break them over the heads of his customers. Then he seized her by the wrist and dragged her before the Band of United Endeavour, then in session around the corner. This was considerate on Frobissaint's part, for he could have dragged her just as well to the police station.

Loka was not beautiful, as she stood in her red calico rags before the scrutinising band. Her coarse, black, unkempt hair framed a broad, swarthy face without a redeeming feature, except eyes that were not bad; slow in their movements, but frank eyes enough. She was big-boned and clumsy.

She did not know how old she was. The minister's wife reckoned she might be sixteen. The judge's wife thought that it made no difference. The doctor's wife suggested that the girl have a bath and change before she be handled, even in discussion. The motion was not seconded. Loka's ultimate disposal was an urgent and difficult consideration.

Someone mentioned a reformatory. Everyone else objected.

Madame Laballière,[172] the planter's wife, knew a respectable family of 'Cadians living some miles below, who, she thought, would give the girl a home, with benefit to all concerned. The 'Cadian woman was a deserving one, with a large family of small children, who had all her own work to do. The husband cropped in a modest way. Loka would not only be taught to work at the Padues', but would receive a good moral training beside.

That settled it. Everyone agreed with the planter's wife that it was a chance in a thousand; and Loka was sent to sit on the steps outside, while the band proceeded to the business next in order.

Loka was afraid of treading upon the little Padues when she first got among them – there were so many of them – and her feet were like leaden weights, encased in the strong brogans with which the band had equipped her.

Madame Padue, a small, black-eyed, aggressive woman, questioned her in a sharp, direct fashion peculiar to herself.

'How come you don't talk French, you?'

Loka shrugged her shoulders. 'I kin talk English good's anybody; an' lit' bit Choctaw, too,' she offered, apologetically.

'*Ma foi*, you kin fo'git yo' Choctaw. Soona the betta for me. Now if you willin', an' ent too lazy an' sassy, we'll git 'long somehow. *Vrai sauvage ça*,'[173] she muttered under her breath, as she turned to initiate Loka into some of her new duties.

She herself was a worker. A good deal more fussy one than her easy-going husband and children thought necessary or agreeable. Loka's slow ways and heavy motions aggravated her. It was in vain Monsieur Padue expostulated: 'She's on'y a chile, rememba, Tontine.'

'She's *vrai sauvage*, that's w'at. It's got to be work out of her,' was Tontine's only reply to such remonstrance.

The girl was indeed so deliberate about her tasks that she had to be urged constantly to accomplish the amount of labour that Tontine required of her. Moreover, she carried to her work a stolid indifference that was exasperating. Whether at the washtub, scrubbing the floors, weeding the garden, or learning her lessons and catechism with the children on Sundays, it was the same.

It was only when entrusted with the care of little Bibine, the baby, that Loka crept somewhat out of her apathy. She grew very fond of him. No wonder; such a baby as he was! So good, so fat, and complaisant! He had such a way of clasping Loka's broad face between his pudgy fists and savagely biting her chin with his hard, toothless gums! Such a way of bouncing in her arms as if he were mounted upon springs! At his antics the girl would laugh a wholesome, ringing laugh that was good to hear.

She was left alone to watch and nurse him one day. An accommodating neighbour who had become the possessor of a fine new spring wagon passed by just after the noon-hour meal, and offered to take the whole family on a jaunt to town. The offer was all the more tempting as Tontine had some long-delayed shopping to do; and the opportunity to equip the children with shoes and summer hats could not be slighted. So away they all went. All but Bibine, who was left swinging in his *branle* with only Loka for company.

This *branle* consisted of a strong circular piece of cotton cloth, securely but slackly fastened to a large, stout hoop suspended by three light cords to a hook in a rafter of the gallery. The baby who has not swung in a *branle* does not know the quintessence of baby luxury. In each of the four rooms of the house was a hook from which to hang this swing.

Often it was taken out under the trees. But today it swung in the shade of the open gallery; and Loka sat beside it, giving it now and then a slight impetus that sent it circling in slow, sleep-inspiring undulations.

Bibine kicked and cooed as long as he was able. But Loka was humming a monotonous lullaby; the *branle* was swaying to and fro, the warm air fanning him deliciously; and Bibine was soon fast asleep.

Seeing this, Loka quietly let down the mosquito net, to protect the child's slumber from the intrusion of the many insects that were swarming in the summer air.

Singularly enough, there was no work for her to do; and Tontine, in her hurried departure, had failed to provide for the emergency. The washing and ironing were over; the floors had been scrubbed, and the rooms righted; the yard swept; the chickens fed; vegetables picked and washed. There was absolutely nothing to do, and Loka gave herself up to the dreams of idleness.

As she sat comfortably back in the roomy rocker, she let her eyes sweep lazily across the country. Away off to the right peeped up, from amid densely clustered trees, the pointed roofs and long pipe of the steam-gin of Laballière's. No other habitation was visible except a few low, flat dwellings far over the river that could hardly be seen.

The immense plantation took up all the land in sight. The few acres that Baptiste Padue cultivated were his own, that Laballière, out of friendly consideration, had sold to him. Baptiste's fine crop of cotton and corn was 'laid by' just now, waiting for rain; and Baptiste had gone with the rest of the family to town. Beyond the river and the field and everywhere about were dense woods.

Loka's gaze, that had been slowly travelling along the edge of the horizon, finally fastened upon the woods, and stayed there. Into her eyes came the absent look of one whose thought is projected into the future or the past, leaving the present blank. She was seeing a vision. It had come with a whiff that the strong south breeze had blown to her from the woods.

She was seeing old Marot, the squaw who drank whiskey and plaited baskets and beat her. There was something, after all, in being beaten, if only to scream out and fight back, as at that time in Natchitoches, when she broke a glass on the head of a man who laughed at her and pulled her hair, and called her 'fool names'.

Old Marot wanted her to steal and cheat, to beg and lie, when they went out with the baskets to sell. Loka did not want to. She did not like to. That was why she had run away – and because she was beaten. But – but ah! the scent of the sassafras leaves hanging to dry in the shade! The pungent camomile! The sound of the bayou tumbling over that old slimy log! Only to lie there for hours and watch the glistening lizards glide in and out was worth a beating.

She knew the birds must be singing in chorus out there in the woods where the grey moss was hanging, and the trumpet-vine trailing from the trees, spangled with blossoms. In spirit she heard the songsters.

She wondered if Choctaw Joe and Sambite played dice every night by the campfire as they used to do; and if they still fought and slashed each other when wild with drink. How good it felt to walk with moccasined feet over the springy turf, under the trees! What fun to trap the squirrels, to skin the otter; to take those swift flights on the pony that Choctaw Joe had stolen from the Texans!

Loka sat motionless; only her breast heaved tumultuously. Her heart was aching with savage homesickness. She could not feel just then that the sin and pain of that life were anything beside the joy of its freedom.

Loka was sick for the woods. She felt she must die if she could not get back to them, and to her vagabond life. Was there anything to hinder her? She stooped and unlaced the brogans that were chafing her feet, removed them and her stockings, and threw the things away from her. She stood up all a-quiver, panting, ready for flight.

But there was a sound that stopped her. It was little Bibine, cooing, sputtering, battling hands and feet with the mosquito net that he had dragged over his face. The girl uttered a sob as she reached down for the baby she had grown to love so, and clasped him in her arms. She could not go and leave Bibine behind.

*

Tontine began to grumble at once when she discovered that Loka was not at hand to receive them on their return.

'*Bon!*' she exclaimed. 'Now w'ere is that Loka? Ah, that girl, she aggravates me too much. Firs' thing she knows I'm goin' sen' her straight back to them ban' of lady w'ere she come frum.'

'Loka!' she called, in short, sharp tones, as she traversed the house and peered into each room. 'Lo-ka!' She cried loudly enough to be heard half a mile away when she got out upon the back gallery. Again and again she called.

Baptiste was exchanging the discomfort of his Sunday coat for the accustomed ease of shirt sleeves.

'*Mais* don't git so excite, Tontine,' he implored. 'I'm sho she's yonda to the crib shellin' co'n, or somew'ere like that.'

'Run, François, you, an' see to the crib,' the mother commanded. 'Bibine mus' be starve! Run to the hen-house an' look, Juliette. Maybe she's fall asleep in some corna. That'll learn me 'notha time to go trus' *une pareille sauvage*[174] with my baby, *va*!'

When it was discovered that Loka was nowhere in the immediate vicinity, Tontine was furious.

'*Pas possible* she's walk to Laballière, with Bibine!' she exclaimed.

'I'll saddle the hoss an' go see, Tontine,' interposed Baptiste, who was beginning to share his wife's uneasiness.

'Go, go, Baptiste,' she urged. 'An' you, boys, run yonda down the road to ole Aunt Judy's cabin an' see.'

It was found that Loka had not been seen at Laballière's, nor at Aunt Judy's cabin; that she had not taken the boat, that was still fastened to its moorings down the bank. Then Tontine's excitement left her. She turned pale and sat quietly down in her room, with an unnatural calm that frightened the children.

Some of them began to cry. Baptiste walked restlessly about, anxiously scanning the country in all directions. A wretched hour dragged by. The sun had set, leaving hardly an afterglow, and in a little while the twilight that falls so swiftly would be there.

Baptiste was preparing to mount his horse, to start out again on the round he had already been over. Tontine sat in the same state of intense abstraction when François, who had perched himself among the lofty branches of a chinaberry tree, called out: 'Ent that Loka 'way yon'a, jis' come out de wood? climbin' de fence down by de melon patch?'

It was difficult to distinguish in the gathering dusk if the figure were that of man or beast. But the family was not left long in suspense. Baptiste sped his horse away in the direction indicated by François, and in a little while he was galloping back with Bibine in his arms, as fretful, sleepy and hungry a baby as ever was.

Loka came trudging on behind Baptiste. He did not wait for explanations; he was too eager to place the child in the arms of its mother. The suspense over, Tontine began to cry; that followed naturally, of course. Through her tears she managed to address Loka, who stood all tattered and dishevelled in the doorway: 'W'ere you been? Tell me that.'

'Bibine an' me,' answered Loka, slowly and awkwardly, 'we was lonesome – we been take lit' 'broad in de wood.'

'You did n' know no betta 'an to take 'way Bibine like that? W'at Ma'ame Laballière mean, anyhow, to sen' me such a objec' like you, I want to know?'

'You go'n' sen' me 'way?' asked Loka, passing her hand in a hopeless fashion over her frowzy hair.

'*Par exemple!* Straight you march back to that ban' w'ere you come from. To give me such a fright like that! *Pas possible.*'

'Go slow, Tontine; go slow,' interposed Baptiste.

'Don' sen' me 'way frum Bibine,' entreated the girl, with a note in her voice like a lament. 'Today,' she went on, in her dragging manner, 'I want to run 'way bad, an' take to de wood; an' go yonda back to Bayou Choctaw to steal an' lie agin. It's on'y Bibine w'at hole me back. I couldn' lef' 'im. I couldn' do dat. An' we jis' go take lit' 'broad in de wood, das all, him an' me. Don' sen' me 'way like dat!'

Baptiste led the girl gently away to the far end of the gallery, and spoke soothingly to her. He told her to be good and brave, and he would right the trouble for her. He left her standing there and went back to his wife.

'Tontine,' he began, with unusual energy, 'you got to listen to the truth – once fo' all.' He had evidently determined to profit by his wife's lachrymose and wilted condition to assert his authority. 'I want to say who's masta in this house – it's me,' he went on. Tontine did not protest; only clasped the baby a little closer, which encouraged him to proceed.

'You been grind that girl too much. She ent a bad girl – I been watch her close, 'count of the chil'ren; she ent bad. All she want, it's li'le mo' rope. You can't drive a ox with the same gearin' you drive a mule. You got to learn that, Tontine.'

He approached his wife's chair and stood beside her.

'That girl, she done tole us how she was temp' today to turn *canaille* – like we all temp' sometime'. W'at was it save her? That li'le chile w'at you hole in yo' arm. An' now you want to take her guarjun angel 'way f'om her? *Non, non, ma femme,*' he said, resting his hand gently upon his wife's head. 'We got to rememba she ent like you an' me, po' thing; she's one Injun, her.'

Boulôt and Boulotte

When Boulôt and Boulotte, the little piny-wood twins, had reached the dignified age of twelve, it was decided in family council that the time had come for them to put their little naked feet into shoes. They were two brown-skinned, black-eyed 'Cadian roly-polies, who lived with father and mother and a troop of brothers and sisters halfway up the hill in a neat log cabin that had a substantial mud chimney at one end. They could well afford shoes now, for they had saved many a picayune through their industry of selling wild grapes, blackberries and 'socoes' to ladies in the village who 'put up' such things.

Boulôt and Boulotte were to buy the shoes themselves, and they selected a Saturday afternoon for the important transaction, for that is the great shopping time in Natchitoches Parish. So upon a bright Saturday afternoon Boulôt and Boulotte, hand in hand, with their quarters, their dimes and their picayunes tied carefully in a Sunday handkerchief, descended the hill, and disappeared from the gaze of the eager group that had assembled to see them go.

Long before it was time for their return, this same small band, with ten-year-old Seraphine at their head, holding a tiny Seraphin in her arms, had stationed themselves in a row before the cabin at a convenient point from which to make quick and careful observation.

Even before the two could be caught sight of, their chattering voices were heard down by the spring, where they had doubtless stopped to drink. The voices grew more and more audible. Then, through the branches of the young pines, Boulotte's blue sun-bonnet appeared, and Boulôt's straw hat. Finally the twins, hand in hand, stepped into the clearing in full view.

Consternation seized the band.

'You bof crazy *donc*, Boulôt an' Boulotte,' screamed Seraphine. 'You go buy shoes, an' come home barefeet like you was go!'

Boulôt flushed crimson. He silently hung his head, and looked sheepishly down at his bare feet, then at the fine stout brogans that he carried in his hand. He had not thought of it.

Boulotte also carried shoes, but of the glossiest, with the highest of heels and brightest of buttons. But she was not one to be disconcerted or to look sheepish; far from it.

'You 'spec' Boulôt an' me we got money fur was'e – us?' she retorted, with withering condescension. 'You think we go buy shoes fur ruin 'em in de dus'? *Comment!*'

And they all walked into the house crestfallen; all but Boulotte, who was mistress of the situation, and Seraphin, who did not care one way or the other.

For Marse Chouchoute 176

'An' now, young man, w'at you want to remember is this – an' take it fer yo' motto: "No monkey-shines with Uncle Sam." You undastan'? You aware now o' the penalties attached to monkey-shinin' with Uncle Sam. I reckon that's 'bout all I got to say; so you be on han' promp' tomorrow mornin' at seven o'clock, to take charge o' the United States mailbag.'

This formed the close of a very pompous address delivered by the postmaster of Cloutierville to young Armand Verchette, who had been appointed to carry the mails from the village to the railway station three miles away.

Armand – or Chouchoute, as everyone chose to call him, following the habit of the Creoles of giving nicknames – had heard the man a little impatiently.

Not so the negro boy who accompanied him. The child had listened with the deepest respect and awe to every word of the rambling admonition.

'How much you gwine git, Marse Chouchoute?' he asked, as they walked down the village street together, the black boy a little behind. He was very black, and slightly deformed; a small boy, scarcely reaching to the shoulder of his companion, whose cast-off garments he wore. But Chouchoute was tall for his sixteen years, and carried himself well.

'W'y, I'm goin' to git thirty dolla' a month, Wash; w'at you say to that? Betta 'an hoein' cotton, ain't it?' He laughed with a triumphant ring in his voice.

But Wash did not laugh; he was too much impressed by the importance of this new function, too much bewildered by the vision of sudden wealth which thirty dollars a month meant to his understanding.

He felt, too, deeply conscious of the great weight of responsibility which this new office brought with it. The imposing salary had confirmed the impression left by the postmaster's words.

'*You* gwine git all dat money? Sakes! W'at you reckon Ma'ame Verchette say? I know she gwine 'mos' take a fit w'en she heah dat.'

But Chouchoute's mother did not ' 'mos' take a fit' when she heard of her son's good fortune. The white and wasted hand which she rested upon the boy's black curls trembled a little, it is true, and tears of emotion came into her tired eyes. This step seemed to her the beginning of better things for her fatherless boy.

They lived quite at the end of this little French village, which was simply two long rows of very old frame houses, facing each other closely across a dusty roadway.

Their home was a cottage, so small and so humble that it just escaped the reproach of being a cabin.

Everyone was kind to Madame Verchette. Neighbours ran in of mornings to help her with her work – she could do so little for herself. And often the good priest, Père Antoine, came to sit with her and talk innocent gossip.

To say that Wash was fond of Madame Verchette and her son is to be poor in language to express devotion. He worshipped her as if she were already an angel in Paradise.

Chouchoute was a delightful young fellow; no one could help loving him. His heart was as warm and cheery as his own southern sunbeams. If he was born with an unlucky trick of forgetfulness – or better, thoughtlessness – no one ever felt much like blaming him for it, so much did it seem a part of his happy, careless nature. And why was that faithful watchdog, Wash, always at Marse Chouchoute's heels, if it were not to be hands and ears and eyes to him, more than half the time?

One beautiful spring night, Chouchoute, on his way to the station, was riding along the road that skirted the river. The clumsy mailbag that lay before him across the pony was almost empty; for the Cloutierville mail was a meagre and unimportant one at best.

But he did not know this. He was not thinking of the mail, in fact; he was only feeling that life was very agreeable this delicious spring night.

There were cabins at intervals upon the road – most of them darkened, for the hour was late. As he approached one of these, which was more pretentious than the others, he heard the sound of a fiddle, and saw lights through the openings of the house.

It was so far from the road that when he stopped his horse and peered through the darkness he could not recognise the dancers who passed before the open doors and windows. But he knew this was Gros-Léon's ball, which he had heard the boys talking about all the week.

Why should he not go and stand in the doorway an instant and exchange a word with the dancers?

Chouchoute dismounted, fastened his horse to the fence-post, and proceeded towards the house.

The room, crowded with people young and old, was long and low, with rough beams across the ceiling, blackened by smoke and time. Upon the high mantelpiece a single coal-oil lamp burned, and none too brightly.

In a far corner, upon a platform of boards laid across two flour barrels, sat Uncle Ben, playing upon a squeaky fiddle, and shouting the 'figures'.

'Ah! *v'là*[177] Chouchoute!' someone called.

'Eh! Chouchoute!'

'Jus' in time, Chouchoute; yere's Miss Léontine waitin' fer a partna.'

'S'lute yo' partnas!' Uncle Ben was thundering forth; and Chouchoute, with one hand gracefully behind him, made a profound bow to Miss Léontine, as he offered her the other.

Now Chouchoute was noted far and wide for his skill as a dancer. The moment he stood upon the floor, a fresh spirit seemed to enter into all present. It was with renewed vigour that Uncle Ben intoned his, 'Balancy all! Fus' fo' fo'ard an' back!'

The spectators drew close about the couples to watch Chouchoute's wonderful performance; his pointing of toes; his pigeon-wings in which his feet seemed hardly to touch the floor.

'It take Chouchoute to show 'em de step, *va*!' proclaimed Gros-Léon, with a fat satisfaction, to the audience at large.

'Look 'im; look 'im yonda! Ole Ben got to work hard' 'an dat, if he want to keep up wid Chouchoute, I tell you!'

So it was; encouragement and adulation on all sides, till, from the praise that was showered on him, Chouchoute's head was soon as light as his feet.

At the windows appeared the dusky faces of negroes, their bright eyes gleaming as they viewed the scene within and mingled their loud guffaws with the medley of sound that was already deafening.

The time was speeding. The air was heavy in the room, but no one seemed to mind this. Uncle Ben was calling the figures now with a rhythmic sing-song: 'Right an' lef' all 'roun'! Swing co'nas!'

Chouchoute turned with a smile to Miss Félicie on his left, his hand extended, when what should break upon his ear but the long, harrowing wail of a locomotive!

Before the sound ceased he had vanished from the room. Miss Félicie stood as he left her, with hand uplifted, rooted to the spot with astonishment.

It was the train whistling for his station, and he a mile and more away! He knew he was too late, and that he could not make the distance; but the sound had been a rude reminder that he was not at his post of duty.

However, he would do what he could now. He ran swiftly to the outer road, and to the spot where he had left his pony.

The horse was gone, and with it the United States mailbag!

For an instant Chouchoute stood half-stunned with terror. Then, in one quick flash, came to his mind a vision of possibilities that sickened him. Disgrace overtaking him in this position of trust; poverty his portion again; and his dear mother forced to share both with him.

He turned desperately to some negroes who had followed him, seeing his wild rush from the house: 'Who saw my hoss? W'at you all did with my hoss, say?'

'Who you reckon tech yo' hoss, boy?' grumbled Gustave, a sullen-looking mulatto. 'You didn' have no call to lef' 'im in de road, fus' place.'

' 'Pear to me like I heahed a hoss a-lopin' down de road jis' now; didn' you, Uncle Jake?' ventured a second.

'Neva heahed nuttin' – nuttin' 't all, 'cep' dat big-mouf Ben yonda makin' mo' fuss 'an a t'unda-sto'm.'

'Boys!' cried Chouchoute, excitedly, 'bring me a hoss, quick, one of you. I'm boun' to have one! I'm boun' to! I'll give two dolla' to the firs' man brings me a hoss.'

Near at hand, in the 'lot' that adjoined Uncle Jake's cabin, was his little Creole pony, nibbling the cool, wet grass that he found along the edges and in the corners of the fence.

The negro led the pony forth. With no further word, and with one bound, Chouchoute was upon the animal's back. He wanted neither saddle nor bridle, for there were few horses in the neighbourhood that had not been trained to be guided by the simple motions of a rider's body.

Once mounted, he threw himself forwards with a certain violent impulse, leaning till his cheek touched the animal's mane.

He uttered a sharp 'Hei!' and at once, as if possessed by sudden frenzy, the horse dashed forwards, leaving the bewildered black men in a cloud of dust.

What a mad ride it was! On one side was the river bank, steep in places and crumbling away; on the other, an unbroken line of fencing: now in straight lines of neat planking, now treacherous barbed wire, sometimes the zigzag rail.

The night was black, with only such faint light as the stars were shedding. No sound was to be heard save the quick thud of the horse's hoofs upon the hard dirt road, the animal's heavy breathing, and the boy's feverish 'hei-hei!' when he fancied the speed slackened.

Occasionally a marauding dog started from the obscurity to bark and give useless chase.

'To the road, to the road, Bon-à-rien!' panted Chouchoute, for the horse in his wild race had approached so closely to the river's edge that the bank crumbled beneath his flying feet. It was only by a desperate lunge and bound that he saved himself and rider from plunging into the water below.

Chouchoute hardly knew what he was pursuing so madly. It was rather something that drove him: fear, hope, desperation.

He was rushing to the station, because it seemed to him, naturally, the first thing to do. There was the faint hope that his own horse had broken rein and gone there of his own accord; but such hope was almost lost in a wretched conviction that had seized him the instant he saw 'Gustave the thief' among the men gathered at Gros-Léon's.

'Hei! hei, Bon-à-rien!'

The lights of the railway station were gleaming ahead, and Chouchoute's hot ride was almost at an end.

With sudden and strange perversity of purpose, Chouchoute, as he drew closer upon the station, slackened his horse's speed. A low fence was in his way. Not long before, he would have cleared it at a bound, for Bon-à-rien could do such things. Now he cantered easily to the end of it, to go through the gate which was there.

His courage was growing faint, and his heart sinking within him as he drew nearer and nearer.

He dismounted, and holding the pony by the mane, approached with some trepidation the young station-master, who was taking note of some freight that had been deposited near the tracks.

'Mr Hudson,' faltered Chouchoute, 'did you see my pony 'roun' yere anywhere? an' – an' the mail-sack?'

'Your pony's safe in the woods, Chou'te. The mailbag's on its way to New Orleans – '

'Thank God!' breathed the boy.

'But that poor little fool darkey of yours has about done it for himself, I guess.'

'Wash? Oh, Mr Hudson! w'at's – w'at's happen' to Wash?'

'He's inside there, on my mattress. He's hurt, and he's hurt bad; that's what's the matter. You see the ten forty-five had come in, and she didn't make much of a stop; she was just pushing out, when bless me if that little chap of yours didn't come tearing along on Spunky as if Old Harry[178] was behind him.

'You know how No. 22 can pull at the start; and there was that little imp keeping abreast of her 'most under the thing's wheels.

'I shouted at him. I couldn't make out what he was up to, when blamed if he didn't pitch the mailbag clean into the car! Buffalo Bill[179] couldn't have done it neater.

'Then Spunky, she shied; and Wash he bounced against the side of that car and back, like a rubber ball, and laid in the ditch till we carried him inside.

'I've wired down the road for Dr Campbell to come up on 14 and do what he can for him.'

Hudson had related these events to the distracted boy while they made their way towards the house.

Inside, upon a low pallet, lay the little negro, breathing heavily, his black face pinched and ashen with approaching death. He had wanted no one to touch him further than to lay him upon the bed.

The few men and coloured women gathered in the room were looking upon him with pity mingled with curiosity.

When he saw Chouchoute he closed his eyes, and a shiver passed through his small frame. Those about him thought he was dead. Chouchoute knelt, choking, at his side and held his hand.

'Oh, Wash, Wash! W'at you did that for? W'at made you, Wash?'

'Marse Chouchoute,' the boy whispered, so low that no one could hear him but his friend, 'I was gwine 'long de big road, pas' Marse Gros-Léon's, an' I seed Spunky tied dah wid de mail. Dar warn't a minute – I 'clar', Marse Chouchoute, dar warn't a minute – to fotch you. W'at makes my head tu'n 'roun' dat away?'

'Neva mine, Wash; keep still; don't you try to talk,' entreated Chouchoute.

'You ain't mad, Marse Chouchoute?'

The lad could only answer with a hand pressure.

'Dar warn't a minute, so I gits top o' Spunky – I neva seed nuttin' cl'ar de road like dat. I come 'longside – de train – an' fling de sack. I seed 'im kotch it, and I don' know nuttin' mo' 'cep' mis'ry, tell I see you – a-comin' frough de do'. Mebby Ma'ame Armand know some'pin,' he murmured faintly, 'w'at gwine make my – head quit tu'nin' 'round dat away. I boun' to git well, 'ca'se who – gwine – watch Marse – Chouchoute?'

A Visit to Avoyelles 180

Everyone who came up from Avoyelles had the same story to tell of Mentine. *Cher Maître!* but she was changed. And there were babies, more than she could well manage; as good as four already. Jules was not kind except to himself. They seldom went to church, and never anywhere upon a visit. They lived as poorly as pine-woods people. Doudouce had heard the story often, the last time no later than that morning.

'Ho-a!' he shouted to his mule plumb in the middle of the cotton row. He had staggered along behind the plough since early morning, and of a sudden he felt he had had enough of it. He mounted the mule and rode away to the stable, leaving the plow with its polished blade thrust deep in the red Cane River soil. His head felt like a windmill with the recollections and sudden intentions that had crowded it and were whirling through his brain since he had heard the last story about Mentine.

He knew well enough Mentine would have married him seven years ago had not Jules Trodon come up from Avoyelles and captivated her with his handsome eyes and pleasant speech. Doudouce was resigned then, for he held Mentine's happiness above his own. But now she was suffering in a hopeless, common, exasperating way for the small comforts of life. People had told him so. And somehow, today, he could not stand the knowledge passively. He felt he must see those things they spoke of with his own eyes. He must strive to help her and her children if it were possible.

Doudouce could not sleep that night. He lay with wakeful eyes watching the moonlight creep across the bare floor of his room; listening to sounds that seemed unfamiliar and weird down among the rushes along the bayou. But towards morning he saw Mentine as he had seen her last in her white wedding gown and veil. She looked at him with appealing eyes and held out her arms for protection – for, rescue, it seemed to him. That dream determined him. The following day Doudouce started for Avoyelles.

Jules Trodon's home lay a mile or two from Marksville. It consisted of three rooms strung in a row and opening upon a narrow gallery. The whole wore an aspect of poverty and dilapidation that summer day, towards noon, when Doudouce approached it. His presence outside the gate aroused the frantic barking of dogs that dashed down the steps as if to attack him. Two little brown barefooted children, a boy and girl, stood upon the gallery staring stupidly at him. 'Call off you' dogs,' he requested; but they only continued to stare.

'Down, Pluto! down, Achille!' cried the shrill voice of a woman who emerged from the house, holding upon her arm a delicate baby of a year or two. There was only an instant of unrecognition.

'*Mais* Doudouce, that ent you, *comment*! Well, if anyone would tole me this mornin'! Git a chair, 'Tit Jules. That's Mista Doudouce, f'om 'way yonda Natchitoches w'ere yo' maman use' to live. *Mais*, you ent change'; you' lookin' well, Doudouce.'

He shook hands in a slow, undemonstrative way, and seated himself clumsily upon the hide-bottomed chair, laying his broad-rimmed felt hat upon the floor beside him. He was very uncomfortable in the cloth Sunday coat which he wore.

'I had business that call' me to Marksville,' he began, 'an' I say to myse'f, "*Tiens*, you can't pass by without tell' 'em all howdy."'

'*Par exemple!* w'at Jules would said to that! *Mais*, you' lookin' well; you ent change', Doudouce.'

'An' you' lookin' well, Mentine. Jis' the same Mentine.' He regretted that he lacked talent to make the lie bolder.

She moved a little uneasily, and felt upon her shoulder for a pin with which to fasten the front of her old gown where it lacked a button. She had kept the baby in her lap. Doudouce was wondering miserably if he would have known her outside her home. He would have known her sweet, cheerful brown eyes, that were not changed; but her figure, that had looked so trim in the wedding gown, was sadly misshapen. She was brown, with skin like parchment, and piteously thin. There were lines, some deep as if old age had cut them, about the eyes and mouth.

'An' how you lef' 'em all, yonda?' she asked, in a high voice that had grown shrill from screaming at children and dogs.

'They all well. It's mighty li'le sickness in the country this yea'. But they been lookin' fo' you up yonda, straight along, Mentine.'

'Don't talk, Doudouce, it's no chance; with that po' wo'-out piece o' lan' w'at Jules got. He say, anotha yea' like that, he's goin' sell out, him.'

The children were clutching her on either side, their persistent gaze always fastened upon Doudouce. He tried without avail to make friends with them. Then Jules came home from the field, riding the mule with which he had worked, and which he fastened outside the gate.

'Yere's Doudouce f'om Natchitoches, Jules,' called out Mentine, 'he stop' to tell us howdy, *en passant*.'[181] The husband mounted to the gallery and the two men shook hands; Doudouce listlessly, as he had done with Mentine; Jules with some bluster and show of cordiality.

'Well, you' a lucky man, you,' he exclaimed with his swagger air, 'able to broad like that, *encore!* You couldn't do that if you had half a dozen mouth' to feed, *allez!*'

'*Non, j'te garantis!*'[182] agreed Mentine, with a loud laugh. Doudouce winced, as he had done the instant before at Jules's heartless implication. This husband of Mentine surely had not changed during the seven years, except to grow broader, stronger, handsomer. But Doudouce did not tell him so.

After the midday dinner of boiled salt pork, corn bread and molasses, there was nothing for Doudouce but to take his leave when Jules did.

At the gate, the little boy was discovered in dangerous proximity to the mule's heels, and was properly screamed at and rebuked.

'I reckon he likes hosses,' Doudouce remarked. 'He take' afta you, Mentine. I got a li'le pony yonda home,' he said, addressing the child, 'w'at ent ne use to me. I'm goin' sen' 'im down to you. He's a good, tough li'le mustang. You jis can let 'im eat grass an' feed 'im a han'ful 'o co'n, once a w'ile. An' he's gentle, yes. You an' yo' ma can ride 'im to church, Sundays. *Hein!* you want?'

'W'at you say, Jules?' demanded the father. 'W'at you say?' echoed Mentine, who was balancing the baby across the gate. ' '*Tit sauvage, va!*'

Doudouce shook hands all around, even with the baby, and walked off in the opposite direction to Jules, who had mounted the mule. He was bewildered. He stumbled over the rough ground because of tears that were blinding him, and that he had held in check for the past hour.

He had loved Mentine long ago, when she was young and attractive, and he found that he loved her still. He had tried to put all disturbing thought of her away, on that wedding-day, and he supposed he had succeeded. But he loved her now as he never had. Because she was no longer beautiful, he loved her. Because the delicate bloom of her existence had been rudely brushed away; because she was in a manner fallen; because she was Mentine, he loved her; fiercely, as a mother loves an afflicted child. He would have liked to thrust that man aside, and gather up her and her children, and hold them and keep them as long as life lasted.

After a moment or two Doudouce looked back at Mentine, standing at the gate with her baby. But her face was turned away from him. She was gazing after her husband, who went in the direction of the field.

A Wizard from Gettysburg[183]

It was one afternoon in April, not long ago, only the other day, and the shadows had already begun to lengthen.

Bertrand Delmandé, a fine, bright-looking boy of fourteen years – fifteen, perhaps – was mounted, and riding along a pleasant country road, upon a little Creole pony, such as boys in Louisiana usually ride when they have nothing better at hand. He had hunted, and carried his gun before him.

It is unpleasant to state that Bertrand was not so depressed as he should have been, in view of recent events that had come about. Within the past week he had been recalled from the college of Grand Coteau to his home, the Bon-Accueil[184] plantation.

He had found his father and his grandmother depressed over money matters, awaiting certain legal developments that might result in his permanent withdrawal from school. That very day, directly after the early dinner, the two had driven to town, on this very business, to be absent till the late afternoon. Bertrand, then, had saddled Picayune and gone for a long jaunt, such as his heart delighted in.

He was returning now, and had approached the beginning of the great tangled Cherokee[185] hedge that marked the boundary line of Bon-Accueil, and that twinkled with multiple white roses.

The pony started suddenly and violently at something there in the turn of the road, and just under the hedge. It looked like a bundle of rags at first. But it was a tramp, seated upon a broad, flat stone.

Bertrand had no maudlin consideration for tramps as a species; he had only that morning driven from the place one who was making himself unpleasant at the kitchen window.

But this tramp was old and feeble. His beard was long, and as white as new-ginned cotton, and when Bertrand saw him he was engaged in stanching a wound in his bare heel with a fistful of matted grass.

'What's wrong, old man?' asked the boy, kindly.

The tramp looked up at him with a bewildered glance, but did not answer.

'Well,' thought Bertrand, 'since it's decided that I'm to be a physician some day, I can't begin to practise too early.'

He dismounted, and examined the injured foot. It had an ugly gash.

Bertrand acted mostly from impulse. Fortunately his impulses were not bad ones. So, nimbly, and as quickly as he could manage it, he had the old man astride Picayune, while he himself was leading the pony down the narrow lane.

The dark green hedge towered like a high and solid wall on one side. On the other was a broad, open field, where here and there appeared the flash and gleam of uplifted, polished hoes that negroes were plying between the even rows of cotton and tender corn.

'This is the State of Louisiana,' uttered the tramp, quaveringly.

'Yes, this is Louisiana,' returned Bertrand cheerily.

'Yes, I know it is. I've been in all of them since Gettysburg. Sometimes it was too hot, and sometimes it was too cold; and with that bullet in my head – you don't remember? No, you don't remember Gettysburg.'

'Well, no, not vividly,' laughed Bertrand.

'Is it a hospital? It isn't a factory, is it?' the man questioned.

'Where we're going? Why, no, it's the Delmandé plantation – Bon-Accueil. Here we are. Wait, I'll open the gate.'

This singular group entered the yard from the rear, and not far from the house. A big black woman, who sat just without a cabin door, picking a pile of rusty-looking moss, called out at sight of them: 'W'at's dat you's bringin' in dis yard, boy, top dat hoss?'

She received no reply. Bertrand, indeed, took no notice of her enquiry.

'Fu' a boy w'at goes to school like you does – whar's yo' sense?' she went on, with a fine show of indignation; then, muttering to herself, 'Ma'ame Delmandé an' Marse St Ange ain't gwine stan' dat, I knows dey ain't. Dah! ef he ain't done sot 'im on de gall'ry, plumb down in his pa's rockin'-cheer!'

Which the boy had done; seated the tramp in a pleasant corner of the veranda, while he went in search of bandages for his wound.

The servants showed high disapproval, the housemaid following Bertrand into his grandmother's room, whither he had carried his investigations.

'W'at you tearin' yo' gra'ma's closit to' pieces dat away, boy?' she complained in her high soprano.

'I'm looking for bandages.'

'Den w'y you don't ax fu' ban'ges, an' lef yo' gra'ma's closit 'lone? You want to listen to me; you gwine git shed o' dat tramp settin' dah naxt to de dinin'-room! W'en de silva be missin', 'tain' you w'at gwine git blame, it's me.'

'The silver? Nonsense, 'Cindy; the man's wounded, and can't you see he's out of his head?'

'No mo' outen his head 'an I is. 'Tain' me w'at want to tres' [trust] 'im wid de sto'-room key, ef he is outen his head,' she concluded with a disdainful shrug.

But Bertrand's protégé proved so unapproachable in his long-worn rags, that the boy concluded to leave him unmolested till his father's return, and then ask permission to turn the forlorn creature into the bath-house, and array him afterwards in clean, fresh garments.

So there the old tramp sat in the veranda corner, stolidly content, when St Ange Delmandé and his mother returned from town.

St Ange was a dark, slender man of middle age, with a sensitive face, and a plentiful sprinkle of grey in his thick black hair; his mother, a portly woman, and an active one for her sixty-five years.

They were evidently in a despondent mood. Perhaps it was for the cheer of her sweet presence that they had brought with them from town a little girl, the child of Madame Delmandé's only daughter, who was married, and lived there.

Madame Delmandé and her son were astonished to find so uninviting an intruder in possession. But a few earnest words from Bertrand reassured them, and partly reconciled them to the man's presence; and it was with wholly indifferent though not unkindly glances that they passed him by when they entered. On any large plantation there are always nooks and corners where, for a night or more, even such a man as this tramp may be tolerated and given shelter.

When Bertrand went to bed that night, he lay long awake thinking of the man, and of what he had heard from his lips in the hushed starlight. The boy had heard of the awfulness of Gettysburg, till it was like something he could feel and quiver at.

On that field of battle this man had received a new and tragic birth. For all his existence that went before was a blank to him. There, in the black desolation of war, he was born again, without friends or kindred; without even a name he could know was his own. Then he had gone forth a wanderer; living more than half the time in hospitals; toiling when he could, starving when he had to.

Strangely enough, he had addressed Bertrand as 'St Ange', not once, but every time he had spoken to him. The boy wondered at this. Was it because he had heard Madame Delmandé address her son by that name, and fancied it?

So this nameless wanderer had drifted far down to the plantation of Bon-Accueil, and at last had found a human hand stretched out to him in kindness.

When the family assembled at breakfast on the following morning, the tramp was already settled in the chair and in the corner which Bertrand's indulgence had made familiar to him.

If he had turned partly around, he would have faced the flower garden, with its gravelled walks and trim parterres, where a tangle of colour and perfume were holding high revelry this April morning; but he liked better to gaze into the back yard, where there was always movement: men and women coming and going, bearing implements of work; little negroes in scanty garments, darting here and there, and kicking up the dust in their exuberance.

Madame Delmandé could just catch a glimpse of him through the long window that opened to the floor near which he sat.

Mr Delmandé had spoken to the man pleasantly; but he and his mother were wholly absorbed by their trouble, and talked constantly of that, while Bertrand went back and forth ministering to the old man's wants. The boy knew that the servants would have done the office with ill grace, and he chose to be cup-bearer himself to the unfortunate creature for whose presence he alone was responsible.

Once, when Bertrand went out to him with a second cup of coffee, steaming and fragrant, the old man whispered: 'What are they saying in there?' pointing over his shoulder to the dining-room.

'Oh, money troubles that will force us to economise for a while,' answered the boy. 'What father and mé-mère[186] feel worst about is that I shall have to leave college now.'

'No, no! St Ange must go to school. The war's over, the war's over! St Ange and Florentine must go to school.'

'But if there's no money,' the boy insisted, smiling like one who humours the vagaries of a child.

'Money! money!' murmured the tramp. 'The war's over – money! money!'

His sleepy gaze had swept across the yard into the thick of the orchard beyond, and rested there.

Suddenly he pushed aside the light table that had been set before him, and rose, clutching Bertrand's arm.

'St Ange, you must go to school!' he whispered. 'The war's over,' looking furtively around. 'Come. Don't let them hear you. Don't let the negroes see us. Get a spade – the little spade that Buck Williams was digging his cistern with.'

Still clutching the boy, he dragged him down the steps as he said this, and traversed the yard with long, limping strides, himself leading the way.

From under a shed where such things were to be found, Bertrand selected a spade, since the tramp's whim demanded that he should, and together they entered the orchard.

The grass was thick and tufted here, and wet with the morning dew. In long lines, forming pleasant avenues between, were peach trees growing, and pear and apple and plum. Close against the fence was the pomegranate hedge, with its waxen blossoms, brick-red. Far down in the centre of the orchard stood a huge pecan tree, twice the size of any other that was there, seeming to rule like an old-time king.

Here Bertrand and his guide stopped. The tramp had not once hesitated in his movements since grasping the arm of his young companion on the veranda. Now he went and leaned his back against the pecan tree, where there was a deep knot, and looking steadily before him he took ten paces forwards. Turning sharply to the right, he made five additional paces. Then pointing his finger downwards, and looking at Bertrand, he commanded: 'There, dig. I would do it myself, but for my wounded foot. For I've turned many a spade of earth since Gettysburg. Dig, St Ange, dig! The war's over; you must go to school.'

Is there a boy of fifteen under the sun who would not have dug, even knowing he was following the insane dictates of a demented man? Bertrand entered with all the zest of his years and his spirit into the curious adventure; and he dug and dug, throwing great spadefuls of the rich, fragrant earth from side to side.

The tramp, with body bent, and fingers like claws clasping his bony knees, stood watching with eager eyes that never unfastened their steady gaze from the boy's rhythmic motions.

'That's it!' he muttered at intervals. 'Dig, dig! The war's over. You must go to school, St Ange.'

Deep down in the earth, too deep for any ordinary turning of the soil with spade or plough to have reached it, was a box. It was of tin, apparently, something larger than a cigar box, and bound round and round with twine, rotted now and eaten away in places.

The tramp showed no surprise at seeing it there; he simply knelt upon the ground and lifted it from its long resting place.

Bertrand had let the spade fall from his hands, and was quivering with the awe of the thing he saw. Who could this wizard be that had come to him in the guise of a tramp, that walked in cabalistic paces upon his own father's ground, and pointed his finger like a divining-rod to the spot where boxes – maybe treasures – lay? It was like a page from a wonder-book.

And walking behind this white-haired old man, who was again leading the way, something of childish superstition crept back into Bertrand's heart. It was the same feeling with which he had often sat, long ago, in the weird firelight of some negro's cabin, listening to tales of witches who came in the night to work uncanny spells at their will.

Madame Delmandé had never abandoned the custom of washing her own silver and dainty china. She sat, when the breakfast was over, with a pail of warm suds before her that 'Cindy had brought to her, with an abundance of soft linen cloths. Her little granddaughter stood beside her playing, as babies will, with the bright spoons and forks, and ranging them in rows on the polished mahogany. St Ange was at the window making entries in a notebook, and frowning gloomily as he did so.

The group in the dining-room were so employed when the old tramp came staggering in, Bertrand close behind him.

He went and stood at the foot of the table, opposite to where Madame Delmandé sat, and let fall the box upon it.

The thing in falling shattered, and from its bursting sides gold came, clicking, spinning, gliding, some of it like oil; rolling along the table and off it to the floor, but heaped up, the bulk of it, before the tramp.

'Here's money!' he called out, plunging his old hand in the thick of it. 'Who says St Ange shall not go to school? The war's over – here's money! St Ange, my boy,' turning to Bertrand and speaking with quick authority, 'tell Buck Williams to hitch Black Bess to the buggy, and go bring Judge Parkerson here.'

Judge Parkerson, indeed, who had been dead for twenty years and more!

'Tell him that – that – ' and the hand that was not in the gold went up to the withered forehead, 'that – Bertrand Delmandé needs him!'

Madame Delmandé, at sight of the man with his box and his gold, had given a sharp cry, such as might follow the plunge of a knife. She lay now in her son's arms, panting hoarsely.

'Your father, St Ange – come back from the dead – your father!'

'Be calm, mother!' the man implored. 'You had such sure proof of his death in that terrible battle, this *may* not be he.'

'I know him! I know your father, my son!' and disengaging herself from the arms that held her, she dragged herself as a wounded serpent might to where the old man stood.

His hand was still in the gold, and on his face was yet the flush which had come there when he shouted out the name Bertrand Delmandé.

'Husband,' she gasped, 'do you know me – your wife?'

The little girl was playing gleefully with the yellow coins.

Bertrand stood, pulseless almost, like a young Actaeon cut in marble.

When the old man had looked long into the woman's imploring face, he made a courtly-bow.

'Madame,' he said, 'an old soldier, wounded on the field of Gettysburg, craves for himself and his two little children your kind hospitality.'

Ma'ame Pélagie

When the war[187] began, there stood on Côte Joyeuse[188] an imposing mansion of red brick, shaped like the Panthéon.[189] A grove of majestic live-oaks surrounded it.

Thirty years later, only the thick walls were standing, with the dull red brick showing here and there through a matted growth of clinging vines. The huge round pillars were intact; so to some extent was the stone flagging of hall and portico. There had been no home so stately along the whole stretch of Côte Joyeuse. Everyone knew that, as they knew it had cost Philippe Valmet sixty thousand dollars to build, away back in 1840. No one was in danger of forgetting that fact, so long as his daughter Pélagie survived. She was a queenly, white-haired woman of fifty. 'Ma'ame Pélagie', they called her, though she was unmarried, as was her sister Pauline, a child in Ma'ame Pélagie's eyes; a child of thirty-five. The two lived alone in a three-roomed cabin, almost within the shadow of the ruin. They lived for a dream, for Ma'ame Pélagie's dream, which was to rebuild the old home.

It would be pitiful to tell how their days were spent to accomplish this end; how the dollars had been saved for thirty years and the picayunes hoarded; and yet, not half enough gathered! But Ma'ame Pélagie felt sure of twenty years of life before her, and counted upon as many more for her sister. And what could not come to pass in twenty – in forty – years?

Often, of pleasant afternoons, the two would drink their black coffee, seated upon the stone-flagged portico whose canopy was the blue sky of Louisiana. They loved to sit there in the silence, with only each other and the sheeny, prying lizards for company, talking of the old times and planning for the new; while light breezes stirred the tattered vines high up among the columns, where owls nested.

'We can never hope to have all just as it was, Pauline,' Ma'ame Pélagie would say; 'perhaps the marble pillars of the salon will have to be replaced by wooden ones, and the crystal candelabra left out. Should you be willing, Pauline?'

'Oh, yes, Sesoeur,[190] I shall be willing.' It was always, 'Yes, Sesoeur,' or 'No, Sesoeur,' 'Just as you please, Sesoeur,' with poor little Mam'selle Pauline. For what did she remember of that old life and that old splendour? Only a faint gleam here and there; the half-consciousness of a young, uneventful existence; and then a great crash. That meant the nearness of war; the revolt of slaves; confusion ending in fire and flame through which she was borne safely in the strong arms of Pélagie, and carried to the log cabin which was still their home. Their brother, Léandre, had known more of it all than Pauline, and not so much as Pélagie. He had left the management of the big plantation with all its memories and traditions to his older sister, and had gone away to dwell in cities. That was many years ago. Now, Léandre's business called him frequently and upon long journeys from home, and his motherless daughter was coming to stay with her aunts at Côte Joyeuse.

They talked about it, sipping their coffee on the ruined portico. Mam'selle Pauline was terribly excited; the flush that throbbed into her pale, nervous face showed it; and she locked her thin fingers in and out incessantly.

'But what shall we do with La Petite, Sesoeur? Where shall we put her? How shall we amuse her? Ah, Seigneur!'

'She will sleep upon a cot in the room next to ours,' responded Ma'ame Pélagie, 'and live as we do. She knows how we live, and why we live; her father has told her. She knows we have money and could squander it if we chose. Do not fret, Pauline; let us hope La Petite is a true Valmet.'

Then Ma'ame Pélagie rose with stately deliberation and went to saddle her horse, for she had yet to make her last daily round through the fields; and Mam'selle Pauline threaded her way slowly among the tangled grasses towards the cabin.

The coming of La Petite, bringing with her as she did the pungent atmosphere of an outside and dimly known world, was a shock to these two, living their dream-life. The girl was quite as tall as her aunt Pélagie, with dark eyes that reflected joy as a still pool reflects the light of stars; and her rounded cheek was tinged like the pink crèpe myrtle. Mam'selle Pauline kissed her and trembled. Ma'ame Pélagie looked into her eyes with a searching gaze, which seemed to seek a likeness of the past in the living present.

And they made room between them for this young life.

2

La Petite had determined upon trying to fit herself to the strange, narrow existence which she knew awaited her at Côte Joyeuse. It went well enough at first. Sometimes she followed Ma'ame Pélagie into the fields to note how the cotton was opening, ripe and white; or to count the ears of corn upon the hardy stalks. But oftener she was with her Aunt Pauline, assisting in household offices, chattering of her brief past, or walking with the older woman arm in arm under the trailing moss of the giant oaks.

Mam'selle Pauline's steps grew very buoyant that summer, and her eyes were sometimes as bright as a bird's, unless La Petite were away from her side, when they would lose all other light but one of uneasy expectancy. The girl seemed to love her well in return, and called her endearingly Tan'tante.[191] But as the time went by, La Petite became very quiet – not listless, but thoughtful, and slow in her movements. Then her cheeks began to pale, till they were tinged like the creamy plumes of the white crèpe myrtle that grew in the ruin.

One day when she sat within its shadow, between her aunts, holding a hand of each, she said: 'Tante Pélagie, I must tell you something, you and Tan'tante.' She spoke low, but clearly and firmly. 'I love you both – please remember that I love you both. But I must go away from you. I can't live any longer here at Côte Joyeuse.'

A spasm passed through Mam'selle Pauline's delicate frame. La Petite could feel the twitch of it in the wiry fingers that were intertwined with her own. Ma'ame Pélagie remained unchanged and motionless. No human eye could penetrate so deep as to see the satisfaction which her soul felt. She said: 'What do you mean, Petite? Your father has sent you to us, and I am sure it is his wish that you remain.'

'My father loves me, Tante Pélagie, and such will not be his wish when he knows. Oh!' she continued with a restless movement, 'it is as though a weight were pressing me backwards here. I must live another life; the life I lived before. I want to know things that are happening from day to day over the world, and hear them talked about. I want my music, my books, my companions. If I had known no other life but this one of privation, I suppose it would be different. If I had to live this life, I should make the best of it. But I do not have to; and you know, Tante Pélagie, you do not need to. It seems to me,' she added in a whisper, 'that it is a sin against myself. Ah, Tan'tante! – what is the matter with Tan'tante?'

It was nothing; only a slight feeling of faintness, that would soon pass. She entreated them to take no notice; but they brought her some water and fanned her with a palmetto leaf.

But that night, in the stillness of the room, Mam'selle Pauline sobbed and would not be comforted. Ma'ame Pélagie took her in her arms.

'Pauline, my little sister Pauline,' she entreated, 'I never have seen you like this before. Do you no longer love me? Have we not been happy together, you and I?'

'Oh, yes, Sesoeur.'

'Is it because La Petite is going away?'

'Yes, Sesoeur.'

'Then she is dearer to you than I!' spoke Ma'ame Pélagie with sharp resentment. 'Than I, who held you and warmed you in my arms the day you were born; than I, your mother, father, sister, everything that could cherish you. Pauline, don't tell me that.'

Mam'selle Pauline tried to talk through her sobs.

'I can't explain it to you, Sesoeur. I don't understand it myself. I love you as I have always loved you; next to God. But if La Petite goes away I shall die. I can't understand – help me, Sesoeur. She seems – she seems like a saviour; like one who had come and taken me by the hand and was leading me somewhere – somewhere I want to go.'

Ma'ame Pélagie had been sitting beside the bed in her *peignoir* and slippers. She held the hand of her sister who lay there, and smoothed down the woman's soft brown hair. She said not a word, and the silence was broken only by Ma'mselle Pauline's continued sobs. Once Ma'ame Pélagie arose to drink of orange-flower water, which she gave to her sister, as she would have offered it to a nervous, fretful child. Almost an hour passed before Ma'ame Pélagie spoke again. Then she said: 'Pauline, you must cease that sobbing, now, and sleep. You will make yourself ill. La Petite will not go away. Do you hear me? Do you understand? She will stay, I promise you.'

Mam'selle Pauline could not clearly comprehend, but she had great faith in the word of her sister, and soothed by the promise and the touch of Ma'ame Pélagie's strong, gentle hand, she fell asleep.

3

Ma'ame Pélagie, when she saw that her sister slept, arose noiselessly and stepped outside upon the low-roofed narrow gallery. She did not linger there, but with a step that was hurried and agitated, she crossed the distance that divided her cabin from the ruin.

The night was not a dark one, for the sky was clear and the moon resplendent. But light or dark would have made no difference to Ma'ame Pélagie. It was not the first time she had stolen away to the ruin at night-time, when the whole plantation slept; but she never before had been there with a heart so nearly broken. She was going there for the last time to dream her dreams; to see the visions that hitherto had crowded her days and nights, and to bid them farewell.

There was the first of them, awaiting her upon the very portal; a robust old white-haired man, chiding her for returning home so late.

There are guests to be entertained. Does she not know it? Guests from
the city and from the near plantations. Yes, she knows it is late. She had
been abroad with Félix, and they did not notice how the time was
speeding. Félix is there; he will explain it all. He is there beside her, but
she does not want to hear what he will tell her father.

Ma'ame Pélagie had sunk upon the bench where she and her sister so
often came to sit. Turning, she gazed in through the gaping chasm of
the window at her side. The interior of the ruin is ablaze. Not with the
moonlight, for that is faint beside the other one – the sparkle from the
crystal candelabra, which negroes, moving noiselessly and respectfully
about, are lighting, one after the other. How the gleam of them reflects
and glances from the polished marble pillars!

The room holds a number of guests. There is old Monsieur Lucien
Santien, leaning against one of the pillars, and laughing at something
which Monsieur Lafirme is telling him, till his fat shoulders shake. His
son Jules is with him – Jules, who wants to marry her. She laughs. She
wonders if Félix has told her father yet. There is young Jerome Lafirme
playing at checkers upon the sofa with Léandre. Little Pauline stands
annoying them and disturbing the game. Léandre reproves her. She
begins to cry, and old black Clémentine, her nurse, who is not far off,
limps across the room to pick her up and carry her away. How sensitive
the little one is! But she trots about and takes care of herself better than
she did a year or two ago, when she fell upon the stone hall floor and
raised a great 'bo-bo' on her forehead. Pélagie was hurt and angry
enough about it; and she ordered rugs and buffalo robes to be brought
and laid thick upon the tiles, till the little one's steps were surer.

'*Il ne faut pas faire mal à Pauline.*'[192]

She was saying it aloud – '*faire mal à Pauline*'.

But she gazes beyond the salon, back into the big dining-hall, where
the white crêpe myrtle grows. Ha! how low that bat has circled. It has
struck Ma'ame Pélagie full on the breast. She does not know it. She is
beyond there in the dining-hall, where her father sits with a group of
friends over their wine. As usual they are talking politics. How tiresome!
She has heard them say 'la guerre'[193] oftener than once. La guerre. Bah!
She and Félix have something pleasanter to talk about, out under the
oaks, or back in the shadow of the oleanders.

But they were right! The sound of a cannon, shot at Sumter,[194] has
rolled across the Southern States, and its echo is heard along the whole
stretch of Côte Joyeuse.

Yet Pélagie does not believe it. Not till La Ricaneuse[195] stands before
her with bare, black arms akimbo, uttering a volley of vile abuse and of

brazen impudence. Pélagie wants to kill her. But yet she will not believe. Not till Félix comes to her in the chamber above the dining-hall – there where that trumpet vine hangs – comes to say goodbye to her. The hurt which the big brass buttons of his new grey uniform pressed into the tender flesh of her bosom has never left it. She sits upon the sofa, and he beside her, both speechless with pain. That room would not have been altered. Even the sofa would have been there in the same spot, and Ma'ame Pélagie had meant all along, for thirty years, all along, to lie there upon it someday when the time came to die.

But there is no time to weep, with the enemy at the door. The door has been no barrier. They are clattering through the halls now, drinking the wines, shattering the crystal and glass, slashing the portraits.

One of them stands before her and tells her to leave the house. She slaps his face. How the stigma stands out red as blood upon his blanched cheek!

Now there is a roar of fire and the flames are bearing down upon her motionless figure. She wants to show them how a daughter of Louisiana can perish before her conquerors. But little Pauline clings to her knees in an agony of terror. Little Pauline must be saved.

'*Il ne faut pas faire mal à Pauline.*'

Again she is saying it aloud – '*faire mal à Pauline*'.

*

The night was nearly spent; Ma'ame Pélagie had glided from the bench upon which she had rested, and for hours lay prone upon the stone flagging, motionless. When she dragged herself to her feet it was to walk like one in a dream. About the great, solemn pillars, one after the other, she reached her arms, and pressed her cheek and her lips upon the senseless brick.

'Adieu, adieu!' whispered Ma'ame Pélagie.

There was no longer the moon to guide her steps across the familiar pathway to the cabin. The brightest light in the sky was Venus, that swung low in the east. The bats had ceased to beat their wings about the ruin. Even the mockingbird that had warbled for hours in the old mulberry tree had sung himself asleep. That darkest hour before the day was mantling the earth. Ma'ame Pélagie hurried through the wet, clinging grass, beating aside the heavy moss that swept across her face, walking on towards the cabin – towards Pauline. Not once did she look back upon the ruin that brooded like a huge monster – a black spot in the darkness that enveloped it.

4

Little more than a year later the transformation which the old Valmet place had undergone was the talk and wonder of Côte Joyeuse. One would have looked in vain for the ruin; it was no longer there; neither was the log cabin. But out in the open, where the sun shone upon it, and the breezes blew about it, was a shapely structure fashioned from woods that the forests of the state had furnished. It rested upon a solid foundation of brick.

Upon a corner of the pleasant gallery sat Léandre smoking his after-noon cigar, and chatting with neighbours who had called. This was to be his *pied à terre*[196] now; the home where his sisters and his daughter dwelt. The laughter of young people was heard out under the trees, and within the house where La Petite was playing upon the piano. With the enthusiasm of a young artist she drew from the keys strains that seemed marvellously beautiful to Mam'selle Pauline, who stood enraptured near her. Mam'selle Pauline had been touched by the recreation of Valmet. Her cheek was as full and almost as flushed as La Petite's. The years were falling away from her.

Ma'ame Pélagie had been conversing with her brother and his friends. Then she turned and walked away; stopping to listen awhile to the music which La Petite was making. But it was only for a moment. She went on around the curve of the veranda, where she found herself alone. She stayed there, erect, holding to the bannister rail and looking out calmly in the distance across the fields.

She was dressed in black, with the white kerchief she always wore folded across her bosom. Her thick, glossy hair rose like a silver diadem from her brow. In her deep, dark eyes smouldered the light of fires that would never flame. She had grown very old. Years instead of months seemed to have passed over her since the night she bade farewell to her visions.

Poor Ma'ame Pélagie! How could it be different! While the outward pressure of a young and joyous existence had forced her footsteps into the light, her soul had stayed in the shadow of the ruin.

At the 'Cadian Ball

Bobinôt, that big, brown, good-natured Bobinôt, had no intention of going to the ball, even though he knew Calixta would be there. For what came of those balls but heartache, and a sickening disinclination for work the whole week through, till Saturday night came again and his tortures began afresh? Why could he not love Ozéina, who would marry him tomorrow; or Fronie, or any one of a dozen others, rather than that little Spanish vixen? Calixta's slender foot had never touched Cuban soil; but her mother's had, and the Spanish was in her blood all the same. For that reason the prairie people forgave her much that they would not have overlooked in their own daughters or sisters.

Her eyes – Bobinôt thought of her eyes, and weakened – the bluest, the drowsiest, most tantalising that ever looked into a man's; he thought of her flaxen hair that kinked worse than a mulatto's close to her head; that broad, smiling mouth and tip-tilted nose, that full figure; that voice like a rich contralto song, with cadences in it that must have been taught by Satan, for there was no one else to teach her tricks on that 'Cadian prairie. Bobinôt thought of them all as he ploughed his rows of cane.

There had even been a breath of scandal whispered about her a year ago, when she went to Assumption[197] – but why talk of it? No one did now. *'C'est Espagnol, ça,'*[198] most of them said with lenient shoulder-shrugs. *'Bon chien tient de race,'*[199] the old men mumbled over their pipes, stirred by recollections. Nothing was made of it, except that Fronie threw it up to Calixta when the two quarrelled and fought on the church steps after mass one Sunday, about a lover. Calixta swore roundly in fine 'Cadian French and with true Spanish spirit, and slapped Fronie's face. Fronie had slapped her back; *'Tiens, cocotte, va!'* *'Espèce de lionèse; prends ça et ça!'*[200] till the curé himself was obliged to hasten and make peace between them. Bobinôt thought of it all, and would not go to the ball.

But in the afternoon, over at Friedheimer's store, where he was buying a trace-chain, he heard someone say that Alcée Laballière[201] would be there. Then wild horses could not have kept him away. He knew how it would be – or rather he did not know how it would be – if the handsome young planter came over to the ball as he sometimes did.

If Alcée happened to be in a serious mood, he might only go to the
card-room and play a round or two; or he might stand out on the
galleries talking crops and politics with the old people. But there was no
telling. A drink or two could put the devil in his head – that was what
Bobinôt said to himself, as he wiped the sweat from his brow with his
red bandana; a gleam from Calixta's eyes, a flash of her ankle, a twirl of
her skirts could do the same. Yes, Bobinôt would go to the ball.

*

That was the year Alcée Laballière put nine hundred acres in rice. It
was putting a good deal of money into the ground, but the returns
promised to be glorious. Old Madame Laballière, sailing about the
spacious galleries in her white *volante*, figured it all out in her head.
Clarisse, her goddaughter, helped her a little, and together they built
more air-castles than enough. Alcée worked like a mule that time; and if
he did not kill himself, it was because his constitution was an iron one.
It was an everyday affair for him to come in from the field well-nigh
exhausted, and wet to the waist. He did not mind if there were visitors;
he left them to his mother and Clarisse. There were often guests: young
men and women who came up from the city, which was but a few hours
away, to visit his beautiful kinswoman. She was worth going a good deal
farther than that to see. Dainty as a lily; hardy as a sunflower; slim, tall,
graceful, like one of the reeds that grew in the marsh. Cold and kind
and cruel by turn, and everything that was aggravating to Alcée.

He would have liked to sweep the place of those visitors, often. Of
the men, above all, with their ways and their manners; their swaying of
fans like women, and dandling about hammocks. He could have pitched
them over the levee into the river, if it hadn't meant murder. That was
Alcée. But he must have been crazy the day he came in from the rice-
field, and, toil-stained as he was, clasped Clarisse by the arms and panted
a volley of hot, blistering love-words into her face. No man had ever
spoken love to her like that.

'Monsieur!' she exclaimed, looking him full in the eyes, without a
quiver. Alcée's hands dropped and his glance wavered before the chill of
her calm, clear eyes.

'*Par exemple!*' she muttered disdainfully, as she turned from him, deftly
adjusting the careful toilet that he had so brutally disarranged.

That happened a day or two before the cyclone came that cut into the
rice like fine steel. It was an awful thing, coming so swiftly, without a
moment's warning in which to light a holy candle or set a piece of
blessed palm burning. Old madame wept openly and said her beads,

just as her son Didier, the New Orleans one, would have done. If such a thing had happened to Alphonse, the Laballière planting cotton up in Natchitoches, he would have raved and stormed like a second cyclone, and made his surroundings unbearable for a day or two. But Alcée took the misfortune differently. He looked ill and grey after it, and said nothing. His speechlessness was frightful. Clarisse's heart melted with tenderness but when she offered her soft, purring words of condolence, he accepted them with mute indifference. Then she and her *nénaine* wept afresh in each other's arms.

A night or two later, when Clarisse went to her window to kneel there in the moonlight and say her prayers before retiring, she saw that Bruce, Alcée's negro servant, had led his master's saddle-horse noiselessly along the edge of the sward that bordered the gravel-path, and stood holding him near by. Presently, she heard Alcée quit his room, which was beneath her own, and traverse the lower portico. As he emerged from the shadow and crossed the strip of moonlight, she perceived that he carried a pair of well-filled saddle-bags which he at once flung across the animal's back. He then lost no time in mounting, and after a brief exchange of words with Bruce, went cantering away, taking no precaution to avoid the noisy gravel as the negro had done.

Clarisse had never suspected that it might be Alcée's custom to sally forth from the plantation secretly, and at such an hour; for it was nearly midnight. And had it not been for the telltale saddle-bags, she would only have crept to bed, to wonder, to fret and dream unpleasant dreams. But her impatience and anxiety would not be held in check. Hastily unbolting the shutters of her door that opened upon the gallery, she stepped outside and called softly to the old negro.

'Gre't Peter, Miss Clarisse! I wasn' sho it was a ghos' o' w'at, stan'in' up dah, plumb in de night, dataway.'

He mounted halfway up the long, broad flight of stairs. She was standing at the top.

'Bruce, w'ere has Monsieur Alcée gone?' she asked.

'W'y, he gone 'bout he business, I reckin,' replied Bruce, striving to be non-committal at the outset.

'W'ere has Monsieur Alcée gone?' she reiterated, stamping her bare foot. 'I won't stan' any nonsense or any lies: mine, Bruce.'

'I don' ric'lic ez I eva tole you lie *yit*, Miss Clarisse. Mista Alcée, he all broke up, sho.'

'W'ere – has – he gone? *Ah, Sainte Vierge! faut de la patience! butor, va!*[202]

'W'en I was in he room, a-breshin' off he clo'es today,' the darkey

began, settling himself against the stair-rail, 'he look dat speechless an'
down, I say, "You 'pear to me like some pussun w'at gwine have a spell
o' sickness, Mista Alcée." He say, "You reckin?" Wi' dat he git up, go
look hisse'f stiddy in de glass. Den he go to de chimbly an' jerk up de
quinine bottle an' po' a gre't hoss-dose on to he han'. An' he swalla dat
mess in a wink, an' wash hit down wid a big dram o' w'iskey w'at he
keep in he room, ag'inst he come all soppin' wet outen de fiel'.

'He 'lows, "No, I ain' gwine be sick, Bruce." Den he square off. He
say, "I kin mak out to stan' up an' gi' an' take wid any man I knows, lessen
hit's John L. Sulvun.[203] But w'en God A'mighty an' a 'oman jines fo'ces
agin me, dat's one too many fur me." I tell 'im, "Jis so," whils' I'se makin'
out to bresh a spot off w'at ain' dah on he coat colla. I tell 'im, "You
wants li'le res', suh." He say, "No, I wants li'le fling; dat w'at I wants; an'
I gwine git it. Pitch me a fis'ful o' clo'es in dem 'ar saddle-bags." Dat w'at
he say. Don't you bodda, missy. He jis' gone a-caperin' yonda to de
Cajun ball. Uh – uh – de skeeters is fair' a-swarmin' like bees roun' yo'
foots!'

The mosquitoes were indeed attacking Clarisse's white feet savagely.
She had unconsciously been alternately rubbing one foot over the other
during the darkey's recital.

'The 'Cadian ball,' she repeated contemptuously. 'Humph! *Par
exemple!* Nice conduc' for a Laballière. An' he needs a saddle-bag, fill'
with clothes, to go to the 'Cadian ball!'

'Oh, Miss Clarisse; you go on to bed, chile; git yo' soun' sleep. He
'low he come back in couple weeks o' so. I kiarn be repeatin' lot o' truck
w'at young mans say, out heah face o' young gal.'

Clarisse said no more, but turned and abruptly re-entered the house.

'You done talk too much wid yo' mouf a'ready, you ole fool nigga,
you,' muttered Bruce to himself as he walked away.

                                      *

Alcée reached the ball very late, of course – too late for the chicken
gumbo which had been served at midnight.

The big, low-ceiled room – they called it a hall – was packed with
men and women dancing to the music of three fiddles. There were
broad galleries all around it. There was a room at one side where sober-
faced men were playing cards. Another, in which babies were sleeping,
was called *le parc aux petits*.[204] Anyone who is white may go to a 'Cadian
ball, but he must pay for his lemonade, his coffee and chicken gumbo.
And he must behave himself like a 'Cadian. Grosboeuf was giving this
ball. He had been giving them since he was a young man, and he was a

middle-aged one, now. In that time he could recall but one disturbance, and that was caused by American railroaders, who were not in touch with their surroundings and had no business there. '*Ces maudits gens du raiderode*',[205] Grosboeuf called them.

Alcée Laballière's presence at the ball caused a flutter even among the men, who could not but admire his 'nerve' after such misfortune befalling him. To be sure, they knew the Laballières were rich – that there were resources East, and more again in the city. But they felt it took a *brave homme*[206] to stand a blow like that philosophically. One old gentleman, who was in the habit of reading a Paris newspaper and knew things, chuckled gleefully to everybody that Alcée's conduct was altogether *chic, mais chic.*[207] That he had more *panache*[208] than Boulanger.[209] Well, perhaps he had.

But what he did not show outwardly was that he was in a mood for ugly things tonight. Poor Bobinôt alone felt it vaguely. He discerned a gleam of it in Alcée's handsome eyes, as the young planter stood in the doorway, looking with rather feverish glance upon the assembly, while he laughed and talked with a 'Cadian farmer who was beside him.

Bobinôt himself was dull-looking and clumsy. Most of the men were. But the young women were very beautiful. The eyes that glanced into Alcée's as they passed him were big, dark, soft as those of the young heifers standing out in the cool prairie grass.

But the belle was Calixta. Her white dress was not nearly so handsome or well made as Fronie's (she and Fronie had quite forgotten the battle on the church steps, and were friends again), nor were her slippers so stylish as those of Ozéina; and she fanned herself with a handkerchief, since she had broken her red fan at the last ball, and her aunts and uncles were not willing to give her another. But all the men agreed she was at her best tonight. Such animation! and abandon! such flashes of wit!

'Hé, Bobinôt! *Mais* w'at's the matta? W'at you standin' *planté là*[210] like ole Ma'ame Tina's cow in the bog, you?'

That was good. That was an excellent thrust at Bobinôt, who had forgotten the figure of the dance with his mind bent on other things, and it started a clamour of laughter at his expense. He joined good-naturedly. It was better to receive even such notice as that from Calixta than none at all. But Madame Suzonne, sitting in a corner, whispered to her neighbour that if Ozéina were to conduct herself in a like manner, she should immediately be taken out to the mule-cart and driven home. The women did not always approve of Calixta.

Now and then were short lulls in the dance, when couples flocked out upon the galleries for a brief respite and fresh air. The moon had gone down pale in the west and in the east was yet no promise of day. After such an interval, when the dancers again assembled to resume the interrupted quadrille, Calixta was not among them.

She was sitting upon a bench out in the shadow, with Alcée beside her. They were acting like fools. He had attempted to take a little gold ring from her finger; just for the fun of it, for there was nothing he could have done with the ring but replace it again. But she clinched her hand tight. He pretended that it was a very difficult matter to open it. Then he kept the hand in his. They seemed to forget about it. He played with her earring, a thin crescent of gold hanging from her small brown ear. He caught a wisp of the kinky hair that had escaped its fastening, and rubbed the ends of it against his shaven cheek.

'You know, last year in Assumption, Calixta?' They belonged to the younger generation, so preferred to speak English.

'Don't come say Assumption to me, M'sieur Alcée. I done yeard Assumption till I'm plumb sick.'

'Yes, I know. The idiots! Because you were in Assumption, and I happened to go to Assumption, they must have it that we went together. But it was nice – *hein*, Calixta? – in Assumption?'

They saw Bobinôt emerge from the hall and stand a moment outside the lighted doorway, peering uneasily and searchingly into the darkness. He did not see them, and went slowly back.

'There is Bobinôt looking for you. You are going to set poor Bobinôt crazy. You'll marry him someday; *hein*, Calixta?'

'I don't say no, me,' she replied, striving to withdraw her hand, which he held more firmly for the attempt.

'But come, Calixta; you know you said you would go back to Assumption, just to spite them.'

'No, I neva said that, me. You mus' dreamt that.'

'Oh, I thought you did. You know I'm going down to the city.'

'W'en?'

'Tonight.'

'Betta make has'e, then, it's mos' day.'

'Well, tomorrow'll do.'

'W'at you goin' do, yonda?'

'I don't know. Drown myself in the lake, maybe; unless you go down there to visit your uncle.'

Calixta's senses were reeling; and they well-nigh left her when she felt Alcée's lips brush her ear like the touch of a rose.

'Mista Alcée! Is dat Mista Alcée?' the thick voice of a negro was asking; he stood on the ground, holding to the bannister-rails near which the couple sat.

'W'at do you want now?' cried Alcée impatiently. 'Can't I have a moment of peace?'

'I ben huntin' you high an' low, suh,' answered the man. 'Dey – dey someone in de road, onda de mulbare tree, want see you a minute.'

'I wouldn't go out to the road to see the Angel Gabriel. And if you come back here with any more talk, I'll have to break your neck.' The negro turned mumbling away.

Alcée and Calixta laughed softly about it. Her boisterousness was all gone. They talked low, and laughed softly, as lovers do.

'Alcée! Alcée Laballière!'

It was not the negro's voice this time; but one that went through Alcée's body like an electric shock, bringing him to his feet.

Clarisse was standing there in her riding-habit, where the negro had stood. For an instant confusion reigned in Alcée's thoughts, as with one who awakes suddenly from a dream. But he felt that something of serious import had brought his cousin to the ball in the dead of night.

'W'at does this mean, Clarisse?' he asked.

'It means something has happen' at home. You mus' come.'

'Happened to maman?' he questioned, in alarm.

'No; *nénaine* is well, and asleep. It is something else. Not to frighten you. But you mus' come. Come with me, Alcée.'

There was no need for the imploring note. He would have followed the voice anywhere.

She had now recognised the girl sitting back on the bench.

'*Ah, c'est vous, Calixta? Comment ça va, mon enfant?*'[211]

'*Tcha va b'en; et vous, mam'zélle?*'[212]

Alcée swung himself over the low rail and started to follow Clarisse, without a word, without a glance back at the girl. He had forgotten he was leaving her there. But Clarisse whispered something to him, and he turned back to say, 'Good-night, Calixta,' and offer his hand to press through the railing. She pretended not to see it.

*

'How come that? You settin' yere by yo'se'f, Calixta?' It was Bobinôt who had found her there alone. The dancers had not yet come out. She looked ghastly in the faint, grey light struggling out of the east.

'Yes, that's me. Go yonda in the *parc aux petits* an' ask Aunt Olisse fu' my hat. She knows w'ere 't is. I want to go home, me.'

'How you came?'

'I come afoot, with the Cateaus. But I'm goin' now. I ent goin' wait fu' 'em. I'm plumb wo' out, me.'

'Kin I go with you, Calixta?'

'I don' care.'

They went together across the open prairie and along the edge of the fields, stumbling in the uncertain light. He told her to lift her dress that was getting wet and bedraggled; for she was pulling at the weeds and grasses with her hands.

'I don' care; it's got to go in the tub, anyway. You been sayin' all along you want to marry me, Bobinôt. Well, if you want, yet, I don' care, me.'

The glow of a sudden and overwhelming happiness shone out in the brown, rugged face of the young Acadian. He could not speak, for very joy. It choked him.

'Oh well, if you don' want,' snapped Calixta, flippantly pretending to be piqued at his silence.

'*Bon Dieu!* You know that makes me crazy, w'at you sayin'. You mean that, Calixta? You ent goin' turn roun' agin?'

'I neva tole you that much *yet*, Bobinôt. I mean that. *Tiens*,' and she held out her hand in the businesslike manner of a man who clinches a bargain with a hand-clasp. Bobinôt grew bold with happiness and asked Calixta to kiss him. She turned her face, that was almost ugly after the night's dissipation, and looked steadily into his.

'I don' want to kiss you, Bobinôt,' she said, turning away again, 'not today. Some other time. *Bonté divine!*[213] ent you satisfy, *yet!*'

'Oh, I'm satisfy, Calixta,' he said.

*

Riding through a patch of wood, Clarisse's saddle became ungirted, and she and Alcée dismounted to readjust it.

For the twentieth time he asked her what had happened at home.

'But, Clarisse, w'at is it? Is it a misfortune?'

'Ah, *Dieu sait*! It's only something that happen' to me.'

'To you!'

'I saw you go away las' night, Alcée, with those saddlebags,' she said, haltingly, striving to arrange something about the saddle, 'an' I made Bruce tell me. He said you had gone to the ball, an' wouldn' be home for weeks an' weeks. I thought, Alcée – maybe you were going to – to Assumption. I got wild. An' then I knew if you didn't come back, *now*, tonight. I couldn't stan' it – again.'

She had her face hidden in her arm that she was resting against the saddle when she said that.

He began to wonder if this meant love. But she had to tell him so, before he believed it. And when she told him, he thought the face of the universe was changed – just like Bobinôt. Was it last week the cyclone had well-nigh ruined him? The cyclone seemed a huge joke, now. It was he, then, who, an hour ago was kissing little Calixta's ear and whispering nonsense into it. Calixta was like a myth, now. The one, only, great reality in the world was Clarisse standing before him, telling him that she loved him.

In the distance they heard the rapid discharge of pistol-shots; but it did not disturb them. They knew it was only the negro musicians who had gone into the yard to fire their pistols into the air, as the custom is, and to announce, '*Le bal est fini*.'[214]

La Belle Zoraïde

The summer night was hot and still; not a ripple of air swept over the *marais*.[215] Yonder, across Bayou St John, lights twinkled here and there in the darkness, and in the dark sky above a few stars were blinking. A lugger that had come out of the lake was moving with slow, lazy motion down the bayou. A man in the boat was singing a song.

The notes of the song came faintly to the ears of old Manna-Loulou, herself as black as the night, who had gone out upon the gallery to open the shutters wide.

Something in the refrain reminded the woman of an old, half-forgotten Creole romance, and she began to sing it low to herself while she threw the shutters open –

> '*Lisett' to kité la plaine,*
> *Mo perdi bonhair à moué;*
> *Ziés à moué semblé fontaine,*
> *Dépi mo pa miré toué.*'[216]

And then this old song, a lover's lament for the loss of his mistress, floating into her memory, brought with it the story she would tell to Madame, who lay in her sumptuous mahogany bed, waiting to be fanned and put to sleep to the sound of one of Manna-Loulou's stories. The old negress had already bathed her mistress's pretty white feet and kissed them lovingly, one, then the other. She had brushed her mistress's beautiful hair, that was as soft and shining as satin, and was the colour of Madame's wedding-ring. Now, when she re-entered the room, she moved softly towards the bed, and seating herself there began gently to fan Madame Delisle.[217]

Manna-Loulou was not always ready with her story, for Madame would hear none but those which were true. But tonight the story was all there in Manna-Loulou's head – the story of la belle Zoraïde – and she told it to her mistress in the soft Creole patois, whose music and charm no English words can convey.

'La belle Zoraïde had eyes that were so dusky, so beautiful, that any man who gazed too long into their depths was sure to lose his head, and even his heart sometimes. Her soft, smooth skin was the colour of *café-au-lait*.[218] As for her elegant manners, her *svelte* and graceful figure, they were the envy of half the ladies who visited her mistress, Madame Delarivière.

'No wonder Zoraïde was as charming and as dainty as the finest lady of la rue Royale:[219] from a toddling thing she had been brought up at her mistress's side; her fingers had never done rougher work than sewing a fine muslin seam; and she even had her own little black servant to wait upon her. Madame, who was her godmother as well as her mistress, would often say to her: "Remember, Zoraïde, when you are ready to marry, it must be in a way to do honour to your bringing up. It will be at the cathedral. Your wedding gown, your *corbeille*, all will be of the best; I shall see to that myself. You know, M'sieur Ambroise is ready whenever you say the word; and his master is willing to do as much for him as I shall do for you. It is a union that will please me in every way."

'M'sieur Ambroise was then the body servant of Dr Langlé. La belle Zoraïde detested the little mulatto, with his shining whiskers like a white man's, and his small eyes, that were cruel and false as a snake's. She would cast down her own mischievous eyes, and say: "Ah, *nénaine*, I am so happy, so contented here at your side just as I am. I don't want to marry now; next year, perhaps, or the next." And Madame would smile indulgently and remind Zoraïde that a woman's charms are not everlasting.

'But the truth of the matter was, Zoraïde had seen le beau Mézor dance the Bamboula[220] in Congo Square. That was a sight to hold one rooted to the ground. Mézor was as straight as a cypress tree and as proud-looking as a king. His body, bare to the waist, was like a column of ebony and it glistened like oil.

'Poor Zoraïde's heart grew sick in her bosom with love for le beau Mézor from the moment she saw the fierce gleam of his eye, lighted by the inspiring strains of the Bamboula, and beheld the stately movements of his splendid body, swaying and quivering through the figures of the dance.

'But when she knew him later, and he came near her to speak with her, all the fierceness was gone out of his eyes, and she saw only kindness in them and heard only gentleness in his voice; for love had taken possession of him also, and Zoraïde was more distracted than ever. When Mézor was not dancing the Bamboula in Congo Square, he was hoeing sugar-cane, barefooted and half naked, in his master's field outside of the city. Dr Langlé was his master as well as M'sieur Ambroise's.

'One day, when Zoraïde kneeled before her mistress, drawing on Madame's silken stockings, that were of the finest, she said: "*Nénaine*, you have spoken to me often of marrying. Now, at last, I have chosen a husband, but it is not M'sieur Ambroise, it is le beau Mézor that I want and no other." And Zoraïde hid her face in her hands when she had said that, for she guessed, rightly enough, that her mistress would be very angry. And, indeed, Madame Delarivière was at first speechless with rage. When she finally spoke it was only to gasp out, exasperated: "That negro! that negro! *Bon Dieu Seigneur*, but this is too much!"

' "Am I white, *nénaine*?" pleaded Zoraïde.

' "You white! *Malheureuse!*[221] You deserve to have the lash laid upon you like any other slave, you have proven yourself no better than the worst."

' "I am not white," persisted Zoraïde, respectfully and gently. "Dr Langlé gives me his slave to marry, but he would not give me his son. Then, since I am not white, let me have from out of my own race the one whom my heart has chosen."

'However, you may well believe that Madame would not hear to that. Zoraïde was forbidden to speak to Mézor, and Mézor was cautioned against seeing Zoraïde again. But you know how the negroes are, Ma'zélle Titite,' added Manna-Loulou, smiling a little sadly. 'There is no mistress, no master, no king, nor priest who can hinder them from loving when they will. And these two found ways and means.

'When months had passed by, Zoraïde, who had grown unlike her-self – sober and preoccupied – said again to her mistress: "*Nénaine*, you would not let me have Mézor for my husband; but I have dis-obeyed you, I have sinned. Kill me if you wish, *nénaine*; forgive me if you will; but when I heard le beau Mézor say to me, '*Zoraïde, mo l'aime toi*,'[222] I could have died, but I could not have helped loving him."

'This time Madame Delarivière was so actually pained, so wounded at hearing Zoraïde's confession, that there was no place left in her heart for anger. She could utter only confused reproaches. But she was a woman of action rather than of words, and she acted promptly. Her first step was to induce Dr Langlé to sell Mézor. Dr Langlé, who was a widower, had long wanted to marry Madame Delarivière, and he would willingly have walked on all fours at noon through the Place d'Armes[223] if she wanted him to. Naturally he lost no time in disposing of le beau Mézor, who was sold away into Georgia, or the Carolinas, or one of those distant countries far away, where he would no longer hear his Creole tongue spoken, nor dance Calinda,[224] nor hold la belle Zoraïde in his arms.

'The poor thing was heartbroken when Mézor was sent away from her, but she took comfort and hope in the thought of her baby that she would soon be able to clasp to her breast.

'La belle Zoraïde's sorrows had now begun in earnest. Not only sorrows but sufferings, and with the anguish of maternity came the shadow of death. But there is no agony that a mother will not forget when she holds her first-born to her heart, and presses her lips upon the baby flesh that is her own, yet far more precious than her own.

'So, instinctively, when Zoraïde came out of the awful shadow she gazed questioningly about her and felt with her trembling hands upon either side of her. "*Où li, mo piti à moin?* Where is my little one?" she asked imploringly. Madame who was there and the nurse who was there both told her in turn, "*To piti à toi, li mouri.* Your little one is dead" – which was a wicked falsehood that must have caused the angels in heaven to weep. For the baby was living and well and strong. It had at once been removed from its mother's side, to be sent away to Madame's plantation, far up the coast. Zoraïde could only moan in reply, "*Li mouri, li mouri,*" and she turned her face to the wall.

'Madame had hoped, in thus depriving Zoraïde of her child, to have her young waiting-maid again at her side, free, happy and beautiful as of old. But there was a more powerful will than Madame's at work – the will of the good God, who had already designed that Zoraïde should grieve with a sorrow that was never more to be lifted in this world. La belle Zoraïde was no more. In her stead was a sad-eyed woman who mourned night and day for her baby. "*Li mouri, li mouri,*" she would sigh over and over again to those about her, and to herself when others grew weary of her complaint.

'Yet, in spite of all, M'sieur Ambroise was still in the notion to marry her. A sad wife or a merry one was all the same to him so long as that wife was Zoraïde. And she seemed to consent, or rather submit, to the approaching marriage as though nothing mattered any longer in this world.

'One day, a black servant entered a little noisily the room in which Zoraïde sat sewing. With a look of strange and vacuous happiness upon her face, Zoraïde arose hastily, "Hush, hush," she whispered, lifting a warning finger, "my little one is asleep; you must not awaken her."

'Upon the bed was a senseless bundle of rags shaped like an infant in swaddling clothes. Over this dummy the woman had drawn the mosquito bar, and she was sitting contentedly beside it. In short, from that day Zoraïde was demented. Night nor day did she lose sight of the doll that lay in her bed or in her arms.

'And now was Madame stung with sorrow and remorse at seeing this terrible affliction that had befallen her dear Zoraïde. Consulting with Dr Langlé, they decided to bring back to the mother the real baby of flesh and blood that was now toddling about, and kicking its heels in the dust yonder upon the plantation.

'It was Madame herself who led the pretty, tiny little *griffe* girl to her mother. Zoraïde was sitting upon a stone bench in the courtyard, listening to the soft splashing of the fountain, and watching the fitful shadows of the palm leaves upon the broad, white flagging.

' "Here," said Madame, approaching, "here, my poor dear Zoraïde, is your own little child. Keep her; she is yours. No one will ever take her from you again."

'Zoraïde looked with sullen suspicion upon her mistress and the child before her. Reaching out a hand she thrust the little one mistrustfully away from her. With the other hand she clasped the rag bundle fiercely to her breast; for she suspected a plot to deprive her of it.

'Nor could she ever be induced to let her own child approach her; and finally the little one was sent back to the plantation, where she was never to know the love of mother or father.

'And now this is the end of Zoraïde's story. She was never known again as la belle Zoraïde, but ever after as Zoraïde la folle, whom no one ever wanted to marry – not even M'sieur Ambroise. She lived to be an old woman, whom some people pitied and others laughed at – always clasping her bundle of rags – her *"piti"*.

'Are you asleep, Ma'zélle Titite?'

'No, I am not asleep; I was thinking. Ah, the poor little one, Man Loulou, the poor little one! Better she had died!'

But this is the way Madame Delisle and Manna-Loulou really talked to each other –

'*Vou pré droumi, Ma'zélle Titite?*'

'*Non, pa pré droumi; mo yapré zongler. Ah, la pauv' piti, Man Loulou. La pauv' piti! Mieux li mouri!*'

It was no wonder Mr Sublet, who was staying at the Hallet plantation, wanted to make a picture of Evariste. The 'Cadian was rather a picturesque subject in his way, and a tempting one to an artist looking for bits of 'local colour' along the Têche.

Mr Sublet had seen the man on the back gallery just as he came out of the swamp, trying to sell a wild turkey to the housekeeper. He spoke to him at once, and in the course of conversation engaged him to return to the house the following morning and have his picture drawn. He handed Evariste a couple of silver dollars to show that his intentions were fair, and that he expected the 'Cadian to keep faith with him.

'He tell' me he want' put my picture in one fine *mag*'zine,' said Evariste to his daughter, Martinette, when the two were talking the matter over in the afternoon.

'W'at fo' you reckon he want' do dat?' They sat within the low, homely cabin of two rooms, that was not quite so comfortable as Mr Hallet's negro quarters.

Martinette pursed her red lips that had little sensitive curves to them, and her black eyes took on a reflective expression.

'Mebbe he yeard 'bout that big fish w'at you ketch las' winta in Carancro Lake. You know it was all wrote about in the *Suga Bowl*.' Her father set aside the suggestion with a deprecatory wave of the hand.

'Well, anyway, you got to fix yo'se'f up,' declared Martinette, dismissing further speculation; 'put on yo' otha pant'loon' an' yo' good coat; an' you betta ax Mr Léonce to cut yo' hair, an' yo' w'sker' a li'le bit.'

'It's w'at I say,' chimed in Evariste. 'I tell dat gent'man I'm goin' make myse'f fine. He say', "No, no," like he ent please'. He want' me like I come out de swamp. So much betta if my pant'loon' an' coat is tore, he say, an' colour' like de mud.' They could not understand these eccentric wishes on the part of the strange gentleman, and made no effort to do so.

An hour later Martinette, who was quite puffed up over the affair, trotted across to Aunt Dicey's cabin to communicate the news to her. The negress was ironing; her irons stood in a long row before the fire of logs that burned on the hearth. Martinette seated herself in the chimney corner and held her feet up to the blaze; it was damp and a little chilly out of doors. The girl's shoes were considerably worn and her garments were a little too thin and scant for the winter season. Her father had given her the two dollars he had received from the artist, and Martinette was on her way to the store to invest them as judiciously as she knew how.

'You know, Aunt Dicey,' she began a little complacently after listening awhile to Aunt Dicey's unqualified abuse of her own son, Wilkins, who was dining-room boy at Mr Hallet's, 'you know that stranger gentleman up to Mr Hallet's? he want' to make my popa's picture; an' he say' he goin' put it in one fine *mag*'zine yonda.' Aunt Dicey spat upon her iron to test its heat. Then she began to snicker. She kept on laughing inwardly, making her whole fat body shake, and saying nothing.

'W'at you laughin' 'bout, Aunt Dice?' enquired Martinette mistrustfully.

'I isn' laughin', chile!'

'Yas, you' laughin'.'

'Oh, don't pay no 'tention to me. I jis studyin' how simple you an' yo' pa is. You is bof de simplest somebody I eva come 'crost.'

'You got to say plumb out w'at you mean, Aunt Dice,' insisted the girl doggedly, suspicious and alert now.

'Well, dat w'y I say you is simple,' proclaimed the woman, slamming down her iron on an inverted, battered pie pan, 'jis like you says, dey gwine put yo' pa's picture yonda in de picture paper. An' you know w'at readin' dey gwine sot down on'neaf dat picture?' Martinette was intensely attentive. 'Dey gwine sot down on'neaf: "Dis heah is one dem low-down 'Cajuns o' Bayeh Têche!" '

The blood flowed from Martinette's face, leaving it deathly pale; in another instant it came beating back in a quick flood, and her eyes smarted with pain as if the tears that filled them had been fiery hot.

'I knows dem kine o' folks,' continued Aunt Dicey, resuming her interrupted ironing. 'Dat stranger he got a li'le boy w'at ain't none too big to spank. Dat li'le imp he come a hoppin' in heah yistiddy wid a kine o' box on'neaf his arm. He says, "Good-mo'nin', madam. Will you be so kine an' stan' jis like you is dah at yo' i'onin', an' lef me take yo' picture?" I 'lowed I gwine make a picture outen him wid dis heah flat-i'on, ef he don' cl'ar hisse'f quick. An' he say he baig my pardon fo' his intrudement. All dat kine o' talk to a ole nigga 'oman! Dat plainly sho' he don' know his place.'

'W'at you want 'im to say, Aunt Dice?' asked Martinette, with an effort to conceal her distress.

'I wants 'im to come in heah an' say: "Howdy, Aunt Dicey! will you be so kine and go put on yo' noo calker dress an' yo' bonnit w'at you w'ars to meetin', an' stan' 'side f'om dat i'onin'-boa'd w'ilse I gwine take yo' photygraph." Dat de way fo' a boy to talk w'at had good raisin'.'

Martinette had arisen, and began to take slow leave of the woman. She turned at the cabin door to observe tentatively: 'I reckon it's Wilkins tells you how the folks they talk, yonda up to Mr Hallet's.'

She did not go to the store as she had intended, but walked with a dragging step back to her home. The silver dollars clicked in her pocket as she walked. She felt like flinging them across the field; they seemed to her somehow the price of shame.

The sun had sunk, and twilight was settling like a silver beam upon the bayou and enveloping the fields in a grey mist. Evariste, slim and slouchy, was waiting for his daughter in the cabin door. He had lighted a fire of sticks and branches, and placed the kettle before it to boil. He met the girl with his slow, serious, questioning eyes, astonished to see her empty-handed.

'How come you didn' bring nuttin' f'om de sto', Martinette?'

She entered and flung her gingham sun-bonnet upon a chair. 'No, I didn' go yonda;' and with sudden exasperation: 'You got to go take back that money; you mus'n' git no picture took.'

'But, Martinette,' her father mildly interposed, 'I promise' 'im; an' he's goin' give me some mo' money w'en he finish.'

'If he give you a ba'el o' money, you mus'n' git no picture took. You know w'at he want to put un'neath that picture, fo' ev'body to read?' She could not tell him the whole hideous truth as she had heard it distorted from Aunt Dicey's lips; she would not hurt him that much. 'He's goin' to write: "This is one 'Cajun' o' the Bayou Têche." '

Evariste winced. 'How you know?' he asked.

'I yeard so. I know it's true.'

The water in the kettle was boiling. He went and poured a small quantity upon the coffee which he had set there to drip. Then he said to her: 'I reckon you jus' as well go care dat two dolla' back, tomo' mo'nin'; me, I'll go yonda ketch a mess o' fish in Carancro Lake.'

*

Mr Hallet and a few masculine companions were assembled at a rather late breakfast the following morning. The dining-room was a big, bare one, enlivened by a cheerful fire of logs that blazed in the wide chimney on massive andirons. There were guns, fishing tackle and other implements of sport lying about. A couple of fine dogs strayed unceremoniously in and out behind Wilkins, the negro boy who waited upon the table. The chair beside Mr Sublet, usually occupied by his little son, was vacant, as the child had gone for an early-morning outing and had not yet returned.

When breakfast was about half over, Mr Hallet noticed Martinette standing outside upon the gallery. The dining-room door had stood open more than half the time.

'Isn't that Martinette out there, Wilkins?' enquired the jovial-faced young planter.

'Dat's who, suh,' returned Wilkins. 'She ben standin' dah sence mos' sun-up; look like she studyin' to take root to de gall'ry.'

'What in the name of goodness does she want? Ask her what she wants. Tell her to come in to the fire.'

Martinette walked into the room with much hesitancy. Her small, brown face could hardly be seen in the depths of the gingham sun-bonnet. Her blue cottonade skirt scarcely reached the thin ankles that it should have covered.

'*Bonjou*,' she murmured, with a little comprehensive nod that took in the entire company. Her eyes searched the table for the 'stranger gentleman', and she knew him at once, because his hair was parted in the middle and he wore a pointed beard. She went and laid the two silver dollars beside his plate and motioned to retire without a word of explanation.

'Hold on, Martinette!' called out the planter, 'what's all this panto-mime business? Speak out, little one.'

'My popa don't want any picture took,' she offered, a little timorously. On her way to the door she had looked back to say this. In that fleeting glance she detected a smile of intelligence pass from one to the other of the group. She turned quickly, facing them all, and spoke out, excitement making her voice bold and shrill: 'My popa ent one low-down 'Cajun. He ent goin' to stan' to have that kine o' writin' put down un'neath his picture!'

She almost ran from the room, half blinded by the emotion that had helped her to make so daring a speech.

Descending the gallery steps she ran full against her father who was ascending, bearing in his arms the little boy, Archie Sublet. The child was most grotesquely attired in garments far too large for his diminutive person – the rough jeans clothing of some negro boy. Evariste himself had evidently been taking a bath without the preliminary ceremony of removing his clothes, that were now half dried upon his person by the wind and sun.

'Yere you' li'le boy,' he announced, stumbling into the room. 'You ought not lef dat li'le chile go by hisse'f *comme ça*[226] in de pirogue.' Mr Sublet darted from his chair; the others following suit almost as hastily. In an instant, quivering with apprehension, he had his little son in his arms. The child was quite unharmed, only somewhat pale and nervous, as the consequence of a recent very serious ducking.

Evariste related in his uncertain, broken English how he had been fishing for an hour or more in Carancro Lake, when he noticed the boy paddling over the deep, black water in a shell-like pirogue. Nearing a clump of cypress trees that rose from the lake, the pirogue became entangled in the heavy moss that hung from the tree limbs and trailed upon the water. The next thing he knew, the boat had overturned; he heard the child scream, and saw him disappear beneath the still, black surface of the lake.

'W'en I done swim to de sho' wid 'im,' continued Evariste, 'I hurry yonda to Jake Baptiste's cabin, an' we rub 'im an' warm 'im up, an' dress 'im up dry like you see. He all right now, M'sieur; but you mus'n lef 'im go no mo' by hisse'f in one pirogue.'

Martinette had followed into the room behind her father. She was feeling and tapping his wet garments solicitously, and begging him in French to come home. Mr Hallet at once ordered hot coffee and a warm breakfast for the two; and they sat down at the corner of the table, making no manner of objection in their perfect simplicity. It was with visible reluctance and ill-disguised contempt that Wilkins served them.

When Mr Sublet had arranged his son comfortably, with tender care, upon the sofa, and had satisfied himself that the child was quite uninjured, he attempted to find words with which to thank Evariste for this service which no treasure of words or gold could pay for. These warm and heartfelt expressions seemed to Evariste to exaggerate the importance of his action, and they intimidated him. He attempted shyly to hide his face as well as he could in the depths of his bowl of coffee.

'You will let me make your picture now, I hope, Evariste,' begged Mr Sublet, laying his hand upon the 'Cadian's shoulder. 'I want to place it among things I hold most dear, and shall call it "A hero of Bayou Têche".' This assurance seemed to distress Evariste greatly.

'No, no,' he protested, 'it's nuttin' hero' to take a li'le boy out de water. I jus' as easy do dat like I stoop down an' pick up a li'le chile w'at fall down in de road. I ent goin' to 'low dat, me. I don't git no picture took, *va*!'

Mr Hallet, who now discerned his friend's eagerness in the matter, came to his aid.

'I tell you, Evariste, let Mr Sublet draw your picture, and you yourself may call it whatever you want. I'm sure he'll let you.'

'Most willingly,' agreed the artist.

Evariste glanced up at him with shy and childlike pleasure. 'It's a bargain?' he asked.

'A bargain,' affirmed Mr Sublet.

'Popa,' whispered Martinette, 'you betta come home an' put on yo' otha pant'loon' an' yo' good coat.'

'And now, what shall we call the much talked-of picture?' cheerily enquired the planter, standing with his back to the blaze.

Evariste in a businesslike manner began carefully to trace on the tablecloth imaginary characters with an imaginary pen; he could not have written the real characters with a real pen – he did not know how.

'You will put on'neat' de picture,' he said, deliberately, ' "Dis is one picture of Mista Evariste Anatole Bonamour, a gent'man of de Bayou Têche." '

A Lady of Bayou St John

The days and the nights were very lonely for Madame Delisle.[227] Gustave, her husband, was away yonder in Virginia somewhere, with Beauregard, and she was here in the old house on Bayou St John, alone with her slaves.

Madame was very beautiful. So beautiful, that she found much diversion in sitting for hours before the mirror, contemplating her own loveliness; admiring the brilliancy of her golden hair, the sweet languor of her blue eyes, the graceful contours of her figure and the peachlike bloom of her flesh. She was very young. So young that she romped with the dogs, teased the parrot and could not fall asleep at night unless old black Manna-Loulou sat beside her bed and told her stories.

In short, she was a child, not able to realise the significance of the tragedy whose unfolding kept the civilised world in suspense. It was only the immediate effect of the awful drama that moved her: the gloom that, spreading on all sides, penetrated her own existence and deprived it of joyousness.

Sépincourt found her looking very lonely and disconsolate one day when he stopped to talk with her. She was pale, and her blue eyes were dim with unwept tears. He was a Frenchman who lived near by. He shrugged his shoulders over this strife between brothers, this quarrel which was none of his; and he resented it chiefly upon the ground that it made life uncomfortable; yet he was young enough to have had quicker and hotter blood in his veins.

When he left Madame Delisle that day, her eyes were no longer dim, and a something of the dreariness that weighted her had been lifted away. That mysterious, that treacherous bond called sympathy, had revealed them to each other.

He came to her very often that summer, clad always in cool, white duck, with a flower in his buttonhole. His pleasant brown eyes sought hers with warm, friendly glances that comforted her as a caress might comfort a disconsolate child. She took to watching for his slim figure, a little bent, walking lazily up the avenue between the double line of magnolias.

They would sit sometimes during whole afternoons in the vine-sheltered corner of the gallery, sipping the black coffee that Manna-

Loulou brought to them at intervals and talking, talking incessantly during the first days when they were unconsciously unfolding themselves to each other. Then a time came – it came very quickly – when they seemed to have nothing more to say to one another.

He brought her news of the war; and they talked about it listlessly, between long intervals of silence, of which neither took account. An occasional letter came by roundabout ways from Gustave – guarded and saddening in its tone. They would read it and sigh over it together.

Once they stood before his portrait that hung in the drawing-room and that looked out at them with kind, indulgent eyes. Madame wiped the picture with her gossamer handkerchief and impulsively pressed a tender kiss upon the painted canvas. For months past the living image of her husband had been receding farther and farther into a mist which she could penetrate with no faculty or power that she possessed.

One day at sunset, when she and Sépincourt stood silently side by side, looking across the *marais*, aflame with the western light, he said to her: '*M'amie*, let us go away from this country that is so *triste*. Let us go to Paris, you and me.'

She thought that he was jesting, and she laughed nervously. 'Yes, Paris would surely be gayer than Bayou St John,' she answered. But he was not jesting. She saw it at once in the glance that penetrated her own; in the quiver of his sensitive lip and the quick beating of a swollen vein in his brown throat.

'Paris, or anywhere – with you – ah, *bon Dieu!*' he whispered, seizing her hands. But she withdrew from him, frightened, and hurried away into the house, leaving him alone.

That night, for the first time, Madame did not want to hear Manna-Loulou's stories, and she blew out the wax candle that till now had burned nightly in her sleeping-room, under its tall, crystal globe. She had suddenly become a woman capable of love or sacrifice. She would not hear Manna-Loulou's stories. She wanted to be alone, to tremble and to weep.

In the morning her eyes were dry, but she would not see Sépincourt when he came. Then he wrote her a letter.

I have offended you and I would rather die! Do not banish me from your presence that is life to me. Let me lie at your feet, if only for a moment, in which to hear you say that you forgive me.

Men have written just such letters before, but Madame did not know it. To her it was a voice from the unknown, like music, awaking in her a delicious tumult that seized and held possession of her whole being.

When they met, he had but to look into her face to know that he
need not lie at her feet craving forgiveness. She was waiting for him
beneath the spreading branches of a live-oak that guarded the gate of
her home like a sentinel.

For a brief moment he held her hands, which trembled. Then he
folded her in his arms and kissed her many times. 'You will go with me,
m'amie? I love you – oh, I love you! Will you not go with me, *m'amie*?'

'Anywhere, anywhere,' she told him in a fainting voice that he could
scarcely hear.

But she did not go with him. Chance willed it otherwise. That night
a courier brought her a message from Beauregard, telling her that
Gustave, her husband, was dead.

When the new year was still young, Sépincourt decided that, all
things considered, he might, without any appearance of indecent haste,
speak again of his love to Madame Delisle. That love was quite as
acute as ever; perhaps a little sharper, from the long period of silence
and waiting to which he had subjected it. He found her, as he had
expected, clad in deepest mourning. She greeted him precisely as she
had welcomed the curé, when the kind old priest had brought to her
the consolations of religion – clasping his two hands warmly, and
calling him '*cher ami*'. Her whole attitude and bearing brought to
Sépincourt the poignant, the bewildering conviction that he held no
place in her thoughts.

They sat in the drawing-room before the portrait of Gustave, which
was draped with his scarf. Above the picture hung his sword, and
beneath it was an embankment of flowers. Sépincourt felt an almost
irresistible impulse to bend his knee before this altar, upon which he
saw foreshadowed the immolation of his hopes.

There was a soft air blowing gently over the *marais*. It came to them
through the open window, laden with a hundred subtle sounds and
scents of the springtime. It seemed to remind Madame of something
far, far away, for she gazed dreamily out into the blue firmament. It
fretted Sépincourt with impulses to speech and action which he found it
impossible to control.

'You must know what has brought me,' he began impulsively, drawing
his chair nearer to hers. 'Through all these months I have never ceased
to love you and to long for you. Night and day the sound of your dear
voice has been with me; your eyes – '

She held out her hand deprecatingly. He took it and held it. She let it
lie unresponsive in his.

'You cannot have forgotten that you loved me not long ago,' he went on eagerly, 'that you were ready to follow me anywhere – anywhere; do you remember? I have come now to ask you to fulfil that promise; to ask you to be my wife, my companion, the dear treasure of my life.'

She heard his warm and pleading tones as though listening to a strange language, imperfectly understood.

She withdrew her hand from his, and leaned her brow thoughtfully upon it.

'Can you not feel – can you not understand, *mon ami*,' she said calmly, 'that now such a thing – such a thought, is impossible to me?'

'Impossible?'

'Yes, impossible. Can you not see that now my heart, my soul, my thought – my very life, must belong to another? It could not be different.'

'Would you have me believe that you can wed your young existence to the dead?' he exclaimed with something like horror. Her glance was sunk deep in the embankment of flowers before her.

'My husband has never been so living to me as he is now,' she replied with a faint smile of commiseration for Sépincourt's fatuity. 'Every object that surrounds me speaks to me of him. I look yonder across the *marais*, and I see him coming towards me, tired and toil-stained from the hunt. I see him again sitting in this chair or in that one. I hear his familiar voice, his footsteps upon the galleries. We walk once more together beneath the magnolias; and at night in dreams I feel that he is there, there, near me. How could it be different! Ah! I have memories, memories to crowd and fill my life, if I live a hundred years!'

Sépincourt was wondering why she did not take the sword from her altar and thrust it through his body here and there. The effect would have been infinitely more agreeable than her words, penetrating his soul like fire. He arose confused, enraged with pain.

'Then, madame,' he stammered, 'there is nothing left for me but to take my leave. I bid you adieu.'

'Do not be offended, *mon ami*,' she said kindly, holding out her hand. 'You are going to Paris, I suppose?'

'What does it matter,' he exclaimed desperately, 'where I go?'

'Oh, I only wanted to wish you *bon voyage*,' she assured him amiably.

Many days after that Sépincourt spent in the fruitless mental effort of trying to comprehend that psychological enigma, a woman's heart.

Madame still lives on Bayou St John. She is rather an old lady now, a very pretty old lady, against whose long years of widowhood there has never been a breath of reproach. The memory of Gustave still fills and satisfies her days. She has never failed, once a year, to have a solemn high mass said for the repose of his soul.

A Night in Acadie

There was nothing to do on the plantation so Telèsphore, having a few dollars in his pocket, thought he would go down and spend Sunday in the vicinity of Marksville.

There was really nothing more to do in the vicinity of Marksville than in the neighbourhood of his own small farm; but Elvina would not be down there, nor Amaranthe, nor any of Ma'me Valtour's daughters to harass him with doubt, to torture him with indecision, to turn his very soul into a weathercock for love's fair winds to play with.

Telèsphore at twenty-eight had long felt the need of a wife. His home without one was like an empty temple in which there is no altar, no offering. So keenly did he realise the necessity that a dozen times at least during the past year he had been on the point of proposing marriage to almost as many different young women of the neighbourhood. Therein lay the difficulty, the trouble which Telèsphore experienced in making up his mind. Elvina's eyes were beautiful and had often tempted him to the verge of a declaration. But her skin was over swarthy for a wife; and her movements were slow and heavy; he doubted she had Indian blood, and we all know what Indian blood is for treachery. Amaranthe presented in her person none of these obstacles to matrimony. If her eyes were not so handsome as Elvina's, her skin was fine, and being slender to a fault, she moved swiftly about her household affairs, or when she walked the country lanes in going to church or to the store. Telèsphore had once reached the point of believing that Amaranthe would make him an excellent wife. He had even started out one day with the intention of declaring himself, when, as the god of chance would have it, Ma'me Valtour espied him passing in the road and enticed him to enter and partake of coffee and *baignés*.[228] He would have been a man of stone to have resisted, or to have remained insensible to the charms and accomplishments of the Valtour girls. Finally there was Ganache's widow, seductive rather than handsome, with a good bit of property in her own right. While Telèsphore was considering his chances of happiness or even success with Ganache's widow, she married a younger man.

From these embarrassing conditions, Telèsphore sometimes felt himself forced to escape; to change his environment for a day or two and thereby gain a few new insights by shifting his point of view.

It was Saturday morning that he decided to spend Sunday in the vicinity of Marksville, and the same afternoon found him waiting at the country station for the southbound train.

He was a robust young fellow with good, strong features and a some-what determined expression – despite his vacillations in the choice of a wife. He was dressed rather carefully in navy-blue 'store clothes' that fitted well because anything would have fitted Telèsphore. He had been freshly shaved and trimmed and carried an umbrella. He wore – a little tilted over one eye – a straw hat in preference to the conventional grey felt; for no other reason than that his uncle Telèsphore would have worn a felt, and a battered one at that. His whole conduct of life had been planned on lines in direct contradistinction to those of his uncle Telèsphore, whom he was thought in early youth greatly to resemble. The elder Telèsphore could not read nor write, therefore the younger had made it the object of his existence to acquire these accomplishments. The uncle pursued the avocations of hunting, fishing and moss-picking; employments which the nephew held in detestation. And as for carrying an umbrella, 'Nonc'[229] Telèsphore would have walked the length of the parish in a deluge before he would have so much as thought of one. In short, Telèsphore, by advisedly shaping his course in direct opposition to that of his uncle, managed to lead a rather orderly, industrious and respectable existence.

It was a little warm for April but the car was not uncomfortably crowded and Telèsphore was fortunate enough to secure the last available window-seat on the shady side. He was not too familiar with railway travel, his expeditions being usually made on horseback or in a buggy, and the short trip promised to interest him.

There was no one present whom he knew well enough to speak to: the district attorney, whom he knew by sight, a French priest from Natchitoches and a few faces that were familiar only because they were native.

But he did not greatly care to speak to anyone. There was a fair stand of cotton and corn in the fields and Telèsphore gathered satisfaction in silent contemplation of the crops, comparing them with his own.

It was towards the close of his journey that a young girl boarded the train. There had been girls getting on and off at intervals and it was perhaps because of the bustle attending her arrival that this one attracted Telèsphore's attention.

She called goodbye to her father from the platform and waved goodbye to him through the dusty, sunlit window pane after entering, for she was compelled to seat herself on the sunny side. She seemed inwardly excited and preoccupied save for the attention which she lavished upon a large parcel that she carried religiously and laid reverentially down upon the seat before her.

She was neither tall nor short, nor stout nor slender; nor was she beautiful, nor was she plain. She wore a figured lawn, cut a little low in the back, that exposed a round, soft *nuque*[230] with a few little clinging circlets of soft, brown hair. Her hat was of white straw, cocked up on the side with a bunch of pansies, and she wore grey lisle-thread[231] gloves. The girl seemed very warm and kept mopping her face. She vainly sought her fan, then she fanned herself with her handkerchief, and finally made an attempt to open the window. She might as well have tried to move the banks of Red River.

Telèsphore had been unconsciously watching her the whole time and perceiving her straight he arose and went to her assistance. But the window could not be opened. When he had grown red in the face and wasted an amount of energy that would have driven the plough for a day, he offered her his seat on the shady side. She demurred – there would be no room for the bundle. He suggested that the bundle be left where it was and agreed to assist her in keeping an eye upon it. She accepted Telèsphore's place at the shady window and he seated himself beside her.

He wondered if she would speak to him. He feared she might have mistaken him for a Western drummer, in which event he knew that she would not; for the women of the country caution their daughters against speaking to strangers on the trains. But the girl was not one to mistake an Acadian farmer for a Western travelling man. She was not born in Avoyelles parish for nothing.

'I wouldn' want anything to happen to it,' she said.

'It's all right w'ere it is,' he assured her, following the direction of her glance, that was fastened upon the bundle.

'The las' time I came over to Foché's ball I got caught in the rain on my way up to my cousin's house, an' my dress! *J' vous réponds!*[232] it was a sight. Li'le mo', I would miss the ball. As it was, the dress looked like I'd wo' it weeks without doin'-up.'

'No fear of rain today,' he reassured her, glancing out at the sky, 'but you can have my umbrella if it does rain; you jus' as well take it as not.'

'Oh, no! I wrap' the dress roun' in *toile-cirée*[233] this time. You goin' to Foché's ball?

Didn' I meet you once yonda on Bayou Derbanne? Looks like I know yo' face. You mus' come f'om Natchitoches pa'ish.'

'My cousins, the Fédeau family, live yonda. Me, I live on my own place in Rapides since '92.'

He wondered if she would follow up her enquiry relative to Foché's ball. If she did, he was ready with an answer, for he had decided to go to the ball. But her thoughts evidently wandered from the subject and were occupied with matters that did not concern him, for she turned away and gazed silently out of the window.

It was not a village; it was not even a hamlet at which they descended. The station was set down upon the edge of a cotton field. Near at hand was the post office and store; there was a section house; there were a few cabins at wide intervals, and one in the distance the girl informed him was the home of her cousin, Jules Trodon. There lay a good bit of road before them and she did not hesitate to accept Telèsphore's offer to bear her bundle on the way.

She carried herself boldly and stepped out freely and easily, like a negress. There was an absence of reserve in her manner; yet there was no lack of womanliness. She had the air of a young person accustomed to decide for herself and for those about her.

'You said yo' name was Fédeau?' she asked, looking squarely at Telèsphore. Her eyes were penetrating – not sharply penetrating, but earnest and dark, and a little searching. He noticed that they were handsome eyes; not so large as Elvina's, but finer in their expression. They started to walk down the track before turning into the lane leading to Trodon's house. The sun was sinking and the air was fresh and invigorating by contrast with the stifling atmosphere of the train.

'You said yo' name was Fédeau?' she asked.

'No,' he returned. 'My name is Telèsphore Baquette.'

'An' my name; it's Zaïda Trodon. It looks like you ought to know me; I don' know w'y.'

'It looks that way to me, somehow,' he replied. They were satisfied to recognise this feeling – almost conviction – of pre-acquaintance, without trying to penetrate its cause.

By the time they reached Trodon's house he knew that she lived over on Bayou de Glaize with her parents and a number of younger brothers and sisters. It was rather dull where they lived and she often came to lend a hand when her cousin's wife got tangled in domestic complications; or, as she was doing now, when Foché's Saturday ball promised to be unusually important and brilliant. There would be people there even from Marksville, she thought; there were often gentlemen from Alexandria. Telèsphore was as unreserved as she, and they appeared like old acquaintances when they reached Trodon's gate.

Trodon's wife was standing on the gallery with a baby in her arms, watching for Zaïda; and four little barefooted children were sitting in a row on the step, also waiting; but terrified and struck motionless and dumb at sight of a stranger. He opened the gate for the girl but stayed outside himself. Zaïda presented him formally to her cousin's wife, who insisted upon his entering.

'Ah, b'en, pour ça!234 you got to come in. It's any sense you goin' to walk yonda to Foché's! Ti Jules, run call yo' pa.' As if Ti Jules could have run or walked even, or moved a muscle!

But Telèsphore was firm. He drew forth his silver watch and looked at it in a businesslike fashion. He always carried a watch; his uncle Telèsphore always told the time by the sun, or by instinct, like an animal. He was quite determined to walk on to Foché's, a couple of miles away, where he expected to secure supper and a lodging, as well as the pleasing distraction of the ball.

'Well, I reckon I see you all tonight,' he uttered in cheerful anticipation as he moved away.

'You'll see Zaïda; yes, an' Jules,' called out Trodon's wife good-humouredly. 'Me, I got no time to fool with balls, J' vous réponds! with all them chil'ren.'

'He's good-lookin'; yes,' she exclaimed, when Telèsphore was out of earshot. 'An' dressed! it's like a prince. I didn' know you knew any Baquettes, you, Zaïda.'

'It's strange you don' know 'em yo'se'f, cousine.' Well, there had been no question from Ma'me Trodon, so why should there be an answer from Zaïda?

Telèsphore wondered as he walked why he had not accepted the invitation to enter. He was not regretting it; he was simply wondering what could have induced him to decline. For it surely would have been agreeable to sit there on the gallery waiting while Zaïda prepared herself for the dance; to have partaken of supper with the family and afterwards accompanied them to Foché's. The whole situation was so novel, and had presented itself so unexpectedly that Telèsphore wished in reality to become acquainted with it, accustomed to it. He wanted to view it from this side and that in comparison with other, familiar situations. The girl had impressed him – affected him in some way; but in some new, unusual way, not as the others always had. He could not recall details of her personality as he could recall such details of Amaranthe or the Valtours, of any of them. When Telèsphore tried to think of her he could not think at all. He seemed to have absorbed her in some way and his brain was not so occupied with her as his senses were. At that moment he was looking forward to the ball; there was no doubt about that. Afterwards, he did not know what he would look forward to; he did not care; afterwards made no difference. If he had expected the crash of doom to come after the dance at Foché's, he would only have smiled in his thankfulness that it was not to come before.

*

There was the same scene every Saturday at Foché's! A scene to have aroused the guardians of the peace in a locality where such commodities abound. And all on account of the mammoth pot of gumbo[235] that bubbled, bubbled, bubbled out in the open air. Foché in shirt-sleeves, fat, red and enraged, swore and reviled, and stormed at old black Douté for her extravagance. He called her every kind of a name of every kind of animal that suggested itself to his lurid imagination. And every fresh invective that he fired at her she hurled it back at him while into the pot went the chickens and the pans-full of minced ham, and the fists-full of onion and sage and *piment rouge* and *piment vert*.[236] If he wanted her to cook for pigs he had only to say so. She knew how to cook for pigs and she knew how to cook for people of les Avoyelles.

The gumbo smelled good, and Telèsphore would have liked a taste of it. Douté was dragging from the fire a stick of wood that Foché had officiously thrust beneath the simmering pot, and she muttered as she hurled it smouldering to one side: '*Vaux mieux y s'mêle ces affairs, lui; si non!*'[237] But she was all courtesy as she dipped a steaming plate for Telèsphore; though she assured him it would not be fit for a Christian or a gentleman to taste till midnight.

Telèsphore having brushed, 'spruced' and refreshed himself, strolled about, taking a view of the surroundings. The house, big, bulky and weather-beaten, consisted chiefly of galleries in every stage of decrepitude and dilapidation. There were a few chinaberry trees and a spreading live-oak in the yard. Along the edge of the fence, a good distance away, was a line of gnarled and distorted mulberry trees; and it was there, out in the road, that the people who came to the ball tied their ponies, their wagons and carts.

Dusk was beginning to fall and Telèsphore, looking out across the prairie, could see them coming from all directions. The little Creole ponies galloping in a line looked like hobby horses in the faint distance; the mule-carts were like toy wagons. Zaïda might be among those people approaching, flying, crawling ahead of the darkness that was creeping out of the far wood. He hoped so, but he did not believe so; she would hardly have had time to dress.

Foché was noisily lighting lamps, with the assistance of an inoffensive mulatto boy whom he intended in the morning to butcher, to cut into sections, to pack and salt down in a barrel, like the Colfax woman did to her old husband – a fitting destiny for so stupid a pig as the mulatto boy. The negro musicians had arrived: two fiddlers and an accordion player, and they were drinking whiskey from a black quart bottle which was passed socially from one to the other. The musicians were really never at their best till the quart bottle had been consumed.

The girls who came in wagons and on ponies from a distance wore, for the most part, calico dresses and sun-bonnets. Their finery they brought along in pillow-slips or pinned up in sheets and towels. With these they at once retired to an upper room; later to appear be-ribboned and be-furbelowed; their faces masked with starch powder, but never a touch of rouge.

Most of the guests had assembled when Zaïda arrived – 'dashed up' would better express her coming – in an open, two-seated buckboard,[238] with her cousin Jules driving. He reined the pony suddenly and viciously before the time-eaten front steps, in order to produce an impression upon those who were gathered around. Most of the men had halted their vehicles outside and permitted their womenfolk to walk up from the mulberry trees.

But the real, the stunning effect was produced when Zaïda stepped upon the gallery and threw aside her light shawl in the full glare of half a dozen kerosene lamps. She was white from head to foot – literally, for her slippers even were white. No one would have believed, let alone suspected that they were a pair of old black ones which she had covered with pieces of her first-communion sash. There is no describing her dress, it was fluffy, like a fresh powder-puff, and stood out. No wonder she had handled it so reverentially! Her white fan was covered with spangles that she herself had sewed all over it; and in her belt and in her brown hair were thrust small sprays of orange blossom.

Two men leaning against the railing uttered long whistles expressive equally of wonder and admiration.

'Tiens! t'es pareille comme ain mariée,[239] Zaïda;' cried out a lady with a baby in her arms. Some young women tittered and Zaïda fanned herself. The women's voices were almost without exception shrill and piercing; the men's, soft and low-pitched.

The girl turned to Telèsphore, as to an old and valued friend: 'Tiens! c'est vous?'[240] He had hesitated at first to approach, but at this friendly sign of recognition he drew eagerly forwards and held out his hand. The men looked at him suspiciously, inwardly resenting his stylish appearance, which they considered intrusive, offensive and demoralising.

How Zaïda's eyes sparkled now! What very pretty teeth Zaïda had when she laughed, and what a mouth! Her lips were a revelation, a promise; something to carry away and remember in the night and grow hungry thinking of next day. Strictly speaking, they may not have been quite all that; but in any event, that is the way Telèsphore thought about them. He began to take account of her appearance: her nose, her eyes, her hair. And when she left him to go in and dance her first dance with cousin Jules, he leaned up against a post and thought of them: nose, eyes, hair, ears, lips and round, soft throat.

Later it was like Bedlam.[241]

The musicians had warmed up and were scraping away indoors and calling the figures. Feet were pounding through the dance; dust was flying. The women's voices were piped high and mingled discordantly, like the confused, shrill clatter of waking birds, while the men laughed boisterously. But if someone had only thought of gagging Foché, there would have been less noise. His good humour permeated everywhere, like an atmosphere. He was louder than all the noise; he was more visible than the dust. He called the young mulatto (destined for the knife) 'my boy' and sent him flying hither and thither. He beamed upon Douté as he tasted the gumbo and congratulated her: *'C'est toi qui s'y connais, ma fille! 'cré tonnerre!'*[242]

Telèsphore danced with Zaïda and then he leaned out against the post; then he danced with Zaïda, and then he leaned against the post. The mothers of the other girls decided that he had the manners of a pig.

It was time to dance again with Zaïda and he went in search of her. He was carrying her shawl, which she had given him to hold.

'W'at time it is?' she asked him when he had found and secured her. They were under one of the kerosene lamps on the front gallery and he drew forth his silver watch. She seemed to be still labouring under some suppressed excitement that he had noticed before.

'It's fo'teen minutes pas' twelve,' he told her exactly.

'I wish you'd fine out w'ere Jules is. Go look yonda in the card-room if he's there, an' come tell me.' Jules had danced with all the prettiest girls. She knew it was his custom after accomplishing this agreeable feat, to retire to the card-room.

'You'll wait yere till I come back?' he asked.

'I'll wait yere; you go on.' She waited but drew back a little into the shadow. Telèsphore lost no time.

'Yes, he's yonda playin' cards with Foché an' some others I don' know,' he reported, when he had discovered her in the shadow. There had been a spasm of alarm when he did not at once see her where he had left her under the lamp.

'Does he look – look like he's fixed yonda fo' good?'

'He's got his coat off. Looks like he's fixed pretty comf'table fo' the nex' hour or two.'

'Gi' me my shawl.'

'You cole?' offering to put it around her.

'No, I ain't cole.' She drew the shawl about her shoulders and turned as if to leave him. But a sudden generous impulse seemed to move her, and she added: 'Come along yonda with me.'

They descended the few rickety steps that led down to the yard. He followed rather than accompanied her across the beaten and trampled sward. Those who saw them thought they had gone out to take the air. The beams of light that slanted out from the house were fitful and uncertain, deepening the shadows. The embers under the empty gumbo-pot glared red in the darkness. There was a sound of quiet voices coming from under the trees.

Zaïda, closely accompanied by Telèsphore, went out where the vehicles and horses were fastened to the fence. She stepped carefully and held up her skirts as if dreading the least speck of dew or of dust.

'Unhitch Jules's ho'se an' buggy there an' turn 'em 'roun' this way, please.' He did as instructed, first backing the pony, then leading it out to where she stood in the half-made road.

'You goin' home?' he asked her. 'Betta let me water the pony.'

'Neva mine.' She mounted and seating herself grasped the reins. 'No, I aint goin' home,' she added. He, too, was holding the reins gathered in one hand across the pony's back.

'W'ere you goin'?' he demanded.

'Neva you mine w'ere I'm goin'.'

'You ain't goin' anyw'ere this time o' night by yo'se'f?'

'W'at you reckon I'm 'fraid of?' she laughed. 'Turn loose that ho'se,' at the same time urging the animal forwards. The little brute started away with a bound and Telèsphore, also with a bound, sprang into the buckboard and seated himself beside Zaïda.

'You ain't goin' anyw'ere this time o' night by yo'se'f.' It was not a question now, but an assertion, and there was no denying it. There was even no disputing it, and Zaïda recognising the fact drove on in silence.

There is no animal that moves so swiftly across a 'Cadian prairie as the little Creole pony. This one did not run nor trot; he seemed to reach out in galloping bounds. The buckboard creaked, bounced, jolted

and swayed. Zaïda clutched at her shawl while Telèsphore drew his
straw hat farther down over his right eye and offered to drive. But he
did not know the road and she would not let him. They had soon
reached the woods.

If there is any animal that can creep more slowly through a wooded
road than the little Creole pony, that animal has not yet been discovered
in Acadie. This particular animal seemed to be appalled by the darkness
of the forest and filled with dejection. His head drooped and he lifted
his feet as if each hoof were weighted with a thousand pounds of lead.
Anyone unacquainted with the peculiarities of the breed would sometimes have fancied that he was standing still. But Zaïda and Telèsphore
knew better. Zaïda uttered a deep sigh as she slackened her hold on the
reins and Telèsphore, lifting his hat, let it swing from the back of his
head.

'How you don' ask me w'ere I'm goin'?' she said finally. These were
the first words she had spoken since refusing his offer to drive.

'Oh, it don' make any diff'ence w'ere you goin'.'

'Then if it don' make any diff'ence w'ere I'm goin', I jus' as well tell
you.' She hesitated, however. He seemed to have no curiosity and did
not urge her.

'I'm goin' to get married,' she said.

He uttered some kind of an exclamation; it was nothing articulate –
more like the tone of an animal that gets a sudden knife thrust. And
now he felt how dark the forest was. An instant before it had seemed a
sweet, black paradise; better than any heaven he had ever heard of.

'W'y can't you get married at home?' This was not the first thing that
occurred to him to say, but this was the first thing he said.

'Ah, *b'en oui*! with perfec' mules fo' a father an' mother! It's good
enough to talk.'

'W'y couldn' he come an' get you? W'at kine of a scound'el is that to
let you go through the woods at night by yo'se'f?'

'You betta wait till you know who you talkin' about. He didn' come
an' get me because he knows I ain't 'fraid; an' because he's got too much
pride to ride in Jules Trodon's buckboard afta he done been put out o'
Jules Trodon's house.'

'W'at's his name an' w'ere you goin' to fine 'im?'

'Yonda on the other side the woods up at ole Wat Gibson's – a kine
of justice the peace or something. Anyhow he's goin' to marry us. An'
afta we done married those *têtes-de-mulets*[243] yonda on Bayou de Glaize
can say w'at they want.'

'W'at's his name?'

'André Pascal.'

The name meant nothing to Telèsphore. For all he knew, André Pascal might be one of the shining lights of Avoyelles; but he doubted it.

'You betta turn 'roun',' he said. It was an unselfish impulse that prompted the suggestion. It was the thought of this girl married to a man whom even Jules Trodon would not suffer to enter his house.

'I done give my word,' she answered.

'W'at's the matte with 'im? W'y don't yo' father and mother want you to marry 'im?'

'W'y? Because it's always the same tune! W'en a man's down eve'y-body's got stones to throw at 'im. They say he's lazy. A man that will walk from St Landry plumb to Rapides lookin' fo' work; an' they call that lazy! Then, somebody's been spreadin' yonda on the Bayou that he drinks. I don' b'lieve it. I neva saw 'im drinkin', me. Anyway, he won't drink afta he's married to me; he's too fon' of me fo' that. He say he'll blow out his brains if I don' marry 'im.'

'I reckon you betta turn roun'.'

'No, I done give my word.' And they went creeping on through the woods in silence.

'W'at time is it?' she asked after an interval. He lit a match and looked at his watch

'It's quarta to one. W'at time did he say?'

'I tole 'im I'd come about one o'clock. I knew that was a good time to get away f'om the ball.'

She would have hurried a little but the pony could not be induced to do so. He dragged himself, seemingly ready at any moment to give up the breath of life. But once out of the woods he made up for lost time. They were on the open prairie again, and he fairly ripped the air; some flying demon must have changed skins with him.

It was a few minutes of one o'clock when they drew up before Wat Gibson's house. It was not much more than a rude shelter, and in the dim starlight it seemed isolated, as if standing alone in the middle of the black, far-reaching prairie. As they halted at the gate a dog within set up a furious barking; and an old negro who had been smoking his pipe at that ghostly hour, advanced towards them from the shelter of the gallery. Telèsphore descended and helped his companion to alight.

'We want to see Mr Gibson,' spoke up Zaïda. The old fellow had already opened the gate. There was no light in the house.

'Marse Gibson, he yonda to ole Mr Bodel's playin' kairds. But he neva' stay atter one o'clock. Come in, ma'am; come in, suh; walk right 'long in.' He had drawn his own conclusions to explain their appearance.

They stood upon the narrow porch waiting while he went inside to light the lamp.

Although the house was small, as it comprised but one room, that room was comparatively a large one. It looked to Telèsphore and Zaïda very large and gloomy when they entered it. The lamp was on a table that stood against the wall, and that held further a rusty looking ink bottle, a pen and an old blank book. A narrow bed was off in the corner. The brick chimney extended into the room and formed a ledge that served as mantelshelf. From the big, low-hanging rafters swung an assortment of fishing tackle, a gun, some discarded articles of clothing and a string of red peppers. The boards of the floor were broad, rough and loosely joined together.

Telèsphore and Zaïda seated themselves on opposite sides of the table and the negro went out to the wood pile to gather chips and pieces of bois-gras[244] with which to kindle a small fire.

It was a little chilly; he supposed the two would want coffee and he knew that Wat Gibson would ask for a cup the first thing on his arrival.

'I wonder w'at's keepin' 'im,' muttered Zaïda impatiently. Telèsphore looked at his watch. He had been looking at it at intervals of one minute straight along.

'It's ten minutes pas' one,' he said. He offered no further comment.

At twelve minutes past one Zaïda's restlessness again broke into speech.

'I can't imagine, me, w'at's become of André! He said he'd be yere sho' at one.' The old negro was kneeling before the fire that he had kindled, contemplating the cheerful blaze. He rolled his eyes towards Zaïda.

'You talkin' 'bout Mr André Pascal? No need to look fo' him. Mr André he b'en down to de P'int all day raisin' Cain.'

'That's a lie,' said Zaïda. Telèsphore said nothing.

'Tain't no lie, ma'am; he b'en sho' raisin' de ole Nick.' She looked at him, too contemptuous to reply.

The negro told no lie so far as his bald statement was concerned. He was simply mistaken in his estimate of André Pascal's ability to 'raise Cain' during an entire afternoon and evening and still keep a rendezvous with a lady at one o'clock in the morning. For André was even then at hand, as the loud and menacing howl of the dog testified. The negro hastened out to admit him.

André did not enter at once; he stayed a while outside abusing the dog and communicating to the negro his intention of coming out to shoot the animal after he had attended to more pressing business that was awaiting him within.

Zaïda arose, a little flurried and excited, when he entered. Telèsphore remained seated.

Pascal was partially sober. There had evidently been an attempt at dressing for the occasion at some early part of the previous day, but such evidences had almost wholly vanished. His linen was soiled and his whole appearance was that of a man who, by an effort, had aroused himself from a debauch. He was a little taller than Telèsphore, and more loosely put together. Most women would have called him a handsomer man. It was easy to imagine that when sober, he might betray, by some subtle grace of speech or manner, evidences of gentle blood.

'W'y did you keep me waitin', André? w'en you knew – ' she got no further, but backed up against the table and stared at him with earnest, startled eyes.

'Keep you waiting, Zaïda? my dear li'le Zaïdé, how can you say such a thing! I started up yere an hour ago an' that – w'ere's that damned ole Gibson?' He had approached Zaïda with the evident intention of embracing her, but she seized his wrist and held him at arm's length away. In casting his eyes about for old Gibson his glance alighted upon Telèsphore.

The sight of the 'Cadian seemed to fill him with astonishment. He stood back and began to contemplate the young fellow and lose himself in speculation and conjecture before him, as if before some unlabelled wax figure. He turned for information to Zaïda.

'Say, Zaïda, w'at you call this? W'at kine of damn fool you got sitting yere? Who let him in? W'at you reckon he's lookin' fo'? Trouble?'

Telèsphore said nothing; he was awaiting his cue from Zaïda.

'André Pascal,' she said, 'you jus' as well take the do' an' go. You might stan' yere till the day o' judgement on yo' knees befo' me; an' blow out yo' brains if you a mine to. I ain't neva goin' to marry you.'

'The hell you ain't!'

He had hardly more than uttered the words when he lay prone on his back. Telèsphore had knocked him down. The blow seemed to complete the process of sobering that had begun in him. He gathered himself together and rose to his feet; in doing so he reached back for his pistol. His hold was not yet steady, however, and the weapon slipped from his grasp and fell to the floor. Zaïda picked it up and laid it on the table behind her. She was going to see fair play.

The brute instinct that drives men at each other's throats was awake and stirring in these two. Each saw in the other a thing to be wiped out of his way – out of existence if need be. Passion and blind rage directed the blows which they dealt, and steeled the tension of muscles and clutch of fingers. They were not skilful blows, however.

The fire blazed cheerily; the kettle which the negro had placed upon the coals was steaming and singing. The man had gone in search of his master. Zaïda had placed the lamp out of harm's way on the high mantle ledge and she leaned back with her hands behind her upon the table.

She did not raise her voice or lift her finger to stay the combat that was acting before her. She was motionless, and white to the lips; only her eyes seemed to be alive and burning and blazing. At one moment she felt that André must have strangled Telèsphore; but she said nothing. The next instant she could hardly doubt that the blow from Telèsphore's doubled fist could be less than a killing one; but she did nothing.

How the loose boards swayed and creaked beneath the weight of the struggling men! The very old rafters seemed to groan; and she felt that the house shook.

The combat, if fierce, was short, and it ended out on the gallery whither they had staggered through the open door – or one had dragged the other – she could not tell. But she knew when it was over, for there was a long moment of utter stillness. Then she heard one of the men descend the steps and go away, for the gate slammed after him. The other went out to the cistern; the sound of the tin bucket splashing in the water reached her where she stood. He must have been endeavouring to remove traces of the encounter.

Presently Telèsphore entered the room. The elegance of his apparel had been somewhat marred; the men over at the 'Cadian ball would hardly have taken exception now to his appearance.

'W'ere is André?' the girl asked.

'He's gone,' said Telèsphore.

She had never changed her position and now when she drew herself up her wrists ached and she rubbed them a little. She was no longer pale; the blood had come back into her cheeks and lips, staining them crimson. She held out her hand to him. He took it gratefully enough, but he did not know what to do with it; that is, he did not know what he might dare to do with it, so he let it drop gently away and went to the fire.

'I reckon we betta be goin', too,' she said. He stooped and poured some of the bubbling water from the kettle upon the coffee which the negro had set upon the hearth.

'I'll make a l'ile coffee firs',' he proposed, 'an' anyhow we betta wait till ole man w'at's-his-name comes back. It wouldn't look well to leave his house that way without some kine of excuse or explanation.'

She made no reply, but seated herself submissively beside the table.

Her will, which had been over-mastering and aggressive, seemed to have grown numb under the disturbing spell of the past few hours. And illusion had gone from her, and had carried her love with it. The absence of regret revealed this to her. She realised, but could not comprehend it, not knowing that the love had been part of the illusion. She was tired in body and spirit, and it was with a sense of restfulness that she sat all drooping and relaxed and watched Telèsphore make the coffee.

He made enough for them both and a cup for old Wat Gibson when he should come in, and also one for the negro. He supposed the cups, the sugar and spoons were in the safe over there in the corner, and that is where he found them.

When he finally said to Zaïda, 'Come, I'm going to take you home now,' and drew her shawl around her, pinning it under the chin, she was like a little child and followed whither he led in all confidence.

It was Telèsphore who drove on the way back, and he let the pony cut no capers, but held him to a steady and tempered gait. The girl was still quiet and silent; she was thinking tenderly – a little tearfully – of those two old *têtes-de-mulets* yonder on Bayou de Glaize.

How they crept through the woods! and how dark it was and how still!

'W'at time it is?' whispered Zaïda. Alas! he could not tell her; his watch was broken. But almost for the first time in his life, Telèsphore did not care what time it was.

Athénaïse

1

Athénaïse went away in the morning to make a visit to her parents, ten miles back on rigolet de Bon Dieu.[245] She did not return in the evening, and Cazeau, her husband, fretted not a little. He did not worry much about Athénaïse, who, he suspected, was resting only too content in the bosom of her family; his chief solicitude was manifestly for the pony she had ridden. He felt sure those 'lazy pigs', her brothers, were capable of neglecting it seriously. This misgiving Cazeau communicated to his servant, old Félicité, who waited upon him at supper.

His voice was low pitched, and even softer than Félicité's. He was tall, sinewy, swarthy, and altogether severe looking. His thick black hair waved, and it gleamed like the breast of a crow. The sweep of his moustache, which was not so black, outlined the broad contour of the mouth. Beneath the underlip grew a small tuft which he was much given to twisting and which he permitted to grow apparently for no other purpose. Cazeau's eyes were dark blue, narrow and overshadowed. His hands were coarse and stiff from close acquaintance with farming tools and implements, and he handled his fork and knife clumsily. But he was distinguished looking, and succeeded in commanding a good deal of respect, and even fear sometimes.

He ate his supper alone, by the light of a single coal-oil lamp that but faintly illuminated the big room, with its bare floor and huge rafters, and its heavy pieces of furniture that loomed dimly in the gloom of the apartment. Félicité, ministering to his wants, hovered about the table like a little, bent restless shadow.

She served him with a dish of sunfish fried crisp and brown. There was nothing else set before him beside the bread and butter and the bottle of red wine, which she locked carefully in the buffet after he had poured his second glass. She was occupied with her mistress's absence, and kept reverting to it after he had expressed his solicitude about the pony.

'Dat beat me! on'y marry two mont', an' got de head turn' a'ready to go 'broad. C'est pas Chrétien, tenez!'[246]

Cazeau shrugged his shoulders for answer, after he had drained his glass and pushed aside his plate. Félicité's opinion of the unchristianlike behaviour of his wife in leaving him thus alone after two months of marriage weighed little with him. He was used to solitude, and did not mind a day or a night or two of it. He had lived alone ten years, since his first wife died, and Félicité might have known better than to suppose that he cared. He told her she was a fool. It sounded like a compliment in his modulated, caressing voice. She grumbled to herself as she set about clearing the table, and Cazeau arose and walked outside on the gallery; his spurs, which he had not removed upon entering the house, jangled at every step.

The night was beginning to deepen, and to gather black about the clusters of trees and shrubs that were grouped in the yard. In the beam of light from the open kitchen door a black boy stood feeding a brace of snarling, hungry dogs; farther away, on the steps of a cabin, someone was playing the accordion; and in still another direction a little negro baby was crying lustily. Cazeau walked around to the front of the house, which was square, squat and one-storey.

A belated wagon was driving in at the gate, and the impatient driver was swearing hoarsely at his jaded oxen. Félicité stepped out on the gallery, glass and polishing towel in hand, to investigate, and to wonder, too, who could be singing out on the river. It was a party of young people paddling around, waiting for the moon to rise, and they were singing 'Juanita',[247] their voices coming tempered and melodious through the distance and the night.

Cazeau's horse was waiting, saddled, ready to be mounted, for Cazeau had many things to attend to before bedtime; so many things that there was not left to him a moment in which to think of Athénaïse. He felt her absence, though, like a dull, insistent pain.

However, before he slept that night he was visited by the thought of her, and by a vision of her fair young face with its drooping lips and sullen and averted eyes. The marriage had been a blunder; he had only to look into her eyes to feel that, to discover her growing aversion. But it was a thing not by any possibility to be undone. He was quite prepared to make the best of it, and expected no less than a like effort on her part. The less she revisited the rigolet, the better. He would find means to keep her at home hereafter.

These unpleasant reflections kept Cazeau awake far into the night, notwithstanding the craving of his whole body for rest and sleep. The moon was shining, and its pale effulgence reached dimly into the room, and with it a touch of the cool breath of the spring night. There was an unusual stillness abroad; no sound to be heard save the distant, tireless, plaintive notes of the accordion.

2

Athénaïse did not return the following day, even though her husband sent her word to do so by her brother, Montéclin, who passed on his way to the village early in the morning.

On the third day Cazeau saddled his horse and went himself in search of her. She had sent no word, no message, explaining her absence, and he felt that he had good cause to be offended. It was rather awkward to have to leave his work, even though late in the afternoon – Cazeau had always so much to do; but among the many urgent calls upon him, the task of bringing his wife back to a sense of her duty seemed to him for the moment paramount.

The Michés, Athénaïse's parents, lived on the old Gotrain place. It did not belong to them; they were 'running' it for a merchant in Alexandria. The house was far too big for their use. One of the lower rooms served for the storing of wood and tools; the person 'occupying' the place before Miché having pulled up the flooring in despair of being able to patch it. Upstairs, the rooms were so large, so bare, that they offered a constant temptation to lovers of the dance, whose importunities Madame Miché was accustomed to meet with amiable indulgence. A dance at Miché's and a plate of Madame Miché's gumbo-*filé* [248] at midnight were pleasures not to be neglected or despised, unless by such serious souls as Cazeau.

Long before Cazeau reached the house his approach had been observed, for there was nothing to obstruct the view of the outer road; vegetation was not yet abundantly advanced, and there was but a patchy, straggling stand of cotton and corn in Miché's field.

Madame Miché, who had been seated on the gallery in a rocking-chair, stood up to greet him as he drew near. She was short and fat, and wore a black skirt and loose muslin sack fastened at the throat with a hair brooch. Her own hair, brown and glossy, showed but a few threads of silver. Her round pink face was cheery, and her eyes were bright and good humoured. But she was plainly perturbed and ill at ease as Cazeau advanced.

Montéclin, who was there too, was not ill at ease, and made no attempt to disguise the dislike with which his brother-in-law inspired him. He was a slim, wiry fellow of twenty-five, short of stature like his mother, and resembling her in feature. He was in shirt-sleeves, half leaning, half sitting, on the insecure railing of the gallery, and fanning himself with his broad-brimmed felt hat.

'*Cochon!*' he muttered under his breath as Cazeau mounted the stairs – '*sacré cochon!*' [249]

'*Cochon*' had sufficiently characterised the man who had once on a time declined to lend Montéclin money. But when this same man had had the presumption to propose marriage to his well-beloved sister, Athénaïse, and the honour to be accepted by her, Montéclin felt that a qualifying epithet was needed fully to express his estimate of Cazeau.

Miché and his oldest son were absent. They both esteemed Cazeau highly, and talked much of his qualities of head and heart, and thought much of his excellent standing with city merchants.

Athénaïse had shut herself up in her room. Cazeau had seen her rise and enter the house at perceiving him. He was a good deal mystified, but no one could have guessed it when he shook hands with Madame Miché. He had only nodded to Montéclin, with a muttered, '*Comment ça va?*'[250]

'Tiens! something tole me you were coming today!' exclaimed Madame Miché, with a little blustering appearance of being cordial and at ease, as she offered Cazeau a chair.

He ventured a short laugh as he seated himself.

'You know, nothing would do,' she went on, with much gesture of her small, plump hands, 'nothing would do but Athénaïse mus' stay las' night fo' a li'le dance. The boys wouldn' year to their sister leaving.'

Cazeau shrugged his shoulders significantly, telling as plainly as words that he knew nothing about it.

'*Comment!* Montéclin didn' tell you we were going to keep Athénaïse?' Montéclin had evidently told nothing.

'An' how about the night befo',' questioned Cazeau, 'an' las' night? It isn't possible you dance every night out yere on the Bon Dieu!'

Madame Miché laughed, with amiable appreciation of the sarcasm; and turning to her son, 'Montéclin, my boy, go tell yo' sister that Monsieur Cazeau is yere.'

Montéclin did not stir except to shift his position and settle himself more securely on the railing.

'Did you year me, Montéclin?'

'Oh yes, I yeard you plain enough,' responded her son, 'but you know as well as me it's no use to tell 'Thénaïse anything. You been talkin' to her yo'se'f since Monday; an' pa's preached himse'f hoa'se on the subject; an' you even had Uncle Achille down yere yesterday to reason with her. W'en 'Thénaïse said she wasn' goin' to set her foot back in Cazeau's house, she meant it.'

This speech, which Montéclin delivered with thorough unconcern, threw his mother into a condition of painful but dumb embarrassment. It brought two fiery red spots to Cazeau's cheeks, and for the space of a moment he looked wicked.

What Montéclin had spoken was quite true, though his taste in the manner and choice of time and place in saying it were not of the best. Athénaïse, upon the first day of her arrival, had announced that she came to stay, having no intention of returning under Cazeau's roof. The announcement had scattered consternation, as she knew it would. She had been implored, scolded, entreated, stormed at, until she felt herself like a dragging sail that all the winds of heaven had beaten upon. Why in the name of God had she married Cazeau? Her father had lashed her with the question a dozen times. Why indeed? It was difficult now for her to understand why, unless because she supposed it was customary for girls to marry when the right opportunity came. Cazeau, she knew, would make life more comfortable for her; and again, she had liked him, and had even been rather flustered when he pressed her hands and kissed them, and kissed her lips and cheeks and eyes, when she accepted him.

Montéclin himself had taken her aside to talk the thing over. The turn of affairs was delighting him.

'Come, now, 'Thénaïse, you mus' explain to me all about it, so we can settle on a good cause, an' secu' a separation fo' you. Has he been mistreating an' abusing you, the *sacré cochon*?' They were alone together in her room, whither she had taken refuge from the angry domestic elements.

'You please to reserve yo' disgusting expressions, Montéclin. No, he has not abused me in any way that I can think.'

'Does he drink? Come 'Thénaïse, think well over it. Does he ever get drunk?'

'Drunk! Oh, mercy, no – Cazeau never gets drunk.'

'I see; it's jus' simply you feel like me; you hate him.'

'No, I don't hate him,' she returned reflectively; adding with a sudden impulse, 'It's jus' being married that I detes' an' despise. I hate being Mrs Cazeau, an' would want to be Athénaïse Miché again. I can't stan' to live with a man; to have him always there, his coats an' pantaloons hanging in my room; his ugly bare feet – washing them in my tub, befo' my very eyes, ugh!' She shuddered with recollections, and resumed, with a sigh that was almost a sob: 'Mon Dieu, mon Dieu! Sister Marie Angélique knew w'at she was saying; she knew me better than myse'f w'en she said God had sent me a vocation an' I was turning deaf ears. W'en I think of a blessed life in the convent, at peace! Oh, w'at was I dreaming of!' and then the tears came.

Montéclin felt disconcerted and greatly disappointed at having obtained evidence that would carry no weight with a court of justice.

The day had not come when a young woman might ask the court's permission to return to her mamma on the sweeping ground of a constitutional disinclination for marriage. But if there was no way of untying this Gordian knot of marriage, there was surely a way of cutting it.

'Well, 'Thénaïse, I'm mighty durn sorry you got no better groun's 'an w'at you say. But you can count on me to stan' by you w'atever you do. God knows I don' blame you fo' not wantin' to live with Cazeau.'

And now there was Cazeau himself, with the red spots flaming in his swarthy cheeks, looking and feeling as if he wanted to thrash Montéclin into some semblance of decency. He arose abruptly, and approaching the room which he had seen his wife enter, thrust open the door after a hasty preliminary knock. Athénaïse, who was standing erect at a far window, turned at his entrance.

She appeared neither angry nor frightened, but thoroughly unhappy, with an appeal in her soft dark eyes and a tremor on her lips that seemed to him expressions of unjust reproach that wounded and maddened him at once. But whatever he might feel, Cazeau knew only one way to act towards a woman.

'Athénaïse, you are not ready?' he asked in his quiet tones. 'It's getting late; we havn' any time to lose.'

She knew that Montéclin had spoken out, and she had hoped for a wordy interview, a stormy scene, in which she might have held her own as she had held it for the past three days against her family, with Montéclin's aid. But she had no weapon with which to combat subtlety. Her husband's looks, his tones, his mere presence, brought to her a sudden sense of hopelessness, an instinctive realisation of the futility of rebellion against a social and sacred institution.

Cazeau said nothing further, but stood waiting in the doorway. Madame Miché had walked to the far end of the gallery, and pretended to be occupied with having a chicken driven from her *parterre*. Montéclin stood by, exasperated, fuming, ready to burst out.

Athénaïse went and reached for her riding skirt that hung against the wall. She was rather tall, with a figure which, though not robust, seemed perfect in its fine proportions. '*La fille de son père*,'[251] she was often called, which was a great compliment to Miché. Her brown hair was brushed all fluffily back from her temples and low forehead, and about her features and expression lurked a softness, a prettiness, a dewiness, that were perhaps too childlike, that savoured of immaturity.

She slipped the riding-skirt, which was of black alpaca, over her head, and with impatient fingers hooked it at the waist over her pink linen-lawn. Then she fastened on her white sun-bonnet and reached for her gloves on the mantelpiece.

'If you don' wan' to go, you know w'at you got to do, 'Thénaïse,' fumed Montéclin. 'You don' set yo' feet back on Cane River, by God, unless you want to – not w'ile I'm alive.'

Cazeau looked at him as if he were a monkey whose antics fell short of being amusing.

Athénaïse still made no reply, said not a word. She walked rapidly past her husband, past her brother; bidding goodbye to no one, not even to her mother. She descended the stairs, and without assistance from anyone mounted the pony, which Cazeau had ordered to be saddled upon his arrival. In this way she obtained a fair start of her husband, whose departure was far more leisurely, and for the greater part of the way she managed to keep an appreciable gap between them. She rode almost madly at first, with the wind inflating her skirt *ballon*-like about her knees, and her sun-bonnet falling back between her shoulders.

At no time did Cazeau make an effort to overtake her until traversing an old fallow meadow that was level and hard as a table. The sight of a great solitary oak tree, with its seemingly immutable outlines, that had been a landmark for ages – or was it the odour of elderberry stealing up from the gully to the south? or what was it that brought vividly back to Cazeau, by some association of ideas, a scene of many years ago? He had passed that old live-oak hundreds of times, but it was only now that the memory of one day came back to him. He was a very small boy that day, seated before his father on horseback. They were proceeding slowly, and Black Gabe was moving on before them at a little dogtrot. Black Gabe had run away, and had been discovered back in the Gotrain swamp. They had halted beneath this big oak to enable the negro to take breath; for Cazeau's father was a kind and considerate master, and everyone had agreed at the time that Black Gabe was a fool, a great idiot indeed, for wanting to run away from him.

The whole impression was for some reason hideous, and to dispel it Cazeau spurred his horse to a swift gallop. Overtaking his wife, he rode the remainder of the way at her side in silence.

It was late when they reached home. Félicité was standing on the grassy edge of the road, in the moonlight, waiting for them.

Cazeau once more ate his supper alone; for Athénaïse went to her room, and there she was crying again.

3

Athénaïse was not one to accept the inevitable with patient resignation, a talent born in the souls of many women; neither was she the one to accept it with philosophical resignation, like her husband. Her sensibilities were alive and keen and responsive. She met the pleasurable things of life with frank, open appreciation, and against distasteful conditions she rebelled. Dissimulation was as foreign to her nature as guile to the breast of a babe, and her rebellious outbreaks, by no means rare, had hitherto been quite open and aboveboard. People often said that Athénaïse would know her own mind someday, which was equivalent to saying that she was at present unacquainted with it. If she ever came to such knowledge, it would be by no intellectual research, by no subtle analyses or tracing the motives of actions to their source. It would come to her as the song to the bird, the perfume and colour to the flower.

Her parents had hoped – not without reason and justice – that marriage would bring the poise, the desirable pose, so glaringly lacking in Athénaïse's character. Marriage they knew to be a wonderful and powerful agent in the development and formation of a woman's character; they had seen its effect too often to doubt it.

'And if this marriage does nothing else,' exclaimed Miché in an outburst of sudden exasperation, 'it will rid us of Athénaïse; for I am at the end of my patience with her! You have never had the firmness to manage her' – he was speaking to his wife – 'I have not had the time, the leisure, to devote to her training; and what good we might have accomplished, that *maudit*²⁵² Montéclin – Well, Cazeau is the one! It takes just such a steady hand to guide a disposition like Athénaïse's, a master hand, a strong will that compels obedience.'

And now, when they had hoped for so much, here was Athénaïse, with gathered and fierce vehemence, beside which her former outbursts appeared mild, declaring that she would not, and she would not, and she would not continue to enact the role of wife to Cazeau. If she had had a reason! as Madame Miché lamented; but it could not be discovered that she had any sane one. He had never scolded, or called names, or deprived her of comforts, or been guilty of any of the many reprehensible acts commonly attributed to objectionable husbands. He did not slight nor neglect her. Indeed, Cazeau's chief offence seemed to be that he loved her, and Athénaïse was not the woman to be loved against her will. She called marriage a trap set for the feet of unwary and unsuspecting girls, and in round, unmeasured terms reproached her mother with treachery and deceit.

'I told you Cazeau was the man,' chuckled Miché, when his wife had related the scene that had accompanied and influenced Athénaïse's departure.

Athénaïse again hoped, in the morning, that Cazeau would scold or make some sort of a scene, but he apparently did not dream of it. It was exasperating that he should take her acquiescence so for granted. It is true he had been up and over the fields and across the river and back long before she was out of bed, and he may have been thinking of something else, which was no excuse, which was even in some sense an aggravation. But he did say to her at breakfast, 'That brother of yo's, that Montéclin, is unbearable.'

'Montéclin? *Par exemple!*'

Athénaïse, seated opposite to her husband, was attired in a white morning wrapper. She wore a somewhat abused, long face, it is true – an expression of countenance familiar to some husbands – but the expression was not sufficiently pronounced to mar the charm of her youthful freshness. She had little heart to eat, only playing with the food before her, and she felt a pang of resentment at her husband's healthy appetite.

'Yes, Montéclin,' he reasserted. 'He's developed into a firs'-class nuisance; an' you better tell him, Athénaïse – unless you want me to tell him – to confine his energies after this to matters that concern him. I have no use fo' him or fo' his interference in w'at regards you an' me alone.'

This was said with unusual asperity. It was the little breach that Athénaïse had been watching for, and she charged rapidly: 'It's strange, if you detes' Montéclin so heartily, that you would desire to marry his sister.' She knew it was a silly thing to say, and was not surprised when he told her so. It gave her a little foothold for further attack, however. 'I don't see, anyhow, w'at reason you had to marry me, w'en there were so many others,' she complained, as if accusing him of persecution and injury. 'There was Marianne running after you fo' the las' five years till it was disgraceful; an' any one of the Dortrand girls would have been glad to marry you. But no, nothing would do; you mus' come out on the rigolet fo' me.' Her complaint was pathetic, and at the same time so amusing that Cazeau was forced to smile.

'I can't see w'at the Dortrand girls or Marianne have to do with it,' he rejoined; adding, with no trace of amusement, 'I married you because I loved you; because you were the woman I wanted to marry, an' the only one. I reckon I tole you that befo'. I thought – of co'se I was a fool fo' taking things fo' granted – but I did think that I might make you

happy in making things easier an' mo' comfortable fo' you. I expected –
I was even that big a fool – I believed that yo' coming yere to me would
be like the sun shining out of the clouds, an' that our days would be like
w'at the storybooks promise after the wedding. I was mistaken. But I
can't imagine w'at induced you to marry me. W'atever it was, I reckon
you foun' out you made a mistake, too. I don' see anything to do but
make the best of a bad bargain, an' shake han's over it.' He had arisen
from the table, and, approaching, held out his hand to her. What he had
said was commonplace enough, but it was significant, coming from
Cazeau, who was not often so unreserved in expressing himself.

Athénaïse ignored the hand held out to her. She was resting her chin
in her palm, and kept her eyes fixed moodily upon the table. He rested
his hand, that she would not touch, upon her head for an instant, and
walked away out of the room.

She heard him giving orders to workmen who had been waiting for
him out on the gallery, and she heard him mount his horse and ride
away. A hundred things would distract him and engage his attention
during the day. She felt that he had perhaps put her and her grievance
from his thoughts when he crossed the threshold; while she . . .

Old Félicité was standing there holding a shining tin pail: asking for
flour and lard and eggs from the storeroom, and meal for the chicks.

Athénaïse seized the bunch of keys which hung from her belt and
flung them at Félicité's feet. '*Tiens! tu vas les garder comme tu as jadis fait.
Je ne veux plus de ce train là, moi!*'[253]

The old woman stooped and picked up the keys from the floor. It was
really all one to her that her mistress returned them to her keeping, and
refused to take further account of the *ménage*.

4

It seemed now to Athénaïse that Montéclin was the only friend left to
her in the world. Her father and mother had turned from her in what
appeared to be her hour of need. Her friends laughed at her, and refused
to take seriously the hints which she threw out – feeling her way to
discover if marriage were as distasteful to other women as to herself.
Montéclin alone understood her. He alone had always been ready to act
for her and with her, to comfort and solace her with his sympathy and
his support. Her only hope for rescue from her hateful surroundings lay
in Montéclin. Of herself she felt powerless to plan, to act, even to
conceive a way out of this pitfall into which the whole world seemed to
have conspired to thrust her.

She had a great desire to see her brother, and wrote asking him to come to her. But it better suited Montéclin's spirit of adventure to appoint a meeting-place at the turn of the lane, where Athénaïse might appear to be walking leisurely for health and recreation, and where he might seem to be riding along, bent on some errand of business or pleasure.

There had been a shower, a sudden downpour, short as it was sudden, that had laid the dust in the road. It had freshened the pointed leaves of the live-oaks, and brightened up the big fields of cotton on either side of the lane till they seemed carpeted with green, glittering gems.

Athénaïse walked along the grassy edge of the road, lifting her crisp skirts with one hand, and with the other twirling a gay sunshade over her bare head. The scent of the fields after the rain was delicious. She inhaled long breaths of their freshness and perfume, that soothed and quieted her for the moment. There were birds splashing and spluttering in the pools, pluming themselves on the fence-rails, and sending out little sharp cries, twitters and shrill rhapsodies of delight.

She saw Montéclin approaching from a great distance – almost as far away as the turn of the woods. But she could not feel sure it was he; it appeared too tall for Montéclin, but that was because he was riding a large horse. She waved her parasol to him; she was so glad to see him. She had never been so glad to see Montéclin before; not even the day when he had taken her out of the convent, against her parents' wishes, because she had expressed a desire to remain there no longer. He seemed to her, as he drew near, the embodiment of kindness, of bravery, of chivalry, even of wisdom; for she had never known Montéclin at a loss to extricate himself from a disagreeable situation.

He dismounted, and, leading his horse by the bridle, started to walk beside her, after he had kissed her affectionately and asked her what she was crying about. She protested that she was not crying, for she was laughing, though drying her eyes at the same time on her handkerchief, rolled in a soft mop for the purpose.

She took Montéclin's arm, and they strolled slowly down the lane; they could not seat themselves for a comfortable chat, as they would have liked, with the grass all sparkling and bristling wet.

Yes, she was quite as wretched as ever, she told him. The week which had gone by since she saw him had in no wise lightened the burden of her discontent. There had even been some additional provocations laid upon her, and she told Montéclin all about them – about the keys, for instance, which in a fit of temper she had returned to Félicité's keeping; and she told how Cazeau had brought them back to her as if they were something she had accidentally lost, and he had recovered; and how he had said, in that aggravating tone of his, that it was not the custom on

Cane River for the negro servants to carry the keys, when there was a mistress at the head of the household.

But Athénaïse could not tell Montéclin anything to increase the disrespect which he already entertained for his brother-in-law; and it was then he unfolded to her a plan which he had conceived and worked out for her deliverance from this galling matrimonial yoke.

It was not a plan which met with instant favour, which she was at once ready to accept, for it involved secrecy and dissimulation, hateful alternatives, both of them. But she was filled with admiration for Montéclin's resources and wonderful talent for contrivance. She accepted the plan; not with the immediate determination to act upon it, rather with the intention to sleep and to dream upon it.

Three days later she wrote to Montéclin that she had abandoned herself to his counsel. Displeasing as it might be to her sense of honesty, it would yet be less trying than to live on with a soul full of bitterness and revolt, as she had done for the past two months.

5

When Cazeau awoke, one morning at his usual very early hour, it was to find the place at his side vacant. This did not surprise him until he discovered that Athénaïse was not in the adjoining room, where he had often found her sleeping in the morning on the lounge. She had perhaps gone out for an early stroll, he reflected, for her jacket and hat were not on the rack where she had hung them the night before. But there were other things absent – a gown or two from the armoire; and there was a great gap in the piles of lingerie on the shelf; and her travelling-bag was missing, and so were her bits of jewellery from the toilet tray – and Athénaïse was gone!

But the absurdity of going during the night, as if she had been a prisoner, and he the keeper of a dungeon! So much secrecy and mystery, to go sojourning out on the Bon Dieu! Well, the Michés might keep their daughter after this. For the companionship of no woman on earth would he again undergo the humiliating sensation of baseness that had overtaken him in passing the old oak tree in the fallow meadow.

But a terrible sense of loss overwhelmed Cazeau. It was not new or sudden; he had felt it for weeks growing upon him, and it seemed to culminate with Athénaïse's flight from home. He knew that he could again compel her return as he had done once before – compel her to return to the shelter of his roof, compel her cold and unwilling submission to his love and passionate transports; but the loss of self-respect seemed to him too dear a price to pay for a wife.

He could not comprehend why she had seemed to prefer him above others; why she had attracted him with eyes, with voice, with a hundred womanly ways, and finally distracted him with love which she seemed, in her timid, maidenly fashion, to return. The great sense of loss came from the realisation of having missed a chance for happiness – a chance that would come his way again only through a miracle. He could not think of himself loving any other woman, and could not think of Athénaïse ever – even at some remote date – caring for him.

He wrote her a letter, in which he disclaimed any further intention of forcing his commands upon her. He did not desire her presence ever again in his home unless she came of her free will, uninfluenced by family or friends; unless she could be the companion he had hoped for in marrying her, and in some measure return affection and respect for the love which he continued and would always continue to feel for her. This letter he sent out to the rigolet by a messenger early in the day. But she was not out on the rigolet, and had not been there.

The family turned instinctively to Montéclin, and almost literally fell upon him for an explanation; he had been absent from home all night. There was much mystification in his answers, and a plain desire to mislead in his assurances of ignorance and innocence.

But with Cazeau there was no doubt or speculation when he accosted the young fellow. 'Montéclin, w'at have you done with Athénaïse?' he questioned bluntly. They had met in the open road on horseback, just as Cazeau ascended the river bank before his house.

'W'at have you done to Athénaïse?' returned Montéclin for answer.

'I don't reckon you've considered yo' conduct by any light of decency an' propriety in encouraging yo' sister to such an action, but let me tell you – '

'*Voyons!* you can let me alone with yo' decency an' morality an' fiddlesticks. I know you mus' 'a' done Athénaïse pretty mean that she can't live with you; an' fo' my part, I'm mighty durn glad she had the spirit to quit you.'

'I ain't in the humour to take any notice of yo' impertinence, Montéclin; but let me remine you that Athénaïse is nothing but a chile in character; besides that, she's my wife, an' I hol you responsible fo' her safety an' welfare. If any harm of any description happens to her, I'll strangle you, by God, like a rat, and fling you in Cane River, if I have to hang fo' it!' He had not lifted his voice. The only sign of anger was a savage gleam in his eyes.

'I reckon you better keep yo' big talk fo' the women, Cazeau,' replied Montéclin, riding away.

But he went doubly armed after that, and intimated that the precaution was not needless, in view of the threats and menaces that were abroad touching his personal safety.

6

Athénaïse reached her destination sound of skin and limb, but a good deal flustered, a little frightened, and altogether excited and interested by her unusual experiences.

Her destination was the house of Sylvie, on Dauphine Street,[254] in New Orleans – a three-storey grey brick, standing directly on the banquette, with three broad stone steps leading to the deep front entrance. From the second-storey balcony swung a small sign, conveying to passers-by the intelligence that within were '*chambres garnies*'.

It was one morning in the last week of April that Athénaïse presented herself at the Dauphine Street house. Sylvie was expecting her, and introduced her at once to her apartment, which was in the second storey of the back ell,[255] and accessible by an open, outside gallery. There was a yard below, paved with broad stone flagging; many fragrant flowering shrubs and plants grew in a bed along the side of the opposite wall, and others were distributed about in tubs and green boxes.

It was a plain but large enough room into which Athénaïse was ushered, with matting on the floor, green shades and Nottingham-lace curtains at the windows that looked out on the gallery, and furnished with a cheap walnut suite. But everything looked exquisitely clean, and the whole place smelled of cleanliness.

Athénaïse at once fell into the rocking-chair, with the air of exhaustion and intense relief of one who has come to the end of her troubles. Sylvie, entering behind her, laid the big travelling-bag on the floor and deposited the jacket on the bed.

She was a portly quadroon of fifty or thereabout, clad in an ample *volante* of the old-fashioned purple calico so much affected by her class. She wore large golden hoop-earrings, and her hair was combed plainly, with every appearance of effort to smooth out the kinks. She had broad, coarse features, with a nose that turned up, exposing the wide nostrils, and that seemed to emphasise the loftiness and command of her bearing – a dignity that in the presence of white people assumed a character of respectfulness, but never of obsequiousness. Sylvie believed firmly in maintaining the colour line, and would not suffer a white person, even a child, to call her 'Madame Sylvie' – a title which she exacted religiously, however, from those of her own race.

'I hope you be please' wid yo' room, madame,' she observed amiably. 'Dat's de same room w'at yo' brother, M'sieur Miché, all time like w'en he come to New Orlean'. He well, M'sieur Miché? I receive' his letter las' week, an' dat same day a gent'man want I give 'im dat room. I say, "No, dat room already ingage." Ev'body like dat room on 'count it so quite. M'sieur Gouvernail,[256] dere in nax' room, you can't pay 'im! He been stay t'ree year' in dat room; but all fix' up fine wid his own furn'ture an' books, 'tel you can't see! I say to 'im plenty time', "M'sieur Gouvernail, w'y you don't take dat t'ree-storey front, now, long it's empty?" He tells me, "Leave me 'lone, Sylvie; I know a good room w'en I fine it, me." '

She had been moving slowly and majestically about the apartment, straightening and smoothing down bed and pillows, peering into ewer[257] and basin, evidently casting an eye around to make sure that everything was as it should be.

'I sen' you some fresh water, madame,' she offered upon retiring from the room. 'An' w'en you want an't'ing, you jus' go out on de gall'ry an' call Pousette: she year you plain – she right down dere in de kitchen.'

Athénaïse was really not so exhausted as she had every reason to be after that interminable and circuitous way by which Montéclin had seen fit to have her conveyed to that city.

Would she ever forget that dark and truly dangerous midnight ride along the 'coast' to the mouth of Cane River! There Montéclin had parted with her, after seeing her aboard the St Louis and Shreveport packet which he knew would pass there before dawn. She had received instructions to disembark at the mouth of Red River, and there transfer to the first southbound steamer for New Orleans; all of which instructions she had followed implicitly, even to making her way at once to Sylvie's upon her arrival in the city. Montéclin had enjoined secrecy and much caution; the clandestine nature of the affair gave it a savour of adventure which was highly pleasing to him. Eloping with his sister was only a little less engaging than eloping with someone else's sister.

But Montéclin did not do the *grand seigneur* by halves. He had paid Sylvie a whole month in advance for Athénaïse's board and lodging. Part of the sum he had been forced to borrow, it is true, but he was not niggardly.

Athénaïse was to take her meals in the house, which none of the other lodgers did; the one exception being that Mr Gouvernail was served with breakfast on Sunday mornings.

Sylvie's clientèle came chiefly from the southern parishes; for the most part, people spending but a few days in the city. She prided herself upon the quality and highly respectable character of her patrons, who came and went unobtrusively.

The large parlour opening upon the front balcony was seldom used. Her guests were permitted to entertain in this sanctuary of elegance – but they never did. She often rented it for the night to parties of respectable and discreet gentlemen desiring to enjoy a quiet game of cards outside the bosom of their families. The second-storey hall also led by a long window out on the balcony. And Sylvie advised Athénaïse, when she grew weary of her back room, to go and sit on the front balcony, which was shady in the afternoon, and where she might find diversion in the sounds and sights of the street below.

Athénaïse refreshed herself with a bath, and was soon unpacking her few belongings, which she ranged neatly away in the bureau drawers and the armoire.

She had revolved certain plans in her mind during the past hour or so. Her present intention was to live on indefinitely in this big, cool, clean back room on Dauphine Street She had thought seriously, for moments, of the convent, with all readiness to embrace the vows of poverty and chastity; but what about obedience? Later, she intended, in some roundabout way, to give her parents and her husband the assurance of her safety and welfare; reserving the right to remain unmolested and lost to them. To live on at the expense of Montéclin's generosity was wholly out of the question, and Athénaïse meant to look about for some suitable and agreeable employment.

The imperative thing to be done at present, however, was to go out in search of material for an inexpensive gown or two; for she found herself in the painful predicament of a young woman having almost literally nothing to wear. She decided upon pure white for one, and some sort of a sprigged muslin for the other.

7

On Sunday morning, two days after Athénaïse's arrival in the city, she went in to breakfast somewhat later than usual, to find two covers laid at table instead of the one to which she was accustomed. She had been to mass, and did not remove her hat, but put her fan, parasol and prayer-book aside. The dining-room was situated just beneath her own apartment, and, like all rooms of the house, was large and airy; the floor was covered with a glistening oil-cloth.

The small, round table, immaculately set, was drawn near the open window. There were some tall plants in boxes on the gallery outside; and Pousette, a little, old, intensely black woman, was splashing and dashing buckets of water on the flagging, and talking loud in her Creole patois to no one in particular.

A dish piled with delicate river-shrimps and crushed ice was on the table; a carafe of crystal-clear water, a few *hors d'oeuvres*,[258] beside a small golden-brown crusty loaf of French bread at each plate. A half-bottle of wine and the morning paper were set at the place opposite Athénaïse.

She had almost completed her breakfast when Gouvernail came in and seated himself at table. He felt annoyed at finding his cherished privacy invaded. Sylvie was removing the remains of a mutton-chop from before Athénaïse, and serving her with a cup of café au lait.

'M'sieur Gouvernail,' offered Sylvie in her most insinuating and impressive manner, 'you please leave me make you acquaint' wid Madame Cazeau. Dat's M'sieur Miché's sister; you meet 'im two t'ree time', you rec'lec', an' been one day to de race wid 'im. Madame Cazeau, you please leave me make you acquaint' wid M'sieur Gouvernail.'

Gouvernail expressed himself greatly pleased to meet the sister of Monsieur Miché, of whom he had not the slightest recollection. He enquired after Monsieur Miché's health, and politely offered Athénaïse a part of his newspaper – the part which contained the Woman's Page and the social gossip.

Athénaïse faintly remembered that Sylvie had spoken of a Monsieur Gouvernail occupying the room adjoining hers, living amid luxurious surroundings and a multitude of books. She had not thought of him further than to picture him a stout, middle-aged gentleman, with a bushy beard turning grey, wearing large gold-rimmed spectacles and stooping somewhat from much bending over books and writing material. She had confused him in her mind with the likeness of some literary celebrity that she had run across in the advertising pages of a magazine.

Gouvernail's appearance was, in truth, in no sense striking. He looked older than thirty and younger than forty, was of medium height and weight, with a quiet, unobtrusive manner which seemed to ask that he be let alone. His hair was light brown, brushed carefully and parted in the middle. His moustache was brown, and so were his eyes, which had a mild penetrating quality. He was neatly dressed in the fashion of the day; and his hands seemed to Athénaïse remarkably white and soft for a man's.

He had been buried in the contents of his newspaper, when he suddenly realised that some further little attention might be due to Miché's sister. He started to offer her a glass of wine, when he was surprised and relieved to find that she had quietly slipped away while he was absorbed in his own editorial on Corrupt Legislation.

Gouvernail finished his paper and smoked his cigar out on the gallery. He lounged about, gathered a rose for his buttonhole, and had his regular Sunday-morning confab with Pousette, to whom he paid a weekly stipend for brushing his shoes and clothing. He made a great pretence of haggling over the transaction, only to enjoy her uneasiness and garrulous excitement.

He worked or read in his room for a few hours, and when he quitted the house, at three in the afternoon, it was to return no more till late at night. It was his almost invariable custom to spend Sunday evenings out in the American Quarter, among a congenial set of men and women – *des esprits forts*,[259] all of them, whose lives were irreproachable, yet whose opinions would startle even the traditional *sapeur*,[260] for whom 'nothing is sacred'. But for all his 'advanced' opinions, Gouvernail was a liberal-minded fellow; a man or woman lost nothing of his respect by being married.

When he left the house in the afternoon, Athénaïse had already ensconced herself on the front balcony. He could see her through the jalousies[261] when he passed on his way to the front entrance. She had not yet grown lonesome or homesick; the newness of her surroundings made them sufficiently entertaining. She found it diverting to sit there on the front balcony watching people pass by, even though there was no one to talk to. And then the comforting, comfortable sense of not being married!

She watched Gouvernail walk down the street, and could find no fault with his bearing. He could hear the sound of her rockers for some little distance. He wondered what the 'poor little thing' was doing in the city, and meant to ask Sylvie about her when he should happen to think of it.

8

The following morning, towards noon, when Gouvernail quitted his room, he was confronted by Athénaïse, exhibiting some confusion and trepidation at being forced to request a favour of him at so early a stage of their acquaintance. She stood in her doorway, and had evidently been sewing, as the thimble on her finger testified, as well as a long-threaded needle thrust in the bosom of her gown. She held a stamped but unaddressed letter in her hand.

And would Mr Gouvernail be so kind as to address the letter to her brother, Mr Montéclin Miché? She would hate to detain him with explanations this morning – another time, perhaps – but now she begged that he would give himself the trouble.

He assured her that it made no difference, that it was no trouble whatever; and he drew a fountain pen from his pocket and addressed the letter at her dictation, resting it on the inverted rim of his straw hat. She wondered a little at a man of his supposed erudition stumbling over the spelling of 'Montéclin' and 'Miché'.

She demurred at overwhelming him with the additional trouble of posting it, but he succeeded in convincing her that so simple a task as the posting of a letter would not add an iota to the burden of the day. Moreover, he promised to carry it in his hand, and thus avoid any possible risk of forgetting it in his pocket.

After that, and after a second repetition of the favour, when she had told him that she had had a letter from Montéclin, and looked as if she wanted to tell him more, he felt that he knew her better. He felt that he knew her *well* enough to join her out on the balcony, one night, when he found her sitting there alone. He was not one who deliberately sought the society of women, but he was not wholly a bear. A little commiseration for Athénaïse's aloneness, perhaps some curiosity to know further what manner of woman she was, and the natural influence of her feminine charm were equal unconfessed factors in turning his steps towards the balcony when he discovered the shimmer of her white gown through the open hall window.

It was already quite late, but the day had been intensely hot, and neighbouring balconies and doorways were occupied by chattering groups of humanity, loath to abandon the grateful freshness of the outer air. The voices about her served to reveal to Athénaïse the feeling of loneliness that was gradually coming over her. Notwithstanding certain dormant impulses, she craved human sympathy and companionship.

She shook hands impulsively with Gouvernail, and told him how glad she was to see him. He was not prepared for such an admission, but it pleased him immensely, detecting as he did that the expression was as sincere as it was outspoken. He drew a chair up within comfortable conversational distance of Athénaïse, though he had no intention of talking more than was barely necessary to encourage Madame . . . He had actually forgotten her name!

He leaned an elbow on the balcony rail, and would have offered an opening remark about the oppressive heat of the day, but Athénaïse did not give him the opportunity. How glad she was to talk to someone, and how she talked!

An hour later she had gone to her room, and Gouvernail stayed smoking on the balcony. He knew her quite well after that hour's talk. It was not so much what she had said as what her half saying had revealed to his quick intelligence. He knew that she adored Montéclin, and he suspected that she adored Cazeau without being herself aware of it. He had gathered that she was self-willed, impulsive, innocent, ignorant, unsatisfied, dissatisfied; for had she not complained that things seemed all wrongly arranged in this world, and no one was permitted to be happy in his own way? And he told her he was sorry she had discovered that primordial fact of existence so early in life.

He commiserated her loneliness, and scanned his bookshelves next morning for something to lend her to read, rejecting everything that offered itself to his view. Philosophy was out of the question, and so was poetry; that is, such poetry as he possessed. He had not sounded her literary tastes, and strongly suspected she had none; that she would have rejected The Duchess[262] as readily as Mrs Humphry Ward.[263] He compromised on a magazine.

It had entertained her passably, she admitted, upon returning it. A New England story had puzzled her, it was true, and a Creole tale had offended her, but the pictures had pleased her greatly, especially one which had reminded her so strongly of Montéclin after a hard day's ride that she was loath to give it up. It was one of Remington's cowboys,[264] and Gouvernail insisted upon her keeping it – keeping the magazine.

He spoke to her daily after that, and was always eager to render her some service or to do something towards her entertainment.

One afternoon he took her out to the lake end. She had been there once, some years before, but in winter, so the trip was comparatively new and strange to her. The large expanse of water studded with pleasure-boats, the sight of children playing merrily along the grassy palisades, the music, all enchanted her. Gouvernail thought her the most beautiful woman he had ever seen. Even her gown – the sprigged muslin – appeared to him the most charming one imaginable. Nor could anything be more becoming than the arrangement of her brown hair under the white sailor hat, all rolled back in a soft puff from her radiant face. And she carried her parasol and lifted her skirts and used her fan in ways that seemed quite unique and peculiar to herself, and which he considered almost worthy of study and imitation.

They did not dine out there at the water's edge, as they might have done, but returned early to the city to avoid the crowd. Athénaïse wanted to go home, for she said Sylvie would have dinner prepared and would be expecting her. But it was not difficult to persuade her to dine instead in the quiet little restaurant that he knew and liked, with its sanded floor, its secluded atmosphere, its delicious menu, and its obsequious waiter wanting to know what he might have the honour of serving to 'monsieur et madame'. No wonder he made the mistake, with Gouvernail assuming such an air of proprietorship! But Athénaïse was very tired after it all; the sparkle went out of her face, and she hung draggingly on his arm in walking home.

He was reluctant to part from her when she bade him good-night at her door and thanked him for the agreeable evening. He had hoped she would sit outside until it was time for him to regain the newspaper office. He knew that she would undress and get into her *peignoir* and lie upon her bed; and what he wanted to do, what he would have given much to do, was to go and sit beside her, read to her something restful, soothe her, do her bidding, whatever it might be. Of course there was no use in thinking of that. But he was surprised at his growing desire to be serving her. She gave him an opportunity sooner than he looked for.

'Mr Gouvernail,' she called from her room, 'will you be so kine as to call Pousette an' tell her she fo'got to bring my ice-water?'

He was indignant at Pousette's negligence, and called severely to her over the banisters. He was sitting before his own door, smoking. He knew that Athénaïse had gone to bed, for her room was dark, and she had opened the slats of the door and windows. Her bed was near a window.

Pousette came flopping up with the ice-water, and with a hundred excuses: '*Mo pa oua vou à tab c'te lanuite, mo cri vou pé gagni déja là-bas; parole! Vou pas cri conté ça Madame Sylvie?*' She had not seen Athénaïse at table, and thought she was gone. She swore to this, and hoped Madame Sylvie would not be informed of her remissness.

A little later Athénaïse lifted her voice again: 'Mr Gouvernail, did you remark that young man sitting on the opposite side from us, coming in, with a grey coat an' a blue ban' aroun' his hat?'

Of course Gouvernail had not noticed any such individual but he assured Athénaïse that he had observed the young fellow particularly.

'Don't you think he looked something – not very much, of co'se – but don't you think he had a little faux-air of Montéclin?'

'I think he looked strikingly like Montéclin,' asserted Gouvernail, with the one idea of prolonging the conversation. 'I meant to call your attention to the resemblance, and something drove it out of my head.'

'The same with me,' returned Athénaïse. 'Ah, my dear Montéclin! I wonder w'at he is doing now?'

'Did you receive any news, any letter from him today?' asked Gouvernail, determined that if the conversation ceased it should not be through lack of effort on his part to sustain it.

'Not today, but yesterday. He tells me that maman was so distracted with uneasiness that finally, to pacify her, he was fo'ced to confess that he knew w'ere I was, but that he was boun' by a vow of secrecy not to reveal it. But Cazeau has not noticed him or spoken to him since he threaten' to throw po' Montéclin in Cane River. You know Cazeau wrote me a letter the morning I lef', thinking I had gone to the rigolet. An' maman opened it, an' said it was full of the mos' noble sentiments, an' she wanted Montéclin to sen' it to me; but Montéclin refuse' poin' blank, so he wrote to me.'

Gouvernail preferred to talk of Montéclin. He pictured Cazeau as unbearable, and did not like to think of him.

A little later Athénaïse called out, 'Good-night, Mr Gouvernail.'

'Good-night,' he returned reluctantly. And when he thought that she was sleeping, he got up and went away to the midnight pandemonium of his newspaper office.

9

Athénaïse could not have held out through the month had it not been for Gouvernail. With the need of caution and secrecy always uppermost in her mind, she made no new acquaintances, and she did not seek out persons already known to her; however, she knew so few, it required little effort to keep out of their way. As for Sylvie, almost every moment of her time was occupied in looking after her house; and, moreover, her deferential attitude towards her lodgers forbade anything like the gossipy chats in which Athénaïse might have condescended sometimes to indulge with her landlady. The transient lodgers, who came and went, she never had occasion to meet. Hence she was entirely dependent upon Gouvernail for company.

He appreciated the situation fully; and every moment that he could spare from his work he devoted to her entertainment. She liked to be out of doors, and they strolled together in the summer twilight through the mazes of the old French Quarter. They went again to the lake end, and stayed for hours on the water; returning so late that the streets through which they passed were silent and deserted. On Sunday morning he arose at an unconscionable hour to take her to the French market, knowing that the sights and sounds there would interest her. And he did not join the intellectual coterie in the afternoon, as he usually did, but placed himself all day at the disposition and service of Athénaïse.

Notwithstanding all, his manner towards her was tactful and evinced intelligence and a deep knowledge of her character surprising upon so brief an acquaintance. For the time he was everything to her that she would have him; he replaced home and friends. Sometimes she wondered if he had ever loved a woman. She could not fancy him loving anyone passionately, rudely, offensively, as Cazeau loved her. Once she was so naive as to ask him outright if he had ever been in love, and he assured her promptly that he had not. She thought it an admirable trait in his character, and esteemed him greatly therefore.

He found her crying one night, not openly or violently. She was leaning over the gallery rail, watching the toads that hopped about in the moonlight, down on the damp flagstones of the courtyard. There was an oppressively sweet odour rising from the cape jessamine. Pousette was down there, mumbling and quarrelling with someone, and seeming to be having it all her own way – as well she might, when her companion was only a black cat that had come in from a neighbouring yard to keep her company.

Athénaïse did admit feeling heart-sick, body-sick, when he questioned her; she supposed it was nothing but homesick. A letter from Montéclin had stirred her all up. She longed for her mother, for Montéclin; she was sick for a sight of the cotton-fields, the scent of the ploughed earth, for the dim, mysterious charm of the woods, and the old tumble-down home on the Bon Dieu.

As Gouvernail listened to her, a wave of pity and tenderness swept through him. He took her hands and pressed them against him. He wondered what would happen if he were to put his arms around her.

He was hardly prepared for what happened, but he stood it courageously. She twined her arms around his neck and wept outright on his shoulder; the hot tears scalding his cheek and neck, and her whole body shaken in his arms. The impulse was powerful to strain her to him; the temptation was fierce to seek her lips; but he did neither.

He understood a thousand times better than she herself understood it that he was acting as substitute for Montéclin. Bitter as the conviction was, he accepted it. He was patient; he could wait. He hoped someday to hold her with a lover's arms. That she was married made no particle of difference to Gouvernail. He could not conceive or dream of it making a difference. When the time came that she wanted him – as he hoped and believed it would come – he felt he would have a right to her. So long as she did not want him, he had no right to her – no more than her husband had. It was very hard to feel her warm breath and tears upon his cheek, and her struggling bosom pressed against him and her soft arms clinging to him and his whole body and soul aching for her, and yet to make no sign.

He tried to think what Montéclin would have said and done, and to act accordingly. He stroked her hair, and held her in a gentle embrace, until the tears dried and the sobs ended. Before releasing herself she kissed him against the neck; she had to love somebody in her own way! Even that he endured like a stoic. But it was well he left her, to plunge into the thick of rapid, breathless, exacting work till nearly dawn.

Athénaïse was greatly soothed, and slept well The touch of friendly hands and caressing arms had been very grateful. Henceforward she would not be lonely and unhappy, with Gouvernail there to comfort her.

10

The fourth week of Athénaïse's stay in the city was drawing to a close. Keeping in view the intention which she had of finding some suitable and agreeable employment, she had made a few tentatives in that direction. But with the exception of two little girls who had promised to take piano lessons at a price that would be embarrassing to mention, these attempts had been fruitless. Moreover, the homesickness kept coming back, and Gouvernail was not always there to drive it away.

She spent much of her time weeding and pottering among the flowers down in the courtyard. She tried to take an interest in the black cat, and a mockingbird that hung in a cage outside the kitchen door, and a disreputable parrot that belonged to the cook next door, and swore hoarsely all day long in bad French.

Beside, she was not well; she was not herself, as she told Sylvie. The climate of New Orleans did not agree with her. Sylvie was distressed to learn this, as she felt in some measure responsible for the health and well-being of Monsieur Miché's sister; and she made it her duty to enquire closely into the nature and character of Athénaïse's malaise.

Sylvie was very wise, and Athénaïse was very ignorant. The extent of her ignorance and the depth of her subsequent enlightenment were bewildering. She stayed a long, long time quite still, quite stunned, after her interview with Sylvie, except for the short, uneven breathing that ruffled her bosom. Her whole being was steeped in a wave of ecstasy. When she finally arose from the chair in which she had been seated, and looked at herself in the mirror, a face met hers which she seemed to see for the first time, so transfigured was it with wonder and rapture.

One mood quickly followed another, in this new turmoil of her senses, and the need of action became uppermost. Her mother must know at once, and her mother must tell Montéclin. And Cazeau must know. As she thought of him, the first purely sensuous tremor of her life swept over her. She half whispered his name, and the sound of it brought red blotches into her cheeks. She spoke it over and over, as if it were some new, sweet sound born out of darkness and confusion, and reaching her for the first time. She was impatient to be with him. Her whole passionate nature was aroused as if by a miracle.

She seated herself to write to her husband. The letter he would get in the morning, and she would be with him at night. What would he say? How would he act? She knew that he would forgive her, for had he not written a letter? – and a pang of resentment towards Montéclin shot through her. What did he mean by withholding that letter? How dared he not have sent it?

Athénaïse attired herself for the street, and went out to post the letter which she had penned with a single thought, a spontaneous impulse. It would have seemed incoherent to most people, but Cazeau would understand.

She walked along the street as if she had fallen heir to some magnificent inheritance. On her face was a look of pride and satisfaction that passers-by noticed and admired. She wanted to talk to someone, to tell some person; and she stopped at the corner and told the oyster-woman, who was Irish, and who God-blessed her, and wished prosperity to the race of Cazeaus for generations to come. She held the oyster-woman's fat, dirty little baby in her arms and scanned it curiously and observingly, as if a baby were a phenomenon that she encountered for the first time in life. She even kissed it!

Then what a relief it was to Athénaïse to walk the streets without dread of being seen and recognised by some chance acquaintance from Red River! No one could have said now that she did not know her own mind.

She went directly from the oyster-woman's to the office of Harding & Offdean,[265] her husband's merchants; and it was with such an air of partnership, almost proprietorship, that she demanded a sum of money on her husband's account, they gave it to her as unhesitatingly as they would have handed it over to Cazeau himself. When Mr Harding, who knew her, asked politely after her health, she turned so rosy and looked so conscious, he thought it a great pity for so pretty a woman to be such a little goose.

Athénaïse entered a dry-goods store and bought all manner of things – little presents for nearly everybody she knew. She bought whole bolts of sheerest, softest, downiest white stuff; and when the clerk, in trying to meet her wishes, asked if she intended it for infant's use, she could have sunk through the floor, and wondered how he might have suspected it.

As it was Montéclin who had taken her away from her husband, she wanted it to be Montéclin who should take her back to him. So she wrote him a very curt note – in fact it was a postal card – asking that he meet her at the train on the evening following. She felt convinced that after what had gone before, Cazeau would await her at their own home; and she preferred it so.

Then there was the agreeable excitement of getting ready to leave, of packing up her things. Pousette kept coming and going, coming and going; and each time that she quitted the room it was with something that Athénaïse had given her – a handkerchief, a petticoat, a pair of stockings with two tiny holes at the toes, some broken prayer-beads and finally a silver dollar.

Next it was Sylvie who came along bearing a gift of what she called a set of pattern' – things of complicated design which never could have been obtained in any new-fangled bazaar or pattern-store, that Sylvie had acquired of a foreign lady of distinction whom she had nursed years before at the St Charles Hotel. Athénaïse accepted and handled them with reverence, fully sensible of the great compliment and favour, and laid them religiously away in the trunk which she had lately acquired.

She was greatly fatigued after the day of unusual exertion, and went early to bed and to sleep. All day long she had not once thought of Gouvernail, and only did think of him when aroused for a brief instant by the sound of his foot-falls on the gallery, as he passed in going to his room. He had hoped to find her up, waiting for him.

But the next morning he knew. Someone must have told him. There was no subject known to her which Sylvie hesitated to discuss in detail with any man of suitable years and discretion.

Athénaïse found Gouvernail waiting with a carriage to convey her to the railway station. A momentary pang visited her for having forgotten him so completely, when he said to her, 'Sylvie tells me you are going away this morning.'

He was kind, attentive and amiable, as usual, but respected to the utmost the new dignity and reserve that her manner had developed since yesterday. She kept looking from the carriage window, silent, and embarrassed as Eve after losing her ignorance. He talked of the muddy streets and the murky morning, and of Montéclin. He hoped she would find everything comfortable and pleasant in the country, and trusted she would inform him whenever she came to visit the city again. He talked as if afraid or mistrustful of silence and himself.

At the station she handed him her purse, and he bought her ticket, secured for her a comfortable section, checked her trunk, and got all the bundles and things safely aboard the train. She felt very grateful. He pressed her hand warmly, lifted his hat, and left her. He was a man of intelligence, and took defeat gracefully; that was all. But as he made his way back to the carriage, he was thinking, 'By heaven, it hurts, it hurts!'

11

Athénaïse spent a day of supreme happiness and expectancy. The fair sight of the country unfolding itself before her was balm to her vision and to her soul. She was charmed with the rather unfamiliar, broad, clean sweep of the sugar plantations, with their monster sugar-houses, their rows of neat cabins, like little villages of a single street, and their impressive homes standing apart amid clusters of trees. There were sudden glimpses of a bayou curling between sunny, grassy banks, or creeping sluggishly out from a tangled growth of wood, and brush, and fern, and poison-vines, and palmettos. And passing through the long stretches of monotonous woodlands, she would close her eyes and taste in anticipation the moment of her meeting with Cazeau. She could think of nothing but him.

It was night when she reached her station. There was Montéclin, as she had expected, waiting for her with a two-seated buggy, to which he had hitched his own swift-footed, spirited pony. It was good, he felt, to have her back on any terms; and he had no fault to find since she came of her own choice. He more than suspected the cause of her coming; her eyes and her voice and her foolish little manner went far in revealing the secret that was brimming over in her heart. But after he had deposited her at her own gate, and as he continued his way towards the rigolet, he could not help feeling that the affair had taken a very disappointing, an ordinary, a most commonplace turn, after all. He left her in Cazeau's keeping.

Her husband lifted her out of the buggy, and neither said a word until they stood together within the shelter of the gallery. Even then they did not speak at first. But Athénaïse turned to him with an appealing gesture. As he clasped her in his arms, he felt the yielding of her whole body against him. He felt her lips for the first time respond to the passion of his own.

The country night was dark and warm and still, save for the distant notes of an accordion which someone was playing in a cabin away off. A little negro baby was crying somewhere. As Athénaïse withdrew from her husband's embrace, the sound arrested her.

'Listen, Cazeau! How Juliette's baby is crying! *Pauvre ti chou*,[266] I wonder w'at is the matter with it?'

After the Winter

1

Trézinie, the blacksmith's daughter, stepped out upon the gallery just as M'sieur Michel passed by. He did not notice the girl but walked straight on down the village street.

His seven hounds skulked, as usual, about him. At his side hung his powder-horn, and on his shoulder a gunny-bag slackly filled with game that he carried to the store. A broad felt hat shaded his bearded face and in his hand he carelessly swung his old-fashioned rifle. It was doubtless the same with which he had slain so many people, Trézinie shudderingly reflected. For Cami, the cobbler's son – who must have known – had often related to her how this man had killed two Choctaws, as many Texans, a free mulatto and numberless blacks, in that vague locality known as 'the hills'.

Older people who knew better took little trouble to correct this ghastly record that a younger generation had scored against him. They themselves had come to half-believe that M'sieur Michel might be capable of anything, living as he had, for so many years, apart from humanity, alone with his hounds in a kennel of a cabin on the hill. The time seemed to most of them fainter than a memory when, a lusty young fellow of twenty-five, he had cultivated his strip of land across the lane from Les Chêniers;[267] when home and toil and wife and child were so many benedictions that he humbly thanked heaven for having given him.

But in the early '60s he went with his friend Duplan[268] and the rest of the 'Louisiana Tigers'.[269] He came back with some of them. He came to find – well, death may lurk in a peaceful valley lying in wait to ensnare the toddling feet of little ones. Then, there are women – there are wives with thoughts that roam and grow wanton with roaming; women whose pulses are stirred by strange voices and eyes that woo; women who forget the claims of yesterday, the hopes of tomorrow, in the impetuous clutch of today.

But that was no reason, some people thought, why he should have cursed men who found their blessings where they had left them – cursed God, who had abandoned him.

Persons who met him upon the road had long ago stopped greeting him. What was the use? He never answered them; he spoke to no one; he never so much as looked into men's faces. When he bartered his game and fish at the village store for powder and shot and such scant food as he needed, he did so with few words and less courtesy. Yet feeble as it was, this was the only link that held him to his fellow-beings.

Strange to say, the sight of M'sieur Michel, though more forbidding than ever that delightful spring afternoon, was so suggestive to Trézinie as to be almost an inspiration.

It was Easter eve and the early part of April. The whole earth seemed teeming with new, green, vigorous life everywhere – except the arid spot that immediately surrounded Trézinie. It was no use; she had tried. Nothing would grow among those cinders that filled the yard; in that atmosphere of smoke and flame that was constantly belching from the forge where her father worked at his trade. There were wagon wheels, bolts and bars of iron, ploughshares and all manner of unpleasant-looking things littering the bleak, black yard; nothing green anywhere except a few weeds that would force themselves into fence corners. And Trézinie knew that flowers belong to Easter time, just as dyed eggs do. She had plenty of eggs; no one had more or prettier ones; she was not going to grumble about that. But she did feel distressed because she had not a flower to help deck the altar on Easter morning. And everyone else seemed to have them in such abundance! There was 'Dame Suzanne among her roses across the way. She must have clipped a hundred since noon. An hour ago Trézinie had seen the carriage from Les Chêniers pass by on its way to church with Mamzelle Euphrasie's[270] pretty head looking like a picture enframed with the Easter lilies that filled the vehicle.

For the twentieth time Trézinie walked out upon the gallery. She saw M'sieur Michel and thought of the pine hill. When she thought of the hill she thought of the flowers that grew there – free as sunshine. The girl gave a joyous spring that changed to a farandole[271] as her feet twinkled across the rough, loose boards of the gallery.

'He, Cami!' she cried, clapping her hands together.

Cami rose from the bench where he sat pegging away at the clumsy sole of a shoe, and came lazily to the fence that divided his abode from Trézinie's.

'Well, w'at?' he enquired with heavy amiability. She leaned far over the railing to better communicate with him.

'You'll go with me yonda on the hill to pick flowers fo' Easter, Cami?

I'm goin' to take La Fringante[272] along, too, to he'p with the baskets. W'at you say?'

'No!' was the stolid reply. 'I'm boun' to finish them shoe', if it is fo' a nigga.'

'Not now,' she returned impatiently; 'tomorrow mo'nin' at sun-up. An' I tell you, Cami, my flowers'll beat all! Look yonda at 'Dame Suzanne pickin' her roses a'ready. An' Mamzelle Euphraisie she's car'ied her lilies an' gone, her. You tell me all that's goin' be fresh tomoro'?'

'Jus' like you say,' agreed the boy, turning to resume his work. 'But you want to mine out fo' the ole possum up in the wood. Let M'sieu Michel set eyes on you!' and he raised his arms as if aiming with a gun. 'Pim, pam, poum! No mo' Trézinie, no mo' Cami, no mo' La Fringante – all stretch'!'

The possible risk which Cami so vividly foreshadowed but added a zest to Trézinie's projected excursion.

2

It was hardly sun-up on the following morning when the three children – Trézinie, Cami and the little negress, La Fringante – were filling big, flat Indian baskets from the abundance of brilliant flowers that studded the hill.

In their eagerness they had ascended the slope and penetrated deep into the forest without thought of M'sieur Michel or of his abode. Suddenly, in the dense wood, they came upon his hut – low, forbidding, seeming to scowl rebuke upon them for their intrusion.

La Fringante dropped her basket, and, with a cry, fled. Cami looked as if he wanted to do the same. But Trézinie, after the first tremor, saw that the ogre himself was away. The wooden shutter of the one window was closed. The door, so low that even a small man must have stooped to enter it, was secured with a chain. Absolute silence reigned, except for the whir of wings in the air, the fitful notes of a bird in the treetop.

'Can't you see it's nobody there!' cried Trézinie impatiently.

La Fringante, distracted between curiosity and terror, had crept cautiously back again. Then they all peeped through the wide chinks between the logs of which the cabin was built.

M'sieur Michel had evidently begun the construction of his house by felling a huge tree, whose remaining stump stood in the centre of the hut, and served him as a table. This primitive table was worn smooth by twenty-five years of use. Upon it were such humble utensils as the man required. Everything within the hovel, the sleeping bunk, the one seat, were as rude as a savage would have fashioned them.

The stolid Cami could have stayed for hours with his eyes fastened to the aperture, morbidly seeking some dead, mute sign of that awful pastime with which he believed M'sieur Michel was accustomed to beguile his solitude. But Trézinie was wholly possessed by the thought of her Easter offerings. She wanted flowers and flowers, fresh with the earth and crisp with dew.

When the three youngsters scampered down the hill again there was not a purple verbena left about M'sieur Michel's hut; not a May apple blossom, not a stalk of crimson phlox – hardly a violet.

He was something of a savage, feeling that the solitude belonged to him. Of late there had been forming within his soul a sentiment towards man, keener than indifference, bitter as hate. He was coming to dread even that brief intercourse with others into which his traffic forced him.

So when M'sieur Michel returned to his hut, and with his quick, accustomed eye saw that his woods had been despoiled, rage seized him. It was not that he loved the flowers that were gone more than he loved the stars, or the wind that trailed across the hill, but they belonged to and were a part of that life which he had made for himself, and which he wanted to live alone and unmolested.

Did not those flowers help him to keep his record of time that was passing? They had no right to vanish until the hot May days were upon him. How else should he know? Why had these people, with whom he had nothing in common, intruded upon his privacy and violated it? What would they not rob him of next?

He knew well enough it was Easter; he had heard and seen signs yesterday in the store that told him so. And he guessed that his woods had been rifled to add to the mummery[273] of the day.

M'sieur Michel sat himself moodily down beside his table – centuries old – and brooded. He did not even notice his hounds that were pleading to be fed. As he revolved in his mind the event of the morning – innocent as it was in itself – it grew in importance and assumed a significance not at first apparent. He could not remain passive under pressure of its disturbance. He rose to his feet, every impulse aggressive, urging him to activity. He would go down among those people all gathered together, blacks and whites, and face them for once and all. He did not know what he would say to them, but it would be defiance – something to voice the hate that oppressed him.

The way down the hill, then across a piece of flat, swampy woodland and through the lane to the village was so familiar that it required no attention from him to follow it. His thoughts were left free to revel in the humour that had driven him from his kennel.

As he walked down the village street he saw plainly that the place was deserted save for the appearance of an occasional negress, who seemed occupied with preparing the midday meal. But about the church scores of horses were fastened; and M'sieur Michel could see that the edifice was thronged to the very threshold.

He did not once hesitate, but obeying the force that impelled him to face the people wherever they might be, he was soon standing with the crowd within the entrance of the church. His broad, robust shoulders had forced space for himself, and his leonine head stood higher than any there.

'Take off yo' hat!'

It was an indignant mulatto who addressed him. M'sieur Michel instinctively did as he was bidden. He saw confusedly that there was a mass of humanity close to him, whose contact and atmosphere affected him strangely. He saw his wild-flowers, too. He saw them plainly, in bunches and festoons, among the Easter lilies and roses and geraniums. He was going to speak out, now; he had the right to and he would, just as soon as that clamour overhead would cease.

'*Bonté divine!* M'sieur Michel!' whispered 'Dame Suzanne tragically to her neighbour. Trézinie heard. Cami saw. They exchanged an electric glance, and tremblingly bowed their heads low.

M'sieur Michel looked wrathfully down at the puny mulatto who had ordered him to remove his hat. Why had he obeyed? That initial act of compliance had somehow weakened his will, his resolution. But he would regain firmness just as soon as that clamour above gave him chance to speak.

It was the organ filling the small edifice with volumes of sound. It was the voices of men and women mingling in the '*Gloria in excelsis Deo!*'[274]

The words bore no meaning for him apart from the old familiar strain which he had known as a child and chanted himself in that same organ-loft years ago. How it went on and on! Would it never cease! It was like a menace; like a voice reaching out from the dead past to taunt him.

'*Gloria in excelsis Deo!*' over and over! How the deep basso rolled it out! How the tenor and alto caught it up and passed it on to be lifted by the high, flutelike ring of the soprano, till all mingled again in the wild paean, '*Gloria in excelsis!*'

How insistent was the refrain! and where, what, was that mysterious, hidden quality in it; the power which was overcoming M'sieur Michel, stirring within him a turmoil that bewildered him?

There was no use in trying to speak, or in wanting to. His throat could not have uttered a sound. He wanted to escape, that was all. '*Bonae voluntatis*'[275] – he bent his head as if before a beating storm. '*Gloria! Gloria! Gloria!*' He must fly; he must save himself, regain his hill where sights and odours and sounds and saints or devils would cease to molest him. '*In excelsis Deo!*' He retreated, forcing his way backward to the door. He dragged his hat down over his eyes and staggered away down the road. But the refrain pursued him – '*Pax! pax! pax!*'[276] – fretting him like a lash. He did not slacken his pace till the tones grew fainter than an echo, floating, dying away in an '*in excelsis!*' When he could hear it no longer he stopped and breathed a sigh of rest and relief.

3

All day long M'sieur Michel stayed about his hut engaged in some familiar employment that he hoped might efface the unaccountable impressions of the morning. But his restlessness was unbounded. A longing had sprung up within him as sharp as pain and not to be appeased. At once, on this bright, warm Easter morning the voices that till now had filled his solitude became meaningless. He stayed mute and uncomprehending before them. Their significance had vanished before the driving want for human sympathy and companionship that had reawakened in his soul.

When night came on he walked through the woods down the slant of the hill again.

'It mus' be all fill' up with weeds,' muttered M'sieur Michel to himself as he went. 'Ah, *bon Dieu!* with trees, Michel, with trees – in twenty-five years, man.'

He had not taken the road to the village, but was pursuing a different one in which his feet had not walked for many days. It led him along the river bank for a distance. The narrow stream, stirred by the restless breeze, gleamed in the moonlight that was flooding the land.

As he went on and on, the scent of the new-ploughed earth that had been from the first keenly perceptible, began to intoxicate him. He wanted to kneel and bury his face in it. He wanted to dig into it; turn it over. He wanted to scatter the seed again as he had done long ago, and watch the new, green life spring up as if at his bidding.

When he turned away from the river, and had walked a piece down the lane that divided Joe Duplan's plantation from that bit of land that had once been his, he wiped his eyes to drive away the mist that was making him see things as they surely could not be.

He had wanted to plant a hedge that time before he went away, but he had not done so. Yet there was the hedge before him, just as he had meant it to be, and filling the night with fragrance. A broad, low gate divided its length, and over this he leaned and looked before him in amazement. There were no weeds as he had fancied; no trees except the scattered live-oaks that he remembered.

Could that row of hardy fig trees, old, squat and gnarled, be the twigs that he himself had set one day into the ground? One raw December day when there was a fine, cold mist falling. The chill of it breathed again upon him; the memory was so real. The land did not look as if it ever had been ploughed for a field. It was a smooth, green meadow, with cattle huddled upon the cool sward, or moving with slow, stately tread as they nibbled the tender shoots.

There was the house unchanged, gleaming white in the moon, seeming to invite him beneath its calm shelter. He wondered who dwelt within it now. Whoever it was he would not have them find him, like a prowler, there at the gate. But he would come again and again like this at nighttime, to gaze and refresh his spirit.

A hand had been laid upon M'sieur Michel's shoulder and someone called his name. Startled, he turned to see who accosted him.

'Duplan!'

The two men who had not exchanged speech for so many years stood facing each other for a long moment in silence.

'I knew you would come back someday, Michel. It was a long time to wait, but you have come home at last.'

M'sieur Michel cowered instinctively and lifted his hands with expressive deprecatory gesture. 'No, no; it's no place for me, Joe; no place!'

'Isn't a man's home a place for him, Michel?' It seemed less a question than an assertion, charged with gentle authority.

'Twenty-five years, Duplan; twenty-five years! It's no use; it's too late.'

'You see, I have used it,' went on the planter, quietly ignoring M'sieur Michel's protestations.

'Those are my cattle grazing off there. The house has served me many a time to lodge guests or workmen, for whom I had no room at Les Chêniers. I have not exhausted the soil with any crops. I had not the right to do that. Yet am I in your debt, Michel, and ready to settle *en bon ami.*'

The planter had opened the gate and entered the enclosure, leading M'sieur Michel with him. Together they walked towards the house.

Language did not come readily to either – one so unaccustomed to hold intercourse with men; both so stirred with memories that would have rendered any speech painful. When they had stayed long in a silence which was eloquent of tenderness, Joe Duplan spoke: 'You know how I tried to see you, Michel, to speak with you, and – you never would.'

M'sieur Michel answered with but a gesture that seemed a supplication.

'Let the past all go, Michel. Begin your new life as if the twenty-five years that are gone had been a long night, from which you have only awakened. Come to me in the morning,' he added with quick resolution, 'for a horse and a plough.' He had taken the key of the house from his pocket and placed it in M'sieur Michel's hand.

'A horse?' M'sieur Michel repeated uncertainly; 'a plough! Oh, it's too late, Duplan; too late.'

'It isn't too late. The land has rested all these years, man; it's fresh, I tell you; and rich as gold. Your crop will be the finest in the land.' He held out his hand and M'sieur Michel pressed it without a word in reply, save a muttered, '*Mon ami*.'

Then he stood there watching the planter disappear behind the high, clipped hedge.

He held out his arms. He could not have told if it was towards the retreating figure, or in welcome to an infinite peace that seemed to descend upon him and envelop him.

All the land was radiant except the hill far off that was in black shadow against the sky

Polydore

It was often said that Polydore was the stupidest boy to be found 'from the mouth of Cane River plumb to Natchitoches'. Hence it was an easy matter to persuade him, as meddlesome and mischievous people some-times tried to do, that he was an overworked and much abused individual.

It occurred one morning to Polydore to wonder what would happen if he did not get up. He hardly expected the world to stop turning on its axis; but he did in a way believe that the machinery of the whole plantation would come to a standstill.

He had awakened at the usual hour – about daybreak – and instead of getting up at once, as was his custom, he resettled himself between the sheets. There he lay, peering out through the dormer window into the grey morning that was deliciously cool after the hot summer night, listening to familiar sounds that came from the barnyard, the fields and woods beyond, heralding the approach of day.

A little later there were other sounds, no less familiar or significant; the roll of the wagon-wheels; the distant call of a negro's voice; Aunt Siney's shuffling step as she crossed the gallery, bearing to Mamzelle Adélaïde and old Monsieur José their early coffee.

Polydore had formed no plan and had thought only vaguely upon results. He lay in a half-slumber awaiting developments, and philo-sophically resigned to any turn which the affair might take. Still he was not quite ready with an answer when Jude came and thrust his head in at the door.

'Mista Polydore! Oh, Mista Polydore! You 'sleep?'

'W'at you want?'

'Dan 'low he ain' gwine wait yonda wid de wagon all day. Say does you inspect 'im to pack dat freight f'om de landing by hisse'f?'

'I reckon he got it to do, Jude. I ain' going to get up, me.'

'You ain' gwine git up?'

'No; I'm sick. I'm going stay in bed. Go 'long and le' me sleep.'

The next one to invade Polydore's privacy was Mamzelle Adélaïde herself. It was no small effort for her to mount the steep, narrow stairway to Polydore's room. She seldom penetrated to these regions under the roof. He could hear the stairs creak beneath her weight, and knew that she was panting at every step. Her presence seemed to crowd the small room; for she was stout and rather tall, and her flowing muslin wrapper swept majestically from side to side as she walked.

Mamzelle Adélaïde had reached middle age, but her face was still fresh with its mignon features; and her brown eyes at the moment were round with astonishment and alarm.

'W'at's that I hear, Polydore? They tell me you're sick!' She went and stood beside the bed, lifting the mosquito bar that settled upon her head and fell about her like a veil.

Polydore's eyes blinked, and he made no attempt to answer. She felt his wrist softly with the tips of her fingers, and rested her hand for a moment on his low forehead beneath the shock of black hair.

'But you don't seem to have any fever, Polydore!'

'No,' hesitatingly, feeling himself forced to make some reply. 'It's a kine of – a kine of pain, like you might say. It kitch me yere in the knee, and it goes 'long like you stickin' a knife clean down in my heel. Aie! Oh, la-la!' expressions of pain wrung from him by Mamzelle Adélaïde gently pushing aside the covering to examine the afflicted member.

'My patience! but that leg is swollen, yes, Polydore.' The limb, in fact, seemed dropsical, but if Mamzelle Adélaïde had bethought her of comparing it with the other one, she would have found the two corresponding in their proportions to a nicety. Her kind face expressed the utmost concern, and she quitted Polydore feeling pained and ill at ease.

For one of the aims of Mamzelle Adélaïde's existence was to do the right thing by this boy, whose mother, a 'Cadian hill woman, had begged her with dying breath to watch over the temporal and spiritual welfare of her son; above all, to see that he did not follow in the slothful footsteps of an over-indolent father.

Polydore's scheme worked so marvellously to his comfort and pleasure that he wondered at not having thought of it before. He ate with keen relish the breakfast which Jude brought to him on a tray. Even old Monsieur José was concerned, and made his way up to Polydore, bringing a number of picture-papers for his entertainment, a palm-leaf fan and a cow-bell, with which to summon Jude when necessary and which he placed within easy reach.

As Polydore lay on his back fanning luxuriously, it seemed to him that he was enjoying a foretaste of paradise. Only once did he shudder with apprehension. It was when he heard Aunt Siney, with lifted voice, recommending to 'wrop the laig up in bacon fat; de oniest way to draw out de misery.'

The thought of a healthy leg swathed in bacon fat on a hot day in

July was enough to intimidate a braver heart than Polydore's. But the suggestion was evidently not adopted, for he heard no more of the bacon fat. In its stead he became acquainted with the not unpleasant sting of a soothing liniment which Jude rubbed into the leg at intervals during the day.

He kept the limb propped on a pillow, stiff and motionless, even when alone and unobserved. Towards evening he fancied that it really showed signs of inflammation, and he was quite sure it pained him.

It was a satisfaction to all to see Polydore appear downstairs the following afternoon. He limped painfully, it is true, and clutched wildly at anything in his way that offered a momentary support. His acting was clumsily overdrawn; and by less guileless souls than Mamzelle Adélaïde and her father would have surely been suspected. But these two only thought with deep concern of means to make him comfortable.

They seated him on the shady back gallery in an easy-chair, with his leg propped up before him.

'He inhe'its dat rheumatism,' proclaimed Aunt Siney, who affected the manner of an oracle. 'I see dat boy's granpap, many times, all twis' up wid rheumatism twell his head sot down on his body, hine side befo'. He got to keep outen de jew in de mo'nin's, and he 'bleege to w'ar red flannen.'

Monsieur José, with flowing white locks enframing his aged face, leaned upon his cane and contemplated the boy with unflagging attention. Polydore was beginning to believe himself a worthy object as a centre of interest.

Mamzelle Adélaïde had but just returned from a long drive in the open buggy, from a mission which would have fallen to Polydore had he not been disabled by this unlooked-for illness. She had thoughtlessly driven across the country at an hour when the sun was hottest, and now she sat panting and fanning herself; her face, which she mopped incessantly with her handkerchief, was inflamed from the heat.

Mamzelle Adélaïde ate no supper that night, and went to bed early, with a compress of *eau sédative* bound tightly around her head. She thought it was a simple headache, and that she would be rid of it in the morning; but she was not better in the morning.

She kept her bed that day, and late in the afternoon Jude rode over to town for the doctor, and stopped on the way to tell Mamzelle Adélaïde's married sister that she was quite ill, and would like to have her come down to the plantation for a day or two.

Polydore made round, serious eyes and forgot to limp. He wanted to go for the doctor in Jude's stead; but Aunt Siney, assuming a brief authority, forced him to sit still by the kitchen door and talked further of bacon fat.

Old Monsieur José moved about uneasily and restlessly, in and out of his daughter's room. He looked vacantly at Polydore now, as if the stout young boy in blue jeans and a calico shirt were a sort of a transparency.

A dawning anxiety, coupled to the inertia of the past two days, deprived Polydore of his usual healthful night's rest. The slightest noises awoke him. Once it was the married sister breaking ice down on the gallery. One of the hands had been sent with the cart for ice late in the afternoon; and Polydore himself had wrapped the huge chunk in an old blanket and set it outside of Mamzelle Adélaïde's door.

Troubled and wakeful, he arose from bed and went and stood by the open window. There was a round moon in the sky, shedding its pale glamour over all the country; and the live-oak branches, stirred by the restless breeze, flung quivering, grotesque shadows slanting across the old roof. A mockingbird had been singing for hours near Polydore's window, and farther away there were frogs croaking. He could see as through a silvery gauze the level stretch of the cotton-field, ripe and white; a gleam of water beyond – that was the bend of the river – and farther yet, the gentle rise of the pine hill.

There was a cabin up there on the hill that Polydore remembered well. Negroes were living in it now, but it had been his home once. Life had been pinched and wretched enough up there for the little chap. The bright days had been the days when his godmother, Mamzelle Adélaïde, would come driving her old white horse over the pine needles and crackling fallen twigs of the deserted hill-road. Her presence was connected with the earliest recollections of whatever he had known of comfort and well-being.

And one day, when death had taken his mother from him, Mamzelle Adélaïde had brought him home to live with her always. Now she was sick down there in her room; very sick, for the doctor had said so, and the married sister had put on her longest face.

Polydore did not think of these things in any connected or very intelligent way. They were only impressions that penetrated him and made his heart swell, and the tears well up to his eyes. He wiped his eyes on the sleeve of his nightgown. The mosquitoes were stinging him and raising great welts on his brown legs. He went and crept back under the mosquito-bar, and soon he was asleep and dreaming that his *nénaine* was dead and he left alone in the cabin upon the pine hill.

In the morning, after the doctor had seen Mamzelle Adélaïde, he went and turned his horse into the lot and prepared to stay with his patient until he could feel it would be prudent to leave her.

Polydore tiptoed into her room and stood at the foot of the bed. Nobody noticed now whether he limped or not. She was talking very loud, and he could not believe at first that she could be as ill as they said, with such strength of voice. But her tones were unnatural, and what she said conveyed no meaning to his ears.

He understood, however, when she thought she was talking to his mother. She was in a manner apologising for his illness; and seemed to be troubled with the idea that she had in a way been the indirect cause of it by some oversight or neglect.

Polydore felt ashamed, and went outside and stood by himself near the cistern till someone told him to go and attend to the doctor's horse.

Then there was confusion in the household, when mornings and afternoons seemed turned around; and meals, which were scarcely tasted, were served at irregular and unseasonable hours. And there came one awful night, when they did not know if Mamzelle Adélaïde would live or die.

Nobody slept. The doctor snatched moments of rest in the hammock. He and the priest, who had been summoned, talked a little together with professional callousness about the dry weather and the crops.

Old monsieur walked, walked, like a restless, caged animal. The married sister came out on the gallery every now and then and leaned up against the post and sobbed in her handkerchief. There were many negroes around, sitting on the steps and standing in small groups in the yard.

Polydore crouched on the gallery. It had finally come to him to comprehend the cause of his *nénaine*'s sickness – that drive in the sweltering afternoon, when he was shamming illness. No one there could have comprehended the horror of himself, the terror that possessed him, squatting there outside her door like a savage. If she died – but he could not think of that. It was the point at which his reason was stunned and seemed to swoon.

*

A week or two later Mamzelle Adélaïde was sitting outside for the first time since her convalescence began. They had brought her own rocker around to the side where she could get a sight and whiff of the flower-garden and the blossom-laden rose-vine twining in and out of the banisters. Her former plumpness had not yet returned, and she looked much older, for the wrinkles were visible.

She was watching Polydore cross the yard. He had been putting up his pony. He approached with his heavy, clumsy walk; his round, simple face was hot and flushed from the ride. When he had mounted to the gallery he went and leaned against the railing, facing Mamzelle Adélaïde, mopping his face, his hands and neck with his handkerchief. Then he removed his hat and began to fan himself with it.

'You seem to be perfec'ly cu'ed of yo' rheumatism, Polydore. It doesn' hurt you any mo', my boy?' she questioned.

He stamped the foot and extended the leg violently, in proof of its perfect soundness.

'You know w'ere I been, *nénaine*?' he said. 'I been to confession.'

'That's right. Now you mus' rememba and not take a drink of water tomorrow morning, as you did las' time, and miss yo' communion, my boy. You are a good child, Polydore, to go like that to confession without bein told.'

'No, I ain' good,' he returned, doggedly. He began to twirl his hat on one finger. 'Père Cassimelle say he always yeard I was stupid, but he never knew befo' how bad I been.'

'Indeed!' muttered Mamzelle Adélaïde, not over well pleased with the priest's estimate of her protégé.

'He gave me a long penance,' continued Polydore. 'The "Litany of the Saint" and the "Litany of the Blessed Virgin", and three "Our Father" and three "Hail Mary" to say ev'ry mo'ning fo' a week. But he say' that ain' enough.'

'My patience! W'at does he expec' mo' from you, I like to know?' Polydore was now creasing and scanning his hat attentively.

'He say' w'at I need, it's to be wo' out with the rawhide. He say' he knows M'sieur José is too ole and feeble to give it to me like I deserve; and if you want, he say' he's willing to give me a good taste of the rawhide himse'f.'

Mamzelle Adélaïde found it impossible to disguise her indignation: 'Père Cassimelle sho'ly fo'gets himse'f, Polydore. Don't repeat to me any further his inconsid'ate remarks.'

'He's right, *nénaine*. Père Cassimelle is right.'

Since the night he crouched outside her door, Polydore had lived with the weight of his unconfessed fault oppressing every moment of existence. He had tried to rid himself of it in going to Father Cassimelle; but that had only helped by indicating the way. He was awkward and unaccustomed to express emotions with coherent speech. The words would not come.

Suddenly he flung his hat to the ground, and falling on his knees, began to sob, with his face pressed down in Mamzelle Adélaïde's lap. She had never seen him cry before, and in her weak condition it made her tremble.

Then somehow he got it out; he told the whole story of his deceit. He told it simply, in a way that bared his heart to her for the first time. She said nothing; only held his hand close and stroked his hair. But she felt as if a kind of miracle had happened. Hitherto her first thought in caring for this boy had been a desire to fulfil his dead mother's wishes.

But now he seemed to belong to herself, and to be her very own. She knew that a bond of love had been forged that would hold them together always.

'I know I can't he'p being stupid,' sighed Polydore, 'but it's no call fo' me to be bad.'

'Neva mine, Polydore; neva mine, my boy,' and she drew him close to her and kissed him as mothers kiss.

Regret

Mamzelle Aurélie possessed a good strong figure, ruddy cheeks, hair that was changing from brown to grey, and a determined eye. She wore a man's hat about the farm, and an old blue army overcoat when it was cold, and sometimes top-boots.

Mamzelle Aurélie had never thought of marrying. She had never been in love. At the age of twenty she had received a proposal, which she had promptly declined, and at the age of fifty she had not yet lived to regret it.

So she was quite alone in the world, except for her dog Ponto, and the negroes who lived in her cabins and worked her crops, and the fowls, a few cows, a couple of mules, her gun (with which she shot chicken-hawks) and her religion.

One morning Mamzelle Aurélie stood upon her gallery, contemplating, with arms akimbo, a small band of very small children who, to all intents and purposes, might have fallen from the clouds, so unexpected and bewildering was their coming, and so unwelcome. They were the children of her nearest neighbour, Odile, who was not such a near neighbour, after all.

The young woman had appeared but five minutes before, accompanied by these four children. In her arms she carried little Elodie; she dragged Ti Nomme[277] by an unwilling hand; while Marcéline and Marcélette followed with irresolute steps.

Her face was red and disfigured from tears and excitement. She had been summoned to a neighbouring parish by the dangerous illness of her mother; her husband was away in Texas – it seemed to her a million miles away; and Valsin was waiting with the mule-cart to drive her to the station.

'It's no question, Mamzelle Aurélie; you jus' got to keep these youngsters fo' me tell I come back. *Dieu sait*, I wouldn' botha you with 'em if it was any otha way to do! Make 'em mine you, Mamzelle Aurélie; don' spare 'em. Me, there, I'm half crazy between the chil'ren, an' Léon not home, an' maybe not even to fine po' maman alive encore! – ' a harrowing possibility which drove Odile to take a final hasty and convulsive leave of her disconsolate family.

She left them crowded into the narrow strip of shade on the porch of the long, low house; the white sunlight was beating in on the white old boards; some chickens were scratching in the grass at the foot of the steps, and one had boldly mounted, and was stepping heavily, solemnly and aimlessly across the gallery. There was a pleasant odour of pinks in the air and the sound of negroes' laughter was coming across the flowering cotton-field.

Mamzelle Aurélie stood contemplating the children. She looked with a critical eye upon Marcéline, who had been left staggering beneath the weight of the chubby Elodie. She surveyed with the same calculating air Marcélette mingling her silent tears with the audible grief and rebellion of Ti Nomme. During those few contemplative moments she was collecting herself, determining upon a line of action which should be identical with a line of duty. She began by feeding them.

If Mamzelle Aurélie's responsibilities might have begun and ended there, they could easily have been dismissed; for her larder was amply provided against an emergency of this nature. But little children are not little pigs; they require and demand attentions which were wholly unexpected by Mamzelle Aurélie, and which she was ill prepared to give.

She was, indeed, very inapt in her management of Odile's children during the first few days. How could she know that Marcélette always wept when spoken to in a loud and commanding tone of voice? It was a peculiarity of Marcélette's. She became acquainted with Ti Nomme's passion for flowers only when he had plucked all the choicest gardenias and pinks for the apparent purpose of critically studying their botanical construction.

' 'Tain't enough to tell 'im, Mamzelle Aurélie,' Marcéline instructed her; 'you got to tie 'im in a chair. It's w'at maman all time do w'en he's bad: she tie 'im in a chair.' The chair in which Mamzelle Aurélie tied Ti Nomme was roomy and comfortable, and he seized the opportunity to take a nap in it, the afternoon being warm.

At night, when she ordered them one and all to bed as she would have shooed the chickens into the hen-house, they stayed uncomprehending before her. What about the little white nightgowns that had to be taken from the pillow-slip in which they were brought over, and shaken by some strong hand till they snapped like ox-whips? What about the tub of water which had to be brought and set in the middle of the floor, in which the little tired, dusty, sun-browned feet had every one to be washed sweet and clean? And it made Marcéline and Marcélette laugh merrily – the idea that Mamzelle Aurélie should for a moment have believed that Ti Nomme could fall asleep without being told the story of Croquemitaine or Loup-garou,[278] or both; or that Elodie could fall asleep at all without being rocked and sung to.

'I tell you, Aunt Ruby,' Mamzelle Aurélie informed her cook in confidence; 'me, I'd rather manage a dozen plantation' than fo' chil'ren. It's *terrassent*! *Bonté!*[279] Don't talk to me about chil'ren!'

' 'Tain' ispected sich as you would know airy thing 'bout 'em, Mamzelle Aurélie. I see dat plainly yistiddy w'en I spy dat li'le chile playin' wid yo' baskit o' keys. You don' know dat makes chillun grow up hard-headed, to play wid keys? Des like it make 'em teeth hard to look in a lookin'-glass. Them's the things you got to know in the raisin' an' manigement o' chillun.'

Mamzelle Aurélie certainly did not pretend or aspire to such subtle and far-reaching knowledge on the subject as Aunt Ruby possessed, who had 'raised five an' bared [buried] six' in her day. She was glad enough to learn a few little mother-tricks to serve the moment's need.

Ti Nomme's sticky fingers compelled her to unearth white aprons that she had not worn for years, and she had to accustom herself to his moist kisses – the expressions of an affectionate and exuberant nature. She got down her sewing-basket, which she seldom used, from the top shelf of the armoire, and placed it within the ready and easy reach which torn slips and buttonless waists demanded. It took her some days to become accustomed to the laughing, the crying, the chattering that echoed through the house and around it all day long. And it was not the first or the second night that she could sleep comfortably with little Elodie's hot, plump body pressed close against her, and the little one's warm breath beating her cheek like the fanning of a bird's wing.

But at the end of two weeks Mamzelle Aurélie had grown quite used to these things, and she no longer complained.

It was also at the end of two weeks that Mamzelle Aurélie, one evening, looking away towards the crib where the cattle were being fed, saw Valsin's blue cart turning the bend of the road. Odile sat beside the mulatto, upright and alert. As they drew near, the young woman's beaming face indicated that her homecoming was a happy one.

But this coming, unannounced and unexpected, threw Mamzelle Aurélie into a flutter that was almost agitation. The children had to be gathered. Where was Ti Nomme? Yonder in the shed, putting an edge on his knife at the grindstone. And Marcéline and Marcélette? Cutting and fashioning doll-rags in the corner of the gallery. As for Elodie, she was safe enough in Mamzelle Aurélie's arms; and she had screamed with delight at sight of the familiar blue cart which was bringing her mother back to her.

The excitement was all over, and they were gone. How still it was when they were gone! Mamzelle Aurélie stood upon the gallery, looking and listening. She could no longer see the cart; the red sunset and the blue-grey twilight had together flung a purple mist across the fields and road that hid it from her view. She could no longer hear the wheezing and creaking of its wheels. But she could still faintly hear the shrill, glad voices of the children.

She turned into the house. There was much work awaiting her, for the children had left a sad disorder behind them; but she did not at once set about the task of righting it. Mamzelle Aurélie seated herself beside the table. She gave one slow glance through the room, into which the evening shadows were creeping and deepening around her solitary figure. She let her head fall down upon her bended arm, and began to cry. Oh, but she cried! Not softly, as women often do. She cried like a man, with sobs that seemed to tear her very soul. She did not notice Ponto licking her hand.

A Matter of Prejudice

Madame Carambeau wanted it strictly understood that she was not to be disturbed by Gustave's birthday party. They carried her big rocking-chair from the back gallery, that looked out upon the garden where the children were going to play, around to the front gallery, which closely faced the green levee bank[280] and the Mississippi coursing almost flush with the top of it.

The house – an old Spanish one, broad, low and completely encircled by a wide gallery – was far down in the French Quarter of New Orleans. It stood upon a square of ground that was covered thick with a semi-tropical growth of plants and flowers. An impenetrable board fence, edged with a formidable row of iron spikes, shielded the garden from the prying glances of the occasional passer-by.

Madame Carambeau's widowed daughter, Madame Cécile Lalonde, lived with her. This annual party, given to her little son, Gustave, was the one defiant act of Madame Lalonde's existence. She persisted in it, to her own astonishment and the wonder of those who knew her and her mother.

For old Madame Carambeau was a woman of many prejudices – so many, in fact, that it would be difficult to name them all. She detested dogs, cats, organ-grinders, white servants and children's noises. She despised Americans, Germans and all people of a different faith from her own. Anything not French had, in her opinion, little right to existence.

She had not spoken to her son Henri for ten years because he had married an American girl from Prytania Street.[281] She would not permit green tea to be introduced into her house, and those who could not or would not drink coffee might drink tisane of *fleur de Laurier* [282] for all she cared.

Nevertheless, the children seemed to be having it all their own way that day, and the organ-grinders were let loose. Old madame, in her retired corner, could hear the screams, the laughter and the music far more distinctly than she liked. She rocked herself noisily, and hummed 'Partant pour la Syrie'.[283]

She was straight and slender. Her hair was white, and she wore it in puffs on the temples. Her skin was fair and her eyes blue and cold.

Suddenly she became aware that footsteps were approaching, and threatening to invade her privacy – not only footsteps, but screams! Then two little children, one in hot pursuit of the other, darted wildly around the corner near which she sat.

The child in advance, a pretty little girl, sprang excitedly into Madame Carambeau's lap, and threw her arms convulsively around the old lady's neck. Her companion lightly struck her a 'last tag', and ran laughing gleefully away.

The most natural thing for the child to do then would have been to wriggle down from madame's lap, without a 'thank you' or a 'by your leave', after the manner of small and thoughtless children. But she did not do this. She stayed there, panting and fluttering, like a frightened bird.

Madame was greatly annoyed. She moved as if to put the child away from her, and scolded her sharply for being boisterous and rude. The little one, who did not understand French, was not disturbed by the reprimand, and stayed on in madame's lap. She rested her plump little cheek, that was hot and flushed, against the soft white linen of the old lady's gown.

Her cheek was very hot and very flushed. It was dry, too, and so were her hands. The child's breathing was quick and irregular. Madame was not long in detecting these signs of disturbance.

Though she was a creature of prejudice, she was nevertheless a skilful and accomplished nurse, and a connoisseur in all matters pertaining to health. She prided herself upon this talent, and never lost an opportunity of exercising it. She would have treated an organ-grinder with tender consideration if one had presented himself in the character of an invalid.

Madame's manner towards the little one changed immediately. Her arms and her lap were at once adjusted so as to become the most comfortable of resting places. She rocked very gently to and fro. She fanned the child softly with her palm-leaf fan, and sang 'Partant pour la Syrie' in a low and agreeable tone.

The child was perfectly content to lie still and prattle a little in that language which madame thought hideous. But the brown eyes were soon swimming in drowsiness, and the little body grew heavy with sleep in madame's clasp.

When the little girl slept Madame Carambeau arose, and treading carefully and deliberately, entered her room, that opened near at hand upon the gallery. The room was large, airy and inviting, with its cool matting upon the floor, and its heavy, old, polished mahogany furniture. Madame, with the child still in her arms, pulled a bell-cord; then she stood waiting, swaying gently back and forth. Presently an old black woman answered the summons. She wore gold hoops in her ears, and a bright bandana knotted fantastically on her head.

'Louise, turn down the bed,' commanded madame. 'Place that small, soft pillow below the bolster. Here is a poor little unfortunate creature whom Providence must have driven into my arms.' She laid the child carefully down.

'Ah, those Americans! Do they deserve to have children? Understanding as little as they do how to take care of them!' said madame, while Louise was mumbling an accompanying assent that would have been unintelligible to anyone unacquainted with the negro patois.

'There, you see, Louise, she is burning up,' remarked madame; 'she is consumed. Unfasten the little bodice while I lift her. Ah, talk to me of such parents! So stupid as not to perceive a fever like that coming on, but they must dress their child up like a monkey to go play and dance to the music of organ-grinders.

'Haven't you better sense, Louise, than to take off a child's shoe as if you were removing the boot from the leg of a cavalry officer?' Madame would have required fairy fingers to minister to the sick. 'Now go to Mamzelle Cécile, and tell her to send me one of those old, soft, thin nightgowns that Gustave wore two summers ago.'

When the woman retired, madame busied herself with concocting a cooling pitcher of orange-flower water, and mixing a fresh supply of *eau sédative* with which agreeably to sponge the little invalid.

Madame Lalonde came herself with the old, soft nightgown. She was a pretty, blonde, plump little woman, with the deprecatory air of one whose will has become flaccid from want of use. She was mildly distressed at what her mother had done.

'But, mamma! But, mamma, the child's parents will be sending the carriage for her in a little while. Really, there was no use. Oh dear! oh dear!'

If the bedpost had spoken to Madame Carambeau, she would have paid more attention, for speech from such a source would have been at least surprising if not convincing. Madame Lalonde did not possess the faculty of either surprising or convincing her mother.

'Yes, the little one will be quite comfortable in this,' said the old lady, taking the garment from her daughter's irresolute hands.

'But, mamma! What shall I say, what shall I do when they send? Oh, dear; oh, dear!'

'That is your business,' replied madame, with lofty indifference. 'My concern is solely with a sick child that happens to be under my roof. I think I know my duty at this time of life, Cécile.'

As Madame Lalonde predicted, the carriage soon came, with a stiff English coachman driving it, and a red-cheeked Irish nursemaid seated inside. Madame would not even permit the maid to see her little charge. She had an original theory that the Irish voice is distressing to the sick.

Madame Lalonde sent the girl away with a long letter of explanation that must have satisfied the parents; for the child was left undisturbed in Madame Carambeau's care. She was a sweet child, gentle and affectionate. And, though she cried and fretted a little throughout the night for her mother, she seemed, after all, to take kindly to madame's gentle nursing. It was not much of a fever that afflicted her, and after two days she was well enough to be sent back to her parents.

Madame, in all her varied experience with the sick, had never before nursed so objectionable a character as an American child. But the trouble was that after the little one went away, she could think of nothing really objectionable against her except the accident of her birth, which was, after all, her misfortune; and her ignorance of the French language, which was not her fault.

But the touch of the caressing baby arms; the pressure of the soft little body in the night; the tones of the voice, and the feeling of the hot lips when the child kissed her, believing herself to be with her mother, were impressions that had sunk through the crust of madame's prejudice and reached her heart.

She often walked the length of the gallery, looking out across the wide, majestic river. Sometimes she trod the mazes of her garden where the solitude was almost that of a tropical jungle. It was during such moments that the seed began to work in her soul – the seed planted by the innocent and undesigning hands of a little child.

The first shoot that it sent forth was Doubt. Madame plucked it away once or twice. But it sprouted again, and with it Mistrust and Dissatisfaction. Then from the heart of the seed, and amid the shoots of Doubt and Misgiving, came the flower of Truth. It was a very beautiful flower, and it bloomed on Christmas morning.

As Madame Carambeau and her daughter were about to enter her carriage on that Christmas morning, to be driven to church, the old lady stopped to give an order to her black coachman, François. François had been driving these ladies every Sunday morning to the French cathedral for so many years – he had forgotten exactly how many, but ever since he had entered their service, when Madame Lalonde was a little girl.

His astonishment may therefore be imagined when Madame Carambeau said to him: 'François, today you will drive us to one of the American churches.'

'*Plait-il, madame?*'[284] the negro stammered, doubting the evidence of his hearing.

'I say, you will drive us to one of the American churches. Any one of them,' she added, with a sweep of her hand. 'I suppose they are all alike,' and she followed her daughter into the carriage.

Madame Lalonde's surprise and agitation were painful to see, and they deprived her of the ability to question, even if she had possessed the courage to do so.

François, left to his fancy, drove them to St Patrick's Church on Camp Street. Madame Lalonde looked and felt like the proverbial fish out of its element as they entered the edifice. Madame Carambeau, on the contrary, looked as if she had been attending St Patrick's Church all her life. She sat with unruffled calm through the long service and through a lengthy English sermon, of which she did not understand a word.

When the mass was ended and they were about to enter the carriage again, Madame Carambeau turned, as she had done before, to the coachman.

'François,' she said, coolly, 'you will now drive us to the residence of my son, M. Henri Carambeau. No doubt Mamzelle Cécile can inform you where it is,' she added, with a sharply penetrating glance that caused Madame Lalonde to wince.

Yes, her daughter Cécile knew, and so did François, for that matter. They drove out to St Charles Avenue – very far out. It was like a strange city to old madame, who had not been in the American Quarter since the town had taken on this new and splendid growth.

The morning was a delicious one, soft and mild; and the roses were all in bloom. They were not hidden behind spiked fences. Madame appeared not to notice them, or the beautiful and striking residences that lined the avenue along which they drove. She held a bottle of smelling-salts to her nostrils, as though she were passing through the most unsavoury instead of the most beautiful quarter of New Orleans.

Henri's house was a very modern and very handsome one, standing a little distance away from the street. A well-kept lawn, studded with rare and charming plants, surrounded it. The ladies, dismounting, rang the bell, and stood out upon the banquette, waiting for the iron gate to be opened.

A white maidservant admitted them. Madame did not seem to mind. She handed her a card with all proper ceremony, and followed with her daughter into the house.

Not once did she show a sign of weakness; not even when her son,

Henri, came and took her in his arms and sobbed and wept upon her neck as only a warm-hearted Creole could. He was a big, good-looking, honest-faced man, with tender brown eyes like his dead father's and a firm mouth like his mother's.

Young Mrs Carambeau came, too, her sweet, fresh face transfigured with happiness. She led by the hand her little daughter, the 'American child' whom madame had nursed so tenderly a month before, never suspecting the little one to be other than an alien to her.

'What a lucky chance was that fever! What a happy accident!' gurgled Madame Lalonde.

'Cécile, it was no accident, I tell you; it was Providence,' spoke madame, reprovingly, and no one contradicted her.

They all drove back together to eat Christmas dinner in the old house by the river. Madame held her little granddaughter upon her lap; her son Henri sat facing her, and beside her was her daughter-in-law.

Henri sat back in the carriage and could not speak. His soul was possessed by a pathetic joy that would not admit of speech. He was going back again to the home where he was born, after a banishment of ten long years.

He would hear again the water beat against the green levee-bank with a sound that was not quite like any other that he could remember. He would sit within the sweet and solemn shadow of the deep and overhanging roof; and roam through the wild, rich solitude of the old garden, where he had played his pranks of boyhood and dreamed his dreams of youth. He would listen to his mother's voice calling him, '*mon fils*', as it had always done before that day he had had to choose between mother and wife. No; he could not speak.

But his wife chatted much and pleasantly – in a French, however, that must have been trying to old madame to listen to.

'I am so sorry, *ma mère*,' she said, 'that our little one does not speak French. It is not my fault, I assure you,' and she flushed and hesitated a little. 'It – it was Henri who would not permit it.'

'That is nothing,' replied madame, amiably, drawing the child close to her. 'Her grandmother will teach her French; and she will teach her grandmother English. You see, I have no prejudices. I am not like my son. Henri was always a stubborn boy. Heaven only knows how he came by such a character!'

Caline

The sun was just far enough in the west to send inviting shadows. In the centre of a small field, and in the shade of a haystack which was there, a girl lay sleeping. She had slept long and soundly, when something awoke her as suddenly as if it had been a blow. She opened her eyes and stared a moment up in the cloudless sky. She yawned and stretched her long brown legs and arms, lazily. Then she arose, never minding the bits of straw that clung to her black hair, to her red bodice, and the blue cotonade skirt that did not reach her naked ankles.

The log cabin in which she dwelt with her parents was just outside the enclosure in which she had been sleeping. Beyond was a small clearing that did duty as a cotton field. All else was dense wood, except the long stretch that curved round the brow of the hill, and in which glittered the steel rails of the Texas and Pacific road.

When Caline emerged from the shadow she saw a long train of passenger coaches standing in view, where they must have stopped abruptly. It was that sudden stopping which had awakened her; for such a thing had not happened before within her recollection, and she looked stupid, at first, with astonishment. There seemed to be something wrong with the engine; and some of the passengers who dismounted went forward to investigate the trouble. Others came strolling along in the direction of the cabin, where Caline stood under an old gnarled mulberry tree, staring. Her father had halted his mule at the end of the cotton row, and stood staring also, leaning upon his plough.

There were ladies in the party. They walked awkwardly in their high-heeled boots over the rough, uneven ground, and held up their skirts mincingly. They twirled parasols over their shoulders, and laughed immoderately at the funny things which their masculine companions were saying.

They tried to talk to Caline, but could not understand the French patois with which she answered them.

One of the men – a pleasant-faced youngster – drew a sketchbook from his pocket and began to make a picture of the girl. She stayed motionless, her hands behind her, and her wide eyes fixed earnestly upon him.

Before he had finished there was a summons from the train; and all went scampering hurriedly away. The engine screeched, it sent a few lazy puffs into the still air, and in another moment or two had vanished, bearing its human cargo with it.

Caline could not feel the same after that. She looked with new and strange interest upon the trains of cars that passed so swiftly back and forth across her vision, each day; and wondered whence these people came, and whither they were going.

Her mother and father could not tell her, except to say that they came from '*loin là bas*', and were going '*Djieu sait é où*'.[285]

One day she walked miles down the track to talk with the old flagman, who stayed down there by the big water tank. Yes, he knew. Those people came from the great cities in the north, and were going to the city in the south. He knew all about the city; it was a grand place. He had lived there once. His sister lived there now; and she would be glad enough to have so fine a girl as Caline to help her cook and scrub, and tend the babies. And he thought Caline might earn as much as five dollars a month, in the city.

So she went; in a new cotonade, and her Sunday shoes; with a sacredly guarded scrawl that the flagman sent to his sister.

The woman lived in a tiny, stuccoed house, with green blinds, and three wooden steps leading down to the banquette. There seemed to be hundreds like it along the street. Over the house tops loomed the tall masts of ships, and the hum of the French market could be heard on a still morning.

Caline was at first bewildered. She had to readjust all her pre-conceptions to fit the reality of it. The flagman's sister was a kind and gentle task-mistress. At the end of a week or two she wanted to know how the girl liked it all. Caline liked it very well, for it was pleasant, on Sunday afternoons, to stroll with the children under the great, solemn sugar sheds; or to sit upon the compressed cotton bales, watching the stately steamers, the graceful boats and noisy little tugs that plied the waters of the Mississippi. And it filled her with agreeable excitement to go to the French market, where the handsome Gascon butchers were eager to present their compliments and little Sunday bouquets to the pretty Acadian girl; and to throw fistfuls of *lagniappes*[286] into her basket.

When the woman asked her again after another week if she were still pleased, she was not so sure. And again when she questioned Caline the girl turned away, and went to sit behind the big, yellow cistern, to cry unobserved. For she knew now that it was not the great city and its crowds of people she had so eagerly sought; but the pleasant-faced boy, who had made her picture that day under the mulberry tree.

A Dresden Lady in Dixie

Madame Valtour had been in the sitting-room some time before she noticed the absence of the Dresden china figure from the corner of the mantelpiece, where it had stood for years. Aside from the intrinsic value of the piece, there were some very sad and tender memories associated with it. A baby's lips that were now for ever still had loved once to kiss the painted 'pitty 'ady'; and the baby arms had often held it in a close and smothered embrace.

Madame Valtour gave a rapid, startled glance around the room, to see perchance if it had been misplaced; but she failed to discover it.

Viny, the housemaid, when summoned, remembered having carefully dusted it that morning, and was rather indignantly positive that she had not broken the thing to bits and secreted the pieces.

'Who has been in the room during my absence?' questioned Madame Valtour, with asperity. Viny abandoned herself to a moment's reflection.

'Pa-Jeff comed in yere wid de mail – ' If she had said St Peter came in with the mail, the fact would have had as little bearing on the case from Madame Valtour's point of view.

Pa-Jeff's uprightness and honesty were so long and firmly established as to have become proverbial on the plantation. He had not served the family faithfully since boyhood and been all through the war with 'old Marse Valtour' to descend at his time of life to tampering with household bric-a-brac.

'Has anyone else been here?' Madame Valtour naturally enquired.

'On'y Agapie w'at brung you some Creole aiggs. I tole 'er to sot 'em down in de hall. I don' know she comed in de settin'-room o' not.'

Yes, there they were; eight, fresh 'Creole eggs' reposing on the muslin in the sewing basket. Viny herself had been seated on the gallery brushing her mistress's gowns during the hours of that lady's absence, and could think of no one else having penetrated to the sitting-room.

Madame Valtour did not entertain the thought that Agapie had stolen the relic. Her worst fear was that the girl, finding herself alone in the room, had handled the frail bit of porcelain and inadvertently broken it.

Agapie came often to the house to play with the children and amuse them – she loved nothing better. Indeed, no other spot known to her on earth so closely embodied her confused idea of paradise as this home with its atmosphere of love, comfort and good cheer. She was, herself, a cheery bit of humanity, overflowing with kind impulses and animal spirits.

Madame Valtour recalled the fact that Agapie had often admired this Dresden figure (but what had she not admired!); and she remembered having heard the girl's assurance that if ever she became possessed of 'fo' bits' to spend as she liked, she would have someone buy her just such a china doll in town or in the city.

Before night, the fact that the Dresden lady had strayed from her proud eminence on the sitting-room mantel became, through Viny's indiscreet babbling, pretty well known on the place.

The following morning Madame Valtour crossed the field and went over to the Bedauts' cabin. The cabins on the plantation were not grouped; each stood isolated upon the section of land which its occupants cultivated. Pa-Jeff's cabin was the only one near enough to the Bedauts to admit of neighbourly intercourse.

Seraphine Bedaut was sitting on her small gallery, stringing red peppers, when Madame Valtour approached.

'I'm so distressed, Madame Bedaut,' began the planter's wife, abruptly. But the 'Cadian woman arose politely and interrupted, offering her visitor a chair.

'Come in, set down, Ma'me Valtour.'

'No, no; it's only for a moment. You know, Madame Bedaut, yester-day when I returned from making a visit, I found that an ornament was missing from my sitting-room mantelpiece. It's a thing I prize very, very much – ' with sudden tears filling her eyes – 'and I would not willingly part with it for many times its value.' Seraphine Bedaut was listening, with her mouth partly open, looking, in truth, stupidly puzzled.

'No one entered the room during my absence,' continued Madame Valtour, 'but Agapie.' Seraphine's mouth snapped like a steel trap and her black eyes gleamed with a flash of anger.

'You wan' say Agapie stole some'in' in yo' house!' she cried out in a shrill voice, tremulous from passion.

'No; oh no! I'm sure Agapie is an honest girl and we all love her; but you know how children are. It was a small Dresden figure. She may have handled and broken the thing and perhaps is afraid to say so. She may have thoughtlessly misplaced it; oh, I don't know what! I want to ask if she saw it.'

'Come in; you got to come in, Ma'me Valtour,' stubbornly insisted Seraphine, leading the way into the cabin. 'I sen' 'er to de house yistiddy wid some Creole aiggs,' she went on in her rasping voice, 'like I all time do, because you all say you can't eat dem sto' aiggs no mo.' Yere de basket w'at I sen' 'em in,' reaching for an Indian basket which hung against the wall – and which was partly filled with cotton seed.

'Oh, never mind,' interrupted Madame Valtour, now thoroughly distressed at witnessing the woman's agitation.

'Ah, *bien non*. I got to show you, Agapie en't no mo' thief 'an yo' own child'en is.' She led the way into the adjoining room of the hut.

'Yere all her things w'at she 'muse herse'f wid,' continued Seraphine, pointing to a soapbox which stood on the floor just beneath the open window. The box was filled with an indescribable assortment of odds and ends, mostly doll-rags. A catechism and a blue-backed speller poked dog-eared corners from out of the confusion; for the Valtour children were making heroic and patient efforts towards Agapie's training.

Seraphine cast herself upon her knees before the box and dived her thin brown hands among its contents. 'I wan' show you; I goin' show you,' she kept repeating excitedly. Madame Valtour was standing beside her.

Suddenly the woman drew forth from among the rags the Dresden lady, as dapper, sound, and smiling as ever. Seraphine's hand shook so violently that she was in danger of letting the image fall to the floor. Madame Valtour reached out and took it very quietly from her. Then Seraphine rose tremblingly to her feet and broke into a sob that was pitiful to hear.

Agapie was approaching the cabin. She was a chubby girl of twelve. She walked with bare, callous feet over the rough ground and bare-headed under the hot sun. Her thick, short, black hair covered her head like a mane. She had been dancing along the path, but slackened her pace upon catching sight of the two women who had returned to the gallery. But when she perceived that her mother was crying she darted impetuously forward. In an instant she had her arms around her mother's neck, clinging so tenaciously in her youthful strength as to make the frail woman totter.

Agapie had seen the Dresden figure in Madame Valtour's possession and at once guessed the whole accusation.

'It en't so! I tell you, maman, it en't so! I neva touch' it. Stop cryin'; stop cryin'!' and she began to cry most piteously herself.

'But Agapie, we fine it in yo' box,' moaned Seraphine through her sobs.

'Then somebody put it there. Can't you see somebody put it there? 'Ten't so, I tell you.'

The scene was extremely painful to Madame Valtour. Whatever she might tell these two later, for the time she felt herself powerless to say anything befitting, and she walked away. But she turned to remark, with a hardness of expression and intention which she seldom displayed: 'No one will know of this through me. But, Agapie, you must not come into my house again; on account of the children; I could not allow it.'

As she walked away she could hear Agapie comforting her mother with renewed protestations of innocence.

Pa-Jeff began to fail visibly that year. No wonder, considering his great age, which he computed to be about one hundred. It was, in fact, some ten years less than that, but a good old age all the same. It was seldom that he got out into the field; and then, never to do any heavy work – only a little light hoeing. There were days when the 'misery' doubled him up and nailed him down to his chair so that he could not set foot beyond the door of his cabin. He would sit there courting the sunshine and blinking, as he gazed across the fields with the patience of the savage.

The Bedauts seemed to know almost instinctively when Pa-Jeff was sick. Agapie would shade her eyes and look searchingly towards the old man's cabin.

'I don' see Pa-Jeff this mo'nin',' or, 'Pa-Jeff en't open his winda,' or, 'I didn' see no smoke yet yonda to Pa-Jeff's.' And in a little while the girl would be over there with a pail of soup or coffee, or whatever there was at hand which she thought the old negro might fancy. She had lost all the colour out of her cheeks and was pining like a sick bird. She often sat on the steps of the gallery and talked with the old man while she waited for him to finish his soup from her tin pail.

'I tell you, Pa-Jeff, its neva been no thief in the Bedaut family. My pa say he couldn' hole up his head if he think I been a thief, me. An' maman say it would make her sick in bed, she don' know she could ever git up. Sosthene tell me the chil'en been cryin' fo' me up yonda. Li'le Lulu cry so hard M'sieur Valtour want sen' afta me, an' Ma'me Valtour say no.'

And with this, Agapie flung herself at length upon the gallery with her face buried in her arms, and began to cry so hysterically as seriously to alarm Pa-Jeff. It was well he had finished his soup, for he could not have eaten another mouthful.

'Hole up yo' head, chile. God save us! W'at you kiarrin' on dat away?' he exclaimed in great distress. 'You gwine to take a fit? Hole up yo' head.'

Agapie rose slowly to her feet, and drying her eyes upon the sleeve of

her josie, reached out for the tin bucket. Pa-Jeff handed it to her, but
without relinquishing his hold upon it.

'War hit you w'at tuck it?' he questioned in a whisper. 'I isn' gwine
tell; you knows I isn' gwine tell.' She only shook her head, attempting
to draw the pail forcibly away from the old man.

'Le' me go, Pa-Jeff. W'at you doin'! Gi' me my bucket!'

He kept his old blinking eyes fastened for a while questioningly upon
her disturbed and tear-stained face. Then he let her go and she turned
and ran swiftly away towards her home.

He sat very still watching her disappear; only his furrowed old face
twitched convulsively, moved by an unaccustomed train of reasoning
that was at work in him.

'She w'ite, I is black,' he muttered calculatingly. 'She young, I is ole;
sho I is ole. She good to Pa-Jeff like I her own kin an' colour.' This line
of thought seemed to possess him to the exclusion of every other. Late
in the night he was still muttering.

'Sho I is ole. She good to Pa-Jeff, yas.'

A few days later, when Pa-Jeff happened to be feeling comparatively
well, he presented himself at the house just as the family had assembled
at their early dinner. Looking up suddenly, Monsieur Valtour was
astonished to see him standing there in the room near the open door.
He leaned upon his cane and his grizzled head was bowed upon his
breast. There was general satisfaction expressed at seeing Pa-Jeff on his
legs once more.

'Why, old man, I'm glad to see you out again,' exclaimed the planter,
cordially, pouring a glass of wine, which he instructed Viny to hand to
the old fellow. Pa-Jeff accepted the glass and set it solemnly down upon
a small table near by.

'Marse Albert,' he said, 'I is come heah today fo' to make a statement
of de rights an' de wrongs w'at is done hang heavy on my soul dis heah
long time. Arter you heahs me an' de missus heahs me an' de chillun an'
ev'body, den ef you says: "Pa-Jeff you kin tech yo' lips to dat glass o'
wine," all well an' right.'

His manner was impressive and caused the family to exchange
surprised and troubled glances. Foreseeing that his recital might be
long, a chair was offered to him, but he declined it.

'One day,' he began, 'w'en I ben hoein' de madam's flower bed close
to de fence, Sosthene he ride up, he say: "Heah, Pa-Jeff, heah de mail."
I takes de mail f'om 'im an' I calls out to Viny w'at settin' on de gallery:
"Heah Marse Albert's mail, gal; come git it."

'But Viny she answer, pert-like – des like Viny: "You is got two laigs,

Pa-Jeff, des well as me." I ain't no han' fo' disputin' wid gals, so I brace up an' I come 'long to de house an' goes on in dat settin'-room dah, naix' to de dinin'-room. I lays dat mail down on Marse Albert's table; den I looks roun'.

'Ev'thing do look putty, sho! De lace cu'tains was a-flappin' an' de flowers was a-smellin' sweet, an' de pictures a-settin' back on de wall. I keep on lookin' roun'. To reckly my eye hit fall on de li'le gal w'at al'ays sets on de een' o' de mantelshelf. She do look mighty sassy dat day, wid 'er toe a-stickin' out, des so; an' holdin' her skirt des dat away; an' lookin' at me wid her head twis'.

'I laff out. Viny mus' heahed me. I say, "G'long 'way f'om dah, gal." She keep on smilin'. I reaches out my han'. Den Satan an' de good Sperrit, dey begins to wrastle in me. De Sperrit say: "You ole fool-nigga, you; mine w'at you about." Satan keep on shovin' my han' – des so – keep on shovin'. Satan he mighty powerful dat day, an' he win de fight. I kiar dat li'le trick home in my pocket.'

Pa-Jeff lowered his head for a moment in bitter confusion. His hearers were moved with distressful astonishment. They would have had him stop the recital right there, but Pa-Jeff resumed, with an effort: 'Come dat night I heah tell how dat li'le trick, wo'th heap money; how madam, she cryin' 'cause her li'le blessed lamb was use' to play wid dat, an' kiar-on ov' it. Den I git scared. I say, "W'at I gwine do?" An' up jump Satan an' de Sperrit a-wrastlin' again.

'De Sperrit say: "Kiar hit back whar it come f'om, Pa-Jeff." Satan 'low: "Fling it in de bayeh, you ole fool." De Sperrit say: "You won't fling dat in de bayeh, whar de madam kain't neva sot eyes on hit no mo'!" Den Satan he kine give in; he 'low he plumb sick o' disputin' so long; tell me go hide it some'eres whar dey nachelly gwine fine it. Satan he win dat fight.

'Des w'en de day g'ine break, I creeps out an' goes 'long de fiel' road. I pass by Ma'me Bedaut's house. I riclic how dey says li'le Bedaut gal ben in de sittin'-room, too, day befo'. De winda war open. Ev'body sleepin'. I tres' in my head, des like a dog w'at shame hisse'f. I sees dat box o' rags befo' my eyes; an' I drops dat li'le imp'dence 'mongst dem rags.

'Mebby yo' all t'ink Satan an' de Sperrit lef' me 'lone, arter dat?' continued Pa-Jeff, straightening himself from the relaxed position in which his members seemed to have settled.

'No, suh; dey ben desputin' straight 'long. Las' night dey come nigh onto en'in' me up. De Sperrit say: "Come 'long, I gittin' tired dis heah, you g'long up yonda an' tell de truf an' shame de devil." Satan 'low: "Stay whar you is; you heah me!" Dey clutches me. Dey twis'es an' twines me. Dey dashes me down an' jerks me up. But de Sperrit he win dat fight in de en', an' heah I is, mist'ess, master, chillun'; heah I is.'

Years later Pa-Jeff was still telling the story of his temptation and fall. The negroes especially seemed never to tire of hearing him relate it. He enlarged greatly upon the theme as he went, adding new and dramatic features which gave fresh interest to its every telling.

Agapie grew up to deserve the confidence and favours of the family. She redoubled her acts of kindness towards Pa-Jeff; but somehow she could not look into his face again.

Yet she need not have feared. Long before the end came, poor old Pa-Jeff, confused, bewildered, believed the story himself as firmly as those who had heard him tell it over and over for so many years.

Nég Créol

At the remote period of his birth he had been named César François Xavier, but no one ever thought of calling him anything but Chicot,[287] or Nég, or Maringouin.[288] Down at the French market, where he worked among the fishmongers, they called him Chicot, when they were not calling him names that are written less freely than they are spoken. But one felt privileged to call him almost anything, he was so black, lean, lame and shrivelled. He wore a head-kerchief, and whatever other rags the fishermen and their wives chose to bestow upon him. Throughout one whole winter he wore a woman's discarded jacket with puffed sleeves.

Among some startling beliefs entertained by Chicot was one that 'Michié St Pierre et Michié St Paul' had created him. Of 'Michié bon Dieu' he held his own private opinion, and not a too flattering one at that. This fantastic notion concerning the origin of his being he owed to the early teaching of his young master, a lax believer, and a great *farceur* in his day. Chicot had once been thrashed by a robust young Irish priest for expressing his religious views, and at another time knifed by a Sicilian. So he had come to hold his peace upon that subject.

Upon another theme he talked freely and harped continuously. For years he had tried to convince his associates that his master had left a progeny, rich, cultured, powerful and numerous beyond belief. This prosperous race of beings inhabited the most imposing mansions in the city of New Orleans. Men of note and position, whose names were familiar to the public, he swore were grandchildren, great-grandchildren, or, less frequently, distant relatives of his master, long deceased. Ladies who came to the market in carriages, or whose elegance of attire attracted the attention and admiration of the fishwomen, were all *des 'tites cousines*[289] to his former master, Jean Boisduré. He never looked for recognition from any of these superior beings, but delighted to discourse by the hour upon their dignity and pride of birth and wealth.

Chicot always carried an old gunny-sack, and into this went his earnings. He cleaned stalls at the market, scaled fish, and did many odd offices for the itinerant merchants, who usually paid in trade for his service. Occasionally he saw the colour of silver and got his clutch upon a coin, but he accepted anything and seldom made terms. He was glad to get a handkerchief from the Hebrew, and grateful if the Choctaws would trade him a bottle of *filé* for it. The butcher flung him a soup bone, and the fishmonger a few crabs or a paper bag of shrimps. It was the big *mulatresse, vendeuse de café*,[290] who cared for his inner man.

Once Chicot was accused by a shoe-vender of attempting to steal a pair of ladies' shoes. He declared he was only examining them. The clamour raised in the market was terrific. Young Dagoes assembled and squealed like rats; a couple of Gascon butchers bellowed like bulls. Matteo's wife shook her fist in the accuser's face and called him incomprehensible names. The Choctaw women, where they squatted, turned their slow eyes in the direction of the fray, taking no further notice; while a policeman jerked Chicot around by the puffed sleeve and brandished a club. It was a narrow escape.

Nobody knew where Chicot lived. A man – even a nég créol – who lives among the reeds and willows of Bayou St John, in a deserted chicken-coop constructed chiefly of tarred paper, is not going to boast of his habitation or to invite attention to his domestic appointments. When, after market hours, he vanished in the direction of St Philip Street, limping, seemingly bent under the weight of his gunny-bag, it was like the disappearance from the stage of some petty actor whom the audience does not follow in imagination beyond the wings, or think of till his return in another scene.

There was one to whom Chicot's coming or going meant more than this. In *la maison grise*[291] they called her La Chouette,[292] for no earthly reason unless that she perched high under the roof of the old rookery and scolded in shrill sudden outbursts. Forty or fifty years before, when for a little while she acted minor parts with a company of French players (an escapade that had brought her grandmother to the grave), she was known as Mademoiselle de Montallaine. Seventy-five years before she had been christened Aglaé Boisduré.

No matter at what hour the old negro appeared at her threshold, Mamzelle Aglaé always kept him waiting till she finished her prayers. She opened the door for him and silently motioned him to a seat, returning to prostrate herself upon her knees before a crucifix, and a shell filled with holy water that stood on a small table; it represented in her imagination an altar. Chicot knew that she did it to aggravate him; he was convinced that she timed her devotions to begin when she heard his footsteps on the stairs. He would sit with sullen eyes contemplating her long, spare, poorly clad figure as she knelt and read from her book or finished her prayers. Bitter was the religious warfare that had raged for years between them, and Mamzelle Aglaé had grown, on her side, as intolerant as Chicot. She had come to hold St Peter and St Paul in such utter detestation that she had cut their pictures out of her prayer-book.

Then Mamzelle Aglaé pretended not to care what Chicot had in his bag. He drew forth a small hunk of beef and laid it in her basket that stood on the bare floor. She looked from the corner of her eye, and went on dusting the table. He brought out a handful of potatoes, some pieces of sliced fish, a few herbs, a yard of calico, and a small pat of butter wrapped in lettuce leaves. He was proud of the butter, and wanted her to notice it. He held it out and asked her for something to put it on. She handed him a saucer, and looked indifferent and resigned, with lifted eyebrows.

'*Pas d'sucre*,[293] *Nég?*'

Chicot shook his head and scratched it, and looked like a black picture of distress and mortification. No sugar! But tomorrow he would get a pinch here and a pinch there, and would bring as much as a cupful.

Mamzelle Aglaé then sat down, and talked to Chicot uninterruptedly and confidentially. She complained bitterly, and it was all about a pain that lodged in her leg; that crept and acted like a live, stinging serpent, twining about her waist and up her spine, and coiling round the shoulder-blade. And then *les rheumatismes* in her fingers! He could see for himself how they were knotted. She could not bend them; she could hold nothing in her hands, and had let a saucer fall that morning and broken it in pieces. And if she were to tell him that she had slept a wink through the night, she would be a liar, deserving of perdition. She had sat at the window *la nuit blanche*,[294] hearing the hours strike and the market-wagons rumble. Chicot nodded, and kept up a running fire of sympathetic comment and suggestive remedies for rheumatism and insomnia: herbs, or *tisanes*,[295] or *grigris*,[296] or all three. As if he knew! There was Purgatory Mary, a perambulating soul whose office in life was to pray for the shades in purgatory – she had brought Mamzelle Aglaé a bottle of *eau de Lourdes*,[297] but so little of it! She might have kept her water of Lourdes, for all the good it did – a drop! Not so much as would cure a fly or a mosquito! Mamzelle Aglaé was going to show Purgatory Mary the door when she came again, not only because of her avarice with the Lourdes water, but, beside that, she brought in on her feet dirt that could only be removed with a shovel after she left.

And Mamzelle Aglaé wanted to inform Chicot that there would be slaughter and bloodshed in *la maison grise* if the people below stairs did not mend their ways. She was convinced that they lived for no other purpose than to torture and molest her. The woman kept a bucket of dirty water constantly on the landing with the hope of Mamzelle Aglaé falling over it or into it. And she knew that the children were instructed to gather in the hall and on the stairway, and scream and make a noise and jump up and down like galloping horses, with the intention of driving her to suicide. Chicot should notify the policeman on the beat, and have them arrested, if possible, and thrust into the parish prison, where they belonged.

Chicot would have been extremely alarmed if he had ever chanced to find Mamzelle Aglaé in an uncomplaining mood. It never occurred to him that she might be otherwise. He felt that she had a right to quarrel with fate, if ever mortal had. Her poverty was a disgrace, and he hung his head before it and felt ashamed.

One day he found Mamzelle Aglaé stretched on the bed, with her head tied up in a handkerchief. Her sole complaint that day was, 'Aïe – aïe – aïe! Aïe – aïe – aïe!' uttered with every breath. He had seen her so before, especially when the weather was damp.

'*Vous pas bézouin tisane, Mamzelle Aglaé? Vous pas veux mo cri gagni docteur?*'[298]

She desired nothing. 'Aïe – aïe – aïe!'

He emptied his bag very quietly, so as not to disturb her; and he wanted to stay there with her and lie down on the floor in case she needed him, but the woman from below had come up. She was an Irishwoman with rolled sleeves.

'It's a shtout shtick I'm afther giving her, Nég, and she do but knock on the flure it's me or Janie or wan of us that'll be hearing her.'

'You too good, Brigitte. Aïe – aïe – aïe! *Une goutte d'eau sucré*,[299] Nég! That Purg'tory Marie – you see hair, ma bonne Brigitte, you tell hair go say li'le prayer là-bas au cathédral.[300] Aïe – aïe – aïe!'

Nég could hear her lamentation as he descended the stairs. It followed him as he limped his way through the city streets, and seemed part of the city's noise; he could hear it in the rumble of wheels and jangle of car-bells, and in the voices of those passing by.

He stopped at Mimotte the Voudou's shanty and bought a *grigri* – a cheap one for fifteen cents. Mimotte held her charms at all prices. This he intended to introduce next day into Mamzelle Anglaé's room – somewhere about the altar – to the confusion and discomfort of 'Michié bon Dieu', who persistently declined to concern himself with the welfare of a Boisduré.

At night, among the reeds on the bayou, Chicot could still hear the woman's wail, mingled now with the croaking of the frogs. If he could have been convinced that giving up his life down there in the water would in any way have bettered her condition, he would not have hesitated to sacrifice the remnant of his existence that was wholly devoted to her. He lived but to serve her. He did not know it himself; but Chicot knew so little, and that little in such a distorted way! He could scarcely have been expected, even in his most lucid moments, to give himself over to self-analysis.

Chicot gathered an uncommon amount of dainties at market the following day. He had to work hard, and scheme and whine a little; but he got hold of an orange and a lump of ice and a *chou-fleur*.[301] He did not drink his cup of *café au lait*, but asked Mimi Lambeau to put it in the little new tin pail that the Hebrew notion-vender had just given him in exchange for a mess of shrimps. This time, however, Chicot had his trouble for nothing. When he reached the upper room of *la maison grise*, it was to find that Mamzelle Aglaé had died during the night. He set his bag down in the middle of the floor, and stood shaking, and whined low like a dog in pain.

Everything had been done. The Irishwoman had gone for the doctor, and Purgatory Mary had summoned a priest. Furthermore, the woman had arranged Mamzelle Aglaé decently. She had covered the table with a white cloth, and had placed it at the head of the bed, with the crucifix and two lighted candles in silver candlesticks upon it; the little bit of ornamentation brightened and embellished the poor room. Purgatory Mary, dressed in shabby black, fat and breathing hard, sat reading half audibly from a prayer-book. She was watching the dead and the silver candlesticks, which she had borrowed from a benevolent society, and for which she held herself responsible. A young man was just leaving – a reporter snuffing the air for items, who had scented one up there in the top room of *la maison grise*.

All the morning Janie had been escorting a procession of street Arabs up and down the stairs to view the remains. One of them – a little girl, who had had her face washed and had made a species of toilet for the occasion – refused to be dragged away. She stayed seated as if at an entertainment, fascinated alternately by the long, still figure of Mamzelle Aglaé, the mumbling lips of Purgatory Mary, and the silver candlesticks.

'Will ye get down on yer knees, man, and say a prayer for the dead!' commanded the woman.

But Chicot only shook his head, and refused to obey. He approached the bed, and laid a little black paw for a moment on the stiffened body of Mamzelle Aglaé. There was nothing for him to do here. He picked up his old ragged hat and his bag and went away.

'The black h'athen!' the woman muttered. 'Shut the dure, child.'

The little girl slid down from her chair, and went on tiptoe to shut the door which Chicot had left open. Having resumed her seat, she fastened her eyes upon Purgatory Mary's heaving chest.

'You, Chicot!' cried Matteo's wife the next morning. 'My man, he read in paper 'bout woman name' Boisduré, use' b'long to big-a famny. She die roun' on St Philip – po', same-a like church rat. It's any them Boisdurés you alla talk 'bout?'

Chicot shook his head in slow but emphatic denial. No, indeed, the woman was not of kin to his Boisdurés. He surely had told Matteo's wife often enough – how many times did he have to repeat it! – of their wealth, their social standing. It was doubtless some Boisduré of Les Attakapas;[302] it was none of his.

The next day there was a small funeral procession passing a little distance away – a hearse and a carriage or two. There was the priest who had attended Mamzelle Aglaé, and a benevolent Creole gentleman whose father had known the Boisdurés in his youth. There was a couple of player-folk, who, having got wind of the story, had thrust their hands into their pockets.

'Look, Chicot!' cried Matteo's wife. 'Yonda go the fune'al. Mus-a be that-a Boisduré woman we talken 'bout yesaday.'

But Chicot paid no heed. What was to him the funeral of a woman who had died in St Philip Street? He did not even turn his head in the direction of the moving procession. He went on scaling his red-snapper.

The Lilies

That little vagabond Mamouche[303] amused himself one afternoon by letting down the fence rails that protected Mr Billy's young crop of cotton and corn. He had first looked carefully about him to make sure there was no witness to this piece of rascality. Then he crossed the lane and did the same with the Widow Angèle's fence, thereby liberating Toto, the white calf who stood disconsolately penned up on the other side.

It was not ten seconds before Toto was frolicking madly in Mr Billy's crop, and Mamouche – the young scamp – was running swiftly down the lane, laughing fiendishly to himself as he went.

He could not at first decide whether there could be more fun in letting Toto demolish things at his pleasure, or in warning Mr Billy of the calf's presence in the field. But the latter course commended itself as possessing a certain refinement of perfidy.

'Ho, the'a, you!' called out Mamouche to one of Mr Billy's hands, when he got around to where the men were at work; 'you betta go yon'a an' see 'bout that calf o' Ma'me Angèle; he done broke in the fiel' an' 'bout to finish the crop, him.' Then Mamouche went and sat behind a big tree, where, unobserved, he could laugh to his heart's content.

Mr Billy's fury was unbounded when he learned that Madame Angèle's calf was eating up and trampling down his corn. At once he sent a detachment of men and boys to expel the animal from the field. Others were required to repair the damaged fence; while he himself, boiling with wrath, rode up the lane on his wicked black charger.

But merely to look upon the devastation was not enough for Mr Billy. He dismounted from his horse, and strode belligerently up to Madame Angèle's door, upon which he gave, with his riding-whip, a couple of sharp raps that plainly indicated the condition of his mind.

Mr Billy looked taller and broader than ever as he squared himself on the gallery of Madame Angèle's small and modest house. She herself half-opened the door, a pale, sweet-looking woman, somewhat bewildered, and holding a piece of sewing in her hands. Little Marie Louise was beside her, with big, enquiring, frightened eyes.

'Well, Madam!' blustered Mr Billy, 'this is a pretty piece of work!

That young beast of yours is a fence-breaker, madam, and ought to be shot.'

'*Oh, non, non, m'sieur*. Toto's too li'le; I'm sho he can't break any fence, him.'

'Don't contradict me, madam. I say he's a fence-breaker. There's the proof before your eyes. He ought to be shot, I say, and – don't let it occur again, madam.' And Mr Billy turned and stamped down the steps with a great clatter of spurs as he went.

Madame Angèle was at the time in desperate haste to finish a young lady's Easter dress, and she could not afford to let Toto's escapade occupy her to any extent, much as she regretted it. But little Marie Louise was greatly impressed by the affair. She went out in the yard to Toto, who was under the fig tree, looking not half so shamefaced as he ought. The child, with arms clasped around the little fellow's white shaggy neck, scolded him roundly.

'Ain't you shame', Toto, to go eat up Mr Billy's cotton an' co'n? W'at Mr Billy ev'a done to you, to go do him that way? If you been hungry, Toto, w'y you did'n' come like always an' put yo' head in the winda? I'm goin' tell yo' maman w'en she come back f'om the woods to 's'evenin', m'sieur.

Marie Louise only ceased her mild rebuke when she fancied she saw a penitential look in Toto's big soft eyes.

She had a keen instinct of right and justice for so young a little maid. And all the afternoon, and long into the night, she was disturbed by the thought of the unfortunate accident. Of course, there could be no question of repaying Mr Billy with money; she and her mother had none. Neither had they cotton and corn with which to make good the loss he had sustained through them.

But had they not something far more beautiful and precious than cotton and corn?

Marie Louise thought with delight of that row of Easter lilies on their tall green stems, ranged thick along the sunny side of the house.

The assurance that she would, after all, be able to satisfy Mr Billy's just anger, was a very sweet one. And soothed by it, Marie Louise soon fell asleep and dreamt a grotesque dream: that the lilies were having a stately dance on the green in the moonlight, and were inviting Mr Billy to join them.

The following day, when it was nearing noon, Marie Louise said to her mamma: 'Maman, can I have some of the Easter lily, to do with like I want?'

Madame Angèle was just then testing the heat of an iron with which to press out the seams in the young lady's Easter dress, and she answered a shade impatiently: 'Yes, yes; *va t'en*,[304] *chérie*,' thinking that her little girl wanted to pluck a lily or two.

So the child took a pair of old shears from her mother's basket, and out she went to where the tall, perfumed lilies were nodding, and shaking off from their glistening petals the raindrops with which a passing cloud had just laughingly pelted them.

Snip, snap, went the shears here and there, and never did Marie Louise stop plying them till scores of those long-stemmed lilies lay upon the ground. There were far more than she could hold in her small hands, so she literally clasped the great bunch in her arms, and staggered to her feet with it.

Marie Louise was intent upon her purpose, and lost no time in its accomplishment. She was soon trudging earnestly down the lane with her sweet burden, never stopping, and only once glancing aside to cast a reproachful look at Toto, whom she had not wholly forgiven.

She did not in the least mind that the dogs barked, or that the darkies laughed at her. She went straight on to Mr Billy's big house, and right into the dining-room, where Mr Billy sat eating his dinner all alone.

It was a finely furnished room, but disorderly – very disorderly, as an old bachelor's personal surroundings sometimes are. A black boy stood waiting upon the table. When little Marie Louise suddenly appeared, with that armful of lilies, Mr Billy seemed for a moment transfixed at the sight.

'Well – bless – my soul! What's all this? What's all this?' he questioned, with staring eyes.

Marie Louise had already made a little curtsey. Her sun-bonnet had fallen back, leaving exposed her pretty round head; and her sweet brown eyes were full of confidence as they looked into Mr Billy's.

'I'm bring some lilies to pay back fo' yo' cotton an' co'n w'at Toto eat all up, m'sieur.'

Mr Billy turned savagely upon Pompey. 'What are you laughing at, you black rascal? Leave the room!'

Pompey, who out of mistaken zeal had doubled himself with merriment, was too accustomed to the admonition to heed it literally, and he only made a pretence of withdrawing from Mr Billy's elbow.

'Lilies! well, upon my – isn't it the little one from across the lane?'

'Dat's who,' affirmed Pompey, cautiously insinuating himself again into favour.

'Lilies! who ever heard the like? Why, the baby's buried under 'em. Set 'em down somewhere, little one; anywhere.' And Marie Louise, glad to be relieved from the weight of the great cluster, dumped them all on the table close to Mr Billy.

The perfume that came from the damp, massed flowers was heavy and almost sickening in its pungency. Mr Billy quivered a little, and drew involuntarily back, as if from an unexpected assailant, when the odour reached him. He had been making cotton and corn for so many years, he had forgotten there were such things as lilies in the world.

'Kiar 'em out? fling 'em 'way?' questioned Pompey, who had observed his master cunningly.

'Let 'em alone! Keep your hands off them! Leave the room, you outlandish black scamp! What are you standing there for? Can't you set the mamzelle a place at table, and draw up a chair?'

So Marie Louise – perched upon a fine old-fashioned chair, supplemented by a *Webster's Unabridged* – sat down to dine with Mr Billy.

She had never eaten in company with so peculiar a gentleman before; so irascible towards the inoffensive Pompey, and so courteous to herself. But she was not ill at ease, and conducted herself properly as her mamma had taught her how.

Mr Billy was anxious that she should enjoy her dinner, and began by helping her generously to jambalaya.[305] When she had tasted it she made no remark, only laid down her fork, and looked composedly before her.

'Why, bless me! what ails the little one? You don't eat your rice.'

'It ain't cook', m'sieur,' replied Marie Louise politely.

Pompey nearly strangled in his attempt to smother an explosion.

'Of course it isn't cooked,' echoed Mr Billy, excitedly, pushing away his plate. 'What do you mean, setting a mess of that sort before human beings? Do you take us for a couple of – of rice-birds? What are you standing there for; can't you look up some jam or something to keep the young one from starving? Where's all that jam I saw stewing a while back, here?'

Pompey withdrew, and soon returned with a platter of black-looking jam. Mr Billy ordered cream for it. Pompey reported there was none.

'No cream, with twenty-five cows on the plantation if there's one!' cried Mr Billy, almost springing from his chair with indignation.

'Aunt Printy 'low she sot de pan o' cream on de winda-sell, suh, an' Unc' Jonah come 'long an' tutn it cl'ar ova; neva lef' a drap in de pan.'

But evidently the jam, with or without cream, was as distasteful to Marie Louise as the rice was; for after tasting it gingerly, she laid away her spoon as she had done before.

'O, no! little one; you don't tell me it isn't cooked this time,' laughed
Mr Billy. 'I saw the thing boiling a day and a half. Wasn't it a day and a
half, Pompey? if you know how to tell the truth.'

'Aunt Printy alluz do cooks her p'esarves tell dey plumb done, sho,'
agreed Pompey.

'It's burn', m'sieur,' said Marie Louise, politely, but decidedly, to the
utter confusion of Mr Billy, who was as mortified as could be at the
failure of his dinner to please his fastidious little visitor.

Well, Mr Billy thought of Marie Louise a good deal after that; as
long as the lilies lasted. And they lasted long, for he had the whole
household employed in taking care of them. Often he would chuckle to
himself: 'The little rogue, with her black eyes and her lilies! And the
rice wasn't cooked, if you please; and the jam was burnt. And the best of
it is, she was right.'

But when the lilies withered finally, and had to be thrown away, Mr
Billy donned his best suit, a starched shirt and fine silk necktie. Thus
attired, he crossed the lane to carry his somewhat tardy apologies to
Madame Angèle and Mamzelle Marie Louise, and to pay them a first
visit.

Azélie

Azélie crossed the yard with slow, hesitating steps. She wore a pink sun-bonnet and a faded calico dress that had been made the summer before, and was now too small for her in every way. She carried a large tin pail on her arm. When within a few yards of the house, she stopped under a chinaberry tree, quite still, except for the occasional slow turning of her head from side to side.

Mr Mathurin, from his elevation upon the upper gallery, laughed when he saw her; for he knew she would stay there, motionless, till someone noticed and questioned her.

The planter was just home from the city, and was therefore in an excellent humour, as he always was, on getting back to what he called *le grand air*,[306] the space and stillness of the country, and the scent of the fields. He was in shirtsleeves, walking around the gallery that encircled the big square white house. Beneath was a brick-paved portico upon which the lower rooms opened. At wide intervals were large whitewashed pillars that supported the upper gallery.

In one corner of the lower house was the store, which was in no sense a store for the general public, but maintained only to supply the needs of Mr Mathurin's 'hands'.

'*Eh bien!* what do you want, Azélie?' the planter finally called out to the girl in French. She advanced a few paces, and, pushing back her sun-bonnet, looked up at him with a gentle, inoffensive face – 'to which you would give the good God without confession,' he once described it.

'*Bon jou', M'si' Mathurin*,' she replied; and continued in English, 'I come git a li'le piece o' meat. We plumb out o' meat home.'

'Well, well, the meat isn' going to walk to you, my chile: it hasn' got feet. Go fine Mr 'Polyte. He's yonda mending his buggy unda the shed.' She turned away with an alert little step, and went in search of Mr 'Polyte.

'That's you again!' the young man exclaimed, with a pretended air of annoyance, when he saw her. He straightened himself, and looked down at her and her pail with a comprehending glance. The sweat was standing in shining beads on his brown, good-looking face. He was in his shirt-sleeves, and the legs of his trousers were thrust into the tops of his fine, high-heeled boots. He wore his straw hat very much on one side, and had an air that was altogether *fanfaron*.[307] He reached to a

back pocket for the store key, which was as large as the pistol that he
sometimes carried in the same place. She followed him across the thick,
tufted grass of the yard with quick, short steps that strove to keep pace
with his longer, swinging ones.

When he had unlocked and opened the heavy door of the store, there
escaped from the close room the strong, pungent odour of the varied
wares and provisions massed within. Azélie seemed to like the odour,
and, lifting her head, snuffed the air as people sometimes do upon
entering a conservatory filled with fragrant flowers.

A broad ray of light streamed in through the open door, illumining
the dingy interior. The double wooden shutters of the windows were all
closed, and secured on the inside by iron hooks.

'Well, w'at you want, Azélie?' asked 'Polyte, going behind the counter
with an air of hurry and importance. 'I ain't got time to fool. Make
has'e; say w'at you want.'

Her reply was precisely the same that she had made to Mr Mathurin.
'I come git a li'le piece o' meat. We plumb out o' meat home.'

He seemed exasperated.

'*Bonté!* w'at you all do with meat yonda? You don't reflec' you about
to eat up yo' crop befo' it's good out o' the groun', you all. I like to
know w'y yo' pa don't go he'p with the killin' once aw'ile, an' git some
fresh meat fo' a change.'

She answered in an unshaded, unmodulated voice that was
penetrating, like a child's: 'Popa he do go he'p wid the killin'; but he say
he can't work 'less he got salt meat. He got plenty to feed – him. He's
got to hire he'p wid his crop, an' he's boun' to feed 'em; they won't year
no diffe'nt. An' he's got gra'ma to feed, an' Sauterelle, an' me – '

'An' all the lazy-bone 'Cadians in the country that know w'ere they
goin' to fine the coffee-pot always in the corna of the fire,' grumbled
'Polyte.

With an iron hook he lifted a small piece of salt meat from the pork
barrel, weighed it, and placed it in her pail. Then she wanted a little
coffee. He gave it to her reluctantly. He was still more loath to let her
have sugar; and when she asked for lard, he refused flatly.

She had taken off her sun-bonnet, and was fanning herself with it, as
she leaned with her elbows upon the counter, and let her eyes travel
lingeringly along the well-lined shelves. 'Polyte stood staring into her
face with the sense of aggravation that her presence, her manner, always
stirred up in him.

The face was colourless but for the red, curved line of the lips. Her
eyes were dark, wide, innocent, questioning eyes, and her black hair was

plastered smooth back from the forehead and temples. There was no trace of any intention of coquetry in her manner. He resented this as a token of indifference towards his sex, and thought it inexcusable.

'Well, Azélie, if it's anything you don't see, ask fo' it,' he suggested, with what he flattered himself was humour. But there was no responsive humour in Azélie's composition. She seriously drew a small flask from her pocket.

'Popa say, if you want to let him have a li'le dram, 'count o' his pains that's 'bout to cripple him.'

'Yo' pa knows as well as I do we don't sell w'iskey. Mr Mathurin don't carry no license.'

'I know. He say if you want to give 'im a li'le dram, he's willin' to do some work fo' you.'

'No! Once fo' all, no!' And 'Polyte reached for the daybook, in which to enter the articles he had given to her.

But Azélie's needs were not yet satisfied. She wanted tobacco; he would not give it to her. A spool of thread; he rolled one up, together with two sticks of peppermint candy, and placed it in her pail. When she asked for a bottle of coal-oil, he grudgingly consented, but assured her it would be useless to cudgel her brain further, for he would positively let her have nothing more. He disappeared towards the coal-oil tank, which was hidden from view behind the piled-up boxes on the counter. When she heard him searching for an empty quart bottle, and making a clatter with the tin funnels, she herself withdrew from the counter against which she had been leaning.

After they quitted the store, 'Polyte, with a perplexed expression upon his face, leaned for a moment against one of the whitewashed pillars, watching the girl cross the yard. She had folded her sun-bonnet into a pad, which she placed beneath the heavy pail that she balanced upon her head. She walked upright, with a slow, careful tread. Two of the yard dogs that had stood a moment before upon the threshold of the store door, quivering and wagging their tails, were following her now, with a little businesslike trot. 'Polyte called them back.

The cabin which the girl occupied with her father, her grandmother and her little brother Sauterelle, was removed some distance from the plantation house, and only its pointed roof could be discerned like a speck far away across the field of cotton, which was all in bloom. Her figure soon disappeared from view, and 'Polyte emerged from the shelter of the gallery, and started again towards his interrupted task.

He turned to say to the planter, who was keeping up his measured tramp above: 'Mr Mathurin, ain't it 'mos' time to stop givin' credit to

Arsene Pauche. Look like that crop o' his ain't goin' to start to pay his account. I don't see, me, anyway, how you come to take that triflin' Li'le River gang on the place.'

'I know it was a mistake, 'Polyte, but *que voulez-vous?*'[308] the planter returned, with a good-natured shrug. 'Now they are yere, we can't let them starve, my frien'. Push them to work all you can. Hole back all supplies that are not necessary, an' nex' year we will let someone else enjoy the privilege of feeding them,' he ended, with a laugh.

'I wish they was all back on Li'le River,' 'Polyte muttered under his breath as he turned and walked slowly away.

Directly back of the store was the young man's sleeping-room. He had made himself quite comfortable there in his corner. He had screened his windows and doors; planted Madeira vines, which now formed a thick green curtain between the two pillars that faced his room; and had swung a hammock out there, in which he liked well to repose himself after the fatigues of the day.

He lay long in the hammock that evening, thinking over the day's happenings and the morrow's work, half dozing, half dreaming, and wholly possessed by the charm of the night, the warm, sweeping air that blew through the long corridor, and the almost unbroken stillness that enveloped him.

At times his random thoughts formed themselves into an almost inaudible speech: 'I wish she would go 'way f'om yere.'

One of the dogs came and thrust his cool, moist muzzle against 'Polyte's cheek. He caressed the fellow's shaggy head. 'I don't know w'at's the matta with her,' he sighed; 'I don' b'lieve she's got good sense.'

It was a long time afterward that he murmured again: 'I wish to God she'd go 'way f'om yere!'

The edge of the moon crept up – a keen, curved blade of light above the dark line of the cotton-field. 'Polyte roused himself when he saw it. 'I didn' know it was so late,' he said to himself – or to his dog. He entered his room at once, and was soon in bed, sleeping soundly.

It was some hours later that 'Polyte was roused from his sleep by – he did not know what; his senses were too scattered and confused to determine at once. There was at first no sound; then so faint a one that he wondered how he could have heard it. A door of his room communicated with the store, but this door was never used, and was almost completely blocked by wares piled up on the other side. The faint noise that 'Polyte heard, and which came from within the store, was followed by a flare of light that he could discern through the chinks, and that lasted as long as a match might burn.

He was now fully aware that someone was in the store. How the intruder had entered he could not guess, for the key was under his pillow with his watch and his pistol.

As cautiously as he could he donned an extra garment, thrust his bare feet into slippers, and crept out into the portico, pistol in hand.

The shutters of one of the store windows were open. He stood close to it, and waited, which he considered surer and safer than to enter the dark and crowded confines of the store to engage in what might prove a bootless struggle with the intruder.

He had not long to wait. In a few moments someone darted through the open window as nimbly as a cat. 'Polyte staggered back as if a heavy blow had stunned him. His first thought and his first exclamation were: 'My God! how close I come to killin' you!'

It was Azélie. She uttered no cry, but made one quick effort to run when she saw him. He seized her arm and held her with a brutal grip. He put the pistol back into his pocket. He was shaking like a man with the palsy. One by one he took from her the parcels she was carrying, and flung them back into the store. There were not many: some packages of tobacco, a cheap pipe, some fishing-tackle, and the flask which she had brought with her in the afternoon. This he threw into the yard. It was still empty, for she had not been able to find the 'key' to the whiskey-barrel.

'So – so, you a thief!' he muttered savagely under his breath.

'You hurtin' me, Mr 'Polyte,' she complained, squirming. He somewhat relaxed, but did not relinquish, his hold upon her.

'I ain't no thief,' she blurted.

'You was stealin',' he contradicted her sharply.

'I wasn' stealin'. I was jus' takin' a few li'le things you all too mean to gi' me. You all treat my popa like he was a dog. It's on'y las' week Mr Mathurin sen' 'way to the city to fetch a fine buckboa'd fo' Son Ambroise, an' he's on'y a nigga, *après tout*.[309] An' w'en my popa he want a picayune tobacca? It's, "No" – ' She spoke loud in her monotonous, shrill voice.

'Polyte kept saying: 'Hush, I tell you! Hush! Somebody'll year you. Hush! It's enough you broke in the sto' – how you got in the sto'?' he added, looking from her to the open window.

'It was w'en you was behine the boxes to the coal-oil tank – I unhook' it,' she explained sullenly.

'An' you don' know I could sen' you to Baton Rouge[310] fo' that?' He shook her as though trying to rouse her to a comprehension of her grievous fault.

'Jus' fo' a li'le picayune o' tobacca!' she whimpered.

He suddenly abandoned his hold upon her, and left her free. She mechanically rubbed the arm that he had grasped so violently.

Between the long row of pillars the moon was sending pale beams of light. In one of these they were standing.

'Azélie,' he said, 'go 'way f'om yere quick; someone might fine you yere. W'en you want something in the sto', fo' yo'se'f or fo' yo' pa – I don' care – ask me fo' it. But you – but you can't neva set yo' foot inside that sto' again. Go 'way f'om yere quick as you can, I tell you!'

She tried in no way to conciliate him. She turned and walked away over the same ground she had crossed before. One of the big dogs started to follow her. 'Polyte did not call him back this time. He knew no harm could come to her, going through those lonely fields, while the animal was at her side.

He went at once to his room for the store key that was beneath his pillow. He entered the store, and refastened the window. When he had made everything once more secure, he sat dejectedly down upon a bench that was in the portico. He sat for a long time motionless. Then, overcome by some powerful feeling that was at work within him, he buried his face in his hands and wept, his whole body shaken by the violence of his sobs.

After that night 'Polyte loved Azélie desperately. The very action which should have revolted him had seemed, on the contrary, to inflame him with love. He felt that love to be a degradation – something that he was almost ashamed to acknowledge to himself; and he knew that he was hopelessly unable to stifle it.

He watched now in a tremor for her coming. She came very often, for she remembered every word he had said; and she did not hesitate to ask him for those luxuries which she considered necessities to her 'popa's' existence. She never attempted to enter the store, but always waited outside, of her own accord, laughing, and playing with the dogs. She seemed to have no shame or regret for what she had done, and plainly did not realise that it was a disgraceful act. 'Polyte often shuddered with disgust to discern in her a being so wholly devoid of moral sense.

He had always been an industrious, bustling fellow, never idle. Now there were hours and hours in which he did nothing but long for the sight of Azélie. Even when at work there was that gnawing want at his heart to see her, often so urgent that he would leave everything to wander down by her cabin with the hope of seeing her. It was even something if he could catch a glimpse of Sauterelle playing in the weeds, or of Arsene lazily dragging himself about, and smoking the pipe which rarely left his lips now that he was kept so well supplied with tobacco.

Once, down the bank of the bayou, when 'Polyte came upon Azélie unexpectedly, and was therefore unprepared to resist the shock of her sudden appearance, he seized her in his arms and covered her face with kisses. She was not indignant; she was not flustered or agitated, as might have been a susceptible, coquettish girl; she was only astonished, and annoyed.

'W'at you doin', Mr 'Polyte?' she cried, struggling. 'Leave me 'lone, I say! Leave me go!'

'I love you, I love you, I love you!' he stammered helplessly over and over in her face.

'You mus' los' yo' head,' she told him, red from the effort of the struggle, when he released her.

'You right, Azélie; I b'lieve I los' my head,' and he climbed up the bank of the bayou as fast as he could.

After that his behaviour was shameful, and he knew it, and he did not care. He invented pretexts that would enable him to touch her hand with his. He wanted to kiss her again, and told her she might come into the store as she used to do. There was no need for her to unhook a window now; he gave her whatever she asked for, charging it always to his own account on the books. She permitted his caresses without returning them, and yet that was all he seemed to live for now. He gave her a little gold ring.

He was looking eagerly forward to the close of the season, when Arsene would go back to Little River. He had arranged to ask Azélie to marry him. He would keep her with him when the others went away. He longed to rescue her from what he felt to be the demoralising influences of her family and her surroundings. 'Polyte believed he would be able to awaken Azélie to finer, better impulses when he should have her apart to himself.

But when the time came to propose it, Azélie looked at him in amazement. 'Ah, b'en, no. I ain't goin' to stay yere wid you, Mr 'Polyte; I'm goin' yonda on Li'le River wid my popa.'

This resolve frightened him, but he pretended not to believe it.

'You jokin', Azélie; you mus' care a li'le about me. It looked to me all along like you cared some about me.'

'An' my popa, *donc*? Ah, b'en, no.'

'You don' rememba how lonesome it is on Li'le River, Azélie,' he pleaded. 'W'enever I think 'bout Li'le River it always make me sad –

like I think about a graveyard. To me it's like a person mus' die, one way or otha, w'en they go on Li'le River. Oh, I hate it! Stay with me, Azélie; don' go 'way f'om me.'

She said little, one way or the other, after that, when she had fully understood his wishes, and her reserve led him to believe, since he hoped it, that he had prevailed with her and that she had determined to stay with him and be his wife.

It was a cool, crisp morning in December that they went away. In a ramshackle wagon, drawn by an ill-mated team, Arsene Pauche and his family left Mr Mathurin's plantation for their old familiar haunts on Little River. The grandmother, looking like a witch, with a black shawl tied over her head, sat upon a roll of bedding in the bottom of the wagon. Sauterelle's bead-like eyes glittered with mischief as he peeped over the side. Azélie, with the pink sun-bonnet completely hiding her round young face, sat beside her father, who drove.

'Polyte caught one glimpse of the group as they passed in the road. Turning, he hurried into his room, and locked himself in.

It soon became evident that 'Polyte's services were going to count for little. He himself was the first to realise this. One day he approached the planter, and said: 'Mr Mathurin, befo' we start anotha year togetha, I betta tell you I'm goin' to quit.' 'Polyte stood upon the steps, and leaned back against the railing. The planter was a little above on the gallery.

'W'at in the name o' sense are you talking about, 'Polyte!' he exclaimed in astonishment.

'It's jus' that; I'm boun' to quit.'

'You had a better offer?'

'No; I ain't had no offa.'

'Then explain yo'se'f, my frien' – explain yo'se'f,' requested Mr Mathurin, with something of offended dignity. 'If you leave me, w'ere are you going?'

'Polyte was beating his leg with his limp felt hat. 'I reckon I jus' as well go yonda on Li'le River – w'ere Azélie,' he said.

Mamouche³¹¹

Mamouche stood within the open doorway, which he had just entered. It was night; the rain was falling in torrents, and the water trickled from him as it would have done from an umbrella, if he had carried one.

Old Dr John-Luis, who was toasting his feet before a blazing hickory-wood fire, turned to gaze at the youngster through his spectacles. Marshall, the old negro who had opened the door at the boy's knock, also looked down at him, and indignantly said: 'G'long back on de gall'ry an' drip yo'se'f! W'at Cynthy gwine say tomorrow w'en she see dat flo' mess' up dat away?'

'Come to the fire and sit down,' said Dr John-Luis.

Dr John-Luis was a bachelor. He was small and thin; he wore snuff-coloured clothes that were a little too large for him, and spectacles. Time had not deprived him of an abundant crop of hair that had once been red, and was not now more than half-bleached.

The boy looked irresolutely from master to man; then went and sat down beside the fire on a splint-bottom chair. He sat so close to the blaze that had he been an apple he would have roasted. As he was but a small boy, clothed in wet rags, he only steamed.

Marshall grumbled audibly, and Dr John-Luis continued to inspect the boy through his glasses.

'Marsh, bring him something to eat,' he commanded, tentatively.

Marshall hesitated, and challenged the child with a speculating look.

'Is you w'ite o' is you black?' he asked. 'Dat w'at I wants ter know 'fo' I kiar' victuals to yo in de settin'-room.'

'I'm w'ite, me,' the boy responded, promptly.

'I ain't disputin'; go ahead. All right fer dem w'at wants ter take yo' wud fer it.'

Dr John-Luis coughed behind his hand and said nothing.

Marshall brought a platter of cold food to the boy, who rested the dish upon his knees and ate from it with keen appetite.

'Where do you come from?' asked Dr John-Luis, when his caller stopped for breath. Mamouche turned a pair of big, soft, dark eyes upon his questioner.

'I come frum Cloutierville this mo'nin'. I been try to git to the twenty-fo'-mile ferry w'en de rain ketch me.'

'What were you going to do at the twenty-four-mile ferry?'

The boy gazed absently into the fire. 'I don' know w'at I was goin' to do yonda to the twenty-fo'-mile ferry,' he said.

'Then you must be a tramp, to be wandering aimlessly about the country in that way!' exclaimed the doctor.

'No; I don' b'lieve I'm a tramp, me.' Mamouche was wriggling his toes with enjoyment of the warmth and palatable food.

'Well, what's your name?' continued Dr John-Luis.

'My name it's Mamouche.'

' "Mamouche". Fiddlesticks! That's no name.'

The boy looked as if he regretted the fact, while not being able to help it.

'But my pa, his name it was Mathurin Peloté,' he offered in some palliation.

'Peloté! Peloté!' mused Dr John-Luis. 'Any kin to Théodule Peloté who lived formerly in Avoyelles parish?'

'W'y, yes!' laughed Mamouche. 'Théodule Peloté, it was my gran'pa.'

'Your grandfather? Well, upon my word!' He looked again, critically, at the youngster's rags. 'Then Stéphanie Galopin must have been your grandmother!'

'Yas,' responded Mamouche, complacently; 'that who was my gran'ma. She die two year ago down by Alexandria.'

'Marsh,' called Dr John-Luis, turning in his chair, 'bring him a mug of milk and another piece of pie!'

When Mamouche had eaten all the good things that were set before him, he found that one side of him was quite dry, and he transferred himself over to the other corner of the fire so as to turn to the blaze the side which was still wet.

The action seemed to amuse Dr John-Luis, whose old head began to fill with recollections.

'That reminds me of Théodule,' he laughed. 'Ah, he was a great fellow, your father, Théodule!'

'My gran'pa,' corrected Mamouche.

'Yes, yes, your grandfather. He was handsome; I tell you, he was good-looking. And the way he could dance and play the fiddle and sing! Let me see, how did that song go that he used to sing when we went out serenading: "*À ta – à ta –*

> *À ta fenêtre*
> *Daignes paraître – tra la la la!*" '[312]

Dr John-Luis's voice, even in his youth, could not have been agreeable;

and now it bore no resemblance to any sound that Mamouche had ever heard issue from a human throat. The boy kicked his heels and rolled sideward on his chair with enjoyment. Dr John-Luis laughed even more heartily, finished the stanza and sang another one through.

'That's what turned the girls' heads, I tell you, my boy,' said he, when he had recovered his breath; 'that fiddling and dancing and tra la la.'

During the next hour the old man lived again through his youth; through any number of alluring experiences with his friend Théodule, that merry fellow who had never done a steady week's work in his life; and Stéphanie, the pretty Acadian girl, whom he had never wholly understood, even to this day.

It was quite late when Dr John-Luis climbed the stairs that led from the sitting-room up to his bedchamber. As he went, followed by the ever attentive Marshall, he was singing:

> '*À ta fenêtre*
> *Daignes paraître,*'

but very low, so as not to awaken Mamouche, whom he left sleeping upon a bed that Marshall at his order had prepared for the boy beside the sitting-room fire.

At a very early hour next morning Marshall appeared at his master's bedside with the accustomed morning coffee.

'What is he doing?' asked Dr John-Luis, as he sugared and stirred the tiny cup of black coffee.

'Who dat, sah?'

'Why, the boy, Mamouche. What is he doing?'

'He gone, sah. He done gone.'

'Gone!'

'Yes, sah. He roll his bed up in de corner; he onlock de do'; he gone. But de silver an' ev'thing dah; he ain't kiar' nuttin' off.'

'Marshall,' snapped Dr John-Luis, ill-humouredly, 'there are times when you don't seem to have sense and penetration enough to talk about! I think I'll take another nap,' he grumbled, as he turned his back upon Marshall. 'Wake me at seven.'

It was no ordinary thing for Dr John-Luis to be in a bad humour, and perhaps it is not strictly true to say that he was now. He was only in a little less amiable mood than usual when he pulled on his high rubber boots and went splashing out in the wet to see what his people were doing.

He might have owned a large plantation had he wished to own one, for a long life of persistent, intelligent work had left him with a comfortable fortune in his old age; but he preferred the farm on which he lived contentedly and raised an abundance to meet his modest wants.

He went down to the orchard, where a couple of men were busying themselves in setting out a line of young fruit trees

'Tut, tut, tut!' They were doing it all wrong; the line was not straight; the holes were not deep. It was strange that he had to come down there and discover such things with his old eyes!

He poked his head into the kitchen to complain to Prudence about the ducks that she had not seasoned properly the day before, and to hope that the accident would never occur again.

He tramped over to where a carpenter was working on a gate; securing it – as he meant to secure all the gates upon his place – with great patent clamps and ingenious hinges, intended to baffle utterly the designs of the evil-disposed persons who had lately been tampering with them. For there had been a malicious spirit abroad, who played tricks, it seemed, for pure wantonness upon the farmers and planters, and caused them infinite annoyance.

As Dr John-Luis contemplated the carpenter at work, and remembered how his gates had recently all been lifted from their hinges one night and left lying upon the ground, the provoking nature of the offence dawned upon him as it had not done before. He turned swiftly, prompted by a sudden determination, and re-entered the house.

Then he proceeded to write out in immense black characters a half-dozen placards. It was an offer of twenty-five dollars' reward for the capture of the person guilty of the malicious offence already described. These placards were sent abroad with the same eager haste that had conceived and executed them.

After a day or two, Dr John-Luis's ill humour had resolved itself into a pensive melancholy.

'Marsh,' he said, 'you know, after all, it's rather dreary to be living alone as I do, without any companion – of my own colour, you understand.'

'I knows dat, sah. It sho' am lonesome,' replied the sympathetic Marshall.

'You see, Marsh, I've been thinking lately,' and Dr John-Luis coughed, for he disliked the inaccuracy of that 'lately', 'I've been thinking that this property and wealth that I've worked so hard to accumulate are after all doing no permanent, practical good to anyone. Now, if I could find some well-disposed boy whom I might train to work, to study, to lead a decent, honest life – a boy of good heart who would care for me in my old age; for I am still comparatively – hem – not old? hey, Marsh?'

'Dey ain't one in de pa'ish hole yo' own like you does, sah.'

'That's it. Now, can you think of such a boy? Try to think. '

Marshall slowly scratched his head and looked reflective.

'If you can think of such a boy,' said Dr John-Luis, 'you might bring him here to spend an evening with me, you know, without hinting at my intentions, of course. In that way I could sound him; study him up, as it were. For a step of such importance is not to be taken without due consideration, Marsh.'

Well, the first whom Marshall brought was one of Baptiste Choupic's boys. He was a very timid child, and sat on the edge of his chair, fearfully. He replied in jerky monosyllables when Dr John-Luis spoke to him, 'Yes, sah – no, sah,' as the case might be; with a little nervous bob of the head.

His presence made the doctor quite uncomfortable. He was glad to be rid of the boy at nine o'clock, when he sent him home with some oranges and a few sweetmeats.

Then Marshall had Theodore over; an unfortunate selection that evinced little judgement on Marshall's part. Not to mince matters, the boy was painfully forward. He monopolised the conversation; asked impertinent questions and handled and inspected everything in the room. Dr John-Luis sent him home with an orange and not a single sweet.

Then there was Hyppolite, who was too ugly to be thought of; and Cami, who was heavy and stupid, and fell asleep in his chair with his mouth wide open. And so it went. If Dr John-Luis had hoped in the company of any of these boys to repeat the agreeable evening he had passed with Mamouche, he was sadly deceived.

At last he instructed Marshall to discontinue the search for that ideal companion he had dreamed of. He was resigned to spend the remainder of his days without one.

Then, one day when it was raining again, and very muddy and chill, a red-faced man came driving up to Dr John-Luis's door in a dilapidated buggy. He lifted a boy from the vehicle, whom he held with a vicelike clutch, and whom he straightway dragged into the astonished presence of Dr John-Luis.

'Here he is, sir,' shouted the red-faced man. 'We've got him at last! Here he is.'

It was Mamouche, covered with mud, the picture of misery. Dr John-Luis stood with his back to the fire. He was startled, and visibly and painfully moved at the sight of the boy.

'Is it possible!' he exclaimed. 'Then it was you, Mamouche, who did

this mischievous thing to me? Lifting my gates from their hinges; letting
the chickens in among my flowers to ruin them; and the hogs and cattle
to trample and uproot my vegetables!'

'Ha! ha!' laughed the red-faced man, 'that game's played out, now;'
and Dr John-Luis looked as if he wanted to strike him.

Mamouche seemed unable to reply. His lower lip was quivering.

'Yes, it's me!' he burst out. 'It's me w'at take yo' gates off the hinge.
It's me w'at turn loose Mr Morgin's hoss, w'en Mr Morgin was passing
veillée[313] wid his sweetheart. It's me w'at take down Ma'ame Angèle's
fence, an' lef her calf loose to tramp in Mr Billy's cotton. It's me w'at
play like a ghos' by the graveyard las' Toussaint[314] to scare the darkies
passin' in the road. It's me w'at – '

The confession had burst out from the depth of Mamouche's heart
like a torrent, and there is no telling when it would have stopped if Dr
John-Luis had not enjoined silence.

'And pray tell me,' he asked, as severely as he could, 'why you left my
house like a criminal, in the morning, secretly?'

The tears had begun to course down Mamouche's brown cheeks.

'I was 'shame' of myself, that's w'y. If you wouldn' gave me no suppa,
an' no bed, an' no fire, I don' say I wouldn' been 'shame' then.'

'Well, sir,' interrupted the red-faced man, 'you've got a pretty square
case against him, I see. Not only for malicious trespass, but for theft.
See this bolt?' producing a piece of iron from his coat pocket. 'That's
what gave him away.'

'I en't no thief!' blurted Mamouche, indignantly. 'It's one piece o'
iron w'at I pick up in the road.'

'Sir,' said Dr John-Luis with dignity, 'I can understand how the
grandson of Théodule Peloté might be guilty of such mischievous
pranks as this boy has confessed to. But I know that the grandson of
Stéphanie Galopin could not be a thief.'

And he at once wrote out the cheque for twenty-five dollars, and
handed it to the red-faced man with the tips of his fingers.

It seemed very good to Dr John-Luis to have the boy sitting again at
his fireside; and so natural, too. He seemed to be the incarnation of
unspoken hopes; the realisation of vague and fitful memories of the past.

When Mamouche kept on crying, Dr John-Luis wiped away the tears
with his own brown silk handkerchief.

'Mamouche,' he said, 'I want you to stay here; to live here with me
always. To learn how to work; to learn how to study; to grow up to be
an honourable man. An honourable man, Mamouche, for I want you
for my own child.'

His voice was pretty low and husky when he said that.

'I shall not take the key from the door tonight,' he continued. 'If you do not choose to stay and be all this that I say, you may open the door and walk out. I shall use no force to keep you.'

*

'What is he doing, Marsh?' asked Dr John-Luis the following morning, when he took the coffee that Marshall had brought to him in bed.

'Who dat, sah?'

'Why, the boy Mamouche, of course. What is he doing?'

Marshall laughed.

'He kneelin' down dah on de flo'. He keep on sayin', "Hail, Mary, full o' grace, de Lord is wid dee. Hail, Mary, full o' grace" – t'ree, fo' times, sah. I tell 'im, "W'at you sayin' yo' prayer dat away, boy?" He 'low dat w'at his gran'ma larn 'im, ter keep outen mischief. W'en de devil say, "Take dat gate offen de hinge; do dis; do dat," he gwine say t'ree Hail Mary, an' de devil gwine tu'n tail an' run.'

'Yes, yes,' laughed Dr John-Luis. 'That's Stéphanie all over.'

'An' I tell 'im, "See heah, boy, you drap a couple o' dem Hail Mary, an' quit studyin' 'bout de devil, an' sot yo'se'f down ter wuk. Dat the oniest way to keep outen mischief."'

'What business is it of yours to interfere?' broke in Dr John-Luis, irritably. 'Let the boy do as his grandmother instructed him.'

'I ain't desputin', sah,' apologised Marshall.

'But you know, Marsh,' continued the doctor, recovering his usual amiability. 'I think we'll be able to do something with the boy. I'm pretty sure of it. For, you see, he has his grandmother's eyes; and his grandmother was a very intelligent woman; a clever woman, Marsh. Her one great mistake was when she married Théodule Peloté.'

A Sentimental Soul

1

Lacodie stayed longer than was his custom in Mamzelle Fleurette's little store that evening. He had been tempted by the vapid utterances of a conservative bell-hanger to voice loudly his radical opinions upon the rights and wrongs of humanity at large and his fellow-workingmen in particular. He was quite in a tremble when he finally laid his picayune down upon Mamzelle Fleurette's counter and helped himself to *l'Abeille*[315] from the top of the diminished pile of newspapers which stood there.

He was small, frail and hollow-chested, but his head was magnificent with its generous adornment of waving black hair, its sunken eyes that glowed darkly and steadily and sometimes flamed, and its moustaches which were formidable.

'*Eh bien, Mamzelle Fleurette, à demain, à demain!*'[316] and he waved a nervous goodbye as he let himself quickly and noiselessly out.

However violent Lacodie might be in his manner towards conservatives, he was always gentle, courteous and low-voiced with Mamzelle Fleurette, who was much older than he, much taller; who held no opinions, and whom he pitied, and even in a manner revered. Mamzelle Fleurette at once dismissed the bell-hanger, with whom, on general principles, she had no sympathy.

She wanted to close the store, for she was going over to the cathedral to confession. She stayed a moment in the doorway watching Lacodie walk down the opposite side of the street. His step was something between a spring and a jerk, which to her partial eyes seemed the perfection of motion. She watched him until he entered his own small low doorway, over which hung a huge wooden key painted red, the emblem of his trade.

For many months now, Lacodie had been coming daily to Mamzelle Fleurette's little notion store to buy the morning paper, which he only read, however, in the afternoon. Once he had crossed over with his box of keys and tools to open a cupboard, which would unlock for no inducements of its owner. He would not suffer her to pay him for the few moments' work; it was nothing, he assured her; it was a pleasure; he would not dream of accepting payment for so trifling a service from a camarade and fellow-worker. But she need not fear that he would lose by it, he told her with a laugh; he would only charge an extra quarter to the rich lawyer around the corner or to the top-lofty druggist down the street, when these might happen to need his services, as they sometimes did. This was an alternative which seemed far from right and honest to Mamzelle Fleurette. But she held a vague understanding that men were wickeder in many ways than women; that ungodliness was constitutional with them, like their sex, and inseparable from it.

Having watched Lacodie until he disappeared within his shop, she retired to her room, back of the store, and began her preparations to go out. She brushed carefully the black alpaca skirt, which hung in long nunlike folds around her spare figure. She smoothed down the brown, ill-fitting basque and readjusted the old-fashioned, rusty black lace collar which she always wore. Her sleek hair was painfully and suspiciously black. She powdered her face abundantly with *poudre de riz* before starting out, and pinned a dotted black lace veil over her straw bonnet. There was little force or character or anything in her withered face, except a pathetic desire and appeal to be permitted to exist.

Mamzelle Fleurette did not walk down Chartres Street with her usual composed tread; she seemed preoccupied and agitated. When she passed the locksmith's shop over the way and heard his voice within, she grew tremulously self-conscious, fingering her veil, swishing the black alpaca and waving her prayer book about with meaningless intention.

Mamzelle Fleurette was in great trouble; trouble which was so bitter, so sweet, so bewildering, so terrifying! It had come so stealthily upon her she had never suspected what it might be. She thought the world was growing brighter and more beautiful; she thought the flowers had redoubled their sweetness and the birds their song, and that the voices of her fellow-creatures had grown kinder and their faces truer.

The day before Lacodie had not come to her for his paper. At six o'clock he was not there, at seven he was not there, nor at eight, and then she knew he would not come. At first, when it was only a little past the time of his coming, she had sat strangely disturbed and distressed in the rear of the store, with her back to the door. When the door opened she turned with fluttering expectancy. It was only an unhappy-looking child, who wanted to buy some foolscap, a pencil and an eraser. The next to come in was an old mulatresse, who was bringing her prayer beads for Mamzelle Fleurette to mend. The next was a gentleman, to buy the *Courier des États Unis*,[317] and then a young girl, who wanted a holy picture for her favourite nun at the Ursulines; it was everybody but Lacodie.

A temptation assailed Mamzelle Fleurette, almost fierce in its intensity, to carry the paper over to his shop herself, when he was not there at seven. She conquered it from sheer moral inability to do anything so daring, so unprecedented. But today, when he had come back and had stayed so long discoursing with the bell-hanger, a contentment, a rapture, had settled upon her being which she could no longer ignore or mistake. She loved Lacodie. That fact was plain to her now, as plain as the conviction that every reason existed why she should not love him. He was the husband of another woman. To love the husband of another woman was one of the deepest sins which Mamzelle Fleurette knew; murder was perhaps blacker, but she was not sure. She was going to confession now. She was going to tell her sin to Almighty God and Father Fochelle, and ask their forgiveness. She was going to pray and beg the saints and the Holy Virgin to remove the sweet and subtle poison from her soul. It was surely a poison, and a deadly one, which could make her feel that her youth had come back and taken her by the hand.

2

Mamzelle Fleurette had been confessing for many years to old Father Fochelle. In his secret heart he often thought it a waste of his time and her own that she should come with her little babblings, her little nothings to him, calling them sins. He felt that a wave of the hand might brush them away, and that it in a manner compromised the dignity of holy absolution to pronounce the act over so innocent a soul.

Today she had whispered all her shortcomings into his ear through the grating of the confessional; he knew them so well! There were many other penitents waiting to be heard, and he was about to dismiss her with a hasty blessing when she arrested him, and in hesitating, faltering accents told him of her love for the locksmith, the husband of another woman. A slap in the face would not have startled Father Fochelle more forcibly or more painfully. What soul was there on earth, he wondered, so hedged about with innocence as to be secure from the machinations of Satan! Oh, the thunder of indignation that descended upon Mamzelle Fleurette's head! She bowed down, beaten to earth beneath it. Then came questions, one, two, three, in quick succession, that made Mamzelle Fleurette gasp and clutch blindly before her. Why was she not a shadow, a vapour, that she might dissolve from before those angry, penetrating eyes; or a small insect, to creep into some crevice and there hide herself for evermore?

'Oh, father! no, no, no!' she faltered, 'he knows nothing, nothing. I would die a hundred deaths before he should know, before anyone should know, besides yourself and the good God of whom I implore pardon.'

Father Fochelle breathed more freely, and mopped his face with a flaming bandana, which he took from the ample pocket of his soutane.[318] But he scolded Mamzelle Fleurette roundly, unpityingly, for being a fool, for being a sentimentalist. She had not committed mortal sin, but the occasion was ripe for it; and look to it she must that she keep Satan at bay with watchfulness and prayer. 'Go, my child, and sin no more.'

Mamzelle Fleurette made a detour in regaining her home by which she would not have to pass the locksmith's shop. She did not even look in that direction when she let herself in at the glass door of her store.

Some time before, when she was yet ignorant of the motive which prompted the act, she had cut from a newspaper a likeness of Lacodie, who had served as foreman of the jury during a prominent murder trial. The likeness happened to be good, and quite did justice to the locksmith's fine physiognomy with its leonine hirsute adornment. This picture Mamzelle Fleurette had kept hitherto between the pages of her prayer book. Here, twice a day, it looked out at her: as she turned the leaves of the holy mass in the morning, and when she read her evening devotions before her own little home altar, over which hung a crucifix and a picture of the Empress Eugénie.[319]

Her first action upon entering her room, even before she unpinned the dotted veil, was to take Lacodie's picture from her prayer book and place it at random between the leaves of a *Dictionnaire de la Langue Française*,[320] which was the undermost of a pile of old books that stood on the corner of the mantelpiece. Between night and morning, when she would approach the holy sacrament, Mamzelle Fleurette felt it to be her duty to thrust Lacodie from her thoughts by every means and device known to her.

The following day was Sunday, when there was no occasion or opportunity for her to see the locksmith. Moreover, after partaking of holy communion, Mamzelle Fleurette felt invigorated; she was conscious of a new, if fictitious, strength to combat Satan and his wiles.

On Monday, as the hour approached for Lacodie to appear, Mamzelle Fleurette became harassed by indecision. Should she call in the young girl, the neighbour who relieved her on occasion, and deliver the store into the girl's hands for an hour or so? This might be well enough for once in a while, but she could not conveniently resort to this subterfuge daily. After all, she had her living to make, which consideration was paramount.

She finally decided that she would retire to her little back room and when she heard the store door open she would call out: 'Is it you, Monsieur Lacodie? I am very busy; please take your paper and leave your cinq sous on the counter.' If it happened not to be Lacodie she would come forward and serve the customer in person. She did not, of course, expect to carry out this performance each day; a fresh device would no doubt suggest itself for tomorrow. Mamzelle Fleurette proceeded to carry out her programme to the letter.

'Is it you, Monsieur Lacodie?' she called out from the little back room, when the front door opened. 'I am very busy; please take your paper – '

'*Ce n'est pas Lacodie, Mamzelle Fleurette. C'est moi, Augustine.*'[321]

It was Lacodie's wife, a fat, comely young woman, wearing a blue veil thrown carelessly over her kinky black hair, and carrying some grocery parcels clasped close in her arms. Mamzelle Fleurette emerged from the back room, a prey to the most contradictory emotions; relief and disappointment struggling for the mastery with her.

'No Lacodie today, Mamzelle Fleurette,' Augustine announced with a certain robust ill-humour; 'he is there at home shaking with a chill till the very window panes rattle. He had one last Friday' (the day he had not come for his paper) 'and now another and a worse one today. God knows, if it keeps on – well, let me have the paper; he will want to read it tonight when his chill is past.'

Mamzelle Fleurette handed the paper to Augustine, feeling like an old woman in a dream handing a newspaper to a young woman in a dream. She had never thought of Lacodie having chills or being ill. It seemed very strange. And Augustine was no sooner gone than all the ague remedies she had ever heard of came crowding to Mamzelle Fleurette's mind; an egg in black coffee – or was it a lemon in black coffee? or an egg in vinegar? She rushed to the door to call Augustine back, but the young woman was already far down the street.

3

Augustine did not come the next day, nor the next, for the paper. The unhappy looking child who had returned for more foolscap, informed Mamzelle Fleurette that he had heard his mother say that Monsieur Lacodie was very sick, and the bell-hanger had sat up all night with him. The following day Mamzelle Fleurette saw Choppin's coupé pass clattering over the cobblestones and stop before the locksmith's door. She knew that with her class it was only in a case of extremity that the famous and expensive physician was summoned. For the first time she thought of death. She prayed all day, silently, to herself, even while waiting upon customers.

In the evening she took an *Abeille* from the top of the pile on the counter, and throwing a light shawl over her head, started with the paper over to the locksmith's shop. She did not know if she were committing a sin in so doing. She would ask Father Fochelle on Saturday, when she went to confession. She did not think it could be a sin; she would have called long before on any other sick neighbour, and she intuitively felt that in this distinction might lie the possibility of sin.

The shop was deserted except for the presence of Lacodie's little boy of five, who sat upon the floor playing with the tools and contrivances which all his days he had coveted, and which all his days had been denied to him. Mamzelle Fleurette mounted the narrow stairway in the rear of the shop which led to an upper landing and then into the room of the married couple. She stood a while hesitating upon this landing before venturing to knock softly upon the partly open door through which she could hear their voices.

'I thought,' she remarked apologetically to Augustine, 'that perhaps Monsieur Lacodie might like to look at the paper and you had no time to come for it, so I brought it myself.'

'Come in, come in, Mamzelle Fleurette. It's Mamzelle Fleurette who comes to enquire about you, Lacodie,' Augustine called out loudly to her husband, whose half consciousness she somehow confounded with deafness.

Mamzelle Fleurette drew mincingly forward, clasping her thin hands together at the waistline, and she peeped timorously at Lacodie lying lost amid the bedclothes. His black mane was tossed wildly over the pillow and lent a fictitious pallor to the yellow waxiness of his drawn features. An approaching chill was sending incipient shudders through his frame, and making his teeth claque. But he still turned his head courteously in Mamzelle Fleurette's direction.

'*Bien bon de votre part, Mamzelle Fleurette – mais c'est fini. J'suis flambé, flambé, flambé!*'[322]

Oh, the pain of it! to hear him in such extremity thanking her for her visit, assuring her in the same breath that all was over with him. She wondered how Augustine could hear it so composedly. She whisperingly enquired if a priest had been summoned.

'*Inutile; il n'en veut pas,*'[323] was Augustine's reply. So he would have no priest at his bedside, and here was a new weight of bitterness for Mamzelle Fleurette to carry all her days.

She flitted back to her store through the darkness, herself like a slim shadow. The November evening was chill and misty. A dull aureole shot out from the feeble gas jet at the corner, only faintly and for an instant illumining her figure as it glided rapidly and noiselessly along the banquette. Mamzelle Fleurette slept little and prayed much that night. Saturday morning Lacodie died. On Sunday he was buried and Mamzelle Fleurette did not go to the funeral, because Father Fochelle told her plainly she had no business there.

It seemed inexpressibly hard to Mamzelle Fleurette that she was not permitted to hold Lacodie in tender remembrance now that he was dead. But Father Fochelle, with his practical insight, made no compromise with sentimentality; and she did not question his authority, or his ability to master the subtleties of a situation utterly beyond reach of her own powers.

It was no longer a pleasure for Mamzelle Fleurette to go to confession as it had formerly been. Her heart went on loving Lacodie and her soul went on struggling; for she made this delicate and puzzling distinction between heart and soul, and pictured the two as set in a very death struggle against each other.

'I cannot help it, father. I try, but I cannot help it. To love him is like breathing; I do not know how to help it. I pray, and pray, and it does no good, for half of my prayers are for the repose of his soul. It surely cannot be a sin, to pray for the repose of his soul?'

Father Fochelle was heartily sick and tired of Mamzelle Fleurette and her stupidities. Oftentimes he was tempted to drive her from the confessional, and forbid her return until she should have regained a rational state of mind. But he could not withhold absolution from a penitent who, week after week, acknowledged her shortcoming and strove with all her faculties to overcome it and atone for it.

4

Augustine had sold out the locksmith's shop and the business, and had removed farther down the street over a bakery. Out of her window she had hung a sign, '*Blanchisseuse de Fin*'.[324] Often, in passing by, Mamzelle Fleurette would catch a glimpse of Augustine up at the window, plying the irons; her sleeves rolled to the elbows, baring her round, white arms, and the little black curls all moist and tangled about her face. It was early spring then, and there was a languor in the air; an odour of jasmine in every passing breeze; the sky was blue, unfathomable, and fleecy white; and people along the narrow street laughed, and sang, and called to one another from windows and doorways. Augustine had set a pot of rose-geranium on her window sill and hung out a birdcage.

Once, Mamzelle Fleurette in passing on her way to confession heard her singing roulades,[325] vying with the bird in the cage. Another time she saw the young woman leaning with half her body from the window, exchanging pleasantries with the baker standing beneath on the banquette.

Still, a little later, Mamzelle Fleurette began to notice a handsome young fellow often passing the store. He was jaunty and debonnaire and wore a rich watchchain, and looked prosperous. She knew him quite well as a fine young Gascon, who kept a stall in the French Market, and from whom she had often bought charcuterie. The neighbours told her the young Gascon was paying his addresses to Mme Lacodie. Mamzelle Fleurette shuddered. She wondered if Lacodie knew! The whole situation seemed suddenly to shift its base, causing Mamzelle Fleurette to stagger. What ground would her poor heart and soul have to do battle upon now?

She had not yet had time to adjust her conscience to the altered conditions when one Saturday afternoon, as she was about to start out to confession, she noticed an unusual movement down the street. The bell-hanger, who happened to be presenting himself in the character of a customer, informed her that it was nothing more nor less than Mme Lacodie returning from her wedding with the Gascon. He was black and bitter with indignation, and thought she might at least have waited for the year to be out. But the charivari[326] was already on foot; and Mamzelle need not feel alarmed if, in the night, she heard sounds and clamour to rouse the dead as far away as Metairie Ridge.

Mamzelle Fleurette sank down in a chair, trembling in all her members. She faintly begged the bell-hanger to pour her a glass of water from the stone pitcher behind the counter. She fanned herself and loosened her bonnet strings. She sent the bell-hanger away.

She nervously pulled off her rusty black kid gloves, and ten times more nervously drew them on again. To a little customer, who came in for chewing gum, she handed a paper of pins.

There was a great, a terrible upheaval taking place in Mamzelle Fleurette's soul. She was preparing for the first time in her life to take her conscience into her own keeping.

When she felt herself sufficiently composed to appear decently upon the street, she started out to confession. She did not go to Father

Fochelle. She did not even go to the cathedral; but to a church which was much farther away, and to reach which she had to spend a picayune for car fare.

Mamzelle Fleurette confessed herself to a priest who was utterly new and strange to her. She told him all her little venial sins, which she had much difficulty in bringing to a number of any dignity and importance whatever. Not once did she mention her love for Lacodie, the dead husband of another woman.

Mamzelle Fleurette did not ride back to her home; she walked. The sensation of walking on air was altogether delicious; she had never experienced it before. A long time she stood contemplative before a shop window in which were displayed wreaths, mottoes, emblems, designed for the embellishment of tombstones. What a sweet comfort it would be, she reflected, on the 1st of November to carry some such delicate offering to Lacodie's last resting place. Might not the sole care of his tomb devolve upon her, after all! The possibility thrilled her and moved her to the heart. What thought would the merry Augustine and her lover-husband have for the dead lying in cemeteries!

When Mamzelle Fleurette reached home she went through the store directly into her little back room. The first thing which she did, even before unpinning the dotted lace veil, was to take the *Dictionnaire de la Langue Française* from beneath the pile of old books on the mantelpiece. It was not easy to find Lacodie's picture hidden somewhere in its depths. But the search afforded her almost a sensuous pleasure; turning the leaves slowly back and forth.

When she had secured the likeness she went into the store and from her showcase selected a picture frame – the very handsomest there; one of those which sold for thirty-five cents.

Into the frame Mamzelle Fleurette neatly and deftly pasted Lacodie's picture. Then she re-entered her room and deliberately hung it upon the wall – between the crucifix and the portrait of Empress Eugènie – and she did not care if the Gascon's wife ever saw it or not.

Dead Men's Shoes

It never occurred to any person to wonder what would befall Gilma now that 'le vieux Gamiche'[327] was dead. After the burial people went their several ways, some to talk over the old man and his eccentricities, others to forget him before nightfall, and others to wonder what would become of his very nice property, the hundred-acre farm on which he had lived for thirty years, and on which he had just died at the age of seventy.

If Gilma had been a child, more than one motherly heart would have gone out to him. This one and that one would have bethought them of carrying him home with them; to concern themselves with his present comfort, if not his future welfare. But Gilma was not a child. He was a strapping fellow of nineteen, measuring six feet in his stockings, and as strong as any healthy youth need be. For ten years he had lived there on the plantation with Monsieur Gamiche; and he seemed now to have been the only one with tears to shed at the old man's funeral.

Gamiche's relatives had come down from Caddo in a wagon the day after his death, and had settled themselves in his house. There was Septime, his nephew, a cripple, so horribly afflicted that it was distressing to look at him. And there was Septime's widowed sister, Ma'me Brozé, with her two little girls. They had remained at the house during the burial, and Gilma found them still there upon his return.

The young man went at once to his room to seek a moment's repose. He had lost much sleep during Monsieur Gamiche's illness; yet, he was in fact more worn by the mental than the bodily strain of the past week.

But when he entered his room, there was something so changed in its aspect that it seemed no longer to belong to him. In place of his own apparel which he had left hanging on the row of pegs, there were a few shabby little garments and two battered straw hats, the property of the Brozé children. The bureau drawers were empty, there was not a vestige of anything belonging to him remaining in the room. His first impression was that Ma'me Brozé had been changing things around and had assigned him to some other room.

But Gilma understood the situation better when he discovered every scrap of his personal effects piled up on a bench outside the door, on the back or 'false' gallery. His boots and shoes were under the bench, while coats, trousers and underwear were heaped in an indiscriminate mass together.

The blood mounted to his swarthy face and made him look for the moment like an Indian. He had never thought of this. He did not know what he had been thinking of; but he felt that he ought to have been prepared for anything; and it was his own fault if he was not. But it hurt. This spot was 'home' to him against the rest of the world. Every tree, every shrub was a friend; he knew every patch in the fences; and the little old house, grey and weather-beaten, that had been the shelter of his youth, he loved as only few can love inanimate things. A great enmity arose in him against Ma'me Brozé. She was walking about the yard, with her nose in the air, and a shabby black dress trailing behind her. She held the little girls by the hand.

Gilma could think of nothing better to do than to mount his horse and ride away – anywhere. The horse was a spirited animal of great value. Monsieur Gamiche had named him Jupiter on account of his proud bearing, and Gilma had nicknamed him Jupe, which seemed to him more endearing and expressive of his great attachment to the fine creature. With the bitter resentment of youth, he felt that Jupe was the only friend remaining to him on earth.

He had thrust a few pieces of clothing in his saddlebags and had requested Ma'me Brozé, with assumed indifference, to put his remaining effects in a place of safety until he should be able to send for them.

As he rode around by the front of the house, Septime, who sat on the gallery all doubled up in his Uncle Gamiche's big chair, called out: 'Hey, Gilma! w'ere you boun' fo'?'

'I'm goin' away,' replied Gilma, curtly, reining his horse.

'That's all right; but I reckon you might jus' as well leave that hoss behine you.'

'The hoss is mine,' returned Gilma, as quickly as he would have returned a blow.

'We'll see 'bout that li'le later, my frien'. I reckon you jus' well turn 'im loose.'

Gilma had no more intention of giving up his horse than he had of parting with his own right hand. But Monsieur Gamiche had taught him prudence and respect for the law. He did not wish to invite disagreeable complications. So, controlling his temper by a supreme effort, Gilma dismounted, unsaddled the horse then and there, and led it back to the stable.

But as he started to leave the place on foot, he stopped to say to Septime: 'You know, Mr Septime, that hoss is mine; I can collec' a hundred aff'davits to prove it. I'll bring them yere in a few days with a statement f'om a lawyer; an' I'll expec' the hoss an' saddle to be turned over to me in good condition.'

'That's all right. We'll see 'bout that. Won't you stay fo' dinna?'

'No, I thank you, sah; Ma'me Brozé already ask' me.' And Gilma strode away, down the beaten footpath that led across the sloping grass-plot towards the outer road.

A definite destination and a settled purpose ahead of him seemed to have revived his flagging energies of an hour before. It was with no trace of fatigue that he stepped out bravely along the wagon-road that skirted the bayou.

It was early spring, and the cotton had already a good stand. In some places the negroes were hoeing. Gilma stopped alongside the rail fence and called to an old negress who was plying her hoe at no great distance.

'Hello, Aunt Hal'fax! see yere.'

She turned, and immediately quitted her work to go and join him,, bringing her hoe with her across her shoulder. She was large-boned and very black. She was dressed in the deshabille[328] of the field.

'I wish you'd come up to yo' cabin with me a minute, Aunt Hally,' he said; 'I want to get an aff'davit f'om you.'

She understood, after a fashion, what an affidavit was; but she couldn't see the good of it.

'I ain't got no aff'davis, boy; you g'long an' don' pesta me.'

' 'Twon't take you any time, Aunt Hal'fax. I jus' want you to put yo' mark to a statement I'm goin' to write to the effec' that my hoss, Jupe, is my own prop'ty; that you know it, an' you are willin' to swear to it.'

'Who say Jupe don' b'long to you?' she questioned cautiously, leaning on her hoe.

He motioned towards the house.

'Who? Mista Septime and them?'

'Yes.'

'Well, I reckon!' she exclaimed, sympathetically.

'That's it,' Gilma went on; 'an' nex' thing they'll be sayin' yo' ole mule, Policy, don't b'long to you.'

She started violently.

'Who say so?'

'Nobody. But I say, nex' thing, that' w'at they'll be sayin'.'

She began to move along the inside of the fence, and he turned to keep pace with her, walking on the grassy edge of the road.

'I'll jus' write the aff'davit, Aunt Hally, an' all you got to do – '

'You know des well as me dat mule mine. I done paid ole Mista

Gamiche fo' 'im in good cotton; dat year you falled outen de puckhorn tree; an' he write it down hisse'f in his 'count book.'

Gilma did not linger a moment after obtaining the desired statement from Aunt Halifax. With the first of those 'hundred affidavits' that he hoped to secure safe in his pocket, he struck out across the country, seeking the shortest way to town.

Aunt Halifax stayed in the cabin door.

' 'Relius,' she shouted to a little black boy out in the road, 'does you see Pol'cy anywhar? G'long, see ef he 'roun' de ben'. Wouldn' s'prise me ef he broke de fence an' got in yo' pa's corn ag'in.' And, shading her eyes to scan the surrounding country, she muttered, uneasily: 'Whar dat mule?'

The following morning Gilma entered town and proceeded at once to Lawyer Paxton's office. He had had no difficulty in obtaining the testimony of blacks and whites regarding his ownership of the horse; but he wanted to make his claim as secure as possible by consulting the lawyer and returning to the plantation armed with unassailable evidence.

The lawyer's office was a plain little room opening upon the street. Nobody was there, but the door was open; and Gilma entered and took a seat at the bare round table and waited. It was not long before the lawyer came in; he had been in conversation with someone across the street.

'Good-morning, Mr Pax'on,' said Gilma, rising.

The lawyer knew his face well enough, but could not place him, and only returned: 'Good-morning, sir – good-morning.'

'I come to see you,' began Gilma plunging at once into business, and drawing his handful of nondescript affidavits from his pocket, 'about a matter of prope'ty, about regaining possession of my hoss that Mr Septime, ole Mr Gamiche's nephew, is holdin' f'om me yonder.'

The lawyer took the papers and, adjusting his eye-glasses, began to look them through.

'Yes, yes,' he said; 'I see.'

'Since Mr Gamiche died on Tuesday' – began Gilma.

'Gamiche died!' repeated Lawyer Paxton, with astonishment. 'Why, you don't mean to tell me that *vieux Gamiche* is dead? Well, well. I hadn't heard of it; I just returned from Shreveport this morning. So *le vieux Gamiche* is dead, is he? And you say you want to get possession of a horse. What did you say your name was?' drawing a pencil from his pocket.

'Gilma Germain is my name, suh.'

'Gilma Germain,' repeated the lawyer, a little meditatively, scanning his visitor closely. 'Yes, I recall your face now. You are the young fellow whom le vieux Gamiche took to live with him some ten or twelve years ago.'

'Ten years ago las' November, suh.'

Lawyer Paxton arose and went to his safe, from which, after unlocking it, he took a legal-looking document that he proceeded to read carefully through to himself.

'Well, Mr Germain, I reckon there won't be any trouble about regaining possession of the horse,' laughed Lawyer Paxton. 'I'm pleased to inform you, my dear sir, that our old friend, Gamiche, has made you sole heir to his property; that is, his plantation, including livestock, farming implements, machinery, household effects, etc. Quite a pretty piece of property,' he proclaimed leisurely, seating himself comfortably for a long talk. 'And I may add, a pretty piece of luck, Mr Germain, for a young fellow just starting out in life; nothing but to step into a dead man's shoes! A great chance – great chance. Do you know, sir, the moment you mentioned your name, it came back to me like a flash, how *le vieux Gamiche* came in here one day, about three years ago, and wanted to make his will – ' And the loquacious lawyer went on with his reminiscences and interesting bits of information, of which Gilma heard scarcely a word.

He was stunned, drunk, with the sudden joy of possession; the thought of what seemed to him great wealth, all his own – his own! It seemed as if a hundred different sensations were holding him at once, and as if a thousand intentions crowded upon him. He felt like another being who would have to readjust himself to the new conditions presenting themselves so unexpectedly. The narrow confines of the office were stifling, and it seemed as if the lawyer's flow of talk would never stop. Gilma arose abruptly, and with a half-uttered apology, plunged from the room into the outer air.

Two days later Gilma stopped again before Aunt Halifax's cabin, on his way back to the plantation. He was walking as before, having declined to avail himself of any one of the several offers of a mount that had been tendered him in town and on the way. A rumour of Gilma's great good fortune had preceded him, and Aunt Halifax greeted him with an almost triumphal shout as he approached.

'God knows you deserve it, Mista Gilma! De Lord knows you does, suh! Come in an' res' yo'se'f, suh. You, 'Relius! git out dis heah cabin; crowdin' up dat away!' She wiped off the best chair available and offered it to Gilma.

He was glad to rest himself and glad to accept Aunt Halifax's proffer of a cup of coffee, which she was in the act of dripping before a small fire. He sat as far as he could from the fire, for the day was warm; he mopped his face, and fanned himself with his broad-rimmed hat.

'I des' can't he'p laughin' w'en I thinks 'bout it,' said the old woman, fairly shaking, as she leaned over the hearth. 'I wakes up in de night, even, an' has to laugh.'

'How's that, Aunt Hal'fax,' asked Gilma, almost tempted to laugh himself at he knew not what.

'G'long, Mista Gilma! like you don' know! It's w'en I thinks 'bout Septime an' them like I gwine see 'em in dat wagon tomor' mo'nin', on dey way back to Caddo. Oh, lawsy!'

'That isn' so ver' funny, Aunt Hal'fax,' returned Gilma, feeling himself ill at ease as he accepted the cup of coffee which she presented to him with much ceremony on a platter. 'I feel pretty sorry for Septime, myse'f.'

'I reckon he know now who Jupe b'long to,' she went on, ignoring his expression of sympathy; 'no need to tell him who Pol'cy b'long to, nuther. An' I tell you, Mista Gilma,' she went on, leaning upon the table without seating herself, 'dey gwine back to hard times in Caddo. I heah tell dey nuva gits 'nough to eat, yonda. Septime, he can't do nuttin' 'cep' set still all twis' up like a sarpint. An' Ma'me Brozé, she do some kine sewin'; but don't look like she got sense 'nough to do dat halfway. An' dem li'le gals, dey 'bleege to run bar'foot mos' all las' winta', twell dat li'les' gal, she got her heel plum fros' bit, so dey tells me. Oh, lawsy! How dey gwine look tomor', all trapsin' back to Caddo!'

Gilma had never found Aunt Halifax's company so intensely disagreeable as at that moment. He thanked her for the coffee, and went away so suddenly as to startle her. But her good humour never flagged. She called out to him from the doorway: 'Oh, Mista Gilma! You reckon dey knows who Pol'cy b'longs to now?'

He somehow did not feel quite prepared to face Septime; and he lingered along the road. He even stopped a while to rest, apparently, under the shade of a huge cottonwood tree that overhung the bayou. From the very first, a subtle uneasiness, a self-dissatisfaction had mingled with his elation, and he was trying to discover what it meant.

To begin with, the straightforwardness of his own nature had inwardly resented the sudden change in the bearing of most people towards himself. He was trying to recall, too, something which the lawyer had said; a little phrase, out of that multitude of words, that had fallen in his consciousness. It had stayed there, generating a little festering sore place that was beginning to make itself irritatingly felt.

What was it, that little phrase? Something about – in his excitement he had only half heard it – something about dead men's shoes.

The exuberant health and strength of his big body; the courage, virility, endurance of his whole nature revolted against the expression in itself, and the meaning which it conveyed to him. Dead men's shoes! Were they not for such afflicted beings as Septime? as that helpless, dependent woman up there? as those two little ones, with their poorly fed, poorly clad bodies and sweet, appealing eyes? Yet he could not determine how he would act and what he would say to them.

But there was no room left in his heart for hesitancy when he came to face the group. Septime was still crouched in his uncle's chair; he seemed never to have left it since the day of the funeral. Ma'me Brozé had been crying, and so had the children – out of sympathy, perhaps.

'Mr Septime,' said Gilma, approaching, 'I brought those aff'davits about the hoss. I hope you about made up yo' mind to turn it over without further trouble.'

Septime was trembling, bewildered, almost speechless.

'W'at you mean?' he faltered, looking up with a shifting, sideward glance. 'The whole place b'longs to you. You tryin' to make a fool out o' me?'

'Fo' me,' returned Gilma, 'the place can stay with Mr Gamiche's own flesh an' blood. I'll see Mr Pax'on again an' make that according to the law. But I want my hoss.'

Gilma took something besides his horse – a picture of *le vieux Gamiche*, which had stood on his mantelpiece. He thrust it into his pocket. He also took his old benefactor's walking-stick and a gun.

As he rode out of the gate, mounted upon his well-beloved Jupe, the faithful dog following, Gilma felt as if he had awakened from an intoxicating but depressing dream.

There was no clumsier looking fellow in church that Sunday morning than Antoine Bocaze – the one they called Tonie. But Tonie did not really care if he were clumsy or not. He felt that he could speak intelligibly to no woman save his mother; but since he had no desire to inflame the hearts of any of the island maidens, what difference did it make?

He knew there was no better fisherman on the Chênière Caminada than himself, if his face was too long and bronzed, his limbs too unmanageable and his eyes too earnest – almost too honest.

It was a midsummer day, with a lazy, scorching breeze blowing from the Gulf straight into the church windows. The ribbons on the young girls' hats fluttered like the wings of birds, and the old women clutched the flapping ends of the veils that covered their heads.

A few mosquitoes, floating through the blistering air, with their nipping and humming fretted the people to a certain degree of attention and consequent devotion. The measured tones of the priest at the altar rose and fell like a song: '*Credo in unum Deum patrem omnipotentem*,'[330] he chanted. And then the people all looked at one another, suddenly electrified.

Someone was playing upon the organ whose notes no one on the whole island was able to awaken; whose tones had not been heard during the many months since a passing stranger had one day listlessly dragged his fingers across its idle keys. A long, sweet strain of music floated down from the loft and filled the church.

It seemed to most of them – it seemed to Tonie standing there beside his old mother – that some heavenly being must have descended upon the Church of Our Lady of Lourdes and chosen this celestial way of communicating with its people.

But it was no creature from a different sphere; it was only a young lady from Grand Isle. A rather pretty young person with blue eyes and nut-brown hair, who wore a dotted lawn of fine texture and fashionable make, and a white Leghorn sailor-hat.

Tonie saw her standing outside the church after mass, receiving the priest's voluble praises and thanks for her graceful service.

She had come over to mass from Grand Isle in Baptiste Beaudelet's

lugger,[331] with a couple of young men, and two ladies who kept a *pension*
over there. Tonie knew these two ladies – the widow Lebrun and her
old mother – but he did not attempt to speak with them; he would not
have known what to say. He stood aside gazing at the group, as others
were doing, his serious eyes fixed earnestly upon the fair organist.

Tonie was late at dinner that day. His mother must have waited an
hour for him, sitting patiently with her coarse hands folded in her lap,
in that little still room with its 'brick-painted' floor, its gaping chimney
and homely furnishings.

He told her that he had been walking – walking he hardly knew
where, and he did not know why. He must have tramped from one end
of the island to the other; but he brought her no bit of news or gossip.
He did not know if the Cotures had stopped for dinner with the
Avendettes; whether old Pierre François was worse, or better, or dead,
or if lame Philibert was drinking again this morning. He knew nothing;
yet he had crossed the village, and passed every one of its small houses
that stood close together in a long jagged line facing the sea; they were
grey and battered by time and the rude buffets of the salt sea winds.

He knew nothing though the Cotures had all bade him 'good-day' as
they filed into Avendette's, where a steaming plate of crab gumbo[332]
was waiting for each. He had heard some woman screaming, and others
saying it was because old Pierre François had just passed away. But he
did not remember this, nor did he recall the fact that lame Philibert had
staggered against him when he stood absently watching a 'fiddler' sidling
across the sunbaked sand. He could tell his mother nothing of all this;
but he said he had noticed that the wind was fair and must have driven
Baptiste's boat, like a flying bird, across the water.

Well, that was something to talk about, and old Ma'me Antoine, who
was fat, leaned comfortably upon the table after she had helped Tonie
to his *courtbouillon*,[333] and remarked that she found Madame was getting
old. Tonie thought that perhaps she was aging and her hair was getting
whiter. He seemed glad to talk about her, and reminded his mother of
old Madame's kindness and sympathy at the time his father and brothers
had perished. It was when he was a little fellow, ten years before, during
a squall in Barataria Bay.[334]

Ma'me Antoine declared that she could never forget that sympathy, if
she lived till Judgement Day; but all the same she was sorry to see that
Madame Lebrun[335] was also not so young or fresh as she used to be.
Her chances of getting a husband were surely lessening every year;
especially with the young girls around her, budding each spring like
flowers to be plucked. The one who had played upon the organ was

Mademoiselle Duvigné, Claire Duvigné, a great belle, the daughter of the famous lawyer who lived in New Orleans, on Rampart Street. Ma'me Antoine had found that out during the ten minutes she and others had stopped after mass to gossip with the priest.

'Claire Duvigné,' muttered Tonie, not even making a pretence to taste his *courtbouillon*, but picking little bits from the half-loaf of crusty brown bread that lay beside his plate. 'Claire Duvigné; that is a pretty name. Don't you think so, mother? I can't think of anyone on the Chênière who has so pretty a one, nor at Grand Isle, either, for that matter. And you say she lives on Rampart Street?'

It appeared to him a matter of great importance that he should have his mother repeat all that the priest had told her.

2

Early the following morning Tonie went out in search of lame Philibert, than whom there was no cleverer workman on the island when he could be caught sober.

Tonie had tried to work on his big lugger that lay bottom upward under the shed, but it had seemed impossible. His mind, his hands, his tools refused to do their office, and in sudden desperation he desisted. He found Philibert and set him to work in his own place under the shed. Then he got into his small boat with the red lateen[336] sail and went over to Grand Isle.

There was no one at hand to warn Tonie that he was acting the part of a fool. He had, singularly, never felt those premonitory symptoms of love which afflict the greater portion of mankind before they reach the age which he had attained. He did not at first recognise this powerful impulse that had, without warning, possessed itself of his entire being. He obeyed it without a struggle, as naturally as he would have obeyed the dictates of hunger and thirst.

Tonie left his boat at the wharf and proceeded at once to Mme Lebrun's *pension*, which consisted of a group of plain, stoutly built cottages that stood in mid-island, about half a mile from the sea.

The day was bright and beautiful with soft, velvety gusts of wind blowing from the water. From a cluster of orange trees a flock of doves ascended, and Tonie stopped to listen to the beating of their wings and follow their flight towards the water oaks whither he himself was moving.

He walked with a dragging, uncertain step through the yellow, fragrant camomile, his thoughts travelling before him. In his mind was always the vivid picture of the girl as it had stamped itself there yesterday, connected in some mystical way with that celestial music which had thrilled him and was vibrating yet in his soul.

But she did not look the same today. She was returning from the beach when Tonie first saw her, leaning upon the arm of one of the men who had accompanied her yesterday. She was dressed differently – in a dainty blue cotton gown. Her companion held a big white sunshade over them both. They had exchanged hats and were laughing with great abandonment.

Two young men walked behind them and were trying to engage her attention. She glanced at Tonie, who was leaning against a tree when the group passed by; but of course she did not know him. She was speaking English, a language which he hardly understood.

There were other young people gathered under the water oaks – girls who were, many of them, more beautiful than Mlle Duvigné; but for Tonie they simply did not exist. His whole universe had suddenly become converted into a glamorous backgound for the person of Mlle Duvigné, and the shadowy figures of men who were about her.

Tonie went to Madame Lebrun and told her he would bring her oranges next day from the Chênière. She was well pleased, and commissioned him to bring her other things from the stores there, which she could not procure at Grand Isle. She did not question his presence, knowing that these summer days were idle ones for the Chênière fishermen. Nor did she seem surprised when he told her that his boat was at the wharf, and would be there every day at her service. She knew his frugal habits, and supposed he wished to hire it, as others did. He intuitively felt that this could be the only way.

And that is how it happened that Tonie spent so little of his time at the Chênière Caminada that summer. Old Ma'me Antoine grumbled enough about it. She herself had been twice in her life to Grand Isle and once to Grand Terre, and each time had been more than glad to get back to the Chênière. And why Tonie should want to spend his days, and even his nights, away from home, was a thing she could not comprehend, especially as he would have to be away the whole winter; and meantime there was much work to be done at his own hearthside and in the company of his own mother. She did not know that Tonie had much, much more to do at Grand Isle than at the Chênière Caminada.

He had to see how Claire Duvigné sat upon the gallery in the big rocking chair that she kept in motion by the impetus of her slender, slippered foot; turning her head this way and that way to speak to the men who were always near her. He had to follow her lithe motions at tennis or croquet, that she often played with the children under the trees. Some days he wanted to see how she spread her bare, white arms, and walked out to meet the foam-crested waves. Even here there were men with her. And then at night, standing alone like a still shadow under the stars, did he not have to listen to her voice when she talked and laughed and sang? Did he not have to follow her slim figure whirling through the dance, in the arms of men who must have loved her and wanted her as he did. He did not dream that they could help it more than he could help it. But the days when she stepped into his boat, the one with the red lateen sail, and sat for hours within a few feet of him, were days that he would have given up for nothing else that he could think of.

3

There were always others in her company at such times, young people with jests and laughter on their lips. Only once she was alone.

She had foolishly brought a book with her, thinking she would want to read. But with the breath of the sea stinging her she could not read a line. She looked precisely as she had looked the day he first saw her, standing outside of the church at Chênière Caminada.

She laid the book down in her lap, and let her soft eyes sweep dreamily along the line of the horizon where the sky and water met. Then she looked straight at Tonie, and for the first time spoke directly to him.

She called him Tonie, as she had heard others do, and questioned him about his boat and his work. He trembled, and answered her vaguely and stupidly. She did not mind, but spoke to him anyhow, satisfied to talk herself when she found that he could not or would not. She spoke French, and talked about the Chênière Caminada, its people and its church. She talked of the day she had played upon the organ there, and complained of the instrument being woefully out of tune.

Tonie was perfectly at home in the familiar task of guiding his boat before the wind that bellied its taut, red sail. He did not seem clumsy and awkward as when he sat in church. The girl noticed that he appeared as strong as an ox.

As she looked at him and surprised one of his shifting glances, a glimmer of the truth began to dawn faintly upon her. She remembered how she had encountered him daily in her path, with his earnest, devouring eyes always seeking her out. She recalled – but there was no need to recall anything. There are women whose perception of passion is very keen; they are the women who most inspire it.

A feeling of complacency took possession of her with this conviction.

There was some softness and sympathy mingled with it. She would have liked to lean over and pat his big, brown hand, and tell him she felt sorry and would have helped it if she could. With this belief he ceased to be an object of complete indifference in her eyes. She had thought, awhile before, of having him turn about and take her back home. But now it was really piquant to pose for an hour longer before a man – even a rough fisherman – to whom she felt herself to be an object of silent and consuming devotion. She could think of nothing more interesting to do on shore.

She was incapable of conceiving the full force and extent of his infatuation. She did not dream that under the rude, calm exterior before her a man's heart was beating clamorously, and his reason yielding to the savage instinct of his blood.

'I hear the angelus[337] ringing at Chênière, Tonie,' she said. 'I didn't know it was so late; let us go back to the island.' There had been a long silence which her musical voice interrupted.

Tonie could now faintly hear the angelus bell himself. A vision of the church came with it, the odour of incense and the sound of the organ. The girl before him was again the celestial being whom our Lady of Lourdes had once offered to his immortal vision.

It was growing dusk when they landed at the pier, and frogs had begun to croak among the reeds in the pools. There were two of Mlle Duvigné's usual attendants anxiously awaiting her return. But she chose to let Tonie assist her out of the boat. The touch of her hand fired his blood again.

She said to him very low and half-laughing, 'I have no money tonight, Tonie; take this instead,' pressing into his palm a delicate silver chain, which she had worn twined about her bare wrist. It was purely a spirit of coquetry that prompted the action, and a touch of the sentimentality which most women possess. She had read in some romance of a young girl doing something like that.

As she walked away between her two attendants she fancied Tonie pressing the chain to his lips. But he was standing quite still, and held it buried in his tightly closed hand; wanting to hold as long as he might the warmth of the body that still penetrated the bauble when she thrust it into his hand.

He watched her retreating figure like a blotch against the fading sky. He was stirred by a terrible, an over-mastering regret, that he had not clasped her in his arms when they were out there alone, and sprung with her into the sea. It was what he had vaguely meant to do when the sound of the angelus had weakened and palsied his resolution. Now she was going from him, fading away into the mist with those figures on either side of her, leaving him alone. He resolved within himself that if ever again she were out there on the sea at his mercy, she would have to perish in his arms. He would go far, far out where the sound of no bell could reach him. There was some comfort for him in the thought.

But as it happened, Mlle Duvigné never went out alone in the boat with Tonie again.

4

It was one morning in January. Tonie had been collecting a bill from one of the fishmongers at the French Market, in New Orleans, and had turned his steps towards St Philip Street. The day was chilly; a keen wind was blowing. Tonie mechanically buttoned his rough, warm coat and crossed over into the sun.

There was perhaps not a more wretched-hearted being in the whole district, that morning, than he. For months the woman he so hopelessly loved had been lost to his sight. But all the more she dwelt in his thoughts, preying upon his mental and bodily forces until his unhappy condition became apparent to all who knew him. Before leaving his home for the winter fishing grounds he had opened his whole heart to his mother, and told her of the trouble that was killing him. She hardly expected that he would ever come back to her when he went away. She feared that he would not, for he had spoken wildly of the rest and peace that could only come to him with death.

That morning when Tonie had crossed St Philip Street he found himself accosted by Madame Lebrun and her mother. He had not noticed them approaching, and, moreover, their figures in winter garb appeared unfamiliar to him. He had never seen them elsewhere than at Grand Isle and the Chênière during the summer. They were glad to meet him, and shook his hand cordially. He stood as usual a little helplessly before them. A pulse in his throat was beating and almost choking him, so poignant were the recollections which their presence stirred up.

They were staying in the city this winter, they told him. They wanted to hear the opera as often as possible, and the island was really too dreary with everyone gone. Madame Lebrun had left her son there to keep order and superintend repairs, and so on.

'You are both well?' stammered Tonie.

'In perfect health, my dear Tonie,' Madame Lebrun replied. She was wondering at his haggard eyes and thin, gaunt cheeks; but possessed too much tact to mention them.

'And – the young lady who used to go sailing – is she well?' he enquired lamely.

'You mean Mlle Favette? She was married just after leaving Grand Isle.'

'No; I mean the one you called Claire – Mamzelle Duvigné – is she well?'

Mother and daughter exclaimed together: 'Impossible! You haven't heard? Why, Tonie,' Madame continued, 'Mlle Duvigné died three weeks ago! But that was something sad, I tell you . . . Her family heartbroken . . . Simply from a cold caught by standing in thin slippers, waiting for her carriage after the opera . . . What a warning!'

The two were talking at once. Tonie kept looking from one to the other. He did not know what they were saying, after Madame had told him, 'Elle est morte.'[338]

As in a dream he finally heard that they said goodbye to him, and sent their love to his mother.

He stood still in the middle of the banquette when they had left him, watching them go towards the market. He could not stir. Something had happened to him – he did not know what. He wondered if the news was killing him.

Some women passed by, laughing coarsely. He noticed how they laughed and tossed their heads. A mockingbird was singing in a cage which hung from a window above his head. He had not heard it before.

Just beneath the window was the entrance to a bar-room. Tonie turned and plunged through its swinging doors. He asked the bartender for whiskey. The man thought he was already drunk, but pushed the bottle towards him nevertheless. Tonie poured a great quantity of the fiery liquor into a glass and swallowed it at a draught. The rest of the day he spent among the fishermen and Barataria oyster men; and that night he slept soundly and peacefully until morning.

He did not know why it was so; he could not understand. But from that day he felt that he began to live again, to be once more a part of the moving world about him. He would ask himself over and over again why it was so, and stay bewildered before this truth that he could not answer or explain, and which he began to accept as a holy mystery.

One day in early spring Tonie sat with his mother upon a piece of driftwood close to the sea.

He had returned that day to the Chênière Caminada. At first she thought he was like his former self again, for all his old strength and courage had returned. But she found that there was a new brightness in

his face which had not been there before. It made her think of the Holy
Ghost descending and bringing some kind of light to a man.

She knew that Mademoiselle Duvigné was dead, and all along had
feared that this knowledge would be the death of Tonie. When she saw
him come back to her like a new being, at once she dreaded that he did
not know. All day the doubt had been fretting her, and she could bear
the uncertainty no longer.

'You know, Tonie – that young lady whom you cared for – well,
someone read it to me in the papers – she died last winter.' She had
tried to speak as cautiously as she could.

'Yes, I know she is dead. I am glad.'

It was the first time he had said this in words, and it made his heart
beat quicker.

Ma'me Antoine shuddered and drew aside from him. To her it was
somehow like murder to say such a thing.

'What do you mean? Why are you glad?' she demanded, indignantly.

Tonie was sitting with his elbows on his knees. He wanted to answer
his mother, but it would take time; he would have to think. He looked
out across the water that glistened gemlike with the sun upon it, but
there was nothing there to open his thought. He looked down into his
open palm and began to pick at the callous flesh that was hard as a
horse's hoof. While he did this his ideas began to gather and take
form.

'You see, while she lived I could never hope for anything,' he began,
slowly feeling his way. 'Despair was the only thing for me. There were
always men about her. She walked and sang and danced with them. I
knew it all the time, even when I didn't see her. But I saw her often
enough. I knew that someday one of them would please her and she
would give herself to him – she would marry him. That thought haunted
me like an evil spirit.'

Tonie passed his hand across his forehead as if to sweep away anything
of the horror that might have remained there.

'It kept me awake at night,' he went on. 'But that was not so bad; the
worst torture was to sleep, for then I would dream that it was all true.

'Oh, I could see her married to one of them – his wife – coming year
after year to Grand Isle and bringing her little children with her! I can't
tell you all that I saw – all that was driving me mad! But now – ' and
Tonie clasped his hands together and smiled as he looked again across
the water – 'she is where she belongs; there is no difference up there;
the curé has often told us there is no difference between men. It is with
the soul that we approach each other there. Then she will know who

has loved her best. That is why I am so contented. Who knows what may happen up there?'

Ma'me Antoine could not answer. She only took her son's big, rough hand and pressed it against her.

'And now, *ma mère*,' he exclaimed, cheerfully, rising, 'I shall go light the fire for your bread; it is a long time since I have done anything for you,' and he stooped and pressed a warm kiss on her withered old cheek.

With misty eyes she watched him walk away in the direction of the big brick oven that stood open-mouthed under the lemon trees.

Odalie Misses Mass

Odalie sprang down from the mule-cart, shook out her white skirts, and firmly grasping her parasol, which was blue to correspond with her sash, entered Aunt Pinky's gate and proceeded towards the old woman's cabin. She was a thick-waisted young thing who walked with a firm tread and carried her head with a determined poise. Her straight brown hair had been rolled up overnight in *papillotes*,[339] and the artificial curls stood out in clusters, stiff and uncompromising beneath the rim of her white chip hat. Her mother, sister and brother remained seated in the cart before the gate.

It was the fifteenth of August, the great feast of the Assumption, so generally observed in the Catholic parishes of Louisiana. The Chotard family were on their way to mass, and Odalie had insisted upon stopping to 'show herself' to her old friend and protégée, Aunt Pinky.

The helpless, shrivelled old negress sat in the depths of a large, rudely-fashioned chair. A loosely hanging unbleached cotton gown enveloped her mite of a figure. What was visible of her hair, beneath the bandana turban, looked like white sheep's wool. She wore round, silver-rimmed spectacles, which gave her an air of wisdom and respectability, and she held in her hand the branch of a hickory sapling, with which she kept mosquitoes and flies at bay, and even chickens and pigs that sometimes penetrated the heart of her domain.

Odalie walked straight up to the old woman and kissed her on the cheek.

'Well, Aunt Pinky, yere I am,' she announced with evident self-complacency, turning herself slowly and stiffly around like a mechanical dummy. In one hand she held her prayer-book, fan and handkerchief, in the other the blue parasol, still open; and on her plump hands were blue cotton mitts. Aunt Pinky beamed and chuckled; Odalie hardly expected her to be able to do more.

'Now you saw me,' the child continued. 'I reckon you satisfied. I mus' go; I ain't got a minute to was'e.' But at the threshold she turned to enquire, bluntly: 'W'ere's Pug?'

'Pug,' replied Aunt Pinky, in her tremulous old-woman's voice. 'She's gone to chu'ch; done gone; she done gone,' nodding her head in seeming approval of Pug's action.

'To church!' echoed Odalie with a look of consternation settling in her round eyes.

'She gone to chu'ch,' reiterated Aunt Pinky. 'Say she kain't miss chu'ch on de fifteent'; de debble gwine pester her twell jedgement, she miss chu'ch on de fifteent'.'

Odalie's plump cheeks fairly quivered with indignation and she stamped her foot. She looked up and down the long, dusty road that skirted the river. Nothing was to be seen save the blue cart with its dejected looking mule and patient occupants.

She walked to the end of the gallery and called out to a negro boy whose black bullet-head showed up in bold relief against the white of the cotton patch: 'Hey, Baptiste! w'ere's yo' ma? Ask yo' ma if she can't come set with Aunt Pinky.'

'Mammy, she gone to chu'ch,' screamed Baptiste in answer.

'*Bonté!* w'at's taken you all darkies with yo' 'church' today? You come along yere Baptiste an' set with Aunt Pinky. That Pug! I'm goin' to make yo' ma wear her out fo' that trick of hers – leavin' Aunt Pinky like that.'

But at the first intimation of what was wanted of him, Baptiste dipped below the cotton like a fish beneath water, leaving no sight nor sound of himself to answer Odalie's repeated calls. Her mother and sister were beginning to show signs of impatience.

'But, I can't go,' she cried out to them. 'It's nobody to stay with Aunt Pinky. I can't leave Aunt Pinky like that, to fall out of her chair, maybe, like she already fell out once.'

'You goin' to miss mass on the fifteenth, you, Odalie! W'at you thinkin' about?' came in shrill rebuke from her sister. But her mother offering no objection, the boy lost not a moment in starting the mule forward at a brisk trot. She watched them disappear in a cloud of dust; and turning with a dejected, almost tearful countenance, re-entered the room.

Aunt Pinky seemed to accept her reappearance as a matter of course; and even evinced no surprise at seeing her remove her hat and mitts, which she laid carefully, almost religiously, on the bed, together with her book, fan and handkerchief.

Then Odalie went and seated herself some distance from the old woman in her own small, low rocking-chair. She rocked herself furiously, making a great clatter with the rockers over the wide, uneven boards of the cabin floor; and she looked out through the open door.

'Puggy, she done gone to chu'ch; done gone. Say de debble gwine pester her twell jedgement – '

'You done tole me that, Aunt Pinky; neva mine; don't le's talk about it.'

Aunt Pinky thus rebuked, settled back into silence and Odalie continued to rock and stare out of the door.

Once she arose, and taking the hickory branch from Aunt Pinky's nerveless hand, made a bold and sudden charge upon a little pig that seemed bent upon keeping her company. She pursued him with flying heels and loud cries as far as the road. She came back flushed and breathless and her curls hanging rather limp around her face; she began again to rock herself and gaze silently out of the door.

'You gwine make yo' fus' c'mmunion?'

This seemingly sober enquiry on the part of Aunt Pinky at once shattered Odalie's ill-humour and dispelled every shadow of it. She leaned back and laughed with wild abandonment.

'Mais w'at you thinkin' about, Aunt Pinky? How you don't remember I made my firs' communion las' year, with this same dress w'at maman let out the tuck,' holding up the altered skirt for Aunt Pinky's inspection. 'An' with this same petticoat w'at maman added this ruffle an' crochet' edge; excep' I had a w'ite sash.'

These evidences proved beyond question convincing and seemed to satisfy Aunt Pinky. Odalie rocked as furiously as ever, but she sang now, and the swaying chair had worked its way nearer to the old woman.

'You gwine git mar'ied?'

'I declare, Aunt Pinky,' said Odalie, when she had ceased laughing and was wiping her eyes, 'I declare, sometime' I think you gittin' plumb foolish. How you expec' me to git married w'en I'm on'y thirteen?'

Evidently Aunt Pinky did not know why or how she expected anything so preposterous; Odalie's holiday attire, that filled her with contemplative rapture, had doubtless incited her to these vagaries.

The child now drew her chair quite close to the old woman's knee after she had gone out to the rear of the cabin to get herself some water and had brought a drink to Aunt Pinky in the gourd dipper.

There was a strong, hot breeze blowing from the river, and it swept fitfully and in gusts through the cabin, bringing with it the weedy smell of cacti that grew thick on the bank, and occasionally a shower of reddish dust from the road. Odalie for a while was greatly occupied in keeping in place her filmy skirt, which every gust of wind swelled balloon-like about her knees. Aunt Pinky's little black, scrawny hand had found its way among the droopy curls and strayed often caressingly to the child's plump neck and shoulders.

'You riclics, honey, dat day yo' granpappy say it wur pinchin' times an' he reckin he bleege to sell Yallah Tom an' Susan an' Pinky? Don' know how come he think 'bout Pinky, 'less caze he sees me playin' an' trapsin' roun' wid you alls, day in an' out. I riclics yit how you tu'n w'ite like milk an' fling yo' arms roun' li'le black Pinky; an' you cries out you don' wan' no saddle-mar'; you don' wan' no silk dresses and fing' rings an' sich; an' don' wan' no idication; des wants Pinky. An' you cries an' screams an' kicks, an' 'low you gwine kill fus' pusson w'at dar come an' buy Pinky an' kiars her off. You riclics dat, honey?'

Odalie had grown accustomed to these flights of fancy on the part of her old friend; she liked to humour her as she chose to sometimes humour very small children; so she was quite used to impersonating one dearly beloved but impetuous 'Paulette', who seemed to have held her place in old Pinky's heart and imagination through all the years of her suffering life.

'I rec'lec' like it was yesterday, Aunt Pinky. How I scream an' kick an' maman gave me some med'cine; an' how you scream en' kick en' Susan took you down to the quarters an' give you "twenty".'

'Des so, honey; des like you says,' chuckled Aunt Pinky. 'But you don' riclic dat time you cotch Pinky cryin' down in de holler behine de gin; an' you say you gwine give me "twenty" ef I don' tell you w'at I cryin' 'bout?'

'I rec'lec' like it happen'd today, Aunt Pinky. You been cryin' because you want to marry Hiram, ole Mr Benitou's servant.'

'Des true like you says, Miss Paulette; an' you goes home an' cries and kiars on an' won' eat, an' breaks dishes, an' pesters yo' gran'pap 'tell he bleege to buy Hi'um f'om de Benitous.'

'Don' talk, Aunt Pink! I can see all that jus' as plain!' responded Odalie sympathetically, yet in truth she took but a languid interest in these reminiscences which she had listened to so often before.

She leaned her flushed cheek against Aunt Pinky's knee.

The air was rippling now, and hot and caressing. There was the hum of bumble bees outside; and busy mud-daubers kept flying in and out through the door. Some chickens had penetrated to the very threshold in their aimless roamings, and the little pig was approaching more cautiously. Sleep was fast overtaking the child, but she could still hear through her drowsiness the familiar tones of Aunt Pinky's voice.

'But Hi'um, he done gone; he nuva come back; an' Yallah Tom nuva come back; an' ole Marster an' de chillun – all gone – nuva come back. Nobody nuva come back to Pinky 'cep you, my honey. You ain' gwine 'way f'om Pinky no mo', is you, Miss Paulette?'

'Don' fret, Aunt Pinky – I'm goin' – to stay with – you.'

'No pussun nuva come back 'cep' you.'

Odalie was fast asleep. Aunt Pinky was asleep with her head leaning back on her chair and her fingers thrust into the mass of tangled brown hair that swept across her lap. The chickens and little pig walked fearlessly in and out. The sunlight crept close up to the cabin door and stole away again.

Odalie awoke with a start. Her mother was standing over her arousing her from sleep. She sprang up and rubbed her eyes. 'Oh, I been asleep!' she exclaimed. The cart was standing in the road waiting. 'An' Aunt Pinky, she's asleep, too.'

'Yes, *chérie*, Aunt Pinky is asleep,' replied her mother, leading Odalie away. But she spoke low and trod softly as gentle-souled women do, in the presence of the dead.

Cavanelle

I was always sure of hearing something pleasant from Cavanelle across the counter. If he was not mistaking me for the freshest and prettiest girl in New Orleans, he was reserving for me some bit of silk, or lace, or ribbon of a nuance marvellously suited to my complexion, my eyes or my hair! What an innocent, delightful humbug Cavanelle was! How well I knew it and how little I cared! For when he had sold me the confection or bit of dry-goods in question, he always began to talk to me of his sister Mathilde, and then I knew that Cavanelle was an angel.

I had known him long enough to know why he worked so faithfully, so energetically and without rest – it was because Mathilde had a voice. It was because of her voice that his coats were worn till they were out of fashion and almost out at elbows. But for a sister whose voice needed only a little training to rival that of the nightingale, one might do such things without incurring reproach.

'You will believe, madame, that I did not know you las' night at the opera? I remark' to Mathilde, "*Tiens!* Mademoiselle Montreville," an' I only rec'nise my mistake when I finally adjust my opera glass . . . I guarantee you will be satisfied, madame. In a year from now you will come an' thank me for having secu' you that bargain in a *poult-de-soie* [340] . . . Yes, yes; as you say, Tolville was in voice. But,' with a shrug of the narrow shoulders and a smile of commiseration that wrinkled the lean olive cheeks beneath the thin beard, 'but to hear that cavatina [341] render' as I have heard it render' by Mathilde is another affair! A quality, madame, that moves, that penetrates. Perhaps not yet enough volume, but that will accomplish itself with time, when she will become more robus' in health. It is my intention to sen' her for the summer to Gran' Isle; that good air an' surf bathing will work miracles. An artiste, *voyez vous*, [342] it is not to be treated like a human being of everyday; it needs *des petits soins*; [343] perfec' res' of body an' mind; good red wine an' plenty . . . oh yes, madame, the stage; that is our intention; but never with my consent in light opera. Patience is what I counsel to Mathilde. A little more stren'th; a little dev'lopment of the chest to give that soupçon [344] of compass which is lacking, an' gran' opera is what I aspire for my sister.'

I was curious to know Mathilde and to hear her sing; and thought it a great pity that a voice so marvellous as she doubtless possessed should not gain the notice that might prove the step towards the attainment of her ambition. It was such curiosity and a half-formed design or desire to interest myself in her career that prompted me to inform Cavanelle that I should greatly like to meet his sister; and I asked permission to call upon her the following Sunday afternoon.

Cavanelle was charmed. He otherwise would not have been Cavanelle. Over and over I was given the most minute directions for finding the house. The green car – or was it the yellow or blue one? I can no longer remember. But it was near Goodchildren Street, and would I kindly walk this way and turn that way? At the corner was an ice dealer's. In the middle of the block, their house – one-storey; painted yellow; a knocker; a banana tree nodding over the side fence. But indeed, I need not look for the banana tree, the knocker, the number or anything, for if I but turn the corner in the neighbourhood of five o'clock I would find him planted at the door awaiting me.

And there he was! Cavanelle himself; but seeming to me not himself; apart from the entourage with which I was accustomed to associate him. Every line of his mobile face, every gesture emphasised the welcome which his kind eyes expressed as he ushered me into the small parlour that opened upon the street.

'Oh, not that chair, madame! I entreat you. This one, by all means. Thousan' times more comfortable.'

'Mathilde! Strange; my sister was here but an instant ago. Mathilde! *Où es tu donc?*'[345] Stupid Cavanelle! He did not know when I had already guessed it – that Mathilde had retired to the adjoining room at my approach, and would appear after a sufficient delay to give an appropriate air of ceremony to our meeting.

And what a frail little piece of mortality she was when she did appear! At beholding her I could easily fancy that when she stepped outside of the yellow house, the zephyrs would lift her from her feet and, given a proper adjustment of the balloon sleeves, gently waft her in the direction of Goodchildren Street, or wherever else she might want to go.

Hers was no physique for grand opera – certainly no stage presence; apparently so slender a hold upon life that the least tension might snap it. The voice which could hope to overcome these glaring disadvantages would have to be phenomenal.

Mathilde spoke English imperfectly, and with embarrassment, and was glad to lapse into French. Her speech was languid, unaffectedly so; and her manner was one of indolent repose; in this respect offering a striking contrast to that of her brother. Cavanelle seemed unable to rest. Hardly was I seated to his satisfaction than he darted from the room and soon returned followed by a limping old black woman bringing in a *sirop d'orgeat* [346] and layer cake on a tray.

Mathilde's face showed feeble annoyance at her brother's want of *savoir vivre* [347] in thus introducing the refreshments at so early a stage of my visit.

The servant was one of those cheap black women who abound in the French Quarter, who speak Creole patois in preference to English, and who would rather work in a *petit ménage* [348] in Goodchildren Street for five dollars a month than for fifteen in the fourth district. Her presence, in some unaccountable manner, seemed to reveal to me much of the inner working of this small household. I pictured her early morning visit to the French market, where picayunes were doled out sparingly, and *lagniappes* [349] gathered in with avidity.

I could see the neatly appointed dinner table; Cavanelle extolling his soup and *bouillie* [350] in extravagant terms; Mathilde toying with her *papabotte* [351] or chicken-wing, and pouring herself a demi-verre [352] from her very own half-bottle of St Julien; Pouponne, as they called her, mumbling and grumbling through habit, and serving them as faithfully as a dog through instinct. I wondered if they knew that Pouponne 'played the lottery' with every spare 'quarter' gathered from a judicious management of *lagniappes*. Perhaps they would not have cared, or have minded, either, that she as often consulted the Voudoo priestess around the corner as her father confessor.

My thoughts had followed Pouponne's limping figure from the room, and it was with an effort I returned to Cavanelle twirling the piano stool this way and that way. Mathilde was languidly turning over musical scores, and the two were warmly discussing the merits of a selection which she had evidently decided upon.

The girl seated herself at the piano. Her hands were thin and anaemic, and she touched the keys without firmness or delicacy. When she had played a few introductory bars, she began to sing. Heaven only knows what she sang; it made no difference then, nor can it make any now.

The day was a warm one, but that did not prevent a creepy chilliness seizing hold of me. The feeling was generated by disappointment, anger, dismay and various other disagreeable sensations which I cannot find names for. Had I been intentionally deceived and misled? Was this some impertinent pleasantry on the part of Cavanelle? Or rather had not the girl's voice undergone some hideous transformation since her brother had listened to it? I dreaded to look at him, fearing to see horror and astonishment depicted on his face. When I did look, his expression was earnestly attentive and beamed approval of the strains to which he measured time by a slow, satisfied motion of the hand.

The voice was thin to attenuation, I fear it was not even true. Perhaps my disappointment exaggerated its simple deficiencies into monstrous defects. But it was an unsympathetic voice that never could have been a blessing to possess or to listen to.

I cannot recall what I said at parting – doubtless conventional things which were not true. Cavanelle politely escorted me to the car, and there I left him with a hand-clasp which from my side was tender with sympathy and pity.

'Poor Cavanelle! poor Cavanelle!' The words kept beating time in my brain to the jingle of the car bells and the regular ring of the mules' hoofs upon the cobblestones. One moment I resolved to have a talk with him in which I would endeavour to open his eyes to the folly of thus casting his hopes and the substance of his labour to the winds. The next instant I had decided that chance would possibly attend to Cavanelle's affair less clumsily than I could. 'But all the same,' I wondered, 'is Cavanelle a fool? is he a lunatic? is he under a hypnotic spell?' And then – strange that I did not think of it before – I realised that Cavanelle loved Mathilde intensely, and we all know that love is blind, but a god just the same.

*

Two years passed before I saw Cavanelle again. I had been absent that length of time from the city. In the meanwhile Mathilde had died. She and her little voice – the apotheosis of insignificance – were no more. It was perhaps a year after my visit to her that I read an account of her death in a New Orleans paper. Then came a momentary pang of commiseration for my good Cavanelle. Chance had surely acted here the part of a skilful though merciless surgeon: no temporising, no half measures. A deep, sharp thrust of the scalpel: a moment of agonising pain; then rest, rest; convalescence; health; happiness! Yes, Mathilde had been dead a year and I was prepared for great changes in Cavanelle.

He had lived like a hampered child who does not recognise the restrictions hedging it about, and lives a life of pathetic contentment in the midst of them. But now all that was altered. He was, doubtless, regaling himself with the half-bottles of St Julien, which were never before for him; with, perhaps, an occasional *petit souper* [353] at Moreau's, and there was no telling what little pleasures beside.

Cavanelle would certainly have bought himself a suit of clothes or two of modern fit and finish. I would find him with a brightened eye, a fuller cheek, as became a man of his years; perchance, even, a waxed moustache! So did my imagination run rampant with me.

And after all, the hand which I clasped across the counter was that of the selfsame Cavanelle I had left. It was no fuller, no firmer. There were even some additional lines visible through the thin, brown beard.

'Ah, my poor Cavanelle! you have suffered a grievous loss since we parted.' I saw in his face that he remembered the circumstances of our last meeting, so there was no use in avoiding the subject. I had rightly conjectured that the wound had been a cruel one, but in a year such wounds heal with a healthy soul.

He could have talked for hours of Mathilde's unhappy taking-off, and if the subject had possessed for me the same touching fascination which it held for him, doubtless, we would have done so, but –

'And how is it now, *mon ami*? Are you living in the same place? running your little *ménage* as before, my poor Cavanelle?'

'Oh, yes, madame, except that my Aunt Félicie is making her home with me now. You have heard me speak of my aunt – No? You never have heard me speak of my Aunt Félicie Cavanelle of Terrebonne! That, madame, is a noble woman who has suffer' the mos' cruel affliction, and deprivation, since the war. – No, madame, not in good health, unfortunately, by any means. It is why I esteem that a blessed privilege to give her declining years those little comforts, *ces petits soins*, that is a woman's right to expec' from men.'

I knew what '*des petits soins*' meant with Cavanelle: doctors' visits, little jaunts across the lake, *friandises* of every description showered upon 'Aunt Félicie', and he himself relegated to the soup and *bouillie* which typified his prosaic existence.

I was unreasonably exasperated with the man for a while, and would not even permit myself to notice the beauty in texture and design of the *mousseline de laine* [354] which he had spread across the counter in tempting folds. I was forced to restrain a brutal desire to say something stinging and cruel to him for his fatuity.

However, before I had regained the street, the conviction that Cavanelle was a hopeless fool seemed to reconcile me to the situation and also afforded me some diversion.

But even this estimate of my poor Cavanelle was destined not to last. By the time I had seated myself in the Prytania Street car and passed up my nickel, I was convinced that Cavanelle was an angel.

Tante Cat'rinette

It happened just as everyone had predicted. Tante Cat'rinette was beside herself with rage and indignation when she learned that the town authorities had for some reason condemned her house and intended to demolish it.

'Dat house w'at Vieumaite[355] gi' me his own se'f, out his own mout', w'en he gi' me my freedom! All wrote down *en régle*[356] befo' de cote! *Bon Dieu Seigneur*, w'at dey talkin' 'bout!'

Tante Cat'rinette stood in the doorway of her home, resting a gaunt black hand against the jamb. In the other hand she held her corncob pipe. She was a tall, large-boned woman of a pronounced Congo type. The house in question had been substantial enough in its time. It contained four rooms: the lower two of brick, the upper ones of adobe. A dilapidated gallery projected from the upper storey and slanted over the narrow banquette, to the peril of passers-by.

'I don't think I ever heard why the property was given to you in the first place, Tante Cat'rinette,' observed Lawyer Paxton, who had stopped in passing, as so many others did, to talk the matter over with the old negress. The affair was attracting some attention in town, and its development was being watched with a good deal of interest. Tante Cat'rinette asked nothing better than to satisfy the lawyer's curiosity.

'Vieumaite all time say Cat'rinette wort' gole to 'im; de way I make dem nigga' walk chalk. But,' she continued, with recovered seriousness, 'w'en I nuss 'is li'le gal w'at all de doctor' 'low it's goin' die, an' I make it well, me, den Vieumaite, he can't do 'nough, him. He name' dat li'le gal Cat'rine fo' me. Das Miss Kitty w'at marry Miché Raymond yon' by Gran' Eco'. Den he gi' me my freedom; he got plenty slave', him; one don' count in his pocket. An' he gi' me dat house w'at I'm stan'in' in de do'; he got plenty house' an' lan', him. Now dey want pay me t'ousan' dolla', w'at I don' axen' fo', an' tu'n me out dat house! I waitin' fo' 'em, Miché Paxtone,' and a wicked gleam shot into the woman's small, dusky eyes. 'I got my axe grine fine. Fus' man w'at touch Cat'rinette fo' tu'n her out dat house, he git 'is head bus' like I bust a gode.

'Dat's nice day, ainty, Miché Paxtone? Fine wedda fo' dry my close.' Upon the gallery above hung an array of shirts, which gleamed white in the sunshine, and flapped in the rippling breeze.

The spectacle of Tante Cattrinette defying the authorities was one which offered much diversion to the children of the neighbourhood. They played numberless pranks at her expense; daily serving upon her fictitious notices purporting to be to the last degree official. One youngster, in a moment of inspiration, composed a couplet, which they recited, sang, shouted at all hours, beneath her windows.

> 'Tante Cat'rinette, she go to town;
> W'en she come back, her house pull' down.'

So ran the production. She heard it many times during the day, but, far from offending her, she accepted it as a warning – a prediction, as it were – and she took heed not to offer to fate the conditions for its fulfilment. She no longer quitted her house even for a moment, so great was her fear and so firm her belief that the town authorities were lying in wait to possess themselves of it. She would not cross the street to visit a neighbour. She waylaid passers-by and pressed them into service to do her errands and small shopping. She grew distrustful and suspicious, ever on the alert to scent a plot in the most innocent endeavour to induce her to leave the house.

One morning, as Tante Cat'rinette was hanging out her latest batch of washing, Eusèbe, a 'free mulatto' from Red River, stopped his pony beneath her gallery.

'*Hé*, Tante Cat'rinette!' he called up to her.

She turned to the railing just as she was, in her bare arms and neck that gleamed ebony-like against the unbleached cotton of her chemise. A coarse skirt was fastened about her waist, and a string of many-coloured beads knotted around her throat. She held her smoking pipe between her yellow teeth.

'How you all come on, Miché Eusèbe?' she questioned, pleasantly.

'We all middlin', Tante Cat'rinette. But Miss Kitty, she putty bad off out yon'a. I see Mista Raymond dis mo'nin' w'en I pass by his house; he say look like de feva don' wan' to quit 'er. She been axen' fo' you all t'rough de night. He 'low he reckon I betta tell you. Nice wedda we got fo' plantin', Tante Cat'rinette.'

'Nice wedda fo' lies, Miché Eusèbe,' and she spat contemptuously down upon the banquette. She turned away without noticing the man further, and proceeded to hang one of Lawyer Paxton's fine linen shirts upon the line.

'She been axen' fo' you all t'rough de night.'

Somehow Tante Cat'rinette could not get that refrain out of her head. She would not willingly believe that Eusèbe had spoken the truth, but – 'She been axen fo' you all t'rough de night – all t'rough de night.' The words kept ringing in her ears, as she came and went about her daily tasks. But by degrees she dismissed Eusèbe and his message from her mind. It was Miss Kitty's voice that she could hear in fancy following her, calling out through the night, 'W'ere Tante Cat'rinette? W'y Tante Cat'rinette don' come? W'y she don' come – w'y she don' come?'

All day the woman muttered and mumbled to herself in her Creole patois; invoking council of 'Vieumaite', as she always did in her troubles. Tante Cat'rinette's religion was peculiarly her own; she turned to heaven with her grievances, it is true, but she felt that there was no one in Paradise with whom she was quite so well acquainted as with 'Vieumaite'.

Late in the afternoon she went and stood on her doorstep, and looked uneasily and anxiously out upon the almost deserted street. When a little girl came walking by – a sweet child with a frank and innocent face, upon whose word she knew she could rely – Tante Cat'rinette invited her to enter.

'Come yere see Tante Cat'rinette, Lolo. It's long time you en't come see Tante Cat'rine; you gittin' proud.' She made the little one sit down, and offered her a couple of cookies, which the child accepted with pretty avidity.

'You putty good li'le gal, you, Lolo. You keep on go confession all de time?'

'Oh, yes. I'm goin' make my firs' communion firs' of May, Tante Cat'rinette.' A dog-eared catechism was sticking out of Lolo's apron pocket.

'Des right; be good li'le gal. Mine yo' maman ev't'ing she say; an' neva tell no story. It's nuttin' bad in dis worl' like tellin' lies. You know Eusèbe?'

'Eusèbe?'

'Yes; dat li'le ole Red River free m'latto. Uh, uh! dat one man w'at kin tell lies, yas! He come tell me Miss Kitty down sick yon'a. You ev' yeard such big story like dat, Lolo?'

The child looked a little bewildered, but she answered promptly, ' 'Tain't no story, Tante Cat'rinette. I yeard papa sayin', dinner time, Mr Raymond sen' fo' Dr Chalon. An' Dr Chalon says he ain't got time to go yonda. An' papa says it's because Dr Chalon on'y want to go w'ere it's rich people; an' he's 'fraid Mista Raymond ain' goin' pay 'im.'

Tante Cat'rinette admired the little girl's pretty gingham dress, and asked her who had ironed it. She stroked her brown curls, and talked of all manner of things quite foreign to the subject of Eusèbe and his wicked propensity for telling lies.

She was not restless as she had been during the early part of the day, and she no longer mumbled and muttered as she had been doing over her work.

At night she lighted her coal-oil lamp, and placed it near a window where its light could be seen from the street through the half-closed shutters. Then she sat herself down, erect and motionless, in a chair.

When it was near upon midnight, Tante Cat'rinette arose, and looked cautiously, very cautiously, out of the door. Her house lay in the line of deep shadow that extended along the street. The other side was bathed in the pale light of the declining moon. The night was agreeably mild, profoundly still, but pregnant with the subtle quivering life of early spring. The earth seemed asleep and breathing – a scent-laden breath that blew in soft puffs against Tante Cat'rinette's face as she emerged from the house. She closed and locked her door noiselessly; then she crept slowly away, treading softly, stealthily as a cat, in the deep shadow.

There were but few people abroad at that hour. Once she ran upon a gay party of ladies and gentlemen who had been spending the evening over cards and anisette.[357] They did not notice Tante Cat'rinette almost effacing herself against the black wall of the cathedral. She breathed freely and ventured from her retreat only when they had disappeared from view. Once a man saw her quite plainly, as she darted across a narrow strip of moonlight. But Tante Cat'rinette need not have gasped with fright as she did. He was too drunk to know if she were a thing of flesh, or only one of the fantastic, maddening shadows that the moon was casting across his path to bewilder him. When she reached the outskirts of the town, and had to cross the broad piece of open country which stretched out towards the pine wood, an almost paralysing terror came over her. But she crouched low, and hurried through the marsh and weeds, avoiding the open road. She could have been mistaken for one of the beasts browsing there where she passed.

But once in the Grand Ecore road that lay through the pine wood, she felt secure and free to move as she pleased. Tante Cat'rinette straightened herself, stiffened herself in fact, and unconsciously assuming the attitude of the professional sprinter, she sped rapidly beneath the Gothic interlacing branches of the pines. She talked constantly to herself as she went, and to the animate and inanimate objects around her. But her speech, far from intelligent, was hardly intelligible.

She addressed herself to the moon, which she apostrophised as an impertinent busybody spying upon her actions. She pictured all manner of troublesome animals, snakes, rabbits, frogs, pursuing her, but she defied them to catch Cat'rinette, who was hurrying towards Miss Kitty. *'Pa capab trapé Cat'rinette, vouzot; mo pé couri vite coté Miss Kitty.'* She called up to a mockingbird warbling upon a lofty limb of a pine tree, asking why it cried out so, and threatening to secure it and put it into a cage. *'Ca to pé crié comme ça, ti céléra? Arete, mo trapé zozos la, mo mété li den ain bon lacage.'* Indeed, Tante Cat'rinette seemed on very familiar terms with the night, with the forest, and with all the flying, creeping, crawling things that inhabit it. At the speed with which she travelled she soon had covered the few miles of wooded road, and before long had reached her destination.

The sleeping-room of Miss Kitty opened upon the long outside gallery, as did all the rooms of the unpretentious frame house which was her home. The place could hardly be called a plantation; it was too small for that. Nevertheless Raymond was trying to plant; trying to teach school between times, in the end room; and sometimes, when he found himself in a tight place, trying to clerk for Mr Jacobs over in Campte, across Red River.

Tante Cat'rinette mounted the creaking steps, crossed the gallery, and entered Miss Kitty's room as though she were returning to it after a few moments' absence. There was a lamp burning dimly upon the high mantelpiece. Raymond had evidently not been to bed; he was in shirt sleeves, rocking the baby's cradle. It was the same mahogany cradle which had held Miss Kitty thirty-five years before, when Tante Cat'rinette had rocked it. The cradle had been bought then to match the bed – the big, beautiful bed on which Miss Kitty lay now in a restless half slumber. There was a fine French clock on the mantel, still telling the hours as it had told them years ago. But there was no carpets or rugs on the floors. There was no servant in the house.

Raymond uttered an exclamation of amazement when he saw Tante Cat'rinette enter.

'How you do, Miché Raymond?' she said, quietly, 'I yeard Miss Kitty been sick; Eusèbe tell me dat dis mo'nin'.'

She moved towards the bed as lightly as though shod with velvet, and seated herself there. Miss Kitty's hand lay outside the coverlet; a shapely hand, which her few days of illness and rest had not yet softened. The negress laid her own black hand upon it. At the touch Miss Kitty instinctively turned her palm upward.

'It's Tante Cat'rinette!' she exclaimed, with a note of satisfaction in her feeble voice. 'W'en did you come, Tante Cat'rinette? They all said you wouldn' come.'

'I'm goin' come ev'y night, *cher coeur*,[358] ev'y night tell you be well. Tante Cat'rinette can't come daytime no mo'.'

'Raymond tole me about it. They doin' you mighty mean in town, Tante Cat'rinette.'

'Nev' mine, *ti chou*.[359] I know how take care dat w'at Vieumaite gi' me. You go sleep now. Cat'rinette goin' set yere an' mine you. She goin' to make you well like she all time do. We don' wan' no *céléra*[360] doctor. We drive 'em out wid a stick, day come roun' yere.

Miss Kitty was soon sleeping more restfully than she had done since her illness began. Raymond had finally succeeded in quieting the baby, and he tiptoed into the adjoining room, where the other children lay, to snatch a few hours of much-needed rest for himself. Cat'rinette sat faithfully beside her charge, administering at intervals to the sick woman's wants.

But the thought of regaining her home before daybreak, and of the urgent necessity of doing so, did not leave Tante Cat'rinette's mind for an instant.

In the profound darkness, the deep stillness of the night that comes before dawn, she was walking again through the woods, on her way back to town.

The mockingbirds were asleep, and so were the frogs and the snakes; and the moon was gone, and so was the breeze. She walked now in utter silence but for the heavy guttural breathing that accompanied her rapid footsteps. She walked with a desperate determination along the road, every foot of which was familiar to her.

When she at last emerged from the woods, the earth about her was faintly, very faintly, beginning to reveal itself in the tremulous, grey, uncertain light of approaching day. She staggered and plunged onward with beating pulses quickened by fear.

A sudden turn, and Tante Cat'rinette stood facing the river. She stopped abruptly, as if at command of some unseen power that forced her. For an instant she pressed a black hand against her tired, burning eyes, and stared fixedly ahead of her.

Tante Cat'rinette had always believed that Paradise was up there overhead where the sun and stars and moon are, and that 'Vieumaite' inhabited that region of splendour. She never for a moment doubted this. It would be difficult, perhaps unsatisfying, to explain why Tante Cat'rinette, on that particular morning, when a vision of the rising day broke suddenly upon her, should have believed that she stood in face of a heavenly revelation. But why not, after all? Since she talked so familiarly herself to the unseen, why should it not respond to her when the time came?

Across the narrow, quivering line of water, the delicate budding branches of young trees were limned black against the gold, orange – what word is there to tell the colour of that morning sky! And steeped in the splendour of it hung one pale star; there was not another in the whole heaven.

Tante Cat'rinette stood with her eyes fixed intently upon that star, which held her like a hypnotic spell.

She stammered breathlessly: '*Mo pé couté, Vieumaite. Cat'rinette pé couté.*' [I am listening, Vieumaite. Cat'rinette hears you.]

She stayed there motionless upon the brink of the river till the star melted into the brightness of the day and became part of it.

When Tante Cat'rinette entered Miss Kitty's room for the second time, the aspect of things had changed somewhat. Miss Kitty was with much difficulty holding the baby while Raymond mixed a saucer of food for the little one. Their oldest daughter, a child of twelve, had come into the room with an apronful of chips from the woodpile, and was striving to start a fire on the hearth, to make the morning coffee. The room seemed bare and almost squalid in the daylight.

'Well, yere Tante Cat'rinette come back,' she said, quietly announcing herself.

They could not well understand why she was back; but it was good to have her there, and they did not question.

She took the baby from its mother, and, seating herself, began to feed it from the saucer which Raymond placed beside her on a chair.

'Yas,' she said, 'Cat'rinette goin' stay; dis time she en't nev' goin' 'way no mo'.'

Husband and wife looked at each other with surprised, questioning eyes.

'Miché Raymond,' remarked the woman, turning her head up to him with a certain comical shrewdness in her glance, 'if somebody want len' you t'ousan' dolla', w'at you goin' say? Even if it's ole nigga 'oman?'

The man's face flushed with sudden emotion. 'I would say that person was our bes' frien', Tante Cat'rinette. An',' he added, with a smile, 'I would give her a mortgage on the place, of co'se, to secu' her f'om loss.'

'Des right,' agreed the woman practically.

'Den Cat'rinette goin' len' you t'ousan' dolla'. Dat w'at Vieumaite give her, dat b'long to her; don' b'long to nobody else. An' we go yon'a to town, Miché Raymond, you an' me. You care me befo' Miché Paxtone. I want 'im fo' put down in writin' befo' de cote dat w'at Cat'rinette got, it fo' Miss Kitty w'en I be dead.'

Miss Kitty was crying softly in the depths of her pillow.

'I en't got no head fo' all dat, me,' laughed Tante Cat'rinette, good humouredly, as she held a spoonful of pap up to the baby's eager lips. 'It's Vieumaite tell me all dat clair an' plain dis mo'nin', w'en I comin' 'long de Gran' Eco' road.'

A Respectable Woman

Mrs Baroda was a little provoked to learn that her husband expected his friend, Gouvernail,[361] up to spend a week or two on the plantation.

They had entertained a good deal during the winter; much of the time had also been passed in New Orleans in various forms of mild dissipation. She was looking forward to a period of unbroken rest, now, and undisturbed tête-à-tête with her husband, when he informed her that Gouvernail was coming up to stay a week or two.

This was a man she had heard much of but never seen. He had been her husband's college friend; was now a journalist, and in no sense a society man or 'a man about town', which were, perhaps, some of the reasons she had never met him. But she had unconsciously formed an image of him in her mind. She pictured him tall, slim, cynical; with eye-glasses, and his hands in his pockets; and she did not like him. Gouvernail was slim enough, but he wasn't very tall nor very cynical; neither did he wear eye-glasses nor carry his hands in his pockets. And she rather liked him when he first presented himself.

But why she liked him she could not explain satisfactorily to herself when she partly attempted to do so. She could discover in him none of those brilliant and promising traits which Gaston, her husband, had often assured her that he possessed. On the contrary, he sat rather mute and receptive before her chatty eagerness to make him feel at home and in face of Gaston's frank and wordy hospitality. His manner was as courteous towards her as the most exacting woman could require; but he made no direct appeal to her approval or even esteem.

Once settled at the plantation he seemed to like to sit upon the wide portico in the shade of one of the big Corinthian pillars, smoking his cigar lazily and listening attentively to Gaston's experience as a sugar planter.

'This is what I call living,' he would utter with deep satisfaction, as the air that swept across the sugar field caressed him with its warm and scented velvety touch. It pleased him also to get on familiar terms with the big dogs that came about him, rubbing themselves sociably against his legs. He did not care to fish, and displayed no eagerness to go out and kill grosbecs when Gaston proposed doing so.

Gouvernail's personality puzzled Mrs Baroda, but she liked him.

Indeed, he was a lovable, inoffensive fellow. After a few days, when she could understand him no better than at first, she gave over being puzzled and remained piqued. In this mood she left her husband and her guest, for the most part, alone together. Then finding that Gouvernail took no manner of exception to her action, she imposed her society upon him, accompanying him in his idle strolls to the mill and walks along the batture.[362] She persistently sought to penetrate the reserve in which he had unconsciously enveloped himself.

'When is he going – your friend?' she one day asked her husband. 'For my part, he tires me frightfully.'

'Not for a week yet, dear. I can't understand; he gives you no trouble.'

'No. I should like him better if he did; if he were more like others, and I had to plan somewhat for his comfort and enjoyment.'

Gaston took his wife's pretty face between his hands and looked tenderly and laughingly into her troubled eyes. They were making a bit of toilet sociably together in Mrs Baroda's dressing-room.

'You are full of surprises, *ma belle*,' he said to her. 'Even I can never count upon how you are going to act under given conditions.' He kissed her and turned to fasten his cravat before the mirror.

'Here you are,' he went on, 'taking poor Gouvernail seriously and making a commotion over him, the last thing he would desire or expect.'

'Commotion!' she hotly resented. 'Nonsense! How can you say such a thing? Commotion, indeed! But, you know, you said he was clever.'

'So he is. But the poor fellow is run down by overwork now. That's why I asked him here to take a rest.'

You used to say he was a man of ideas,' she retorted unconciliated. 'I expected him to be interesting, at least. I'm going to the city in the morning to have my spring gowns fitted. Let me know when Mr Gouvernail is gone; I shall be at my Aunt Octavie's.'

That night she went and sat alone upon a bench that stood beneath a live-oak tree at the edge of the gravel walk.

She had never known her thoughts or her intentions to be so confused. She could gather nothing from them but the feeling of a distinct necessity to quit her home in the morning.

Mrs Baroda heard footsteps crunching the gravel; but could discern in the darkness only the approaching red point of a lighted cigar. She knew it was Gouvernail, for her husband did not smoke. She hoped to remain unnoticed, but her white gown revealed her to him. He threw away his cigar and seated himself upon the bench beside her; without a suspicion that she might object to his presence.

'Your husband told me to bring this to you, Mrs Baroda,' he said, handing her a filmy white scarf with which she sometimes enveloped her head and shoulders. She accepted the scarf from him with a murmur of thanks, and let it lie in her lap.

He made some commonplace observation upon the baneful effect of the night air at that season. Then, as his gaze reached out into the darkness, he murmured, half to himself:

'Night of south winds – night of the large few stars!
Still nodding night – '363

She made no reply to this apostrophe to the night, which indeed, was not addressed to her.

Gouvernail was in no sense a diffident man, for he was not a self-conscious one. His periods of reserve were not constitutional, but the result of moods. Sitting there beside Mrs Baroda, his silence melted for the time.

He talked freely and intimately in a low, hesitating drawl that was not unpleasant to hear. He talked of the old college days when he and Gaston had been a good deal to each other; of the days of keen and blind ambitions and large intentions. Now there was left with him, at least, a philosophic acquiescence to the existing order – only a desire to be permitted to exist, with now and then a little whiff of genuine life, such as he was breathing now.

Her mind only vaguely grasped what he was saying. Her physical being was for the moment predominant. She was not thinking of his words, only drinking in the tones of his voice. She wanted to reach out her hand in the darkness and touch him with the sensitive tips of her fingers upon the face or the lips. She wanted to draw close to him and whisper against his cheek – she did not care what – as she might have done if she had not been a respectable woman.

The stronger the impulse grew to bring herself near him, the farther, in fact, did she draw away from him. As soon as she could so do without an appearance of too great rudeness, she rose and left him there alone.

Before she reached the house, Gouvernail had lighted a fresh cigar and ended his apostrophe to the night.

Mrs Baroda was greatly tempted that night to tell her husband – who was also her friend – of this folly that had seized her. But she did not yield to the temptation. Beside being a respectable woman she was a very sensible one; and she knew there are some battles in life which a human being must fight alone.

When Gaston arose in the morning, his wife had already departed.

She had taken an early-morning train to the city. She did not return till Gouvernail was gone from under her roof.

There was some talk of having him back during the summer that followed. That is, Gaston greatly desired it; but this desire yielded to his wife's strenuous opposition.

However, before the year ended, she proposed, wholly from herself, to have Gouvernail visit them again. Her husband was surprised and delighted with the suggestion coming from her.

'I am glad, *chère amie*, to know that you have finally overcome your dislike for him; truly he did not deserve it.'

'Oh,' she told him, laughingly, after pressing a long, tender kiss upon his lips, 'I have overcome everything! you will see. This time I shall be very nice to him.'

Ripe Figs

Maman-Nainaine said that when the figs were ripe Babette might go to visit her cousins down on Bayou-Boeuf, where the sugar cane grows. Not that the ripening of figs had the least thing to do with it, but that is the way Maman-Nainaine was.

It seemed to Babette a very long time to wait; for the leaves upon the trees were tender yet, and the figs were like little hard, green marbles.

But warm rains came along and plenty of strong sunshine; and though Maman-Nainaine was as patient as the statue of la Madone,[364] and Babette as restless as a hummingbird, the first thing they both knew it was hot summertime. Every day Babette danced out to where the fig trees were in a long line against the fence. She walked slowly beneath them, carefully peering between the gnarled, spreading branches. But each time she came disconsolate away again. What she saw there finally was something that made her sing and dance the whole day long.

When Maman-Nainaine sat down in her stately way to breakfast, the following morning, her muslin cap standing like an aureole about her white, placid face, Babette approached. She bore a dainty porcelain platter, which she set down before her godmother. It contained a dozen purple figs, fringed around with their rich, green leaves.

'Ah,' said Maman-Nainaine, arching her eyebrows, 'how early the figs have ripened this year!'

'Oh,' said Babette, 'I think they have ripened very late.'

'Babette,' continued Maman-Nainaine, as she peeled the very plumpest figs with her pointed silver fruit-knife, 'you will carry my love to them all down on Bayou-Boeuf. And tell your Tante Frosine I shall look for her at Toussaint[365] – when the chrysanthemums are in bloom.'

Ozème's Holiday

Ozème often wondered why there was not a special dispensation of providence to do away with the necessity for work. There seemed to him so much created for man's enjoyment in this world, and so little time and opportunity to profit by it. To sit and do nothing but breathe was a pleasure to Ozème; but to sit in the company of a few choice companions, including a sprinkling of ladies, was even a greater delight; and the joy which a day's hunting or fishing or picnicking afforded him is hardly to be described. Yet he was by no means indolent. He worked faithfully on the plantation the whole year long, in a sort of methodical way; but when the time came around for his annual week's holiday, there was no holding him back. It was often decidedly inconvenient for the planter that Ozème usually chose to take his holiday during some very busy season of the year.

He started out one morning in the beginning of October. He had borrowed Mr Laballière's[366] buckboard and Padue's old grey mare, and a harness from the negro Sevérin. He wore a light blue suit which had been sent all the way from St Louis, and which had cost him ten dollars; he had paid almost as much again for his boots; and his hat was a broad-rimmed grey felt which he had no cause to be ashamed of. When Ozème went 'broading', he dressed – well, regardless of cost. His eyes were blue and mild; his hair was light, and he wore it rather long; he was clean shaven, and really did not look his thirty-five years.

Ozème had laid his plans weeks beforehand. He was going visiting along Cane River; the mere contemplation filled him with pleasure. He counted upon reaching the Fédeaus' about noon, and he would stop and dine there. Perhaps they would ask him to stay all night. He really did not hold to staying all night, and was not decided to accept if they did ask him. There were only the two old people, and he rather fancied the notion of pushing on to the Beltrans', where he would stay a night, or even two, if urged. He was quite sure that there would be something agreeable going on at the Beltrans', with all those young people – perhaps a fish-fry, or possibly a ball!

Of course he would have to give a day to Tante Sophie and another to Cousine Victoire; but none to the St Annes unless entreated – after St Anne reproaching him last year with being a *fainéant*[367] for broading at such a season! At Cloutierville, where he would linger as long as possible, he meant to turn and retrace his course, zigzagging back and forth across Cane River so as to take in the Duplans,[368] the Velcours, and others that he could not at the moment recall. A week seemed to Ozème a very, very little while in which to crowd so much pleasure.

There were steam-gins at work; he could hear them whistling far and near. On both sides of the river the fields were white with cotton, and everybody in the world seemed busy but Ozème. This reflection did not distress or disturb him in the least; he pursued his way at peace with himself and his surroundings.

At Lamérie's crossroads store, where he stopped to buy a cigar, he learned that there was no use heading for the Fédeaus', as the two old people had gone to town for a lengthy visit, and the house was locked up. It was at the Fédeaus' that Ozème had intended to dine.

He sat in the buckboard,[369] given up to a moment or two of reflection. The result was that he turned away from the river, and entered the road that led between two fields back to the woods and into the heart of the country. He had determined upon taking a short cut to the Beltrans' plantation, and on the way he meant to keep an eye open for old Aunt Tildy's cabin, which he knew lay in some remote part of this cut-off. He remembered that Aunt Tildy could cook an excellent meal if she had the material at hand. He would induce her to fry him a chicken, drip a cup of coffee, and turn him out a pone of corn bread,[370] which he thought would be sumptuous enough fare for the occasion.

Aunt Tildy dwelt in the not unusual log cabin, of one room, with its chimney of mud and stone, and its shallow gallery formed by the jutting of the roof. In close proximity to the cabin was a small cotton-field, which from a long distance looked like a field of snow. The cotton was bursting and overflowing foam-like from bolls on the drying stalk. On the lower branches it was hanging ragged and tattered, and much of it had already fallen to the ground. There were a few chinaberry trees in the yard before the hut, and under one of them an ancient and rusty-looking mule was eating corn from a wood trough. Some common little Creole chickens were scratching about the mule's feet and snatching at the grains of corn that occasionally fell from the trough.

Aunt Tildy was hobbling across the yard when Ozème drew up before the gate. One hand was confined in a sling; in the other she carried a tin pan, which she let fall noisily to the ground when she recognised him. She was broad, black and misshapen, with her body lent forward almost at an acute angle. She wore a blue cottonade of large plaids, and a bandana awkwardly twisted around her head.

'Good God A'mighty, man! Whar you come from?' was her startled exclamation at beholding him.

'F'om home, Aunt Tildy; w'ere else do you expec'?' replied Ozème, dismounting composedly.

He had not seen the old woman for several years – since she was cooking in town for the family with which he boarded at the time. She had washed and ironed for him, atrociously, it is true, but her intentions were beyond reproach if her washing was not. She had also been clumsily attentive to him during a spell of illness. He had paid her with an occasional bandana, a calico dress or a checked apron, and they had always considered the account between themselves square, with no sentimental feeling of gratitude remaining on either side.

'I like to know,' remarked Ozème, as he took the grey mare from the shafts, and led her up to the trough where the mule was – 'I like to know w'at you mean by makin' a crop like that an' then lettin' it go to was'e? Who you reckon's goin' to pick that cotton? You think maybe the angels goin' to come down an' pick it to' you, an' gin it an' press it, an' then give you ten cents a poun' fo' it, *hein*?'

'Ef de Lord don' pick it, I don' know who gwine pick it, Mista Ozème. I tell you, me an' Sandy we wuk dat crap day in an' day out; it's him done de mos' of it.'

'Sandy? That little – '

'He ain' dat li'le Sandy no mo' w'at you rec'lec's; he 'mos' a man, an' he wuk like a man now. He wuk mo' 'an fittin' fo' his strenk, an' now he layin' in dah sick – God A'mighty knows how sick. An' me wid a risin' twell I bleeged to walk de flo' o' nights, an' don' know ef I ain' gwine to lose de han' after all.'

'W'y, in the name o' conscience, you don' hire somebody to pick?'

'Whar I got money to hire? An' you knows well as me ev'y chick an' chile is pickin' roun' on de plantations an' gittin' good pay.'

The whole outlook appeared to Ozème very depressing, and even menacing, to his personal comfort and peace of mind. He foresaw no prospect of dinner unless he should cook it himself. And there was that Sandy – he remembered well the little scamp of eight, always at his grandmother's heels when she was cooking or washing. Of course he would have to go in and look at the boy, and no doubt dive into his travelling-bag for quinine, without which he never travelled.

Sandy was indeed very ill, consumed with fever. He lay on a cot covered up with a faded patchwork quilt. His eyes were half closed, and he was muttering and rambling on about hoeing and bedding and cleaning and thinning out the cotton; he was hauling it to the gin, wrangling about weight and bagging and ties and the price offered per pound. That bale or two of cotton had not only sent Sandy to bed, but had pursued him there, holding him through his fevered dreams, and threatening to end him. Ozème would never have known the black boy, he was so tall, so thin, and seemingly so wasted, lying there in bed.

'See yere, Aunt Tildy,' said Ozème, after he had, as was usual with him when in doubt, abandoned himself to a little reflection; 'between us – you an' me – we got to manage to kill an' cook one o' those chickens I see scratchin' out yonda, fo' I'm jus' about starved. I reckon you ain't got any quinine in the house? No; I didn't suppose an instant you had. Well, I'm goin' to give Sandy a good dose o' quinine tonight, an' I'm goin' stay an' see how that'll work on 'im. But sun-up, min' you, I mus' get out o' yere.'

Ozème had spent more comfortable nights than the one passed in Aunt Tildy's bed, which she considerately abandoned to him.

In the morning Sandy's fever was somewhat abated, but had not taken a decided enough turn to justify Ozème in quitting him before noon, unless he was willing 'to feel like a dog', as he told himself. He appeared before Aunt Tildy stripped to the undershirt, and wearing his second-best pair of trousers.

'That's a nice pickle o' fish you got me in, ol' woman. I guarantee, nex' time I go abroad, 'tain't me that'll take any cut-off. W'ere's that cotton-basket an' cotton-sack o' yo's?'

'I knowed it!' chanted Aunt Tildy – 'I knowed de Lord war gwine sen' somebody to holp me out. He warn' gwine let de crap was'e atter he give Sandy an' me de strenk to make hit. De Lord gwine shove you 'long de row, Mista Ozème. De Lord gwine give you plenty mo' fingers an' han's to pick dat cotton nimble an' clean.'

'Neva you min' w'at the Lord's goin' to do; go get me that cotton-sack. An' you put that poultice like I tol' you on yo' han', an' set down there an' watch Sandy. It looks like you are 'bout as helpless as a' ol' cow tangled up in a potato-vine.'

Ozème had not picked cotton for many years, and he took to it a little awkwardly at first; but by the time he had reached the end of the first row the old dexterity of youth had come back to his hands, which flew rapidly back and forth with the motion of a weaver's shuttle; and his ten fingers became really nimble in clutching the cotton from its dry shell. By noon he had gathered about fifty pounds. Sandy was not then quite so well as he had promised to be, and Ozème concluded to stay that day and one more night. If the boy were no better in the morning, he would go off in search of a doctor for him, and he himself would continue on down to Tante Sophie's; the Beltrans' was out of the question now.

Sandy hardly needed a doctor in the morning. Ozème's doctoring was beginning to tell favourably; but he would have considered it criminal indifference and negligence to go away and leave the boy to Aunt Tildy's awkward ministrations just at the critical moment when there was a turn for the better; so he stayed that day out, and picked his hundred and fifty pounds.

On the third day it looked like rain, and a heavy rain just then would mean a heavy loss to Aunt Tildy and Sandy, and Ozème again went to the field, this time urging Aunt Tildy with him to do what she might with her one good hand.

'Aunt Tildy,' called out Ozème to the bent old woman moving ahead of him between the white rows of cotton, 'if the Lord gets me safe out o' this ditch, 't ain't tomorro' I'll fall in anotha with my eyes open, I bet you.'

'Keep along, Mista Ozème; don' grumble, don' stumble; de Lord's a-watchin' you. Look at yo' Aunt Tildy; she doin' mo' wid her one han' 'an you doin' wid yo' two, man. Keep right along, honey. Watch dat cotton how it fallin' in yo' Aunt Tildy's bag.'

'I am watchin' you, ol' woman; you don' fool me. You got to work that han' o' yo's spryer than you doin', or I'll take the rawhide. You done fo'got w'at the rawhide tas'e like, I reckon – ' a reminder which amused Aunt Tildy so powerfully that her big negro-laugh resounded over the whole cotton-patch, and even caused Sandy, who heard it, to turn in his bed.

The weather was still threatening on the succeeding day, and a sort of dogged determination or characteristic desire to see his undertakings carried to a satisfactory completion urged Ozème to continue his efforts to drag Aunt Tildy out of the mire into which circumstances seemed to have thrust her.

One night the rain did come, and began to beat softly on the roof of the old cabin. Sandy opened his eyes, which were no longer brilliant with the fever flame. 'Granny,' he whispered, 'de rain! Des listen, granny; de rain a-comin', an' I ain' pick dat cotton yit. W'at time it is? Gi' me my pants – I got to go – '

'You lay whar you is, chile alive. Dat cotton put aside clean and dry. Me an' de Lord an' Mista Ozème done pick dat cotton.'

Ozème drove away in the morning looking quite as spick and span as the day he left home in his blue suit and his light felt drawn a little over his eyes.

'You want to take care o' that boy,' he instructed Aunt Tildy at parting, 'an' get 'im on his feet. An', let me tell you, the nex' time I start out to broad, if you see me passin' in this yere cut-off, put on yo' specs an' look at me good, because it won't be me; it'll be my ghos', ol' woman.'

Indeed, Ozème, for some reason or other, felt quite shame-faced as he drove back to the plantation. When he emerged from the lane which he had entered the week before, and turned into the river road, Lamérie, standing in the store door, shouted out: 'He, Ozème! you had good times yonda? I bet you danced holes in the sole of them new boots.'

'Don't talk, Lamérie!' was Ozème's rather ambiguous reply, as he flourished the remainder of a whip over the old grey mare's sway-back, urging her to a gentle trot.

When he reached home, Bode, one of Padue's boys, who was assisting him to unhitch, remarked: 'How come you didn' go yonda down de coas' like you said, Mista Ozème? Nobody didn' see you in Cloutierville, an' Mailitt say you neva cross' de twenty-fo'-mile ferry, an' nobody didn' see you no place.'

Ozème returned, after his customary moment of reflection: 'You see, it's 'mos' always the same thing on Cane Riva, my boy; a man gets tired o' that *à la fin*.[371] This time I went back in the woods, 'way yonda in the Fédeau cut-off; kin' o' campin' an' roughin' like, you might say. I tell you, it was sport, Bode.'

Wiser Than a God

To love and be wise is scarcely granted even to a god.[372]

Latin proverb

'You might at least show some distaste for the task, Paula,' said Mrs Von Stoltz, in her querulous invalid voice, to her daughter who stood before the glass bestowing a few final touches of embellishment upon an otherwise plain toilet.

'And to what purpose, *Mutterchen*?[373] The task is not entirely to my liking, I'll admit; but there can be no question as to its results, which you even must concede are gratifying.'

'Well, it's not the career your poor father had in view for you. How often he has told me when I complained that you were kept too closely at work, "I want that Paula shall be at the head," ' with an appealing look through the window and up into the grey November sky, into that far 'somewhere' which might be the abode of her departed husband.

'It isn't a career at all, mamma; it's only a makeshift,' answered the girl, noting the happy effect of an amber pin that she had thrust through the coils of her lustrous yellow hair. 'The pot must be kept boiling at all hazards, pending the appearance of that hoped-for career. And you forget that an occasion like this gives me the very opportunities I want.'

'I can't see the advantages of bringing your talent down to such banal servitude. Who are those people, anyway?'

The mother's question ended in a cough which shook her into speechless exhaustion.

'Ah! I have let you sit too long by the window, mother,' said Paula, hastening to wheel the invalid's chair nearer the grate fire that was throwing genial light and warmth into the room, turning its plainness to beauty as by a touch of enchantment. 'By the way,' she added, having arranged her mother as comfortably as might be, 'I haven't yet qualified for that "banal servitude", as you call it.' And approaching the piano which stood in a distant alcove of the room, she took up a roll of music that lay curled up on the instrument and straightened it out before her. Then, seeming to remember the question which her mother had asked, turned on the stool to answer it. 'Don't you know? The Brainards, very swell people, and awfully rich. The daughter is that girl whom I once told you about, how she went to the Conservatory to cultivate her voice and old Engfelder told her in his brusque way to go back home, that his system was not equal to overcoming impossibilities.'

'Oh, those people.'

'Yes; this little party is given in honour of the son's return from Yale or Harvard, or some place or other.' And turning to the piano she softly ran over the dances, while the mother gazed into the fire with unresigned sadness, which the bright music seemed to deepen.

'Well, there'll be no trouble about *that*,' said Paula, with comfortable assurance, having ended the last waltz. 'There's nothing here to tempt me into flights of originality; there'll be no difficulty in keeping to the hand-organ effect.'

'Don't leave me with those dreadful impressions, Paula; my poor nerves are on edge.'

'You are too hard on the dances, mamma. There are certain strains here and there that I thought not bad.'

'It's your youth that finds it so; I have outlived such illusions.'

'What an inconsistent little mother it is!' the girl exclaimed, laughing. 'You told me only yesterday it was my youth that was so impatient with the commonplace happenings of everyday life. That age, needing to seek its delights, finds them often in unsuspected places, wasn't that it?'

'Don't chatter, Paula; some music, some music!'

'What shall it be?' asked Paula, touching a succession of harmonious chords. 'It must be short.'

'The *Berceuse*,[374] then; Chopin's. But soft, soft and a little slowly as your dear father used to play it.'

Mrs Von Stoltz leaned her head back among the cushions, and with eyes closed, drank in the wonderful strains that came like an ethereal voice out of the past, lulling her spirit into the quiet of sweet memories.

When the last soft notes had melted into silence, Paula approached her mother and looking into the pale face saw that tears stood beneath the closed eyelids. 'Ah! mamma, I have made you unhappy,' she cried, in distress.

'No, my child, you have given me a joy that you don't dream of. I have no more pain. Your music has done for me what Faranelli's[375] singing did for poor King Philip of Spain; it has cured me.'

There was a glow of pleasure on the warm face and the eyes with almost the brightness of health. 'While I listened to you, Paula, my soul went out from me and lived again through an evening long ago. We were in our pretty room at Leipzig. The soft air and the moonlight came through the open-curtained window, making a quivering fretwork

along the gleaming waxed floor. You lay in my arms and I felt again the
pressure of your warm, plump little body against me. Your father was at
the piano playing the *Berceuse*, and all at once you drew my head down
and whispered, "*Ist es nicht wonderschen, mama?*"[376] When it ended, you
were sleeping and your father took you from my arms and laid you
gently in bed.'

Paula knelt beside her mother, holding the frail hands which she
kissed tenderly.

'Now you must go, *liebchen*.[377] Ring for Berta, she will do all that is
needed. I feel very strong tonight. But do not come back too late.'

'I shall be home as early as possible; likely in the last car, I couldn't
stay longer or I should have to walk. You know the house in case there
should be need to send for me?'

'Yes, yes; but there will be no need.'

Paula kissed her mother lovingly and went out into the drear
November night with the roll of dances under her arm.

2

The door of the stately mansion at which Paula rang was opened by a
footman, who invited her to 'kindly walk upstairs'.

'Show the young lady into the music room, James,' called from some
upper region a voice, doubtless the same whose impossibilities had been
so summarily dealt with by Herr Engfelder, and Paula was led through
a suite of handsome apartments, the warmth and mellow light of which
were very grateful, after the chill outdoor air.

Once in the music room, she removed her wraps and seated herself
comfortably to await developments. Before her stood the magnificent
Steinway[378] on which her eyes rested with greedy admiration, and her
fingers twitched with a desire to awaken its inviting possibilities. The
odour of flowers impregnated the air like a subtle intoxicant and over
everything hung a quiet smile of expectancy, disturbed by an occasional
feminine flutter above stairs, or muffled suggestions of distant household sounds.

Presently, a young man entered the drawing-room – no doubt, the
college student, for he looked critically and with an air of proprietorship
at the festive arrangements, venturing the bestowal of a few improving
touches. Then, gazing with pardonable complacency at his own handsome, athletic figure in the mirror, he saw reflected Paula looking at
him, with a demure smile lighting her blue eyes.

'By Jove!' was his startled exclamation. Then, approaching, 'I beg
pardon, Miss – Miss – '

'Von Stoltz.'

'Miss Von Stoltz,' drawing the right conclusion from her simple toilet and the roll of music. 'I hadn't seen you when I came in. Have you been here long? and sitting all alone, too? That's certainly rough.'

'Oh, I've been here but a few moments, and was very well entertained.'

'I dare say,' with a glance full of prognostic complimentary utterances, which a further acquaintance might develop.

As he was lighting the gas of a side bracket, that she might better see to read her music, Mrs Brainard and her daughter came into the room, radiantly attired and both approached Paula with sweet and polite greeting.

'George, in mercy!' exclaimed his mother, 'put out that gas, you are killing the effect of the candlelight.'

'But Miss Von Stoltz can't read her music without it, mother.'

'I've no doubt Miss Von Stoltz knows her pieces by heart,' Mrs Brainard replied, seeking corroboration from Paula's glance.

'No, madame; I'm not accustomed to playing dance music, and this is quite new to me,' the girl rejoined, touching the loose sheets that George had conveniently straightened out and placed on the rack.

'Oh, dear! "not accustomed"?' said Miss Brainard. 'And Mr Sohmeir told us he knew you would give satisfaction.'

Paula hastened to reassure the thoroughly alarmed young lady on the point of her ability to give perfect satisfaction.

The doorbell now began to ring incessantly. Up the stairs, tripped fleeting opera-cloaked figures, followed by their black-robed attendants. The rooms commenced to fill with the pretty hubbub that a bevy of girls can make when inspired by a close masculine proximity; and Paula, not waiting to be asked, struck the opening bars of an inspiring waltz.

Some hours later, during a lull in the dancing, when the men were making vigorous applications of fans and handkerchiefs; and the girls beginning to throw themselves into attitudes of picturesque exhaustion – save for the always indefatigable few – a proposition was ventured, backed by clamourous entreaties, which induced George to bring forth his banjo. And an agreeable moment followed, in which that young man's skill met with a truly deserving applause. Never had his audience beheld such proficiency as he displayed in the handling of his instrument, which was now behind him, now overhead, and again swinging in mid-air like the pendulum of a clock and sending forth the sounds of stirring melody. Sounds so inspiring that a pretty little black-eyed fairy, an acknowledged votary of Terpsichore,[379] and the object of George's particular admiration, was moved to contribute a few passes of a Virginia breakdown, as she had studied it from life on a Southern plantation. The act closed amid a spontaneous babel of hand-clapping and admiring bravos.

It must be admitted that this little episode, however graceful, was hardly a fitting prelude to the magnificent 'Jewel Song' from *Faust*,[380] with which Miss Brainard next consented to regale the company. That Miss Brainard possessed a voice was a fact that had existed as matter of tradition in the family as far back almost as the days of that young lady's baby utterances, in which loving ears had already detected the promise which time had so recklessly fulfilled.

True genius is not to be held in abeyance, though a host of Engfelders would rise to quell it with their mundane protests!

Miss Brainard's rendition was a triumphant achievement of sound, and with the proud flush of success moving her to kind condescension, she asked Miss Von Stoltz to 'please play something'.

Paula amiably consented, choosing a selection from the *Modern Classic*. How little did her auditors appreciate in the performance the results of a life study, of a drilling that had made her among the knowing an acknowledged mistress of technique. But to her skill she added the touch and interpretation of the artist; and in hearing her, even Ignorance paid to her genius the tribute of a silent emotion.

When she arose there was a moment of quiet, which was broken by the black-eyed fairy, always ready to cast herself into a breach, observing, flippantly, 'How pretty!' 'Just lovely!' from another; and, 'What wouldn't I give to play like that.' Each inane compliment fell like a dash of cold water on Paula's ardour.

She then became solicitous about the hour, with reference to her car, and George who stood near looked at his watch and informed her that the last car had gone by a full half-hour before.

'But,' he added, 'if you are not expecting anyone to call for you, I will gladly see you home.'

'I expect no one, for the car that passes here would have set me down at my door,' and in this avowal of difficulties, she tacitly accepted George's offer.

The situation was new. It gave her a feeling of elation to be walking through the quiet night with this handsome young fellow. He talked so freely and so pleasantly. She felt such a comfort in his strong protective nearness. In clinging to him against the buffets of the staggering wind she could feel the muscles of his arms, like steel.

He was so unlike any man of her acquaintance. Strictly unlike Poldorf, the pianist, the short rotundity of whose person could have been less objectionable if she had not known its cause to lie in an inordinate consumption of beer. Old Engfelder, with his long hair, his spectacles and his loose, disjointed figure, was *hors de combat*[381] in comparison. And as for Max Kuntzler, the talented composer, her teacher of harmony, she could at that moment think of no positive point of objection against him, save the vague, general, serious one of his unlikeness to George.

Her new-awakened admiration, though, was not deaf to a little inexplicable wish that he had not been so proficient with the banjo.

On they went chatting gaily, until turning the corner of the street in which she lived, Paula saw that before the door stood Dr Sinn's buggy.

Brainard could feel the quiver of surprised distress that shook her frame, as she said, hurrying along, 'Oh! mamma must be ill – worse, they have called the doctor.'

Reaching the house, she threw open wide the door that was unlocked, and he stood hesitatingly back. The gas in the small hall burned at its full, and showed Berta at the top of the stairs, speechless, with terrified eyes, looking down at her. And coming to meet her was a neighbour, who strove with well-meaning solicitude to keep her back, to hold her yet a moment in ignorance of the cruel blow that fate had dealt her while she had in happy unconsciousness played her music for the dance.

3

Several months had passed since the dreadful night when death had deprived Paula for the second time of a loved parent.

After the first shock of grief was over, the girl had thrown all her energies into work, with the view of attaining that position in the musical world which her father and mother had dreamed might be hers.

She had remained in the small home occupying now but the half of it; and here she kept house with the faithful Berta's aid.

Friends were both kind and attentive to the stricken girl. But there had been two whose constant devotion spoke of an interest deeper than mere friendly solicitude.

Max Kuntzler's love for Paula was something that had taken hold of his sober middle age with an enduring strength which was not to be lessened or shaken by her rejection of it. He had asked leave to remain her friend, and while holding the tender, watchful privileges which that comprehensive title may imply, had refrained from further thrusting a warmer feeling on her acceptance.

Paula one evening was seated in her small sitting-room, working over some musical transpositions, when a ring at the bell was followed by a footstep in the hall which made her hand and heart tremble.

George Brainard entered the room, and before she could rise to greet him, had seated himself in the vacant chair beside her.

'What an untiring worker you are,' he said, glancing down at the scores before her. 'I always feel that my presence interrupts you; and yet I don't know that a judicious interruption isn't the wholesomest thing for you sometimes.'

'You forget,' she said, smiling into his face, 'that I was trained to it. I must keep myself fitted to my calling. Rest would mean deterioration.'

'Would you not be willing to follow some other calling?' he asked, looking at her with unusual earnestness in his dark, handsome eyes.

'Oh, never!'

'Not if it were a calling that asked only for the labour of loving?'

She made no answer, but kept her eyes fixed on the idle traceries that she drew with her pencil on the sheets before her.

He arose and made a few impatient turns about the room, then coming again to her side, said abruptly: 'Paula, I love you. It isn't telling you something that you don't know, unless you have been without bodily perceptions. Today there is something driving me to speak it out in words. Since I have known you,' he continued, striving to look into her face that bent low over the work before her, 'I have been mounting into higher and always higher circles of paradise, under a blessed illusion that you – cared for me. But today, a feeling of dread has been forcing itself upon me – dread that with a word you might throw me back into a gulf that would now be one of everlasting misery. Say if you love me, Paula. I believe you do, and yet I wait with indefinable doubts for your answer.'

He took her hand which she did not withdraw from his. 'Why are you speechless? Why don't you say something to me!' he asked desperately.

'I am speechless with joy and misery,' she answered. 'To know that you love me, gives me happiness enough to brighten a lifetime. And I am miserable, feeling that you have spoken the signal that must part us.'

'You love me, and speak of parting. Never! You will be my wife. From this moment we belong to each other. Oh, my Paula,' he said, drawing her to his side, 'my whole existence will be devoted to your happiness.'

'I can't marry you,' she said shortly, disengaging his hand from her waist.

'Why?' he asked abruptly. They stood looking into each other's eyes.

'Because it doesn't enter into the purpose of my life.'

'I don't ask you to give up anything in your life. I only beg you to let me share it with you.'

George had known Paula only as the daughter of the undemonstrative American woman. He had never before seen her with the father's emotional nature aroused in her. The colour mounted into her cheeks, and her blue eyes were almost black with intensity of feeling.

'Hush,' she said; 'don't tempt me further.' And she cast herself on her knees before the table near which they stood, gathering the music that lay upon it into an armful, and resting her hot cheek upon it.

'What do you know of my life,' she exclaimed passionately. 'What can you guess of it? Is music anything more to you than the pleasing distraction of an idle moment? Can't you feel that with me it courses with the blood through my veins? That it's something dearer than life, than riches, even than love?' with a quiver of pain.

'Paula listen to me; don't speak like a madwoman.'

She sprang up and held out an arm to ward away his nearer approach.

'Would you go into a convent, and ask to be your wife a nun who has vowed herself to the service of God?'

'Yes, if that nun loved me; she would owe to herself, to me and to God to be my wife.'

Paula seated herself on the sofa, all emotion seeming suddenly to have left her; and he came and sat beside her.

'Say only that you love me, Paula,' he urged persistently.

'I love you,' she answered low and with pale lips.

He took her in his arms, holding her in silent rapture against his heart and kissing the white lips back into red life.

'You will be my wife?'

'You must wait. Come back in a week and I will answer you.' He was forced to be content with the delay.

The days of probation being over, George went for his answer, which was given him by the old lady who occupied the upper storey.

'*Ach Gott! Fräulein Von Stoltz ist schon im Leipzig gegangen!*'[382]

All that has not been many years ago. George Brainard is as handsome as ever, though growing a little stout in the quiet routine of domestic life. He has quite lost a pretty taste for music that formerly distinguished him as a skilful banjoist. This loss his little black-eyed wife deplores; though she has herself made concessions to the advancing years, and abandoned Virginia breakdowns as incompatible with the serious offices of wifehood and matrimony.

You may have seen in the morning paper that the renowned pianist, Fräulein Paula Von Stoltz, is resting in Leipzig, after an extended and remunerative concert tour. Professor Max Kuntzler is also in Leipzig – with the ever persistent will, the dogged patience that so often wins in the end.

A Point at Issue!

MARRIED – On Tuesday, May 11, Eleanor Gail to Charles Faraday

Nothing bearing the shape of a wedding announcement could have been less obtrusive than the foregoing hidden in a remote corner of the Plymdale *Promulgator*, clothed in the palest and smallest of type, and modestly wedged in between the big, black-lettered offer of the *Promulgator* to mail itself free of extra charge to subscribers leaving home for the summer months, and an equally sombre-clad notice (doubtless astray as to place and application) that Hammersmith & Co. were carrying a large and varied assortment of marble and granite monuments!

Yet notwithstanding its sandwiched condition, that little marriage announcement seemed to Eleanor to parade the whole street.

Whichever way she turned her eyes, it glowered at her with scornful reproach.

She felt it to be an indelicate thrusting of herself upon the public notice; and at the sight she was plunged in regret at having made to the proprieties the concession of permitting it.

She hoped now that the period for making concessions was ended. She had endured long and patiently the trials that beset her path when she chose to diverge from the beaten walks of female Plymdaledom. Had stood stoically enough the questionable distinction of being relegated to a place amid that large and ill-assorted family of 'cranks', feeling the discomfort and attending opprobrium to be far out-balanced by the satisfying consciousness of roaming the heights of free thought and tasting the sweets of a spiritual emancipation.

The closing act of Eleanor's young ladyhood, when she chose to be married without pre-announcement, without the paraphernalia of accessories so dear to a curious public – had been in keeping with previous methods distinguishing her career. The disappointed public, cheated of its entertainment, was forced to seek such compensation for the loss as was offered in reflections that, while condemning her present, were unsparing of her past and full with damning prognostic of her future.

Charles Faraday, who added to his unembellished title that of Professor of Mathematics of the Plymdale University, had found in Eleanor Gail his ideal woman.

Indeed, she rather surpassed that ideal, which had of necessity been but an adorned picture of woman as he had known her. A mild emphasising of her merits, a soft toning down of her defects had served to offer to his fancy a prototype of that bequoted creature.

'Not too good for human nature's daily food,' yet so good that he had cherished no hope of beholding such a one in the flesh. Until Eleanor had come, supplanting his idea, and making of that fanciful creation a very simpleton by contrast. In the beginning he had found her extremely good to look at, with her combination of graceful womanly charms, unmarred by self-conscious mannerisms that was as rare as it was engaging. Talking with her, he had caught a look from her eyes into his that he recognised at once as a freemasonry of intellect. And the longer he knew her, the greater grew his wonder at the beautiful revelations of her mind that unfurled itself to his, like the curling petals of some hardy blossom that opens to the inviting warmth of the sun. It was not that Eleanor knew many things. According to her own modest estimate of herself, she knew nothing. There were schoolgirls in Plymdale who surpassed her in the amount of their positive knowledge. But she was possessed of a clear intellect: sharp in its reasoning, strong and un-prejudiced in its outlook. She was that *rara avis*,[383] a logical woman – something which Faraday had not encountered in his life before. True, he was not hoary with age. At thirty the types of women he had met with were not legion; but he felt safe in doubting that the hedges of the future would grow logical women for him, more than they had borne such prodigies in the past.

He found Eleanor ready to take broad views of life and humanity; able to grasp a question and anticipate conclusions by a quick intuition which he himself reached by the slower, consecutive steps of reason.

During the months that shaped themselves into the cycle of a year these two dwelt together in the harmony of a united purpose.

Together they went looking for the good things of life, knocking at the closed doors of philosophy; venturing into the open fields of science, she, with uncertain steps, made steady by his help.

Whithersoever he led she followed, oftentimes in her eagerness taking the lead into unfamiliar ways in which he, weighted with a lingering conservatism, had hesitated to venture.

So did they grow in their oneness of thought to belong each so absolutely to the other that the idea seemed not to have come to them that this union might be made faster by marriage. Until one day it broke upon Faraday, like a revelation from the unknown, the possibility of making her his wife.

When he spoke, eager with the new awakened impulse, she laughingly replied: 'Why not?' She had thought of it long ago.

In entering upon their new life they decided to be governed by no precedential methods. Marriage was to be a form that, while fixing legally their relation to each other, was in no wise to touch the individuality of either; that was to be preserved intact. Each was to remain a free integral of humanity, responsible to no dominating exactions of so-called marriage laws. And the element that was to make possible such a union was trust in each other's love, honour, courtesy, tempered by the reserving clause of readiness to meet the consequences of reciprocal liberty.

Faraday appreciated the need of offering to his wife advantages for culture which had been of impossible attainment during her girlhood.

Marriage, which marks too often the closing period of a woman's intellectual existence, was to be in her case the open portal through which she might seek the embellishments that her strong, graceful mentality deserved.

An urgent desire with Eleanor was to acquire a thorough speaking knowledge of the French language. They agreed that a lengthy sojourn in Paris could be the only practical and reliable means of accomplishing such an end.

Faraday's three months of vacation were to be spent by them in the idle happiness of a loitering honeymoon through the continent of Europe, then he would leave his wife in the French capital for a stay that might extend indefinitely – two, three years – as long as should be found needful, he returning to join her with the advent of each summer, to renew their love in a fresh and re-strengthened union.

And so, in May, they were married, and in September we find Eleanor established in the *pension* of the old couple Clairegobeau and comfortably ensconced in her pretty room that opened on to the Rue Rivoli, her heart full of sweet memories that were to cheer her coming solitude.

On the wall, looking always down at her with his quiet, kind glance, hung the portrait of her husband. Beneath it stood the fanciful little desk at which she hoped to spend many happy hours.

Books were everywhere, giving character to the graceful furnishings which their united taste had evolved from the paucity of the Clairegobeau germ, and out of the window was Paris!

Eleanor was supremely satisfied amid her new and attractive

surroundings. The pang of parting from her husband seeming to lend sharp zest to a situation that offered the fulfilment of a cherished purpose.

Faraday, with the stronger man-nature, felt more keenly the discomfort of giving up a companionship that in its brief duration had been replete with the duality of accomplished delight and growing promise.

But to him also was the situation made acceptable by its involving a principle which he felt it incumbent upon him to uphold. He returned to Plymdale and to his duties at the university, and resumed his bachelor existence as quietly as though it had been interrupted but by the interval of a day.

The small public with which he had acquaintance, and which had forgotten his existence during the past few months, was fired anew with indignant astonishment at the effrontery of the situation which his singular coming back offered to their contemplation.

That two young people should presume to introduce such innovations into matrimony!

It was uncalled for!

It was improper!

It was indecent!

He must have already tired of her idiosyncrasies, since he had left her in Paris.

And in Paris, of all places, to leave a young woman alone! Why not at once in Hades![384]

She had been left in Paris forsooth to learn French. And since when was Mme Belaire's French, as it had been taught to select generations of Plymdalions, considered insufficient for the practical needs of existence as related by that foreign tongue?

But Faraday's life was full with occupation and his brief moments of leisure were too precious to give to heeding the idle gossip that floated to his hearing and away again without holding his thoughts an instant.

He lived uninterruptedly a certain existence with his wife through the medium of letters. True, an inadequate substitute for her actual presence, but there was much satisfaction in this constant communion of thought between them.

They told such details of their daily lives as they thought worth the telling.

Their readings were discussed. Opinions exchanged. Newspaper cuttings sent back and forth, bearing upon questions that interested them. And what did not interest them?

Nothing was so large that they dared not look at it. Happenings, small in themselves, but big in their psychological comprehensiveness, held them with strange fascination. Her earnestness and intensity in such matters were extreme; but happily, Faraday brought to this union humorous instincts, and an optimism that saved it from a too monotonous sombreness.

The young man had his friends in Plymdale. Certainly none that ever remotely approached the position which Eleanor held in that regard. She stood pre-eminent. She was himself.

But his nature was genial. He invited companionship from his fellow beings, who, however short that companionship might be, carried always away a gratifying consciousness of having made their personalities felt.

The society in Plymdale which he most frequented was that of the Beatons.

Beaton *père* was a fellow professor, many years older than Faraday, but one of those men with whom time, after putting its customary stamp upon his outward being, took no further care.

The spirit of his youth had remained untouched, and formed the nucleus around which the family gathered, drawing the light of their own cheerfulness.

Mrs Beaton was a woman whose aspirations went not further than the desire for her family's good, and her bearing announced, in its every feature, the satisfaction of completed hopes.

Of the daughters, Margaret, the eldest, was looked upon as slightly erratic, owing to a timid leaning in the direction of Woman's Suffrage.

Her activity in that regard, taking the form of a desultory correspondence with members of a certain society of protest; the fashioning and donning of garments of mysterious shape, which, while stamping their wearer with the distinction of a quasi-emancipation, defeated the ultimate purpose of their construction by inflicting a personal discomfort that extended beyond the powers of long endurance. Miss Kitty Beaton, the youngest daughter, and just returned from boarding-school, while clamouring for no privileges doubtful of attainment and of remote and questionable benefit, with a Napoleonic grip possessed herself of such rights as were at hand and exercised them in keeping the household under her capricious command.

She was at that age of blissful illusion when a girl is in love with her own youth and beauty and happiness. That age which heeds no purpose in the scope of creation further than may touch her majesty's enjoyment. Who would not smilingly endure with that charming selfishness of youth, knowing that the rough hand of experience is inevitably descending to disturb the short-lived dream?

They were all clever people, bright and interesting, and in this family circle Faraday found an acceptable relaxation from work and enforced solitude.

If they ever doubted the wisdom or expediency of his domestic relations, courtesy withheld the expression of any such doubts. Their welcome was always complete in its friendliness, and the interest which they evinced in the absent Eleanor proved that she was held in the highest esteem.

With Beaton Faraday enjoyed that pleasant intercourse which may exist between men whose ways, while not too divergent, are yet divided by an appreciable interval.

But it remained for Kitty to touch him with her girlish charms in a way, which, though not too usual with Faraday, meant so little to the man that he did not take the trouble to resent it.

Her laughter and song, the restless motions of her bubbling happiness, he watched with the casual pleasure with which one follows the playful gambols of a graceful kitten.

He liked the soft shining light of her eyes. When she was near him the velvet smoothness of her pink cheeks stirred him with a feeling that could have found satisfying expression in a kiss.

It is idle to suppose that even the most exemplary men go through life with their eyes closed to woman's beauty and their senses steeled against its charm.

Faraday thought little of this feeling (and so should we if it were not outspoken).

In writing one day to his wife, with the cold-blooded impartiality of choosing a subject which he thought of neither more nor less prominence than the next, he descanted at some length upon the interesting emotions which Miss Kitty's pretty femininity aroused in him.

If he had given serious thought to the expediency of touching upon such a theme with one's wife, he still would not have been deterred. Was not Eleanor's large comprehensiveness far above the littleness of ordinary women?

Did it not enter into the scheme of their lives, to keep free from prejudices that hold their sway over the masses?

But he thought not of that, for, after all, his interest in Kitty and his interest in his university class bore about an equal reference to Eleanor and his love for her.

His letter was sent, and he gave no second thought to the matter of its contents.

The months went by for Faraday with few distinctive features to mark them outside the enduring desire for his wife's presence.

There had been a visit of sharp disturbance once when her customary letter failed him, and the tardy missive coming, carried an inexplicable coldness that dealt him a pain which, however, did not long survive a little judicious reflection and a very deluge of letters from Paris that shook him with their unusual ardour.

May had come again, and at its approach Faraday with the impatience of a hundred lovers hastened across the seas to join his Eleanor.

It was evening and Eleanor paced to and fro in her room, making the last of a series of efforts that she had been putting forth all day to fight down a misery of the heart, against which her reason was in armed rebellion. She had tried the strategy of simply ignoring its presence, but the attempt had failed utterly. During her daily walk it had embodied itself in every object that her eyes rested upon. It had enveloped her like a smoke mist, through which Paris looked more dull than the desolation of the Sahara.

She had thought to displace it with work, but, like the disturbing element in the chemist's crucible, it rose again and again overspreading the surface of her labour.

Alone in her room, the hour had come when she meant to succeed by the unaided force of reason – proceeding first to make herself bodily comfortable in the folds of a majestic flowing gown, in which she looked a distressed goddess.

Her hair hung heavy and free about her shoulders, for those reasoning powers were to be spurred by a plunging of white fingers into the golden mass.

In this dishevelled state Eleanor's presence seemed too large for the room and its delicate furnishings. The place fitted well an Eleanor in repose but not an Eleanor who swept the narrow confines like an incipient cyclone.

Reason did good work and stood its ground bravely, but against it were the too great odds of a woman's heart, backed by the soft prejudices of a far-reaching heredity.

She finally sank into a chair before her pretty writing desk. The golden head fell upon the outspread arms waiting to receive it, and she burst into a storm of sobs and tears. It was the signal of surrender.

It is a gratifying privilege to be permitted to ignore the reason of such unusual disturbance in a woman of Eleanor's high qualifications. The cause of that abandonment of grief will never be learned unless she chooses to disclose it herself.

When Faraday first folded his wife in his arms he saw but the Eleanor of his constant dreams. But he soon began to perceive how more beautiful she had grown; with a richness of colouring and fullness of health that Plymdale had never been able to bestow. And the object of her stay in Paris was gaining fast to accomplishment, for she had already acquired a knowledge of French that would not require much longer to perfect.

They sat together in her room discussing plans for the summer, when a timid knock at the door caused Eleanor to look up, to see the little housemaid eyeing her with the glance of a fellow conspirator and holding in her hand a card that she suffered to be but partly visible.

Eleanor hastily approached her, and reading the name upon the card thrust it into her pocket, exchanging some whispered words with the girl, among which were audible, 'excuse me', 'engaged', 'another time'. She came back to her husband looking a little flustered, to resume the conversation where it had been interrupted and he offered no enquiries about her mysterious caller.

Entering the salon not many days later he found that in doing so he interrupted a conversation between his wife and a very striking looking gentleman who seemed on the point of taking his leave.

They were both disconcerted; she especially, in bowing, almost thrusting him out, had the appearance of wanting to run away; to do anything but meet her husband's glance.

He asked with assumed indifference who her friend might be.

'Oh, no one special,' with a hopeless attempt at brazenness.

He accepted the situation without protest, only indulging the reflection that Eleanor was losing something of her frankness.

But when his wife asked him on another occasion to dispense with her company for a whole afternoon, saying that she had an urgent call upon her time, he began to wonder if there might not be modifications to this marital liberty of which he was so staunch an advocate.

She left him with a hundred little endearments that she seemed to have acquired with her French.

He forced himself to the writing of a few urgent letters, but his restlessness did not permit him to do more.

It drove him to ugly thoughts, then to the means of dispelling them.

He gazed out of the window, wondered why he was remaining indoors, and followed up the reflection by seizing his hat and plunging out into the street.

The Paris boulevards of a day in early summer are calculated to dispel almost any ache but one of that nature, which was making itself incipiently felt with Faraday.

It was at that stage when it moves a man to take exception at the inadequacy of everything that is offered to his contemplation or entertainment.

The sun was too hot.

The shop windows were vulgar; lacking artistic detail in their make-up.

How could he ever have found the Paris women attractive? They had lost their chic. Most of them were scrawny – not worth looking at.

He thought to go and stroll through the galleries of art. He knew Eleanor would wish to be with him; then he was tempted to go alone.

Finally, more tired from inward than outward restlessness, he took refuge at one of the small tables of a café, called for a 'Mazarin',[385] and, so seated for an unheeded time, let the panorama of Paris pass before his indifferent eyes.

When suddenly one of the scenes in this shifting show struck him with stunning effect.

It was the sight of his wife riding in a fiacre[386] with her caller of a few days back, both conversing and in high spirits.

He remained for a moment enervated, then the blood came tingling back into his veins like fire, making his finger ends twitch with a desire (full worthy of anyone of the 'prejudiced masses') to tear the scoundrel from his seat and paint the boulevard red with his villainous blood.

A rush of wild intentions crowded into his brain.

Should he follow and demand an explanation? Leave Paris without ever looking into her face again? and more not worthy of the man.

It is right to say that his better self and better senses came quickly back to him.

That first revolt was like the unwilling protest of the flesh against the surgeon's knife before a man has steeled himself to its endurance.

Everything came back to him from their short, common past – their dreams, their large intentions for the shaping of their lives. Here was the first test, and should he be the one to cry out, 'I cannot endure it.'

When he returned to the *pension*, Eleanor was impatiently waiting for him in the entry, radiant with gladness at his coming.

She was under a suppressed excitement that prevented her noting his disturbed appearance.

She took his listless hand and led him into the small drawing-room that adjoined their sleeping chamber.

There stood her companion of the fiacre, smiling as was she at the pleasure of introducing him to another Eleanor disposed on the wall in the best possible light to display the gorgeous radiance of her wonderful beauty and the skill of the man who had portrayed it.

The most sanguine hopes of Eleanor and her artist could not have anticipated anything like the rapture with which Faraday received this surprise.

'Monsieur l'Artiste' went away with his belief in the undemonstrativeness of the American very much shaken; and in his pocket substantial evidence of American appreciation of art.

Then the story was told how the portrait was intended as a surprise for his arrival. How there had been delay in its completion. The artist had required one more sitting, which she gave him that day, and the two had brought the picture home in the fiacre, he to give it the final advantages of a judicious light; to witness its effect upon M. Faraday and finally the excusable wish to be presented to the husband of the lady who had captivated his deepest admiration and esteem.

'You shall take it home with you,' said Eleanor

Both were looking at the lovely creation by the soft light of a reckless expenditure of bougie.[387]

'Yes, dearest,' he answered, with feeble elation at the prospect of returning home with that exquisite piece of inanimation.

'Have you engaged your return passage?' she asked.

She sat at his knee, arrayed in the gown that had one evening clothed such a goddess in distress.

'Oh, no. There's plenty of time for that,' was his answer. 'Why do you ask?'

'I'm sure I don't know,' and after a while, 'Charlie, I think – I mean, don't you think – I have made wonderful progress in French?'

'You've done marvels, Nellie. I find no difference between your French and Mme Clairegobeau's, except that yours is far prettier.'

'Yes?' she rejoined, with a little squeeze of the hand.

'I mayn't be right and I want you to give me your candid opinion. I believe Mme Belaire – now that I have gone so far – don't you think – hadn't you better engage passage for two?'

His answer took the form of a pantomimic rapture of assenting gratefulness, during which each gave speechless assurance of a love that could never more take a second place.

'Nellie,' he asked, looking into the face that nestled in close reach of his warm kisses, 'I have often wanted to know, though you needn't tell it if it doesn't suit you,' he added, laughing, 'why you once failed to write to me, and then sent a letter whose coldness gave me a week's heart trouble?'

She flushed, and hesitated, but finally answered him bravely, 'It was when – when you cared so much for that Kitty Beaton.'

Astonishment for a moment deprived him of speech.

'But Eleanor! In the name of reason! It isn't possible!'

'I know all you would say,' she replied. 'I have been over the whole ground myself, over and over, but it is useless. I have found that there are certain things which a woman can't philosophise about, any more than she can about death when it touches that which is near to her.'

'But you don't think – '

'Hush! don't speak of it ever again. I think nothing!' closing her eyes, and with a little shudder drawing closer to him.

As he kissed his wife with passionate fondness, Faraday thought, 'I love her none the less for it, but my Nellie is only a woman, after all.'

With man's usual inconsistency, he had quite forgotten the episode of the portrait.

Mrs Mobry's Reason

1

It was in the springtime and under the blossom-laden branches of an apple tree that Editha Payne finally accepted John Mobry for her husband.

For three years she had been refusing him, with an obstinacy that made people wonder only a little less than they marvelled at the persistence of his desire to marry her. She was simply a nobody – an English girl with antecedents shrouded in obscurity; a governess, moreover; not in her first youth, and none too handsome. But John Mobry was of that class of men who, when they want something, usually keep on wanting it and striving for it so long as there is possibility of attainment in view.

Chance brought him to her that spring day out under the blossoms, at a moment when inward forces were at work with her to weaken and undo the determination of a lifetime.

She looked away from him, far away from him, far away across the green hills that the sun had touched and quickened, and beyond, into the impenetrable mist. Her tired face wore the look of the conquered who has made a brave fight and would rest.

'Well, John, if you want it,' she said, placing her hand in his.

And as she did so she formed the inward resolve that her eyes should never again look into the impenetrable mist. But why she had ever rejected him was something which people kept on asking themselves and each other for the length of time that people will ask such things.

The answer came slowly – twenty-five years later. Most people had forgotten by that time that they ever wanted to know why.

2

Again it was springtime.

A young man who had been trying to read, where he lounged in the deep embrasure[388] of a window, turned to say to the girl who sat playing at the piano: 'Naomi, why is it the spring always comes like a revelation – a delicious surprise?'

'Wait, Sigmund,' and she played the closing bars of the piece of music that was open before her, then rising, went to join him at the window.

She was a splendid type of physical health and beauty, lithe, supple, firm of flesh, wearing youth's colours in cheek and lip, youth's gloss and glow in the waves of her thick brown hair. Her brown eyes drowsed and gleamed alternately, and questioned often.

'The spring?' she said, 'why does it come like a revelation? How should I know? This is surely reversing roles when you question.'

She took the book from his hand to glance carelessly through its pages.

'Do you know, you are a very curious young woman,' he said, looking at her with something of admiration, but yet superciliously, for he was young, and a college student. 'You gave me the same reply this morning when I asked you – what was it, now, I asked you?'

'To define the quality in Chopin's music that charms me. Well,' she continued, 'I don't know the "why" of things. That certain sounds, scenes, impressions move me I know, because I feel it. I don't bother about reasons. Remember, Sigmund, I know so little.'

'Oh, you want training, no doubt, and it's an immense pity you've never received it. Let us go through a course together this summer. Do you agree to it?'

He was the lordly collegiate, sure of his weapons.

'I don't believe I do, Sigmund,' Naomi laughed. 'And if I did it would be useless, for mamma never would consent. You know what she thinks of ologies and isms and all that for women.'

'Oh, isms and ologies do not constitute solely the training I have in mind.'

'Why, my recollection never goes back to any time when books formed an important feature of my life,' she interrupted. 'I've lived more than half my days under the sky, galloping over the hills, as often as not with the rain stinging my face. Oh, the open air and all that it teems with! There's nothing like it, Sigmund. What colour! Look, now, at the purple wrapping those hills away to the east. See the hundred shades of green spreading before us, with the new-ploughed fields between making brown dashes and patches. And then the sky, so blue where it frames those white velvet clouds. They'll be red and gold this evening.'

'What a greedy eye you have – a veritable savage eye for pure colour. Do you know how to use it? to make it serve you?'

'Oh, no, Sigmund,' she said. 'Music's the only thing I've studied and learned. Mamma couldn't have prevented that if she'd wanted to, I believe. There's nothing that has the meaning for me in this world that sound has. I feel as if the Truth were going to come to me, someday, through the harmony of it. I wonder if anyone else has an ear so tuned and sharpened as I have, to detect the music, not of the spheres, but of earth, subtleties of major and minor chord that the wind strikes upon the tree branches. Have you ever heard the earth breathe, Sigmund?' she asked, with wide eyes that filled with merriment when she saw the astonishment in his.

Then, half laughing, half singing the gay refrain of a comic-opera air, she sprang with quick catlike movement to her feet, and seizing a foil from against the wall, whirled with it into position in the centre of the room.

Her companion had been as quick to follow. They measured their distances with stately grace, and looked a continuous challenge into each other's eyes. Then for five long minutes, as they stood face to face exchanging skilful thrust and parry, no sound was heard but the clink and scrape of the slender steels; on the hardwood floor, the stamp of advancing feet in the charge. It was only when Mrs Mobry's long, pale face looked in at the cautiously opened door that the engagement ended.

'Why, Naomi,' she said, a little apologetically, coming into the room, 'I didn't hear the piano and – '

'And you wondered what disaster could have happened,' the girl replied, flushed and amused as she replaced her weapon upon the wall. 'I was only giving Cousin Sigmund a lesson with the foils, mamma.'

'You know your father comes on the early train today, Naomi; he'll be disappointed if you're not at the station to meet him, dear.'

'And a perfect right he'd have to be disappointed, and bewildered, too. When have I ever failed him?'

And she quitted the room, making, as she left it, a pass at Sigmund with an imaginary weapon, and laughing gaily as she did so.

Mrs Mobry went to the piano and gathered together the sheets of music that Naomi had left there in some disorder, and arranged them upon the stand. She had the appearance of seeking occupation; a house full of servants left her little or none of a manual sort, for wealth was one of the things which John Mobry had persistently wanted, long ago.

Mrs Mobry was past fifty, with her hair, that was turning grey, carefully parted and brushed smooth down upon her temples. When she seated herself and began to rock gently, she drew the cape which she wore closely about her thin shoulders.

'Don't you find it chill, Sigmund,' she said, 'with that window open? I dare say not, though; young blood is warm.'

But Sigmund went and closed the window, making no boast that his veins were scintillant. He only said: 'You're right, Aunt Editha; this early spring air is treacherous.'

'I wanted to speak with you a moment alone, dear,' she commenced at once, coughing uneasily behind her hand. 'It may be, and I trust it is, wholly unnecessary, this caution; but it's best to be open, so far as we can be, in this world. And, of course, when young people are thrown together – '

Sigmund, to quote his thoughts, literally, wondered what his aunt was driving at.

'I only want to say – as you perhaps are not aware of it – that it's our intention, and Naomi's, too, that she shall never marry. As you will be with us all summer I thought it best to acquaint you at once with such little family arrangements, so that we may all feel comfortable and avoid unpleasant consequences.' Mrs Mobry smiled feebly as she said this, and smoothed down the hair on her temples with her long thin hands.

'Has Naomi made you such a promise?' Sigmund asked, thinking it a great pity if she had.

'Oh, there's been no promise, but it has been always understood. I've impressed upon her since she was a little child that she is to remain with me always. It looks selfish – I know it looks selfish; your Uncle John even thinks so, though he has never opposed my wish.'

'I see rather a natural instinct in this wish of yours than cold selfishness, Aunt Editha. Something you can't overcome, perhaps. I remember now hearing how fearfully cut up you were two years ago when Edward married.'

Mrs Mobry grew a shade paler, and her voice trembled when she said: 'I can't pardon Edward. It was treacherous, marrying in that way, knowing how I opposed it. It was unfortunate that your uncle should have sent him to take charge of the business in Middleburg. That marriage could not have come about if he had been here at my side, where his place was.'

'But, Aunt Editha, it isn't such a calamity after all. He has married a charming woman, and seems perfectly happy. If you would consent to visit him, and were to see his content with your bodily eyes, I think you would be reconciled to his *coup d'état*.'

Sigmund thought his Aunt Editha rather stupidly set in her ideas. But as he had already recognised the possibility of falling in love with his cousin, Naomi, he was not ill-pleased that Mrs Mobry had so considerately warned him. If he walked into the fire now it would be with open eyes.

Sigmund was the son of Mr Mobry's sister; a student of medicine, twenty-two years of age, a little run down and overworked, and hoping for recuperation amid these Western hills. He had visited his uncle's family often as a child, when he and his cousin Edward – two years his senior – had been friends. But his absence this time had lasted four years. He had left Naomi an awkward, boisterous girl of fourteen. When he returned he found that she had undergone a seeming recreation.

He himself was a good-looking young blond fellow, full of hope and belief in his future; though he tried hard to cultivate an interesting cynicism, which he could never succeed in making anyone believe in.

3

Had Mrs Mobry's intention been that Sigmund should fall in love with her daughter she could not have designed a plan more Machiavellian[389] than the one she employed. But her only thought had been a caution against marriage. Thus there was no cause to grumble, for she had done her work well and surely.

This caution served Sigmund as his only shield – poor fool; all others, he set aside at once. It was more than a shield. It was a licence, drawn, signed, stamped and delivered to his conscience, which permitted him to live at Naomi's side with his young nature all unbridled to wound itself after the manner of young unbridled natures.

They lived such a joyous life during those spring and summer days, and did so many things that were delightful! For must it not have been a delight to rise when the morning was yet grey, and to tramp – high-booted both of them – through the brush of the hillside, crisp and silvered with dew? Silently to wait with ready rifle for the young covey to start with sudden whirr from the fence corners? To watch the east begin to fire and set the wet earth sparkling?

But perhaps they liked it better, or certainly as well, when they sat side by side in Naomi's wagonette and went jogging to town, three miles away, behind the fat, lazy pony who always wanted to stop and drink when they crossed the shallow ford of the Meramec, where the water ran like liquid crystal over the shining pebbles beneath. He always wanted to stop, too, and rest under the branches of the big walnut tree that marked the limit of the Mobry's field. It was a whim of Naomi's to let her pony do what he wanted to, and as often as not he wanted to nibble the grass that grew tender along the edges of the road.

It is no wonder then that their little jogs to town consumed an incredible length of time. Yet what had they to do with time but to waste it? And this they did from morning till night. Sometimes upon

the river that twines like a silver ribbon through the green slopes of
Southern Missouri, seated in Naomi's slender boat, they floated in
midstream when the stars or moon were over them. They skirted the
banks, gliding under the shade of hanging willows when the sun grew
hot and lurid, as it did often when the summer days came.

Then Sigmund's blue eyes saw nothing in all the world so good to
look upon as Naomi's brown ones, that filled with wonder at the sweet
trouble which stirred her when she caught his gaze and answered it.

There was much reading in books, too, during that summertime.
There are many things in books beside isms and ologies. The world has
always its poets who sing. And, strangely enough, Sigmund could think
of no training so fit for Naomi's untrammelled thought as to follow
Lancelot[390] in his loves or Juliet[391] in her hot despair. And Naomi often
sighed over such tales, and wept sometimes, for Sigmund told them
from his heart, and they seemed very real.

Mrs Mobry's first care – and John Mobry's, too, for that matter – was
always Naomi's health; then, Naomi's happiness. These had been from
babyhood so fixed and well established that the mother could surely
have been forgiven had she permitted her solicitude to wane sometimes.
But this she never did. The colour must be always there in Naomi's
cheek, or she must know why it was not. When the girl grew languid
and dreamy – the summer being hot – the mother must know why it
was so.

'I'm sure I don't know, mamma. This heavy heat would make anyone's blood run a little sluggishly, I think.'

4

One morning when the family arose and assembled at an early breakfast,
it was to find that Naomi had been up long before and had gone for one
of her tramps. The gardener had seen her pass when he left his cottage
just at daybreak, and she had called to him: 'We are no sluggards to lie
abed, Heinrich, when the earth has waked up,' so he said.

They thought at every moment she would enter, flushed and dishevelled, to take her place at table. Sigmund was restless because she
was not there; Mrs Mobry anxious, as she gazed constantly from the
window and listened to every sound. When the meal ended, and John
Mobry was forced to leave for the station without giving Naomi the
accustomed morning farewell, it was plainly a thing that gave him
annoyance and pain, for that early kiss from the daughter he loved was a
day's inspiration to him.

Sigmund went in search of her. He was quite sure she would be up on the summit of that nearest hill, seated upon the rocky plateau that he knew. But she was not there, nor in the oak grove, nor in any of the places where he looked. The time was speeding, and the sun had grown fierce. He retraced his steps, sure that he would find her at home when he reached there. Passing an opening in the wood that led down to the river, and where it was narrow, he turned instinctively, thinking that she might be there by the water, where she loved to sit. And there he found her. But she was across the stream in her boat, resting motionless under the willow branches, her big straw hat hanging down over the side of her face.

'Naomi! oh, Naomi!' Sigmund called.

At the sound of his voice she looked up, then seizing the oars she pulled with vigorous strokes across the water towards the spot where he stood waiting for her. She sprang from the boat, heedless of the aid which he offered, and passing him quickly, hastened up the slope, where she seated herself, when she had reached its summit, upon the huge trunk of a fallen tree.

Sigmund followed in some surprise, and went to sit beside her.

'We mustn't linger here too long, Naomi; Aunt Editha is worried about your absence. Why did you stay so long away? You shouldn't do such cruel things.'

'Sigmund,' she whispered, and drawing nearer to him twined her arms around his neck. 'I want you to kiss me, Sigmund.'

Had the earth trembled, that Sigmund shook like that? And had the sky and the air grown red before his eyes? Were his arms turned wooden that they should hang at his side, when hers were around him? He was hoping a senseless hope for strength when she kissed him. Then his arms did their office. He could not help it; he was young and so human. But he sought no further kiss. He only sat motionless with Naomi in his arms; her head resting upon his heart where his pulses had gone mad.

'Ah, Sigmund, this is just as I was dreaming it this morning when I awoke. Then I was angry because you were sleeping off there in your room like a senseless log, when I was awake and wanted you. And you slept on and never came to me. How could you do it? I was angry and went away and walked over the hills. I thought you would come after me, but you never did. I wouldn't go back till you came. And just now, I went in the boat, and when I was out there in the middle of the stream – listen, Sigmund – the sun struck me upon the head, with something in his hand – no, no, not in his hand –'

'Naomi –'

'And after that I didn't care, for I know everything now. I know what the birds are saying up in the trees – '

'Naomi, look at me!'

'Like Siegfried when he played upon his pipe under a tree, last winter in town. I can tell you everything that the fishes say in the water. They were talking under the boat when you called me – '

'Naomi! Oh, God – Naomi, look at me!'

He did look into her eyes then – her eyes that he loved so, and there was no more light in them.

'Aunt Editha,' said Sigmund, entering his aunt's room, where she was in restless movement, as she had been all morning – 'Aunt Editha, Naomi is in the library. I left her there. She must have been chilled by the early-morning air, I'm afraid. And the sun seems to have made her ill – wait – Aunt Editha – ' for Mrs Mobry had clutched Sigmund's arm with fingers like steel, and was staggering towards the library.

'How dare you tell me Naomi's ill? She can't be ill,' she gasped; 'she was never ill in all her life.'

They had reached the library, and facing the door through which they entered Naomi sat upon a lounge. She was playing like a little child, with scraps of paper that she was tearing and placing in rows upon the cushion beside her. An instant more, and Mrs Mobry lay in Sigmund's arms like one dead.

But when night came she kneeled, sobbing as a culprit might, at her husband's feet, telling him a broken story that he scarcely heeded in his anguish.

'It has been in the blood that is mine for generations, John, and I knew it, and I married you.

'Oh, God! if it might end with me and with her – my stricken dove! But, John,' she whispered with a new terror in her eyes, 'Edward has already a child. Others will be born to him, and I see the crime of my marriage[392] reaching out to curse me through the lips of generations that will come.'

The Maid of Saint Phillippe 393

Marianne was tall, supple and strong. Dressed in her worn buckskin trappings she looked like a handsome boy rather than like the French girl of seventeen that she was. As she stepped from the woods the glimmer of the setting sun dazzled her. An instant she raised her hand – palm outward – to shield her eyes from the glare, then she continued to descend the gentle slope and make her way towards the little village of Saint Phillippe that lay before her, close by the waters of the Mississippi.

Marianne carried a gun across her shoulder as easily as a soldier might. Her stride was as untrammelled as that of the stag who treads his native hillside unmolested. There was something stag-like, too, in the poise of her small head as she turned it from side to side, to snuff the subtle perfume of the Indian summer. But against the red western sky curling columns of thin blue smoke began to ascend from chimneys in the village. This meant that housewives were already busy preparing the evening meal; and the girl quickened her steps, singing softly as she strode along over the tufted meadow where sleek cattle were grazing in numbers.

Less than a score of houses formed the village of Saint Phillippe, and they differed in no wise from one another except in the matter of an additional room when the prosperity of the owner admitted of such. All were of upright logs, standing firmly in the ground, or rising from a low foundation of stone, with two or more rooms clustering round a central stone chimney. Before each was an inviting porch, topped by the projection of the shingled roof.

Gathered upon such a porch, when Marianne walked into the village, were groups of men talking eagerly and excitedly together with much gesture and intensity of utterance.

The place was Sans-Chagrin's tavern; and Marianne stopped beside the fence, seeing that her father, Picoté Laronce, was among the number who crowded the gallery. But it was not he, it was young Jacques Labrie who when he saw her there came down to where she stood.

'Well, what luck, Marianne?' he asked, noting her equipment.

'Oh, not much,' she replied, slapping the gamebag that hung rather slack at her side. 'Those idle soldiers down at the fort have no better employment than to frighten the game away out of reach. But what

does this talk and confusion mean? I thought all the trouble with
Monsieur le Curé was settled. My father stands quiet there in a corner;
he seems to be taking no part. What is it all about?'

'The old grievance of a year ago, Marianne. We were content to
grumble only so long as the English did not come to claim what is theirs.
But we hear today they will soon be at Fort Chartres[394] to take possession.'

'Never!' she exclaimed. 'Have not the Natchez[395] driven them back
each time they attempted to ascend the river? And do you think that
watchful tribe will permit them now to cross the line?'

'They have not attempted the river this time. They have crossed the
great mountains and are coming from the east.'

'Ah,' muttered the girl with pale exasperation, 'that is a monarch to be
proud of! Your Louis who sits in his palace at Versailles[396] and gives away
his provinces and his people as if they were baubles! Well, what next?'

'Come, Marianne,' said the young man as he joined her outside. 'Let
me walk to your home with you, I will tell you as we go along. Sans-
Chagrin, you know, returned this morning from the West Illinois, and
he tells astonishing things of the new trading post over there – Laclède's
village.'[397]

'The one they call Saint Louis?' she asked half-heartedly, 'where old
Toussaint of Kaskaskia[398] has taken his family to live?'

'Old Toussaint is far seeing, Marianne, for Sans-Chagrin says the
town across the water is growing as if by enchantment. Already it is
double the size of Saint Phillippe and Kaskaskia put together. When
the English reach Fort Chartres, St Ange de Bellerive[399] will relinquish
the fort to them, and with his men will cross to Laclède's village – all
but Captain Vaudry, who has leave to return to France.'

'Captain Alexis Vaudry[400] will return to France!' she echoed in tones
that rose and fell like a song of lamentation. 'The English are coming
from the east! And all this news has come today while I hunted in the
forest.'

'Do you not see what is in the air, Marianne?' he asked, giving her a
sideward cautious glance.

They were at her portal now, and as he followed her into the house
she half turned to say to him: 'No, Jacques, I can see no way out of it.'
She sat down languidly at the table, as though heavy fatigue had
suddenly weighted her limbs.

'We hate the English,' Jacques began emphatically, leaning upon the
table as he stood beside her.

'To be sure, we hate the English,' she returned, as though the fact
were a self-evident one that needed no comment.

'Well, it is only the eastern province of Louisiana that has been granted to England. There is hardly a man in Saint Phillippe who would not rather die than live subject to that country. But there is no reason to do either,' he added smiling. 'In a week from now, Marianne, Saint Phillippe will be deserted.'

'You mean that the people will abandon their homes, and go to the new trading post?'

'Yes, that is what I mean.'

'But I have heard – I am sure I have heard, long ago, that King Louis made a gift of his Louisiana possessions to his cousin of Spain;[401] that they jointly granted the East Illinois to England. So that leaves the West under the Spanish dominion, Jacques.'

'But Spain is not England,' he explained, a little disconcerted. 'No Frenchman who respects himself will live subject to England,' he added fiercely. 'All are of one mind – to quit Saint Phillippe at once. All save one, Marianne.'

'And that one?'

'Your father.'

'My father! Ah, I might have known. What does he say?' she questioned eagerly.

'He says he is old, that he has dwelt here many years – '

'That is true,' the girl mused. 'I was born here in Saint Phillippe; so were you, Jacques.'

'He says,' continued the young man, 'that he could not dispose of his mill and that he would not leave it.'

'His mill – his mill! no!' exclaimed Marianne, rising abruptly, 'it is not that. Would you know why my father will never leave Saint Phillippe?' approaching as she said this a rear window whose shutters were partly closed, and throwing them wide open. 'Come here, Jacques. That is the reason,' pointing with her strong shapely arm to where a wooden cross marked the presence of a grave out under the wide-spreading branches of a maple.

They both stood for a while silently gazing across the grassy slope that reflected the last flickering gleams of the setting sun. Then Jacques muttered as if in answer to some unspoken thought: 'Yes, he loved her very dearly. Surely the better part of himself went with her. And you, Marianne?' he questioned gently.

'I, Jacques? Oh, it is only the old whose memories dwell in graves,' she replied a little wearily. 'My life belongs to my father. I have but to follow his will, whatever that may be.'

Then Marianne left Jacques standing by the open window, and went into the adjoining room to divest herself of her hunting raiment. When she returned she was dressed in the garments that had been her mother's once – a short camlet skirt of sober hue; a green laced bodice whose scantiness was redeemed by a muslin kerchief laid in deep folds across the bosom; and upon her head was the white cap of the French working woman.

Jacques had lighted the fire for her in the big stone chimney, and gone silently away.

It was indeed true. During that autumn of 1765, a handful of English, under command of Captain Sterling of the Highlanders, crossed the Alleghanies and were coming to take peaceful possession of their hitherto inaccessible lands in the Illinois.

To none did this seem a more hated intrusion than to the people of Saint Phillippe. After the excited meeting at Sans-Chagrin's tavern, all went to work with feverish haste to abandon the village which had been the only home that many of them had ever known. Men, women, and children seemed suddenly possessed with demoniac strength to demolish. Doors, windows and flooring, everything that could serve in building up the new, was rifled from the old. For days there was gathering together and hauling away in rough carts constructed for the sole purpose. Cattle were called from the pasture lands and driven in herds to the northward.

When the last of these rebellious spirits was gone, Saint Phillippe stood like the skeleton of its former self; and Picoté Laronce with his daughter found themselves alone amid the desolate hearthstones.

'It will be a dreary life, my child, for you,' said the old man, gathering Marianne in a close embrace.

'It will not be dreary,' she assured him, disengaging herself to look into his eyes. 'I shall have much work to do. We shall forget – try to forget – that the English are at our door. And sometime when we are rich in peltries, we will go to visit our friends in that great town that they talk so much about. Do not ever think that I am sad, father, because we are alone.'

But the silence was very desolate. So was the sight of those abandoned homes, where smiling faces no longer looked from windows, and where the music of children's laughter was heard no more.

Marianne worked and hunted and grew strong and stronger. The old man was more and more like a child to her. When she was not with him, he would sit for hours upon a rude seat under the maple tree, with a placid look of content in his old, dim eyes.

One day when Captain Vaudry rode up from Fort Chartres, fine as could be in his gay uniform of a French officer, he found Picoté and Marianne sitting in the solitude hand in hand. He had heard how they had remained alone in Saint Phillippe, and he had come to know if it was true, and to persuade them, if he could, to return with him to France – to La Rochelle, where Picoté had formerly lived. But he urged in vain. Picoté knew no home save that in which his wife had dwelt with him, and no resting place on earth except where she lay. And Marianne said always the same thing – that her father's will was hers.

But when she came in from her hunt one evening and found him stretched in the eternal sleep out under the maple, at once she felt that she was alone, with no will to obey in the world but her own. Then her heart was as strong as oak and her nerves were like iron. Lovingly she carried him into the house. And when she had wept because he was dead, she lit two blessed candles and placed them at his head and she watched with him all through the still night.

At the break of day she barred the doors and windows, and mounting her fleet Indian pony, away she galloped to the fort, five miles below, to seek the aid she needed.

Captain Vaudry, and others as well, made all haste to Saint Phillippe when they learned this sad thing that had befallen Marianne. Word was sent to the good curé of Kaskaskia, and he came too, with prayer and benediction. Jacques was in Kaskaskia when the tidings of Picoté's death reached there, and with all the speed at his command he hurried to Marianne to help her in her need.

So Marianne was not alone. Good and staunch friends were about her. When Picoté had been laid to rest – under the maple – and the last blessing had been spoken, the good curé turned to Marianne and said: 'My daughter, you will return with me to Kaskaskia. Your father had many friends in that village, and there is not a door but will open to receive you. It would be unseemly, now he is gone, to live alone in Saint Phillippe.'

'I thank you, my father,' she answered, 'but I must pass this night alone, and in thought. If I decide to go to my good friends in Kaskaskia, I shall ride into town early, upon my pony.'

Jacques, too, spoke to her, with gentle persuasion: 'You know, Marianne, what I want to say, and what my heart is full of. It is not I alone but my father and mother as well to whom you are dear, and who long to have you with us – one of us. Over there in the new village of Saint Louis a new life has begun for all of us. Let me beg that you will not refuse to share it till you have at least tried.'

She held up her hand in token than she had heard enough and turned resolutely from him. 'Leave me, my friend,' she said, 'leave me alone. Follow the curé, there where he goes. If I so determine, you shall hear from me; if not, then think no longer of Marianne.'

So another silent night fell upon Saint Phillippe, with Marianne alone in her home. Not even the dead with her now. She did not know that under the shelter of a neighbouring porch Captain Vaudry lay like a sentinel, wrapped in his mantle.

Near the outer road, but within the enclosure of Marianne's home, was 'the great tree of Saint Phillippe', under which a rude table and benches stood. Here Picoté and his daughter had often taken their humble meals, shared with any passer-by that chose to join them.

Seated there in the early morning was Captain Vaudry when Marianne stepped from her door, in her jerkin of buckskin and her gun across her shoulder.

'What are you doing here, Captain Vaudry?' she asked with startled displeasure when she saw him there.

'I have waited, Marianne. You cannot turn me from you as lightly as you have the others.'

And then with warm entreaty in his voice he talked to her of France: 'Ah, Marianne, you do not know what life is, here in this wild America. Let the curé of Kaskaskia say the words that will make you my wife, and I will take you to a land, child, where men barter with gold, and not with hides and peltries. Where you shall wear jewels and silks and walk upon soft and velvet carpets. Where life can be a round of pleasure. I do not say these things to tempt you; but to let you know that existence holds joys you do not dream of – that may be yours if you will.'

'Enough, Captain Alexis Vaudry! I have sometimes thought I should like to know what it is that men call luxury; and sometimes have felt that I should like to live in sweet and gentle intercourse with men and women. Yet these have been but fleeting wishes. I have passed the night in meditation and my choice is made.'

'I love you, Marianne.' He sat with hands clasped upon the table, and his handsome enraptured eyes gazing up into her face, as she stood before him.

But she went on unheedingly: 'I could not live here in Saint Phillippe or there in Kaskaskia. The English shall never be masters of Marianne. Over the river it is no better. The Spaniards may any day they choose give a rude awakening to those stolid beings who are living on in a half-slumber of content.'

'I love you; oh, I love you, Marianne!'

'Do you not know, Captain Vaudry,' she said with savage resistance,

'I have breathed the free air of forest and stream, till it is in my blood now. I was not born to be the mother of slaves.'[402]

'Oh, how can you think of slaves and motherhood! Look into my eyes, Marianne, and think of love.'

'I will not look into your eyes, Captain Vaudry,' she murmured, letting the quivering lids fall upon her own, 'with your talk and your looks of love – of love! You have looked it before, and you have spoken it before till the strength would go from my limbs and leave me feeble as a little child, till my heart would beat like that of one who has been stricken. Go away, with your velvet and your jewels and your love. Go away to your France and to your treacherous kings; they are not for me.'

'What do you mean, Marianne?' demanded the young man, grown pale with apprehension. 'You deny allegiance to England and Spain; you spurn France with contempt; what is left for you?'

'Freedom is left for me!' exclaimed the girl, seizing her gun that she lifted upon her shoulder. 'Marianne goes to the Cherokees! You cannot stay me; you need not try to. Hardships may await me, but let it be death rather than bondage.'

While Vaudry sat dumb with pain and motionless with astonishment; while Jacques was hoping for a message; while the good curé was looking eagerly from his doorstep for signs of the girl's approach, Marianne had turned her back upon all of them.

With gun across her shoulder she walked up the gentle slope, her brave, strong face turned to the rising sun.

Dr Chevalier's Lie

The quick report of a pistol rang through the quiet autumn night. It was no unusual sound in the unsavoury quarter where Dr Chevalier had his office. Screams commonly went with it. This time there had been none.

Midnight had already rung in the old cathedral tower.

The doctor closed the book over which he had lingered so late, and awaited the summons that was almost sure to come.

As he entered the house to which he had been called he could not but note the ghastly sameness of detail that accompanied these oft-recurring events. The same scurrying; the same groups of tawdry, frightened women bending over banisters – hysterical, some of them; morbidly curious, others; and not a few shedding womanly tears; with a dead girl stretched somewhere, as this one was.

And yet it was not the same. Certainly she was dead: there was the hole in the temple where she had sent the bullet through. Yet it was different. Other such faces had been unfamiliar to him, except so far as they bore the common stamp of death. This one was not.

Like a flash he saw it again amid other surroundings. The time was little more than a year ago. The place, a homely cabin down in Arkansas, in which he and a friend had found shelter and hospitality during a hunting expedition.

There were others beside. A little sister or two; a father and mother – coarse, and bent with toil, but proud as archangels of their handsome girl, who was too clever to stay in an Arkansas cabin, and who was going away to seek her fortune in the big city.

'The girl is dead,' said Dr Chevalier. 'I knew her well, and charge myself with her remains and decent burial.'

The following day he wrote a letter. One, doubtless, to carry sorrow, but no shame to the cabin down there in the forest.

It told that the girl had sickened and died. A lock of hair was sent and other trifles with it. Tender last words were even invented.

Of course it was noised about that Dr Chevalier had cared for the remains of a woman of doubtful repute.

Shoulders were shrugged. Society thought of cutting him. Society did not, for some reason or other, so the affair blew over.

The Story of an Hour

Knowing that Mrs Mallard was afflicted with heart trouble, great care was taken to break to her as gently as possible the news of her husband's death.

It was her sister Josephine who told her, in broken sentences; veiled hints that revealed in half concealing. Her husband's friend Richards was there, too, near her. It was he who had been in the newspaper office when intelligence of the railroad disaster[403] was received, with Brently Mallard's name leading the list of 'killed'. He had only taken the time to assure himself of its truth by a second telegram, and had hastened to forestall any less careful, less tender friend in bearing the sad message.

She did not hear the story, as many women have heard the same, with a paralysed inability to accept its significance. She wept at once, with sudden, wild abandonment, in her sister's arms. When the storm of grief had spent itself she went away to her room alone. She would have no one follow her.

There stood, facing the open window, a comfortable, roomy arm-chair. Into this she sank, pressed down by a physical exhaustion that haunted her body and seemed to reach into her soul.

She could see in the open square before her house the tops of trees that were all aquiver with the new spring life. The delicious breath of rain was in the air. In the street below a peddler was crying his wares. The notes of a distant song which someone was singing reached her faintly, and countless sparrows were twittering in the eaves.

There were patches of blue sky showing here and there through the clouds that had met and piled one above the other in the west facing her window.

She sat with her head thrown back upon the cushion of the chair, quite motionless, except when a sob came up into her throat and shook her, as a child who has cried itself to sleep continues to sob in its dreams.

She was young, with a fair, calm face, whose lines bespoke repression and even a certain strength. But now there was a dull stare in her eyes, whose gaze was fixed away off yonder on one of those patches of blue sky. It was not a glance of reflection, but rather indicated a suspension of intelligent thought.

There was something coming to her and she was waiting for it, fearfully. What was it? She did not know; it was too subtle and elusive to name. But she felt it, creeping out of the sky, reaching towards her through the sounds, the scents, the colour that filled the air.

Now her bosom rose and fell tumultuously. She was beginning to recognise this thing that was approaching to possess her, and she was striving to beat it back with her will – as powerless as her two white slender hands would have been.

When she abandoned herself a little whispered word escaped her slightly parted lips. She said it over and over under her breath: 'Free, free, free!' The vacant stare and the look of terror that had followed it went from her eyes. They stayed keen and bright. Her pulses beat fast, and the coursing blood warmed and relaxed every inch of her body.

She did not stop to ask if it were or were not a monstrous joy that held her. A clear and exalted perception enabled her to dismiss the suggestion as trivial.

She knew that she would weep again when she saw the kind, tender hands folded in death; the face, that had never looked save with love upon her, fixed and grey and dead. But she saw beyond that bitter moment a long procession of years to come that would belong to her absolutely. And she opened and spread her arms out to them in welcome.

There would be no one to live for her[404] during those coming years; she would live for herself. There would be no powerful will bending hers in that blind persistence with which men and women believe they have a right to impose a private will upon a fellow-creature. A kind intention or a cruel intention made the act seem no less a crime as she looked upon it in that brief moment of illumination.

And yet she had loved him – sometimes. Often she had not. What did it matter! What could love, the unsolved mystery, count for in face of this possession of self-assertion which she suddenly recognised as the strongest impulse of her being!

'Free! Body and soul free!' she kept whispering.

Josephine was kneeling before the closed door with her lips to the keyhole, imploring for admission. 'Louise, open the door, I beg! Open the door – you will make yourself ill. What are you doing, Louise? For heaven's sake open the door.'

'Go away. I am not making myself ill.' No; she was drinking in a very elixir of life through that open window.

Her fancy was running riot along those days ahead of her. Spring days, and summer days, and all sorts of days that would be her own. She breathed a quick prayer that life might be long. It was only yesterday she had thought with a shudder that life might be long.

She arose at length and opened the door to her sister's importunities. There was a feverish triumph in her eyes, and she carried herself unwittingly like a goddess of Victory.[405] She clasped her sister's waist, and together they descended the stairs. Richards stood waiting for them at the bottom.

Someone was opening the front door with a latchkey. It was Brently Mallard who entered, a little travel-stained, composedly carrying his grip-sack and umbrella. He had been far from the scene of accident, and did not even know there had been one. He stood amazed at Josephine's piercing cry; at Richards's quick motion to screen him from the view of his wife.

But Richards was too late.

When the doctors came they said she had died of heart disease – of joy that kills.

Lilacs

Mme Adrienne Farival never announced her coming; but the good nuns knew very well when to look for her. When the scent of the lilac blossoms began to permeate the air, Sister Agathe would turn many times during the day to the window; upon her face the happy, beatific expression with which pure and simple souls watch for the coming of those they love.

But it was not Sister Agathe; it was Sister Marceline who first espied her crossing the beautiful lawn that sloped up to the convent. Her arms were filled with great bunches of lilacs which she had gathered along her path. She was clad all in brown; like one of the birds that come with the spring, the nuns used to say. Her figure was rounded and graceful, and she walked with a happy, buoyant step. The cabriolet which had conveyed her to the convent moved slowly up the gravel drive that led to the imposing entrance. Beside the driver was her modest little black trunk, with her name and address printed in white letters upon it: 'Mme A. Farival, Paris'. It was the crunching of the gravel which had attracted Sister Marceline's attention. And then the commotion began.

White-capped heads appeared suddenly at the windows; she waved her parasol and her bunch of lilacs at them. Sister Marceline and Sister Marie Anne appeared, fluttered and expectant at the doorway. But Sister Agathe, more daring and impulsive than all, descended the steps and flew across the grass to meet her. What embraces, in which the lilacs were crushed between them! What ardent kisses! What pink flushes of happiness mounting the cheeks of the two women!

Once within the convent Adrienne's soft brown eyes moistened with tenderness as they dwelt caressingly upon the familiar objects about her, and noted the most trifling details. The white, bare boards of the floor had lost nothing of their lustre. The stiff, wooden chairs, standing in rows against the walls of hall and parlour, seemed to have taken on an extra polish since she had seen them, last lilac time. And there was a new picture of the Sacré-Coeur[406] hanging over the hall table. What had they done with Ste Catherine de Sienne,[407] who had occupied that position of honour for so many years? In the chapel – it was no use trying to deceive her – she saw at a glance that St Joseph's mantle had been embellished with a new coat of blue, and the aureole about his head freshly gilded. And the Blessed Virgin there neglected! Still wearing her garb of last spring, which looked almost dingy by contrast. It was not just – such partiality! The Holy Mother had reason to be jealous and to complain.

But Adrienne did not delay to pay her respects to the Mother Superior, whose dignity would not permit her to so much as step outside the door of her private apartments to welcome this old pupil. Indeed, she was dignity in person: large, uncompromising, unbending She kissed Adrienne without warmth, and discussed conventional themes learnedly and prosaically during the quarter of an hour which the young woman remained in her company.

It was then that Adrienne's latest gift was brought in for inspection. For Adrienne always brought a handsome present for the chapel in her little black trunk. Last year it was a necklace of gems for the Blessed Virgin, which the Good Mother was only permitted to wear on extra occasions, such as great feast days of obligation. The year before it had been a precious crucifix – an ivory figure of Christ suspended from an ebony cross, whose extremities were tipped with wrought silver. This time it was a linen embroidered altar cloth of such rare and delicate workmanship that the Mother Superior, who knew the value of such things, chided Adrienne for the extravagance.

'But, dear Mother, you know it is the greatest pleasure I have in life – to be with you all once a year, and to bring some such trifling token of my regard.'

The Mother Superior dismissed her with the rejoinder: 'Make yourself at home, my child. Sister Thérèse will see to your wants. You will occupy Sister Marceline's bed in the end room, over the chapel. You will share the room with Sister Agathe.'

There was always one of the nuns detailed to keep Adrienne company during her fortnight's stay at the convent. This had become almost a fixed regulation. It was only during the hours of recreation that she found herself with them all together. Those were hours of much harmless merry-making under the trees or in the nuns' refectory.

This time it was Sister Agathe who waited for her outside the Mother Superior's door. She was taller and slenderer than Adrienne, and perhaps ten years older. Her fair blond face flushed and paled with every passing emotion that visited her soul. The two women linked arms and went together out into the open air.

There was so much which Sister Agathe felt that Adrienne must see. To begin with, the enlarged poultry yard, with its dozens upon dozens of new inmates. It took now all the time of one of the lay sisters to attend to them. There had been no change made in the vegetable garden, but – yes there had; Adrienne's quick eye at once detected it. Last year old Phillippe had planted his cabbages in a large square to the right. This year they were set out in an oblong bed to the left. How it made Sister Agathe laugh to think Adrienne should have noticed such a trifle! And old Phillippe, who was nailing a broken trellis not far off, was called forward to be told about it.

He never failed to tell Adrienne how well she looked, and how she was growing younger each year. And it was his delight to recall certain of her youthful and mischievous escapades. Never would he forget that day she disappeared; and the whole convent in a hubbub about it! And how at last it was he who discovered her perched among the tallest branches of the highest tree on the grounds, where she had climbed to see if she could get a glimpse of Paris! And her punishment afterwards! – half of the Gospel of Palm Sunday to learn by heart!

We may laugh over it, my good Phillippe, but we must remember that Madame is older and wiser now.'

'I know well, Sister Agathe, that one ceases to commit follies after the first days of youth.' And Adrienne seemed greatly impressed by the wisdom of Sister Agathe and old Phillippe, the convent gardener.

A little later when they sat upon a rustic bench which overlooked the smiling landscape about them, Adrienne was saying to Sister Agathe, who held her hand and stroked it fondly: 'Do you remember my first visit, four years ago, Sister Agathe? and what a surprise it was to you all!'

'As if I could forget it, dear child!'

'And I! Always shall I remember that morning as I walked along the boulevard with a heaviness of heart – oh, a heaviness which I hate to recall. Suddenly there was wafted to me the sweet odour of lilac blossoms. A young girl had passed me by, carrying a great bunch of them. Did you ever know, Sister Agathe, that there is nothing which so keenly revives a memory as a perfume – an odour?'

'I believe you are right, Adrienne. For now that you speak of it, I can feel how the odour of fresh bread – when Sister Jeanne bakes – always makes me think of the great kitchen of *ma tante* de Sierge,[408] and crippled Julie, who sat always knitting at the sunny window. And I never smell the sweet-scented honeysuckle without living again through the blessed day of my first communion.'

'Well, that is how it was with me, Sister Agathe, when the scent of the lilacs at once changed the whole current of my thoughts and my despondency. The boulevard, its noises, its passing throng, vanished from before my senses as completely as if they had been spirited away. I was standing here with my feet sunk in the green sward as they are now. I could see the sunlight glancing from that old white stone wall, could hear the notes of birds, just as we hear them now, and the humming of insects in the air. And through all I could see and could smell the lilac blossoms, nodding invitingly to me from their thick-leaved branches. It seems to me they are richer than ever this year, Sister Agathe. And do you know, I became like an *enragée*;[409] nothing could have kept me back. I do not remember now where I was going; but I turned and retraced my steps homeward in a perfect fever of agitation: "Sophie! My little trunk – quick – the black one! A mere handful of clothes! I am going away. Don't ask me any questions. I shall be back in a fortnight." And every year since then it is the same. At the very first whiff of a lilac blossom, I am gone! There is no holding me back.'

'And how I wait for you, and watch those lilac bushes, Adrienne! If you should once fail to come, it would be like the spring coming without the sunshine or the song of birds.

'But do you know, dear child, I have sometimes feared that in moments of despondency such as you have just described, I fear that you do not turn as you might to our Blessed Mother in heaven, who is ever ready to comfort and solace an afflicted heart with the precious balm of her sympathy and love.'

'Perhaps I do not, dear Sister Agathe. But you cannot picture the annoyances which I am constantly submitted to. That Sophie alone, with her detestable ways! I assure you she of herself is enough to drive me to St Lazare.'[410]

'Indeed, I do understand that the trials of one living in the world must be very great, Adrienne; particularly for you, my poor child, who have to bear them alone, since Almighty God was pleased to call to himself your dear husband. But on the other hand, to live one's life along the lines which our dear Lord traces for each one of us must bring with it resignation and even a certain comfort. You have your household duties, Adrienne, and your music, to which, you say, you continue to devote yourself. And then, there are always good works – the poor – who are always with us – to be relieved; the afflicted to be comforted.'

'But, Sister Agathe! Will you listen! Is it not La Rose that I hear moving down there at the edge of the pasture? I fancy she is reproaching me with being an ingrate, not to have pressed a kiss yet on that white forehead of hers. Come, let us go.'

The two women arose and walked again, hand in hand this time, over the tufted grass down the gentle decline where it sloped towards the broad, flat meadow, and the limpid stream that flowed cool and fresh from the woods. Sister Agathe walked with her composed, nunlike tread; Adrienne with a balancing motion, a bounding step, as though the earth responded to her light footfall with some subtle impulse all its own.

They lingered long upon the footbridge that spanned the narrow stream which divided the convent grounds from the meadow beyond. It was to Adrienne indescribably sweet to rest there in soft, low converse with this gentle-faced nun, watching the approach of evening. The gurgle of the running water beneath them; the lowing of cattle approaching in the distance, were the only sounds that broke upon the stillness, until the clear tones of the angelus bell pealed out from the convent tower. At the sound both women instinctively sank to their knees, signing themselves with the sign of the cross. And Sister Agathe repeated the customary invocation, Adrienne responding in musical tones:

> 'The Angel of the Lord declared unto Mary,
> And she conceived by the Holy Ghost – '

and so forth, to the end of the brief prayer, after which they arose and retraced their steps towards the convent.

It was with subtle and naïve pleasure that Adrienne prepared herself that night for bed. The room which she shared with Sister Agathe was immaculately white. The walls were a dead white, relieved only by one florid print depicting Jacob's dream at the foot of the ladder, upon which angels mounted and descended. The bare floors, a soft yellow-white, with two little patches of grey carpet beside each spotless bed. At the head of the white-draped beds were two *bénitiers* [411] containing holy water absorbed in sponges.

Sister Agathe disrobed noiselessly behind her curtains and glided into bed without having revealed, in the faint candlelight, as much as a shadow of herself. Adrienne pattered about the room, shook and folded her garments with great care, placing them on the back of a chair as she had been taught to do when a child at the convent. It secretly pleased Sister Agathe to feel that her dear Adrienne clung to the habits acquired in her youth.

But Adrienne could not sleep. She did not greatly desire to do so. These hours seemed too precious to be cast into the oblivion of slumber.

'Are you not asleep, Adrienne?'

'No, Sister Agathe. You know it is always so the first night. The excitement of my arrival – I don't know what – keeps me awake.'

'Say your "Hail, Mary", dear child, over and over.'

'I have done so, Sister Agathe; it does not help.'

'Then lie quite still on your side and think of nothing but your own respiration. I have heard that such inducement to sleep seldom fails.'

'I will try. Good-night, Sister Agathe.'

'Good-night, dear child. May the Holy Virgin guard you.'

An hour later Adrienne was still lying with wide, wakeful eyes, listening to the regular breathing of Sister Agathe. The trailing of the passing wind through the treetops, the ceaseless babble of the rivulet were some of the sounds that came to her faintly through the night.

The days of the fortnight which followed were in character much like the first peaceful, uneventful day of her arrival, with the exception only that she devoutly heard mass every morning at an early hour in the convent chapel, and on Sundays sang in the choir in her agreeable, cultivated voice, which was heard with delight and the warmest appreciation.

When the day of her departure came, Sister Agathe was not satisfied to say goodbye at the portal as the others did. She walked down the drive beside the creeping old cabriolet, chattering her pleasant last words. And then she stood – it was as far as she might go – at the edge of the road, waving goodbye in response to the fluttering of Adrienne's handkerchief. Four hours later Sister Agathe, who was instructing a class of little girls for their first communion, looked up at the classroom clock and murmured: 'Adrienne is at home now.'

Yes, Adrienne was at home. Paris had engulfed her.

At the very hour when Sister Agathe looked up at the clock, Adrienne, clad in a charming *négligé*, was reclining indolently in the depths of a luxurious armchair. The bright room was in its accustomed state of picturesque disorder. Musical scores were scattered upon the open piano. Thrown carelessly over the backs of chairs were puzzling and astonishing-looking garments.

In a large gilded cage near the window perched a clumsy green parrot. He blinked stupidly at a young girl in street dress who was exerting herself to make him talk.

In the centre of the room stood Sophie, that thorn in her mistress's side. With hands plunged in the deep pockets of her apron, her white starched cap quivering with each emphatic motion of her grizzled head, she was holding forth, to the evident ennui of the two young women.

She was saying: 'Heaven knows I have stood enough in the six years I have been with Mademoiselle; but never such indignities as I have had to endure in the past two weeks at the hands of that man who calls himself a manager! The very first day – and I, good enough to notify him at once of Mademoiselle's flight – he arrives like a lion; I tell you, like a lion. He insists upon knowing Mademoiselle's whereabouts. How can I tell him any more than the statue out there in the square? He calls me a liar! Me, me – a liar! He declares he is ruined. The public will not stand La Petite Gilberta in the role which Mademoiselle has made so famous – La Petite Gilberta, who dances like a jointed wooden figure and sings like a *traînée*[412] of a *café chantant*.[413] If I were to tell La Gilberta that, as I easily might, I guarantee it would not be well for the few straggling hairs which he has left on that miserable head of his!

'What could he do? He was obliged to inform the public that Mademoiselle was ill; and then began my real torment! Answering this one and that one with their cards, their flowers, their dainties in covered dishes! which, I must admit, saved Florine and me much cooking. And all the while having to tell them that the physician had advised for Mademoiselle a rest of two weeks at some watering-place, the name of which I had forgotten!'

Adrienne had been contemplating old Sophie with quizzical, half-closed eyes, and pelting her with hot-house roses which lay in her lap, and which she nipped off short from their graceful stems for that purpose. Each rose struck Sophie full in the face; but they did not disconcert her or once stem the torrent of her talk.

'Oh, Adrienne!' entreated the young girl at the parrot's cage. 'Make her hush; please do something. How can you ever expect Zozo to talk? A dozen times he has been on the point of saying something! I tell you, she stupefies him with her chatter.'

'My good Sophie,' remarked Adrienne, not changing her attitude, 'you see the roses are all used up. But I assure you, anything at hand goes,' carelessly picking up a book from the table beside her. 'What is this? Mons. Zola![414] Now I warn you, Sophie, the weightiness, the heaviness of Monsieur Zola's works are such that they cannot fail to prostrate you; thankful you may be if they leave you with energy to regain your feet.'

'Mademoiselle's pleasantries are all very well; but if I am to be shown the door for it – if I am to be crippled for it – I shall say that I think Mademoiselle is a woman without conscience and without heart. To torture a man as she does! A man? No, an angel!

'Each day he has come with sad visage and drooping mien. "No news, Sophie?"

' "None, Monsieur Henri." "Have you no idea where she has gone?" "Not any more than the statue in the square, monsieur." "Is it perhaps possible that she may not return at all?" with his face blanching like that curtain.

'I assure him you will be back at the end of the fortnight. I entreat him to have patience. He drags himself, *désolé*,[415] about the room, picking up Mademoiselle's fan, her gloves, her music, and turning them over and over in his hands. Mademoiselle's slipper, which she took off to throw at me in the impatience of her departure, and which I purposely left lying where it fell on the chiffonier[416] – he kissed it – I saw him do it – and thrust it into his pocket, thinking himself unobserved.

'The same song each day. I beg him to eat a little good soup which I have prepared. "I cannot eat, my dear Sophie." The other night he came and stood long gazing out of the window at the stars. When he turned he was wiping his eyes; they were red. He said he had been riding in the dust, which had inflamed them. But I knew better; he had been crying.

'*Ma foi!* in his place I would snap my finger at such cruelty. I would go out and amuse myself. What is the use of being young!'

Adrienne arose with a laugh. She went and seizing old Sophie by the shoulders shook her till the white cap wobbled on her head.

'What is the use of all this litany, my good Sophie? Year after year the same! Have you forgotten that I have come a long, dusty journey by rail, and that I am perishing of hunger and thirst? Bring us a bottle of Château Yquem and a biscuit and my box of cigarettes.' Sophie had freed herself, and was retreating towards the door. 'And, Sophie! If Monsieur Henri is still waiting, tell him to come up.'

*

It was precisely a year later. The spring had come again, and Paris was intoxicated.

Old Sophie sat in her kitchen discoursing to a neighbour who had come in to borrow some trifling kitchen utensil from the old *bonne*.

'You know, Rosalie, I begin to believe it is an attack of lunacy which seizes her once a year. I wouldn't say it to everyone, but with you I know it will go no further. She ought to be treated for it; a physician should be consulted; it is not well to neglect such things and let them run on.

'It came this morning like a thunder clap. As I am sitting here, there had been no thought or mention of a journey. The baker had come into the kitchen – you know what a gallant he is – with always a girl in his eye. He laid the bread down upon the table and beside it a bunch of lilacs. I didn't know they had bloomed yet. "For Mam'selle Florine, with my regards," he said with his foolish simper.

'Now, you know I was not going to call Florine from her work in

order to present her the baker's flowers. All the same, it would not do to
let them wither. I went with them in my hand into the dining-room to
get a majolica pitcher which I had put away in the closet there, on an
upper shelf, because the handle was broken. Mademoiselle, who rises,
early, had just come from her bath, and was crossing the hall that opens
into the dining-room. Just as she was, in her white *peignoir*, she thrust
her head into the dining-room, snuffling the air and exclaiming, "What
do I smell?"

'She espied the flowers in my hand and pounced upon them like a cat
upon a mouse. She held them up to her, burying her face in them for
the longest time, only uttering a long, "Ah!"

"Sophie, I am going away. Get out the little black trunk; a few of the
plainest garments I have; my brown dress that I have not yet worn.'

' "But, Mademoiselle," I protested, "you forget that you have ordered
a breakfast of a hundred francs for tomorrow."

' "Shut up!" she cried, stamping her foot.

' "You forget how the manager will rave," I persisted, "and vilify me.
And you will go like that without a word of adieu to Monsieur Paul,
who is an angel if ever one trod the earth."

'I tell you, Rosalie, her eyes flamed.

' "Do as I tell you this instant," she exclaimed, "or I will strangle
you – with your Monsieur Paul and your manager and your hundred
francs!" '

'Yes,' affirmed Rosalie, 'it is insanity. I had a cousin seized in the same
way one morning, when she smelled calf's liver frying with onions.
Before night it took two men to hold her.'

'I could well see it was insanity, my dear Rosalie, and I uttered not
another word as I feared for my life. I simply obeyed her every command
in silence. And now – whiff, she is gone! God knows where. But between
us, Rosalie – I wouldn't say it to Florine – but I believe it is for no good.
I, in Monsieur Paul's place, should have her watched. I would put a
detective upon her track.

'Now I am going to close up; barricade the entire establishment.
Monsieur Paul, the manager, visitors, all – all may ring and knock and
shout themselves hoarse. I am tired of it all. To be vilified and called a
liar – at my age, Rosalie!'

*

Adrienne left her trunk at the small railway station, as the old cabriolet
was not at the moment available; and she gladly walked the mile or two
of pleasant roadway which led to the convent. How infinitely calm,

peaceful, penetrating was the charm of the verdant, undulating country spreading out on all sides of her! She walked along the clear smooth road, twirling her parasol; humming a gay tune; nipping here and there a bud or a waxlike leaf from the hedges along the way; and all the while drinking deep draughts of complacency and content.

She stopped, as she had always done, to pluck lilacs in her path.

As she approached the convent she fancied that a white-capped face had glanced fleetingly from a window; but she must have been mistaken. Evidently she had not been seen, and this time would take them by surprise. She smiled to think how Sister Agathe would utter a little joyous cry of amazement, and in fancy she already felt the warmth and tenderness of the nun's embrace. And how Sister Marceline and the others would laugh, and make game of her puffed sleeves! For puffed sleeves had come into fashion since last year; and the vagaries of fashion always afforded infinite merriment to the nuns. No, they surely had not seen her.

She ascended lightly the stone steps and rang the bell. She could hear the sharp metallic sound reverberate through the halls. Before its last note had died away the door was opened very slightly, very cautiously by a lay sister who stood there with downcast eyes and flaming cheeks. Through the narrow opening she thrust forward towards Adrienne a package and a letter, saying, in confused tones: 'By order of our Mother Superior.' After which she closed the door hastily and turned the heavy key in the great lock.

Adrienne remained stunned. She could not gather her faculties to grasp the meaning of this singular reception. The lilacs fell from her arms to the stone portico on which she was standing. She turned the note and the parcel stupidly over in her hands, instinctively dreading what their contents might disclose.

The outlines of the crucifix were plainly to be felt through the wrapper of the bundle, and she guessed, without having courage to assure herself, that the jewelled necklace and the altar cloth accompanied it.

Leaning against the heavy oaken door for support, Adrienne opened the letter. She did not seem to read the few bitter reproachful lines word by word – the lines that banished her for ever from this haven of peace, where her soul was wont to come and refresh itself. They imprinted themselves as a whole upon her brain, in all their seeming cruelty – she did not dare to say injustice.

There was no anger in her heart; that would doubtless possess her later, when her nimble intelligence would begin to seek out the origin of this treacherous turn. Now, there was only room for tears. She leaned her forehead against the heavy oaken panel of the door and wept with the abandonment of a little child.

She descended the steps with a nerveless and dragging tread. Once as she was walking away, she turned to look back at the imposing façade of the convent, hoping to see a familiar face, or a hand, even, giving a faint token that she was still cherished by some one faithful heart. But she saw only the polished windows looking down at her like so many cold and glittering and reproachful eyes.

In the little white room above the chapel, a woman knelt beside the bed on which Adrienne had slept. Her face was pressed deep in the pillow in her efforts to smother the sobs that convulsed her frame. It was Sister Agathe.

After a short while, a lay sister came out of the door with a broom, and swept away the lilac blossoms which Adrienne had let fall upon the portico.

The Kiss

It was still quite light out of doors, but inside with the curtains drawn and the smouldering fire sending out a dim, uncertain glow, the room was full of deep shadows.

Brantain sat in one of these shadows; it had overtaken him and he did not mind. The obscurity lent him courage to keep his eyes fastened as ardently as he liked upon the girl who sat in the firelight.

She was very handsome, with a certain fine, rich colouring that belongs to the healthy brune type. She was quite composed, as she idly stroked the satiny coat of the cat that lay curled in her lap, and she occasionally sent a slow glance into the shadow where her companion sat. They were talking low, of indifferent things which plainly were not the things that occupied their thoughts. She knew that he loved her – a frank, blustering fellow without guile enough to conceal his feelings, and no desire to do so. For two weeks past he had sought her society eagerly and persistently. She was confidently waiting for him to declare himself and she meant to accept him. The rather insignificant and unattractive Brantain was enormously rich; and she would like and required the entourage which wealth could give her.

During one of the pauses between their talk of the last tea and the next reception the door opened and a young man entered whom Brantain knew quite well. The girl turned her face towards him. A stride or two brought him to her side, and bending over her chair – before she could suspect his intention, for she did not realise that he had not seen her visitor – he pressed an ardent, lingering kiss upon her lips.

Brantain slowly arose; so did the girl arise, but quickly, and the newcomer stood between them, a little amusement and some defiance struggling with the confusion in his face.

'I believe,' stammered Brantain, 'I see that I have stayed too long. I – I had no idea – that is, I must wish you goodbye.' He was clutching his hat with both hands, and probably did not perceive that she was extending her hand to him, her presence of mind had not completely deserted her; but she could not have trusted herself to speak.

'Hang me if I saw him sitting there, Nattie! I know it's deuced awkward for you. But I hope you'll forgive me this once – this very first break. Why, what's the matter?'

'Don't touch me; don't come near me,' she returned angrily. 'What do you mean by entering the house without ringing?'

'I came in with your brother, as I often do,' he answered coldly, in self-justification. 'We came in the side way. He went upstairs and I came in here hoping to find you. The explanation is simple enough and ought to satisfy you that the misadventure was unavoidable. But do say that you forgive me, Nathalie,' he entreated, softening.

'Forgive you! You don't know what you are talking about. Let me pass. It depends upon – a good deal whether I ever forgive you.'

At that next reception which she and Brantain had been talking about she approached the young man with a delicious frankness of manner when she saw him there.

'Will you let me speak to you a moment or two, Mr Brantain?' she asked with an engaging but perturbed smile. He seemed extremely unhappy; but when she took his arm and walked away with him, seeking a retired corner, a ray of hope mingled with the almost comical misery of his expression. She was apparently very outspoken.

'Perhaps I should not have sought this interview, Mr Brantain; but – but, oh, I have been very uncomfortable, almost miserable since that little encounter the other afternoon. When I thought how you might have misinterpreted it, and believed things – ', hope was plainly gaining the ascendancy over misery in Brantain's round, guileless face, ' – of course, I know it is nothing to you, but for my own sake I do want you to understand that Mr Harvy is an intimate friend of long standing. Why, we have always been like cousins – like brother and sister, I may say. He is my brother's most intimate associate and often fancies that he is entitled to the same privileges as the family. Oh, I know it is absurd, uncalled for, to tell you this; undignified even,' she was almost weeping, 'but it makes so much difference to me what you think of – of me.' Her voice had grown very low and agitated. The misery had all disappeared from Brantain's face.

'Then you do really care what I think, Miss Nathalie? May I call you Miss Nathalie?' They turned into a long, dim corridor that was lined on either side with tall, graceful plants. They walked slowly to the very end of it. When they turned to retrace their steps Brantain's face was radiant and hers was triumphant.

*

Harvy was among the guests at the wedding; and he sought her out in a rare moment when she stood alone.

'Your husband,' he said, smiling, 'has sent me over to kiss you.'

A quick blush suffused her face and round polished throat.

'I suppose it's natural for a man to feel and act generously on an occasion of this kind. He tells me he doesn't want his marriage to interrupt wholly that pleasant intimacy which has existed between you and me. I don't know what you've been telling him,' with an insolent smile, 'but he has sent me here to kiss you.'

She felt like a chess player who, by the clever handling of his pieces, sees the game taking the course intended. Her eyes were bright and tender with a smile as they glanced up into his; and her lips looked hungry for the kiss which they invited.

'But, you know,' he went on quietly, 'I didn't tell him so, it would have seemed ungrateful, but I can tell you. I've stopped kissing women; it's dangerous.'

Well, she had Brantain and his million left. A person can't have everything in this world; and it was a little unreasonable of her to expect it.

Her Letters

She had given orders that she wished to remain undisturbed and more-over had locked the doors of her room.

The house was very still. The rain was falling steadily from a leaden sky in which there was no gleam, no rift, no promise. A generous wood fire had been lighted in the ample fireplace and it brightened and illumined the luxurious apartment to its furthermost corner.

From some remote nook of her writing desk the woman took a thick bundle of letters, bound tightly together with strong, coarse twine, and placed it upon the table in the centre of the room.

For weeks she had been schooling herself for what she was about to do. There was a strong deliberation in the lines of her long, thin sensitive face; her hands, too, were long and delicate and blue-veined.

With a pair of scissors she snapped the cord binding the letters together. Thus released the ones which were topmost slid down to the table and she, with a quick movement thrust her fingers among them, scattering and turning them over till they quite covered the broad surface of the table.

Before her were envelopes of various sizes and shapes, all of them addressed in the handwriting of one man and one woman. He had sent her letters all back to her one day when, sick with dread of possibilities, she had asked to have them returned. She had meant, then, to destroy them all, his and her own. That was four years ago, and she had been feeding upon them ever since – they had sustained her, she believed, and kept her spirit from perishing utterly.

But now the days had come when the premonition of danger could no longer remain unheeded. She knew that before many months were past she would have to part from her treasure, leaving it unguarded. She shrank from inflicting the pain, the anguish which the discovery of those letters would bring to others – to one, above all, who was near to her, and whose tenderness and years of devotion had made him, in a manner, dear to her.

She calmly selected a letter at random from the pile and cast it into the roaring fire. A second one followed almost as calmly, with the third her hand began to tremble; whereupon, in a sudden paroxysm, she cast a fourth, a fifth and a sixth into the flames in breathless succession.

Then she stopped and began to pant – for she was far from strong, and she stayed staring into the fire with pained and savage eyes. Oh, what had she done! What had she not done! With feverish apprehension she began to search among the letters before her. Which of them had she so ruthlessly, so cruelly put out of her existence? Heaven grant, not the first, that very first one written before they had learned or dared to say to each other, 'I love you.' No, no; there it was, safe enough. She laughed with pleasure, and held it to her lips. But what if that other most precious and most imprudent one were missing! in which every word of untempered passion had long ago eaten its way into her brain; and which stirred her still today, as it had done a hundred times before when she thought of it. She crushed it between her palms when she found it. She kissed it again and again. With her sharp white teeth she tore the far corner from the letter, where the name was written; she bit the torn scrap and tasted it between her lips and upon her tongue like some god-given morsel.

What unbounded thankfulness she felt at not having destroyed them all! How desolate and empty would have been her remaining days without them; with only her thoughts, illusive thoughts that she could not hold in her hands and press, as she did these, to her cheeks and her heart.

This man had changed the water in her veins to wine, whose taste had brought delirium to both of them. It was all one and past now, save for these letters that she held encircled in her arms. She stayed breathing softly and contentedly, with the hectic cheek resting upon them.

She was thinking; thinking of a way to keep them without possible ultimate injury to that other one whom they would stab more cruelly than keen knife blades.

At last she found the way. It was a way that frightened and bewildered her to think of at first, but she had reached it by deduction too sure to admit of doubt. She meant, of course, to destroy them herself before the end came. But how does the end come and when? Who may tell? She would guard against the possibility of accident by leaving them in charge of the very one who, above all, should be spared a knowledge of their contents.

She roused herself from the stupor of thought and gathered the scattered letters once more together, binding them again with the tough twine. She wrapped the compact bundle in a thick sheet of white polished paper. Then she wrote in ink upon the back of it, in large, firm characters: 'I leave this package to the care of my husband. With perfect faith in his loyalty and his love, I ask him to destroy it unopened.'

It was not sealed; only a bit of string held the wrapper, which she could remove and replace at will whenever the humour came to her to pass an hour in some intoxicating dream of the days when she felt she had lived.

2

If he had come upon that bundle of letters in the first flush of his poignant sorrow there would not have been an instant's hesitancy. To destroy it promptly and without question would have seemed a welcome expression of devotion – a way of reaching her, of crying out his love to her while the world was still filled with the illusion of her presence. But months had passed since that spring day when they had found her stretched upon the floor, clutching the key of her writing desk, which she appeared to have been attempting to reach when death overtook her.

The day was much like that day a year ago when the leaves were falling and the rain pouring steadily from a leaden sky which held no gleam, no promise. He had happened accidentally upon the package in that remote nook of her desk And just as she herself had done a year ago, he carried it to the table and laid it down there, standing, staring with puzzled eyes at the message which confronted him: 'I leave this package to the care of my husband. With perfect faith in his loyalty and his love, I ask him to destroy it unopened.' She had made no mistake; every line of his face – no longer young – spoke loyalty and honesty, and his eyes were as faithful as a dog's and as loving. He was a tall, powerful man, standing there in the firelight, with shoulders that stooped a little, and hair that was growing somewhat thin and grey, and a face that was distinguished, and must have been handsome when he smiled. But he was slow. 'Destroy it unopened,' he reread, half aloud, 'but why unopened?'

He took the package again in his hands, and turning it about and feeling it, discovered that it was composed of many letters tightly packed together.

So here were letters which she was asking him to destroy unopened. She had never seemed in her lifetime to have had a secret from him. He knew her to have been cold and passionless, but true, and watchful of his comfort and his happiness. Might he not be holding in his hands the secret of some other one, which had been confided to her and which she had promised to guard? But, no, she would have indicated the fact by some additional word or line. The secret was her own, something contained in these letters, and she wanted it to die with her.

If he could have thought of her as on some distant shadowy shore waiting for him throughout the years with outstretched hands to come and join her again, he would not have hesitated. With hopeful confidence he would have thought: 'In that blessed meeting-time, soul to soul, she will tell me all; till then I can wait and trust.' But he could not think of her in any far-off paradise awaiting him. He felt that there was no smallest part of her anywhere in the universe, more than there had been before she was born into the world. But she had embodied herself with terrible significance in an intangible wish, uttered when life still coursed through her veins; knowing that it would reach him when the annihilation of death was between them, but uttered with all confidence in its power and potency. He was moved by the splendid daring, the magnificence of the act, which at the same time exalted him and lifted him above the head of common mortals.

What secret save one could a woman choose to have die with her? As quickly as the suggestion came to his mind, so swiftly did the man-instinct of possession creep into his blood. His fingers cramped about the package in his hands, and he sank into a chair beside the table. The agonising suspicion that perhaps another had shared with him her thoughts, her affections, her life, deprived him for a swift instant of honour and reason. He thrust the end of his strong thumb beneath the string which, with a single turn would have yielded – 'with perfect faith in your loyalty and your love'. It was not the written characters addressing themselves to the eye; it was like a voice speaking to his soul. With a tremor of anguish he bowed his head down upon the letters.

He had once seen a clairvoyant hold a letter to his forehead and purport in so doing to discover its contents. He wondered for a wild moment if such a gift, for force of wishing it, might not come to him. But he was only conscious of the smooth surface of the paper, cold against his brow, like the touch of a dead woman's hand.

A half-hour passed before he lifted his head. An unspeakable conflict had raged within him, but his loyalty and his love had conquered. His face was pale and deep-lined with suffering, but there was no more hesitancy to be seen there.

He did not for a moment think of casting the thick package into the flames to be licked by the fiery tongues, and charred and half-revealed to his eyes. That was not what she meant. He arose, and taking a heavy bronze paperweight from the table, bound it securely to the package. He walked to the window and looked out into the street below. Darkness had come, and it was still raining. He could hear the rain dashing against the window-panes, and could see it falling through the dull yellow rim of light cast by the lighted street lamp.

He prepared himself to go out, and when quite ready to leave the house thrust the weighted package into the deep pocket of his top-coat.

He did not hurry along the street as most people were doing at that hour, but walked with a long, slow, deliberate step, not seeming to mind the penetrating chill and rain driving into his face despite the shelter of his umbrella.

His dwelling was not far removed from the business section of the city; and it was not a great while before he found himself at the entrance of the bridge that spanned the river – the deep, broad, swift, black river dividing two states. He walked on and out to the very centre of the structure. The wind was blowing fiercely and keenly. The darkness where he stood was impenetrable. The thousands of lights in the city he had left seemed like all the stars of heaven massed together, sinking into some distant mysterious horizon, leaving him alone in a black, boundless universe.

He drew the package from his pocket and leaning as far as he could over the broad stone rail of the bridge, cast it from him into the river. It fell straight and swiftly from his hand. He could not follow its descent through the darkness, nor hear its dip into the water far below. It vanished silently; seemingly into some inky unfathomable space. He felt as if he were flinging it back to her in that unknown world whither she had gone.

3

An hour or two later he sat at his table in the company of several men whom he had invited that day to dine with him. A weight had settled upon his spirit, a conviction, a certitude that there could be but one secret which a woman would choose to have die with her. This one thought was possessing him, it occupied his brain, keeping it nimble and alert with suspicion. It clutched his heart, making every breath of existence a fresh moment of pain.

The men about him were no longer the friends of yesterday; in each one he discerned a possible enemy. He attended absently to their talk. He was remembering how she had conducted herself towards this one and that one; striving to recall conversations, subtleties of facial expression that might have meant what he did not suspect at the moment, shades of meaning in words that had seemed the ordinary interchange of social amenities.

He led the conversation to the subject of women, probing these men for their opinions and experiences. There was not one but claimed some infallible power to command the affections of any woman whom his fancy might select. He had heard the empty boast before from the same group and had always met it with good-humoured contempt. But tonight every flagrant, inane utterance was charged with a new meaning, revealing possibilities that he had hitherto never taken into account.

He was glad when they were gone. He was eager to be alone, not from any desire or intention to sleep. He was impatient to regain her room, that room in which she had lived a large portion of her life, and where he had found those letters. There must surely be more of them somewhere, he thought; some forgotten scrap, some written thought or expression lying unguarded by an inviolable command.

At the hour when he usually retired for the night he sat himself down before her writing desk and began the search of drawers, slides, pigeonholes, nooks and corners. He did not leave a scrap of anything unread. Many of the letters which he found were old: some he had read before; others were new to him. But in none did he find the faintest evidence that his wife had not been the true and loyal woman he had always believed her to be. The night was nearly spent before the fruitless search ended. The brief, troubled sleep which he snatched before his hour for rising was freighted with feverish, grotesque dreams, through all of which he could hear and could see dimly the dark river rushing by, carrying away his heart, his ambitions, his life.

But it was not alone in letters that women betrayed their emotions, he thought. Often he had known them, especially when in love, to mark fugitive, sentimental passages in books of verse or prose, thus expressing and revealing their own hidden thought. Might she not have done the same?

Then began a second and far more exhausting and arduous quest than the first, turning, page by page, the volumes that crowded her room – books of fiction, poetry, philosophy. She had read them all; but nowhere, by the shadow of a sign, could he find that the author had echoed the secret of her existence – the secret which he had held in his hands and had cast into the river.

He began cautiously and gradually to question this one and that one, striving to learn by indirect ways what each had thought of her. Foremost he learned she had been unsympathetic because of her coldness of manner. One had admired her intellect; another her accomplishments; a third had thought her beautiful before disease claimed her, regretting, however, that her beauty had lacked warmth of colour and expression. She was praised by some for gentleness and kindness, and by others for cleverness and tact. Oh, it was useless to try to discover anything from men! he might have known. It was women who would talk of what they knew.

They did talk, unreservedly. Most of them had loved her; those who had not had held her in respect and esteem.

4

And yet, and yet, 'there is but one secret which a woman would choose to have die with her', was the thought which continued to haunt him and deprive him of rest. Days and nights of uncertainty began slowly to unnerve him and to torture him. An assurance of the worst that he dreaded would have offered him peace most welcome, even at the price of happiness.

It seemed no longer of any moment to him that men should come and go; and fall or rise in the world; and wed and die. It did not signify if money came to him by a turn of chance or eluded him. Empty and meaningless seemed to him all devices which the world offers for man's entertainment. The food and the drink set before him had lost their flavour. He did not longer know or care if the sun shone or the clouds lowered about him. A cruel hazard had struck him there where he was weakest, shattering his whole being, leaving him with but one wish in his soul, one gnawing desire, to know the mystery which he had held in his hands and had cast into the river.

One night when there were no stars shining he wandered, restless, upon the streets. He no longer sought to know from men and women what they dared not or could not tell him. Only the river knew. He went and stood again upon the bridge where he had stood many an hour since that night when the darkness then had closed around him and engulfed his manhood.

Only the river knew. It babbled, and he listened to it, and it told him nothing, but it promised all. He could hear it promising him, with caressing voice, peace and sweet repose. He could hear the sweep, the song of the water inviting him.

A moment more and he had gone to seek her, and to join her and her secret thought in the immeasurable rest.

Fedora

Fedora had determined upon driving over to the station herself for Miss Malthers.

Though one or two of them looked disappointed – notably her brother – no one opposed her. She said the brute was restive, and shouldn't be trusted to the handling of the young people.

To be sure Fedora was old enough, from the standpoint of her sister Camilla and the rest of them. Yet no one would ever have thought of it but for her own persistent affectation and idiotic assumption of superior years and wisdom. She was thirty.

Fedora had too early in life formed an ideal and treasured it. By this ideal she had measured such male beings as had hitherto challenged her attention, and needless to say she had found them wanting. The young people – her brothers' and sisters' guests, who were constantly coming and going that summer – occupied her to a great extent, but failed to interest her. She concerned herself with their comforts – in the absence of her mother – looked after their health and well-being; contrived for their amusements, in which she never joined. And, as Fedora was tall and slim, and carried her head loftily, and wore eye-glasses and a severe expression, some of them – the silliest – felt as if she were a hundred years old. Young Malthers thought she was about forty.

One day when he stopped before her out in the gravel walk to ask her some question pertaining to the afternoon's sport, Fedora, who was tall, had to look up into his face to answer him. She had known him eight years, since he was a lad of fifteen, and to her he had never been other than the lad of fifteen.

But that afternoon, looking up into his face, the sudden realisation came home to her that he was a man – in voice, in attitude, in bearing, in every sense – a man.

In an absorbing glance, and with unaccountable intention, she gathered in every detail of his countenance as though it were a strange, new thing to her, presenting itself to her vision for the first time. The eyes were blue, earnest, and at the moment a little troubled over some trivial affair that he was relating to her. The face was brown from the sun, smooth, with no suggestion of ruddiness, except in the lips, that were strong, firm and clean. She kept thinking of his face, and every trick of it after he passed on.

From that moment he began to exist for her. She looked at him when he was near by, she listened for his voice, and took notice and account of what he said. She sought him out; she selected him when occasion permitted. She wanted him by her, though his nearness troubled her. There was uneasiness, restlessness, expectation when he was not there within sight or sound. There was redoubled uneasiness when he was by – there was inward revolt, astonishment, rapture, self-contumely; a swift, fierce encounter betwixt thought and feeling.

Fedora could hardly explain to her own satisfaction why she wanted to go herself to the station for young Malthers's sister. She felt a desire to see the girl, to be near her; as unaccountable, when she tried to analyse it, as the impulse which drove her, and to which she often yielded, to touch his hat, hanging with others upon the hall pegs, when she passed it by. Once a coat which he had discarded hung there too. She handled it under pretence of putting it in order. There was no one near, and, obeying a sudden impulse, she buried her face for an instant in the rough folds of the coat.

Fedora reached the station a little before train time. It was in a pretty nook, green and fragrant, set down at the foot of a wooded hill. Off in a clearing there was a field of yellow grain, upon which the sinking sunlight fell in slanting, broken beams. Far down the track there were some men at work, and the even ring of their hammers was the only sound that broke upon the stillness. Fedora loved it all – sky and woods and sunlight; sounds and smells. But her bearing – elegant, composed, reserved – betrayed nothing emotional as she tramped the narrow platform, whip in hand, and occasionally offered a condescending word to the mailman or the sleepy agent.

Malthers's sister was the only soul to disembark from the train. Fedora had never seen her before; but if there had been a hundred, she would have known the girl. She was a small thing; but aside from that, there was the colouring; there were the blue, earnest eyes; there, above all, was the firm, full curve of the lips; the same setting of the white, even teeth. There was the subtle play of feature, the elusive trick of expression, which she had thought peculiar and individual in the one, presenting themselves as family traits.

The suggestive resemblance of the girl to her brother was vivid, poignant even to Fedora, realising, as she did with a pang, that familiarity and custom would soon blur the image.

Miss Malthers was a quiet, reserved creature, with little to say. She had been to college with Camilla, and spoke somewhat of their friendship and former intimacy. She sat lower in the cart than Fedora, who drove, handling whip and rein with accomplished skill.

'You know, dear child,' said Fedora, in her usual elderly fashion, 'I want you to feel completely at home with us.' They were driving through a long, quiet, leafy road, into which the twilight was just beginning to creep. 'Come to me freely and without reserve – with all your wants; with any complaints. I feel that I shall be quite fond of you.'

She had gathered the reins into one hand, and with the other free arm she encircled Miss Malthers's shoulders.

When the girl looked up into her face, with murmured thanks, Fedora bent down and pressed a long, penetrating kiss upon her mouth.

Malthers's sister appeared astonished, and not too well pleased. Fedora, with seemingly unruffled composure, gathered the reins, and for the rest of the way stared steadily ahead of her between the horse's ears.

A Pair of Silk Stockings

Little Mrs Sommers one day found herself the unexpected possessor of fifteen dollars. It seemed to her a very large amount of money, and the way in which it stuffed and bulged her worn old *porte-monnaie* gave her a feeling of importance such as she had not enjoyed for years.

The question of investment was one that occupied her greatly. For a day or two she walked about apparently in a dreamy state, but really absorbed in speculation and calculation. She did not wish to act hastily, to do anything she might afterwards regret. But it was during the still hours of the night when she lay awake revolving plans in her mind that she seemed to see her way clearly towards a proper and judicious use of the money.

A dollar or two should be added to the price usually paid for Janie's shoes, which would ensure their lasting an appreciable time longer than they usually did. She would buy so and so many yards of percale for new shirt waists for the boys and Janie and Mag. She had intended to make the old ones do by skilful patching. Mag should have another gown. She had seen some beautiful patterns, veritable bargains in the shop windows. And still there would be left enough for new stockings – two pairs apiece – and what darning that would save for a while! She would get caps for the boys and sailor-hats for the girls. The vision of her little brood looking fresh and dainty and new for once in their lives excited her and made her restless and wakeful with anticipation.

The neighbours sometimes talked of certain 'better days' that little Mrs Sommers had known before she had ever thought of being Mrs Sommers. She herself indulged in no such morbid retrospection. She had no time – no second of time to devote to the past. The needs of the present absorbed her every faculty. A vision of the future like some dim, gaunt monster sometimes appalled her, but luckily tomorrow never comes. Mrs Sommers was one who knew the value of bargains; who could stand for hours making her way inch by inch towards the desired object that was selling below cost. She could elbow her way if need be; she had learned to clutch a piece of goods and hold it and stick to it with persistence and determination till her turn came to be served, no matter when it came.

But that day she was a little faint and tired. She had swallowed a light luncheon – no! when she came to think of it, between getting the children fed and the place righted, and preparing herself for the shopping bout, she had actually forgotten to eat any luncheon at all!

She sat herself upon a revolving stool before a counter that was comparatively deserted, trying to gather strength and courage to charge through an eager multitude that was besieging breast-works of shirting and figured lawn. An all-gone-limp feeling had come over her and she rested her hand aimlessly upon the counter. She wore no gloves. By degrees she grew aware that her hand had encountered something very soothing, very pleasant to touch. She looked down to see that her hand lay upon a pile of silk stockings. A placard near by announced that they had been reduced in price from two dollars and fifty cents to one dollar and ninety-eight cents; and a young girl who stood behind the counter asked her if she wished to examine their line of silk hosiery. She smiled, just as if she had been asked to inspect a tiara of diamonds with the ultimate view of purchasing it. But she went on feeling the soft, sheeny luxurious things – with both hands now, holding them up to see them glisten, and to feel them glide serpent-like through her fingers.

Two hectic blotches came suddenly into her pale cheeks. She looked up at the girl.

'Do you think there are any eight-and-a-halfs among these?'

There were any number of eight-and-a-halfs. In fact, there were more of that size than any other. Here was a light-blue pair; there were some lavender, some all black and various shades of tan and grey. Mrs Sommers selected a black pair and looked at them very long and closely. She pretended to be examining their texture, which the clerk assured her was excellent.

'A dollar and ninety-eight cents,' she mused aloud. 'Well, I'll take this pair.' She handed the girl a five-dollar bill and waited for her change and for her parcel. What a very small parcel it was. It seemed lost in the depths of her shabby old shopping-bag.

Mrs Sommers after that did not move in the direction of the bargain counter. She took the elevator, which carried her to an upper floor into the region of the ladies' waiting-rooms. Here, in a retired corner, she exchanged her cotton stockings for the new silk ones which she had just bought. She was not going through any acute mental process or reasoning with herself, nor was she striving to explain to her satisfaction the motive of her action. She was not thinking at all. She seemed for the time to be taking a rest from that laborious and fatiguing function and to have abandoned herself to some mechanical impulse that directed her actions and freed her of responsibility.

How good was the touch of the raw silk to her flesh! She felt like lying back in the cushioned chair and revelling for a while in the luxury of it. She did for a little while. Then she replaced her shoes, rolled the cotton stockings together and thrust them into her bag. After doing this she crossed straight over to the shoe department and took her seat to be fitted.

She was fastidious. The clerk could not make her out; he could not reconcile her shoes with her stockings, and she was not too easily pleased. She held back her skirts and turned her feet one way and her head another way as she glanced down at the polished, pointed-tipped boots. Her foot and ankle looked very pretty. She could not realise that they belonged to her and were a part of herself. She wanted an excellent and stylish fit, she told the young fellow who served her, and she did not mind the difference of a dollar or two more in the price so long as she got what she desired.

It was a long time since Mrs Sommers had been fitted with gloves. On rare occasions when she had bought a pair they were always 'bargains', so cheap that it would have been preposterous and unreasonable to have expected them to be fitted to the hand.

Now she rested her elbow on the cushion of the glove counter, and a pretty, pleasant young creature, delicate and deft of touch, drew a long-wristed 'kid' over Mrs Sommers's hand. She smoothed it down over the wrist and buttoned it neatly, and both lost themselves for a second or two in admiring contemplation of the little symmetrical gloved hand. But there were other places where money might be spent.

There were books and magazines piled up in the window of a stall a few paces down the street. Mrs Sommers bought two high-priced magazines such as she had been accustomed to read in the days when she had been accustomed to other pleasant things. She carried them without wrapping. As well as she could she lifted her skirts at the crossings. Her stockings and boots and well-fitting gloves had worked marvels in her bearing – had given her a feeling of assurance, a sense of belonging to the well-dressed multitude.

She was very hungry. Another time she would have stilled the cravings for food until reaching her own home, where she would have brewed herself a cup of tea and taken a snack of anything that was available. But the impulse that was guiding her would not suffer her to entertain any such thought.

There was a restaurant at the corner. She had never entered its doors; from the outside she had sometimes caught glimpses of spotless damask and shining crystal, and soft-stepping waiters serving people of fashion.

When she entered her appearance created no surprise, no

consternation, as she had half feared it might. She seated herself at a small table alone, and an attentive waiter at once approached to take her order. She did not want a profusion; she craved a nice and tasty bite – a half-dozen blue-points,[417] a plump chop with cress, a something sweet – a *crème-frappée*,[418] for instance; a glass of Rhine wine, and after all a small cup of black coffee.

While waiting to be served she removed her gloves very leisurely and laid them beside her. Then she picked up a magazine and glanced through it, cutting the pages with the blunt edge of her knife. It was all very agreeable. The damask was even more spotless than it had seemed through the window, and the crystal more sparkling. There were quiet ladies and gentlemen, who did not notice her, lunching at the small tables like her own. A soft, pleasing strain of music could be heard, and a gentle breeze was blowing through the window. She tasted a bite, and she read a word or two, and she sipped the amber wine and wiggled her toes in the silk stockings. The price of it made no difference. She counted the money out to the waiter and left an extra coin on his tray, whereupon he bowed before her as before a princess of royal blood.

There was still money in her purse, and her next temptation presented itself in the shape of a matinée poster.

It was a little later when she entered the theatre, the play had begun and the house seemed to her to be packed. But there were vacant seats here and there, and into one of them she was ushered, between brilliantly dressed women who had gone there to kill time and eat candy and display their gaudy attire. There were many others who were there solely for the play and acting. It is safe to say there was no one present who bore quite the attitude which Mrs Sommers did to her surroundings. She gathered in the whole – stage and players and people in one wide impression, and absorbed it and enjoyed it. She laughed at the comedy and wept – she and the gaudy woman next to her wept over the tragedy. And they talked a little together over it. And the gaudy woman wiped her eyes and sniffled on a tiny square of filmy, perfumed lace and passed little Mrs Sommers her box of candy.

The play was over, the music ceased, the crowd filed out. It was like a dream ended. People scattered in all directions. Mrs Sommers went to the corner and waited for the cable car.

A man with keen eyes, who sat opposite to her, seemed to like the study of her small, pale face. It puzzled him to decipher what he saw there. In truth, he saw nothing – unless he were wizard enough to detect a poignant wish, a powerful longing that the cable car would never stop anywhere, but go on and on with her for ever.

An Egyptian Cigarette

My friend the architect, who is something of a traveller, was showing us various curios which he had gathered during a visit to the Orient.

'Here is something for you,' he said, picking up a small box and turning it over in his hand. 'You are a cigarette-smoker; take this home with you. It was given to me in Cairo by a species of fakir,[419] who fancied I had done him a good turn.'

The box was covered with glazed, yellow paper, so skilfully gummed as to appear to be all one piece. It bore no label, no stamp – nothing to indicate its contents.

'How do you know they are cigarettes?' I asked, taking the box and turning it stupidly around as one turns a sealed letter and speculates before opening it.

'I only know what he told me,' replied the architect, 'but it is easy enough to determine the question of his integrity.' He handed me a sharp, pointed paper-cutter, and with it I opened the lid as carefully as possible.

The box contained six cigarettes, evidently hand-made. The wrappers were of pale-yellow paper, and the tobacco was almost the same colour. It was of finer cut than the Turkish or ordinary Egyptian, and threads of it stuck out at either end.

'Will you try one now, madame?' asked the architect, offering to strike a match.

'Not now and not here,' I replied; 'after the coffee, if you will permit me to slip into your smoking-den. Some of the women here detest the odour of cigarettes.'

The smoking-room lay at the end of a short, curved passage. Its appointments were exclusively oriental. A broad, low window opened out upon a balcony that overhung the garden. From the divan upon which I reclined, only the swaying treetops could be seen. The maple leaves glistened in the afternoon sun. Beside the divan was a low stand which contained the complete paraphernalia of a smoker. I was feeling quite comfortable, and congratulated myself upon having escaped for a while the incessant chatter of the women that reached me faintly.

I took a cigarette and lit it, placing the box upon the stand just as the tiny clock, which was there, chimed in silvery strokes the hour of five.

I took one long inspiration of the Egyptian cigarette. The grey-green smoke arose in a small puffy column that spread and broadened, that seemed to fill the room. I could see the maple leaves dimly, as if they were veiled in a shimmer of moonlight. A subtle, disturbing current passed through my whole body and went to my head like the fumes of disturbing wine. I took another deep inhalation of the cigarette.

*

Ah! the sand has blistered my cheek! I have lain here all day with my face in the sand. Tonight, when the everlasting stars are burning, I shall drag myself to the river.

He will never come back.

Thus far I followed him; with flying feet; with stumbling feet; on hands and knees, crawling; and outstretched arms, and here I have fallen in the sand.

The sand has blistered my cheek; it has blistered all my body, and the sun is crushing me with hot torture. There is shade beneath yonder cluster of palms.

I shall stay here in the sand till the hour and the night comes.

I laughed at the oracles and scoffed at the stars when they told that after the rapture of life I would open my arms inviting death, and the waters would envelop me.

Oh! how the sand blisters my cheek! and I have no tears to quench the fire. The river is cool and the night is not far distant.

I turned from the gods and said: 'There is but one; Bardja is my god.' That was when I decked myself with lilies and wove flowers into a garland and held him close in the frail, sweet fetters.

He will never come back. He turned upon his camel as he rode away. He turned and looked at me crouching here and laughed, showing his gleaming white teeth.

Whenever he kissed me and went away he always came back again. Whenever he flamed with fierce anger and left me with stinging words, he always came back. But today he neither kissed me nor was he angry. He only said: 'Oh! I am tired of fetters, and kisses, and you. I am going away. You will never see me again. I am going to the great city where men swarm like bees. I am going beyond, where the monster stones are rising heavenward in a monument for the unborn ages. Oh! I am tired. You will see me no more.'

And he rode away on his camel. He smiled and showed his cruel white teeth as he turned to look at me crouching here.

How slow the hours drag! It seems to me that I have lain here for days in the sand, feeding upon despair. Despair is bitter and it nourishes resolve.

I hear the wings of a bird flapping above my head, flying low, in circles.

The sun is gone. The sand has crept between my lips and teeth and under my parched tongue.

If I raise my head, perhaps I shall see the evening star.

Oh! the pain in my arms and legs! My body is sore and bruised as if broken. Why can I not rise and run as I did this morning? Why must I drag myself thus like a wounded serpent, twisting and writhing?

The river is near at hand. I hear it – I see it – Oh! the sand! Oh! the shine! How cool! how cold!

The water! the water! In my eyes, my ears, my throat! It strangles me! Help! will the gods not help me?

Oh! the sweet rapture of rest! There is music in the temple. And here is fruit to taste. Bardja came with the music – The moon shines and the breeze is soft – A garland of flowers – let us go into the king's garden and look at the blue lily, Bardja.

*

The maple leaves looked as if a silvery shimmer enveloped them. The grey-green smoke no longer filled the room. I could hardly lift the lids of my eyes. The weight of centuries seemed to suffocate my soul as it struggled to escape, to free itself and breathe.

I had tasted the depths of human despair.

The little clock upon the stand pointed to a quarter past five. The cigarettes still reposed in the yellow box. Only the stub of the one I had smoked remained. I had laid it in the ashtray.

As I looked at the cigarettes in their pale wrappers, I wondered what other visions they might hold for me; what might I not find in their mystic fumes? Perhaps a vision of celestial peace; a dream of hopes fulfilled; a taste of rapture, such as had not entered into my mind to conceive.

I took the cigarettes and crumpled them between my hands. I walked to the window and spread my palms wide. The light breeze caught up the golden threads and bore them writhing and dancing far out among the maple leaves.

My friend the architect lifted the curtain and entered, bringing me a second cup of coffee.

'How pale you are!' he exclaimed, solicitously. 'Are you not feeling well?'

'A little the worse for a dream,' I told him.

GLOSSARY

The following notes do not attempt to gloss Chopin's use of regional dialects, which is generally easy enough to follow, neither do they include those expressions already explained by Chopin in the text. The Glossary provides a translation of recurrent French and regional terms.

Allez! Go away!

ami / amie; en bon ami friend (male and female); like a good friend

au revoir goodbye

banquette pavement (usually a wooden platform)

beau / belle beautiful (masculine and feminine)

bien well

blaguer tease, joker

bon / bonne good (masculine and feminine)

bon à rien good for nothing

bon voyage have a good journey

chambres garnies furnished rooms

cher / chère; chéri / chérie dear; darling (masculine and feminine)

comment! what! (exclamation)

coup d'état the sudden, often violent, overthrow of a government

coupé a short, four-wheeled, closed carriage, typically for two passengers and with an outside seat for the driver

croquignoles crunchy biscuits made with flour, butter, eggs and sugar

curé priest

Dieu God

Dieu sait God knows

donc then

eau sédative calming water

encore still, again

farceur joker, buffoon

femme woman, wife

fils / fille son / daughter

friandises sweet delicacies

garçon boy

grif / griffe	the child of a mulatto and a black person (male and female)
grosbec	a large-beaked bird
hein!	eh!
ma foi!	indeed! (literally 'my faith!')
mais	but
maître	master (also in the sense of Lord/God, when capitalised)
maman	mummy, mama
mignon(ne)	sweet, cute (masculine and feminine)
mon / ma	my (masculine and feminine)
mulatresse / mulâtresse	mulatto woman
(Maman-)Nainaine / nénaine	godmother
oui	yes
par example!	really!
parbleu!	by Jove!
parterre	flower bed, arranged ornamentally on a level surface, typical of formal gardens
pauvre	poor
peignoir	a woman's dressing gown; etymologically, a garment worn when combing one's hair (from the French *peigner*)
pension	boarding house
petit / petite	small, little (masculine and feminine)
picayune	a small coin
porte-monnaie / portemonnaie	coin purse
poudre de riz	face powder
reine	queen
sapristi!	for God's sake! / good heavens!
sauvage	savage
(en) grand seigneur	like a great lord
soirée musicale	evening of musical entertainment
(bien) souffrant	unwell
tiens!	well!
tignon	a handkerchief tied up and used as a headdress
'Tit / 'Tite	abbreviation for Petit / Petite
tonnerre!	thunder!
triste	sad
va!	go away!

NOTES

THE AWAKENING

1 (p. 1) *Allez vous-en! Allez vous-en! Sapristi!*   Go away! Go away! For God's sake!

2 (p. 1) *Grand Isle*   a barrier island located at the mouth of Barataria Bay in the Gulf of Mexico, approximately fifty miles south of New Orleans. Its first recorded settlements date back to the 1780s, when the Louisiana Territory was a Spanish colony. Its local population were mostly fishermen, but by the 1870s Grand Isle had become a fashionable summer resort for New Orleans residents, including Kate Chopin and her young family. On 1 October 1893, the island was devastated by a hurricane.

3 (p. 1) *Zampa*   or *La fiancée de marbre* ('The marble fiancée'), an opera by the French composer Ferdinand Hérold (1791–1833), first performed in Paris in 1831. Its eponymous protagonist is a pirate.

4 (p. 1) *Madame Lebrun*   a character first featured in 'Tonie' (1893), the short story later included in *A Night in Acadie* (1897) with the title 'At Chênière Caminada'

5 (p. 2) *telling her beads*   saying her prayers, using rosary beads

6 (p. 2) *Chênière Caminada*   a small coastal settlement opposite Grand Isle, named after Francisco Caminada, the Spanish merchant who owned the land in the late eighteenth century. A *chênière* is a ridge emerging from a swamp and covered with oaks (*chênes* in French).

7 (p. 2) *lugger*   a small sailing vessel, typically used as a fishing boat. Beaudelet first featured in 'Tonie' (1893). See Note 4 above.

8 (p. 2) *quadroon*   a person of one-quarter black ancestry

9 (p. 3) *The Poet and the Peasant*   an operetta by the Austrian composer Franz von Suppé (1819–95), first performed in 1846

10 (p. 4) *Quartier Français*   the French Quarter in New Orleans. Also known as Vieux Carré (Old Quarter), it was home to the Creole elite of French and Spanish descent.

11 (p. 5) *mules*   closed-toe, backless slippers

12 (p. 6) *rockaway*   a light, low four-wheel carriage with open sides

13 (p. 6) *Carondelet Street*   the financial centre of the city and home to the New Orleans Cotton Exchange (built in 1871). Oscar Chopin had his office in 65 Carondelet Street.

14 (p. 9) *Creole*   Louisiana people of pure French descent. See Introduction.

15 (p. 9) *accouchements*   confinements (during childbirth)

16 (p. 10) *Mademoiselle Duvigné*   first featured in 'Tonie' (1893). See Note 4 above.

17 (p. 10) *Daudet*   the French novelist Alphonse Daudet (1840–97)

18 (p. 10) *Passez! Adieu! Allez vous-en!*   Go on! Goodbye! Go away!

19 (p. 10) *Blaguer – farceur – gros bête, va!*   Tease – buffoon – big idiot, run along!

20 (p. 11) *Mais ce n'est pas mal! Elle s'y connait, elle a de le force, oui*   Not bad! She knows what she's doing, she has some talent, yes

21 (p. 11) *befurbelowed*   dressed in frilly clothing

22 (p. 14) *crash*   rough cotton or linen fabric

23 (p. 15) *lateen*   triangular

24 (p. 15) *Cat Island*   Pamela Knights (p. 362) points out that, according to the Louisiana writer G. W. Cable (1844–1925), this was the site of an encounter between a warship of the British Navy and two privateers. It is therefore one of the earliest allusions to pirates in the text.

25 (p. 16) *Her most intimate friend at school*   this friendship is reminiscent of the relationship between Kate Chopin and Kitty Garesché. The two met as fellow pupils at the Sacred Heart Academy in St Louis and became lifelong friends. Kitty would later join the Sacred Heart convent as a nun.

26 (p. 16) *Napoleon*   the French general Napoleon Bonaparte (1769–1821). He was emperor of France from 1804 to 1814, and again in 1815.

27 (p. 18) *Iberville*   Iberville parish (county), located north-west of New Orleans along the Mississippi. Throughout the nineteenth century, Louisiana was the leading producer of sugar in the United States, and Iberville was at the heart of its sugar-cane industry. The Mississippi River also boosted the local timber manufacture and trade.

28 (p. 18) *Tiens! . . . Voilà que Madame Ratignolle est jalousie!*   Ah! So Madame Ratignolle is jealous!

29 (p. 19) *Alcée Arobin*   Kate Chopin's biographer Emily Toth suggests that Alcée Arobin is based on Albert Sampite, the Cloutierville plantation owner with whom Chopin is rumoured to have had an affair (see Introduction and also Note 201 for another possibility).

30 (p. 19) *Biloxi*   a seaside resort on the Mississippi coast

31 (p. 20) *Angostura*   a blend of aromatic herbs and spices, used to flavour drinks

32 (p. 20) *Goncourt*   the French brothers Edmond (1822–96) and Jules (1830–70) de Goncourt, who wrote several novels together

33 (p. 21) *tête montée*   hothead

34 (p. 21) *Vera Cruz*   a major city and port on the Gulf of Mexico, in the Mexican state of Veracruz. In the second half of the nineteenth century, it underwent a period of significant decline.

35 (p. 22) *Allez vous-en! Sapristi!*   Go away! For God's sake! See Note 1 above.

36 (p. 24) *'Solitude'*   Kate Chopin's working title for the novel was *A Solitary Soul*, perhaps an echo of Guy de Maupassant's story 'Solitude' (1884). Chopin's translation of that story was published in the *St Louis Life* on 28 December 1895.

37 (p. 25) *Chopin*   the celebrated Polish composer and virtuoso pianist Frédéric François Chopin (1810–49)

38 (p. 33) *Spanish moss*   also referred to as 'grey beard'. It is an air plant which does not have roots, and grows instead around a host tree, capturing moisture from the atmosphere. Its trailing stems, hanging down from branches, are associated with Southern States gothic imagery in literature.

39 (p. 33) *Grande Terre*   a small island, east of Grand Isle

40 (p. 34) *Bayou Brulow*   one of the fishing villages built on stilts above the marshy water of the bay

41 (p. 34) *Tonie*   the eponymous protagonist of 'Tonie' (1893). See Note 7 above.

42 (p. 34) *the pirate gold*   Grand Isle, Grande Terre and the other neighbouring islands are associated with the French privateer Jean Lafitte (*c.*1780–*c.*1826), who led a colony of pirates and smugglers in the Barataria Bay.

43 (p. 35) *Madame Antoine*   first featured in 'Tonie' (1893). See Note 4 above.

44 (p. 35) *Acadian*   the descendants of French Canadian settlers who, driven away from Nova Scotia by the British in 1755, had relocated to Louisiana

45 (p. 35) *cot*   cottage

46 (p. 38) *Baratarians*   Jean Lafitte's band of pirates. See Note 42 above.

47 (p. 39) *Si tu savais*   If you knew

48 (p. 40) *Bedlam*   a lunatic asylum (after the Bethlehem Royal Hospital in London)

49 (p. 41) *courtbouillon*   a fish broth or stew

50 (p. 41) *tamales*   traditional Mexican food

51 (p. 48) *Esplanade Street*   the most prestigious address in the French Quarter in New Orleans

52 (p. 49) *reception day*   the day, once a week, when women of Edna Pontellier's social class were expected to be at home to receive visitors

53 (p. 50) *le convenances*   social conventions

54 (p. 50) *free-lunch stand*   a stand with a selection of free food, common in drinking establishments of New Orleans, designed to lure businessmen in at lunchtime

55 (p. 50) *Carrolton*   a village to the west of New Orleans, incorporated into the city in the 1880s

56 (p. 53) *porte cochère*   large covered entrance for carriages. It provided sheltered access to and from the house to those alighting or boarding the vehicle.

57 (p. 55) *Better a dinner of herbs*   Proverbs 15:17

58 (p. 55) *en bonne ménagère*   as a good housewife

59 (p. 56) *atelier*   studio

60 (p. 56) *Ah! si tu savais!*   Robert's song. See Note 47 above.

61 (p. 58) *the old régime*   the Spanish rule (officially from 1766 to 1803). See Introduction.

62 (p. 60) *prunella gaiter*   an overshoe with a cloth top

63 (p. 61) *la belle dame*   literally 'the beautiful lady', but also a possible reference to the figure of the *femme fatale* in John Keats's ballad 'La Belle Dame sans Merci' (1819)

64 (p. 62) *that Impromptu of Chopin's*   Chopin (see Note 37 above) composed three pieces with this title. The name suggests a composition of passionate, spontaneous character.

65 (p. 63) *Isolde's song* from the opera *Tristan und Isolde* (1865) by the German composer Richard Wagner (1813–83). The legend of the doomed lovers dates back to twelfth-century French courtly romances.

66 (p. 64) *Canal Street* a major thoroughfare in New Orleans. It marked the boundary between the French Quarter and the newer, 'American' section, inhabited by more recent immigrants to the city, following the Louisiana Purchase in 1803. Despite their French ancestry, Kate and Oscar Chopin lived in three different houses in the American section during their nine years of married life in New Orleans.

67 (p. 65) *à jeudi* until Thursday

68 (p. 66) *Confederate army* the army of the pro-slavery, secessionist Southern States during the American Civil War (1861–5). Louisiana was one of the first seven states to secede from the Union and join the Confederation in 1861. Kentucky tried to maintain its precarious neutrality in the Civil War but, following its occupation by Confederate troops, it sought the intervention of the Union military forces.

69 (p. 67) *bourgeois* middle-class

70 (p. 68) *Lecompte stables* New Orleans had several racetracks, and Lecompte was the name of one of the most famous Louisiana racehorses of the antebellum period.

71 (p. 69) *Baratarian Islands* See Notes 2 and 42 above.

72 (p. 71) *à point* just right

73 (p. 71) *marron glacé* glazed chestnuts

74 (p. 71) *Emerson* the Transcendentalist philosopher, critic and writer Ralph Waldo Emerson (1803–82), one of the most eminent American thinkers of the nineteenth century. The fact that Edna finds him soporific might indicate what Chopin herself thought of his support for the theory of 'separate spheres' (different, complementary gender roles). See Toth, pp. 52–3.

75 (p. 72) *drag* a coach drawn by four horses

76 (p. 73) *Dante* the Italian poet Dante Alighieri (1265–1321), author of *The Divine Comedy*

77 (p. 73) *Grieg* the Norwegian composer Edvard Grieg (1843–1907)

78 (p. 77) *Beethoven* the German composer Ludwig van Beethoven (1770–1827)

79 (p. 79) *grand esprit* great mind

80 (p. 81) *tabouret*   stool

81 (p. 85) *lorgnettes*   spectacles with a handle to hold them in place

82 (p. 85) *nom de guerre*   a pseudonym under which one engages in war, or any other enterprising activity

83 (p. 85) *Gouvernail*   the bachelor journalist who also features in 'Athénaïse' (1896) and 'A Respectable Woman' (1894)

84 (p. 86) *the mets, the entre-mets*   the main courses, the side dishes

85 (p. 86) *pompono*   an expensive fish (usually spelled 'pompano')

86 (p. 86) *Perdido Street*   a street in the American Quarter. The name literally means 'lost'.

87 (p. 87) *Bonne nuit, ma reine; soyez sage*   Good night, my queen; be wise

88 (p. 88) *There was a graven image . . . ground of gold*   the opening lines of 'A Cameo', a sonnet by the English Decadent poet Algernon Charles Swinburne (1837–1909)

89 (p. 88) *Ah! si tu savais / Ce que tes yeux me disent*   Ah! if you knew, what your eyes are telling me

90 (p. 91) *ménage*   household

91 (p. 91) *snuggery*   a small, cosy room

92 (p. 94) *vingt-et-un*   twenty-one, a card game

93 (p. 98) *patois*   a version of French spoken by the black population of Louisiana

94 (p. 104) *being able to smoke*   Chopin herself enjoyed smoking, although women were not supposed to smoke in public.

95 (p. 110) *scantling*   a timber beam

96 (p. 110) *Lucullan feast*   a lavish banquet (after the first-century Roman general Lucius Licinus Lucullus, renowned for his hospitality)

97 (p. 110) *Venus*   the Roman equivalent of Aphrodite, the Greek goddess of love and beauty. Venus was born out of the foam of the sea.

98 (p. 110) *houris*   beautiful young women in the Muslim paradise

BAYOU FOLK

The volume was published on 24 March 1894 by Houghton, Mifflin & Company (Boston and New York). Of the twenty-three stories in the collection, only five had not previously appeared in print.

A No-Account Creole

First published in *Century*, January 1894

99 (p. 115) *Canal Street*   See Note 66 above.

100 (p. 115) *Harding & Offdean*   the office of the two agents is mentioned again in 'Athénaïse' (1896)

101 (p. 116) *Red River*   a major tributary of the Mississippi. In Natchitoches parish, in north-west Louisiana, it forms the Cane River Lake and is known as the Cane River.

102 (p. 116) *Natchitoches parish*   'pronounced Nack-e-tosh' (Chopin's own note). Louisiana is divided into parishes, rather than counties; Natchitoches was founded in 1714 and is therefore the oldest permanent settlement in Louisiana.

103 (p. 116) *Santien*   Members of the Santien family appear in Chopin's first novel *At Fault* (1890), as well as in 'In and Out of Old Natchitoches' (1893), 'In Sabine' (1894) and 'Ma'ame Pélagie' (1893), all included in *Bayou Folk* (1894).

104 (p. 117) *extinguisher*   'a hollow conical cap for extinguishing the light of a candle or lamp' (*OED*)

105 (p. 117) *gloire-de-Dijon*   a climbing rose, also known as 'Old Glory Rose'

106 (p. 118) *Mme Duplan*   owner of the plantation Les Chêniers. She also features in 'A Rude Awakening' (1893). The Duplans are the neighbours of M'sieur Michel in 'After the Winter' (1896), where Euphrasie makes a brief appearance. Their plantation is mentioned in 'Ozème's Holiday' (1896) too.

107 (p. 120) *Les Chêniers*   The Oak Grove, Mme Duplan's plantation

108 (p. 121) *Mardi Gras*   Shrove Tuesday or, literally, Fat Tuesday. The day before the beginning of Lent on Ash Wednesday, it is the culmination of the carnival season, which is typically celebrated through parades, masquerade balls and street parties in Catholic countries. New Orleans was, and still is, particularly famous for its Mardi Gras celebrations.

109 (p. 123) *La Chatte*   The She-Cat

110 (p. 124) *Pres'dent Hayes* Rutherford Birchard Hayes (1822–93), 19th President of the United States, from 1877 to 1881. The year of his election marks the end of the Reconstruction Era following the American Civil War (1861–5).

111 (p. 126) *had not 'crossed Canal Street'* had not left the French Quarter

112 (p. 129) *maigre-échine* thin, lanky man

In and Out of Old Natchitoches

First published in *Two Tales*, 8 April 1893

113 (p. 137) *Mr Alphonse Laballière* Members of the Laballière family appear in other stories in this collection, such as 'Loka' (1892) and 'At the 'Cadian Ball' (1892), in 'Ozème's Holiday' (1896) and in *A Night in Acadie* (1897), as well as in a couple of uncollected pieces not included in the present volume.

114 (p. 137) *free mulattoes* 'A term still applied in Louisiana to mulattoes who were never in slavery and whose families in most instances were themselves slave owners' (Kate Chopin's note).

115 (p. 138) *the Empress Eugénie* wife of Napoleon III, emperor of France from 1852 to 1870

116 (p. 139) *Choctaw Indians* Native American people living to the east of the Mississippi River

117 (p. 139) *South Sea* the area of the Pacific Ocean typically identified with Polynesia

118 (p. 140) *Et toi, mon petit Numa, j'espère qu'un autre* And you, my little Numa, I hope that another –

119 (p. 141) *l'Isle des Mulâtres* the Island of the Mulattoes

120 (p. 142) *un ange du bon Dieu* an angel of the good Lord

121 (p. 142) *sauterne* a sweet wine

122 (p. 142) *charcuterie* cured and cooked pork meat

123 (p. 143) *Ah, la bonne tante* Ah, the good aunt

124 (p. 143) *Kyrie eleison* part of the Christian liturgy, meaning 'Lord have mercy' (in Greek)

125 (p. 143) *can-cans* gossip

126 (p. 143) *Athénaïse Miché* Athénaïse will be the protagonist of the eponymous story, first published in 1896 and later included in *A Night in Acadie* (1897).

127 (p. 144) *Figurez vous . . . pensez donc* Imagine . . . think about it

128 (p. 144) *boudin blanc* white blood sausage

129 (p. 148) *volante* frilly garment

In Sabine

First published in *Bayou Folk*

130 (p. 150) *'Pike's Magnolia'*   a kind of liquor

131 (p. 154) *a pone of corn bread*   corn mixed with water and fried in a flat cake on a griddle

132 (p. 155) *Cloutierville*   a small village on the Cane River, in Natchitoches parish. Chopin lived there from 1879 to 1884. (See Introduction).

133 (p. 155) *gumbo-filé*   a traditional stew, thickened with powdered dried sassafras leaves instead of okra

A Very Fine Fiddle

First published in *Harper's Young People*, 16 February 1892

134 (p. 157) *Italien*   Italian. Italy numbers several prestigious violin-makers.

135 (p. 157) *Dieu merci!* God have mercy!

Beyond the Bayou

First published in *Youth's Companion*, 15 June 1893

136 (p. 159) *La Folle*   the madwoman

137 (p. 159) *Bellissime*   The Most Beautiful

138 (p. 160) *Non, non!*   No, no!

139 (p. 161) *mon bébé, mon Chéri!*   my baby, my Chéri!

140 (p. 161) *Dr Bonfils*   the doctor had already featured in 'The Bênitous' Slave' (1892)

141 (p. 161) *Venez donc! Au secours!*   Come here! Help!

142 (p. 161) *Bon Dieu, ayez pitié La Folle! Bon Dieu, ayez pitié moi!* Good God, have mercy on La Folle! Good God, have mercy on me!

Old Aunt Peggy

First published in *Bayou Folk*

143 (p. 165) *the war*   the American Civil War (1861–5)

The Return of Alcibiade

First published in *St Louis Life*, 17 December 1892

144 (p. 167) *À la fin! mon fils! À la fin!*   At last! my son! At last!

145 (p. 167) *chapelet*   rosary

146 (p. 168) *il est malin, oui*   he is shrewed, yes

147 (p. 170) *aux truffles*   stuffed with truffles

148 (p. 170) *négrillon*   black child (diminutive of 'negre')

A Rude Awakening

First published in *Youth's Companion*, 2 February 1893

149 (p. 174) *Marse Duplan* He is the owner of Les Chêniers, the plantation mentioned in 'A No-Account Creole' (1894) and in 'After the Winter' (1896). (See Notes 106 and 107 above.)

150 (p. 174) *Brahma chickens* a breed of large chickens

151 (p. 176) *Malédiction!* Damn!

The Bênitous' Slave

First published in *Harper's Young People*, 16 February 1892

152 (p. 180) *Dr Bonfils* also featured in 'Beyond the Bayou' (1893)

153 (p. 180) *extinguisher fashion* See Note 104.

Désirée's Baby

First published as 'The Father of Désirée's Baby' in *Vogue*, 14 January 1893

154 (p. 182) *L'Abri* The Shelter

155 (p. 182) *corbeille* wedding present from the groom to the bride

156 (p. 183) *cochon de lait* piglet

157 (p. 183) *La Blanche* The White Woman

158 (p. 186) *layette* clothing for a newborn baby

A Turkey Hunt

First published in *Harper's Young People*, 16 February 1892

159 (p. 187) *Polisson* literally, disobedient

Madame Célestin's Divorce

First published in *Bayou Folk*

160 (p. 189) *Watteau fold* a fold of the kind worn by the women painted by the French artist Jean-Antoine Watteau (1684–1721)

161 (p. 189) *pourtant* furthermore

162 (p. 190) *je vous garantis* I assure you

163 (p. 190) *empressement* eagerness

Love on the Bon-Dieu

First published in *Two Tales*, 23 July 1892

164 (p. 192) *Père Antoine* Father Antoine

165 (p. 192) *barège* a sheer fabric

166 (p. 192) *'josie'* girl's jacket

167 (p. 195) *mull* a soft, fine fabric

168 (p. 196) *canaille* scoundrel

169 (p. 197) *endimanchés* dressed up (with Sunday clothes)

170 (p. 197) *garde manger* pantry

Loka

First published in *Youth's Companion*, 22 December 1892

171 (p. 202) *Band of the United Endeavour* a Christian charitable society

172 (p. 202) *Madame Laballière* See Note 113 above.

173 (p. 203) *Vrai sauvage ça* A real savage, this one

174 (p. 206) *une pareille sauvage* such a savage

Boulôt and Boulotte

First published in *Harper's Young People*, 8 December 1891

175 (p. 208) *Boulôt and Boulotte* plump, chubby (masculine and feminine)

For Marse Chouchoute

First published in *Youth's Companion*, 20 August 1891

176 (p. 210) *Chouchoute* Sweetie

177 (p. 212) *v'là* here it is

178 (p. 214) *Old Harry* the devil

179 (p. 215) *Buffalo Bill* nickname of William Frederick Cody (1846–1917). A former rider for the Pony Express, soldier in the Union army and civilian scout, in 1883 Cody founded Buffalo Bill's Wild West Show, which staged episodes of frontier life and of the Indian Wars throughout the United States and Europe.

A Visit to Avoyelles

First published in *Vogue*, 14 January 1893

180 (p. 216) *Avoyelles* a parish about a hundred miles down the Red River from Natchitoches

181 (p. 218) *en passant* when passing, while on his way

182 (p. 218) *Non, j'te garantis!* No, I assure you!

A Wizard from Gettysburg

First published in *Youth's Companion*, 7 July 1892

183 (p. 219) *Gettysburg* a town in Pennsylvania. In July 1863, it was the location of one of the most famous battles of the American Civil War, where the Union forces won a historic victory against General Robert E. Lee's Confederate troops.

184 (p. 219) *Bon-Accueil* Welcome

185 (p. 219) *Cherokee* a Native American tribe, indigenous to the south-eastern United States

186 (p. 222) *mé-mère* grandmother

Ma'ame Pèlagie

First published in *New Orleans Times–Democrat*, 24 December 1893

187 (p. 226) *the war* the American Civil War (1861–5)

188 (p. 226) *Côte Joyeuse* Happy Coast

189 (p. 226) *Panthéon* an imposing building in Paris. Formerly a church, it is now used as a mausoleum and houses the remains of notable French citizens.

190 (p. 226) *Sesoeur* Sister

191 (p. 228) *Tan'tante* Aunt

192 (p. 230) *Il ne faut pas faire mal à Pauline* We must not let Pauline get hurt

193 (p. 230) *la guerre* the war

194 (p. 230) *Sumter* Fort Sumter, South Carolina. The shots that started the Civil War were fired there on 12 April 1861.

195 (p. 230) *La Ricaneuse* The Mocking/Disrespectful Woman

196 (p. 232) *pied à terre* second residence

At the 'Cadian Ball

First published in *Two Tales*, 22 October 1892

197 (p. 233) *Assumption* a parish in south-eastern Louisiana

198 (p. 233) *C'est Espagnol, ça* She's Spanish

199 (p. 233) *Bon chien tient de race* a French proverb, roughly equivalent to the English 'the apple doesn't fall far from the tree', meaning that children take after their parents

200 (p. 233) *Tiens . . . Espèce de lionèse; prends ça, et ça!* Take this, you slut! You lioness [meant as an insult], take this and this!

201 (p. 233) *Alcée Laballiére* his brother Alphonse features in 'In and Out of Old Natchitoches' (1893). Kate Chopin's biographer Emily Toth suggests that Alcée Laballiére is based on Albert Sampite, the Cloutierville plantation owner with whom Chopin is rumoured to have had an affair. (See Introduction and also Note 29 for another possibility.)

202 (p. 235) *Ah, Sainte Vierge! faut de la patience! butor, va!* Ah, Holy Virgin Mary! Give me patience! Go away, you oaf!

203 (p. 236) *John L. Sulvun* the boxing champion John L. Sullivan (1858–1918)

204 (p. 236) *le parc aux petits*   the children's room, a regular feature at Acadian balls

205 (p. 237) *Ces maudits gens du raiderode*   These damned people from the railroad

206 (p. 237) *brave homme*   a good man

207 (p. 237) *chic, mais chic*   classy, very classy

208 (p. 237) *panache*   flair, courage

209 (p. 237) *Boulanger*   the extremely popular French general and politician George Boulanger (1837–91)

210 (p. 237) *planté là*   planted there

211 (p. 239) *Ah, c'est vous, Calixta? Comment ça va, mon enfant?*   Ah, it's you, Calixta? How are you, my child?

212 (p. 239) *Tcha va b'en; et vous, mam'zélle?*   I'm fine; and you, miss?

213 (p. 240) *Bonté divine!*   Good God!

214 (p. 241) *Le bal est fini*   The ball is over

La Belle Zoraïde

First published in *Vogue*, 4 January 1894

215 (p. 242) *marais*   swamp

216 (p. 242) *Lisett'* . . . *toué*   Lisette has left / I've lost my happiness / My eyes are like fountains / Since they can't look at you

217 (p. 242) *Madame Delisle*   She is also the title character of 'A Lady of Bayou St John' (1894).

218 (p. 242) *café-au-lait*   coffee with milk

219 (p. 243) *la rue Royale*   a street in the French Quarter of New Orleans

220 (p. 243) *Bamboula*   an African dance. For about a hundred years, until the Civil War, African dancing would take place every Sunday afternoon in Congo Square (officially known as Place des Nègres) in New Orleans.

221 (p. 244) *Malheureuse!*   Wretch!

222 (p. 244) *mo l'aime toi*   I love you

223 (p. 244) *Place d'Armes*   The name typically indicates a big square, large enough for military parades.

224 (p. 244) *Calinda*   another dance of African origins

A Gentleman of Bayou Têche

First published in *Bayou Folk*

225 (p. 247) *Bayou Têche* a major waterway in southern Louisiana. It runs through the area settled by the Acadians after their expulsion from Nova Scotia in 1755.

226 (p. 251) *comme ça* like this

A Lady of Bayou St John

First published in *Vogue*, 4 January 1894

227 (p. 253) *Madame Delisle* It is to her that Manna-Loulou tells the tragic story of la belle Zoraïde in the eponymous story.

A NIGHT IN ACADIE

The volume was published in November 1897 by Way & Williams (Chicago). Of the twenty-one tales and sketches in the collection, only the title story had not previously appeared in print.

A Night in Acadie

First published in the eponymous collection. Chopin's working title for this story had been 'In the Vicinity of Marksville' (see Introduction).

228 (p. 257) *baignés* sweet pastries

229 (p. 258) *Nonc* Uncle

230 (p. 259) *nuque* nape

231 (p. 259) *lisle-thread* a fine cotton thread

232 (p. 259) *J' vous réponds!* I tell you!

233 (p. 259) *toile-cirée* oilcloth

234 (p. 261) *Ah, b'en, pour ça!* Ah, well, really!

235 (p. 262) *gumbo* a traditional stew. See Note 133 above.

236 (p. 262) *piment rouge and piment vert* red and green peppers

237 (p. 262) *Vaux mieux y s'mêle ces affairs, lui; si non!* He'd better mind his own business, or else!

238 (p. 263) *buckboard* a simple vehicle whose seating is attached to a board stretching between the front and rear axles

239 (p. 263) *t'es pareille comme ain mariée* you look just like a bride

240 (p. 263) *c'est vous?* is that you?

241 (p. 264) *Bedlam* See Note 48 above.

242 (p. 264) *C'est toi . . . tonnerre!* You really are the best, my girl! By Jove!

243 (p. 266) *têtes-de-mulets* stubborn mules (literally, 'mule-headed' people)

244 (p. 268) *bois-gras* bits of tree stump

Athénaïse

First published in August and September 1896 in *Atlantic Monthly*

245 (p. 272) *rigolet de Bon Dieu* A 'rigolet' is a small stream off a bayou. The Bon-Dieu is also the setting of 'Love on the Bon-Dieu' (1892).

246 (p. 272) *C'est pas Chrétien, ténez!* It's not Christian, see!

247 (p. 273) *Juanita* a song by the English social reformer Caroline Norton (1808–77), set to a traditional Spanish melody. Norton caused scandal when she left her husband in 1836. She was a campaigner for divorce and for women's rights in marital law. The lyrics to 'Juanita', however, appear to echo Cazeau's predicament as the lover pleads to Juanita, 'Be my own fair bride.'

248 (p. 274) *gumbo-filé* See Note 133 above.

249 (p. 274) *Cochon . . . sacré cochon!* Swine . . . bloody swine!

250 (p. 275) *Comment ça va?* How are you?

251 (p. 277) *La fille de son père* Her father's daughter

252 (p. 279) *maudit* damned

253 (p. 281) *Tiens! Tu va . . . là, moi!* Here! You are going to look after them as you used to. I don't want anything more to do with this now.

254 (p. 285) *Dauphine Street* a street in the French Quarter

255 (p. 285) *the back ell* the back extension, at a right angle to the main building, which therefore looks like the letter 'L'

256 (p. 286) *Gouvernail* See Note 83 above.

257 (p. 286) *ewer* a vase-shaped pitcher

258 (p. 288) *hors d'oeuvres* starters, appetisers

259 (p. 289) *des esprits forts* free spirits, free thinkers, radicals

260 (p. 289) *sapeur* sapper: a soldier who performs military engineering duties, such as digging trenches, building bridges or disarming mines

261 (p. 289) *jalousies* shutters

262 (p. 291) *The Duchess* the Irish writer of light romantic fiction Margaret Wolfe Hungerford, née Hamilton (1855–97). She was popular in the United States under the pen-name 'The Duchess'.

263 (p. 291) *Mrs Humphry Ward*   the English writer Mary Augusta
     Arnold (1851–1920), who published her work under her married
     name. While The Duchess's novels provided light entertainment,
     Ward's fiction dealt with weightier social and moral issues.

264 (p. 291) *Remington's cowboys*   Frederic Remington (1861–1909)
     was an American artist, most famous for his paintings and
     magazine illustrations about the Old West.

265 (p. 296) *Harding & Offdean*   agents mentioned in 'A No-Account
     Creole'. See Note 100 above.

266 (p. 298) *Pauvre ti chou*   Poor little cabbage

After the Winter

First published in *New Orleans Times–Democrat*, 5 April 1896

267 (p. 299) *Les Chêniers*   See Note 107 above.

268 (p. 299) *Duplan*   See Note 106 above.

269 (p. 299) *Louisiana Tigers*   the nickname given to the Louisiana
     Brigade in the Confederate Army of Northern Virginia

270 (p. 300) *Mamzelle Euphrasie*   the protagonist of 'A No-Account
     Creole' (1893)

271 (p. 300) *farandole*   a traditional French dance

272 (p. 301) *La Fringante*   The Frisky Woman

273 (p. 302) *mummery*   a dumb show, a pantomime

274 (p. 303) *Gloria in excelsis Deo!*   Glory to God in the highest! (Latin)

275 (p. 304) *Bonae voluntatis*   Of good will (Latin)

276 (p. 304) *Pax! pax! pax!*   Peace! peace! peace! (Latin)

Polydore

First published in *Youth's Companion*, 23 April 1896

Regret

First published in *Century*, May 1894

277 (p. 314) *Ti Nomme*   Little Man

278 (p. 316) *Croque-mitaine or Loup-garou*   traditional tales, one about
     an ogre and one about a werewolf

279 (p. 316) *It's terrassent! Bonté!*   It's exhausting! Goodness!

A Matter of Prejudice

First published in *Youth's Companion*, 25 September 1895

280 (p. 318) *levee bank*   embankment

281 (p. 318) *Prytania Street* one of the most affluent streets in the American Quarter in New Orleans

282 (p. 318) *fleur de Laurier* the poisonous tisane of laurel flowers

283 (p. 318) *Partant pour la Syrie!* 'Leaving for Syria', a traditional patriotic French song

284 (p. 322) *Plait-il, madame?* Excuse me, madam?

Caline

First published in *Vogue*, 20 May 1893

285 (p. 325) *loin . . . sait é où* far away . . . God knows where

286 (p. 325) *lagniappe* a small gift given by a merchant to a customer together with a purchase

A Dresden Lady in Dixie

First published in *Catholic Home Journal*, 3 March 1895

Nég Créol

First published in *Atlantic Monthly*, July 1897

287 (p. 333) *Chicot* stump

288 (p. 333) *Maringouin* mosquito

289 (p. 333) *des 'tites cousines* little girl cousins

290 (p. 334) *vendeuse de café* a woman who sells coffee

291 (p. 334) *la maison grise* the grey house

292 (p. 334) *La Chouette* The Owl

293 (p. 335) *Pas d'sucre* No sugar

294 (p. 335) *la nuit blanche* the sleepless night

295 (p. 335) *tisanes* herbal teas

296 (p. 335) *grisgris* charms

297 (p. 335) *eau de Lourdes* water from the French city of Lourdes, thought to be able to cure ailments

298 (p. 336) *Vous pas . . . gagni docteur?* Don't you want your tea, Miss Aglaé? Don't you want me to call the doctor?

299 (p. 336) *une goutte d'eau sucré* a drop of sugared water

300 (p. 336) *là-bas au cathédral* over there at the cathedral

301 (p. 337) *chou-fleur* cauliflower

302 (p. 338) *les Attakapas* a region in central Louisiana

The Lilies

First published in *Wide Awake*, April 1893

303 (p. 339) *Mamouche* also features as the protagonist of 'Mamouche' (1894)

304 (p. 341) *va t'en* go on

305 (p. 342) *jambalaya* a rich Cajun dish

Azélie

First published in *Century*, December 1894

306 (p. 344) *le grand air* fresh air

307 (p. 344) *fanfaron* a boaster, somebody full of himself

308 (p. 347) *que voulez-vous?* what can you do?

309 (p. 348) *après tout* after all

310 (p. 348) *Baton Rouge* the capital of Louisiana, on the east bank of the Mississippi River

Mamouche

First published in *Youth's Companion*, 19 April 1894

311 (p. 352) *Mamouche* first featured in 'The Lilies' (1893)

312 (p. 353) *À ta . . . tra la la la!* Please be good enough to come to your window – tra la la la!

313 (p. 357) *veillée* the evening

314 (p. 357) *Toussaint* All Saints' Day (1 November)

A Sentimental Soul

First published in *New Orleans Times–Democrat*, 22 December 1895

315 (p. 359) *l'Abeille* *The Bee*, a French newspaper published in the United States

316 (p. 359) *à demain!* see you tomorrow!

317 (p. 360) *Courier des États Unis* *United States Courier*, a French newspaper published in the United States

318 (p. 362) *soutane* cassock

319 (p. 362) *Empress Eugénie* See Note 115 above.

320 (p. 362) *Dictionnaire de la Langue Française* *Dictionary of the French Language*

321 (p. 363) *C'est ne pas . . . Augustine* It's not Lacodie, Miss Fleurette. It's me, Augustine.

322 (p. 364) *Bien bon . . . flambé!* It's very kind of you, Miss Fleurette – but it's over. I'm dying, dying, dying!

323 (p. 365) *Inutile; il n'en veut pas*   There's no point; he doesn't want one

324 (p. 365) *Blanchisseuse de Fin*   Laundress of Fine Fabrics

325 (p. 366) *roulades*   a musical embellishment

326 (p. 366) *charivari*   a mock serenade for a newly-wedded couple

Dead Man's Shoes

First published in the *Independent*, 11 February 1897

327 (p. 368) *le vieux Gamiche*   Old Gamiche

328 (p. 370) *deshabille*   the scant clothes

At Chênière Caminada

First published in *New Orleans Times–Democrat*, 23 December 1894

329 (p. 375) *Chênière Caminada*   See Note 6 above.

330 (p. 375) *Credo . . . omnipotentem*   I believe in one God, the Father Almighty (from the Latin liturgy of the Catholic Mass)

331 (p. 376) *Beaudelet's lugger*   See Note 7 above.

332 (p. 376) *gumbo*   See Note 133 above.

333 (p. 376) *courtbouillon*   See Note 49 above.

334 (p. 376) *Barataria Bay*   See Note 42 above.

335 (p. 376) *Madame Lebrun*   See Note 4 above.

336 (p. 377) *lateen*   See Note 23 above.

337 (p. 380) *angelus*   a Catholic devotion

338 (p. 382) *Elle est morte*   She is dead

Odalie Misses Mass

First published in *Shreveport Times*, 1 July 1895

339 (p. 385) *papillottes*   curlers

Cavanelle

First published in *American Jewess*, April 1895

340 (p. 390) *poult-de-soie*   silky fabric

341 (p. 390) *cavatina*   a short, simple song

342 (p. 390) *voyez vous*   you see

343 (p. 390) *des petits soins*   small attentions

344 (p. 390) *soupçon*   little bit

345 (p. 391) *Où es tu donc?*   Where are you?

346 (p. 392) *sirop d'orgeat*   a sweet, almond drink

347 (p. 392) *savoir vivre*   knowledge of the world, and of polite society

348 (p. 392) *petit ménage*   small household
349 (p. 392) *lagniappe*   See Note 286 above.
350 (p. 392) *bouillie*   gruel
351 (p. 392) *papabotte*   small plover (a game bird)
352 (p. 392) *demi-verre*   half glass
353 (p. 393) *petit souper*   small supper
354 (p. 394) *mousseline de laine*   wool chiffon

Tante Cat'rinette

First published in *Athlantic Monthly*, September 1894

355 (p. 395) *Vieumaite*   Old Master
356 (p. 395) *en règle*   according to the law
357 (p. 398) *anisette*   anise-flavoured liqueur
358 (p. 400) *cher coeur*   dear heart
359 (p. 400) *ti chou*   little cabbage
360 (p. 400) *céléra*   terrible

A Respectable Woman

First published in *Vogue*, 15 February 1894

361 (p. 403) *Gouvernail*   See Note 83 above.
362 (p. 404) *batture*   the alluvial land between a river at low-water stage and an embankment
363 (p. 405) *Night of south . . . nodding night* – lines from 'Song of Myself', section 21 of the 1892 edition of *Leaves of Grass* by the American poet Walt Whitman (1819–92). Whitman's poetry is characterised by very sensuous passages. The words that immediately follow those murmured by Gouvernail are 'mad naked summer night'.

Ripe Figs

First published in *Vogue*, 19 August 1893

364 (p. 407) *la Madone*   the Virgin Mary
365 (p. 407) *Toussaint*   All Saints' Day (1 November)

Ozème's Holiday

First published in *Century*, August 1896

366 (p. 408) *Mr Laballière*   See Note 113 above.
367 (p. 408) *fainéant*   a lazy, ineffective person
368 (p. 409) *Duplans*   See Note 106 above.
369 (p. 409) *buckboard*   See Note 238 above.

370 (p. 409) *a pone of corn bread*   See Note 131 above.

371 (p. 413) *à la fin*   in the end, eventually

UNCOLLECTED STORIES

Wiser Than a God

Published in the *Philadelphia Musical Journal*, December 1889

372 (p. 414) *To love . . . even to a god*   Latin proverb from the *Sentantiae* of Publilius Syrus (first century BC)

373 (p. 414) *Mutterchen*   literally, 'little Mother' (German)

374 (p. 415) *Berceuse*   a lullaby

375 (p. 415) *Faranelli*   a misspelling of Farinelli, the stage name of Carlo Maria Broschi (1705–82), the famous Italian castrato who worked at the court of King Philip V of Spain

376 (p. 416) *Ist est nicht . . . mama?*   Isn't it wonderful, mother? (German)

377 (p. 416) *liebchen*   darling (German)

378 (p. 416) *Steinway*   a prestigious make of pianos

379 (p. 417) *Terpsichore*   the muse of dancing and poetry

380 (p. 418) *Jewel Song from Faust*   an aria from the opera *Faust* (1859), written by the French composer Charles François Gounod (1818-93)

381 (p. 419) *hors de combat*   literally, 'outside the fight' (French); out of the running

382 (p. 421) *Ach Gott! . . . gegangen!*   Oh God! Miss Von Stoltz has already left for Leipzig! (German)

A Point at Issue!

Published in *St Louis Post–Dispatch*, 27 October 1889, with the subtitle 'A Story of Love and Reason in which Love Triumphs'

383 (p. 423) *rara avis*   literally, a 'rare bird' (Latin); a wonder

384 (p. 425) *Hades*   the Greek underworld, the abode of the dead

385 (p. 430) *Mazarin*   almond cake

386 (p. 430) *fiacre*   a horse-drawn four-wheeled carriage

387 (p. 431) *bougie*   candle

Mrs Mobry's Reason

Published in *New Orleans Times–Democrat*, 23 April 1893

388 (p. 433) *embrasure*   outward splay of a window

389 (p. 437) *Machiavellian*   cunning and duplicitous

390 (p. 438) *Lancelot*   one of the Knights of the Round Table in the Arthurian legends, known for his prowess and his love for Queen Guinevere

391 (p. 438) *Juliet*   the heroine of William Shakespeare's tragedy of doomed love, *Romeo and Juliet*

392 (p. 440) *the crime of my marriage*   the implication is that Mrs Mobry is the carrier of congenital syphilis which she has passed on to her children.

The Maid of Saint Phillippe
Published in *Short Stories* in November 1892

393 (p. 441) *Saint Phillippe*   a small trading post founded along the Mississippi River, in what is now southern Illinois, by the French explorer Philip François Renault in 1720. As part of the French territory located to the east of the Mississippi, the village came under British domination following their victory in the French and Indian War (as the Seven Years' War of 1754–63 came to be called on its North-American front). The city of New Orleans was excluded from the territories to be ceded by the French to the British.

394 (p. 442) *Fort Chartres*   another small trading post on the French frontier, located about three miles away from Saint Phillippe

395 (p. 442) *Natchez*   a Native American tribe. As the story makes clear, they sided against the earlier French settlers and against the British in the French and Indian Wars.

396 (p. 442) *Louis . . . at Versailles*   the King of France, Louis XV (1710–74), who had been on the throne since 1715. The royal palace of Versailles, where Louis XV was born, is virtually synonymous with the absolute power of the French monarchy at the time.

397 (p. 442) *Laclède's village*   the city of St Louis, as Chopin makes clear immediately afterwards. Named after the French king Louis IX, the city was founded in 1764 by Pierre Laclède and Auguste Chouteau (the latter was at one point the guardian of Marianne Victoire Richelet, Kate Chopin's great-great-grandmother). As Emily Toth explains, the founders of St Louis were part of an unconventional family set-up: Madame Chouteau, Auguste's mother, left her abusive husband for Pierre Laclède, who unofficially became the boy's adoptive father. The four children born in this common-law marriage all took the name Chouteau, after their mother's estranged husband (see Toth, pp. 38–9).

398 (p. 442) *Kaskaskia* initially a Native American village, Kaskaskia became a multicultural trading post with the arrival of French settlers, who made it the capital of Upper Louisiana in the early eighteenth century. In 1733, the French built an eponymous fort nearby, which was destroyed thirty years later by the British in the French and Indian War.

399 (p. 442) *St Ange de Bellerive* a French military commander, he oversaw the surrender of the lands east of the Mississippi to the British troops

400 (p. 442) *Captain Alexis Vaudry* Pamela Knights suggests that this might be an echo of 'Vaudreil', the Canadian governor-general during the French and Indian War (see also Note 393).

401 (p. 443) *his cousin of Spain* in a secret agreement (the Treaty of Fontainebleau) in 1762, Louis XV did cede Louisiana (New France) to his cousin Charles III of Spain. The following year, as already mentioned, the territories east of the Mississippi were ceded to Britain with the Treaty of Paris, which marked the end of the Seven Years' War.

402 (p. 447) *the mother of slaves* Emily Toth points out that 'Saint Phillippe was the first village in the "Illinois country" in which slavery was instituted' (p. 40)

Doctor Chevalier's Lie
Published in *Vogue* on 5 October 1893

The Story of an Hour
Published in *Vogue* on 6 December 1894 as 'The Dream of an Hour'

403 (p. 449) *railroad disaster* Chopin's own father was killed in a train accident in 1855.

404 (p. 450) *live for her* the original version published in *Vogue* reads 'live for during'. Chopin added 'her' on her clipping of *Vogue*.

405 (p. 451) *Victory* in Greek mythology, Nike/Victory is the winged goddess of Triumph

Lilacs
Published in *New Orleans Times–Democrat* on 20 December 1896

406 (p. 452) *Sacré-Coeur* the Sacred Heart of Jesus

407 (p. 452) *Ste Catherine de Sienne* Saint Catherine of Siena (*c.*1347–80). One of the doctors of the Church, she is perhaps most famous for her work in bringing the Papacy back to Rome from the

French city of Avignon. Her spiritual writings and political engagement made her an unusual female figure for her time.

408 (p. 454) *ma tante de Sierge*   my aunt from Sierge

409 (p. 455) *enragée*   the Enraged Ones, a radical group during the French Revolution (1789–99)

410 (p. 455) *St Lazare*   the madhouse

411 (p. 456) *bénitiers*   vessels for holy water

412 (p. 458) *traînée*   trainee

413 (p. 458) *café chantant*   literally, a 'singing café' (French); an establishment with music and entertainment

414 (p. 458) *Mons. Zola*   the French naturalist writer Monsieur Émile Zola (1840–1902)

415 (p. 459) *désolé*   desolate

416 (p. 459) *chiffonier*   an ornate chest of drawers

The Kiss

Published in *Vogue* on 17 January 1895

Her Letters

Published in *Vogue* on 11 and 18 April 1895

Fedora

Published in *Criterion* (St Louis) on 20 February 1897 as 'The Falling in Love of Fedora', under the pseudonym of 'La Tour' ('The Tower')

A Pair of Silk Stockings

Published in *Vogue* on 16 September 1897

417 (p. 479) *blue-points*   small oysters

418 (p. 479) *crème-frappée*   a creamy dessert

An Egyptian Cigarette

Published in *Vogue* on 21 October 1897

419 (p. 480) *fakir*   a religious ascetic